Acclaim for **RICHARD FORD's**

Independence Day

"With a mastery second to none, Richard Ford has created, and continues to develop in *Independence Day*, a character we know as well as we know our next-door neighbors. Frank Bascombe has earned himself a place beside Willy Loman and Harry Angstrom in our literary landscape, but he has done so with a wry wit and a fin de siècle wisdom that is very much his own." —*The New York Times Book Review*

"Exhilarating. . . . Ford brings back the sportswriter . . . elevating him to a great mythic American character." —*Newsweek*

"Ford combines the rare talent of a great storyteller with that of a writer who has mastered the means for laying bare the most revealing and compelling nuances of his characters. That he carefully creates only the most human and realistic of characters is a further example of his genius." —*Detroit Free Press*

"*Independence Day* is an astonishing accomplishment, richly detailed, peopled with compelling and realistic characters, and constructed with heartbreaking care by an enviably gifted writer." —*San Francisco Examiner & Chronicle*

"*Independence Day* is a wonderful book, a literary event, and Frank Bascombe is a man not only of our times but one to masterfully interpret them." —*New York Daily News*

"*Independence Day* is a bold, clear-eyed, ambitious, original and wickedly funny take on American life. . . . This is a major American novel."
—*Washington Times*

"Richard Ford [is] one of the finest curators of the great American living museum."
—*Washington Post Book World*

"Ford writes with terrific subtlety, deftly capturing unspoken sentiments. *Independence Day* is a vivid celebration not just of the textures of daily life, but also of the epiphanies that punctuate the most ordinary moments."
—*People*

"Here is the definitive novel of the postwar generation."
—*Pittsburgh Post-Gazette*

"It is Richard Ford's great gift as a novelist that makes the details matter. *Independence Day* is a fully realized portrait of modern American life as filtered through the mind and heart of a unique yet typical American man."
—*Christian Science Monitor*

"*Independence Day* is deeply, emotionally involving, with superbly drawn characters."
—*New York Newsday*

"*Independence Day* is a beautiful, enriching book."
—*Milwaukee Journal Sentinel*

"There are many pleasures to be found in *Independence Day*. . . . It is the author's portrait of America as it and his protagonist evolve and change that Ford fixes so well."
—*Chicago Tribune*

"A tour de force, with wonderful characterizations . . . a thoughtful look at the dilemma of modern Americans."
—*Cleveland Plain Dealer*

RICHARD FORD

Independence Day

Richard Ford is the author of *Rock Springs*, a collection of stories, and four previous novels: *A Piece of My Heart*, *The Ultimate Good Luck*, *The Sportswriter*, and *Wildlife*.

Books by **RICHARD FORD**

A Piece of My Heart

The Ultimate Good Luck

The Sportswriter

Rock Springs

Wildlife

Independence Day

Independence Day

Independence Day

RICHARD FORD

VINTAGE CONTEMPORARIES

Vintage Books

A Division of Random House, Inc.

New York

I wish to thank the Lyndhurst Foundation and the Echoing
Green Foundation for their generous support while I wrote this book.
I wish also to express great gratitude to my friends Angela and
Rea Hederman, Pam and Carl Navarre, Amanda Urban
and, again, Gary Fisketjon. —RF

FIRST VINTAGE CONTEMPORARIES EDITION, JULY 1996

Copyright © 1995 by Richard Ford

All rights reserved under International and Pan-American Copyright Conventions.
Published in the United States by Vintage Books, a division of Random
House, Inc., New York. Originally published in hardcover by
Alfred A. Knopf, Inc., New York, in 1995.

Portions of this work were originally published
in *Antaeus*, *Esquire*, and *The New Yorker*.

Grateful acknowledgment is made to Famous Music Corporation for
permission to reprint an excerpt from "Isn't It Romantic?" by Lorenz Hart
and Richard Rodgers, copyright © 1932 by Famous Music Corporation,
copyright renewed 1959 by Famous Music Corporation.

The Library of Congress has cataloged the Knopf edition as follows:
Ford, Richard, [*date*]
Independence day / by Richard Ford.
p. cm.
ISBN 0-679-49265-8
1. Real estate agents—New Jersey—Fiction.
2. Fathers and sons—New Jersey—Fiction.
3. Divorced men—New Jersey—Fiction.
I. Title.
PS 3556.O713I53 1995
813'.54—DC20 95-3126
CIP
Vintage ISBN: 0-679-73518-6

Random House Web address: http://www.randomhouse.com/

Printed in the United States of America
10 9 8 7 6 5

KRISTINA

Independence Day

I

In Haddam, summer floats over tree-softened streets like a sweet lotion balm from a careless, languorous god, and the world falls in tune with its own mysterious anthems. Shaded lawns lie still and damp in the early a.m. Outside, on peaceful-morning Cleveland Street, I hear the footfalls of a lone jogger, tramping past and down the hill toward Taft Lane and across to the Choir College, there to run in the damp grass. In the Negro trace, men sit on stoops, pants legs rolled above their sock tops, sipping coffee in the growing, easeful heat. The marriage enrichment class (4 to 6) has let out at the high school, its members sleepy-eyed and dazed, bound for bed again. While on the green gridiron pallet our varsity band begins its two-a-day drills, revving up for the 4th: "Boom-Haddam, boom-Haddam, boom-boom-ba-boom. Haddam-Haddam, up'n-at-'em! Boom-boom-ba-boom!"

Elsewhere up the seaboard the sky, I know, reads hazy. The heat closes in, a metal smell clocks through the nostrils. Already the first clouds of a summer T-storm lurk on the mountain horizons, and it's hotter where *they* live than where we live. Far out on the main line the breeze is right to hear the Amtrak, "The Merchants' special," hurtle past for Philly. And along on the same breeze, a sea-salt smell floats in from miles and miles away, mingling with shadowy rhododendron aromas and the last of the summer's staunch azaleas.

Though back on my street, the first shaded block of Cleveland, sweet silence reigns. A block away, someone patiently bounces a driveway ball: squeak . . . then breathing . . . then a laugh, a cough . . . "All riiight, that's the *waaay*." None of it too loud. In front of the Zumbros', two doors down, the streets crew is finishing a quiet smoke before cranking their machines and unsettling the dust again. We're repaving this summer, putting in a new "line," resodding the neutral ground, setting new curbs, using our proud new tax dollars—the workers all Cape Verdeans and wily Hondurans from poorer towns north of here. Sergeantsville and Little York. They sit and stare silently beside their yellow front-loaders, ground flatteners and backhoes, their sleek private cars—Camaros and Chevy low-riders—parked around the corner, away from the dust and where it will be shady later on.

And suddenly the carillon at St. Leo the Great begins: gong, gong, gong, gong, gong, gong, then a sweet, bright admonitory matinal air by old Wesley himself: "Wake the day, ye who would be saved, wake the day, let your souls be laved."

*T*hough all is not exactly kosher here, in spite of a good beginning. (When is anything *exactly* kosher?)

I myself, Frank Bascombe, was mugged on Coolidge Street, one street over, late in April, spiritedly legging it home from a closing at our realty office just at dusk, a sense of achievement lightening my step, still hoping to catch the evening news, a bottle of Roederer—a gift from a grateful seller I'd made a bundle for—under my arm. Three young boys, one of whom I thought I'd seen before—an Asian—yet couldn't later name, came careering ziggy-zaggy down the sidewalk on minibikes, conked me in the head with a giant Pepsi bottle, and rode off howling. Nothing was stolen or broken, though I was knocked silly on the ground, and sat in the grass for ten minutes, unnoticed in a whirling daze.

Later, in early May, the Zumbros' house and one other were burgled twice in the same week (they missed some things the first time and came back to get them).

And then, to all our bewilderment, Clair Devane, our one black agent, a woman I was briefly but intensely "linked with" two years ago, was murdered in May inside a condo she was showing out the Great Woods Road, near Hightstown: roped and tied, raped and stabbed. No good clues left—just a pink while-you-were-out slip lying in the parquet entry, the message in her own looping hand: "Luther family. Just started looking. Mid-90's. 3 p.m. Get key. Dinner with Eddie." Eddie was her fiancé.

Plus, falling property values now ride through the trees like an odorless, colorless mist settling through the still air where all breathe it in, all sense it, though our new amenities—the new police cruisers, the new crosswalks, the trimmed tree branches, the buried electric, the refurbished band shell, the plans for the 4th of July parade—do what they civically can to ease our minds off worrying, convince us our worries aren't worries, or at least not ours alone but everyone's—no one's—and that staying the course, holding the line, riding the cyclical nature of things are what this country's all about, and thinking otherwise is to drive optimism into retreat, to be paranoid and in need of expensive "treatment" out-of-state.

And practically speaking, while bearing in mind that one event rarely causes another in a simple way, it must mean *something* to a town, to the local *esprit*, for its values on the open market to fall. (Why else would real estate prices be an index to the national well-being?) If, for instance, some otherwise healthy charcoal briquette firm's stock took a nosedive, the *company* would react ASAP. Its "people" would stay at their desks an extra hour past dark (unless they were fired outright); men would go home more dog-tired than usual, carrying no flowers, would stand longer in the violet evening hours staring up at the tree limbs in need of trimming, would talk less kindly to their kids, would opt for an extra Pimm's before dinner alone with the wife, then wake oddly at four with nothing much, but nothing good, in mind. Just restless.

And so it is in Haddam, where all around, our summer swoon notwithstanding, there's a new sense of a wild world being just beyond our perimeter, an untallied apprehension among our residents, one I believe they'll never get used to, one they'll die before accommodating.

A sad fact, of course, about adult life is that you see the very things you'll never adapt to coming toward you on the horizon. You see them as the problems they are, you worry like hell about them, you make provisions, take precautions, fashion adjustments; you tell yourself you'll have to change your way of doing things. Only you don't. You can't. Somehow it's already too late. And maybe it's even worse than that: maybe the thing you see coming from far away is not the real thing, the thing that scares you, but its aftermath. And what you've feared will happen has already taken place. This is similar in spirit to the realization that all the great new advances of medical science will have no benefit for us at all, though we cheer them on, hope a vaccine might be ready in time, think things could still get better. Only it's too late there too. And in that very way our life gets over before we know it. We miss it. And like the poet said: "The ways we miss our lives are life."

*T*his morning I am up early, in my upstairs office under the eaves, going over a listing logged in as an "Exclusive" just at closing last night, and for which I may already have willing buyers later today. Listings frequently appear in this unexpected, providential way: An owner belts back a few Manhattans, takes an afternoon trip around the yard to police up bits of paper blown from the neighbors' garbage, rakes the last of the winter's damp, fecund leaves from under the forsythia beneath which lies buried his old Dalmatian, Pepper, makes a close inspection of the hemlocks he and his wife planted as a hedge when they were young marrieds long ago, takes a nostalgic walk back through rooms he's painted, baths grouted far past midnight, along the way has two more stiff ones followed hard by a sudden great welling and suppressed heart's cry for a long-lost life we must all (if we care to go on living) let go of . . . And boom: in two minutes more he's on the phone, interrupting some realtor from a quiet dinner at home, and in ten more minutes the whole deed's done. It's progress of a sort. (By lucky coincidence, my clients the Joe Markhams will have driven down from Vermont this very night, and conceivably I could complete the circuit—listing to sale—in a single day's time. The record, not mine, is four minutes.)

My other duty this early morning involves writing the editorial for our firm's monthly "Buyer vs. Seller" guide (sent free to every breathing freeholder on the Haddam tax rolls). This month I'm fine-tuning my thoughts on the likely real estate fallout from the approaching Democratic Convention, when the uninspirational Governor Dukakis, spirit-genius of the sinister Massachusetts Miracle, will grab the prize, then roll on to victory in November—my personal hope, but a prospect that paralyzes most Haddam property owners with fear, since they're almost all Republicans, love Reagan like Catholics love the Pope, yet also feel dumbfounded and double-crossed by the clownish spectacle of Vice President Bush as their new leader. My arguing tack departs from Emerson's famous line in *Self-Reliance*, "To be great is to be misunderstood," which I've rigged into a thesis that claims Governor Dukakis has in mind more "pure pocketbook issues" than most voters think; that economic insecurity is a plus for the Democrats; and that interest rates, on the skids all year, will hit 11% by New Year's no matter if William Jennings Bryan is elected President and the silver standard reinstituted. (These sentiments also scare Republicans to death.) "So what the hell," is the essence of my clincher, "things could get worse in a hurry. Now's the time to test the realty waters. Sell! (or Buy)."

*I*n these summery days my own life, at least frontally, is simplicity's model. I live happily if slightly bemusedly in a forty-four-year-old bachelor's way in my former wife's house at 116 Cleveland, in the "Presidents Streets" section of Haddam, New Jersey, where I'm employed as a Realtor Associate by the Lauren-Schwindell firm on Seminary Street. I should say, perhaps, the house formerly owned by formerly my wife, Ann Dykstra, now Mrs. Charley O'Dell of 86 Swallow Lane, Deep River, CT. Both my children live there too, though I'm not certain how happy they are or even should be.

The configuration of life events that led me to this profession and to this very house could, I suppose, seem unusual if your model for human continuance is some *Middletown* white paper from early in the century and geared to Indiana, or an "ideal American family life" profile as promoted by some right-wing think tank—several of whose directors live here in Haddam—but that are just propaganda for a mode of life no one could live without access to the very impulse-suppressing, nostalgia-provoking drugs they don't want you to have (though I'm sure *they* have them by the tractor-trailer loads). But to anyone reasonable, my life will seem more or less normal-under-the-microscope, full of contingencies and incongruities none of us escapes and which do little harm in an existence that otherwise goes unnoticed.

This morning, however, I'm setting off on a weekend trip with my only son, which promises, unlike most of my seekings, to be starred by weighty life events. There is, in fact, an odd feeling of *lasts* to this excursion, as if some signal period in life—mine *and* his—is coming, if not to a full close, then at least toward some tightening, transforming twist in the kaleidoscope, a change I'd be foolish to take lightly and don't. (The impulse to read *Self-Reliance* is significant here, as is the holiday itself—my favorite secular one for being public and for its implicit goal of leaving us only as it found us: free.) All of this comes—in surfeit—near the anniversary of my divorce, a time when I routinely feel broody and insubstantial, and spend days puzzling over that summer seven years ago, when life swerved badly and I, somehow at a loss, failed to right its course.

Yet prior to all that I'm off this afternoon, south to South Mantoloking, on the Jersey Shore, for my usual Friday evening rendezvous with my lady friend (there aren't any politer or better words, finally), blond, tall and leggy Sally Caldwell. Though even here trouble may be brewing.

For ten months now, Sally and I have carried on what's seemed to me a perfect "your place and mine" romance, affording each other generous portions of companionship, confidence (on an as-needed basis), within-reason reliability and plenty of spicy, untranscendent transport—all with ample "space" allotted and the complete presumption of laissez-faire (which I don't have much use for), while remaining fully respectful of the high-priced lessons and vividly catalogued mistakes of adulthood.

Not love, it's true. Not exactly. But closer to love than the puny goods most married folks dole out.

And yet in the last weeks, for reasons I can't explain, what I can only call a strange *awkwardness* has been aroused in each of us, extending all the way to our usually stirring lovemaking and even to the frequency of our visits; as if the hold we keep on the other's attentions and affections is changing and loosening, and it's now our business to form a new grip, for a longer, more serious attachment—only neither of us has yet proved quite able, and we are perplexed by the failure.

Last night, sometime after midnight, when I'd already slept for an hour, waked up twice twisting my pillow and fretting about Paul's and my journey, downed a glass of milk, watched the Weather Channel, then settled back to read a chapter of *The Declaration of Independence*—Carl Becker's classic, which, along with *Self-Reliance*, I plan to use as key "texts" for communicating with my troubled son and thereby transmitting to him important info—Sally called. (These volumes by the way aren't a bit grinding, stuffy or boring, the way they seemed in school, but are brimming with useful, insightful lessons applicable directly or metaphorically to the ropy dilemmas of life.)

"Hi, hi. What's new?" she said, a tone of uneasy restraint in her usually silky voice, as if midnight calls were not our regular practice, which they aren't.

"I was just reading Carl Becker, who's terrific," I said, though on alert. "He thought that the whole Declaration of Independence was an attempt to prove rebellion was the wrong word for what the founding fathers were up to. It was a war over a word choice. That's pretty amazing."

She sighed. "What was the right word?"

"Oh. Common sense. Nature. Progress. God's will. Karma. Nirvana. It pretty much all meant the same thing to Jefferson and Adams and those guys. They were smarter than we are."

"I thought it was more important than that," she said. Then she said, "Life seems congested to me. Just suddenly tonight. Does it to you?" I was aware coded messages were being sent, but I had no idea how to translate them. Possibly, I thought, this was an opening gambit to an announcement that she never wanted to see me again—which has happened. ("Congested" being used in its secondary meaning as: "unbearable.") "Something's crying out to be noticed, I just don't know what it is," she said. "But it must have to do with you and I. Don't you agree?"

"Well. Maybe," I said. "I don't know." I was propped up by my bed lamp, under my favorite framed map of Block Island, the musty old annotated Becker on my chest, the window fan (I've opted for no air-conditioning) drawing cool, sweet suburban midnight onto my bedcovers. Nothing I could think of was missing right then, besides sleep.

"I just feel things are congested and I'm missing something," Sally said again. "Are you sure you don't feel that way?"

"You have to miss some things to have others." This was an idiotic answer. I felt I might possibly be asleep but tomorrow still have a hard time convincing myself this conversation hadn't happened—which is also not that infrequent with me.

"I had a dream tonight," Sally said. "We were in your house in Haddam, and you kept neatening everything up. I was your wife somehow, but I felt terrible anxiety. There was blue water in our toilet bowl, and at some point you and I shook hands, standing on your front steps—just like you'd sold me your own house. And then I saw you shooting away out across the middle of a big cornfield with your arms stretched out like Christ or something, just like back in Illinois." Where she's from, the stolid, Christian corn belt. "It was peaceful in a way. But the whole effect was that everything was very, very busy and hectic and no one could get anything done right. And I felt this anxiety right in my dream. Then I woke up and I wanted to call you."

"I'm glad you did," I said. "It doesn't sound like anything that bad, though. You weren't being chased by wild animals who looked like me, or getting pushed out of airplanes."

"No," she said, and seemed to consider those fates. Far away in the night I could hear a train. "Except I felt so anxious. It was very vivid. I don't usually have vivid dreams."

"I try to forget my dreams."

"I know. You're very proud of it."

"No I'm not. But they don't ever seem mysterious enough. I'd remember them if they seemed very interesting. Tonight I dreamed I was reading, and I *was* reading."

"You don't seem too engaged. Maybe now isn't a good time to talk seriously." She sounded embarrassed, as if I was making fun of her, which I wasn't.

"I'm glad to hear your voice, though," I said, thinking she was right. It was the middle of the night. Little good begins then.

"I'm sorry I got you up."

"You didn't get me up." At this point, though, and unbeknownst to her, I turned out my light and lay breathing, listening to the train in the cool dark. "You just want something you're not getting, is my guess. It's not unusual." In Sally's case, it could be any one of a number of things.

"Don't you ever feel that way?"

"No. I feel like I have a lot as it is. I have you."

"That's very nice," she said, not so warmly.

"It *is* nice."

"I guess I'll be seeing you tomorrow, won't I?"

"You bet. I'll be there with bells on."

"Great," she said. "Sleep tight. Don't dream."

"I will. I won't." And I put the phone down.

It would be untruthful to pretend that what Sally was wrestling with last night was some want or absence I didn't feel myself. And perhaps I'm simply a poor bet for her or anybody, since I so like the tintinnabulation of early romance yet lack the urge to do more than ignore it when that sweet sonority threatens to develop into something else. A successful practice of my middle life, a time I think of as the Existence Period, has been to ignore much of what I don't like or that seems worrisome and embroiling, and then usually see it go away. But I'm as aware of "things" as Sally is, and imagine this may be the first signal (or possibly it's the thirty-seventh) that we might soon no longer "see" each other. And I feel regret, would like to find a way of reviving things. Only, as per my practice, I'm willing to let matters go as they go and see what happens. Perhaps they'll even get better. It's as possible as not.

*T*he matter of greater magnitude and utmost importance, though, involves my son, Paul Bascombe, who is fifteen. Two and a half months ago, just after tax time and six weeks before his school year ended in Deep River, he was arrested for shoplifting three boxes of 4X condoms ("Magnums") from a display-dispenser in the Finast down in Essex. His acts were surveilled by an "eye in the sky" camera hidden above the male hygiene products. And when a tiny though uniformed Vietnamese security person (a female) approached him just beyond the checkout, where as a diversionary tactic he'd bought a bottle of Grecian Formula, he bolted but was wrestled to the ground, whereupon he screamed that the woman was "a goddamned spick asshole," kicked her in the thigh, hit her in the mouth (conceivably by accident) and pulled out a fair amount of hair before she could apply a police stranglehold and with the help of a pharmacist and another customer get the cuffs on him. (His mother had him out in an hour.)

The security guard naturally enough has pressed criminal charges of assault and battery, as well as for the violation of some of her civil rights, and there have even been "hate crime" and "making an example" rumblings out of the Essex juvenile authorities. (I consider this only as election-year bluster plus community rivalry.)

Meanwhile, Paul has been through myriad pretrial interviews, plus hours of tangled psychological evaluations of his personality, attitudes and mental state—two of which sessions I attended, found unremarkable but fair, though I have not yet seen the results. For these proceedings he has had not a lawyer but an "ombudsman," who's a social worker trained in legal matters, and who his mother has talked to but I haven't. His first actual court date is to be this Tuesday morning, the day after the 4th of July.

Paul for his part has admitted everything yet has told me he feels not very guilty, that the woman rushed him from behind and scared the shit out of him so that he thought he might be being murdered and needed to defend himself; that he shouldn't have said what he said, that it was a mistake, but he's promised he has nothing against any other races or genders and in fact feels "betrayed" himself—by what, he hasn't said. He's claimed to have had no specific use in mind for the condoms (a relief if true) and probably would've used them only in a practical joke against Charley O'Dell, his mother's husband, whom he, along with his father, dislikes.

For a brief time I thought of taking a leave from the realty office, sub-letting a condo somewhere down the road from Deep River and keeping in touch with Paul on a daily basis. But his mother disapproved. She didn't want me around, and said so. She also believed that unless things got worse, life should remain as "normal" as possible until his hearing. She and I have continued to talk it over every bit—Haddam to Deep River—and she is of the belief that all this will pass, that he is simply going through a phase and doesn't, in fact, have a syndrome or a mania, as someone might think. (It is her Michigan stoicism that allows her to equate endurance with progress.) But as a result, I've seen less of him than I'd like in the last two months, though I have now proposed bringing him down to Haddam to live with me in the fall, which Ann has so far been leery of.

She has, however—because she isn't crazy—hauled him to New Haven to be "privately evaluated" by a fancy shrink, an experience Paul claims he enjoyed and lied through like a pirate. Ann even went so far as to send him for twelve days in mid-May to an expensive health camp in the Berkshires, Camp Wanapi (called "Camp Unhappy" by the inmates), where he was judged to be "too inactive" and therefore encouraged to wear mime makeup and spend part of every day sitting in an invisible chair with an invisible pane of glass in front of him, smiling and looking surprised and grimacing at passersby. (This was, of course, also videotaped.) The camp counselors, who were all secretly "milieu therapists" in mufti—loose white tee-shirts, baggy khaki shorts, muscle-bound calves, dog whistles, lanyards, clipboards, preternaturally geared up for unstructured heart-to-hearts—expressed the opinion that Paul was intellectually beyond his years (language and reasoning skills off the Stanford charts) but was emotionally underdeveloped (closer to age twelve), which in their view posed "a problem." So that even though he acts and talks like a shrewd sophomore in the honors program at Beloit, full of sly jokes and double entendres (he has also recently shot up to

5'8", with a new layer of quaky pudge all over), his feelings still get hurt in the manner of a child who knows much less about the world than a Girl Scout.

Since Camp Unhappy, he has also begun exhibiting an unusual number of unusual symptoms: he has complained about an inability to yawn and sneeze properly; he has remarked about a mysterious "tingling" at the end of his penis; he has complained about not liking how his teeth "line up." And he has from time to time made unexpected barking noises—leering like a Cheshire, afterwards—and for several days made soft but audible *eeeck-eeecking* sounds by drawing breath back down his throat with his mouth closed, usually with a look of dismay on his face. His mother has tried to talk to him about this, has re-consulted the shrink (who's advised many more sessions), and has even gotten Charley to "step in." Paul at first claimed he couldn't imagine what anybody was talking about, that all seemed normal to him, then later he said that making noises satisfied a legitimate inner urge and didn't bother others, and that they should get over their problems with it, and him.

In these charged months I have tried, in essence, to increase my own ombudsman's involvement, conducting early-morning phone conversations with him (one of which I'm awaiting hopefully this morning) and taking him and now and then his sister, Clarissa, on fishing trips to the Red Man Club, an exclusive anglers' hideaway I joined for this very purpose. I have also taken him once to Atlantic City on a boys-only junket to see Mel Tormé at TropWorld, and twice to Sally's seashore house, there to be idle-hours bums, swimming in the ocean when syringes and solid human waste weren't competing for room, walking the beach and talking over affairs of the world and himself in a nondirected way until way after dark.

In these talks, Paul has revealed much: most notably, that he's waging a complex but losing struggle to forget certain things. He remembers, for instance, a dog we had years ago when we were all a nuclear family together in Haddam, a sweet, wiggly, old basset hound named Mr. Toby, who none of us could love enough and all doted on like candy, but who got flattened late one summer afternoon right in front of our house during a family cookout. Poor Mr. Toby actually clambered up off the Hoving Road pavement and in a dying dash galumphed straight to Paul and leaped into his arms before shuddering, wailing once and croaking. Paul has told me in these last weeks that even then (at only age six) he was afraid the incident would stay in his mind, possibly even for the rest of his life, and ruin it. For weeks and weeks, he said, he lay awake in his room thinking about Mr. Toby and worrying about the fact that he was thinking about it. Though eventually the memory had gone away, until just after the Finast rubber incident, when it came back, and now he thinks about Mr. Toby "a lot" (possibly constantly), thinks that Mr. Toby should be alive still and we should have him—and by extension, of course, that his poor brother, Ralph, who died of Reye's, should also be alive (as he surely should) and we should all still be we. There are even ways, he's said, in which all this is not that unpleasant to think about, since he remembers much of that early time, before bad things happened, as having been "fun." And in that sense, his is a rare species of nostalgia.

He has also told me that as of recently he has begun to picture the thinking process, and that his seems to be made of "concentric rings," bright like hula hoops, one of which is memory, and that he tries but can't make them all "fit down flush on top of each other" in the congruent way he thinks they should—except sometimes just before the precise moment of sleep, when he can briefly forget about everything and feel happy. He has likewise told me about what he refers to as "thinking he's thinking," by which he tries to maintain continuous monitorship of all his thoughts as a way of "understanding" himself and being under control and therefore making life better (though by doing so, of course, he threatens to drive himself nuts). In a way his "problem" is simple: he has become compelled to figure out life and how to live it far too early, long before he's seen a sufficient number of unfixable crises cruise past him like damaged boats and realized that fixing one in six is a damn good average and the rest you have to let go—a useful coping skill of the Existence Period.

All this is not a good recipe, I know. In fact, it's a bad recipe: a formula for a life stifled by ironies and disappointments, as one little outer character tries to make friends with or exert control over another, submerged, one, but can't. (He could end up as an academic, or a U.N. translator.) Plus, he's left-handed and so is already threatened by earlier-than-usual loss of life, by greater chances of being blinded by flying objects, scalded by pans of hot grease, bitten by rabid dogs, hit by cars piloted by other left-handers, of deciding to live in the Third World, of not getting the ball over the plate consistently and of being divorced like his Dad and Mom.

My fatherly job, needless to say, is not at all easy at this enforced distance of miles: to coax by some middleman's charm his two foreign selves, his present and his childish past, into a better, more robust and outward-tending relationship—like separate, angry nations seeking one government—and to sponsor self-tolerance as a theme for the future. This, of course, is what any father should do in any life, and I have tried, despite the impediments of divorce and time and not always knowing my adversary. Only it seems plain to me now, and as Ann believes, I have not been completely successful.

But bright and early tomorrow I am picking him up all the way in Connecticut and staging for both our benefits a split-the-breeze father-and-son driving campaign in which we will visit as many sports halls of fame as humanly possible in one forty-eight-hour period (this being only two), winding up in storied Cooperstown, where we'll stay in the venerable Deerslayer Inn, fish on scenic Lake Otsego, shoot off safe and ethical fireworks, eat like castaways, and somehow along the way I'll work (I hope) the miracle only a father can work. Which is to say: if your son begins suddenly to fall at a headlong rate, you must through the agency of love and greater age throw him a line and haul him back. (All this somehow before delivering him to his mother in NYC and getting myself back here to Haddam, where I myself, for reasons of familiarity, am best off on the 4th of July.)

And yet, and yet. Even a good idea can be misguided if embarked on in ignorance. And who could help wondering: is my surviving son already out of reach and crazy as a betsy bug, or headed fast in that dire direction? Are his problems the product of haywire neurotransmitters, only solvable by preemptive chemicals? (This was the New Haven guy's, Dr. Stopler's, initial view.) Will he turn gradually into a sly recluse with a bad complexion, rotten teeth, bitten nails, yellow eyes, who abandons school early, hits the road, falls in with the wrong bunch, tries drugs, and finally becomes convinced *trouble* is his only dependable friend, until one sunny Saturday it, too, betrays him in some unthought-of and unbearable way, after which he stops off at a suburban gun store, then spirits on to some quilty mayhem in a public place? (This I frankly don't expect, since he has

yet to exhibit any of the "big three" of childhood homicidal dementia: attraction to fire, the need to torture helpless animals, or bed-
wetting; and because he is in fact quite softhearted and mirthful, and
always has been.) Or, and in the best-case scenario, is he—as happens to us all and as his mother hopes—merely going through a
phase, so that in eight weeks he'll be trying out for lonely end on the
Deep River JV?

God only knows, right? *Really* knows?

For me, alone without him most of the time, truly the worst part
is that I believe he should now be at an age when he cannot imagine
one bad thing happening to him, ever. And yet he can. And sometimes at the Shore or standing streamside at the Red Man Club as
the sun dies and leaves the water black and bottomless, I have
looked into his sweet, pale, impermanent boy's face and known that
he squints out at a future he's unsure of, from a vantage point he
already knows he doesn't like, but toward which he soldiers on
because he thinks he should and because even though in his heart of
hearts he knows we're not alike, he wishes we were and for that likeness to give him assurance.

Naturally enough, I can explain almost nothing to him. Father-
hood by itself doesn't provide wisdom worth imparting. Though in
preparation for our trip, I've sent him copies of *Self-Reliance* and the
Declaration, and suggested he take a browse. These are not your
ordinary fatherly offerings, I admit; yet I believe his instincts are
sound and he will help himself if he can, and that independence is, in
fact, what he lacks—independence from whatever holds him captive:
memory, history, bad events he struggles with, can't control, but
feels he should.

A parent's view of what's wrong or right with his kid is probably
less accurate than even the next-door neighbor's, who sees the child's
life perfectly through a gap in the curtain. I, of course, would like to
tell him how to live life and do better in a hundred engaging ways,
just as I tell myself: that nothing ever neatly "fits," that mistakes must
be made, bad things forgotten. But in our short exposures I seem only
able to talk glancingly, skittishly before shying away, cautious not to
be wrong, not to quiz or fight him, not to be his therapist but his
Dad. So that in all likelihood I will never provide good cure for his
disease, will never even imagine correctly what his disease is, but will
only suffer it with him for a time and then depart.

The worst of being a parent is my fate, then: being an adult. Not owning the right language; not dreading the same dreads and contingencies and missed chances; the fate of knowing much yet having to stand like a lamppost with its lamp lit, hoping my child will see the glow and venture closer for the illumination and warmth it mutely offers.

Outside in the still, quiet morning, I hear a car door close, then the muffled voice (softened to the early hour) of Skip McPherson, my neighbor across the street. He is returning from his summer hockey league in East Brunswick (ice time available only before daylight). Many mornings I've seen him and his bachelor CPA chums lounging on his front steps drinking a quiet beer, still in their pads and jerseys, their skates and sticks piled on the sidewalk. Skip's team has adopted the ruddy Indian-warrior insignia and hard-check skating style of the '70 Chicago Blackhawks (Skip hails from Aurora), and Skip himself has taken the number 21 in honor of his hero, Stan Mikita. Sometimes when I'm up early and out picking up the Trenton *Times*, we'll talk sports curb to curb. He frequently has a butterfly bandage over his eye, or a gummy fat lip, or a complicated knee brace that stiffens his leg, but he's always high-spirited and acts as if I'm the best neighbor in the world, though he has little notion of me other than that I'm a realtor—some older guy. He is typical of the young professionals who bought into the Presidents Streets in the middle Eighties and paid a big price, and who are sticking it out now, gradually fixing up their houses, sitting on their equity and waiting for the market to fire up.

In my "Buyer vs. Seller" editorial I've noted that even though most people won't be happy with *whoever* wins the election, 54 percent of them still expect to be better off this time next year. (I've omitted the companion statistic, cribbed from the *New York Times*, that only 24 percent feel the *country* will be better off. Why these numbers shouldn't be the same, is anybody's guess.)

And then suddenly, it is seven-thirty. My phone comes alive. It is my son.

"Hi," Paul says lamely.

"Hi, son," I say, the model of upbeat father-at-a-remove. Music is playing somewhere, and I think for a moment it's outside my window—the streets crew, possibly, or Skip—then I recognize the heavy, fuzzed-out *thunga-thyunga-thunga-thyunga* and realize Paul has his headphones on and is listening to Mammoth Deth or some such group he likes while he's also listening to me. "What's going on up there, son? Everything okay?"

"Yeah." *Thunga-thyunga.* "Everything's okay."

"Are we all set? Canton, Ohio, tomorrow, the Cowgirl Hall of Fame by Sunday?" We have compiled a list of all the halls of fame there are, including the Anthracite Hall of Fame in Scranton, the Clown Hall of Fame in Delavan, Wisconsin, the Cotton Hall of Fame in Greenwood, Mississippi, and the Cowgirl in Beaton, Texas. We've vowed to visit them all in two days, though of course we can't and will have to satisfy ourselves with basketball, in Springfield (it's close to his house), and Cooperstown—which I'm counting on to be the *ur*-father-son meeting ground, offering the assurances of a spiritually neutral spectator sport made seemingly meaningful by its context in idealized male history. (I have never been there, but the brochures suggest I'm right.)

"Yeah. We're all set." *Thunga-thyunga-thunga-thyunga.* Paul has turned it up.

"Are you still pretty keen to be going?" Two days are paltry, we both recognize but pretend we don't.

"Yeah," Paul says noncommittally.

"Are you still in bed, son?"

"Yeah. I am. Still in bed." This doesn't seem like a great sign, though of course it's only seven-thirty.

There is really nothing for us to talk about every morning. In any normal life, we would pass each other going this way and that, to and fro, exchange pleasantries or casual bits of wry or impertinent information, feel varyingly in touch with each other or out in harmless ways. But under the terms of our un-normal life we have to make extra efforts, even if they're wastes of time.

"Did you have any good dreams last night?" I sit forward in my chair, stare straight into the cool mulberry leaves out my window. This way it is possible to concentrate totally. Paul sometimes has wacky dreams, though it may be he invents them to have something to tell.

"Yeah, I did." He sounds distracted, but then the *thunga-thyunga-thunga-thyunga* goes very low. (Last night was apparently a good one for dreaming.)

"Want to tell me about it?"

"I was a baby, right?"

"Right."

He is tampering with something metallic. I hear a metal *snap!* "But I was a really ugly baby? *Really* ugly. And my parents were not you or Mom, but they kept leaving me at home and going off to parties. Veddy, veddy posh parties."

"Where was this?"

"Here. I don't know. Somewhere."

"In Deep Water?" Deep Water is his wisenheimer's name for Deep River, calculated precisely to make Charley O'Dell feel as unappreciated as possible. He conceivably has less use for Charley than even I do.

"Yep. Deep Water. And that's the *way* it is." He adopts his perfect-pitch Walter Cronkite voice. A headshrinker, I'm confident, would read signs of dread and fear in Paul's dream and be right. Fear of abandonment. Of castration. Of death—all solid fears, the same ones I entertain. He at least seems willing to make a joke out of it.

"Anything else going on?"

"Mom and Charley had a big fight last night."

"Sorry to hear that. About what?"

"Stuff, I guess. I don't know." I hear the weatherman on *Good Morning America* giving us the good news for the weekend. Paul has activated his TV now and doesn't want to talk more about his mother's marital dustup; he simply wants to announce it so he can refer to it usefully on our trip. For a while I've sensed (with an acuity unique to ex-husbands) that something wasn't right with Ann. Early menopause, early nostalgia all her own, late-breaking regret. All are possible. Or maybe Charley has a honey, some little busty button-nosed waitress from the boatyard diner in Old Saybrook. Their union, though, has lasted four years, which seems long enough under the circumstances—since its chief frailty is that Charley's nobody anyone in her right mind should ever marry in the first place.

"So look. Your ole Dad's got to go sell a house this morning. Slam home my pitch. Reel in the big fish."

"D. O. Volente," Paul says.

"You got it. The Volente family from Upper High Point, North Carolina." He has decided, from his one year of Latin, that D. O.

Volente is the patron saint of realtors and must be courted like a good Samaritan—shown every house, given the best deals, accorded every courtesy, made to pay no vigorish—or bad things will happen. Since the rubber incident our life has largely been conducted as a reticule of jokes, quips, double entendres, horse laughs, whose excuse for being, of course, is love. "Be a pal to your mother today, okay, pal?" I say.

"I'm her pal. She's just a bitch."

"No she's not. Her life's harder than yours, believe it or not. She has to deal with you. How's your sister?"

"Great." His sister Clary is twelve and as sage as Paul is callow.

"Tell her I'll see her tomorrow, okay?"

The volume suddenly zooms up on the TV, another man's voice blabbing at a high-decibel level about Mike Tyson making 22 mil for beating Michael Spinks in ninety-one seconds. "I'd let him sock *me* in the kisser for half that much," the man says. "Did you hear that?" Paul says. "He'd let him 'sock him in the kisser.' " He loves this kind of tricky punning talk, thinks it's hilarious.

"Yeah. But you be ready to go when I get there tomorrow, okay? We have to hit the ground running if we expect to get to Beaton, Texas."

"He was Beaton to the punch, then socked in the kisser. Are you gonna get married again?" He says this shyly. Why, I don't know.

"No, never. I love you, okay? Did you look at the Declaration of Independence and those brochures? I expect you to have your ducks in a row."

"No," he says. "But I've got one, okay?" This refers to a real joke.

"Tell me. I'll use it on my clients."

"A horse comes into a bar and orders a beer," Paul says, deadpan. "What does the bartender say?"

"I give up."

" 'Gee, why the long face?' "

Silence on his end of the line, a silence that says we each know what the other is thinking and are splitting our sides in silent laughter—the best, giddiest laughter of all. My right eyelid gives a predictable flicker. Now would be a perfect moment—with silent laughter as sad counterpoint—to think a melancholy thought, ponder a lost something or other, conduct a quick review of life's misread menu of what's important and what's not. But what I feel instead is acceptance hedging on satisfaction and a faint promise for the day just beginning. There is no such thing as a false sense of well-being.

"Great," I say. "That's great. But what's a horse doing in a bar?"

"I don't know," Paul says. "Maybe dancing."

"Having a drink," I say. "Somebody led him to it."

Outside, on the warming lawns of Cleveland Street, Skip McPherson shouts, "He shoots, he *scooooores!*" Restrained laughter floats up, a beer can goes *kee-runch*, another manly voice says, "Old slapshot, ooold slapshot, yesssireeobert." Down the block I hear a diesel growl to life like a lion waking. The streets crew is up and going.

"I'll catch you tomorrow, son," I say. "Okay?"

"Yeah," Paul says, "catch you tomorrow. Okay." And then we hang up.

2

On Seminary Street at 8:15, Independence Day is the mounting spirit of the weekend, and all outward signs of life mean to rise with it. The 4th is still three days off, but traffic is jamming into Frenchy's Gulf and through the parking lot at Pelcher's Market, citizens shouting out greetings from the dry cleaners and Town Liquors, as the morning heat is drumming up. Plenty of our residents are already taking off for Blue Hill and Little Compton; or, like my neighbors the Zumbros, with time on their hands, to dude ranches in Montana or expensive trout water in Idaho. Everyone's mind-set reads the same: avoid the rush, get a jump, hit the road, put pedal to the metal. Exit is the seaboard's #1 priority.

My first order of business is to make an early stop at one of two rental houses I own, with a mind to collecting the rent, then do a quick sweep through the realty office to drop off my editorial, pick up the key for the house I'm showing in Penns Neck and have a last-minute map-out session with the Lewis twins, Everick and Wardell, the agency's "utility men," regarding our planned participation in Monday's holiday events. As it happens, our part simply amounts to handing out free hot dogs and root beer from a portable "dogs-on-wheels" stand I myself own and am lending to the cause (all proceeds to Clair Devane's two orphaned children).

Up Seminary, which since the boom has become a kind of Miracle Mile "main street" none of us ever wished for, all merchants are staging sidewalk "firecracker sales," setting out derelict merchandise they haven't moved since Christmas and draping sun racks with patriotic bunting and gimmicky signs that say wasting hard-earned money is the American way. Virtual Profusion has laid in extra bunches of low-quality daisies and red bachelor buttons to draw the bushed businessman or seminarian hiking home in a funk but determined to seem festive ("Say it with cheap flowers"). Brad Hulbert, our gay shoe-store owner, has stacked boxes of one-size-only oddities along his front window and stationed his tanned and bored little catamite, Todd, on a stool behind an open-air cash register. And the bookstore has hauled out its overstocks—piles of cheap dictionaries, atlases and unsellable '88 calendars, plus last season's computer games, all of it heaped high on a banquet table to be eyed and picked over by larcenous teens like my son.

For the first time, though, since I moved here in 1970, two businesses on Seminary have left their stores standing empty, their management clearing out under cover of darkness, owing people money and merchandise. One has since resurfaced in the Nutley Mall, the other hasn't been heard from. Indeed, many of the high-dollar franchises—places that never staged a sale—have now gone through takeovers and Chapter 11 reorganizations and given way to second-echelon high-dollar places where sales are a way of life. This spring, Pelcher's postponed a grand reopening of its specialty meat-and-cheese boutique; a Japanese car dealership suddenly went belly-up and now sits empty on Route 27. And on the weekend streets there's even a different crowd of visitors. In the early Eighties, when the Haddam population ballooned from twelve to twenty thousand, and I was still writing for a flashy sports magazine, our typical weekenders were suave New Yorkers—rich SoHo residents in bizarre get-ups and well-heeled East Siders come down to "the country" for the day, having heard it was a quaint little village here, one worth seeing, still unspoiled, approximately the way Greenwich or New Canaan used to be fifty years ago, which was at least partly true, then.

Now those same people are either staying at home in their cement-and-burglar-barred pillboxes and getting into urban pioneering or whatever their checkbooks allow; or else they've sold out and gone back to KC or decided to make a new start in the Twin Cities or Portland, where life's slower (and cheaper). Though plenty, I'm sure, are lonely and bored silly wherever they are and are wishing someone would try to rob them.

But in Haddam, their place has been taken by, of all things, more Jerseyites, down from Baleville and Totowa or up the dogleg from Vineland and Millville—day-trippers driving 206 "just to remember where it goes" and who stop in here (unhappily rechristened "Haddam the Pleasant" by the village council) for a snack and a look-around. These people—I've watched them through the office window when I've been "on point" on the weekend—all seem to be a less purposeful lot of humans. They have more kids that're noisier, drive rattier cars with exterior parts missing and don't mind parking in handicap spaces or across a driveway or beside a fire hydrant as though they didn't have fire hydrants where they come from. They keep the yogurt franchise jumping and bang down truckloads of chocolate-chip cookies, but few of them ever sit down at The Two Lawyers for an actual lunch, fewer still spend a night in the August Inn, and none get interested in houses—though sometimes they'll waste half your day larky-farking around looking at places they'll forget the instant they're back in their Firebirds and Montegos, beetle-browing it down to Manahawkin. (Shax Murphy, who took over the agency when old man Otto Schwindell passed on, tried instituting a credit check before allowing a house to be shown over 400K. But the rest of us did some lobbying after a rock star got turned away, then spent two million at Century 21.)

I turn off Seminary out of the holiday traffic, coast down Constitution Street behind downtown, past the library, across Plum Road at the blinker, and cruise along outside the metal-picket fence behind which my son Ralph Bascombe lies buried, out as far as Haddam Medical Center, where I make a left at Erato, then over to Clio, where my two rental houses sit in their quiet neighborhood.

It might seem unusual that a man my age and nature (unadventuresome) would get involved in potentially venal landlording, chockablock as it is with shady, unreliable tenants, vicious damage-deposit squabbles, dishonest repair persons, bad checks, hectoring late-night phone calls over roof leaks, sewage backups, sidewalk repairs, barking dogs, crummy water heaters, falling plaster and noisy parties requiring the police being called, often eventuating in lengthy lawsuits. The quick and simple answer is that I decided none of these potential nightmares would be my story, which is how it's mostly happened. The two houses I own, side by side, are on a quiet, well-treed street in the established black neighborhood known as Wallace Hill, snugged in between our small CBD and the richer white demesnes on the west side, more or less behind the hospital. Reliable, relatively prosperous middle-aged and older Negro families have lived here for decades in small, close-set homes they keep in much better than average condition and whose values (with a few eyesore exceptions) have gone steadily up—if not keeping exact pace with the white sections, at least approximating them but also not suffering price slippage related to recent sags in white-collar employment. It's America like it used to be, only blacker.

Most of the residents on these streets are blue-collar professionals—plumbers or small-engine mechanics or lawn-care partners who work out of garage setups that come right off their taxes. There are a couple of elderly Pullman porters and several working moms who're teachers, plus plenty of retirees whose mortgages are paid off and who are perfectly happy to be going nowhere. Lately a few black dentists and internists and three trial lawyer couples have decided to move back to a neighborhood similar to where they grew up, or at least where they might've grown up if their families hadn't been trial lawyers and dentists themselves, and they hadn't gone to Andover and Brown. Eventually, of course, as in-town property becomes more valuable (they aren't making any more of it), all the families here will realize big profits and move away to Arizona or down South, where their ancestors were once property themselves, and the whole area will be gentrified by incoming whites and rich blacks, after which my small investment, with its few-but-bearable headaches, will turn into a gold mine. (This demographic shifting is, in fact, slower-moving in the stable black neighborhoods, since there aren't that many places for a well-heeled black American to go that's better than where he or she already is.)

Though that isn't the whole picture.

Since my divorce and, more pointedly, after my former life came to a sudden end and I suffered what must've been a kind of survivable "psychic detachment" and took off in a fugue for Florida and afterward to as far away as France, I had been uneasily aware that I had never done very much in my life that was honestly good except for myself and my loved ones (and not all of them would agree even with that). Writing sports, as anyone can tell you who's ever done it or read it, is at best offering a harmless way to burn up a few unpromising brain cells while someone eats breakfast cereal, waits nervously in the doctor's office for CAT-scan results or mulls away dreamy, solitary minutes in the can. And as far as my own hometown was concerned, apart from transporting the occasional half-flattened squirrel to the vet, or calling the fire department once when my elderly neighbors the Deffeyes let their gas barbecue set their back porch on fire and threatened the neighborhood, or some other act of tepid suburban heroism, I'd probably contributed as little to the commonweal as it was possible for a busy man to contribute without being plain evil. This, though I'd lived in Haddam fifteen years, ridden the prosperity curve right through the roof, enjoyed its civic amenities, sent my kids to its schools, made frequent and regular use of the streets, curb cuts, sewers, water mains, police and fire, plus various other departments dedicated to my well-being. Almost two years ago, however, while driving home in a weary semi-daze after a long, unproductive morning of house showings, I took a wrong turn and ended up behind Haddam Medical Center on little Clio Street, where most of our town's Negro citizens were sitting out on their porches in the late August heat, fanning themselves and chatting porch to porch, pitchers of iced tea and jars of water at their feet and little oscillating fans connected with cords through the windows to keep the air moving. As I drove past they all looked out at me serenely (or so I judged). One elderly woman waved. A group of boys stood on the street corner wearing baggy athletic shorts, holding basketballs, smoking cigarettes and talking, their arms draped around each other's shoulders. None of them seemed to notice me, or do anything menacing. So that for some reason I felt compelled to make the block and do the whole tour over, which I did—complete with the old woman waving as if she'd never laid eyes on me or my car in her life, much less two minutes before.

And what I thought, when I'd driven around a third time, was that I'd passed down this street and the four or five others like it in the darktown section of Haddam at least *five hundred* times in the decade and a half I'd lived here, and didn't know a single soul; I had been invited into no one's home, had paid no social calls, never sold a house here, had probably never even walked down a single sidewalk (though I had no fear about doing it day or night). And yet I considered this to be a bedrock, first-rate neighborhood and these souls its just and sovereign protectors.

On my fourth trip around the block, naturally no one waved at me (two people in fact came to the top of their porch steps and frowned, and the boys with the basketballs glowered with their hands on their hips). However, I had seen two identical next-door houses—single-storey, American-vernacular frame structures in slightly run-down condition, with keyboard awnings, brick-veneer half-fronts, raised, roofed porches and a fenced alley in between, both with a Trenton realty company's FOR SALE sign out front. I discreetly jotted down the phone number, then went straight to the office and put in a call to investigate price and the possibility of buying both places. I hadn't been in the realty business long and was happy to think about diversifying my assets and stashing money away where it'd be hard to get at. And I thought that if I could buy both houses at a bargain, I could then rent them to whoever wanted to live there—black retirees on fixed incomes, or not-entirely-healthy elderlies still able to look after their affairs and not be a burden on their kids, or young-marrieds in need of a sensibly priced but sturdy leg up in life—people I could assure a comfortable existence in the face of housing costs going sky-high and until such time as they could move into a perpetual-care facility or buy a starter home of their own. All of which would bestow on me the satisfaction of reinvesting in my community, providing affordable housing options, maintaining a neighborhood integrity I admired, while covering my financial backside and establishing a greater sense of connectedness, something I'd lacked since before Ann moved to Deep River two years before.

I would, I felt, be the perfect modern landlord: a man of superior sympathies and sound investments, with something to donate from years of accumulated life led thoughtfully if not always at complete peace. Everybody on the street would be happy to see my car come cruising by, because they'd know I was probably stopping in to install a new faucet kit in the kitchen, or to service the washer-dryer, or was just paying a visit to see if everybody was feeling good about things, which they always, I felt sure, would be. (Most people with an urge to diversify, I knew, would've checked with their accountant, bought beachfront condos on Marco Island, limited their loss exposure, set aside one unit for themselves, one for their grandchildren, put the others with a management company, then cleared the whole business out of their mind April to April.)

What I thought I had to offer was a deep appreciation for the sense of belonging and permanence the citizens of these streets might totally lack in Haddam (through no fault of their own), yet might long for the way the rest of us long for paradise. When Ann and I—expecting the arrival of our son, Ralph—first came to Haddam from New York and moved into our Tudor-style house on Hoving Road, we landed with the uneasy immigrant sense that everybody but the two of us had been here since before Columbus and they all damn well wanted us to feel that way; that there was some secret insider knowledge we didn't have simply because we'd shown up when we did—too late—yet unfortunately it was knowledge we could also never acquire, for more or less the same reasons. (This is total baloney, of course. Most people are late arrivals wherever they live, as selling real estate makes clear in fifteen minutes, though for Ann and me the uneasy feeling lasted a decade.)

But the residents of Haddam's black neighborhood, I concluded, had possibly never felt at home where they were either, even though they and their relatives might've been here a hundred years and had never done anything but make us white late-arrivers feel welcome at their own expense. And so what I thought I could do was at least help make two families feel at home and let the rest of the neighbors observe it.

Therefore, with a relatively small down, I quickly snapped up the two houses on Clio Street, presented myself at the front door of each as the new owner and gave my pledge to the two startled families inside that I intended to keep the houses as rental properties, all reliances and responsibilities to be meticulously honored, and that they could feel confident about staying put as long as they wanted.

The first family, the Harrises, immediately asked me in for coffee and carrot cake, and we got started on a good relationship that has lasted to the present—though they've since retired and moved in with their children in Cape Canaveral.

The other family, however, the McLeods, were unfortunately miles different. They are a mixed-race family—man and wife with two small children. Larry McLeod is a middle-aged former black militant who's married to a younger white woman and works in the mobile-home construction industry in nearby Englishtown. The day I came to his door he opened it wearing a tight red tee-shirt that had *Keep on shooting 'til the last motherfucker be dead* stenciled across the front. A big automatic pistol was lying just inside the door on a table, and not surprisingly it was the second thing my eyes lit on. Larry has long arms and bulging, venous biceps, as if he might've been an athlete once (a kick boxer, I decided), and acted surly as hell, wanting to know why I was bothering him during the part of the day when he was usually asleep, and even going so far as to tell me he didn't believe I owned the house and was just there to hassle him. Inside on the couch I could see his skinny little white wife, Betty, watching TV with their kids—all three of them looking wan and drugged in the watery light. There was also an odd, bestilled odor inside the house, something I could almost identify but not quite, though it was like the air in a closet full of shoes that has been shut up for years.

Larry kept on seeming mad as a bulldog and glaring at me through the latched screen. I told him exactly what I'd told the elderly Harrises—all responsibilities and reliances meticulously honored, etc., etc., though I specifically mentioned to him the requirement of keeping up the rent, which I spontaneously decided to drop by ten dollars. I added that I wanted the neighborhood to stay intact, with housing available and affordable for the people who lived there, and while I intended to make needed capital improvements to both houses he should feel confident these would not be reflected in rent increases. I explained that with this plan I could realistically foresee a net gain just by keeping the property in excellent condition, deducting expenses from my taxes, keeping my tenants happy and possibly selling out when I was ready to retire—though I allowed that seemed a long way off.

I smiled at Larry through the metal screen. "Uh-huh," was the total of what he had to say, though he glanced over his shoulder once as if he was about to instruct his wife to come interpret something I'd said. Then he returned his gaze to me and looked down at the pistol on the table. "That's registered," he said. "Check it out." The pistol was big and black, looked well oiled and completely bursting with bullets—able to do an innocent world irretrievable damage. I wondered what he needed it for.

"That's good," I said cheerfully. "I'm sure we'll be seeing each other."

"Is that it?" Larry said.

"That's about it."

"All right then," he said, and closed the door in my face.

Since this first meeting nearly two years ago, Larry McLeod and I have not much enriched or broadened each other's world-views. After a few months of sending his rent check by mail he simply stopped, so that I now have to go by the house every first of the month and ask for it. If he's there, Larry always acts menacing and routinely asks me when I plan to get something fixed—though I've kept everything in both houses in good condition the entire time and have never let longer than a day go by to have a drain unplugged or a ball float replaced. On the other hand, if Betty McLeod happens to answer the door she simply stares out at me as if she's never seen me before and has in any case stopped communicating with words. She almost never has the rent check herself, so when I see her pale, scraggly-haired little pointy-nosed face appear like a specter behind the screen, I know I'm out of luck. Sometimes neither of us even speaks. I just stand on the porch trying to look pleasant, while she peers silently out as if she were staring not at me but at the street beyond. Finally she just shakes her head, begins pushing the door closed, and I understand I am not getting paid that day.

This morning when I park at 44 Clio it is eight-thirty and already a third way up the day's heat ladder and as still and sticky as a summer morning in New Orleans. Parked cars line both sides, and a few birds are chirping in the sycamores planted in the neutral ground decades ago. Two elderly women stand farther down the sidewalk chatting at the corner of Erato, leaning on brooms. A radio plays somewhere behind a window screen—an old Bobby Bland tune I knew all the words to when I was in college but now can't even remember the title of. A somber mix of vernal lethargy and minor domestic tension fills the air like a funeral dirge.

The Harrises' house sits still empty, our agency's green-and-gray FOR RENT sign in the yard, the new white metal siding and new three-way windows with plastic screens glistening dully in the sunlight. The aluminum flashing I installed below the chimney and above the eaves makes the house look spanking new, which in most ways it is, since I also installed soffit vents, roll-in insulation in the attic (upping the R factor to 23), refooted half the foundation and still mean to put up crime bars as soon as I find a tenant. The Harrises have been gone now for half a year, and I frankly don't understand my failure to attract a tenant, since rentals are tight as a drumhead and I have priced it fairly at $575, utilities included. A young black mortuarial student from Trenton came close, but his wife felt the commute was too long. Then two sexy black legal secretaries came frisking through, though for some reason felt the neighborhood wasn't safe enough. I of course had a long explanation ready for why it was probably the safest neighborhood in town:

our one black policeman lives within shouting distance, the hospital is only three blocks away, people on the block get to know one another and pay attention as a matter of course; and how in the one break-in in anybody's memory, citizen-neighbors charged out of their houses and brought the crook to ground before he got to the corner. (That the crook turned out to be the son of the black police-man, I didn't mention.) But it was no use.

For reasons of my restricted access, the McLeods' house isn't yet as spiffy as the former Harrises'. The seedy brick veneer's still in place, and a couple of porch boards will soon begin "weathering" if nothing's done. Though hiking up the front steps I can hear the new window unit humming on the side (Larry demanded it, though I got it *used* out of one of our management properties), and I'm sure someone's home.

I give the doorbell one short ring, then stand back and put a businesslike but altogether friendly smile on my face. Anyone inside knows who's out here, as do all the neighbors. I glance around and down the hot, shaded street. The two women are still talking beside their brooms, the radio is still playing blues in some hot indoors. "Honey Bee," I remember, is the Bobby Bland song, but can't yet think of the words. I notice the grass in both yards is long and yel-lowed in spots, and the spirea Sylvania Harris planted and kept watered to a fare-thee-well are scrawny and dry and brown and probably rotten at the roots. I lean around and take a quick look down the fenced side yard between houses. Pink and blue hydrangeas are barely blooming along the foundation walls where they conceal the gas and water meters, and both areas seem deserted and unused, inviting to a burglar.

I ring the bell again, suddenly conscious that no one's answering and that I'll have to come back after the weekend, when the rent will be more in arrears and possibly in jeopardy of being forgotten. Ever since I became the owner here, I've wondered if I shouldn't just move out of my house on Cleveland—put it up for sale—and trans-fer into my rental unit as a cost-cutting, future-securing measure, and as a way of putting my money where my mouth is in the human-relations arena. Eventually the McLeods would take off out of pure dislike for me, and I could then locate new tenants to be my neigh-bors (possibly a Hmong family to spice the mix). Though under cur-rent market stresses my house on Cleveland could conceivably sit empty for months, after which I could get lowballed and sustain a major whomping—even acting as my own agent and carrying the paper. Whereas, on the other hand, finding a quality, short-term renter for a larger house like mine, even in Haddam, is a tricky proposition and rarely works out happily.

I ring the doorbell one more time, stand back to the top of the steps, listen for sounds within—footfalls, a back door closing, a muffled voice, the sound of kids' bare feet running. But nothing. This has happened before. Someone's, of course, inside, but no one's answering, and short of using my landlord's key or calling the police and saying I'm "worried" about the inhabitants, I have nothing to do but fold my tents and come again, possibly later in the day.

*B*ack up on busy Seminary Street, I park in front of the Lauren-Schwindell building and make a fast turn through the office, where the usual holiday realty-office languor hangs over the still-empty desks, blank Real-trom consoles and copy machines. Almost everyone, including the younger agents, has stood steadfastly in bed an extra hour, pretending the holiday exodus means no one's doing any real business and that anybody who needs to can just jolly well call them at home. Only Everick and Wardell are glimpsable, passing in and out of the back storage room, the outside door to the parking lot left standing open. They're returning FOR SALE signs retrieved from the ditches and woodlots where our local teenagers toss them once they're tired of having them on their walls at home or when their mothers won't stand for it any longer. (We offer a no-questions-asked, three-dollar "capture fee" for every one brought in, and Everick and Wardell—grave-faced, gangly, beanpole bachelor twins in their late fifties, who are lifelong Haddamites and oddly enough Trenton State graduates—have made a science out of knowing exactly where to search.) The Lewises, who I usually find impossible to tell apart, live around the corner from my two rentals in a duplex left them by their parents, and in fact are tight-fisted, no-nonsense landlords in their own right, owning a block of senior-citizen units in Neshanic, from which they enjoy a nice profit. Yet they still work part-time for the agency and regularly do minor upkeep chores for me on Clio Street, duties they perform with a severe, distinctly put-upon efficiency that might make someone out

of the know conclude they resented me. Though that is not at all
the case, since they have both told me on more than one occasion
that by being born in Mississippi, even with all the heavy baggage
that brings along, I naturally possess a truer instinct for members of
their race than any white northerner could ever approximate. This
is, of course, not one bit true, though theirs is an old-style racial sta-
tionlessness that forever causes baseless "verities" to persist on with
the implacable force of truth.

Our receptionist, Miss Vonda Lusk, has I see exited the ladies
room and parked herself halfway down the row of empty desks, with
a smoke and a Coke, and is sitting, one leg crossed and swinging,
happily answering the phones and leafing through *Time* magazine
till we shut down in earnest at noon. She is a big, tall, bulgy-busted,
wry-humored blonde who wears a ton of makeup, bright-colored,
ludicrously skimpy cocktail dresses to work, and lives in nearby
Grovers Mills where she was head majorette back in 1980. She was
also best friends with Clair Devane, our murdered agent, and regularly wants to discuss "the case" with me because she seems to know
Clair and I once had a discreet special something of our own. "I
think they're not pushing this thing hard enough," is her persistent
view of the police attitude. "If she'd been a local white girl you'd
have seen a big difference. You'd have FBI here out your butt."
Three white men, in fact, were taken into custody for a day, though
they were let go, and in the weeks since then it's true that no apparent progress has been made, though Clair's boyfriend is a well-
connected black bond lawyer in a good firm in town, and the realty
board along with his partners have established a $5,000 reward. Yet
it's also true that the FBI made inquiries before deciding Clair's
death was not a federal crime but a simple murder.

In the office we've at least officially left her desk unoccupied
until the murderer is found (though in fact business hasn't been
good enough to hire somebody in her place). And Vonda for her
part has kept a piece of black ribbon taped across Clair's chair and a
single rose in a murky bud vase on the empty wood-grain top. We
are all warned against forgetting.

This morning, though, Vonda has global matters more in mind.
She is a current-events buff, reads all the magazines in the office and
has her *Time* folded over on her amply exposed thigh. "Look here,
Frank, are you a single-warhead guy or a ten-warhead guy?" She

sings this out when she sees me and flashes me her big okay-what's-up-with-you smile. She's wearing an outlandish red, white and blue off-the-shoulder taffeta getup that wouldn't let her pick a dime up off a countertop and stay decent. There is nothing between us but banter.

"I'm still a single-warhead guy," I say, heading for the front now with three listing sheets, Everick and Wardell having taken one look at me and ducked out the back (not unusual), so that I've deposited in their message box some already prepared instructions for where and when to park the dogs-on-wheels stand beside the Haddam Green once they've trailered it Monday from Franks, the root beer stand I own west of town on Route 31. This is the way they prefer to conduct all affairs—indirectly and at a distance. "I think there're too many warheads around these days," I say, heading toward the door.

"Well then, you're in deep doo-doo on your vision thing, according to *Time*." She's twirling a strand of golden hair around her little finger. She's a yellow-dog Democrat and knows I'm one too, and thinks—unless I miss my guess—that we could have some fun together.

"We'll have to talk about it," I say.

"That's quite all right," she says archly. "I'm sure you're busy. Did you know Dukakis speaks fluent Spanish?" This is not for me but for whoever might be listening, as if the empty office were jammed with interested people. Only I'm out *la puerta* seeming not to hear and as quick as possible back to the cool serenity of my Crown Victoria.

*B*y nine I'm on my way out King George Road toward the Sleepy Hollow Motel on Route 1, to pick up Joe and Phyllis Markham and (it's my hope) sell them our new listing by noon.

Haddam out this woodsy way doesn't seem like a town in the throes of a price decline. An old and wealthy settlement, founded in 1795 by disgruntled Quaker merchants who split off from their more liberal Long Island neighbors, traveled south and set up things the right way, Haddam looks prosperous and confidently single-minded about its civic expectations. The housing stock boasts plenty of big 19th-century Second Empires and bracketed villas (now owned by high-priced lawyers and software CEOs) with cupolas and belvederes and oriels punctuating the basic architectural *lingua*, which is Greek with Federalist details, and post-Revolutionary stone houses fitted with fanlights, columned entries and Roman-y flutings. These houses were all big-ticket items the day the last door got hung in 1830, and hardly any turn up on the market except in vindictive divorces in which a spouse wants a big FOR SALE sign stuck out front of a former love nest to get the goat of the party of the second part. Even the few "village-in" Georgian row houses have in the last five years become prestige addresses and are all owned by rich widows, privacy-hungry gay husbands and surgeons from Philadelphia who keep them as country places they can hie off to with their nurse-anesthetists during the color season.

Though looks, of course, can be deceiving and usually are. Asking prices have yet to reflect it, but banks have slowly begun rationing money and coming back to us realtors with "problems" about appraisals. Many sellers who'd nailed down early-retirement plans at Lake of the Ozarks or for a "more intimate" place in Snowmass, now that the kids are finished at UVA, are taking a wait-and-see attitude and deciding Haddam's a lot better place to live than they'd imagined when they thought their houses were worth a fortune. (I didn't get into the residential housing business at exactly the optimum moment; in fact, I got in at almost the worst possible moment—a year before the big gut-check of last October.)

Yet like most people I remain optimistic, and feel the boom paid off no matter what things feel like at the moment. The Village of Haddam was able to annex the Township of Haddam, which deepened our tax base and gave us a chance to lift our building moratorium and reinvest in infrastructure (the excavation in front of my house is a good illustration). And because of the influx of stockbrokers and rich entertainment lawyers early in the decade, several village landmarks were spared, as well as some late-Victorian residences that were falling in because their owners had grown old, moved to Sun City or died. At the same time, in the moderate-to-low range, where I've shown house after house to the Markhams, prices have gone on rising slowly, as they have since the beginning of the century; so that most of our median-incomers, including our African Haddamites, can still sell out once they're ready to quit paying high taxes, take a fistful of dollars along with a sense of accomplishment, and move back to Des Moines or Port-au-Prince, buy a house and live off their savings. Prosperity is not always bad news.

At the end of King George Road, where sod farms open out wide like a green hayfield in Kansas, I make the turn onto once-countrified Quakertown Road, then a hard left back onto Route 1, then through the jug handle at Grangers Mill Road, which lets me work back to the Sleepy Hollow and avoid a half hour of pre-4th get-away traffic. Off on the right, Quakertown Mall sits desolated on its wide plain of parking lot, now mostly empty, a smattering of cars at either end, where the anchors—a Sears and a Goldbloom's—are still hanging on, the original developers now doing business out of a federal lockup in Minnesota. Even the Cinema XII on the backside is down to one feature, showing on only two screens. The marquee says: *B. Streisand: A Star Is Bored ** Return engagement ** Congradulations Bertie and Stash.*

My clients the Markhams, whom I'm meeting at nine-fifteen, are from tiny Island Pond, Vermont, in the far northeast corner, and their dilemma is now the dilemma of many Americans. Sometime in the indistinct Sixties, each with a then-spouse, they departed unpromising flatlander lives (Joe was a trig teacher in Aliquippa, Phyllis a plump, copper-haired, slightly bulgy-eyed housewife from the D.C. area) and trailered up to Vermont in search of a sunnier, less predictable *Weltansicht.* Time and fate soon took their unsurprising courses: spouses wandered off with other people's spouses; their kids got busily into drugs, got pregnant, got married, then disappeared to California or Canada or Tibet or Wiesbaden, West Germany. Joe and Phyllis each floated around uneasily for two or three years in intersecting circles of neighborhood friends and off-again, on-again *Weltansicht*s, taking classes, starting new degrees, trying new mates and eventually giving in to what had been available and obvious all along: true and eyes-open love for each other. Almost immediately, Joe Markham—who's a stout, aggressive little bullet-eyed, short-armed, hairy-backed Bob Hoskins type of about my age, who played nose guard for the Aliquippa Fighting Quips and who's not obviously "creative"—started having good luck with the pots and sand-cast sculptures in abstract forms he'd been making, projects he'd only fiddled around with before and that his first wife, Melody, had made vicious fun of before moving back to Beaver Falls, leaving him alone with his regular job for the Department of

Social Services. Phyllis meanwhile began realizing she, in fact, had an untapped genius for designing slick, lush-looking pamphlets on fancy paper she could actually make herself (she designed Joe's first big mailing). And before they knew it they were shipping Joe's art and Phyllis's sumptuous descriptive booklets all over hell. Joe's pots began showing up in big department stores in Colorado and California and as expensive specialty items in ritzy mail order catalogues, and to both their amazement were winning prizes at prestigious crafts fairs the two of them didn't even have time to attend, they were so busy.

Pretty soon they'd built themselves a big new house with cantilevered cathedral ceilings and a hand-laid hearth and chimney, using stones off the place, the whole thing hidden at the end of a private wooded road behind an old apple orchard. They started teaching free studio classes to small groups of motivated students at Lyndon State as a way of giving something back to the community that had nurtured them through assorted rough periods, and eventually they had another child, Sonja, named for one of Joe's Croatian relatives.

Both of them, of course, realized they'd been lucky as snake charmers, given the mistakes they'd made and all that had gone kaflooey in their lives. Though neither did they view "the Vermont life" as necessarily the ultimate destination. Each of them had pretty harsh opinions about professional dropouts and trust-fund hippies who were nothing more than nonproducers in a society in need of new ideas. "I didn't want to wake up one morning," Joe said to me the first day they came in the office, looking like bedraggled, wide-eyed missionaries, "and be a fifty-five-year-old asshole with a bandanna and a goddamn earring and nothing to talk about but how Vermont's all fucked up since a lot of people just like me showed up to ruin it."

Sonja needed to go to a better school, they decided, so she could eventually get into an even better school. Their previous batch of kids had all trooped off in serapes and Sorels and down jackets to the local schools, and that hadn't worked out very well. Joe's oldest boy, Seamus, had already done time for armed robbery, toured three detoxes and was learning-disabled; a girl, Dot, got married to a Hell's Commando at sixteen and hadn't been heard from in a long time. Another boy, Federico, Phyllis's son, was making the Army a career. And so, based on these sobering but instructive experiences, they understandably wanted something more promising for little Sonja.

They therefore made a study of where schools were best and the lifestyle pretty congenial, and where they could have some access to NYC markets for Joe's work, and Haddam came at the top in every category. Joe blanketed the area with letters and résumés and found a job working on the production end for a new textbook publisher, Leverage Books in Hightstown, a job that took advantage of his math and computer background. Phyllis found out there were several paper groups in town, and that they could go on making pots and sculptures in a studio Joe would build or renovate or rent, and could keep sending his work out with Phyllis's imaginative brochures, yet embark on a whole new adventure where schools were good, streets safe and everything basked in a sunny drug-free zone.

Their first visit was in March—which they correctly felt was when "everything" came on the market. They wanted to take their time, survey the whole spectrum, work out a carefully reasoned decision, make an offer on a house by May first and be out watering the lawn by the 4th. They realized, of course, as Phyllis Markham told me, that they'd probably need to "scale back" some. The world had changed in many ways while they were plopped down in Vermont. Money wasn't worth as much, and you needed more of it. Though all told they felt they'd had a good life in Vermont, saved some money over the past few years and wouldn't have done anything—divorce, wandering alone at loose ends, kid troubles—one bit differently.

They decided to sell their own new hand-built house at the first opportunity, and found a young movie producer willing to take it on a ten-year balloon with a small down. They wanted, Joe told me, to create a situation with no fallback. They put their furniture in some friends' dry barn, took over some other friends' cabin while they were away on vacation, and set off for Haddam in their old Saab one Sunday night, ready to present themselves as home buyers at somebody's desk on Monday morning.

Only they were in for the shock of their lives!

What the Markhams were in the market for—as I told them— was absolutely clear and they were dead right to want it: a modest three-bedroom with charm and maybe a few nice touches, though in keeping with the scaled-back, education-first ethic they'd opted for. A house with hardwood floors, crown moldings, a small carved mantel, plain banisters, mullioned windows, perhaps a window seat. A Cape or a converted saltbox set back on a small chunk of land bordering some curmudgeonly old farmer's cornfield or else a little pond or stream. Pre-war, or just after. Slightly out of the way. A lawn with maybe a healthy maple tree, some mature plantings, an attached garage possibly needing improvement. Assumable note or owner-finance, something they could live with. Nothing ostentatious: a sensible home for the recast nuclear family commencing life's third quartile with a kid on board. Something in the 148K area, up to three thousand square feet, close to a middle school, with a walk to the grocery.

The only problem was, and is, that houses like that, the ones the Markhams still google-dream about as they plow down the Taconic, mooning out at the little woods-ensconced rooftops and country lanes floating past, with mossy, overgrown stone walls winding back to mysterious-wondrous home possibilities in Columbia County—those houses are history. Ancient history. And those prices quit floating around at about the time Joe was saying good-bye to Melody and turning his attentions to plump, round-breasted and winsome Phyllis. Say 1976. Try four-fifty today if you can find it.

And I *maybe* could come close if the buyer weren't in a big hurry and didn't faint when the bank appraisal came in at thirty-under-asking, and the owner wanted 25% as earnest money and hadn't yet heard of a concept called owner finance.

The houses I *could* show them all fell significantly below their dream. The current median Haddam-area house goes for 149K, which buys you a builder-design colonial in an almost completed development in not-all-that-nearby Mallards Landing: 1,900 sq ft, including garage, three-bedroom, two-bath, expandable, no fplc, basement or carpets, sited on a 50-by-200-foot lot "clustered" to preserve the theme of open space and in full view of a fiberglass-bottom "pond." All of which cast them into a deep gloom pit and, after three weeks of looking, made them not even willing to haul out of the car and walk through most of the houses where I'd made appointments.

Other than that, I showed them an assortment of older village-in houses inside their price window—mostly small, dark two-bedrooms with vaguely Greek facades, originally built for the servants of the rich before the turn of the century and owned now either by descendants of immigrant Sicilians who came to New Jersey to be stonemasons on the chapel at the Theological Institute, or else by service-industry employees, shopkeepers or Negroes. For the most part those houses are unkempt, shrunken versions of grander homes across town—I know because Ann and I rented one when we moved in eighteen years ago—only the rooms are square with few windows, low-ceilinged and connected in incongruous ways so that inside you feel as closed in and on edge as you would in a cheap chiropractor's office. Kitchens are all on the back, rarely is there more than one bath (unless the place has been fixed up, in which case the price is double); most of the houses have wet basements, old termite damage, unsolvable structural enigmas, cast-iron piping with suspicions of lead, subcode wiring and postage-stamp yards. And for this you pay full price just to get anybody to break wind in your direction. Sellers are always the last line of defense against reality and the first to feel their soleness threatened by mysterious market corrections. (Buyers are the second.)

On two occasions I actually ended up showing houses to *Sonja* (who's my daughter's age!) in hopes she'd see something she liked (a primly painted "pink room" that could be hers, a particularly nifty place to snug a VCR, some kitchen built-ins she thought were neat), then go traipsing back down the walk burbling that this was the place she'd dreamed of all her little life and her Mom and Dad simply had to see it.

Only that never happened. On both of these charades, as Sonja went clattering around the empty rooms, wondering, I'm sure, how a twelve-year-old is supposed to buy a house, I peeked through the curtains and saw Joe and Phyllis waging a corrosive argument inside my car—something that'd been brewing all day—both of them facing forward, he in the front, she in the back, snarling but not actually looking at each other. Once or twice Joe'd whip his head around, focus-in his dark little eyes as intent as an ape, growl something withering, and Phyllis would cross her plump arms and stare out hatefully at the house and shake her head without bothering to answer. Pretty soon we were out and headed to our next venue.

Unhappily, the Markhams, out of ignorance and pigheadedness, have failed to intuit the one gnostic truth of real estate (a truth impossible to reveal without seeming dishonest and cynical): that people never find or buy the house they say they want. A market economy, so I've learned, is not even remotely premised on anybody getting what he wants. The premise is that you're presented with what you might've thought you didn't want, but what's available, whereupon you give in and start finding ways to feel good about it and yourself. And not that there's anything wrong with that scheme. Why should you only get what you think you want, or be limited by what you can simply plan on? Life's never like that, and if you're smart you'll decide it's better the way it is.

My own approach in all these matters and specifically so far as the Markhams are concerned has been to make perfectly clear who pays my salary (the seller) and that my job is to familiarize them with our area, let them decide if they want to settle here, and then use my accumulated goodwill to sell them, in fact, a house. I've also impressed on them that I go about selling houses the way I'd want one sold to me: by not being a realty wind sock; by not advertising views I don't mostly believe in; by not showing clients a house they've already said they won't like by pretending the subject never came up; by not saying a house is "interesting" or "has potential" if I think it's a dump; and finally by not trying to make people believe in *me* (not that I'm untrustworthy—I simply don't invite trust) but by asking them to believe in whatever they hold dearest—themselves, money, God, permanence, progress, or just a house they see and like and decide to live in—and to act accordingly.

All told today, the Markhams have looked at forty-five houses— dragging more and more grimly down from and back to Vermont— though many of these listings were seen only from the window of my car as we rolled slowly along the curbside. "I wouldn't live in that particular shithole," Joe would say, fuming out at a house where I'd made an appointment. "Don't waste your time here, Frank," Phyllis would offer, and away we'd go. Or Phyllis would observe from the back seat: "Joe can't stand stucco construction. He doesn't want to be the one to say so, so I'll just make it easier. He grew up in a stucco house in Aliquippa. Also, we'd rather not share a driveway."

And these weren't bad houses. There wasn't a certifiable "fixer-upper," "handyman special," or a "just needs love" in the lot (Haddam doesn't have these anyway). I haven't shown them one yet that the three of them couldn't have made a damn good fresh start in with a little elbow grease, a limited renovation budget and some spatial imagination.

Since March, though, the Markhams have yet to make a purchase, tender an offer, write an earnest-money check or even see a house twice, and consequently have become despondent as we've entered the dog days of midsummer. In my own life during this period, I've made eight satisfactory home sales, shown a hundred other houses to thirty different people, gone to the Shore or off with my kids any number of weekends, watched (from my bed) the Final 4, opening day at Wrigley, the French Open and three rounds of Wimbledon; and on the more somber side, I've watched the presidential campaigns grind on in disheartening fashion, observed my forty-fourth birthday, and sensed my son gradually become a source of worry and pain to himself and me. There have also been, in this time frame, two fiery jetliner crashes far from our shores; Iraq has poisoned many Kurdish villagers, President Reagan has visited Russia; there's been a coup in Haiti, drought has crippled the country's midsection and the Lakers have won the NBA crown. Life, as noted, has gone on.

Meanwhile, the Markhams have begun "eating into their down" from the movie producer now living in their dream house and, Joe believes, producing porn movies using local teens. Likewise Joe's severance pay at Vermont Social Services has come and gone, and he's nearing the end of his piled-up vacation money. Phyllis, to her dismay, has begun suffering painful and possibly ominous female problems that have required midweek trips to Burlington for testing, plus two biopsies and a discussion of surgery. Their Saab has started overheating and sputtering on the daily commutes Phyllis makes to Sonja's dance class in Craftsbury. And as if that weren't enough, their friends are now home from their geological vacation to the Great Slave Lake, so that Joe and Phyllis are having to give thought to moving into the original and long-abandoned "home place" on their own former property and possibly applying for welfare.

Beyond all that, the Markhams have had to face the degree of unknown involved in buying a house—unknown likely to affect their whole life, even if they were rich movie stars or the keyboardist for the Rolling Stones. Buying a house will, after all, partly determine what they'll be worrying about but don't yet know, what consoling window views they'll be taking (or not), where they'll have bitter arguments and make love, where and under what conditions they'll feel trapped by life or safe from the storm, where those spirited parts of themselves they'll eventually leave behind (however over-prized) will be entombed, where they might die or get sick and wish they were dead, where they'll return after funerals or after they're divorced, like I did.

After which all these unknown facts of life to come have then to be figured into what they still don't know about a house itself, right along with the potentially grievous certainty that they *will* know a *great* deal the instant they sign the papers, walk in, close the door and it's theirs; and then later will know even a great deal more that's possibly not good, though they want none of it to turn out badly for them or anyone they love. Sometimes I don't understand why any-body buys a house, or for that matter does anything with a tangible downside.

As part of my service to the Markhams, I've tried to come up with some stop-gap accommodations. Addressing that feeling of not knowing *is*, after all, my job, and I'm aware what fears come quaking and quivering into most clients' hearts after a lengthy, unsatisfactory realty experience: Is this guy a crook? Will he lie to me and steal my money? Is this street being rezoned C-1 and he's in on the ground floor of a new chain of hospices or drug rehab centers? I know also that the single biggest cause of client "jumps" (other than realtor rudeness or blatant stupidity) is the embittering suspicion that the agent isn't paying any attention to your wishes. "He's just showing us what he hasn't already been able to unload and trying to make us like it"; or "She's never shown us anything like what we said we were interested in"; or "He's just pissing away our time driving us around town and letting us buy him lunch."

In early May I came up with a furnished condominium in a remodeled Victorian mansion on Burr Street, behind the Haddam Playhouse, complete with utilities and covered off-street parking. It was steep at $1,500, but it was close to schools and Phyllis could've managed without a second car if they'd stayed put till Joe started work. Joe, though, swore he'd lived in his last "shitty cold-water flat" in 1964, when he was a sophomore at Duquesne, and didn't intend to start Sonja off in some oppressive new school environment with a bunch of rich, neurotic suburban kids while the three of them lived like transient apartment rats. She'd never outlive it. He'd rather, he said, forget the whole shittaree. A week later I turned up a perfectly workable brick-and-shingle bungalow on a narrow street behind Pelcher's—a bolt-hole, to be sure, but a place they could get into with some lease-to-buy furniture and a few odds and ends of their own, exactly the way Ann and I and everybody else used to live when we were first married and thought everything was great and getting greater. Joe, however, refused to even drive by.

Since early June, Joe has grown increasingly sullen and mean-spirited, as though he's begun to see the world in a whole new way he doesn't like and is working up some severe defense mechanisms. Phyllis has called me twice late at night, once when she'd been crying, and hinted Joe was not an easy man to live with. She said he'd begun disappearing for parts of the day and had started throwing pots at night over in a woman artist friend's studio, drinking a lot of beer and coming home after midnight. Among her other worries, Phyllis is convinced he might just forget the whole damn thing—the move, Sonja's schooling, Leverage Books, even their marriage—and sink back into an aimless nonconformist's life he lived before they got together and charted a new path to the waterfall. It was possible, she said, that Joe couldn't stand the consequences of real intimacy, which to her meant sharing your troubles as well as your achievements with the person you loved, and it seemed also possible that the act of trying to buy a house had opened the door on some dark corridors in herself that she was fearful of going down, though she thankfully seemed unready to discuss which these might be.

In so many sad words, the Markhams are faced with a potentially calamitous careen down a slippery socio-emotio-economic slope, something they could never have imagined six months ago. Plus, I know they have begun to brood about all the other big missteps they've taken in the past, the high cost of these, and how they don't want to make any more like that. As regret goes, theirs, of course, is not unusual in kind. Though finally the worst thing about regret is that it makes you duck the chance of suffering new regret just as you get a glimmer that nothing's worth doing unless it has the potential to fuck up your whole life.

A tangy metallic fruitiness filters through the Jersey ozone—the scent of overheated motors and truck brakes on Route 1—reaching clear back to the rolly back road where I am now passing by an opulent new pharmaceutical world headquarters abutting a healthy wheat field managed by the soil-research people up at Rutgers. Just beyond this is Mallards Landing (two ducks coasting-in on a colonial-looking sign made to resemble wood), its houses-to-be as yet only studded in on skimpy slabs, their bald, red-dirt yards awaiting sod. Orange and green pennants fly along the roadside: "Models Open." "Pleasure You Can Afford!" "New Jersey's Best-Kept Secret." But there are still long ragged heaps of bulldozed timber and stumps piled up and smoldering two hundred yards to one side, more or less where the community center will be. And a quarter mile back and beyond the far wall of third-growth hardwoods where no animal is native, a big oil-storage depot lumps up and into what's becoming thickened and stormy air, the beacons on its two great canisters blinking a red and silver *steer clear*, *steer clear* to the circling gulls and the jumbo jets on Newark approach.

When I make the final right into the Sleepy Hollow, two cars are nosed into the potholed lot, though only one has the tiresome green Vermont plate—a rusted-out, lighter-green Nova, borrowed from the Markhams' Slave Lake friends, and with a muddy bumper sticker that says ANESTHETISTS ARE NOMADS. A cagier realtor would've already phoned up with some manufactured "good news" about an unexpected price reduction in a previously out-of-reach house, and left this message at the desk last night as a form of torture and enticement. But the truth is I've become a little sick of the Markhams—given our long campaign—and have fallen into a not especially hospitable mood, so that I simply stop midway in the lot, hoping some emanations of my arrival will penetrate the flimsy motel walls and expel them both out the door in grateful, apologetic humors, fully ready to slam down their earnest money the instant they set eyes on this house in Penns Neck that, of course, I have yet to tell them about.

A thin curtain does indeed part in the little square window of room #7. Joe Markham's round, rueful face—which looks changed (though I can't say how)—floats in a small sea of blackness. The face turns, its lips move. I make a little wave, then the curtain closes, followed in five seconds by the banged-up pink door opening, and

Phyllis Markham, in the uncomfortable gait of a woman not accustomed to getting fat, strides out into the midmorning heat. Phyllis, I
see from the driver's seat, has somehow amplified her red hair's cop-
pery color to make it both brighter and darker, and has also bobbed
it dramatically into a puffy, mushroomy bowl favored by sexless
older moms in better-than-average suburbs, and which in Phyllis's
case exposes her tiny ears and makes her neck look shorter. She's
dressed in baggy khaki culottes, sandals and a thick damask Mexican
pullover to hide her extra girth. Like me, she is in her forties,
though unclear where, and she carries herself as if there were a new
burden of true woe on the earth and only she knows about it.

"All set?" I say, my window down now, cracking a smile into the
new pre-storm breeze. I think about Paul's horse joke and consider
telling it, as I said I would.

"He says he's not going," Phyllis says, her bottom lip slightly
enlarged and dark, making me wonder if Joe has given her a stiff
smack this morning. Though Phyllis's lips are her best feature and
it's more likely Joe has gifted himself with a manly morning's
woogling to take his mind off his realty woes.

I'm still smiling. "What's the problem?" I say. Paper trash and
parking lot grit are kicking around on the hot breeze now, and when
I peek in the rearview there's a dark-purple thunderhead closing fast
from the west, toiling the skies and torquing up winds, making
ready to dump a big bucket of rain on us. Not a good augury for a
home sale.

"We had an argument on the way down." Phyllis lowers her eyes,
then casts an unhappy look back at the pink door, as if she expects
Joe to come bursting through it in camo gear, screaming expletives
and commands and locking and loading an M-16. She takes a self-
protective look at the teeming sky. "I wonder if you'd mind just
talking to him." She says this in a clipped, back-of-the-mouth voice,
then elevates her small nose and stiffens her lips as two tears teeter
inside her eyelids. (I've forgotten how much Joe's gooby western PA
accent has rubbed off on her.)

Most Americans will eventually transact at least some portion of
their important lives in the presence of realtors or as a result of
something a realtor has done or said. And yet my view is, people
should get their domestic rhubarbs, verbal fisticuffs and emotional
jugular-snatching completely out of the way *before* they show up for
a house tour. I'm more or less at ease with steely silences, bitter

cryptic asides, eyes rolled to heaven and dagger stares passed between prospective home buyers, signaling but not actually putting on display more dramatic after-midnight wrist-twistings, shoutings and real rock-'em, sock-'em discord. But the client's code of conduct ought to say: Suppress all important horseshit by appointment time so I can get on with my job of lifting sagging spirits, opening fresh, unexpected choices, and offering much-needed assistance toward life's betterment. (I haven't said so, but the Markhams are on the brink of being written off, and I in fact feel a strong temptation just to run up my window, hit reverse, shoot back into the traffic and head for the Shore.)

But instead I simply say, "What would you like me to say?"

"Just tell him there's a great house," she says in a tiny, defeated voice.

"Where's Sonja?" I'm wondering if she's inside, alone with her dad.

"We had to leave her home." Phyllis shakes her head sadly. "She was showing signs of stress. She's lost weight, and she wet the bed night before last. This has been pretty tough for all of us, I guess." (She has yet to torch any animals, apparently.)

I reluctantly push open my door. Occupying the lot beside the Sleepy Hollow, inside a little fenced and razor-wire enclosure, is a shabby hubcap emporium, its shiny silvery wares nailed and hung up everywhere, all of it clanking and stuttering and shimmering in the breeze. Two old white men stand inside the compound in front of a little clatter-board shack that's completely armored with shiny hubcaps. One of them is laughing about something, his arms crossed over his big belly, swaying side to side. The other seems not to hear, just stares at Phyllis and me as if some different kind of transaction were going on.

"That's exactly what I was going to tell him anyway," I say, and try to smile again. Phyllis and Joe are obviously nearing a realty meltdown, and the threat is they may just dribble off elsewhere, feeling the need for an unattainable fresh start, and end up buying the first shitty split-level they see with another agent.

Phyllis says nothing, as if she hasn't heard me, and just looks morose and steps out of the way, hugging her arms as I head for the pink door, feeling oddly jaunty with the breeze at my back.

I half tap, half push on the door, which is ajar. It's dark and warm inside and smells like roach dope and Phyllis's coconut shampoo.

"Howzit goin' in here?" I say into the gloom, my voice, if not full of confidence, at least half full of false confidence. The door to a lighted bathroom is open; a suitcase and some strewn clothes are on top of an unmade bed. I have the feeling Joe might be on the crapper and I may have to conduct a serious conversation about housing possibilities with him there.

Though I make him out then. He's sitting in a big plastic-covered recliner chair back in a shadowed corner between the bed and the curtained window where I saw his face before. He's wearing—I can make out—turquoise flip-flops, tight silver Mylar-looking stretch shorts and some sort of singlet muscle shirt. His short, meaty arms are on the recliner's arms, his feet on the elevated footrest and his head firmly back on the cushion, so that he looks like an astronaut waiting for the first big G thrust to drive him into oblivion.

"*Sooou,*" Joe says meanly in his Aliquippa accent. "You got a house you want to sell me? Some dump?"

"Well, I do think I've got something you ought to see, Joe, I really do." I am just addressing the room, not specifically Joe. I would sell a house to anyone who happened to be here.

"Like what?" Joe is unmoving in his spaceship chair.

"Well. Like pre-war," I say, trying to bring back to memory what Joe wants in a house. "A yard on the side and in back and in front too. Mature plantings. Inside, I think you'll like it." I've never been inside, of course. My info comes from the rap sheet. Though I may have driven past with an agents' cavalcade, in which case you can pretty well guess about the inside.

"It's just your shitty job to say that, Bascombe." Joe has never called me "Bascombe" before, and I don't like it. Joe, I notice, has the beginnings of an aggressive little goatee encircling his small red mouth, which makes it seem both smaller and redder, as though it served some different function. Joe's muscle shirt, I also see, has *Potters Do It With Their Fingers* stenciled on the front. It's clear he and Phyllis are suffering some pronounced personality and appearance alterations—not that unusual in advanced stages of house hunting.

I'm self-conscious peeking in the dark doorway with the warm, blustery storm breeze whipping at my backside. I wish Joe would just get the hell on with what we're all here for.

"D'you know what *I* want?" Joe's begun to fiddle for something on the table beside him—a package of generic cigarettes. As far as I know, Joe hasn't been a smoker until this morning. He lights up now though, using a cheap little plastic lighter, and blows a huge cloud of smoke into the dark. I'm certain Joe considers himself a ladies' man in this outfit.

"I thought you came down here to buy a house," I say.

"What I want is for reality to set in," Joe says in a smug voice, setting his lighter down. "I've been kidding myself about all this bullshit down here. The whole goddamn mess. I feel like my whole goddamn life has been in behalf of bullshit. I figured it out this morning while I was taking a dump. You don't get it, do you?"

"What's that?" Holding this conversation with Joe is like consulting a cut-rate oracle (something I in fact once did).

"You think your life's leading someplace, Bascombe. You *do* think that way. But I saw myself this morning. I closed the door to the head and there I was in the mirror, looking straight at myself in my most human moment in this bottom-feeder motel I wouldn't have taken a whore to when I was in college, just about to go look at some house I would never have wanted to live in in a hundred years. Plus, I'm taking a fucked-up job just to be able to afford it. That's something, isn't it? There's a sweet scenario."

"You haven't seen the house yet." I glance back and see that Phyllis has climbed into the back seat of my car before the rain starts but is staring at me through the windshield. She's worried Joe's scotching their last chance at a good house, which he may be.

Big, noisy splats of warm rain all at once begin thumping the car roof. The wind gusts up dirty. It is truly a bad day for a showing, since ordinary people don't buy houses in a rainstorm.

Joe takes a big, theatrical drag on his generic and funnels smoke expertly out his nostrils. "Is it a Haddam address?" he asks (ever a prime consideration).

I'm briefly bemused by Joe's belief that I'm a man who believes life's leading someplace. I *have* thought that way other times in life, but one of the fundamental easements of the Existence Period is not letting whether it is or whether it isn't worry you—as loony as that might be. "No," I say, recollecting myself. "It's not. It's in Penns Neck."

"I see." Joe's stupid half-bearded red mouth rises and lowers in the dark. "Penns Neck. I live in Penns Neck, New Jersey. What does that mean?"

"I don't know," I say. "Nothing, I guess, if you don't want it to."

(Or better yet if the bank doesn't want you to, or if you've got a mean Chapter 7 lurking in your portfolio, or a felony conviction, or too many late payments on your Trinitron, or happen to enjoy the services of a heart valve. In that case it's back to Vermont.) "I've shown you a lot of houses, Joe," I say, "and you haven't liked any of them. But I don't think you'd say I tried to force you into any of them."

"You don't offer advice, is that it?" Joe is still cemented to his lounge chair, where he obviously feels in a powerful command modality.

"Well. Shop around for a mortgage," I say. "Get a foundation inspection. Don't budget more than you can pay. Buy low, sell high. The rest isn't really my business."

"Right," Joe says, and smirks. "I know who pays your salary."

"You can always offer six percent less than asking. That's up to you. I'll still get paid, though."

Joe takes another drastic slag-down on his weed. "You know, I like to have a view of things from above," he says, absolutely mysteriously.

"Great," I say. Behind me, air is changing rapidly with the rain, cooling my back and neck as the front passes by. A sweet rain aroma envelops me. Thunder is rumbling over Route 1.

"You remember what I said when you first came in here?"

"You said something about reality setting in. That's all I remember." I'm staring at him impatiently through the murk, in his flip-flops and Mylar shorts. Not your customary house-hunting attire. I take a surreptitious look at my watch. Nine-thirty.

"I've completely quit becoming," Joe says, and actually smiles. "I'm not out on the margins where new discoveries take place anymore."

"I think that's probably too severe, Joe. You're not doing plasma research, you're just trying to buy a house. You know, it's my experience that it's when you don't think you're making progress that you're probably making plenty." This is a faith I in fact hold—the Existence Period notwithstanding—and one I plan to pass on to my son if I can ever get where he is, which at the moment seems out of the question.

"When I got divorced, Frank, and started trying to make pots up in East Burke, Vermont"—Joe crosses his short legs and cozies down authoritatively in his lounger—"I didn't have the foggiest idea about what I was doing. Okay? I was out of control, actually. But things just worked out. Same when Phyllis and I got together—just slammed into each other one day. But I'm not out of control any-more."

"Maybe you are more than you think, Joe."

"Nope. I'm *in* control way too much. That's the problem."

"I think you're confusing things you're already sure about, Joe. All this has been pretty stressful on you."

"But I'm on the verge of something here, I think. That's the important part."

"Of what?" I say. "I think you're going to find this Houlihan house pretty interesting." Houlihan is the owner of the Penns Neck property.

"I don't mean *that*." He pops both his chunky little fists on the plastic armrests. Joe may be verging on a major disorientation here—a legitimate rent in the cloth. This actually appears in text-books: Client abruptly begins to see the world in some entirely new way he feels certain, had he only seen it earlier, would've directed him down a path of vastly greater happiness—only (and this, of course, is the insane part) he inexplicably senses that way's still open to him; that the past, just this once, doesn't operate the way it usu-ally operates. Which is to say, irrevocably. Oddly enough, only home buyers in the low to middle range have these delusions, and for the most part all they bring about is trouble.

Joe suddenly bucks up out of his chair and goes slappety-slap through the dark little room, taking big puffs on his cigarette, look-ing into the bathroom, then crossing and peeping out between the curtains to where Phyllis waits in my car. He then turns like an undersized gorilla in a cage and stalks past the TV to the bathroom door, his back to me, and stares out the frosted, louvered window that reveals the dingy motel rear alley, where there's a blue garbage lugger, full to brimming with white PVC piping, which I sense Joe finds significant. Our talk now has the flavor of a hostage situation.

"What do you think you mean, Joe?" I say, because I detect that what he's looking for, like anybody on the skewers of dilemma, is *sanction*: agreement from beyond himself. A nice house he could both afford and fall in love with the instant he sees it could be a per-fect sanction, a sign some community recognizes him in the only way communities ever recognize anything: financially (tactfully expressed as a matter of compatibility).

"What I mean, Bascombe," Joe says, leaning against the door-jamb and staring pseudo-casually through the bathroom at the blue load lugger (the mirror where he's caught himself on the can must be just behind the door), "is that the reason we haven't bought a house in four months is that I don't *want* to goddamned buy one. And the reason for that is I don't want to get trapped in some shitty life I'll never get out of except by dying." Joe swivels toward me—a small, round man with hirsute butcher's arms and a little sorcerer's beard, who's come to the sudden precipice of what's left of life a little quicker than he knows how to cope with. It's not what I was hoping for, but anyone could appreciate his predicament.

"It *is* a big decision, Joe," I say, wanting to sound sympathetic. "If you buy a house, you own it. That's for sure."

"So are you giving up on me? Is that it?" Joe says this with a mean sneer, as if he's observed now what a shabby piece of realty dreck I am, only interested in the ones that sell themselves. He is probably indulging in the idyll of what it'd be like to be a realtor himself, and what superior genius strategies he'd choose to get his point across to a crafty, interesting, hard-nut-to-crack guy like Joe Markham. This is another well-documented sign, but a good one: when your client begins to see things as a realtor, half the battle's won.

My wish of course is that after today Joe will spend a sizable portion if not every minute of his twilight years in Penns Neck, NJ, and it's even possible he believes it'll happen, himself. My job, therefore, is to keep him on the rails—to supply sanction *pro tempore*, until I get him into a buy-sell agreement and cinch the rest of his life around him like a saddle on a bucking horse. Only it's not that simple, since Joe at the moment is feeling isolated and scared through no fault of anyone but him. So that what I'm counting on is the phenomenon by which most people will feel they're not being strong-armed if they're simply allowed to advocate (as stupidly as they please) the position opposite the one they're really taking. This is just another way we create the fiction that we're in control of anything.

"I'm not giving up on you, Joe," I say, feeling a less pleasant dampness on my back now and inching forward into the room. Traffic noise is being softened by the rain. "I just go about selling houses the way I'd want one sold to me. And if I bust my ass showing you property, setting up appointments, checking out this and that till I'm purple in the face, then you suddenly back out, I'll be ready to say you made the right decision if I believe it."

"Do you believe it this time?" Joe is still sneering, but not quite as much. He senses we're getting to the brassier tacks now, where I take off my realtor's hat and let him know what's right and what's wrong in the larger sphere, which he can then ignore.

"I sense your reluctance pretty plainly, Joe."

"Right," Joe says adamantly. "If you feel like you're tossing your life in the ter-let, why go through with it, right?"

"You'll have plenty more opportunities before you're finished."

"Yup," Joe says. I hazard another look toward Phyllis, whose mushroom head is in motionless silhouette inside my car. The glass has already fogged up from her heavy body exhalations. "These things aren't easy," he says, and tosses his stubby cigarette directly into the toilet he was no doubt referring to.

"If we're not going to do this, we better get Phyllis out of the car before she suffocates in there," I say. "I've got some other things to do today. I'm going away with my son for the holiday."

"I didn't know you had a son," Joe says. He, of course, has never asked me one question about me in four months, which is fine, since it's not his business.

"And a daughter. They live in Connecticut with their mother." I smile a friendly, not-your-business smile.

"Oh yeah."

"Let me get Phyllis," I say. "She'll need a little talking to by you, I think."

"Okay, but let me just ask one thing." Joe crosses his short arms and leans against the doorjamb, feigning even greater casualness. (Now that he's off the hook, he has the luxury of getting back on it of his own free and misunderstood will.)

"Shoot."

"What do you think's going to happen to the realty market?"

"Short term? Long term?" I'm acting ready to go.

"Let's say short."

"Short? More of the same's my guess. Prices are soft. Lenders are pretty retrenched. I expect it to last the summer, then rates'll probably bump up around ten-nine or so after Labor Day. Course, if one high-priced house sells way under market, the whole structure'll adjust overnight and we'll all have a field day. It's pretty much a matter of perception out there."

Joe stares at me, trying to act as though he's mulling this over and fitting his own vital data into some new mosaic. Though if he's smart he's also thinking about the cannibalistic financial forces gnashing and churning the world he's claiming he's about to march back into—instead of buying a house, fixing his costs onto a thirty-year note and situating his small brood behind its solid wall. "I see," he says sagely, nodding his fuzzy little chin. "And what about the long term?"

I take another stagy peek at Phyllis, though I can't see her now. Possibly she's started hitchhiking down Route 1 to Baltimore.

"The long term's less good. For you, that is. Prices'll jump after the first of the year. That's for sure. Rates'll spurt up. Property really doesn't go down in the Haddam area as a whole. All boats pretty much rise on a rising whatever." I smile at him blandly. In realty, all boats most certainly *do* rise on a rising whatever. But it's still being right that makes you rich.

Joe, I'm sure, has been brooding all over again this morning about his whopper miscues—miscues about marriage, divorce, remarriage, letting Dot marry a Hell's Commando, whether he should've quit teaching trig in Aliquippa, whether he should've joined the Marines and right now be getting out with a fat pension and qualifying for a VA loan. All this is a natural part of the aging process, in which you find yourself with less to do and more opportunities to eat your guts out regretting everything you *have* done. But Joe doesn't want to make another whopper, since one more big one might just send him to the bottom.

Except he doesn't know bread from butter beans about which is the fatal miscue and which is the smartest idea he ever had.

"Frank, I've just been standing here thinking," he says, and peers back out the dirty bathroom louvers as if he'd heard someone call his name. Joe may at this moment be close to deciding what he actually thinks. "Maybe I need a new way to look at things."

"Maybe you ought to try looking at things across a flat plain, Joe," I say. "I've always thought that looking at things from above, like you said, forced you to see all things as the same height and made decisions a lot harder. Some things are just bigger than others. Or smaller. And I think another thing too."

"What's that?" Joe's brows give the appearance of knitting together. He is vigorously trying to fit my "viewpoint" metaphor into his own current predicament of homelessness.

"It really won't hurt you to take a quick run over to this Penns Neck house. You're already down here. Phyllis is in the car, scared to death you're not going to look at it."

"Frank, what do you think about me?" Joe says. At some point of dislocatedness, this is what all clients start longing to know. Though it's almost always insincere and finally meaningless, since once their business is over they go right back to thinking you're either a crook or a moron. Realty is not a friendly business. It only seems to be.

"Joe, I may just queer my whole deal here," I say, "but what I think is you've done your best to find a house, you've stuck to your principles, you've put up with anxiety as long as you know how. You've acted responsibly, in other words. And if this Penns Neck house is anywhere close to what you like, I think you ought to take the plunge. Quit hanging onto the side of the pool."

"Yeah, but you're paid to think that, though," Joe says, sulky again in the bathroom door. "Right?"

But I'm ready for him. "Right. And if I can get you to spend a hundred and fifty on this house, then I can quit working and move to Kitzbühel, and you can thank me by sending me a bottle of good gin at Christmas because you're not freezing your nuts off in a barn while Sonja gets further behind in school and Phyllis files fucking divorce papers on you because you can't make up your mind."

"Point taken," Joe says, moodily.

"I really don't want to go into it any further," I say. There's no place further to go, of course, realty being not a very complex matter. "I'm going to take Phyllis on up to Penns Neck, Joe. And if she likes it we'll come get you and you can make up your mind. If she doesn't I'll bring her back anyway. It's a win-win proposition. In the meantime you can stay here and look at things from above."

Joe stares at me guiltily. "Okay, I'll just come along." He virtually blurts this out, having apparently blundered into the sanction he was looking for: the win-win, the sanction not to be an idiot. "I've come all this fucking way."

With my damp right arm I give a quick thumbs-up wave out to Phyllis, who I hope is still in the car.

Joe begins picking up change off the dresser top, stuffing a fat wallet into the tight waistband of his shorts. "I should let you and Phyllis figure this whole goddamn thing out and follow along like a goddamn pooch."

"You're still looking at things from above." I smile at Joe across the dark room.

"You just see everything from the fucking middle, that's all," Joe says, scratching his bristly, balding head and looking around the room as though he'd forgotten something. I have no idea what he means by this and am fairly sure he couldn't explain it either. "If I died right now, you'd go on about your business."

"What else should I do?" I say. "I'd be sorry I hadn't sold you a house, though. I promise you that. Because you at least could've died at home instead of in the Sleepy Hollow."

"Tell it to my widow out there," Joe Markham says, and stalks by me and out the door, leaving me to pull it shut and to get out to my car before I'm soaked to my toes. All this for the sake of what? A sale.

3

In my air-conditioned Crown Vic heading up Route 1 both Markhams sit, Joe in front, Phyllis in back, staring out at the rainy morning bustle and rush as though they were in a funeral cortege for a relative neither of them liked. Any rainy summer morning, of course, has the seeds of gloomy alienation sown in. But a rainy summer morning far from home—when your personal clouds don't move but hang—can easily produce the feeling of the world as seen from the grave. This I know.

My own view is that the realty dreads (which is what the Markhams have, pure and simple) originate not in actual house buying, which could just as easily be one of life's most hopeful optional experiences; or even in the fear of losing money, which is not unique to realty; but in the cold, unwelcome, built-in-America realization that we're just like the other schmo, wishing his wishes, lusting his stunted lusts, quaking over his idiot frights and fantasies, all of us popped out from the same unchinkable mold. And as we come nearer the moment of closing—when the deal's sealed and written down in a book in the courthouse—what we sense is that we're being tucked even deeper, more anonymously, into the weave of culture, and it's even less likely we'll make it to Kitzbühel. What we all want, of course, is all our best options left open as long as possible; we want not to have taken any obvious turns, but also not to have misread the correct turn the way some other boy-o would. As a unique strain of anxiety, it makes for a vicious three-way split that drives us all crazy as lab rats.

If I, for instance, were to ask the Markhams, staring stonily now at rain-drenched exurbia, cartage trucks and Mercedes wagons sluicing by, spewing water right into their mute faces—ask them if they were self-conscious about leaving homespun Vermont and copping an easier, more conventional life of curbs, reliable fire protection, garbage pickup three days a week, they'd be irate. *Jesus, no,* they'd shout. *We simply discovered we had some pretty damn unique needs that could only be met by some suburban virtues we'd never even heard about before.* (Good schools, malls, curbs, adequate fire protection, etc.) I'm sure, in fact, the Markhams feel like pioneers, reclaiming the suburbs from people (like me) who've taken them for granted for years and given them their bad name. Though I'd be surprised if the distaste they feel about being in the wagon with everybody else isn't teamed with the usual pioneer conservatism about not venturing *too* far—in this case toward a glut of too many cinemas, too-safe streets, too much garbage pickup, too-clean water—the suburban experiential ante raised to dizzier and dizzier heights.

My job—and I often succeed—is to draw them back toward a chummier feeling, make them less anxious both about the unknown *and* the obvious: the ways they're like their neighbors (all insignificant) and the happy but crucial ways they're not. When I fail at this task, when I sell a house but leave the buyers with an intact pioneer anxiety, it usually means they'll be out and on the road again in 3.86 years instead of settling in and letting time slip past the way people (that is, the rest of us) do who have nothing that pressing on their minds.

I turn off Route 1 onto NJ 571 at Penns Neck and hand Phyllis and Joe two fresh listing sheets so they can begin placing the Houlihan house into a neighborhood context. Neither of them has had much to say on the drive up—I assume they're letting their early-morning emotional bruises heal in silence. Phyllis has posed one question about "the radon problem," which she said was more serious than a lot of their Vermont neighbors would ever admit. Her blue, exophthalmic eyes grew hooded, as if radon was only one item in a Pandora's box of North-country menace and grimness she'd grown prematurely old worrying about. Among them: asbestos in the school heating system, heavy metals in the well water, B. coli bacteria, wood smoke, hydrocarbons, rabid foxes, squirrels, voles, plus cluster flies, black ice, frozen mud—the wilderness experience up the yin-yang.

I, however, assured her radon wasn't a big problem in central New Jersey, owing to our sandy-loamy soil, and most people I knew had had their houses "crawled" and sealed around 1981, when the last scare swept through.

Joe has had even less to say. As we neared the 571 turnoff he peered back once through his side mirror at the streaming roadway behind and asked in a mumbling voice where Penns Neck *was*. "It's in the Haddam area," I said, "but across Route 1 nearer the train line, which is a plus."

He was silent for a while, then said, "I don't want to live in an area."

"You don't what?" Phyllis said. She was leafing through the green-jacketed *Self-Reliance* I have brought along for Paul (my old, worn, individually bound copy from college).

"The Boston area, the tristate area, the New York area. Nobody ever said the Vermont area, or the Aliquippa area," Joe said. "They just said the places."

"Some people said the Vermont area," Phyllis answered, flipping pages smartly.

"The D.C. area," Joe said as a reproach. Phyllis said nothing. "Chicagoland," Joe continued. "The Metro area. The Dallas area."

"I guess you have to chalk it up to perception again," I said, passing the little metal Penns Neck sign, which looked like a license plate, nearly hidden by some clumpy yew trees. "We're in Penns Neck now," I said, though no one answered.

Penns Neck is not in fact much of a town, much less an area: a few tidy, middle-rank residential streets situated on either side of busy 571, which connects the serenely tree-studded and affluent groves of nearby Haddam with the gradually sloping, light-industrial, overpopulous coastal plain where housing is abundant and affordable but the Markhams aren't interested. In decades past, Penns Neck would've boasted a spruced-up, Dutchy-Quakery village character, islanded by fertile cornfields, well-tended stone walls, maple and hickory farmsteads teeming with wildlife. Only now it's become just one more aging bedroom community for other larger, newer bedroom communities, in spite of the fact that its housing stock has withstood modernity's rush, leaving it with an earnest old-style-suburban appeal. There is, however, no intact town center left, only a couple of at-home antique shops, a lawn-mower repair and a gas station–deli hard by the state road. The town office (I've checked into this) has actually been moved to the next town down Route 1 and into a mini-mall. At the Haddam Realty Board I've heard the sentiment bruited that the state should unincorporate Penns Neck and drop it onto the county tax rolls, which would sweeten the rates. In the past three years I've sold two houses here, though both families have since departed for better jobs in upstate New York.

But in truth I'm showing the Markhams a Penns Neck house not because I think it'll be the house they've waited for me to show them all along, but because what's here is what they can afford and because I think they may be dejected enough to buy it.

Once we turn left off 571 onto narrow Friendship Lane, pass a series of intersecting residential streets to the north, ending up at Charity Street, the beating-whomping hum of Route 1 traffic fades out of earshot and the silken, seamless ambience of quiet houses all in neat, close rows amid tall trees, nice-ish shrubberies and edged lawns with morning sprinklers hissing, plus no overnight parking— all this begins to fill the space that worry likes to occupy.

The Houlihan house, at 212 Charity, is forthright and not even so little, a remodeled gable-roofed American farmhouse set back on a shaded and shrubbed double lot among some old hardwoods and younger pines, farther from the street than any of its neighbors, and also elevated enough in its siting to suggest it once meant more than it means now. It has, in fact, the nicer, larger, slightly out-of-place look of having been the "original farmhouse" when all this was nothing but cow pastures and farmland, and pheasants and unrabid foxes coursed the turnip rows and real estate meant zip. It also has a new bright-green shingled roof, a solid-looking brick front stoop, and white wooden siding a generation older but of more or less the same material as the other houses on the street, which are smaller one-storey, design-book ranches with attached pole garages and little concrete walks straight to the curb, where mailboxes are posted house after house after house.

But here—and to my complete surprise, since I see I've, in fact, never seen it before—here might be the house the Markhams have been hoping for; the fabled long-shot house, the one I'd never shown them, the little Cape set too far back, with too many trees, the old caretaker's cottage from the once-grand manor now gone, a place requiring "imagination," a place no other clients could quite "visualize," a house with "a story" or "a ghost," but which might have a *je-ne-sais-quoi* attraction for a couple as amusingly offbeat as the Markhams. (Again, such houses do exist. They've usually just been retrofitted into single-practice laser-gynecological clinics run by doctors with Costa Rican M.D.'s and are most often found along older, major thoroughfares and not in actual neighborhoods in towns like Penns Neck.)

Our "Lauren-Schwindell Exclusive" sign is staked out front on the sloping lawn with *Julie Loukinen*, the listing agent's name, dangling from the bottom. The grass has been newly trimmed, shrubbery pruned, the driveway swept clear to the back. There are lights inside, glowing humidly in the post-storm gloom. A car, an older Merc, sits in the driveway, and the door behind the front screen is standing open (aka no central air). This could be Julie's car, though we haven't planned to show the house as a team, so that it probably belongs to owner Houlihan, who (I've arranged this with Julie) is right now supposed to be eating a late breakfast at Denny's courtesy of me.

The Markhams sit silent, noses first in their listing sheets then to the windows. This has often been the point when Joe announces he's seen quite enough.

"Is that it?" Phyllis says.

"It's our sign," I say, turning in the driveway and pulling up halfway. Rain has stopped now. Beyond the old Merc, at the end of the drive behind the house, a detached wooden garage is visible, plus an enticing angle-slice of green from the shaded back yard. No crime bars are on any windows or doors.

"What's the heating?" Joe—veteran Vermonter—says, squinting out the windshield, his listing sheet in his lap.

"Circulating hot water, electric baseboards in the den," I say verbatim from the same sheet.

"How old?"

"Nineteen twenty-four. Not in the floodplain, and the side lot's buildable if you ever want to sell or add on."

Joe casts a dark frown of ecological betrayal at me, as if the very idea of parceling off vacant lots was a crime of rain-forest-type gravity which no one should even be allowed to conceptualize. (He himself would more than conceptualize it if he ever needed the money, or were getting divorced. I of course conceptualize it all the time.)

"It has a nice front yard," I say. "Shade's your hidden asset."

"What kind of trees?" Joe says, scowling and concentrating on the side yard.

"Let's see," I say, leaning and looking out past his thick, hair-matte chest. "One's a copper beech. That one's a split-leaf maple, I'd say. One's a sugar maple—which you should like. There's a red oak. And one may be a ginkgo. It's a good mix soilwise."

"Ginkgoes stink," Joe says, fixed in his seat, as is Phyllis, neither one offering to get out. "What's it border on the back side?"

"We'll need to look at that," I say, though of course I know.

"Is that the owner?" Phyllis says, looking out.

A figure has come to the door and is rubbernecking from behind the shadowy screen: a man—not large—in a shirt and tie with no jacket. I'm not sure he even sees us.

"We'll just have to find that out," I say, hoping not, but easing the car a notch farther up the drive before shutting it off and immediately opening my door to the summer heat.

*O*nce out, Phyllis steams right up the walk, moving with the same wobble-gaited unwieldiness as before, toes slightly out, arms working, intent on loving as much as possible before Joe can weigh in with the bad news.

Joe, though, in his silver shorts, flip-flops and pathetic muscle shirt, hangs back with me, then stops stock-still on the walk to survey the lawn, the street and the neighboring houses, which are Fifties constructions and cheaper, but with fewer maintenance worries and more modest, less burdensome lawns. The Houlihans' is in fact the nicest house on the street, which can become a scratchy price issue with an experienced buyer but probably will not be today.

I have grabbed my clipboard and put on my red nylon windbreaker from the back seat. The jacket has the Lauren-Schwindell *Societas Progressioni Commissa* crest on the breast and a big white stenciled REALTOR across the back, like an FBI agent's. I'm wearing it today in spite of the heat and humidity to get a point across to the Markhams: I'm not their friend; it's business, not a hobby; there's something at issue. Time's a-wastin'.

"It ain't Vermont, is it?" Joe muses as we stand side by side in the last drippy moments of the morning's wet weather. This is exactly what he's said at similar moments outside any number of other houses in the last four months, though he probably doesn't remember. And what he means is: *Well, fuck this. If you can't show me Ver-*

mont, then why the hell are you showing me a goddamned thing? After which, often before Phyllis has even made it to the front door, we've turned around and left. This is why Phyllis caught fire to get inside. I, however, am frankly glad just to get Joe out of the car and this far, no matter what his objections might later be.

"It's New Jersey, Joe," I say as always. "And it's pretty nice, too. You got tired of Vermont."

Which has usually prompted Joe to say ruefully, "Yeah, and what a stupid fuck I am." Only this time he says "Yeah" and looks at me soulfully, his little flat brown irises gone flatter, as if some essential lambency has droozled out and he has faced certain facts.

"That's not a net loss," I say, zipping my jacket halfway up and feeling my toes, damp from standing in the rain back at the Sleepy Hollow. "You don't have to buy this house." Which is a hell of a thing for a realtor to say, instead of: "You goddamn *do* have to buy it. It's God's patent will that you buy it. He'll be furious at you if you don't. Your wife'll leave you and take your daughter to Garden Grove and enroll her in an Assembly of God school, and you'll never see her again if you don't buy this son of a bitch by lunchtime." Yet what I go on airily to say is: "You can always head back to Island Pond tonight and be there in time to watch the crows come home to roost."

Joe is not susceptible to other people's witticisms and looks up at me strangely (I'm a few inches taller than he is, though he's a little bullock). He clearly starts to say one thing in one tone of voice (sarcastic, without doubt), then just lets it go and stares out at the unpretentious row of hip-roofed, frame-with-brick-facade houses (some *with* crime bars), all built when he was a teenager, and where now, across Charity Street at 213, a young, shockingly red-haired woman—brighter red even than Phyllis's—is pushing a big black-plastic garbage-can-on-wheels to the curb for the last pickup before the 4th.

The woman is obviously a young mom, in blue jeans cut off midthigh, sockless tennies and a blue work shirt sloppily but calculatedly cinched in a Marilyn Monroe knot just below her breasts. When she squares her plastic can up beside her mailbox, she looks at us and waves a cheery, careless wave that means she knows who we are—new-neighbor candidates, more lively maybe than the current owner.

I wave back, but Joe doesn't. Possibly he is thinking about seeing things across a flat plain.

"I was just thinking as we were driving over here . . . ," he says, watching young Marilyn flounce back up the driveway and disappear into an empty carport. A door closes, a screen slams. " . . . that wherever you took us today was going to be where I was going to live for the rest of my life." (I was right.) "A decision almost entirely in other people's hands. And that in fact my judgment's no good anymore." (Joe hasn't tumbled to my telling him he didn't have to buy this place.) "I don't know what the hell's the right thing anymore. All I do is hold out as long as I can in hopes the really fucked-up choices will start to *look* fucked up, and I'll be saved at least that much. You know what I mean?"

"I guess so." I can hear Phyllis yakking inside, introducing herself to whoever was at the front door—not, I still hope, Houlihan himself. I would like to get inside, but I can't leave Joe here under the dripping oaks in a brown study whose net yield might be double-decker despair and a botched chance at an offer.

Across in 213, the redhead we've watched suddenly whips open the draw drapes in a far-end bedroom window. I see only her head, but she is watching us brazenly. Joe is still lost in his bad-judgment funk.

"The other day Phyl and Sonja were off in Craftsbury," he says, somberly, "and I got on the phone and called a woman I used to know. Just called her up. Out in Boise. I had a little—really a not so little—thing with her after my first marriage went south. Just before that happened, actually. She's a potter too. Makes finished-looking stuff she sells to Nordstrom's. And after we'd talked a while, just past events and whatnot, she said she had to get off the phone and wanted to know my number. But when I told her she laughed. She said, 'God, Joe, there were a whole lot of pay-phone numbers for you in my book, but none of the *M*'s are you now.' " Joe stuffs his little hands up under his damp armpits and ponders this, staring in the direction of 213.

"She didn't mean anything by that," I say, still wanting to get a move on. Phyllis has not gone much farther than inside the door yet. I can hear her sing-songy voice exclaiming that everything in sight's the nicest she ever saw. "You probably ended it on a good note way back then, didn't you? Otherwise you wouldn't have called her."

"Oh, absolutely." Joe's little goatee works first this way and then that, as if he is double-checking his memory on all counts. "No blood let. Ever. But I really thought she'd call me later to say we needed to get together—which I was willing to do, to be honest. This house-buying business pushes you to extremes." Willing-wife-deceiver Joe looks at me importantly.

"Right," I say.

"But she never called. At least I never knew if she did." He nods, still staring across at 213, which is painted a not very bright green on the wood above the brick and has a faded red front door no one ever uses. The bedroom curtain zips closed. Joe hasn't been paying attention there. Some somnolent quality in the moment or the place or the misty rain or the distant rumble of Route 1 has rendered him unexpectedly capable of thinking a whole thought through.

"I don't think it's that meaningful, though, Joe," I say.

"And I don't even care a goddamned thing about this woman," he says. "If she'd called me and said she was flying out to Burlington and wanted to meet me in a Holiday Inn and fuck me to death, I'd have most likely begged off." Joe is not aware he has contradicted himself inside of a minute.

"Maybe she just figured that out and decided to let it go herself. Saved you the trouble."

"But I'm just struck about my judgment," Joe says sadly. "I was sure she'd call. That's all. It was something *she* did, not something I did, or was even right about. Everything happened without me. Just like what's going on here."

"Maybe you'll like this house," I say lamely. The big front picture-window curtain at 213 now goes slashing back, and young red-haired Marilyn is standing in the middle, fixing us with what seems to me from here to be an accusing frown, as if whatever she took us for was making her mad enough to flash us the evil eye.

"You must've had this happen." Joe looks toward me but not at me, in fact, looks right straight back over my left shoulder, which is his usual and most comfortable mode of address. "We're the same age. You've been divorced. Had lots of women."

"We need to go on inside, Joe," I say. Though I am sympathetic. Not trusting your judgment—and, worse, *knowing* you shouldn't trust it for some damn substantial reasons—can be one of the major causes and also one of the least tolerable ongoing features of the

Existence Period, one you have to fine-tune out by the use of caution. "But let me just try to say this to you." I cross my hands in front of my fly, holding my clipboard down there like an insurance adjuster. "When I got divorced, I was sure things had all happened *to* me and that I hadn't really acted and was probably a coward and at least an asshole. Who knows if I was right? But I made one promise to myself, and that was that I'd never complain about my life, and just go on and try to do my best, mistakes and all, since there's only so much anybody can do to make things come out right, judgment or no judgment. And I've kept my promise. And I don't think you're the kind of guy to fashion a life by avoiding mistakes. You make choices and live with them, even if you don't feel like you've chosen a damn thing." Joe may think, and I hope he does, that I've paid him a compliment of the rarest kind for being untranslatable.

His little bristle-mouth again makes a characteristic O, which he is totally oblivious to, his eyes going narrow as razor cuts. "Sounds like you're telling me to shut up."

"I just want us to have a look at this house so you and Phyllis can think about what you want to do. And I don't want you to worry about making a mistake before you even have a chance to make one."

Joe shakes his head, sneers, then sighs—a habit I intensely dislike, and for that reason I hope he buys the Houlihan house and discovers an eyelash too late that it's sitting over a sinkhole. "My profs at Duquesne always said I overintellectualized too much." He sneers again.

"That's what I was trying to suggest," I say, just as the flame-haired woman in 2 1 3 whisks across the picture-window space, north to south, totally in the buff, a big protuberant pair of white breasts leading the way, her arms out Isadora Duncan style, her good, muscular legs leaping and striding like a painting on an antique urn. "Wow, look at that," I say. Joe, though, has shaken his head again over what a brainy guy he is, chuckled and ambled on off, and is already mounting the steps of what might be his last home on earth. Though what he's just missed is a neighbor's neighborly way of letting the prospective buyer know what he's getting into out here, and frankly it's a sight that causes my estimation of Penns Neck to go up and off the charts. It has mystery and the unexpected as its hidden assets—much better than shade—and Joe, had he seen it, might also have seen where his own interests lay and known exactly what to do.

Stepping inside the little arched front foyer, I can hear Phyllis far in the back already having an important-sounding conversation about gypsy moths, and about what her recent experience has been in Vermont. She is having this, I feel sure, with Ted Houlihan, who shouldn't be here haunting his own house, badgering the shit out of my clients, satisfying himself they're the kind of "solid" (meaning white) folks he'll be comfortable passing his precious fee simple on to.

All the table lamps have been turned on. The floors are shiny, ashtrays cleaned, radiator tops dusted, floor moldings scrubbed, doorknobs polished. A welcome waxy smell deodorizes all—a sound selling strategy for creating the illusion that nobody actually lives here.

Joe, without even offering to greet the owner, goes right into his inspection modality, which he conducts with a brusque and speechless air of military thoroughness. In his smushed-pecker shorts, he takes a quick turn through the living room, which contains mint-condition Fifties couches, sturdy upholstered wing chairs, polished end tables, a sky-blue area rug and some elderly, store-bought prints of bird dogs, parrots in trees and lovers by a peaceful sylvan lake. He leans into the dining room, scans its heavy, polished eight-piece mahogany table-and-chairs ensemble. His beady eyes survey the crown moldings, the chair rails, the swinging kitchen door. He twists the rheostat, brightening then dimming the pink salad-bowl globe, then turns and heads back through the living room and down the central hall, where lights are also on and there's a security panel with a keypad of oversized cartoon numbers, friendly to older users. With me right behind, Joe strides slappety-slap into each bedroom, takes an unimpressed look around, slides open then closed a closet door, mentally adds up the number of grounded wall sockets, steps to the window, takes in the view, gives each window a little lift to determine if it's hung correctly or painted shut, then makes for the bathrooms.

In the pink-tiled master bath, he goes for the sink, twists on both taps full blast and waits, assessing the flow, how long the hot takes, how efficiently the drain drains. He flushes the toilet and stares at the bowl to time the "retrieval." In the "little" bath he raises the thin, new-style venetian blinds and stares out again at the park-like yard, as though contemplating the peaceful vista he would have *après le bain* or during another prolonged nature call. (Once a client, an eminent German economist from one of the local think tanks, actually dropped trou and plopped down for a real test.)

During all such inspections, over nearly four months, and with me in attendance, Joe has stopped looking the instant he recorded three major demerits: too few sockets, more than two squishy floorboards, any unrepaired ceiling water stain, any kind of crack or odd wall angle indicating settling or "pulling away." Customarily he has also spoken very little, making only infrequent, undesignated hums. In one split-level in Pennington, he wondered out loud about the possibility of undetected root damage from an older linden tree planted close to the foundation; another time, in Haddam, he mumbled the words "lead-based paint" as he strode through a daylight basement, checking for seepage. In each case no response was asked from me, since he'd already found plenty not to like, starting with the price, which he later said, in both instances, indicated the owners needed to have their heads uncorked from their asses.

When Joe makes his plunge into the basement (where I'm happy not to go), flipping the light switch on at the top and then off again at the bottom, I take my opportunity to wander back where Phyllis stands with, indeed, Ted Houlihan at the glass door to the back yard. Here, an afterthought rumpus room *cum* live-in kitchen gives pleasingly onto a neat brick patio surrounded by luau torches, viewable through a big picture window (a neighborhood staple) that also exhibits some seepage discoloration around its frame—a defect Joe won't miss if he gets this far.

Ted Houlihan is a recently widowed engineer, not long retired from the R & D division of a nearby kitchen appliance firm. He is a sharp-eyed little white-haired seventy-plus-year-old, in faded chinos, penny loafers, an old short-sleeved, nicely frayed blue oxford shirt and a blue-and-red rep tie, and looks like the happiest man in Penns Neck. (He looks, in fact, eerily like the old honey-voiced chorister Fred Waring, who was a favorite of mine in the Fifties but in private was a martinet and a bully despite having an old softy's reputation.)

Ted gives me a big sincere back-over-his-shoulder smile when I arrive in my REALTOR windbreaker. It is our first meeting, and he would make me happy if he'd take this opportunity to head for Denny's. Noisy *boom, boom, boom* racketing has begun below-floors, as if Joe were breaking through the foundation with a sledgehammer.

"I was just about to explain to Mrs. Markham, Mr. Bascombe," Ted Houlihan says as we shake hands—his is small and tough as a walnut, mine pulpy and for some reason damp. "I've been diagnosed with testicular cancer here just last month, and I've got a son out in Tucson who's a surgeon, and he's going to do the operation himself. I'd sort of been mulling over selling for months, but just decided yesterday enough was enough." (Which it certainly is.)

Phyllis (and who wouldn't?) has reacted to this cancer news with a look of pale distress. No doubt it puts her in mind of her own problems—which is reason # fourteen to keep owners miles away from clients: they inevitably heave murky, irresolvable personal issues into the sales arena, often making my job all but impossible.

Though unless I'm way off, Phyllis is already well dazzled and charmed by everything. The back yard is a grassy little mini-Watteau, with carpets of deep-green pachysandra ringing the large trees. Rhodies, wisterias and peonies are set out all over everywhere. A good-size Japanese rock garden containing a little toy maple has been artfully situated under a big dripping oak that looks thoroughly robust and in no danger of falling over into the house. Plus, against the side of the garage is an actual pergola, clustered all over with dense, ropy grapevines and honeysuckle, with a little rustic English-looking iron settee placed underneath like a wedding bower—just the setting for renewing your sacred oaths on a clear late-summer's evening, followed by some ardent alfresco love-making.

"I was just saying to Mr. Houlihan what a lovely yard it is," Phyllis says, recovering herself and smiling a little dazedly at the thought of the man in front of her having his nuts snipped by his own son. Joe has stopped banging on whatever he was banging on downstairs, though I hear other metal-to-metal scraping and prying coming up through the floorboards.

"I've got a bunch of old pictures someplace of the house and the yard back in 1955 when we bought it. My wife thought it was the prettiest place she'd ever seen *then*. There was a farmer's field and a big stone silo out back and a cow lot and a milk parlor." Ted points a leathery finger toward the back property line, where there's a thick tropical-bamboo stand backed by a high plank fence painted the exact same shade of unnoticeably dark green. The fence continues in both directions behind the next-door neighbors' houses until it goes out of sight.

"What's back there, now?" Phyllis says. She has the look of "this is the one, this is the place" written all over her flushed, puffy face. Joe is currently clumping up the basement steps, his excavations and explorings now complete. I picture him as a miner in a metal-cage elevator rising miles and miles out of the deep Pennsylvania earth, his face caked, his eye sockets white, a bunged-up lunch pail under his ham-hock arm and a dim beacon light on his helmet. I am betting the next thing Ted Houlihan says isn't going to faze Phyllis Markham one iota.

"Oh, the state put its little facility back there," Ted Houlihan says genially. "Though they're pretty good neighbors."

"What kind of facility?" Phyllis says, smiling.

"Mmm. It's a little minimum security unit," Ted says. "It's just one of these country clubs. Nothing serious."

"For what?" Phyllis says, still happy. "What kind of security?"

"For you and me, I guess," Ted says, and looks over at me. "Isn't that right, Mr. Bascombe?"

"It's the State of New Jersey's minimum security facility," I say chummily. "It's where they put the mayor of Burlington, and bankers, and ordinary people like Ted and me. And Joe." I smile a little co-conspirator's smile.

"*It's* back there?" Phyllis says. Her eyes find Joe, who has emerged from down under—no coal-dust tan or headlamp or lunchbox, just his flip-flops, jersey shirt and shorts with his wallet stuck in his belt—come in to be cordial. He's seen some things he likes and is thinking about possibilities. "Did you hear what Frank said?" Her full and curvaceous mouth shows a slight sign of stiffening concern. For some reason she puts her palm flat on top of her bobbed red hair and blinks, as though she were holding something down inside her skull.

"I missed it," Joe says, rubbing his hands together. There is in fact a black dust smudge on his naked shoulder, where he's been rooting around. He looks happily at the three of us—his first on-record pleased expression in weeks. He again makes no effort to introduce himself to Ted.

"There's a prison behind that fence." Phyllis points out the picture window, across the little spruced-up lawn.

"Is that right?" Joe says, still smiling. He sort of ducks so he can see out the window. "What's that mean?" He has yet to notice the seepage.

"There's criminals in cells behind the back yard," Phyllis says. She looks at Ted Houlihan and tries to seem agreeable, as if this were just an irksome little sticking point to be worked out as a contingency in a contract ("Owner agrees to remove state prison on or before date of closing"). "Isn't that right," she asks, her blue eyes larger and intenser than usual.

"Not really cells, per se," Ted says, thoroughly relaxed. "It's more like a campus atmosphere—tennis courts, swimming pools, college classes. You can attend classes there yourself. A good many of the residents go home on weekends. I really wouldn't call it a prison."

"That's interesting," Joe Markham says, nodding out at the bamboo curtain and the green plank wall behind it. "You can't really see it, can you?"

"Did you know about this?" Phyllis says to me, still agreeable.

"Absolutely," I say, sorry to be involved. "It's on the listing sheet." I scan down my page. "Adjoins state land on north property line."

"I thought that meant something else," Phyllis says.

"I've actually never even been over there," Ted Houlihan says, Mr. Upbeat. "They have their own fence behind ours, which you can't see. And you never hear a sound. Bells or sirens or anything. They do have nice chimes on Christmas Day. I know the gal across the street works there. It's the biggest employer in Penns Neck."

"I just think it might be a problem for Sonja," Phyllis says quietly to everyone.

"I don't think there's a threat to anything or anyone," I say, thinking about Marilyn Monroe across the way, strapping on her hogleg and heading off to work every morning. What must the prisoners think? "I mean, Machine Gun Kelly's not in there. It's probably just people we all voted for and will again." I smile around, thinking this might be a correct time for Ted to walk us through his own security setup.

"We've come up quite a bit in value since they built it," Ted says. "The rest of the area—including Haddam, I should say—has lost some ground. I feel like I'm probably really leaving at the wrong time." He gives all three of us a sad-but-foxy Fred Waring grin.

"You're sure leaving a goddamned good house, I'll just tell you that," Joe says self-importantly. "I had a look at the floor joists and the sills. They don't cut 'em that wide anymore, except in Vermont." He gives Phyllis a narrow-eyed, approving frown meant to announce he's found a house he likes even if Alcatraz is next door. Joe has turned a corner now—a mysterious transit no man can chart for another. "The pipes and the wiring are all copper. The sockets are all three-prongs. You don't see that in an older home." Joe stares at Ted Houlihan almost irritably. I'm sure he would like to dope out the entire house plan in detail.

"My wife liked everything up to code," Ted says, a little sheepish.

"Where's she now?" Joe has the listing sheet out and is giving it a good perusing.

"She's dead," Ted says, and lets his gaze for an instant slip out to his bosky lawn to glide among the white peonies and yew shrubs, up under the pergola and through the wisterias. A little glistening and chartless passage has been glimpsed open and he's wandered in, and there is a golden cornfield beyond, and he and the missus are in their wondrous primes. (It is not foreign ground to me, this passage, though under my strict rules of existence it opens but rarely.)

Joe is running his stubby finger and snapping eyes over some listing sheet fine points, undoubtedly pertaining to "extras" and "rm sz," and "schls." Noting the "sq ftge" for his new work space. He is house-buying Joe now, death on the scent of a good deal.

"Joe, you asked Mr. Houlihan about his wife, and she's dead," Phyllis says.

"Hm?" Joe says.

"She's lying right there in the kitchen floor, bleeding out her ears, in fact." I'd like to say this in old reverie-lost Ted's defense, but I don't.

"Oh yeah, I know, I'm sorry to know that," Joe says. He holds the listing sheet down and frowns at Phyllis and me and lastly at Ted Houlihan, as if we'd all been shouting at him "She's dead, she's dead, you asshole, she's dead," while he's been sound asleep. "I am, I really am," he says. "When did this happen?" Joe gives me a look of incredulity.

"Two years ago," Ted says, back from the past and regarding Joe kindly. His is an honest face of life's sad dwindling. Joe shakes his head as if there were things in life you just couldn't explain.

"Let's see the rest of the house," Phyllis says, weary with letdown. "I'd still like to see it."

"You bet," I say.

"I am *very* interested in the house," Joe says to no one. "It's got a lot of features I like. I really do."

"I'll stay with Mr. Markham here," Ted Houlihan says, still unintroduced. "Let's go out and have a look at the garage." He opens the glass door to the sweet, past-besotted yard, while Phyllis and I head moodily back into the house for what, I'm afraid, will now be only a hollow formality.

*P*hyllis, as expected, takes only polite interest, barely poking her head into the staid little bedrooms and baths, taking pleasant but brief notice of the plastic-decor laundry hampers and pink cotton bath mats, emitting an occasional "I see" or "That's nice" toward a tub-and-shower that looks brand-new. Once she murmurs, "I haven't seen that in years," toward a phone nook built into the end of the hall.

"It's been taken care of," she says, standing in the front foyer but stealing a look through to the back to where Joe is now out by the bamboo wall, short arms crossed, listing sheet in hand, jawing with Ted in a pool of midmorning sunlight. She would like to leave. "I liked it so much at first," she says, turning to gaze out the front, where sexy Marilyn-the-prison-guard's garbage can waits at the curb.

"My advice is just to think about it," I say, sounding insipid even to myself. My job, though, is to place a light finger on the scale of judgment when I sense the moment requires, when a potential buyer has a gold-plated chance to make herself happy by becoming an owner. "What I wonder about, Phyllis, when I sell a house is whether a client's getting his or her money's worth." I say this as I feel it—truly. "You might think I'd wonder about whether he or she gets their dream house, or if they get the house they originally wanted. Getting your money's worth, though, getting value, is frankly more important—particularly in the current economy. When the correction comes, value will be what things stand on. And in this house"—I cast a theatrical look around and up at the ceiling as if that was where value generally staked its pennant—"in this house I think you've got the value." And I do. (My windbreaker is beginning to stoke up inside, but I don't want to take it off just yet.)

"I don't want to live next door to a prison," Phyllis says almost pleadingly, and walks to the screen and looks out, her pudgy hands stuffed in her culotte pockets. (It may be she is attempting one simulated act of ownership—the innocent pause of an everyday to stare out a front door—trying to feel where the "catch" comes and *if* it comes, the needling thought that somewhere nearby's a TV-room full of carefree tax cheats, randy priests and scheming pension-fund CEOs who are her leering neighbors, and whether that's as intolerable as she's thought.)

Phyllis shakes her head, as if an unsavory taste had just been located. "I always felt I was a liberal. But I guess I'm not," she says. "I think there ought to be these types of institutions for certain types of criminals, but I shouldn't have to live next to one and raise my daughter there."

"We're all a little less flexible as we get older," I say. I should tell her about Clair Devane being murdered in a condo, and me being bopped to the pavement by larking Orientals. A convenient good-neighbor prison wouldn't be all that bad.

I hear Joe and Ted laugh like Rotarians out back, Joe going "Ho-ho-ho." A greasy, gassy fragrance has wafted out from the kitchen, supplanting the clean, furniture-wax smell. (I'm surprised Joe could've missed it.) Ted and his wife may have mooned around here half gassed and happy as goats for decades, never knowing quite why.

"What do you do about your testicles? Is that bad?" Phyllis says, still solemn.

"I'm not much of an expert," I say. I need to haul Phyllis back from life's darker corridor, where she seems to be venturing, and push us on to the more positive aspects of close-by prison living.

"I was just thinking about getting old." Phyllis gives her little mushroom top a one-finger scratching. "And how fucked up it is." She, for this moment, is seeing all God's children as a dying breed (possibly the gas leak is responsible), killed off not by disease but by

MRIs, biopsies, sonograms and cold, blunt instruments unsoothingly entered into our most unwelcoming recesses. "I guess I have to have a hysterectomy," she says, facing the front yard but speaking serenely. "I haven't even told Joe yet."

"I'm sorry to hear that," I say, unclear whether that's the correct and wished-for sympathy.

"Yeah. So. Ho-hum," she says sadly, her wide backside to me. She may be dousing tears. But I'm frozen in my saddle. A less advertised part of the realtor's job is overcoming natural client morbidity—the quickening, queasy realization that by buying a house you're taking over someone else's decays and lurking problems, troubles you'll be responsible for till doomsday and that do nothing more than replace troubles of your own, old ones you've finally gotten used to. There are tricks of the trade to deal with this sort of recoil: stressing value (I just did it); stressing workmanship (Joe did that); stressing an older home's longevity, its being finished with settling pains, blah, blah, blah (Ted did exactly that); stressing general economic insecurity (I did that in my editorial this morning and will see that Phyllis gets a copy by sundown).

Only for Phyllis's particular distress and dismay I have no antidote, except to wish for a kinder world. It hardly counts.

"The whole country seems in a mess to me, Frank. We really can't afford to live in Vermont, if you want to know the truth. But now we can't live down here either. And with my health concerns, we need to put down some roots." Phyllis sniffs, as if the tears she's been fighting have retreated. "I'm riding a hormonal roller coaster today. I'm sorry. I just see everything black."

"I don't think things are that bad, Phyllis. I think, for instance, this is a good house with good value, just the way I've said, and you and Joe would be happy here, and so would Sonja, and you'd never worry about your neighbors at all. No one knows his neighbors in the suburbs anyway. It's not like Vermont." I peek down at my listing sheet to see if there's anything new and diverting I can stress: "fplc," "gar/cpt," "lndry," priced right at 155K. Solid value considerations but nothing to bring the hormonal roller coaster into the station.

I gaze in puzzlement at her ill-defined posterior and have a sudden, fleeting curiosity about, of all things, her and Joe's sex life. Would it be jolly and jokey? Prayerful and restrained? Rowdy, growling and obstreperous? Phyllis has an indefinite milky allure that is not always obvious—encased and bundled as she is, and slightly bulge-eyed in her fitless, matron-designer clothes—some yielding, unmaternal *abundance* that could certainly get a rise out of some lonely PTA dad in corduroys and a flannel shirt, encountered by surprise in the chilly intimacy of the grade-school parking lot after parents' night.

The truth is, however, we know little and can find out precious little more about others, even though we stand in their presence, hear their complaints, ride the roller coaster with them, sell them houses, consider the happiness of their children—only in a flash or a gasp or the slam of a car door to see them disappear and be gone forever. Perfect strangers.

And yet, it is one of the themes of the Existence Period that interest can mingle successfully with uninterest in this way, intimacy with transience, caring with the obdurate uncaring. Until very recently (I'm not sure when it stopped) I believed this was the *only* way of the world; maturity's balance. Only more things seem to need sorting out now: either in favor of complete uninterest (ending things with Sally might be an example) or else going whole hog (not ending things with Sally might be another example).

"You know, Frank . . ." Her misty moment past, Phyllis has walked by me into the Houlihans' living room, stepped to the front window beside a little leafed butler's table and, just like the redhead across the street, pulled open the drapes, letting in a warm, mid-morning light, which defeats the room's funeral stillness by causing its fussy couches and feminine mint dishes, its antimacassars and polished knickknacks (all of which Ted has left sentimentally in place), to seem to shine from within. "I was just standing there thinking that maybe no one gets the house they want." Phyllis glances around the room in an interested, friendly way, as if she liked the new light but thought the furniture needed rearranging.

"Well, if I can find it for them they do. And if they can afford it. You *are* best off coming as close as you can and trying to bring life to a place, not just depending on the place to supply it for you." I give her my own version of a willing smile. This is a positive sign, though of course we're not really addressing each other now; we're merely setting forth our points of view, and everything depends on whose act is better. It is a form of strategizing pseudo-communication I've gotten used to in the realty business. (Real talk—the kind you have with a loved one such as your former wife back when you were her husband—real talk is out of the question.)

"Do you have a prison behind your house?" Phyllis says bluntly. She gazes at her toes, which are pinched into her sandals, their nails painted scarlet. They seem to imply something to her.

"No, but I *do* live in my ex-wife's former house," I say, "and I live alone, and my son's an epileptic who has to wear a football helmet all day, and I've decided to live in her house just to give him a little semblance of continuity when he comes to visit, since his life expectancy's not so great. So I've made *some* adjustments to necessity." I blink at her. This is about her, not about me.

Phyllis was not expecting this, and looks stunned, suddenly acknowledging how much everything up to now has been usual salesmanship, usual aggravating clienthood; but that now everything is suddenly *down to it*: her and Joe's *actual situation* being attended to diligently by a man with even bigger woes than they have, who sleeps less well, visits more physicians, has more worrisome phone calls, during which he spends more anxious time on hold while gloomy charts are being read, and whose life generally matters more than theirs by his being closer to the grave (not necessarily his own).

"Frank, I don't mean to compare wounds with bruises," Phyllis says abjectly. "I'm sorry. I'm just feeling a lot of pressure along with everything else." She gives me a sad Stan Laurel smile and lowers her chin just like old Stan. Her face, I see, is a malleable and sweet putty face, perfect for alternative children's theater in the Northeast Kingdom. But no less right for Penns Neck, where a thespian group she might head up could do *Peter Pan* or *The Fantasticks* (minus the "Rape" song) for the lonely, sticky-fingered ex-comptrollers and malpractitioners across the fence, leaving them with at least a temporary feeling that life isn't all that ruined, that there's still hope on the outside, that there are a lot of possibilities left—even if there aren't.

I hear Ted and Joe scraping their damp dogs on the back steps, then stamping the welcome mat and Joe saying, "Now that'd be a *real* reality check, I'll tell you," while gentle, clever Ted says, "I've just decided for the time I have left, Joe, to let go all the nonessentials."

"I envy that, don't think I don't," Joe says. "Boy-oh-boy, I could get rid of some of those, all right."

Phyllis and I both hear this. Each of us knows that one of us is the first nonessential Joe would like to put behind him.

"Phyllis, I figure we've all got scars and bruises," I say, "but I just don't want them to cause you to miss a damn good deal on a wonderful house when it's in your grasp here."

"Is there anything else we can see today?" Phyllis says dispiritedly.

I sway back slightly on my heels, arms enfolding my clipboard. "I could show you a new development." I'm thinking of Mallards Landing, of course, where slash is smoldering and maybe two units are finished and the Markhams will go out of their gourds the minute they lay eyes on the flapping pennants. "The young developer's a heck of a good guy. They're all in your range. But you indicated you didn't want to consider new homes."

"No," Phyllis says darkly. "You know, Frank, Joe's a manic-depressive."

"No, I didn't know that." I hug my clipboard tighter. (I'm beginning to cook like a cabbage in my windbreaker.) I mean, though, to hold my ground. Manic-depressives, convicted felons, men and women with garish tattoos over every inch of their skin: all are entitled to a hook to hang their hats on if they've got the scratch. This claim for Joe's looniness is probably a complete lie, a ploy to let me know she's a worthy opponent in the realty struggle (for some reason her female troubles still seem legit). "Phyllis, you and Joe need to do some serious thinking about this house." I stare profoundly into her obstinate blue eyes, which I realize for the first time must have contacts, since no blue nearly similar to that occurs in nature.

She is framed by the window, her small hands clasped in front like a schoolmarm lording a trick question over a schoolboy dunce. "Do you feel sometimes"—the light glowing around Phyllis seems to have brought her in contact with the forces of saintliness—"that no one's looking out for you anymore?" She smiles faintly. The creases at the corners of her mouth make weals in her cheeks.

"Every day." I try to beam back a martyrish look.

"I had that feeling when I got married the first time. When I was twenty and a sophomore at Towson. And I had it this morning again at the motel—the first time in years." She rolls her eyes in a zany way.

Joe and Ted are making a noisy second trek over the floor plan now. Ted's unscrolling some old blueprints he's kept squirreled away. They will soon barge into Phyllis's and my little séance.

"I think that feeling's natural, Phyllis, and I think you and Joe take care of each other just fine." I peek to see if the orienteers are here yet. I hear them tromping over the defunct floor furnace, talking importantly about the attic.

Phyllis shakes her head and smiles a beatified smile. "The trick's changing the water to wine, isn't it?"

I have no idea what this might mean, though I give her a lawyerly-brotherly look that says this competition's over. I could even give her a pat on her plump shoulder, except she'd get wary. "Phyllis, look," I say. "People think there're just two ways for things to go. A worked-out way and a not-worked-out way. But I think most things start one way, then we steer them where we want them to go. And no matter how you feel at the time you buy a house—even if you don't buy this one or don't buy one from me at all—you're going to have to—"

And then our séance *is* over. Ted and Joe come trooping back down the hall from where they've decided not to take a cobwebby tour up the "disappearing" stairway to eyeball some metal rafter gussets Ted installed when Hurricane Lulu passed by in '58, blowing hay straw through tree trunks, moving yachts miles inland and leveling grander houses than Ted's. It's too hot upstairs.

"God's in the details," one of the new best friends observes. But adds, "Or is it the devil?"

Phyllis looks peacefully at the entry, into which the two of them go first one way and then the other before locating us in the l/r. Ted, coming into view with his blueprints, looks to my estimation satisfied with everything. Joe, in his immature goatee, his vulgar shorts and *Potters Do It With Their Fingers* shirt, seems on the verge of some form of hysteria.

"I've seen enough," Joe shouts like a railroad conductor, taking a quick estimation of the living room as if he'd never seen it in his life. He jams his thick knuckles together in satisfaction. "I can make up my mind on what I've seen."

"Okay," I say. "We'll take a drive, then." (Code for: We'll go to breakfast and write up a full-price offer and be back in an hour.) I give Ted Houlihan an assuring nod. Unexpectedly he's proved a key player in an ad hoc divide-and-conquer scheme. His memories, his poor dead wife, his faulty *cojones*, his Milquetoast Fred Waring soft-shoe worldview and casual attire, are first-rate selling tools. He could be a realtor.

"This place won't stay on the market long," Joe shouts to anyone in the neighborhood who's interested. He swivels around and starts for the front door in some kind of beehive panic.

"Well, we'll see," Ted Houlihan says, and gives me and Phyllis a doubtful smile, scrolling his blueprints tighter. "I know that place across the fence disturbs you, Mrs. Markham. But I've always felt it made the whole neighborhood safer and more cohesive. It's not much different from having AT & T or RCA, if you get what I mean."

"I understand," Phyllis says, unmoved.

Joe is already through the front door, down the steps and out onto the lawn, scoping out the roofline, the fascial boards, the soffits, his hair-framed mouth gaped open as he searches for sags in the ridgeboard or ice damage under the eaves. Possibly it is manic-depression medicine that causes his lips to be so red. Joe, I think, needs a bit of tending to.

I find a *Frank Bascombe, Realtor Associate* card in my windbreaker pocket and slip it onto the umbrella stand outside the living-room door, where I've spent the last ten minutes keeping Phyllis in the corral.

"We'll be in touch," I say to Ted. (More code. Less specific.)

"Yes, indeed," Ted says, smiling warmly.

And then out Phyllis goes, hips swaying, sandals clicking, shaking Ted's little hand on the fly and saying something about its being a lovely house and a pity he has to sell it, but heading right out to where Joe's trying to get a clear bead on things through whatever fog it's his bewildered lot to see through.

"They'll never buy it," Ted says gamely as I head toward the door. His is not disappointment but possibly misplaced satisfaction at having foreign elements turned away, permitting a brief retreat into the comfortable bittersweet domesticity that's still his. Joe out the door would be a relief for anyone.

"I can't tell, Ted," I say. "You don't know what other people will do. If I did, I'd be in another line of work."

"It'd be nice to think that the place was valuable to others. I'd feel good about that. There's not a lot of corroboration there for us anymore."

"Not what we'd like. But that's my part in this." Phyllis and Joe are standing beside my car, looking at the house as though it were an ocean liner just casting off for open seas. "Just don't underestimate your own house, Ted," I say, and once again grab his little hard-biscuit hand and give it an affirming shake. I take a last whiff of gas leak. (I'll hear Joe out on this subject inside of five minutes.) "Don't be surprised if I come back with an offer this morning. They won't see a house as good as yours, and I mean to make that clear as Christmas."

"A guy once climbed over the fence while I was out back sacking leaves," Ted says. "Susan and I took him inside, gave him some coffee and an egg salad sandwich. Turned out he was an alderman from West Orange. He'd just gotten in over his head. But he ended up helping me bag leaves for an hour, then going back over. We got a Christmas card from him for a while."

"He's probably back in politics," I say, happy Ted has spared Phyllis this anecdote.

"Probably."

"We'll be in touch."

"I'll be right here," Ted says. He closes the front door behind me.

*I*nside the car, the Markhams seem to want to get rid of me as fast as possible, and, more important, neither one makes a peep about an offer.

As we're pulling out the drive we all notice another realtor's car slowing to a stop, a young couple front and back—the woman videotaping the Houlihan place through the passenger window. The driver's-side sign on the big shiny Buick door says BUY AND LARGE REALTY—*Freehold, NJ.*

"This place'll be history by sundown," Joe says flatly, seated beside me, his get-up-and-go oddly got-up-and-gone. No mention of any gas odor. Phyllis has had no real chance to browbeat him, but a look can raze cities.

"Could be," I say, staring knives at the BUY AND LARGE Buick. Ted Houlihan may have already reneged on our *exclusive*, and I'm tempted to step out and explain some things to everybody involved. Though the sight of competing buyers could put a special, urgent onus to act on Phyllis and Joe, who watch these new people in disapproving silence as I drive us back down Charity Street.

On the way to Route 1, Phyllis—who has now put on dark glasses and looks like a diva—suddenly insists I drive them "around" so she can see the prison. Consequently, I negotiate us back through the less nice, bordering neighborhoods, curve in behind a new Sheraton and a big Episcopal church with a wide, empty parking lot, then merge out onto Route 1 north of Penns Neck, where, a half mile down the road in what looks like a mowed hayfield, there sits, three hundred yards back, a complex of low, indistinct flat-green buildings fenced all around and refenced closer in, which altogether constitutes the offending "big house." We can see basketball backboards, a baseball diamond, several fenced and lighted tennis courts, a high-dive platform over what might very well be an Olympic-size pool, some paved and winding "reflection paths" leading out into open stretches of field where pairs of men—some apparently elderly and limping—are strolling and chatting and wearing street clothes instead of prison monkey garb. There's also, apparently for atmosphere, a large flock of Canada geese milling and nosing around a flat, ovoid pond.

I, naturally, have passed this place incalculable times but have paid it only the briefest attention (which is what the prison planners expected, the whole shebang as unremarkable as a golf course). Though looked at now, a grassy, summery compound with substantial trees ranked beyond its boundaries, where an inmate can do any damn thing he wants but leave—read a book, watch color TV, think about the future—and where one's debts to society can be unobtrusively retired in a year or two, it seems like a place anyone might be glad to pause just to get things sorted out and cut through the crap.

"It looks like some goddamn junior college," Joe Markham says, still talking in the higher decibels but seeming calmer now. We're stopped on the opposite shoulder, with traffic booming past, and are rubbernecking the fence and the official silver-and-black sign that reads: N.J. MEN'S FACILITY—A MINIMUM SECURITY ENVIRONMENT, behind which New Jersey, American and Penal System flags all rustle on separate poles in the faint, damp breezes. There's no guardhouse here, no razor wire, no electric fences, no watchtowers with burp guns, stun grenades, searchlights, no leg-chewing canines—

just a discreet automatic gate with a discreet speaker box and a small security camera on a post. No biggie.

"It doesn't look that bad, does it?" I say.

"Where's our house from here?" Joe says, still loudly, leaning to see across me.

We study the row of big trees which is Penns Neck, the Houlihan house on Charity Street invisible within.

"You can't see it," Phyllis says, "but it's back there."

"Out of sight, out of mind," Joe says. He flashes a look back at Phyllis in her shades. A giant dump truck blows past, rocking the car on its chassis. "They have a gap in the fence where you can trade recipes." He snorts.

"A cake with a file in it," Phyllis says, her face unresigned. I try to catch her eye in the rearview, but can't. "I don't see it."

"I goddamned see it," Joe growls.

We sit staring for thirty more seconds, and then it's off we go.

*A*s a negative inducement and a double cincher, I drive us out past Mallards Landing, where everything is as it was two hours ago, only wetter. A few workmen are moving inside the half-studded homes. A crew of black men is loading wads of damp sod off a flatbed and stacking them in front of the MODEL that's supposedly OPEN but isn't and in fact looks like a movie façade where a fictionalized American family would someday pay the fictionalized mortgage. It puts me and, I'm sure, the Markhams in mind of the prison we just left.

"Like I was saying to Phyllis," I say to Joe, "these are in your price window, but they're not what you described."

"I'd rather have AIDS than live in that junk," Joe snarls, and doesn't look at Phyllis, who sits in the back, peering out toward the strobing oil-storage depot and the bulldozed piles of now unsmoldering trees. *Why have I come here?* she is almost certainly thinking. *How long a ride back is it by Vermont Transit?* She could be down at the Lyndonville Farmers' Co-op at this very moment, a clean red kerchief on her head, she and Sonja blithely but responsibly shopping for the holiday—surprise fruits for the "big fruit bowl" she'll take to the Independence Day bash. Chinese kites would be tethered above the veggie stalls. Someone would be playing a dulcimer and singing quirky mountain tunes full up with sexual double meanings. Labs and goldens by the dozens would be scratching and lounging around, wearing colorful bandanna collars of their own. Where has that all disappeared to, she is wondering. What have I done?

Suddenly *crash-boom!* Somewhere miles aloft in the peaceful atmosphere, invisible to all, a war jet breaks the barrier of harmonious sound and dream, reverbs rumbling toward mountaintops and down the coastal slope. Phyllis jumps. "Oh fuck," she says. "What was that?"

"I broke wind. Sorry," Joe says, smirking at me, and then we say no more.

At the Sleepy Hollow, the Markhams, who have ridden the rest of the way in total motionless silence, seem now reluctant to depart my car. The scabby motel lot is empty except for their ancient borrowed Nova with its mismatched tires and moronic anesthetists' sticker caked with Green Mountain road dirt. A small, pinkly dressed maid wearing her dark hair in a bun is flickering in and out the doorway to #7, loading a night's soiled linen and towels into a cloth hamper and carting in stacks of fresh.

The Markhams would both rather be dead than anywhere that's available to them, and for a heady, unwise moment I consider letting them follow me home, setting them up for a weekend of house discussion on Cleveland Street—a safe, depression-free base from which they could walk to a movie, eat a decent bluefish or manicotti dinner at the August Inn, window-shop down Seminary Street till Phyllis can't stand not to live here, or at least nearby.

Though that is simply not in the cards, and my heart strikes two and a half sharp, admonitory beats at the very thought. Not only do I not like the idea of them rummaging around in my life's accoutrements (which they would absolutely do, then lie about it), but since we're not talking offer, I want them left as solitary as Siberia so they can get their options straight. They could always, of course, move themselves up to the new Sheraton or the Cabot Lodge and pay the freight. Though in its own way each of these is as dismal as the Sleepy Hollow. In my former sportswriter's life I often sought shelter and even exotic romance in such spiritless hideaways, and often, briefly, found it. But no more. No way.

Joe has gone all the way through his list of questions left unanswered on the listing sheet, which he has spindled, then folded, his former lion's certainty now beginning to wane. "Any chance of a lease option back there at Houlihan's?" he says, as we all three just sit.

"No."

"Any chance Houlihan might come off a buck fifty-five?"

"Make an offer."

"When can Houlihan vacate?"

"Minimum time. He has cancer."

"Would you negotiate the commission down to four percent?"

(This comes as no surprise.) "No."

"What's the bank renting money for these days?"

(Again.) "Ten-four on a thirty-year fixed, plus a point, plus an application fee."

We skirl down through everything Joe can dredge up. I have turned the a/c vent into my face until I almost decide again to let them move into my house. Except, forty-five showings is the statistical point of no return, and the Markhams have today gone to forty-six. Clients, after this point, frequently don't buy a house but shove off to other locales, or else do something nutty like take a freighter to Bahrain or climb the Matterhorn. Plus, I might have a hard time getting them to leave. (In truth, I'm ready to cut the Markhams loose, let them set off toward a fresh start in the Amboys.)

Though of course they might just as well say, "Okay. Let's just get the sonofabitch bought and quit niggly-pigglying around. We're in for the full boat. Let's get an offer sheet filled out." I've got a boxful in my trunk. "Here's five grand. We're moving into the Sheraton Tara. You get your sorry ass back over to Houlihan's, tell him to get his bags packed for Tucson or go fuck himself, because one fifty's all we're offering because that's all we've got. Take an hour to decide."

People do that. Houses get sold on the spot; checks get written, escrow accounts opened, moving companies called from windy pay phones outside HoJo's. It makes my job one hell of a lot easier. Though when it happens that way it's usually rich Texans or maxillary surgeons or political operatives fired for financial misdealings and looking for a place to hide out until they can be players again.

Rarely does it happen with potters and their pudgy paper-making wives who wander back to civilization from piddly-ass Vermont with emaciated wallets and not a clue about what makes the world go around but plenty of opinions about how it ought to.

Joe sits in the front seat grinding his molars, breathing audibly and staring out at the foreign national swamping out their soiled room with a mop and a bottle of Pine-Sol. Phyllis, in her Marginalia shades, sits thinking—what? It's anybody's guess. There's no question left to ask, no worry to express, no resolve or ultimatum worth enunciating. They've reached the point where nothing's left to do but act. Or not.

But by God, Joe doesn't like it even in spite of loving the house, and sits inventorying his brain for something more to say, some barrier to erect. Likely it will have to do with "seeing from above" again, or wanting to make some great discovery.

"Maybe we *should* think about renting," Phyllis says vacantly. I have her in my mirror, keeping to herself like a bereaved widow. She has been staring at the hubcap bazaar next door, where no one's visible in the rain-soaked yard, though the hubcaps sparkle and clank in the breeze. She may be seeing something as a metaphor for something else.

Unexpectedly, though, she sits forward and lays a consolidating mitt on Joe's bare, hairy shoulder, which causes him to jump like he'd been stabbed. Though he quickly detects this as a gesture of solidarity and tenderness, and lumpily reaches round and grubs her hand with his. All patrols and units are now being called in. A unified response is imminent. It is the bedrock gesture of marriage, something I have somehow missed out on, and rue.

"Most of your better rentals turn up when the Institute term ends and people leave. That was last month," I say. "You didn't like anything then."

"Is there anything we might get into temporarily?" Joe says, limply holding Phyllis's plump fingers as though she were laid out beside him in a hospital bed.

"I've got a place *I* own," I say. "It might not be what you want."

"What's wrong with it?" Joe and Phyllis say in suspicious unison.

"Nothing's wrong with it," I say. "It happens to be in a black neighborhood."

"Oh Je-sus. Here we go," Joe says, as if this was a long-foreseeable and finally sprung trap. "That's all I need. Spooks. Thanks for nothin'." He shakes his head in disgust.

"That's not how we look at things in Haddam, Joe," I say coolly. "That's not how I practice realty."

"Well, good for you," he says, seething but still holding Phyllis's hand, probably tighter than she likes. "You don't live there," he fumes. "And you don't have kids."

"I do have kids," I say. "And I'd happily live there with them if I didn't already live someplace else." I give Joe a hard, iron-browed frown meant to say that beyond what he already doesn't know about, the world he left behind in nineteen seventy-whatever is an empty crater, and he'll get no sympathy here if it turns out he doesn't like the present.

"What you got, some shotgun shacks you collect rent on every Saturday morning?" Joe says this in a mealy, nasty way. "My old man ran that scam in Aliquippa. He ran it with Chinamen. He carried a pistol in his belt where they could see it. I used to sit in the car."

"I don't have a pistol," I say. "I'm just doing you a favor by mentioning it."

"Thanks. Forget about it."

"We could go look at it," Phyllis says, squeezing Joe's hairy knuckles, which he's balled up now into a menacing little fist.

"In a million years, maybe. But only maybe." Joe yanks up the door latch, letting hot Route 1 whoosh in.

"The Houlihan house is worth thinking about," I say to the car seat Joe is vacating, giving a sidelong look to Phyllis in the back.

"You realty guys," Joe says from outside, where I can just see his ball-packer shorts. "You're always nosing after the fucking sale." He then just stalks off in the direction of the cleaning woman, who's standing beside her laundry hamper and his very room, looking at Joe as if he were a strange sight (which he is).

"Joe's not a good compromiser," Phyllis says lamely. "He may be having dosage problems too."

"He's free to do whatever he wants, as far as I'm concerned."

"I know," Phyllis says. "You're very patient with us. I'm sorry we're so much trouble." She pats me on *my* shoulder, just the way she did asshole Joe. A victory pat. I don't much appreciate it.

"It's my job," I say.

"We'll be in touch with you, Frank," Phyllis says, struggling to exit her door to the hot morning heading toward eleven.

"That's just great, Phyllis," I say. "Call me at the office and leave a message. I'll be in Connecticut with my son. I don't get to spend that much time with him. We can do pretty much everything on the phone if there's anything to talk about."

"We're trying, Frank," Phyllis says, blinking pathetically at the idea of my son who's an epileptic, but not wanting to mention it. "We're really trying here."

"I can tell," I lie, and turn and give her a contrite smile, which for some reason drives her right out of the doorway and across the hot little crumbling motel lot in search of her unlikely husband.

I now find myself in a whir to get back into town, and so split the breeze over the steamy pavement up Route 1, retaking King George Road for the directest route to Seminary Street. I have more of the day returned to me than I'd expected, and I mean to put it to use by making a second stop by the McLeods', before driving out to Franks on Route 31, then heading straight down to South Mantoloking for some earlier than usual quality time with Sally, plus dinner.

I'd hoped, of course, to be back in the office, running the numbers on an offer or already delivering same to Ted Houlihan, hustling to get various balls rolling—calling a contractor for a structural inspection, getting the earnest money deposited, vetting the termite contract, dialing up Fox McKinney at Garden State Savings for a fast track through to the mortgage board. There's absolutely nothing an owner likes better than a quick, firm reply to his sell decision. Philosophically, as Ted said, it indicates the world is more or less the way we best feature it. (Most of what we unhappily hear back from the world being: "Boy, we're back-ordered on that one, it'll take six weeks"; or, "I thought they quit making those gizmos in '58"; or, "You'll have to have that part milled special, and the only guy who does it is on a walking trip through Swaziland. Take a vacation, we'll call you.") And yet if an agent can pry loose a well-conceived offer on an entirely new listing, the likelihood of clear sailing all the way to closing is geometrically increased by the simple weight of seller satisfaction, confidence, a feeling of corroboration and a sense of immanent meaning. *Real* closure in other words.

Consequently, it's a good strategy to set the Markhams adrift as I just did, let them wheeze around in their clunker Nova, brooding about all the houses in all the neighborhoods they've sneered at, then crawl back for a nap in the Sleepy Hollow—one in which they doze off in daylight but awake startled, disoriented and demoralized after dark, lying side by side, staring at the greasy motel walls, listening to the traffic drum past, everyone but them bound for cozy seaside holiday arrangements where youthful, happy, perfect-toothed loved ones wave greetings from lighted porches and doorways, holding big pitchers of cold gin. (I myself hope shortly to be arriving for just such a welcome—to be a cheerful, eagerly awaited addition to the general store of holiday fun, having a million laughs, feeling the world's woe rise off me someplace where the Markhams can't reach me. Possibly bright and early tomorrow there'll either be a frantic call from Joe wanting to slam a bid in by noon, or else no call—confoundment having taken over and driven them back to Vermont and public assistance—in which case I'll be rid of them. Win-win again.)

It's perfectly evident that the Markhams haven't looked in life's mirror in a while—forget about Joe's surprise look this morning. Vermont's spiritual mandate, after all, is that you don't look at your-*self*, but spend years gazing at everything *else* as penetratingly as possible in the conviction that everything out there more or less stands for you, and everything's pretty damn great because you are. (Emerson has some different opinions about this.) Only, with home buying as your goal, there's no real getting around a certain self-viewing.

Right about now, unless I miss my guess, Joe and Phyllis are lying just as I pictured them, stiff as planks, side by side, fully clothed on their narrow bed, staring up into the dim, flyspeck ceiling with all the lights off, realizing as silent as corpses that they can't *help* seeing themselves. They are the lonely, haunted people soon to be seen standing in a driveway or sitting on a couch or a cramped patio chair (wherever they land next), peering disconcertedly into a TV camera while being interviewed by the six o'clock news not merely as average Americans but as people caught in the real estate crunch, indistinct members of an indistinct class they don't want to be members of—the frustrated, the ones on the bubble, the ones who suffer, those forced to live anonymous and glum on short cul-de-sac streets named after the builder's daughter or her grade-school friends.

And the only thing that'll save them is to figure out a way to think about themselves and most everything else *differently*; formulate fresh understandings based on the faith that for new fires to kindle, old ones have to be dashed; and based less on isolating, boneheaded obstinance and more, for instance, on the wish to make each other happy without neutralizing the private self—which was why they showed up in New Jersey in the first place instead of staying in the mountains and becoming smug casualties of their own idiotic miscues.

With the Markhams, of course, it's hard to believe they'll work it out. A year from now Joe would be the first person to kick back at a summer solstice party in some neighbor's new-mown hay meadow, sipping homemade lager and grazing a hand-fired plate full of vegetarian lasagna—naked kids a-frolic in the twilight, the smell of compost, the sound of a brook and a gas generator in the background—and hold forth on the subject of change and how anybody's a coward who can't do it: a philosophy naturally honed on his and Phyllis's own life experiences (which include divorce, inadequate parenting practices, adultery, self-importance, and spatial dislocation).

Though it's change that's driving him crackers *now*. The Markhams say they won't compromise on their ideal. But they aren't compromising! They can't afford their ideal. And not buying what you can't afford's not a compromise; it's reality speaking English. To get anywhere you have to learn to speak the same language back.

And yet they may find hidden strengths: their fumbling, lurching Sistine Chapel touch across the car seat was a promising signal, but it's one they'll need to elaborate over the weekend, when they're on their own. And inasmuch as I'm not in possession of their check, on their own's where they'll be—sweating it but also, I hope, commencing the process of self-seeing as a sacred initiation to a fuller later life.

4

It might be of some interest to say how I came to be a Residential Specialist, distant as it is from my prior vocations of failed short-story writer and sports journalist. A good *liver* would be a man or woman who'd distilled all of life that's important down to a few inter-related principles and events, which are easy to explain in fifteen minutes and don't require a lot of perplexed pauses and apologies for this or that being hard to understand exactly if you weren't there. (Finally, almost nobody else *is* ever able to "be there," and in many cases it's too bad *you* have to be.) And it is in this streamlined, distilled sense that it's possible to say my former wife's getting remarried and moving to Connecticut is what brought me to where I am.

Five years ago, at the end of a bad season that my friend Dr. Catherine Flaherty described as "maybe a kind of major crisis," or "the end of something stressful followed by the beginning of something indistinct," I one day simply quit my job at a large sports magazine in New York and moved myself to Florida, and then in the following year to France, where I had never been but decided I needed to go.

In the ensuing winter, the previously mentioned Dr. Flaherty, then age twenty-three and not yet a doctor, interrupted her medical studies at Dartmouth and flew to Paris to spend "a season" with me—entirely against her father's best judgment (who could blame him?) and without the slightest expectance that the world held out any future for her and me together or that the future even needed to be taken into account. The two of us struck off on a driving tour in a rented Peugeot to wherever seemed interesting on the European map, with me paying the freight from the proceeds of my magazine-stock buyout and Catherine doing all the complicated map reading, food ordering, direction seeking, bathroom locating, phone calling, and bellman paying. She had, naturally, been to Europe at least twenty times before she was out of Choate and could in all instances remember and easily lead us straight to a "neat little hilltop restaurant" above the Dordogne, or "an interesting place for very late lunch" near the Palacio in Madrid, or find the route to a house that was once Strindberg's wife's home outside Helsinki. The whole trip had for her the virtue of an aimless, nostalgic return to past triumphs in the company of a non-traditional "other," just before life—serious adult life—began in earnest and fun was forgotten forever; while for me it was more of an anxious dash across a foreign but thrilling *exterior* landscape, commenced in hopes of arriving at a temporary refuge where I'd feel rewarded, revived, less anxious, possibly even happy and at peace.

It's not necessary to say much of what we did. (Such pseudo-romantic excursions must all be more or less alike and closed-ended.) We eventually "settled" in the town of Saint-Valéry-sur-Somme, in Channel-side Picardy. There we passed the better part of two months together, spent a great deal of my money, rode bicycles, read plenty of books, visited battlefields and cathedrals, tried sculling on the canals, walked pensively along the grassy verge of the old estuarial river, watching French fishermen catch perch, walked pensively around the bay to the alabaster village of Le Crotoy, then walked back, made much love. I also practiced my college French, chatted up the English tourists, stared at sailboats, flew kites, ate many gritty *moules meunières*, listened to much "traditional" jazz, slept when I wanted to and even when I didn't, woke at midnight and stared at the sky as though I needed to get a clearer view of something but wasn't sure what it was. I did all this until I felt perfectly okay, not in love with Catherine Flaherty but not unhappy, although also futureless, disused and bored—the way, I imagine, extended time in Europe makes any American who cares to stay an American feel (possibly similar to how a larcenous small-town road commissioner feels during the latter part of his stay in the Penns Neck minimum security facility).

Though what I in time began to sense in France was actually a kind of disguised urgency (disguised, as urgency often is, as un-urgency), a feeling completely different from the old clicking, whirly, suspenseful perturbations I'd felt in my last days as a sportswriter: of being divorced, full of regret, and needing to pursue women just to keep myself pacified, amused and slightly dreamy. This new variety was more a deep-beating urgency having to do with me and me only, not me *and* somebody. It was, I now believe, the profound low thrum of my middle life seeking to be seized rather than painlessly avoided. (There's nothing like spending eight weeks alone with a woman two decades your junior to make you wise to the fact that you'll someday disappear, make you bored daffy by the concept of youth, and dismally aware how impossible it is ever to be "with" another human being.)

One evening then, over a plate of *ficelle picarde* and one more glass of tolerable Pouilly-Fumé, it occurred to me that being there with winsome, honey-haired, sweetly ironic Catherine was indeed a kind of dream and a dream I'd wanted to have, only it was now a dream that was holding me back—from what, I wasn't sure, but I needed to find out. Needless to say, she had to have been bored silly by me but had gone on acting, in a vaguely amused way, as if I was a "pretty funny ole guy" with pretty interesting, eccentric habits, not one bit to be taken lightly "as a man," and that being in Saint-Valéry with me had made all the difference in getting her young life started in the most properly seasoned way, and she would remember it all forever. She didn't, however, mind if I left or if she stayed, or if we both left or stayed. She already had plans to leave, which she hadn't thought to tell me about yet; and in any case, when I was seventy and in adult Pampers, she'd have been fiftyish, in a surly mood from all she'd missed and in no rush to humor me—which by then would be all I'd want. So that there was no thought of a long haul for the two of us.

But in just that short an order and on that very evening, and without a harsh word, we kissed and broke camp—she back to Dartmouth, and me back to . . .

Haddam. Where I landed not only with a new feeling of great purpose and a fury to suddenly *do* something serious for my own good and possibly even others', but also with the feeling of renewal I'd gone far to look for and that immediately translated into a homey connectedness to Haddam itself, which felt at that celestial moment like my spiritual residence more than any place I'd ever been, inasmuch as it *was* the place I instinctively and in a heat came charging back to. (Of course, having come first to life in a true *place*, and one as monotonously, lankly *itself* as the Mississippi Gulf Coast, I couldn't be truly surprised that a simple *setting* such as Haddam— willing to be so little itself—would seem, on second look, a great relief and damned easy to cozy up to.)

Before, when I was in town writing sports, as a married, then latter, divorced man, I'd always fancied myself a spectral presence, like a ship cruising foggy banks, hoping to hang near and in hearing distance of the beach but without ever bashing into it. Now, though, by reason of Haddam's or any suburb's capacity to accommodate any but the rankest outsider (a special lenience which can make us miss even the most impersonal housing tract or condo development), I felt *towny:* a guy who shares a scuzzy joke with the Neapolitan produce man, who knows exactly the haircut he'll get at Barber's barbershop but goes there anyway, who's voted for more than three mayors and can remember how things used to be before something else happened and as a result feels right at home. These feelings of course ride the froth of one's sense of hope and personal likelihood.

Every age of life has its own little pennant to fly. And mine upon returning to Haddam was decidedly two-sided. On one side was a feeling of bright synchronicity in which everything I thought about—regaining a close touch with my two children after having flown the coop for a while, getting my feet wet in some new life's enterprise, possibly waging a campaign to reclaim lost ground with Ann—all these hopeful activities seemed to be, as though guided by a lightless beam, what my whole life was all about. I was in a charmed state in which nothing was alien and nothing could resist me if I turned my mind to it. (Psychiatrists like the one my son visits warn us about such feelings, flagging us all away from the poison of euphoria and hauling us back to flat earth, where they want us to be.)

The other feeling, the one that balanced the first, was a sensation that everything I then contemplated was limited or at least underwritten by the "plain fact of my existence": that I was after all only a human being, as untranscendent as a tree trunk, and that everything I might do had to be calculated against the weight of the practical and according to the standard considerations of: Would it work? and, What good would it do for me or anybody?

I now think of this balancing of urgent forces as having begun the Existence Period, the high-wire act of normalcy, the part that comes *after* the big struggle which led to the big blow-up, the time in life when whatever was going to affect us "later" actually affects us, a period when we go along more or less self-directed and happy, though we might not choose to mention or even remember it later were we to tell the story of our lives, so steeped is such a time in the small dramas and minor adjustments of spending quality time simply with ourselves.

Certain crucial jettisonings, though, seemed necessary for this passage to be a success—just as Ted Houlihan mentioned to Joe Markham an hour ago but which probably didn't register. Most people, once they reach a certain age, troop through their days struggling like hell with the concept of completeness, keeping up with all the things that were ever part of them, as a way of maintaining the illusion that they bring themselves fully to life. These things usually amount to being able to remember the birthday of the first person they "surrendered" to, or the first calypso record they ever bought, or the poignant line in *Our Town* that seemed to sum life up back in 1960.

Most of these you just have to give up on, along with the whole idea of completeness, since after a while you get so fouled up with all you did and surrendered to and failed at and fought and didn't like, that you can't make any progress. Another way of saying this is that when you're young your opponent is the future; but when you're not young, your opponent's the past and everything you've done in it and the problem of getting away from it. (My son Paul may be an exception.)

My own feelings were that since I'd jettisoned employment, marriage, nostalgia and swampy regret, I was now rightfully a man a-quiver with possibility and purpose—similar to a way you might feel just prior to taking up the sport of, say, glacier skiing; and not for sharpening your acuities or tempting grisly death, but simply to celebrate the hum of the human spirit. (I could not, of course, have told you what my purpose actually was, which probably meant my purpose was just to have a purpose. Though I'm certain I was afraid that if I didn't use my life, even in a ridiculous way, I'd lose it—what people used to say about your dick when I was a kid.)

My qualifications for a new undertaking were, first, that I was not one bit preoccupied with how things *used to be*. You're usually wrong about how things used to be anyway, except that you used to be happier—only you may not have known it at the time, or might've been unable to seize it, so stuck were you in life's gooeyness; or, as is often the case, you might never have been quite as happy as you like to believe you were.

The second of my qualifications was that intimacy had begun to matter less to me. (It had been losing ground since my marriage came to a halt and other attractions failed.) And by intimacy I mean the real kind, the kind you have with only one person (or maybe two or three) in a lifetime; not the kind where you're willing to talk to someone you're close to about laxative choices or your dental problems; or, if it's a woman, about her menstrual cycle, or your aching prostate. These are private, not intimate. But I mean the real stuff— *silent intimacies*—when spoken words, divulgences, promises, oaths are almost insignificant: the intimacy of the fervently understood and sympathized with, having nothing to do with being a "straight shooter" or a truth teller, or with being able to be "open" with strangers (these don't mean anything anyway). To *none* of these, though, was I in debt, and in fact I felt I could head right into my new frame of reference—whatever was beginning—pretty well prepared and buttoned up.

Third, but not last, I wasn't actually worried that I was a coward. (This seemed important and still does.) Years earlier, in my sportswriting days, Ann and I were once walking out of a Knicks–Bullets night game at the Garden, when some loony up ahead began brandishing a pistol and threatening to open up on everybody all around. Word went back like a windstorm over wheat stalks. "Gun! He's got a GUN! Watch it!" I quickly pulled Ann inside a men's room door, hoping to get some concrete between the gun muzzle and us. Though in twenty seconds the gunman was tackled and kicked to sawdust by a squad of New York's quick-witted finest, and thank God no one was hurt.

But Ann said to me when we were in the car, waiting in a drizzle to enter the bleak tunnel back to New Jersey, "Did you realize you jumped *behind* me when that guy had his gun?" She smiled at me in a tired but sympathetic way.

"That's not what I did!" I said. "I jumped in the rest room and pulled you in with me."

"You did that too. But you also grabbed me by my shoulders and got behind me. Not that I blame you. It happened in a hurry." She drew a wavy vertical line in the window fog and put a dot at the bottom.

"It did happen in a hurry. But you're wrong about *what* happened," I said, flustered because in fact it *had* all happened fast, I'd acted solely on instinct and couldn't remember much.

"Well, if that's what happened," she said confidently, "then tell me if the man—if it was a man—was colored or white." Ann has never gotten over her old man's Michigan racial epithets.

"I don't know," I said as we made the curve down into the lurid world of the tunnel. "It was too crowded. He was too far up ahead. We couldn't see him."

"*I* could," she said, sitting straighter and flattening her skirt across her knees. "He wasn't actually that far. He might've shot one of us. He was a small brown-colored man, and he had a small black revolver. If we passed him on the street I'd recognize him again. Not that it matters. You were trying to do the right thing. I'm happy I was no less than the second person you thought to protect when you thought you were in danger." She smiled at me again and patted my leg infuriatingly, and we were all the way to Exit 9 before I could think of anything to say.

But for years it bothered me (who wouldn't be bothered?). My belief had always been with the ancient Greeks, that the most important events in life are physical events. And it bothered me that in (I now realize) the last opportunity I might've had to throw myself in front of my dearest loved one, it appeared I'd pushed my dearest loved one in front of myself as cravenly as a slinking cur (appearances are just as bad when cowardliness is at issue).

And yet I found that when Ann and I divorced because she couldn't put up with me and my various aberrations of grief and longing owing to the death of our first son, and just flew the coop (a physical act if there ever was one), I quit worrying about cowardice almost immediately and decided she'd been wrong. Though even if she'd been right, I felt it was braver to live with the specific knowledge of cowardice and look for improvements than never to know anything about myself on that front; and better, too, to go on believing, as we all do in our daydreams, that when the robber jumps out of the alley brandishing the skinning knife or the large-caliber pistol, terrorizing you and your wife and plenty of innocent bystanders (old people in wheelchairs, your high-school math teacher, Miss Hawthorne, who was patient when you couldn't get the swing of plane geometry and thus changed your life forever), that there'll be time for you (me) to act heroically ("I just don't think you've got nuts big enough to use that thing, mister, so you might as well hand it over and get out of here"). Better to wish the best for yourself; better also (and this isn't easy) that others wish it too.

*I*t would be of no great interest to hear me expound on all I tried and started out to do during this time—1984, the Orwellian year, when Reagan was reelected to the term soon to end, the one he has more or less napped through when he wasn't starting wars or lying about it and getting the country into plenty of trouble.

For the first few months, I spent three mornings a week reading to the blind down at WHAD-FM (98.6). Michener novels and *Doctor Zhivago* were the blind people's favorites, and it is still something I occasionally stop off and do when I have time, and take real satisfaction in. I also looked briefly into the possibility of becoming a court reporter (my mother had always thought that would be a wonderful job because it served a useful purpose and you'd always be in demand). Later, and for one entire week, I attended classes in heavy-equipment operation, which I enjoyed but didn't finish (I was determined to aim at less predictable choices for a man with my background). I likewise tried getting a contract to write an "as told to" book but couldn't get my former literary agency interested since I had no particular subject in mind and they by then were only interested in young writers with surefire projects. And for three weeks I actually worked as an inspector for a company that certified as "excellent" crummy motels and restaurants across the Middle West, though that didn't work because of all the lonely time spent in the car.

At this same time, I also got busy shoring up my responsibilities with my two children (then ages eleven and eight), who were living with their mother on Cleveland Street and growing up between our two households in ordinary divorced-family style, which they seemed reconciled to, if not completely happy about. I joined the high-priced Red Man Club during this period, with a mind to teaching the two of them respect for nature's bounty; and I was also planning a nostalgic update trip to Mississippi, for my old military school's class reunion, as well as a trip to the Catskills for a murder-mystery weekend, a hike up the Appalachian Trail and a guided float down the Wading River. (I was, as I said, fully conscious that taking an extended flier to Florida, then France, had not been scrupulous fathering practice and I needed to do better; though I felt it was arguable that if one of my parents had done the same thing I'd have understood, as long as they said they loved me and hadn't both vamoosed at once.)

All told, I felt I was positioning myself well for whatever good might come along and was even giving tentative thought to approaching Ann for an older-but-wiser reconsideration of the marriage option, when one evening in early June Ann herself called up and announced that she and Charley O'Dell were getting married, she was selling her house, quitting her job, putting the children in new schools, moving kit and caboodle, lock, stock and barrel, the whole nine yards up to Deep River and not coming back. She hoped I wouldn't be upset.

And I simply didn't know what in the hell to say or think, much less feel, and for several seconds I just stood holding the receiver to my ear as if the line had gone dead, or as if some lethal current had connected through my ear to my brain and struck me cold as a haddock.

Anybody, of course, could've seen it coming. I'd met Charley O'Dell, age fifty-seven (tall, prematurely white-haired, rich, big-boned, big-schnozzed, big-jawed, literal-as-a-dictionary architect), on various occasions having to do with the delivery and pickup of my children, and had at that time officially declared him a "no-threat." O'Dell is commandant of his own pretentious one-man design firm, housed in a converted seamen's chapel built on stilts (!) at the marsh edge in Deep River, and of course pilots his own 25-foot Alerion, built with his own callused hands and fitted with sails sewn at night while listening to Vivaldi, yakkedy, yakkedy, yak. We once stood one spring night, on the little front stoop of Ann's house—now mine—and yammered for thirty minutes with not one grain of sincerity or goodwill about diplomatic strategies for corraling the Scandinavians into the EEC, something I knew not a fig about and cared less. "Now if you ask me, Frank, the Danes are the key to the whole square-headed pack out there"—one tanned, naked knobby knee hiked up on Ann's stoop railing, one bespoke deck shoe dangling half off his long big toe, chin balanced pseudo-judiciously on big fist. Charley's usual attire when he isn't wearing a bow tie and a blazer is a big white tee-shirt and khaki canvas walking shorts, something they must hand out at graduation at Yale. I, that night, stared him straight in the eyes as if I were paying rapt attention, though in fact I was sucking one of my molars where I'd discovered a randy taste in an area I couldn't floss, and was also thinking that if I could hypnotize him and will him into disappearing I could have some time alone with my ex-wife.

Ann, however (suspiciously), wouldn't give in on the several evenings she and I paused together by my car in the silent dark of divorced former mates who still love each other, wouldn't crack smirky jokes at Charley's expense, the way she always had about all her other suitors—jokes about their taste in suits or their dreary jobs, their breath, the reported savage personalities of their ex-wives. Mum was always the word where Charley was concerned. (I guessed wrongly it was respect for his age.) But I should've paid closer attention and torpedoed him the way any man would who's in charge of his senses.

As a result, though, when Ann gave me the bad news on the phone that June evening just at cocktail hour—the sun having cleared the yardarm in butler's pantries all over Haddam, and trays of ice were being cracked into crystal buckets, leaded tumblers and slender Swedish pitchers, the vermouth hauled out wryly, the smell of juniper flaring the nostrils of many a bushed but deserving ex-hubby—I was kicked square in the head.

And my first on-record thought was of course that I had been bitterly, scaldingly betrayed just at a critical point—the point at which I'd gotten things almost "turned around" for the long canter back to the barn—the commencing point of life's gentle ameliora-tion, all sins forgiven, all lesions healed.

"Married?" I, in essence, shouted, my heart making one palpable, possibly audible clunk at the bottom of its cavity. "Married to who?"

"To Charley O'Dell," Ann said, unduly calm in the face of calamitous news.

"You're marrying the bricklayer!" I said. "Why?"

"I guess because I want somebody to make love to me more than three times after which I never see them again." She said this calmly too. "You just go to France and I don't hear from you for months"—which wasn't true—"I actually think the children need a better life than that. And also because I don't want to die in Had-dam, and because I'd like to see the Connecticut in the morning mist and go sailing in a skiff. I guess, in more traditional terms, I'm in love with him. What'd you think?"

"Those seem like good reasons," I said, light-headed.

"I'm happy you approve."

"I don't approve," I said, breathless, as if I'd come straight inside from a long run. "You're moving the kids away too?"

"It's not in our decree that I can't," she said.

"What do *they* think?" I felt my heart thunk-a-thunk again at the thought of the children. This, of course, was a serious issue, and one that becomes urgent decades beyond divorce itself: the issue of what the children think of their father if their mother remarries. (He almost never fares well. There are books about this, and they aren't funny: the father is seen either as a stooge wearing goat horns or a brute betrayer who forced Mom into marrying a hairy outsider who invariably treats the kids with irony, ill-disguised contempt and annoyance. Either way, insult is glommed onto injury.)

"They think it's wonderful," Ann said. "Or they should. I think they expect me to be happy."

"Sure, why not?" I said numbly.

"Right. Why not."

And then there was a long, cold silence, which we both knew to be the silence of the millennium, the silence of divorce, of being fatigued by love parceled out and withheld in the unfair ways it had been, by love lost when something should've made it not be lost but didn't, the silence of death—long before death might even be winked at.

"That's all I really have to say now," she said. A heavy curtain had parted briefly, then closed again.

I was *in fact* standing in the butler's pantry at 19 Hoving Road, staring out the little round nautically paned fo'c'sle window into my side yard, where the big copper beech cast ominous puddles of purple, pre-dark shadow over the green grasses and shrubs of late-spring evening.

"When's all this happening?" I said almost apologetically. I put my hand to my cheek, and my cheek was cold.

"In two months."

"What about the club?" Ann had stayed on as a part-time teaching pro at Cranbury Hills and had once briefly been an aspirant to the state ladies' pro-am. She'd actually met Charley there, on the cadge with his reciprocating membership from the Old Lyme Country Club. She had told me (I thought) all about him: a sort of nice older man she felt comfortable with.

"I've taught enough women to play golf now," she said briskly, then paused. "I put my house on the market this morning with Lauren-Schwindell."

"Maybe I'll buy it," I said rashly.

"That'd certainly be novel."

I had no idea why I'd say anything so preposterous, except to have something bold to say instead of breaking into hysterical laughter or howls of grief. But then I said, "Maybe I'll sell this place and move into your house."

And as quick as the words left my mouth I had the dead-eyed conviction that I was going to do exactly that, and in a hurry—perhaps so she could never get rid of me. (That may be what marriage means in laymen's terms: a relation you have with the one person in the world you can't get rid of except by dying.)

"I think I'll leave the real estate ventures to you," Ann said, ready to get off the phone.

"Is Charley there?" It seemed conceivable I might just storm over right then and bust him up, bloody his tee-shirt, put some extra years on him.

"No, he's not, and don't come over here, please. I'm crying now, and you don't get to see that." I hadn't *heard* her crying and concluded she was lying to make me feel like a louse, which was how I felt even though I hadn't done anything lousy. *She* was getting married. I was the one getting left behind like a cripple.

"Don't worry," I said, "I don't want to spoil any of the fun."

And then suddenly, the receiver pressed to my ear, another even more inert silence filled the optic lines connecting us. And I had the sharpest pain that Ann *was* going to die, not in Haddam and not immediately, not even soon, but not so long from then either—at the end of a period of time that, because she was abandoning me for the arms of another, would pass almost imperceptibly, her life's extinguishment paying out beyond my knowing via a series of small, exquisite doctors' appointments, anxieties, dismays, unhappy lab reports, gloomy X rays, tiny struggles, tiny victories, reprieves, then failures (life's inventory of morose happenstance), at the sudden, misty conclusion of which a call would come or a voice mail or a fax or a mailgram, saying: "Ann Dykstra died Tuesday morning. Services yesterday. Thought you'd want to know. Condolences. C. O'Dell." After which my own life would be ruined and over with, big time! (It's a matter of my age that all new events threaten to ruin my precious remaining years. Nothing like this feeling happens when you're thirty-two.)

And of course it was just cheap sentimentalism—the kind the gods frown down on from Olympus and send avengers to punish the small-time con men of emotion for practicing. Only sometimes you can't feel anything about a subject without hypothesizing its extinction. And that *is* how I felt: full of sadness that Ann was going away to start the part of her life that would end in her death; at which time I'd be elsewhere, piddling around at nothing very important, the way I had since coming back from Europe or—depending on your point of view—the way I had for twenty years. I'd be unthought of or worse, thought of only as "a man Ann was once married to. . . . I'm not sure where he is now. He was strange."

Yet I felt, if I was to have a part, any part in it at all, it would have to be spoken right then—on the phone, streets away but different neighborhoods (the geography of divorce), me alone in my house, feeling, as recently as ten minutes prior, hopeful about my unruined prospects but suddenly feeling as divorced as a man can be.

"Don't marry him, sweetheart! Marry me! Again! Let's sell both our shitty houses and move to Quoddy Head, where I'll buy a small newspaper from the proceeds. You can learn to sail your skiff off Grand Manan, and the kids can learn to set type by hand, be wary little seafarers, grow adept with lobster pots, trade in their Jersey accents, go to Bowdoin and Bates." These are words I *didn't* say into the dense millennial silence available to me. They would've been laughed at, since I'd had years to say them before then and hadn't—which Dr. Stopler of New Haven will tell you means I didn't really want to.

"I think I understand all this," I said instead, in a convinced voice, as I poured myself a convincing amount of gin, bypassing the vermouth. "And I love you, by the way."

"Please," Ann said. "Just please. You love me? What difference does that make? I'm finished with what I had to tell you, anyway." She was and is the kind of bedrock literalist who takes no interest in the far-fetched (the things I sometimes feel I'm *only* interested in), which is I'm sure why she married Charley.

"To say that some important truths are founded on flimsy evidence really isn't saying much." I voiced this view meekly.

"That's your philosophy, Frank, not mine. I've heard it for years. It only matters to you how long some improbable thing holds up, right?"

I took my first sip of just-cold-enough gin. I could feel the slow exhilaration of a long, honing talk coming. There aren't very many better feelings. "For some people the improbable can last long enough to become true," I said.

"And for other people it can't. And if you were about to ask me to marry you instead of Charley, don't. I won't. I don't want to."

"I was just trying to speak to an ephemeral truth at a moment of transition and trudge on beyond it."

"Trudge on, then," Ann said. "I've got to cook dinner for the children. I do want to admit this, though: I thought that it'd be you who'd get married again after we got divorced. To some bimbo. I admit I was wrong."

"Maybe you don't know me very well."

"I'm sorry."

"Thanks for calling me," I said. "Congratulations."

"Sure. It was nothing." Then she said good-bye and hung up.

*B*ut . . . nothing? It was nothing? It was something!

I bolted my gin in one shuddering, breathless gulp, to wash down frothing bitterness. Nothing? It was epochal. And I didn't care if it was blue-blood Charley from Deep River, pencil-neck, breast-pocket-penholder Waldo from Bell Labs or tattooed Lonnie down at the car wash: I'd have felt the same. Like shit!

Up to that moment, Ann and I had had a nice, cozy-efficient system worked out, one by which we lived separate lives in separate houses in one small, tidy, peril-free town. We had flings, woes, despairs, joys, a whole gearbox full of life's meshings and unmeshings, on and on, but fundamentally we were the same two people who'd gotten married and divorced, only set in different equipoise: same planets, different orbits, same solar system. But in a pinch, a real pinch, say a head-on car crash requiring extended life support or a prolonged bout of chemo, no one but the other would've been in attendance, buttonholing the doctors, chatting up the nurses, judiciously closing and opening heavy curtains, monitoring the game shows through the long, silent afternoons, shooing away prying neighbors and long-ignored relatives, former boyfriends, girlfriends, old nemeses come to make up—shepherding them all back down the long hallways, speaking in confidential whispers, saying "She had a good night," or "He's resting now." All this while the patient dozed, and the necessary machines clicked and whirred and sighed. And all just so we could be alone. Which is to say we had standing in the other's dire moments, even if not in the happy ones.

Eventually, after a long recovery during which one or the other would have had to relearn some basic human life functions up to now taken for granted (walking, breathing, pissing), certain key conversations would've taken place, certain dour admissions been offered if not already offered in moments of extremis, and important truths reconciled so that a new and (this time) binding union could be forged.

Or maybe not. Maybe we would simply have parted again, though with new strengths and insights and respects achieved through the fragile life experiences of the other.

But all of that was gone like a fart in a skillet. And jeez Louise! If I'd thought back in '81 that Ann would get remarried, I'd have fought it like a Viking instead of giving in to divorce like a queasy, uninspired saint. And I'd have fought it for a damn good reason: because no matter where she held the mortgage papers, she completely supposed my existence. My life was (and to some vague extent still is) played out on a stage in which she's continually in the audience (whether she's paying attention or not). All my decent, reasonable, patient, loving components were developed in the experimental theater of our old life together, and I realized that by moving house up to Deep River she was striking most of the components, dismembering the entire illusion, intending to hook up with another, leaving me with only faint, worn-out costumes to play myself with.

Naturally enough, I fell into a deep, sulfurous, unsynchronous gloom, stayed at home, called no one for days, drank a lot more gin, reconsidered heavy-equipment-operator's class and becoming an unwieldy embarrassment to people who knew me, and overall felt myself becoming significantly less substantial.

I spoke once or twice to my children, who seemed to calculate their mother's marriage to Charley O'Dell with the alacrity with which a small investor notices a gain in a stock he feels certain he'll eventually lose money on. Though he'd later change his mind, Paul uncomfortably declared Charley to be an "okay" guy and admitted having gone to a Giants game with him in November (something I hadn't heard about because I was in Florida and contemplating going to France). Clarissa seemed more interested in the wedding itself than in the conception of remarriage, which didn't seem to worry her much. She was concerned with what she was going to wear, where everyone would stay (the Griswold Inn in Essex) and if I could be invited ("No"), plus whether she could be a bridesmaid if I got married in the future (which she said she hoped I would). All three of us talked about all these matters for a while via extension phones. I tried to calm fears, sweeten prospects and simplify growing confusions about my own and their possible unhappiness, until there was nothing left to say, after which we parted company, never to speak under those exact circumstances or in those same innocent voices again. Gone. Poof.

*T*he wedding itself was an intimate though elegant "on the grounds" affair at Charley's house—"The Knoll" (pretentious hand-hewn post-and-beam Nantucket cottage adaptation: giant windows, wood from Norway and Mongolia, everything built-in flush, rabbeted, solar panels, heated floors, Finnish sauna, on and on and on). Ann's mother flew in from Mission Viejo, Charley's aged parents somehow motored down from Blue Hill or Northeast Harbor or some such magnate's enclave, with the happy couple flying off to the Huron Mountain Club, where Ann's father had left her his membership.

But no sooner had Ann solemnized her retreaded vows than I plunged forward with my own plans (founded on my previously explained sense of practicality, since high-spirited synchronicity hadn't fared well) to purchase her house on Cleveland Street for four ninety-five, and to get rid of my big old soffit-sagging half-timber on Hoving Road, where I'd lived nearly every minute of my life in Haddam and where I mistakenly thought I could live forever, but which now seemed to be one more commitment holding me back. Houses can have this almost authorial power over us, seeming to ruin or make perfect our lives just by persisting in one place longer than we can. (In either case it's a power worth defeating.)

Ann's house was a crisp, well-kept freestanding Greek Revival town house of a style and 1920s vintage typical of the succinct, nice-but-not-finicky central Jersey architectural temper—a place she'd bought on the cheap (with my help) after our divorce and done some modernizing work on ("opening out" the back, adding skylights and crown moldings, repointing some basement piers, finishing off the third floor to be Paul's lair, then giving the clapboards a new white paint job and new green shutters).

In truth, the house was a natural for me, since I'd already spent a three-years collection of sleepless nights there when a child was sick or when, in the early days of our sad divorced limbo, I'd sometimes gotten the jimjams so bad Ann would take pity on me and let me slip in and sleep on the couch.

It felt like home, in other words; and if not my home, at least my kids' home, *someone's* home. Whereas since Ann's announcement, my old place had begun to feel barny and murky, murmurous and queer, and myself strangely outdistanced as its owner—in the yard cranking away on the Lawn-Boy, or standing in my driveway, hands on hips, supervising from below the patching of a new squirrel hole under the chimney flashing. I was no longer, I felt, preserving anything *for* anything, even for myself, but was just going through the motions, joining life's rough timbers end to end.

Consequently, I got promptly over to Lauren-Schwindell and threw my hat in both rings at once: hers to buy, mine to sell. My thinking was, if lightning struck and Charley and his new bride came unglued during week one, Ann and I could forge our new beginning in her house (then later move to Maine more or less as newlyweds).

So, before the O'Dells returned home (no annulment was pending), I'd entered a full-price cash offer on 116 Cleveland and, through a savvy intercession by old man Otto Schwindell himself, reached an extremely advantageous deal with the Theological Institute to take over my house for the purpose of converting it into the Ecumenical Center where guests like Bishop Tutu, the Dalai Lama and the head of the Icelandic Federation of Churches could hold high-level confabs about the fate of the world's soul, and still find accommodations homey enough to slip down after midnight for a snack.

The Institute's Board of Overseers was, in fact, highly sensitive to my tax situation, since my house appraised out at an eye-popping million two, near the peak of the boom. Their lawyers were able to set up a healthy annuity which earns interest for me and later passes on to Paul and Clarissa, and by whose terms I in essence donated my house as an outright gift, claimed a whopper deduction and afterward received a generous "consultant's" fee in what I think of as temporal affairs. (This tax loophole has since been closed, but too late, since what's done's done.)

One bright and green August day, I simply walked out the door and down the steps of my house, leaving all my furniture except for books and nostalgic attachments (my map of Block Island, a hatch-cover table, a leather chair I liked, my marriage bed), drove over to Ann's house on Cleveland, with all her old-new furniture sitting exactly where she'd left it, and took up residence. I was allowed to keep my old phone number.

And truth to tell I hardly noticed the difference, so often had I lain awake nights in my old place or roamed the rooms and halls of hers when all were sleeping—searching, I suppose, for where I fit in, or where I'd gone wrong, or how I could breathe air into my ghostly self and become a recognizable if changed-for-the-better figure in their sweet lives or my own. One house is as good as another for this kind of private enterprise. And the poet was right again: "Let the wingèd Fancy roam, / Pleasure never is at home."

Getting going in the realty business followed as a natural off-spring of selling my house and buying Ann's. Once all was set-tled and I was "at home" on Cleveland Street, I started thinking again about new enterprises, about diversification and stashing my new money someplace smart. A ministorage in New Sharon, a train-station lobster house rehab, a chain of low-maintenance self-serv car washes—all rose as possibles. Though none did I immediately bite for, since I still somehow felt frozen in place, unable or unwilling or just uninspired to move into action. Without Ann and my kids nearby, I, in fact, felt as lonely and inessential and exposed as a lighthouse keeper in broad daylight.

Unmarried men in their forties, if we don't subside entirely into the landscape, often lose important credibility and can even attract unwholesome attention in a small, conservative community. And in Haddam, in my new circumstances, I felt I was perhaps becoming the personage I least wanted to be and, in the years since my divorce, had feared being: the suspicious bachelor, the man whose life has no mystery, the graying, slightly jowly, slightly too tanned and trim middle-ager, driving around town in a cheesy '58 Chevy ragtop polished to a squeak, always alone on balmy summer nights, wearing a faded yellow polo shirt and green suntans, elbow over the window top, listening to progressive jazz, while smiling and pretending to have everything under control, when in fact there was nothing *to* control.

One morning in November, though, Rolly Mounger, one of the broker-agents at Lauren-Schwindell, and the one who had walked me through my buyout with the Institute and who is a big ex–Fairleigh Dickinson nose-tackle out of Plano, Texas, called up to advise me about some tax forms I needed to get hold of after New Year's and to fill me in on some "investment entities" dealing with government refinance grants for a bankrupt apartment complex in Kendall Park that he was putting together with "other principals"—just in case I wanted a first crack (I didn't). He said, however, as if in passing, that he himself was just before pulling up stakes and heading to Seattle to get involved with some lucrative commercial concepts he didn't want to get particular about; and would I like to come over and talk to some people about coming on there as a residential specialist. My name, he said, had come up "seriously" any number of times from several different sources (why, and who, I couldn't guess and never found out and I'm sure now it was a total lie). It was generally thought, he said, I had strong natural credentials "per se" for their line of work: which was to say I was looking to get into a new situation; I wasn't hurting for dough (a big plus in any line of work); I knew the area, was single and had a pleasant personality. Plus, I was mature—meaning over forty—and I didn't seem to have a lot of attachments in the community, a factor that made selling houses one hell of a lot easier.

What did I think?

Training, paperwork and "all that good boool dukie," Rolly said, could be plowed under right on the job while I went nights to a three-month course up at the Weiboldt Realty Training Institute in New Brunswick, after which I could take the state boards and start printing money like the rest of them.

And the truth was, having parted with or been departed from by most everything, until I was left almost devoid of all expectation, I thought it was a reasonable idea. In those last three months I'd begun to feel that living through the consequences of my various rash acts and bad decisions had had its downsides as well as its purported rewards, and if it was possible to be at a complete loss without being miserable about it, that's what I was. I'd started going fishing alone at the Red Man Club three afternoons a week, sometimes staying overnight in the little beaverboard cabin meant for keeping elderly members out of the rain, taking a book up with me but ultimately just lying there in the dark listening to big fish kerplunking and mosquitoes bopping the screen, while not very far away the bangety-bang of I-80 soothed the night and, out east, Gotham shone like a temple set to fire by infidels. I still registered a faint tingle of the synchronicity I'd felt when I got back from France. I was still dead set on taking the kids to Mississippi and the Pine Barrens once they were settled, and had even joined AAA and gotten color-coded maps with sidebars to various attractions down side roads (Cooperstown and the Hall of Fame was in fact one of them).

But tiny things—things I'd never even noticed when Ann lived in Haddam and we shared responsibilities and I held down my sportswriting job—had begun to get the better of me. Some little worry, some little anything, would settle into my thinking—for instance, how was I going to get my car serviced on Tuesday but also get to the airport to sign for a Greek rug I'd ordered from Thessaloníki and had been waiting on for months and was sure some thieving airport worker would steal if I wasn't there to lay hands on it the instant it came down the conveyer? Should I rent a car? Should I send someone? Who? And would that person even be willing to go if I could think of who he or she was, or would that person think I was an idiot? Should I call the broker in Greece and tell him to delay the shipping? Should I call the freight company and say I'd be a day late getting up there and would they please see to it the rug was kept in a safe place until my car was ready? I'd wake up right in the Red Man Club cabin, my heart booming, or in my own new house, brooding about such things, sweating, clenching my fists, scheming how to get this plus a hundred *other* simple, ordinary things done, as if everything were a crisis as big as my health. Later I'd start to think about how stupid it was to carry such things around all day. I'd decide then to trust fate, go up and get it when I could or maybe never, or to forget the fucking rug and just go fishing. Though then I'd start to fear I was letting everything go, that my life was spinning crazy-out-of-azimuth, proportion and common sense flying out the window like pie plates. Then I'd realize that years later I'd look back on this period as a "bad time," when I was "*waaaa*y out there at the edge," my everyday conduct as erratic and zany as a roomful of chimps, only I was the last to notice (again, one's neighbors would be the first: "He really sort of stayed to himself a lot, though he seemed like a pretty nice guy. I wouldn't have expected anything like *this*!").

Now, of course, in 1988, driving into sunny Haddam with better hopes for the day squirreling around my belly, I know the source of that devilment. I'd paid handsome dues to the brotherhood of consolidated mistake-makers, and having survived as well as I had, I wanted my goddamned benefits: I wanted *everything* to go my way and to be happy *all the time*, and I was wild it wouldn't work out like that. I wanted the Greek rug delivery not to interfere with getting my windshield washer pump replaced. I wanted the fact that I had left France and Catherine Flaherty and come home in the best spirit of enterprise and good works to still somehow reward me in big numbers. I wanted the fact that my wife had managed to divorce me *again* and *worse*, and even divorce my kids from me, to become a fact of life I got smoothly used to and made the most of. I wanted a lot of things, in other words (these are just samples). And I'm not in fact sure all this didn't constitute another "kind of major crisis," though it may also be how you feel when you survive one.

But what I wanted more than anything was to quit being deviled so I could have a chance for the rest, and it occurred to me once I'd listened to Rolly Mounger's idea that I might try out a new thought (since I wasn't making any other headway): I might just take seriously his list of my "qualifications" and let them lead me toward the unexpected—instead of going on worrying about how happy I was all the time—after which worries and contingencies might glide away like leaves on a slack tide, and I might find myself, if not in the warp of many highly dramatic events, reckless furies and rocketing joie de vivre, still as close to day-to-day happy as I could be. This code of conduct, of course, is the most self-preserving and salubrious tenet of the Existence Period and makes real estate its ideal occupation.

I told Rolly Mounger I'd give his suggestion some serious thought, even though I said the idea pretty much came out of left field. He said there was no hurry to make a decision about becoming a realtor, that down at their office everyone had gotten there by different routes and timetables, and there were no two alike. He himself, he said, had been a supermarket developer and before that a policy strategist for a Libertarian state senate candidate. One person had a Ph.D. in American literature; another had left a seat on the Exchange; a third was a dentist! They all worked as independents but acted in concert whenever possible, which gave everybody a damn good feeling. Everybody had made a "ton of money" in the last few years and expected to make a ton more before the big correction came ("the whole industry" knew it was coming). From his point of view, which he admitted favored the commercial side, all you needed to do to wake up rich was "get with your money people, put some key factors and some financing on the table," locate some unimproved parcels your group can handle the debt service and taxes on for twelve to eighteen months, then once the time's up sell out the whole trunkload to some Johnny-come-lately Arabs or Japs and start cashing in your chips. "Let your money people run the risk gauntlet," Rolly said. "You just sit tight in the middle seat and take your commissions." (You could always, of course, "participate" yourself, and he admitted he had. But the exposure could be substantial.)

To figure all this out took me no time at all. If everybody came at it from all angles, I thought maybe I could find one of my own to work—relying on the concept that you don't sell a house to someone, you sell a life (this had so far been my experience). In this way I could still pursue my original plan to do for others while looking after Number One, which seemed a good aspiration as I entered a part of life when I'd decided to expect less, hope for modest improvements and be willing to split the difference.

I went down to the office in three days and got introduced around to everybody—a crew of souls who seemed like people you wouldn't mind working out of the same office with. A short, bunchy-necked, thick-waisted dyke in a business suit and wing tips, named Peg, with Buick-bumper breasts, braces on her teeth and hair bleached silver (she was the Ph.D.). There was a tall, salt-and-pepper, blue-blazer Harvard grad in his late fifties—this was Shax Murphy, who's since bought the agency and who'd retired out of some brokerage firm and still owned a house in Vinalhaven. He had his long, gray-flanneled legs stretched out in the aisle between desks, one big shiny cordovan oxford on top of the other, his face red as a western sunset from years of gentlemanly drinking, and I took to him instantly because when I shook his hand he had just put down a dog-eared copy of *Paterson*, which made me think he probably had life in pretty much the right perspective. "You just need to remember the three most important words in the 'relaty budnus,' Frank, and you'll do fine in this shop," he said, jiggering his heavy brows up and down mock seriously. 'Locution, locution, locution.'" He sniffed loudly through his big ruby nose, rolled his eyes and went right back to reading.

Everyone else in the office at that time—two or three young realtor associates and the dentist—has left since the '86 slide began to seem like a long fall-off. All of them were people without solid stakes in town or capital to back them up, and they quickly scattered back out of sight—to vet school at Michigan State, back home to New Hampshire, one in the Navy, and of course Clair Devane, who came later and met an unhappy end.

Old man Schwindell accorded me only the briefest, most cursory of interviews. He was an old, palely grim, wispy-haired, flaking-skinned little tyrant in an out-of-season seersucker suit and whom I'd seen in town for years, knew nothing about and viewed as a curio—though it was he who'd done the behind-the-scenes knitting of my deal with the Institute. He was also the "dean" of New Jersey realtors and had thirty plaques on his office wall saying as much, along with framed photos of himself with movie stars and generals and prizefighters he'd sold homes to. No longer officially active, he held forth in the back office, hunched behind a cluttered old glass-topped desk with his coat always on, smoking Pall Malls.

"Do you believe in progress, Bascombe?" Old man Schwindell squinted his almost hueless blue eyes up at me. He had a big mustache yellowed by eight million Pall Malls, and his grizzled hair was thick on the sides and growing out his ears but was thin on top and falling out in clusters. He suddenly groped behind himself without looking, clutched at the clear plastic hose attached to a big oxygen cylinder on wheels, yanked it and strapped a little elastic band around his head so that a tiny clear nozzle fit up into his nose and fed him air. "You know that's our motto," he gasped, routing his eyes down to monkey with his lifeline.

"That's what Rolly's told me," I said. Rolly had never mentioned word one about progress, had talked only about risk gauntlets, capital gains taxes and exposure, all of which he was dead against.

"I'm not going to ask you about it now. Don't worry," old man Schwindell said, not entirely satisfied with his flow, straining around to twist a green knob on the cylinder and succeeding only in getting half a good breath. "When you've been around here and know something," he said with difficulty, "I'll ask you to tell me *your* definition of progress. And if you give me the wrong answer, I'll get rid of you on the spot." He swiveled back around and gave me a mean little ocher-toothed leer, his air apparatus getting in the way of his mouth, though his breathing was going much more smoothly, so that he might've felt like he wasn't about to die that very minute. "How's that? Is that fair?"

"I think that's fair," I said. "I'll try to give you a good answer."

"Don't give me a good answer. Give me the right answer!" he shouted. "Nobody should graduate the sixth grade without an idea of what progress is all about. Don't you think so?"

"I agree completely," I said, and I did, though mine had been suffering some setbacks.

"Then you're good enough to start. You don't have to be any good anyway. Realty sells itself in this town. Or it used to." He started fiddling more furiously with his breathing tubes, trying to get the holes to line up better with his old hairy nostrils. And my interview was over, though I stood there for almost another minute before I recognized he wasn't going to say anything else, so that I just eventually let myself out.

And for all practical purposes I was on my sweet way after that. Rolly Mounger took me to lunch at The Two Lawyers. I'd have a "break-in period," he told me, of about three months, when I'd be on salary (no insurance or benefits). Everybody would chip in and rotate me around the office, see to it I learned the MLS hardware and the office lingo. I'd go on *"beaucoup"* house showings and closings and inspections and realty caravans, "just to get to know whatever," all this while I was going to class at my own expense—"three hundred bucks *más o menos*." At the end of the course I'd take the state exam at the La Quinta in Trenton, then "jump right in on the commission side and start root-hoggin'."

"I wish I could tell you there was one goddamn hard thing about any of this, Frank," Rolly said in amazement. "But"—and he shook his jowly, buzz-cut head—"if it was *so* goddamned hard why would I be doing it? Hard work's what the other asshole does." And with that he cut a big bracking fart right into his Naugahyde chair and looked all around at the other lunchers, grinning like a farm boy. "You know, your soul's not supposed to be in this," he said. "This is realty. *Reality's* something else—that's when you're born and you die. This is the in-between stuff here."

"I get it," I said, though I thought my personal take on the job probably wouldn't be just like Rolly's.

And that was that. In six months old man Schwindell gorked off in the front seat of his Sedan de Ville, stopped at the light at the corner of Venetian Way and Lipizzaner Road, a man-and-wife ophthalmologist team in the car, on their way to the preclosing walkthrough at the retired New Jersey Supreme Court Justice's house, down the street from my former home on Hoving (the deal naturally fell through). By then Rolly Mounger was steaming along selling time-shares to Seattleites, most of the young people in our office had taken off for better pickings in distant area codes, and I'd passed the board and was out hawking listings.

Though based on strict cash flow and forgetting about taxes, it was already true by then that a person could rent for half the cost of buying, and a lot of our clients were beginning to wise up. In addition—as I have ever so patiently told the Markhams, fidgeting now out in the Sleepy Hollow—housing costs were rising faster than incomes, at about 4.9 percent. Plus, plenty of other signs were bad. Employment was down. Expansion was way out of balance. Building permits were taking a nosedive. It was "what the monkey does on the other side of the stick," Shax Murphy said. And those who had no choice or, like me, had choices but no wish to pursue them, all dug in for the long night that becomes winter.

But truth to say, I was as happy as I expected to be. I enjoyed being on the periphery of the business community and having the chance to stay up with trends—trends I didn't even know existed back when I was writing sports. I liked the feeling of earning a living by the sweat of my brow, even if I didn't need the money, still don't work that hard and don't always earn a great deal. And I managed to achieve an even fuller appreciation of the Existence Period; began to see it as a good, permanent and adaptable strategy for meeting life's contingencies other than head-on.

For a brief time I took some small interest in forecast colloquia, attended the VA and FHA update meetings and a few taking-control-of-the-market seminars. I attended the state Realty Roundtable, sat in on the Fair Housing Panel down in Trenton. I delivered Christmas packages to the elderly, helped coach the T-ball team, even dressed up like a clown and rode from Haddam to New Brunswick in a circus wagon to try to spruce up the public perception of realtors as being, if not a bunch of crooks, at least a bunch of phonies and losers.

But eventually I let most of it slide. A couple of young hotshot associates have come in since I signed on, and they're fired up to put on clown suits to prove a point. Whereas I don't feel like I'm trying to prove a point anymore.

And yet I still like the sunny, paisley-through-the-maples exhilaration of exiting my car and escorting motivated clients up some new and strange walkway and right on into whatever's waiting—an unoccupied house on a summer-warm morning when it's chillier indoors than out, even if the house isn't much to brag about, or even if I've shown it twenty-nine times and the bank's got it on the foreclosure rolls. I enjoy going into other people's rooms and nosing around at their things, while hoping to hear a groan of pleasure, an "Ahhh, now *this*, this is more like it," or a whispered approval between a man and wife over some waterfowl design worked into the fireplace paneling, then surprisingly repeated in the bathroom tiles; or share the satisfaction over some small grace note—a downstairs-upstairs light switch that'll save a man possible injury when he's stumbling up to bed half sloshed, having gone to sleep on the couch watching the Knicks long after his wife has turned in because she can't stand basketball.

Beyond all that, since two years ago I've bought no new houses on Clio Street or elsewhere. I ride herd on my small hot dog empire. I write my editorials and have as always few friends outside of work. I take part in the annual Parade of Homes, standing in the entryway of our fanciest listings with a big smile on my chops. I play an occasional game of volleyball behind St. Leo's with the co-ed teams from other businesses. And I go fishing as much as I can at the Red Man Club, where I sometimes take Sally Caldwell in violation of Rule 1 but never see other members, and where I've learned over time to catch a fish, to marvel a moment at its opaline beauties and then to put it back. And of course I act as parent and guardian to my two children, though they are far away now and getting farther.

I try, in other words, to keep something finite and acceptably doable on my mind and not disappear. Though it's true that sometimes in the glide, when worries and contingencies are floating off, I sense I myself am afloat and cannot always feel the sides of where I am, nor know what to expect. So that to the musical question "What's it all about, Alfie?" I'm not sure I'd know the answer. Although to the old taunt that says, "Get a life," I can say, "I already have an existence, thanks."

And this may perfectly well constitute progress the way old man Schwindell had it in mind. His wouldn't have been some philosopher's enigma about human improvement over the passage of time used frugally, or an economist's theorem about profit and loss, or the greater good for the greater number. He wanted, I believe, to hear something from me to convince him I was simply *alive*, and that by doing whatever I was doing—selling houses—I was extending life and my own interest in it, strengthening my tolerance for it and the tolerance of innocent, unnamed others. That was undoubtedly what made him "dean" and kept him going. He wanted me to feel a little every day—and a little would've been enough—like I felt the day after I speared a liner bare-handed in the right-field stands at Veterans Stadium, hot off the bat of some black avenger from Chicago, with my son and daughter present and awed to silence with admiration and astoundment for their Dad (everyone around me stood up and applauded as my hand began to swell up like a tomato). How I felt at that moment was that life would never get better than that—though later what I thought, upon calmer reflection, was that it had merely been just a damn good thing to happen, and my life wasn't a zero. I'm certain old Otto would've been satisfied if I'd come in and said something along those lines: "Well, Mr. Schwindell, I don't know very much about progress, and truthfully, since I became a realtor my life hasn't been totally transformed; but I don't feel like I'm in jeopardy of disappearing into thin air, and that's about all I have to say." He would, I'm certain, have sent me back to the field with a clap on the back and a hearty go-get-'em.

And this in fact may be how the Existence Period helps create or at least partly stimulates the condition of honest independence:

inasmuch as when you're in it you're visible as you are, though not necessarily very noticeable to yourself or others, and yet you maintain reason enough and courage in a time of waning urgency to go toward where your interests lie as though it mattered that you get there.

*T*he rain that dumped buckets on Route 1 and Penns Neck has missed Wallace Hill, so that all the hot, neat houses are shut up tight as nickels with their window units humming, the pavement already giving off wavy lines no one's willing to tread through at eleven-thirty. Later, when I'm long gone to South Mantoloking and shade inches beyond the eaves and sycamores, all the front porches will be full, laughter and greetings crisscrossing the way as on my first drive-by. Though now everyone who's not at work or in summer school or in jail is sitting in the TV darkness watching game shows and waiting for lunch.

The McLeods' house looks as it did at 8:30, though someone in the last three hours has removed my FOR RENT sign from in front of the Harrises', and I pull to a halt there, careful not to stop in front of the McLeods' and alert them. I climb out into the clammy heat, ditch my windbreaker and hike up onto the dry lawn and take a look around. I check down both sides of the house, behind the hydrangeas and the rose of Sharon bush and up on the tiny porch as if the sign stealers had just uprooted the thing and tossed it, which according to Everick and Wardell is what usually happens. Only it's not here now.

I step back out to my car, open the trunk for another sign from the several (FOR SALE, OPEN HOUSE, REDUCED, CONTRACT PENDING) that're stacked there with my box of offer sheets, along with my suitbag and fishing rods, three Frisbees, two ball mitts, baseballs and the fireworks I've ordered special from relatives in Florida—all important paraphernalia for my trip with Paul.

I bring the new FOR RENT up onto the lawn, find the two holes the previous sign occupied, waggle the stiff metal legs in until they stop, and with my toe mash some grassy ground around so that everything looks as it did. Then I close up the trunk, wipe the sweat off my arms and brow, using my handkerchief, and walk straight to the McLeods' front door, where, though I mean to ring the bell, I like a criminal step to the side and peer through the front window into the living room, where it's murky as twilight. I can make out both McLeod kids huddled on a couch, eyes glued like zombies to the TV (little Winnie is clutching a stuffed bunny in her tiny hands). Neither one of them seems to see me, though suddenly the older one, Nelson, jerks his curly head around and stares at the window as if it were just another TV screen, and I was in the picture.

I wave a little friendly wave and grin. I would like to get this over with and get going to Franks and on to Sally's.

Nelson continues staring at me out of the dark room's dreamy light as though he expects me to disappear in a few more seconds. He and his sister are watching Wimbledon, and I suddenly realize that I have no business whatsoever gawking in the window and am actually running a serious risk hothead Larry will blow my head off.

Little Nelson gazes at me until I wave again, step away from the window, move back to the door and ring the bell. Like a shot, his bare feet hit the floor and pound out of the room, heading I hope to get his lazy parents up out of bed. An interior door slams, and far, far away I hear a voice below the a/c hum, a voice I can't make out, saying what, I'm not sure, though it's certainly about me. I look out at the street of white, green, blue and pink frame houses with green and red roofs and neat little cemetery-plot yards—some with overgrown tomato plants along the foundation walls, others with sweetpea vines running up side lattices and porch poles. It could be a neighborhood in the Mississippi Delta, though the local cars at the curb are all snazzy van conversions and late-model Fords and Chevys (Negroes are among the most loyal advocates of "Buy American").

A large elderly black woman, pushing an aluminum walker over which a yellow tea towel is draped, stumps out the screen door of the house directly across the street. When she sees me on the McLeods' porch she stops and stares. This is Myrlene Beavers, who waved at me hospitably the first two times I cruised the block, back in 1986, when I was deciding to buy into her neighborhood. Her husband, Tom, has died within the year, and Myrlene—the Harrises tell me by letter—has gone into a decline.

"Who you lookin' fo'?" Myrlene shouts out at me across the street.

"I'm just looking for Larry, Myrlene," I shout back and wave amiably. She and Mr. Beavers were both diabetics, and Myrlene is losing the rest of her sight to milky cataracts. "It's me, Myrlene," I call out. "It's Frank Bascombe."

"Sho' better not be," Myrlene says, her steely hair all tufted out in crazy stalks. "I'm tellin' you right now." She's wearing a bright-orange Hawaiian-print muumuu, and her ankles are swollen and bound up in bandages. I am aware she may fall slap over dead if she gets excited.

"It's all right, Myrlene," I call out. "I'm just visiting Larry. Don't worry. Everything's all right."

"I'm callin' the po-lice," Mrs. Beavers says, and goes stumping around so she can get back through her front door, the walker scraping the porch boards ahead of her.

"No, don't call the police," I shout. I should jog across and let her see it's me, that I'm not a burglar or a process server, only a rent collector—more or less the way Joe Markham said. Myrlene and I had several cordial conversations when the Harrises were still here—she from her porch, me going to and from my car. But something has happened now.

Though just as I'm about to hustle across and stop her from calling the cops, more bare feet come thundering toward the door, which suddenly quakes with locks and bolts being keyed and thrown, then opens to reveal Nelson in the crack, sandy-curly headed and light tan skin, a little mulatto Jackie Cooper. His face is below the nail latch on the screen, and staring down on him I feel like a giant. He says nothing, just peers up at me with his small, brown, skeptical eyes. He is six, bare-chested and wearing only a pair of purple-and-gold Lakers shorts. A draft of air-conditioned air slips past my face, which again is sweating. "Advantage, Miss Navratilova," an English woman's bland voice says, after which spectators applaud. (It's a replay from yesterday.)

"Nelson, how you doin'?" I say enthusiastically. We have never spoken, and Nelson just stares up at me and blinks as if I were speaking Swahili. "Your folks home today?"

He takes a look over his shoulder, then back at me. "Nelson, why don't you tell your folks Mr. Bascombe's at the front door, okay? Tell 'em I'm just here for the rent, not to murder anybody." This may be the wrong brand of humor for Nelson.

I would like not to peek in farther. It's, after all, my house, and I have a right to see in under extraordinary circumstances. But Nelson and Winnie may be home by themselves, and I wouldn't want to be inside alone with them. I have the sensation from behind me of Myrlene Beavers yelling inside her house: an unidentified white man is trying to break into Larry McLeod's private home in broad daylight. "Nelson," I say, sweating through my shirt and feeling unexpectedly trapped, "why don't you let me lean inside and call your Dad? Okay?" I offer him a big persuasive nod, then pull back the screen door, which surprisingly isn't latched, and push my face into the cool, swimming air. "Larry," I say fairly loudly into the dark room. "I'm just here for the rent." Winnie, clutching her stuffed rabbit, seems asleep. The TV's showing the deep greens of the All England Club.

Nelson looks straight up at me still (I'm leaning directly over him), then turns and goes and reseats himself on the couch by his sister, whose eyes open slowly, then close.

"Larry!" I call in again. "Are you in here?" Larry's big pistol is absent from the table, which may mean, of course, he has it in his possession.

I hear what sounds like a drawer opening and shutting in a back room; then a door slams. What would a panel of eight blacks and four whites—a jury of my peers—say if because of wishing to collect my rent I turned out to be a pre-holiday homicide statistic? I'm sure I'd be found at fault.

I step back from the door and turn a wary look over at the Beavers' house. Myrlene's orange muumuu is swimming like a mirage behind the screen, where she's watching me.

"It's all right, Myrlene," I say at nothing, which causes the muumuu specter to recede into the shadows.

"What's the matter?"

I turn quickly, and Betty McLeod is behind the screen, which she is this instant latching. She looks out at me with an unwelcoming frown. She's wearing a quilted pink housecoat and holding its scalloped collar closed with her skinny papery fingers.

"Nothing's the *matter*," I say, shaking my head in a way that probably makes me look deranged. "I think Mrs. Beavers just called the cops on me. I'm just trying to collect the rent." I'd like to look amused about it, but I'm not.

"Larry isn't here. He'll be home tonight, so you'll have to come back." Betty says this as though I'd been yelling in her face.

"Okay," I say, and smile mirthlessly. "Just tell him I came by like every other month. And the rent's due."

"He'll pay you," she says in a sour voice.

"That's great, then." Far back in the house, I hear a toilet flushing, water slackly then more vigorously touring the new pipes I had installed less than a year ago and paid a pretty penny for. Larry has no doubt just waked up, had his long morning piss and is holing up in the bathroom until I'm dispensed with.

Betty McLeod blinks at me defiantly as we both listen to the water trickle. She is a sallow, pointy-faced little Grinnell grad, off the farm near Minnetonka, who married Larry while she was doing a social work M.A. at Columbia and he was working himself through trade school at some uptown community college. He'd been a Green Beret and was searching for a way out of the city hell (all this I learned from the Harrises). Betty's Zion Lutheran parents naturally had a conniption when she and Larry came home their first Christmas with baby Nelson in a bassinet, though they've reportedly recovered. But since moving to Haddam, the McLeods have lived an increasingly reclusive life, with Betty staying inside all the time, Larry going off to his night job at the mobile-home factory and the kids being their only outward signs. It's not so different from many people's lives.

In truth I don't much like Betty McLeod, despite wanting to rent the house to her and Larry because I think they're probably courageous. To my notice she's always worn a perpetually disappointed look that says she regrets all her major life choices yet feels absolutely certain she made the right moral decision in every instance, and is better than you because of it. It's the typical three-way liberal paradox: anxiety mingled with pride and self-loathing. The McLeods are also, I'm afraid, the kind of family who could someday go paranoid and barricade themselves in their (my) house, issue confused manifestos, fire shots at the police and eventually torch everything, killing all within. (This, of course, is no reason to evict them.)

"Well," I say, moving back to the top step as if to leave, "I hope everything's A-okay around the house." Betty looks at me reproachfully. Though just then her eyes leave mine, move to the side, and I turn around to see one of our new black-and-white police cruisers stopping behind my car. Two uniformed officers are inside. One—the passenger—is talking into a two-way radio.

"He's still over there!" Myrlene Beavers bawls from inside her house, totally lost from sight. "That white man! Go on and git him. He's breakin' in."

The policeman who was talking on the radio says something to his partner-driver that makes them both laugh, then he gets out without his hat on and begins to stroll up the walk.

The cop, of course, is an officer I've known since I arrived in Haddam—Sergeant Balducci, who is only answering disturbance calls today because of the holiday. He is from a large local family of Sicilian policemen, and he and I have often passed words on street corners or chatted reticently over coffee at the Coffee Spot, though we've actually never "met." I have tried to talk him out of a half-dozen parking tickets (all unsuccessfully), and he once assisted me when I'd locked my keys in my car outside Town Liquors. He has also cited me for three moving violations, come into my house to investigate a burglary years ago when I was married, once stopped me for questioning and patted me down not long after my divorce, when I was given to long midnight rambles on my neighborhood streets, during which I often admonished myself in a loud, desperate voice. In all these dealings he has stayed as abstracted as a tax collector, though always officially polite. (Frankly, I've always thought of him as an asshole.)

Sergeant Balducci approaches almost to the bottom of the porch steps without having looked at either Betty McLeod or me. He hitches up on the heavyweight black belt containing all his police gear—Mace canister, radio, cuffs, a ring of keys, blackjack, his big service automatic. He is wearing his iron-creased blue and black HPD uniform with its various quasi-military markings, stripes and insignia, and either he has gained weight around his thick midsection or he's wearing a flak vest under his shirt.

He looks up at me as if he'd never laid eyes on me before. He is five-ten with a heavy-browed, large-pored face as vacant as the moon, his hair cut in a regimental flattop.

"We got a problem out here, folks?" Sergeant Balducci says, setting one polished police boot on the bottom step.

"Nothing's wrong," I say, and for some reason am breathless, as if more's wrong here than could ever meet the eye. I mean, of course, to look guilt-free. "Mrs. Beavers just got the wrong idea in her head." I know she's watching everything like an eagle, her mind apparently departed for elsewhere.

"Is that right?" Sergeant Balducci says and looks at Betty McLeod.

"Nothing's wrong," she says inertly, behind her screen.

"We have a reported break-in in progress at this address." Sergeant Balducci's voice is his official voice. "Do you live here, ma'am?" He says this to Betty.

Betty nods but adds nothing helpful.

"And did anybody break into your house or attempt to?"

"Not that I know of," she says.

"What's *your* business here?" Officer Balducci says to me, gazing around at the yard to see if he can notice anything out of the everyday—a broken pane of glass, a bloody ball-peen hammer, a gun with a silencer.

"I'm the owner," I say. "I was just stopping by on some business." I don't want to say I'm here hawking the rent, as if collecting rent were a crime.

"You're the owner of *this* house?" Officer Balducci's still glancing casually around but finally settles his gaze back on me.

"Yes, and that one too." I motion toward the Harrises' empty exhome.

"What's your name again?" he says, producing a little yellow spiral notebook and a ballpoint from his back pocket.

"Bascombe," I say. "Frank Bascombe."

"Frank . . . ," he says as he writes, "Bascombe. Owner."

"Right," I say.

"I think I've seen you before, haven't I?" He looks slowly down, then up at me.

"Yes," I say, and immediately picture myself in a lineup with a lot of unshaven sex-crime suspects, being given the once-over by Betty McLeod behind a two-way mirror. He has known a great deal about my life, once, but has simply let it recede.

"Did I arrest you one time for D and D?"

"I don't know what D and D is, but you didn't arrest me for it. You gave me a ticket twice"—three times, actually—"for turning right on red on Hoving Road after not making a full stop. Once when I didn't do it and once when I did."

"That's a pretty good average." Sergeant Balducci smiles, mocking me as he's writing in his notebook. He asks Betty McLeod her name, too, and enters that in his little book.

Myrlene Beavers comes scraping out onto her porch, a yellow cordless phone to her ear. A few neighbors have appeared on their porches to see what's what. One of them also has a cordless. She and Myrlene are doubtless connected up.

"Well," Sergeant Balducci says, dotting a few *i*'s and shoving his notebook back in his pocket. He is still smiling mockingly. "We'll check this out."

"Fine," I say, "but I didn't try to break into this house." And I'm breathless again. "That old lady's nuts across the street." I glare over at the traitorous Myrlene, gabbling away like a goose to her neighbor two houses down.

"People all watch out for each other in this neighborhood, Mr. Bascombe," Sergeant Balducci says, and looks up at me pseudo-seriously, then looks at Betty McLeod. "They have to. If you have any more trouble, Mrs. McLeod, just give us a call."

"All right," is all Betty McLeod says.

"She didn't have any trouble *this* time!" I say, and give Betty a betrayed look.

Sergeant Balducci takes a semi-interested glance up at me from the concrete walk of my house. "I could give you some time to cool off," he says in an uninflected way.

"I *am* cooled off," I say angrily. "I'm not mad at anything."

"That's good," he says. "I wouldn't want you to get your bowels in an uproar."

On the tip of my tongue are these words: "Gee thanks. And how would you like to bite my ass?" Only the look of his short, stout arms stuffed like fat salamis into his short blue shirtsleeves makes me suspect Sergeant Balducci is probably a specialist in broken collarbones and deadly chokeholds of the type practiced on my son. And I literally bite the tip of my tongue and look bleakly across Clio Street at Myrlene Beavers, blabbing on her cheap Christmas phone and watching me—or some blurry image of a white devil she's identified me to be—as if she expected me to suddenly catch flame and explode in a sulfurous flash. It's too bad her husband's gone, is what I know. The good Mr. Beavers would've made this all square.

Sergeant Balducci begins ambling back toward his cruiser Plymouth, his waist radio making fuzzy, meaningless crackles. When he opens the door, he leans in and says something to his partner and they both laugh as the Sarge squeezes in and notes something on a clipboard stuck to the dash. I hear the word "owner," and another laugh. Then the door shuts and they ease away, their big duals murmuring importantly.

Betty McLeod has not moved behind her screen, her two little mulatto kids now peeping around each side of her housecoat. Her face reveals no sympathy, no puzzlement, no bitterness, not even a memory of these.

"I'll just come back when Larry's home," I say hopelessly.

"All right then."

I fasten a firm, accusing look on her. "Who else is here?" I say. "I heard the toilet running."

"My sister," Betty says. "Is that any of your business?"

I look hard at her, trying to read truth in her beaky little features. A sibling from Red Cloud? A willowy, big-handed Sigrid, taking a holiday from her own Nordic woes to commiserate with her ethical sis. Conceivable, but not likely. "No," I say, and shake my head.

And then Betty McLeod, on no particular cue, simply shuts her front door, leaving me on the porch empty-handed with the equatorial sun beating on my head. Inside, she goes through the relocking-the-locks ritual, and for a long moment I stand listening and feeling forlorn; then I just start off toward my car with nothing left of good to do. I will now be after the 4th getting my rent, if I get it then.

Myrlene Beavers is still on the porch of her tiny white abode with sweet peas twirling up the posts, her hair frazzled and damp, her big fingers clenching the rubber walker like handholds on a roller coaster. Other neighbors have now gone back inside.

"Hey!" she calls out at me. "Did they catch that guy?" Her little yellow phone is hooked to her walker with a plastic coat-hanger rig-up. No doubt her kids have bought it so they can all keep in touch. "They was tryin' to break in over at Larry's. You musta scared him off."

"They caught him," I say. "He's not a threat anymore."

"That's good!" she says, a big falsey-toothy smile opening onto her face. "You do a wonderful job for us. We're all grateful to you."

"We just do our best," I say.

"Did you never know my husband?"

I put my hands on my doorframe and look consolingly at poor

fast-departing Myrlene, soon to join her beloved in the other place. "I sure did," I say.

"Now he was a wonderful man," Mrs. Beavers says, taking the words from my very thought. She shakes her head at his lost visage.

"We all miss him," I say.

"I guess we do," she says, and starts her halting, painful way back inside her house. "I guess we sho 'nuf do."

5

I drive windingly out Montmorency Road into Haddam horse country—our little Lexington—where fences are long, white and orthogonal, pastures wide and sloping, and roads (Rickett's Creek Close, Drumming Log Way, Peacock Glen) slip across shaded, rocky rills via wooden bridges and through the quaking aspens back to rich men's domiciles snugged deep in summer foliage. Here, the Fish & Game quietly releases hatchery trout each spring so well-furnished sportsmen/home owners with gear from Hardy's can hike down and wet a line; and here, wedges of old-growth hardwoods still loom, trees that saw Revolutionary armies rumble past, heard the bugles, shouts and defiance cries of earlier Americans in their freedom swivet, and beneath which now tawny-haired heiresses in jodhpurs stroll to the paddock with a mind for a noon ride alone. Occasionally I've shown houses out this way, though their owners, fat and bedizened as pharaohs, and who should be giddy with the world's gifts, always seem the least pleasant people in the world and the most likely to treat you like part-time yard help when you show up to "present their marvelous home." Mostly, Shax Murphy handles these properties for our office, since by nature he possesses the right brand of inbred cynicism to find it all hilarious, and likes nothing more than peeling the skin off rich clients a centimeter at a time. I, on the other hand, cleave to the homier market, whose homespun spirit I prize.

I think now, with regard to the disagreeable McLeods, that my mistake has been pretty plain: I should've hauled them over for a cookout the minute I closed on their house, gotten them into some lawn chairs on the deck, slammed a double margarita in both of them, served up a rack of ranch-style ribs, corn on the cob, tomato and onion salad and a key lime pie, and all after would've been jake. Later, when matters took a sour turn (as always happens between landlord and tenant, unless the tenants are inclined toward gratitude, or the landlord's a fool), we'd have had some instant history for ballast against suspicion and ill will, which are now unhappily the status quo. Why I didn't I don't know, except that it's not my nature.

I literally bashed right into Franks one summer night a year ago, driving home tired and foggy-eyed from the Red Man Club, where I'd fished till ten. In its then incarnation as Bemish's Birch Beer Depot, it rose appealingly up out of the night as I rounded a curve on Route 31, my eyes smarting and heavy, my mouth dry as burlap, the perfect precondition for a root beer.

Everybody over forty (unless they were born in the Bronx) has pristine and uncomplicated memories of such places: low, orange-painted wooden bunker boxes with sliding-screen customers' windows, strings of yellow bulbs outside, whitewashed tree trunks and trash barrels, white car tires designating proper parking etiquette, plenty of instructional signs on the trees and big frozen mugs of too-cold root beer you could enjoy on picnic tables by a brook or else drink off metal trays with your squeeze in the dark, radio-lit sanctity of your '57 Ford.

As soon as I saw this one I angled straight toward the lot, though at the precise moment I turned I apparently dozed off and drove right across the white-tire barrier, over a petunia bed, and gave one of the green picnic tables a board-cracking whack, which brought the owner, Karl Bemish, booming out the side door in his paper cap and his apron, wanting to know what in the hell I featured myself doing, and pretty sure I was drunk and in need of being arrested.

None of it came to anything unhappy (far from it). I was naturally enough awakened by the crash, climbed out apologizing at a high rate of speed, offered to take a breathalyzer, peeled off three hundred bucks to cover all damages and explained I'd been fishing, not closing down some gin mill in Frenchtown, and had veered into the lot because I thought the place was so goddamned irresistible out here by the brook with strings of bulbs and white trees, and in fact still wanted a root beer if he could see his way clear to selling me one.

Karl let himself be talked out of being mad by stuffing my wad of money in his apron pocket and relying on good character to concede that sometimes innocent things happen and sometimes (if rarely) the stated cause of an event is the real cause.

With my root beer in hand, I took a table that wasn't cracked and sat smilingly beside babbling Trendle Brook, my thoughts on my father stopping with me in just such places in the long-ago Fifties, in the far-away South, when as a Navy purchasing officer he had taken me on trips so my mother could recover from the chaos of being home alone with me night and day.

After a while Karl Bemish came out, having switched off all but one string of bulbs. He was carrying another root beer for me and a real suds for himself, and sat down across the table, happy to have a late-night chit-chat with a stranger who in spite of some initial suspiciousness seemed to be a good person to end the day with by virtue of being the only one around.

Karl, of course, did all the talking. (There were apparently insufficient opportunities to talk to his customers through the sliding window.) He was a widower, he said, and had been employed in the ergonomics field up in Tarrytown for almost thirty years. His wife, Millie, had died three years before, and he'd just decided to take his retirement, cash in his company stock and go looking for something imaginative to do (this sounded familiar). He knew plenty about ergonomics, a science I'd never even heard of, but nothing about retail trade or the food service industry or dealing with the public. And he admitted he'd bought the birch beer stand totally on a whim, after seeing it advertised in an entrepreneurs magazine. Where he had grown up, in the little upstate Polish community of Pulaski, New York, there'd been a place just like his right by a little stream that ran into Lake Ontario, and it of course was the "real meeting place" for all the kids and the grownups too. He'd met his wife there and even remembered working in the place and wearing a brown cotton smock with his name stitched in darker brown script on the front and a brown paper cap, though he admitted he could never find any actual evidence he'd worked there and had probably just dreamed it up as a way better to furnish his past. He remembered that place and time, though, as the best of his life, and his own birch beer stand served, he felt, to commemorate it.

"Of course, things haven't worked out exactly perfect here now," Karl said, taking his white paper cap off and setting it on the sticky planks of the picnic table, revealing his smooth, lacquered-looking dome, shiny under the string of lights strung back to the Depot. He was sixty-five and a big sausage-handed, small-eared guy who looked more like he might've loaded bricks for a living.

"It sure seems awful good to me," I said, taking an admiring look around. Everything was newly painted, washed, picked up, as GI'd as a hospital grounds. "I'd think you pretty much had a gold mine out here." I nodded approvingly, full to the gills with rich and creamy root beer.

"Super my first year and a half. I did super," Karl Bemish said. "The previous guy had let the place run down. And I put some money in it and fixed everything up. People in the little communities out here said it was great to see an old place restored and wanted to see it catch on again, and people like you stopped by late. It became a meeting place again, or started to. And I guess I got overexcited, 'cause I added a machine to make these slush puppies. I had some cash flow. Then I bought a yogurt machine. Then I bought a trailer kitchen to cater parties with. Then I got this idea from the entrepreneurs magazine to buy an old railroad dining car to fix up as a restaurant and put it beside here; maybe have a waiter out there, a limited menu, rig it up with chrome fixtures, original tables, bud vases, carpets. For special occasions." Karl looked over his shoulder in the direction of the brook and frowned. "It's all back there. I bought the goddamn thing from a place in Lackawanna and had it trucked down here in two pieces and set up right on a length of track. That's about when I ran out of money." Karl shook his head and brushed at a mosquito camped out on his pate.

"That's a shame," I said, peering into the dark and making out a blacker-than-normal hulk sitting still and ominous in the night. The original bad idea.

"I had big plans going," Karl Bemish said, and smiled across the table in a defeated way meant to suggest again that innocent things happen but that big ideas are inherently big mistakes.

"But you're still doing fine," I said. "You can just hold off on expansion till you renew your capital base." These were expressions I'd only recently learned in the realty business and hardly knew the meaning of.

"I'm carrying pretty stiff debt," Karl said dolefully, as if that were equivalent to toting around a hunk of lead in his heart. With his flat pink thumbnail he stabbed at a hardened root beer droplet bonded to the tabletop. "I'm about, oh, six months from two tits up out here." He sniffed and dug away at the scab of sweetness, baked on by a long summer of shitty luck.

"Can't you recapitalize?" I said. "Sell off the dining car, maybe take out an equity loan?" More realty lingo.

"Don't got the equity," Karl said. "And no one wants a goddamned dining car in central Jersey."

I was ready to drag myself home by then, have a real drink and pile into bed. But I said, "So what do you think you're going to do?"

"I need an investor to come in and clear my debt, then maybe trust me not to run us into the ground again. You know anybody like that? 'Cause I'm going to lose this pop stand before I have a chance to prove I'm not a complete asshole. It'll be too bad." Karl was not making an attempt at a joke, as my son would've.

I looked around behind Karl Bemish, at his little orange birch beer outlet—neat, hand-lettered signs all over the trees: "Walk dogs here ONLY!" "PLEASE don't litter." "Our customers are our BEST FRIENDS." "THANKS, come again." "BIRCH BEER is GOOD for YOU." It was a sweet little operation, with, I imagine, plenty of local goodwill and a favorable suburban-semi-rural location—a few old farms nearby, with small but prospering vegetable patches, the odd nursery *cum* cider mill, some decades-old hippie pottery operations and one or two mediocre, mostly treeless golf courses. New housing soon would be sprouting up in the open pastures. Traffic flow was good at the intersection of 518 and 31, where there was already a two-way stop and as growth continued there would have to be a light, since 31, if no longer the main road, was at least the scenic *former* main road from the northwestern counties down to the state house in Trenton. All of which spelled money.

It might really be, I thought, that all Karl Bemish needed was a little debt relief, a partner to consult with and oversee capital decisions while he ran the day-to-day. And for some reason (partly, I'm sure, because I shared a slice of nostalgic past with old Karl) I just couldn't say no.

I said to him right out under the gum trees, with mosquitoes thickening around our two heads, that I myself might be interested in some sort of partnership possibility. He seemed not the least bit surprised at this and immediately started spieling about several great ideas he had, all of which I thought would never work and told him so as a way of letting him know (and myself too) that I could be firm on some things. We talked for another hour, till nearly one, then I gave him my card, told him to call me at the office the next day and said if I didn't wake up feeling like I needed to have my brain replaced, maybe we could sit down again, go over his books and records, lay out his debts versus his assets, income and cash flow and if there weren't any tax problems or black holes (like boozing or a gambling problem), maybe I'd buy in for a piece of his birch beer action.

All of which seemed to please the daylights out of Karl, from the evidence of how many times he nodded his head solemnly and said, "Yep, sure, okee, yep, sure, okee. Right, right, right."

But who wouldn't be happy! A man comes crashing out of the night into your place of business, apparently drunk and wrecking the shit out of your picnic table and petunia beds. Yet before the dust even settles, you and he are making plans to be partners and to haul you out of a mud hole you'd gotten yourself in by a combination of dumb optimism, ineptitude and greed. Who wouldn't think the horn of plenty had been laid, big end forward, right outside his door?

And in fact inside of a month everything was pretty much in place, as the high rollers say. I bought into Karl's operation at the agreed-to amount of 35 thousand, which in essence zero-balanced his creditor debt, and also—because Karl was completely broke—took a controlling interest.

I immediately got busy selling off the slush puppy and yogurt machines to a restaurant wholesaler over in Allentown. I got in touch with the company up in Lackawanna that sold Karl the dining car, "The Pride of Buffalo," and they agreed to return a fifth of what they could get from reselling it, plus they'd haul it away. I sold off the copy and fax machines Karl had bought expecting eventually to further diversify by offering his roadway clients a wider variety of services than just birch beer. I eliminated several novelty food items Karl had also bought equipment for but never got operational because of space and money problems—a machine for making pronto pups; another, almost identical machine for (and only for) making New Orleans–style beignets. Karl had catalogues for daiquiri makers (in case he got a liquor license), a six-burner crepe stove and a lot of other crap no one in central New Jersey had ever heard of. It occurred to me during this time that after his wife's death Karl may have suffered a nervous breakdown or possibly a series of small strokes that left his decision-making faculty slightly bent.

Yet pretty soon, by application of nothing but common sense, I had things under control and was able to split the proceeds of the equipment sales with Karl and to put back half of mine into working capital (I decided, on a lark, to keep the kitchen-on-wheels). I also filled Karl in on some of my own newly minted, common-sense-rooted business acumen, all of which I'd picked up around the realty office. The biggest mistake, I told him, was an impulse to replicate a good thing so as to try to make it twice as good (this almost never works). And the second was that people failed not simply because they were greedy but because they got bored with regular life and with what they were doing—even things they liked—and farted away their hard-won gains just trying to stay amused. My view was, keep your costs down, make it simple, don't permit yourself the luxury of boredom, build up a clientele, then later sell to some doofus who can go broke making your idea "better." (None of this had I ever done, of course: all I'd done was buy two rental houses and sell my own house to buy my ex-wife's— hardly qualifying me for the trading pit.) I expounded these maxims to Karl while two enormous black men from Allentown Restaurant Outfitters were fork-lifting his slush puppy and yogurt machines out the back door onto a rental truck. It was, I thought, a vivid object lesson.

The last alterations I made in our business strategies were, first, to change the name of the place from Bemish's Birch Beer Depot (too big a mouthful) to Franks, no apostrophe (I liked the pun plus the straightforward appeal). And on top of that I declared that only two things would a human being buy when he pulled off the road at our sign: a frosty mug of root beer and a hell of a good Polish wurst-dog of the sort everyone always dreams about and wishes they could find while driving through some semi-scenic backwater with a hunger on. Karl Bemish, a saved man now in his white, mono-grammed tunic, paper cap and shiny dome, was of course promptly established as owner-operator, yukking it up with his old customers, making crude, half-assed jokes about the "bun man" and generally feeling like he'd gotten his life back on track since the much-too-early death of his precious wife. And for me, for whom it was all pretty simple and amusing, our transaction was more or less what I'd been searching for when I came back from France but didn't find: a chance to help another, do a good deed well and diversify in a way that would pay dividends (as it's begun to) without driving myself crazy. We should all be so lucky.

I emerge out of the woodsy Haddam back roads to the intersection with 31, over which a state utility crew with a cherry picker is just suspending the prophesied new stoplight, the crew members standing around in white hard hats and work clothes, watching the procedure as if it were an act of legerdemain. A temporary sign says "Your highway taxes at work—SLOW." A few cars are pulling cautiously around, then heading off south toward Trenton.

Franks, with its new brown and orange mug-with-frothy-bubbles sign, sits kitty-cornered from the yellow highway truck. A lone customer car sits off to one side on the newly re-asphalted lot, its driver cool behind tinted windows. Karl's old red VW Beetle is parked by the back door, the red OPEN card in the window. And as I park I admit I unreservedly admire all, including the silver kitchen-on-wheels converted now into a dogs-on-wheels, glistening in the corner of the lot, all polished up by Everick and Wardell and ready to be hauled into Haddam early Monday. Some quality of its single-use efficiency, its compactness and portability, make it seem like the best purchase I've ever made, including even my house, though of course I have scarcely any use for it and should probably sell it before it depreciates out of existence.

Karl and I have forged an unwritten agreement that at least once a week I drive out and troop the colors, a practice I enjoy and especially today after my disconcerting wire-crossings with the Markhams and Betty McLeod—neither one typical of my days, which are almost always pleasant. Karl, during our first year together, which included the market sinkhole last fall (we coasted through unfazed), has begun treating me like a spirited but slightly too headstrong young maverick boss and has reinvented himself as an eccentric but faithful lifelong employee whose job it is to snipe at me in a salty, Walter Brennanish way, thereby keeping me on a true compass course. (He is much happier being an employee than running the show, which I'm sure comes from years in the ergonomics industry; though I have never thought of myself as anyone's boss, since at times I feel I'm hardly my own.)

When I step inside the "Employees only" side door, Karl is behind the sliding window, reading the Trenton *Times*, perched on two stacked red plastic milk cartons from the days when he made malts. It is hot as a broiler back here, and Karl has a little rubber-bladed Hammacher Schlemmer fan trained on his face. As usual, everything is spotless, since Karl has dark worries of getting what he calls a "C card" from the county health officer and so spends hours every night scouring and polishing, mopping and rinsing, until you could sit right down on the concrete and eat a four-course meal and never give one thought to salmonella.

"I'll tell you, I'm getting goddamn anxious about my economic future now, aren't you?" he says in a loud, scoffing voice. Karl has on his plastic reading specs and hasn't otherwise remarked my arrival. He's dressed in his summer issue: short-sleeved white tunic, laundry-supplied black-and-white checkered knee shorts that let his thick, mealy, sausage-veined calves "breathe," short black nylon socks and black crepe-soled brogans. An ancient transistor, tuned to the all-polka station in Wilkes-Barre, is playing "There Is No Beer in Heaven" at a low volume.

"I'm just interested in the Democrats to see how they'll fuck up next," I say, as though we'd been talking for hours, walking back to open the rear door onto the brookside picnic area to get some breeze going. (Karl is a lifelong Democrat who began voting Republican in the last decade but still thinks of himself as a noncon-forming Jacksonian. To me, these are the true turncoats, though Karl in most ways is not a bad citizen.)

Since I have no special mission here today, I begin counting packages of hot dog buns, cans of condiments (spice relish, mustard, mayo, ketchup, diced onions), checking the meat delivery and the extra kegs of root beer I've ordered for the "Firecracker Weenie Firecracker" concession.

"Looks like housing starts fell *way* off last month again, twelve point two from May. The dumb fucks. It's gotta mean trouble to the realty business, right?" Karl gives the *Times* a good snapping as though to get the words lined up straighter. It pleases him for us to talk in this quasi-familial way (he is finally an old nostalgian where I'm concerned), as if we had come a long ways together and learned the same hard human lessons of decency and need. He peers at me over the newspaper, removes his half glasses, then stands and looks out the window as the car that's been parked by the picnic tables idles out onto Route 31 and slowly starts north toward Ringoes. The backup bell on the highway department truck starts dinging away and a heavy, black man's voice sings out, "Come-awn-back, nah, come-awn-back."

"Units sold is down five from a year ago, though." I say, while I estimate packages of Polish weenies in the cold box, frigid air hitting my face like a bright light. "Maybe it means people are going to buy houses already built. That's my guess." In fact that *is* what'll happen, and the sorry-ass Markhams better be getting in touch with me and their brains *toute de suite*.

"Dukakis takes credit for the big Massachusetts Miracle, it's only right he takes it for the big Taxachusetts Fuck-up. I'm glad I live in *Joisey* now." Karl says this listlessly, still mooning out the window at the newly lined lot.

"Well." I turn back toward him, ready to quote him my "Buyer vs. Seller" column eye-to-eye, but I confront his big checkered behind and two pale, meaty legs underneath. The rest of him is geezering around, watching the workers and their cherry picker and the new stoplight going up.

"And hot dogs," Karl observes, having heard me say something I haven't said, his voice faint for most of it being directed into the hot day, and making it easier for me to hear the polka music, which is pleasing. I am as ever always pleased to be here. "I don't think anybody gives a shit about this election anyway," Karl says, still facing out. "It's just like the fuckin' all-star game. Big buildup, then nothin'." Karl makes a juicy fart noise with his mouth for proper emphasis. "We're all distanced from government. It don't mean anything in our lives. We're in limbo." He is undoubtedly quoting some right-wing columnist he read exactly two minutes ago in the Trenton *Times*. Karl couldn't care less about government or limbo.

I, however, have nothing more I can do now, and my gaze wanders through the side door, back out to the lot, where the portable silver dog stand sits in the sun on its shiny new tires, its collapsible green-and-white awning furled above its delivery window, the whole outfit chained to a fifty-gallon oil drum filled with concrete that is itself bolted to a slab set in the ground (Karl's idea for discouraging thievery). Seeing outside from this angle, though, and particularly viewing the feasible but also in most ways sweetly ridiculous hot dog trailer, makes me feel suddenly, unexpectedly distanced from all except what's here, as though Karl and I were all each other had in the world. (Which of course isn't true: Karl has nieces in Green Bay; I have two children in Connecticut, an ex-wife, and a girlfriend I'm right now keen to see.) Why this feeling, why now, why here, I couldn't tell you.

"You know, I was just reading in the paper yesterday . . ." Karl pulls his bulk off the counter and swivels around toward me. He reaches down and switches off the polka festival. " . . . that there's a decline in songbirds now that's directly credited to the suburbs."

"I didn't know that." I stare at his smooth, pink features.

"It's true. Predatory animals that thrive in disturbed areas eat the songbird eggs and young. Vireos. Flycatchers. Warblers. Thrushes. They're all taking a real beating."

"That's too bad," I say, not knowing what else to offer. Karl is a facts man. His idea of a worthwhile give-and-take is to confront you with something you've never dreamed of, an obscure koan of history, a rash of irrefutable statistics such as that New Jersey has the highest effective property-tax rate in the nation, or that one of every three Latin Americans lives in Los Angeles, something that explains nothing but makes any except the most banal response inescapable, and then to look at you for a reply—which can only ever amount to: "Well, what d'you know," or "Well, I'll be goddamned." Actual, speculative, unprogrammed dialogue between human beings is unappetizing to him, his ergonomic training notwithstanding. I am, I realize, ready to leave now.

"Listen," Karl says, forgetting the dark fate of vireos, "I think we might be being cased out here."

"What do you mean?" A trickle of oily, hot-doggy sweat leaves my hairline and heads underground into my left ear before I can finger it stopped.

"Well, last night, see, just at eleven"—Karl has both hands on the counter edge behind him, as if he were about to propel himself upward—"I was scrubbin' up. And these two Mexicans drove in. Real slow. Then they drove off down Thirty-one, and in about ten minutes here they come back. Just pulled through slow again, and then left again."

"How do you know they were Mexicans?" I feel myself squinting at him.

"They *were* Mexicans. They were Mexican-*looking*," Karl says, exasperated. "Two small guys with black hair and GI haircuts, driving a blue Monza, lowered, with tinted windows and those red and green salsa lights going around the license tag? Those weren't Mexicans? Okay. Hondurans then. But that doesn't really make a lot of difference, does it?"

"Did you know them?" I give a worried look out the open customer window, as though the suspicious foreigners were there now.

"No. But they came back about an hour ago and bought birch beers. Pennsylvania plates. CEY 146. I wrote it all down."

"Did you let the sheriff know?"

"They said there's still no law yet against driving through a drive-in. If there were, we wouldn't be in business."

"Well." Again I don't know what else to say. In most ways it is a statement like the one about songbird decline. Though I'm not happy to hear about suspicious lurkers in lowered Monzas. It's news no small businessman wants to hear. "Did you ask the sheriff to check by special?" A little more oily sweat slides down my cheek.

"I'm not supposed to worry, just pay attention." Karl picks up his rubber-bladed fan and holds it so it blows warm air at my face. "I just hope if the little cocksuckers decide to rob us, they don't kill me. Or half kill me."

"Just fork over all the money," I say seriously. "We can replace that. No heroics." I wish Karl would put the fan away.

"I want a chance to protect myself," he says, and makes his own quick assessment outside, via the customer window. I'd never considered protecting myself until I got bonked in the head by the Asian kid with the big Pepsi bottle. Though what I thought of doing then was concealing a handgun, lying in wait at the same place the next evening and blasting all three of them—which was not a workable idea.

Behind Karl I see the gang of state stoplight installers swaggering in a scattered group across the highway and on into our parking lot, still wearing their hard hats and thick insulated gloves. A couple are animatedly dusting off their thick pants, a couple are laughing. Half are black and half white, though they're taking their break together as if they are best of friends. "I'll have the big weenie," I hear one say from a distance, making the others laugh some more. " 'She said *hungrily*,' " someone else says. And they all laugh again (too boisterous to be sincere).

I, though, want to get out of here, get back in my car, jack the a/c to the max and lickety-split head to the Shore before I get corralled into building Polish dogs and serving up root beer and watching out for stickup artists. I occasionally hold down the fort when Karl takes off for some medical checkup or to have his choppers adjusted, but I don't like it and feel like an asshole every time. Karl, however, loves nothing better than the idea of "the boss" donning a paper cap.

He has already started lining up cold mugs out of the freezer box. "How's old Paul?" he says, forgetting about the Mexicans. "You oughta bring him out here and leave him with me a couple of days. I'll shape him up." Karl knows all about Paul's brush with the law over filched condoms, and his view is that all fifteen-year-olds need shaping up. I'm sure Paul would pay big money to spend two free-wheeling days out here with Karl, cracking jokes and double entendres, garbaging down limitless root beers and Polish dogs and generally driving Karl nuts.

But not a chance. The vision of Karl's little second-floor bachelor apartment over in Lambertville, with all his old furniture from his prior Tarrytown life, his pictures of his dead wife, his closets full of elderly "man's" things, odorous old toiletries on dressertop doilies, the green rubber drain rack, all the strange smells of lonely habits—I'd be grateful if Paul lived an entire life without having to experience that firsthand. And for fear of a hundred things: that a set of "mature" snapshots might just get left on a table, or a "funny magazine" turn up among the *Time*s and *Argosy*s under the TV stand, possibly an odd pair of "novelty undershorts" Karl might wear only at home and decide my son would think was "a gas." Such notions come to solitary older men, happen without plan, and then boom—piggy's in the soup before you know it! So that with all due respect to Karl, whom I'm happy to be in the hot dog business with and who has never given a hint something might be fishy about himself, a parent has to be vigilant (though it's unarguable I have not been as vigilant as I should've been).

All the state workers are standing outside now, staring at the closed sliding window as if they expected it to speak to them. There are seven or so, and they're digging into their pockets for lunch money. "So how's it going out there? You guys ready for a dog?" Karl shouts through the little window, as much to me as the state guys, as though we both know what we know—that this place is a friggin' gold mine.

"I think I'll sneak on out," I say.

"Yeah, okay," Karl says brightly, but now busily.

"Got a hamburg?" someone outside says to the screen.

"No burgs, just dogs," Karl answers, and viciously slides back the screen. "Just dogs and birch beer, boys," he says, turning cheery, leaning into the window, his big damp haunch hoisted once again into the air.

"I'll see you, Karl," I say. "Everick and Wardell will be here early Monday."

"Right. You bet," Karl shouts. He has no idea what I've said. He has entered his medium—dogs 'n' sweet suds—and his happy abstraction from life is my welcome cue to leave.

I make a southerly diversion below Haddam now, take streaming 295 up from Philadelphia, bypass Trenton and skirt the campus of De Tocqueville Academy, where Paul could attend when and if he comes to live with me and had the least interest, even though I would personally prefer the public schools. Then I head off onto the spanky new I-195 spur for more or less a bullet shot across the wide, subsident residential plain (Imlaystown, Jackson Mills, Squankum— all viewed from freeway level), toward the Shore.

I have not gone far before I pass above Pheasant Meadow, sprawled along the "old" Great Woods Road directly in the corridor of great silver high-voltage towers made in the shape of tuning forks. An older dilapidated sign just off the freeway announces: AN ATTRACTIVE RETIREMENT WAITS JUST AHEAD.

Pheasant Meadow, not old but already gone visibly to seed, is the condo community where our black agent, Clair Devane, met her grim, still unsolved and inexplicable death. And in fact, as I watch it drift by below me, its low, boxy, brown-shake buildings set in what was once a farmer's field, now abutting a strip of pastel medical arts plazas and a half-built Chi-Chi's, it seems so plainly the native architecture of lost promise and early death (though it's possible I'm being too harsh, since not even so long ago, I—arch-ordinary American—was a suitor to love there myself, wooing, in its tiny paper-walled, nubbly-ceilinged rooms, its dimly lit entryways and parking desert, a fine Texas girl who liked me some but finally had more sense than I did).

Clair was a fresh young realty associate from Talladega, Alabama, who'd gone to Spelman, married a hotshot computer whiz from Morehouse working his way up through an aggressive new software company in Upper Darby, and who for a sweet moment thought her life had locked into a true course. Except before she knew it she'd ended up with no husband, two kids to raise and no work experience except once having been an RA in her dormitory and, later, having kept the books for Zeta Phi Beta imaginatively enough that at year's end a big surplus was available to stage a carnival for underprivileged Atlanta kids and also to have a mixer with the Omegas at Georgia Tech.

On a fall Sunday in 1985, during an afternoon drive "in the country," which included a mosey through Haddam, she and her husband, Vernell, fell into a ferocious, screaming fight right in the middle of after-church traffic on Seminary Street. Vernell had just announced in the car that he had somehow fallen into true love with a female colleague at Datanomics and was the very next morning (!) moving out to L.A. to "be with her" while she started a new company of her own, designing educational packages targeted for the DIY home-repair industry. He allowed to Clair that he might drift back in a few months, depending on how things went and on how much he missed her and the kids, though he couldn't be sure.

Clair, however, just opened the car door, stepped out right at the stoplight at Seminary and Bank, across from the First Presbyterian (where I occasionally "worship") and simply started walking, looking in store windows as she went and smilingly whispering, "Die, Vernell, die right now," to all the white, contrite Presbyterians whose eyes she met. (She told me this story at an Appleby's out on Route 1, when we were at the height of our ardent but short-lived amours.)

Later that afternoon she checked into the August Inn and called her sister-in-law in Philadelphia, revealing Vernell's treachery and telling her to go get the kids at the baby-sitter's and put them on the first flight to Birmingham, where her mother would be waiting to take them back to Talladega.

And the next morning—Monday—Clair simply hit the bricks, looking for work. She told me she felt that even though she didn't see many people who looked like her, Haddam seemed as good a town as any and a damn sight better than the City of Brotherly Love, where life had come unstitched, and that the measure of any human being worthy of the world's trust and esteem was her ability to make something good out of something shitty by reading the signs right: the signs being that some strong force had crossed Vernell off the list and at the same time put her down in Haddam across from a church. This she considered to be the hand of God.

In no time she found a job as a receptionist in our office (this was less than a year after I came on board). In a few weeks she'd started the agent's course I took up at the Weiboldt school. And in two months she had her kids back, had bought a used Honda Civic and was set up in an apartment in Ewingville with a manageable rent, a pleasant, tree-lined drive to Haddam and a new and unexpected sense of possibility wrought from disaster. If she wasn't a hundred percent free and clear, she was at least free and making ends meet, and before long she started seeing me on the Q.T., and when that didn't seem to work she got together with a nice, somewhat older Negro attorney from a good local firm, whose wife had died and whose bad-tempered kids were all grown and gone.

It is a good story: human enterprise and good character triumphing over adversity and bad character, and everybody in our office coming to love her like their sister (though she never really sold much to the moneyed white clientele Haddam attracts like sheep, but came to specialize in rentals and condo turnarounds, which are not much of our market).

And yet completely mysteriously, in a routine showing of one of her condos right out here below me in Pheasant Meadow, a condo she'd shown ten times before and to which she arrived early to turn on lights, flush the toilets and open the windows—all normal chores—she was confronted by what the state police believe were at least three men. (As I said before, indications were that they were white, though I couldn't say what those indications were.) For two days, Everick and Wardell were extensively questioned, due to their access to keys, but they were completely exonerated. The unknown men, though, bound Clair hand and foot, gagged her with clear plastic tape, then raped and murdered her, slashing her throat with a packing knife.

Drugs were at first thought to be a motive, not that she was in any way implicated. It was speculated the unnamed men could've been repackaging bricks of cocaine, and Clair just walked unluckily in. The police know that empty condos in remote or declining locations, developments where good times have come and gone or never even came, often serve as havens for illicit transactions of all kinds—drug deals, the delivery of kidnapped Brazilian babies to rich childless Americans, the storage of various contrabands including dead bodies and auto parts, cigarettes and animals—anything that might profit from the broad-daylight anonymity condos are designed to provide. Our receptionist, Vonda, has a private-public theory that the owners, some young Bengali businessmen from New York, are at the bottom of everything and have a secret interest in pushing condo prices down for tax reasons (several agencies, including ours, have stopped showing property there). But there's no proof nor any reason to imagine anyone would *need* to kill as sweet a soul as Clair was for their purposes to win out. Only they did.

Immediately after Clair's murder, the women in our office, along with most of the other female realtors in town, formed mutual-protection groups. Some have begun to carry guns and Mace canisters and Tasers to work and right on out to houses they are showing. Women realtors now go around only in twos. Several have enrolled in martial arts classes, and "grieving and coping" sessions are still going on in different offices after business hours. (We men were encouraged to come, but I felt I already knew plenty about grieving and enough about coping.) There is even a clearinghouse number whereby any female agent can ask for and be given a male escort to any showing she feels uneasy about; and twice I've gone out just to be there when the clients show up, in case there was any funny business (there hasn't been any). None of these precautions, needless to say, can be discussed with the clients, who would hot-foot it out of town at the first sniff of danger. In both instances I was simply introduced as Ms. So-and-so's "associate," no explanations given; and when the coast proved clear, I inconspicuously departed.

Since May, all the realtors in Haddam have contributed to the Clair Devane Fund for her kids' education ($3,000 has so far been raised, enough for two full days at Harvard). Yet in spite of all the gloominess and hollow feeling, and the practical realization that "this kind of thing *can* happen here, and did," that no one is very far from a crime statistic, and the general recognition of how much we take our safety for granted—in spite of all that, no one talks about Clair much now, other than Vonda, whose cause she somehow is. Clair's kids have moved out with Vernell in Canoga Park, her fiancé, Eddie, is in quiet mourning (though he has already been seen lunching with one of the legal secretaries who considered renting my house). Even I have made my peace, having said my explicit adieus long before, when she was alive. Eventually her desk will be manned by someone else and business will go on—sad to say, but true—which is the way people want it. And in that regard, as well as respecting the most private of evidence, it can sometime already seem as though Clair Devane had not fully existed in anyone's life but her very own.

Nowadays I end up driving over once a week to pass a jolly-intimate evening with Sally Caldwell. We often attend a movie, later slip out to some little end-of-a-pier place for an amber-jack steak, a pitcher of martinis, sometimes a stroll along a beach or out some jetty, following which events take care of themselves. Though often as not I end up driving home in the moonlight alone, my heart pulsing regularly, my windows wide open, a man in charge of his own tent stakes and personal equipment, my head full of vivid but fast-disappearing memories and no anxious expectancies for a late-night phone call (like this morning's) full of longing and confusion, or demands that I spell out my intentions and come back immediately, or bitter accusations that I have not been forthright in every conceivable way. (I may not have, of course; forthright being a greater challenge than would seem, though my intentions are always good if few.) Our relationship, in fact, hasn't seemed to need more attention to theme or direction but has proceeded or at least persisted on autopilot, like a small plane flying out over a peaceful ocean with no one exactly in command.

Not of course that this is *best*—life's paradigm mapped out to perfection. It's simply what is: *fine* in the eternity of the here and now.

Best would be . . . well, *good* for a time was Cathy Flaherty in a wintry, many-windowed flat overlooking the estuary in Saint-Valéry (walks along the cold Picardy coast, fishermen fishing, foggy views across foggy bays, etc., etc.). *Good* was the early days (even the middle to late days) of my unrequited love for Nurse Vicki Arcenault of Pheasant Meadow and Barnegat Pines (now a Catholic mother of two in Reno, where she heads the trauma unit at Reno St. Veronica's). *Good* was even much of my sportswriting work (for a time, at least), my days back then happily dedicated to giving voice to the inarticulate and inane in order that an abstracted-but-still-yearning readership be painlessly diverted.

All that was *good*, sometimes even mysterious, sometimes so outwardly complicated as to *seem* interesting and even transporting, which is what most life gets by on and what we'll take as scrip against what's eternally due us.

But *best?* There's no use going through that card sort. Best's a concept without reference once you're married and have loused that up; maybe even once you've had your first banana split at age five and find, upon finishing it off, that you could handle another one. Forget best, in other words. Best's gone.

*M*y lady friend Sally Caldwell is the widow of a boy I attended Gulf Pines Military Academy with, Wally "Weasel" Caldwell of Lake Forest, Illinois; and for that reason Sally and I sometimes act as if we have a long, bittersweet history together of love lost and fate reconciled—which we don't. Sally, who's forty-two, merely saw my snapshot, address and a short personal reminiscence of Wally in the *Pine Boughs* alumni book printed for our 20th Gulf Pines reunion, which I didn't attend. At the time she didn't know me from Bela Lugosi's ghost. Only in trying to dream up a good reminiscence and skimming through my old yearbook for somebody I could attribute something amusing to, I chose Wally and sent in a mirthful but affectionate account that made fleeting reference to his having once drunkenly washed his socks in a urinal (a complete fabrication; I, in fact, chose him because I discovered from another school publication that he was deceased). But it was my "reminiscence" that Sally happened to see. I barely, in fact, had any memory of Wally, except that he was a fat, bespectacled boy with blackheads who was always trying to smoke Chesterfields using a cigarette holder—a character who, in spite of a certain likeness, turned out not to be Wally Caldwell at all but somebody else, whose name I never could remember. I have since explained my whole gambit to Sally, and we have had a good laugh about it.

I learned later from Sally that Wally had gone to Vietnam about the time I enlisted in the Marines, had come damn close to getting blown to bits in some ridiculous Navy mishap which left him intermittently distracted, though he came home to Chicago (Sally and two kids waiting devotedly), unpacked his bags, talked about studying biology, but after two weeks simply disappeared. Completely. Gone. The End. A nice boy who would've made a better than average horticulturist, became forever a mystery.

Sally, however, unlike the calculating Ann Dykstra, never remarried. Finally, for IRS reasons, she was forced to obtain a divorce by having Wally declared a croaker. But she went right on and raised her kids as a single mom in the Chicago suburb of Hoffman Estates, earned her B.A. in marketing administration from Loyola while holding down a full-time job in the adventure-travel industry. Wally's well-heeled Lake Forest parents provided her with make-ends-meet money and moral support, having realized she was not the cause of their son's going loony and that some human conditions are beyond love's reach.

Years went by.

But as quick as the kids were old enough to be safely dumped out of the nest, Sally put into motion her plan for setting sail with whatever fresh wind was blowing. And in 1983, on a rental-car trip to Atlantic City, she happened to turn off the Garden State in search of a clean rest room, stumbled all at once upon the Shore, South Mantoloking and the big old Queen-Anne-style double-gallery beach house facing the sea, a place she could afford with her parents' and in-laws' help, and where her kids would be happy coming home to with their friends and spouses, while she got her feet wet in some new business enterprise. (As it happened, as marketing director and later owner of an agency that finds tickets to Broadway shows for people in the later stages of terminal illness but who somehow think that seeing a revival of *Oliver* or the original London cast of *Hair* will make life—discolored by impending death—seem brighter. Curtain Call is her company's name.)

I luckily enough got into the picture when Sally read my bio and reminiscence about ersatz Wally in the *Pine Boughs*, saw I was a realtor in central New Jersey and tracked me down, thinking I might help her find bigger space for her business.

I came over one Saturday morning almost a year ago, and got a look at her—angularly pretty, frosted-blond, blue-eyed, tall in the extreme, with long, flashing model's legs (one an inch shorter than the other from a freak tennis accident, but not an issue) and the occasional habit of looking at you out the corner of her eyes as though most of what you were talking about was mighty damn silly. I took her to lunch at Johnny Matassa's in Point Pleasant, a lunch that lasted well past dark and moved over subjects far afield of office space—Vietnam, the coming election prospects for the Democrats, the sad state of American theater and elder care, and how lucky we were to have kids who weren't drug addicts, young litigators-to-be or maladjusted sociopaths (my luck there may be waning). And from there the rest was old hat: the inevitable usual, with a weather eye out for health concerns.

*A*t Lower Squankum I turn off then slide over to NJ 34, which becomes NJ 35, the beach highway, and head into the steamy swarm of 4th of July early-bird traffic, those who so love misery and wall-to-wall car companionship that they're willing to rise before dawn and drive ten hours from Ohio. (Many of these Buckeye Staters, I notice, are Bush supporters, which makes the holiday spirit seem meanly expropriated.)

Along the beach drag through Bay Head and West Mantoloking, patriotic pennants and American flags are snapping along the curbside, and down the short streets past the seawall I can see sails tilting and springing at close quarters on a hazy blue-steel sea. Though there's no actual feel of shimmery patriot fervor, just the everyday summery wrangle of loud Harleys, mopeds, topless Jeeps with jutting surfboards, squeezed in too close to Lincolns and Prowlers with stickers saying TRY BURNING THIS ONE! Here the baked sidewalks are cluttered with itchy, skinny bikini'd teens waiting on line for saltwater taffy and snow cones, while out on the beach the wooden lifeguard stands are occupied by brawny hunks and hunkettes, their arms folded, staring thoughtlessly at the waves. Parking lots are all full; motels, efficiencies and trailer hookups on the landward side have been booked for months, their renter-occupants basking in lawn chairs brought from home, or stretched out reading on skimpy porches bordered by holly shrubs. Others simply stand on old, Thirties shuffleboard pavements, sticks in hand, wondering: Wasn't this once—summer—a time of inner joy?

Though off to the right the view inland opens behind the town toward the broad reach of cloudy, brackish estuarial veldt, wintry and sprouted with low-tide pussy willows, rose hips and rotting boat husks stuck in the muck; and, overseeing all, farther and across, a great water tower, pink as a primrose, beyond which regimented housing takes up again. Silver Bay this is, its sky fletched with darkened gulls gliding to sea behind the morning's storm. I pass a lone and leathered biker, standing on the shoulder beside his broken-down chopper just watching, taking it all in across the panoramic estuary, trying, I suppose, to imagine how to get from here to there, where help might be.

And I am then into South Mantoloking and am almost "home."

I stop along the beach road at a store where LIQUOR is sold, buy two bottles of Round Hill Fumé Blanc '83, eat a candy bar (my last bite was at six), then walk out onto the windy, salty sidewalk to call for messages, unwilling not to know if the Markhams have resurfaced.

Message one of five, in fact, is Joe Markham, at noon in the full dudgeon of his helpless state. "Yeah. Bascombe? Joe Markham speaking. Gimme a call. Area code 609 259–6834. That's it." Clunk. Words like bullets. Perhaps he can wait a bit.

Message two. A cold call. "Right. Mr. Bascombe? My name is Fred Koeppel. Maybe Mr. Blankenship mentioned my name." (Mr. Who?) "I'm considering putting my house on the market up in Griggstown. I'm sure it'll go pretty quick. It's a sellers' market, so I'm told. Anyway, I'd like to discuss it with you. Maybe let you list it if we can work a fair commission. It'll sell itself, is my view. It'll just be paperwork for you. My number is . . ." A commission, fair or unfair, is 6%. Click.

Message three. "Joe Markham." (Basically the same news.) "Yeah. Bascombe. Gimme a call. Area code 609 259–6834." Clunk. "Oh yeah, it's one or whatever on Friday."

Message four. Phyllis Markham. "Hi, Frank. Try to get in touch with us." Bright as a sprite. "We have some questions. Okay? Sorry to bother you." Clunk.

Message five. A voice I don't recognize though briefly imagine to be Larry McLeod: "Look, chump! Ah-mo-ha-tuh-fuck-you-up, unu-stan-where-ahm-cummin-frum? Cause"—more distinct now, as if somebody else was talking—"I'm like sicka *yo* shit. Got it, chump? Fuckah?" Clunk. We get used to these in the realty biz. The police philosophy is, if they're calling, they're harmless. Larry, however, wouldn't leave such a message no matter how hot under the collar he'd gotten at my thinking I deserve to be paid money for letting him live in my house. Some part of him, I believe, is too dignified.

I'm relieved there's no call from Ann or Paul, or worse. When Paul was hauled away to juvenile detention by the Essex P.D. and Ann had to go get him out, it was Charley O'Dell who called to say, "Look, Frank, this'll all parse out right. Just hold steady. We'll be in touch." Parse out. Hold steady. *WE?* I haven't wanted to hear such niceness again, but been touchy I might have to. Charley, though (obviously at Ann's request), has since then been mum about Paul's problems, leaving them for his real parents to hassle over and try to fix.

Charley, of course, owns his own probs: a big, dirty-blond, overweight, bad-tempered, pimply-faced daughter named Ivy (who Paul refers to as IV), a student in an experimental writing program in NYC, who's currently living with her professor, aged sixty-six (older even than Charley), while writing a novel surgerying her parents' breakup when she was thirteen, a book that (according to Paul, who's had parts read to him) boasts as its first lines: "An orgasm, Lulu believed, was like God—something she'd heard was good but didn't really believe in. Though her father had very different ideas." In another life I might be sympathetic to Charley, but not in this one.

Sally's rambling dark-green beach house at the end of narrow Asbury Street is, when I hike up the old concrete seawall steps alongside and attain the beach-level promenade, locked, and she surprisingly gone, though all the side-opening windows upstairs and down are thrown out to catch a breeze. I am still early.

I, for a while, have had my own set of keys, though for a moment I simply stand on the shaded porch (plastic wine sack in hand) and gaze at the quiet, underused stretch of beach, the silent, absolute Atlantic and the gray-blue sky against which more near-in sailboats and Windsurfers joust in the summer haze. Farther out, a dark freighter inches north on the horizon. It is not so far from here that in my distant, postdivorce days I set sail for many a night's charter cruise with the Divorced Men's Club, all of us drinking grappa and angling for weakfish off Manasquan, a solemn, hopeful, joyless crew, mostly scattered now, most remarried, two dead, a couple still in town. Back in '83 we'd come over as a group, using the occasion of a midnight fishing excursion to put an even firmer lock on our complaints and sorrows—important training for the Existence Period, and good practice if your resolve is never to complain about life.

On the beach, beyond the sandy concrete walk, moms under beach umbrellas lie fast asleep on their heavy sides, arms flung over sleeping babies. Secretaries with a half day off to start the long weekend are lying on their bellies, shoulder to shoulder, chatting, winking and smoking cigarettes in their two-pieces. Tiny, stick-figure boys stand bare-chested at the margins of the small surf, shading their eyes as dogs trot by, tanned joggers jog and elderlies in pastel garb stroll behind them in the fractured light. Here is human hum in the barely moving air and surf-sigh, the low scrim of radio notes and water subsiding over words spoken in whispers. Something in it moves me as though to a tear (but not quite); some sensation that I have been here, or nearby, been at dire pains here time-ago and am here now again, sharing the air just as then. Only nothing signifies, nothing gives a nod. The sea closes up, and so does the land.

I am not sure what chokes me up: either the place's familiarity or its rigid reluctance to act familiar. It is another useful theme and exercise of the Existence Period, and a patent lesson of the realty profession, to cease sanctifying places—houses, beaches, hometowns, a street corner where you once kissed a girl, a parade ground where you marched in line, a courthouse where you secured a divorce on a cloudy day in July but where there is now no sign of you, no mention in the air's breath that you were there or that you were ever, importantly you, or that you even *were*. We may feel they *ought* to, *should* confer something—sanction, again—because of events that transpired there once; light a warming fire to animate us when we're well nigh inanimate and sunk. But they don't. Places never cooperate by revering you back when you need it. In fact, they almost always let you down, as the Markhams found out in Vermont and now New Jersey. Best just to swallow back your tear, get accustomed to the minor sentimentals and shove off to whatever's next, not whatever was. Place means nothing.

D own the wide, cool center hall I head to the shadowy, high, tin-ceilinged kitchen that smells of garlic, fruit and refrigerator freon, where I unload my wine into the big Sub-Zero. A "Curtain Call" note is stuck on the door: "FB. Go jump in the ocean. See you at 6. Have fun. S." No words about where she might be, or why it's necessary to use both the "F" and the "B." Perhaps another "F" lurks in the wings.

Sally's house, as I make my way up toward a nap, always reminds me of my own former family pile on Hoving Road—too many big wainscoted downstairs rooms with bulky oak paneling, pocket doors and thick chair rails, too much heavy plaster and a God's own excess of storage and closet space. Plus murky, mildewy back stairways, floors worn smooth and creaky with use, dented crown moldings, medallions, escutcheons, defunct gas wall fixtures from a bygone era, leaded glass, carved newel posts and the odd nipple button for a bell only servants (like canines) could hear—a house to raise a family in a bygone fashion or retire to if you've got the scratch to keep it up.

But for me, Sally's is a place of peculiar unease on account of its capacity to create a damned unrealistic, even scary, illusion of the future—which is one more reason I couldn't stand my own, could barely even sleep in it when I got back from France, in spite of high hopes. Suddenly I couldn't bear its woozy, fusty, weighted clubbiness, its heavy false promise that since the appearance of things can stay the same, life'll take care of itself too. (I knew better.) This is why I couldn't wait to get my hands on Ann's, with its re-habbed everything—clean sheetrock, new, sealed skylights made in Minnesota, polyurethaned floors, thermopanes, level-headed aluminum siding—nothing consecrated by or for all time, only certified as a building serviceable enough to live in for an uncertain while. Sally, though, who's already as cut off from her past as an amnesia victim, doesn't see things this way. She is calmer, smarter than I am, less a creature of extremes. Her house, to her, is just a nice old house she sleeps in, a comfortably convincing stage set for a life played out in the foreground, which is a quality she's perfected and that I find admirable, since it so matches what I would have be my own.

Up the heavy oak stairs, I make straight for the brown-curtained and breezy bedroom on the front of the house. It has become a point of policy with Sally—whether she's here or in New York with a vanload of Lou Gehrig's sufferers seeing *Carnival*—that I have my own space when I show up. (So far there's been no quibbling about where I sleep once the sun goes down—her room on the back). But this small, eave-shaded, semi-garret overlooking the beach and the end of Asbury Street has been designated mine, though it would otherwise be a spare: brown gingham wallpaper, an antique ceiling fan, a few tasteful but manly grouse-hunting prints, an oak dresser, a double bed with brass rainbow headboard, an armoire converted to a TV closet, a mahogany clotheshorse, all serviced by its own demure small forest-green and oak bathroom—a layout perfect for someone (a man) you don't know too well but sort of like.

I draw the curtains, strip down and crawl between the cool blue-paisley sheets, my feet still clammy from being rained on. Only when I reach to turn off the bedside lamp, I notice on the table a book that was not here last week, a red hand-me-down paperback of *Democracy in America*, a book I defy anyone to read who is not on some form of life support; and beside it, conspicuously, is a set of gold cuff links engraved with the anchor, ball and chain of the USMC, my old service branch (though I didn't last long). I pluck up one cuff link—it has a nice jeweler's heft in my palm. I try, leaning on my bare elbow, to remember through the haze of time if these are Marine issue, or just some trinket an old leatherneck had "crafted" to memorialize a burnished valiance far from home.

Except I don't want to wonder over the origin of cuff links, or whose starchy cuffs they might link; or if they were left for my private perusal, or pertain to Sally calling up last night to complain about life's congestions. If I were married to Sally Caldwell, I would wonder about that. But I'm not. If "my room" on Fridays and Saturdays becomes Colonel Rex "Knuckles" Trueblood's on Tuesdays and Wednesdays, I only hope that we never cross paths. This is a matter to be filed under "laissez-faire" in our arrangement. Divorce, if it works, should rid you of these destination-less stresses, or at least that's the way I feel now that welcome sleep approaches.

I thumb quickly back through the old, soft-sided de Tocqueville, Vol. II, check its yellowed title page for ownership, note any under-linings, margin notes (nothing), then remember my experiment from college: supine, holding the book up at a proper viewing dis-tance, I open it at random and begin to read, testing how many sec-onds will pass before my eyes close, the book sinks and I fall off the cushiony cliff to dreamland.

I commence: "How Democratic Institutions and Manners Tend to Raise Rents and Shorten the Terms of Leases." Too boring even to sleep through. Outside I hear girls giggling on the beach, hear the tame surf as a soft, sleep-bringing ocean breeze raises and floats the window curtain.

I thumb back farther and start again: "What Causes Almost All Americans to Follow Industrial Callings." Nothing.

Again: "Why So Many Ambitious Men and So Little Lofty Ambitions Are to Be Found in the United States." Possibly I can get my teeth into this at least for eight seconds: "The first thing that strikes a traveler to the United States is the innumerable multitudes of those who seek to emerge from their original condition; and the second is the rarity of lofty ambition to be observed in the midst of universally ambitious stir of society. No Americans are devoid of a yearning desire to rise but hardly any appear to entertain hopes of great magnitude or to pursue lofty aims. . . ."

I set the book back on the table beside the Marine cuff links and lie now more awake than asleep, listening to the children's voices and, farther away, nearer the continent's sandy crust, a woman's voice saying, "I'm not hard to understand. Why are you so goddamn difficult?" Followed by a man's evener voice, as if embarrassed: "I'm *not*," he says, "I'm not. I'm really, really not." They talk more, but their sounds fade in the light airishness of Jersey seaside.

Then, suddenly, peering up at the brassy fan listlessly turning, I for some reason wince—*whing-crack!*—as though a rock or a scary shadow or a sharp projectile had flashed close and just missed maim-ing me, making my whole head whip to the right, setting my heart to pounding thunk-a, thunk-a, thunk-a, thunk-a, exactly the way it did the summer evening Ann announced she was marrying Frank Lloyd O'Dell and moving to Deep River and stealing my kids.

But why now?

There are winces, of course, and there are other winces. There is the "love wince," the shudder—often with accompanying animal groan—of hot-rivet sex imagined, followed frequently by a sense of loss thick enough to upholster a sofa. There is the "grief wince," the one you experience in bed at 5 a.m., when the phone rings and some stranger tells you your mother or your first son has "regretfully" expired; this is normally attended by a chest-emptying sorrow which is almost like relief but not quite. There is the "wince of fury," when your neighbor's Irish setter, Prince Sterling, has been barking at squirrels' shadows for months, night after night, keeping you awake and in an agitation verging on dementia, though unexpectedly you confront the neighbor at the end of his driveway at dusk, only to be told you're blowing the whole dog-barking thing way out of proportion, that you're too tightly wrapped and need to smell the roses. This wince is often followed by a shot to the chops and can also be called "the Billy Budd."

What I have just suffered, though, is none of these and has left me light-headed and tingling, as if an electrical charge had been administered via terminals strapped to my neck. Black spots wander my vision, my ears feel as though glass tumblers were pressed over them.

But then, just as quickly, I can hear the beach voices again, the slap of a book being closed, a feathery laugh, somebody's sandy sandals being slapped together, a palm being smacked on someone's tender red back and the searing "owwwweeee," while the tide fondly chides the ever-retreating shingle.

What I feel rising in me now (a consequence of my "big-time wince") is a strange curiosity as to what exactly in the hell I'm doing here; and its stern companion sensation that I really ought to be somewhere else. Though where? Where I'm wanted more than just expected? Where I fit in better? Where I'm more purely ecstatic and not just glad? At least someplace where meeting the terms, conditions and limitations set on life are not so front and center. Where the rules are not the game.

Time was when a moment like this one—stretched out in a cool, inviting house not my own, drifting toward a nap, but also thrillingly awaiting the arrival of a sweet, wonderful and sympathetic visitor, eager to provide what I need because she needs it too—time was when this state was the best damned feeling on God's earth, in fact was the very feeling the word "life" was coined for, plus all the more intoxicating and delectable because I recognized it even as it was happening, and knew with certainty no one else did or could, so that I could have it all, all, all to myself, the way I had nothing else.

Here, now, all the props are in place, light and windage set; Sally is doubtless on her way at this instant, eager (or at least willing) to run up, jump in bed, find once more the key to my heart and give it a good cranking-up turn, thereby routing last night's entire squadron of worries.

Only the old giddyup (mine) is vanished, and I'm not lying here a-buzz and a-thrill but listening haphazard to voices on the beach— the way I used to feel, would like to feel, gone. Left is only some ether of its presence and a hungrified wonder about where it might be and will it ever come back. Nullity, in other words. Who the hell wouldn't wince?

Possibly this is one more version of "disappearing into your life," the way career telephone company bigwigs, overdutiful parents and owners of wholesale lumber companies are said to do and never know it. You simply reach a point at which everything looks the same but nothing matters much. There's no evidence you're dead, but you act that way.

But to dispel this wan, cavern-of-winds feeling, I try fervently now to picture the first girl I ever "went" with, willing like a high-schooler to project lurid mind-pictures and arouse myself into taking matters in hand, after which sleep's a cinch. Except my film's a blank; I can't seem to remember my first sexual conduction, though experts swear it's the one act you *never* forget, long after you've forgotten how to ride a bicycle. It's there on your mind when you're parked on a porch in your diaper at the old folks home, lost in a row of other dozing seniors, hoping to get a little color in your cheeks before lunch is served.

My hunch, though, is that it was a little pasty brunette named Brenda Patterson, whom a military-school classmate and I convinced to go "golfing" with us on the hot Bermuda-grass links at Keesler AFB, in Mississippi, then half-pleaded, half-teased and almost certainly browbeat into taking her pants down in a stinking little plywood men's room beside the 9th green, this in exchange for our—me and my pal "Angle" Carlisle—grim-facedly returning the favor (we were fourteen; the rest is hazy).

Otherwise it was years later in Ann Arbor, when, nuzzling under some cedar shrubs in the Arboretum, below the New York Central trestle, I made an effort in full watery daylight to convince a girl named Mindy Levinson to let me do it just with our pants half down, our young tender flesh all over stickers and twigs. I remember she said yes, though, as uninspired as it now seems, I'm not even certain if I went through with it.

Abruptly now my mind goes electric with sentences, words, strings of unrelateds running on in semi-syntactical disarray. I sometimes can go to sleep this way, in a swoony process of returning sense to nonsense (the pressure to make sense is for me always an onerous, sometimes sleepless one). In my brain I hear: *Try burning life's congested Buckeye State biker . . . There is a natural order of things in the cocktail dress . . . I'm fluent in the hysterectomy warhead (don't I?) . . . Give them the Locution, come awn back, nah, come awn, the long term's less good for you . . . The devil's in the details, or is it God . . .*

Not this time, apparently. (What kinship these bits enjoy is a brainteaser for Dr. Stopler, not me.)

Sometimes, though not *that* often, I wish I were still a writer, since so much goes through anybody's mind and right out the window, whereas, for a writer—even a shitty writer—so much less is lost. If you get divorced from your wife, for instance, and later think back to a time, say, twelve years before, when you almost broke up the first time but didn't because you decided you loved each other too much or were too smart, or because you both had gumption and a shred of good character, then later after everything *was* finished, you decided you actually *should've* gotten divorced long before because you think now you missed something wonderful and irreplaceable and as a result are filled with whistling longing you can't seem to shake—*if you were a writer*, even a half-baked short-story writer, you'd have someplace to put that fact buildup so you wouldn't have to think about it all the time. You'd just write it all down, put quotes around the most gruesome and rueful lines, stick them in somebody's mouth who doesn't exist (or better, a thinly disguised enemy of yours), turn it into pathos and get it all off your ledger for the enjoyment of others.

Not that you ever truly *lose* anything, of course—as Paul is finding out with pain and difficulty—no matter how careless you are or how skilled at forgetting, or even if you're a writer as good as Saul Bellow. Though you do have to teach yourself not to cart it all around inside until you rot or explode. (The Existence Period, let me say, is made special for this sort of adjusting.)

For example. I never worry about whether or not my parents felt rewarded because they only had me or if they might've wanted another child (a memory-based anxiety that could drive the right person nuts). And it's simply because I once wrote a story about a small, loving family living on the Mississippi Gulf Coast who have one child but sort of want another one, ya-ta-ya-ta-ya-ta—ending with the mother taking a solitary boat ride on a hot windy day (very much like this one) out to Horn Island, where she walks on the sand barefoot, picks up a few old beer cans and stares back at the mainland until she realizes, due to something being said by a nun to some nearby crippled children, that wishing for things that can't be is—you guessed it—like being on an island with strangers and picking up old beer cans, when what she needs to do is get back to the boat (which is just whistling) and return to her son and husband, who are that day on a bass-fishing trip but will soon be back, wanting supper, and who that very morning have told her how much they both love her, but which has succeeded only in making her sad and lonely as a hermit and in need of a boat ride. . . .

This story, of course, is in a book of stories I wrote, under the title, "Waiting Offshore." Though since I stopped writing stories eighteen years ago I've had to find other ways to cope with unpleasant and worrisome thoughts. (Ignoring them is one way.)

When Ann and I were first married and living in NYC, in 1969, and I was scribbling away like a demon, hanging around my agent's office on 35th Street and showing Ann my precious pages every night, she used to stand at the window pouting because she could never find, she felt, much direct evidence of herself in my work—no cameos, no tall, slouchingly athletic golfer types of strong, resolute Dutch extraction, saying calamitously witty or incisive things to take the starch out of lesser women or men, who, naturally, would all be sluts or bores. What I used to tell her was—and God smite me if I'm lying almost twenty years later—that if I could encapsulate her in words, it would mean I'd rendered her less complex than she was and would therefore signify I was already living at a distance from her, which would eventuate in my setting her aside like a memory or a worry (which happened anyway, but not for that reason and not with complete success).

Indeed, I often tried telling her that her contribution was not to be a character but to make my little efforts at creation *urgent* by being so wonderful that I loved her; stories being after all just words giving varied form to larger, compelling but otherwise speechless mysteries such as love and passion. In that way, I explained, she was my muse; muses being not comely, playful feminine elves who sit on your shoulder suggesting better word choices and tittering when you get one right, but powerful life-and-death forces that threaten to suck you right out the bottom of your boat unless you can heave enough crates and boxes—words, in a writer's case—into the breach. (I have not found a replacement for this force as yet, which may explain how I've been feeling lately and especially here today.)

Ann, of course, in her overly factual, Michigan-Dutch way, didn't like the part that seemed to be my secret, and always assumed I was simply bullshitting her. If we were to have a heart-to-heart at this very minute, she would finally get around to asking me why I never wrote about her. And my answer would be that it was because I didn't want to use her up, bind her in words, set her aside, consign her to a "place" where she would be known, but always as less than she was. (She still wouldn't believe me.)

I try running all this end to end as I watch the ceiling fan baffle light around my room's shadowy atmosphere: *Ann wishes for . . . Horn Island . . . God smite my Round Hill elves . . . try burning this one . . .*

Someplace far, far away I seem to hear footsteps, then the softened sound of a wine cork being squeezed, then popped, a spoon set down gently on a metal stovetop, a hushed radio playing the theme music of the news broadcast I regularly tune to, a phone ringing and being answered in a grateful voice, followed by condoning laughter—a sweet and precious domestic sonority I so rarely feel these days that I would lie here and listen till way past dark if I only, only could.

I lumber down the stairs, my teeth brushed, my face washed, though groggy and misaligned in time. My teeth in fact don't feel they're in the right occlusion either, as if I'd gnashed them in some dream (no doubt a dismal "night guard" is in my future).

It is twilight. I've slept for hours without believing I slept at all, and feel no longer fuguish but exhausted, as though I'd dreamed of running a race, my legs heavy and achy clear up to my groin.

When I come around the newel post I can see, out the open front doorway, a few darkened figures on the beach and, farther out, the lights of a familiar oil platform that can't be seen in the hazy daytime, its tiny white lights cutting the dark eastern sky like diamonds. I wonder where the freighter is, the one I saw before—no doubt well into harbor.

A lone, dim candle burns in the kitchen, though the little security panel—just as in Ted Houlihan's house—blinks a green all-clear from down the hall. Sally usually maintains lights-off till there's none left abroad, then sets scented candles through the house and goes barefoot. It is a habit I've almost learned to respect, along with her cagey sidelong looks that let you know she's got your number.

No one is in the kitchen, where the beige candle flickers on the counter for my sake. A shadowy spray of purple irises and white wisteria have been arranged in a ceramic vase to dress up the table. A green crockery bowl of cooling bow ties sits beside a loaf of French bread, my bottle of Round Hill in its little chilling sleeve. Two forks, two knives, two spoons, two plates, two napkins.

I pour a glass and head for the porch.

"I don't think I hear you with your bells on," Sally says, while I'm still trooping down the hall. Outside, to my surprise it is almost full dark, the beach apparently empty, as if the last two minutes had occupied a full hour. "I'm just taking in the glory of the day's end," she continues, "though I came up an hour ago and watched you sleep." She smiles around at me from the porch shadows and extends her hand back, which I touch, though I stay by the door, overtaken for a moment by the waves breaking white-crested out of the night. Part of our "understanding" is not to be falsely effusive, as though unmeant effusiveness was what got our whole generation in trouble somewhere back up the line. I wonder forlornly if she will take up where she left off last night, with me flying across cornfields looking like Christ almighty, and her odd feelings of things being congested—both of which are encrypted complaints about me that I understand but don't know how to answer. I have yet to speak. "I'm sorry I woke you up last night. I just felt so odd," she says. She's seated in a big wood rocker, in a long white caftan slit up both sides to let her hike her long legs and bare feet up. Her yellow hair is pulled back and held with a silver barrette, her skin brown from beach life, her teeth luminous. A damp perfume of sweet bath oil floats away on the porch air.

"I hope I wasn't snoring," I say.

"Nope. Nope. You're a wife's dream. You never snore. I hope you saw I put de Tocqueville out for you since you're taking a trip and also reading history in the middle of the night. I always liked him."

"Me too," I lie.

She gives me the look then. Her features are narrow, her nose is sharp, her chin angular and freckled—a sleek package. She is wearing thin silver earrings and heavy turquoise bracelets. "You *did* say something about Ann—speaking of wives, or former wives." This is the reason for the look, not my lying about de Tocqueville.

"I only remember dreaming about somebody not getting his insurance premiums paid on time, and then about if it was better to be killed or tortured and then killed."

"I know what I'd choose." She takes a sip of wine, holding the round glass in both palms and focusing into the dark that has taken over the beach. New York's damp glow brightens the lusterless sky. Out on the main drag cars are racing; tires squeal, one siren goes *woop*.

Whenever Sally turns ruminant, I assume she's brooding over Wally, her long-lost, now roaming the ozone, somewhere amongst these frigid stars, "dead" to the world but (more than likely) not to her. Her situation is much like mine—divorced in a generic sense—with all of divorce's shaky unfinality, which, when all else fails, your mind chews on like a piece of sour meat you just won't swallow.

I sometimes imagine that one night right at dusk she'll be here on her porch, wondering away as now, and up'll stride ole Wal, a big grin on his kisser, more slew-footed than she remembered, softer around center field, wide-eyed and more pudding-faced, but altogether himself, having suddenly, in the midst of a thriving florist's career in Bellingham or his textile manufacturer's life in downstate Pekin, just waked up in a movie, say, or on a ferry, or midway of the Sunshine Bridge, and immediately begun the journey

back to where he'd veered off on that long-ago morning in Hoffman
Estates. (I'd rather not be present for this reunion.) In my story they
embrace, cry, eat dinner in the kitchen, drink too much vino, find it
easier to talk than either of them would've thought, later head back
to the porch, sit in the dark, hold hands (optional), start to get cozy,
consider a trek up the flight of stairs to the bedroom, where another
candle's lit—thinking as they consider this what a strange but not
altogether supportable thrill it would be. Then they just snap out of
it, laugh a little, grow embarrassed at the mutually unacknowledged
prospect, then grow less chummy, in fact cold and impatient, until
it's clear there's not enough language to fill the space of years and
absence, plus Wally (aka Bert, Ned, whatever) is needed back in
Pekin or the Pacific Northwest by his new/old wife and semi-grown
kids. So that shortly past midnight off he goes, down the walkway to
oblivion with all the other court-appointed but not-quite dead (not
that much different from what Sally and I do together, though I
always show up again).

Anything more, of course, would be too complex and rueful: the
whole bunch of them ending up on TV, dressed in suits, sitting
painfully on couches—the kids, the wives, the boyfriend, a family
priest, the psychiatrist, all there to explain what they're feeling to
bleachers full of cakey fat women eager to stand up and say they
themselves "would prolly have to feel a lot of jealousy, you know?"
if they were in either wife's place, and really "no one could be sure if
Wally was telling the truth about where . . ." True, true, true. And
who cares?

Somewhere on the water a boat neither of us can see suddenly
becomes a launch pad for a bright, fusey, sparkly projectile that arcs
into the inky air and explodes into luminous pink and green effusions that brighten the whole sky like creation's dawn, then pops
and fizzles as other, minor detonations go off, before the whole
gizmo weakens and dies out of view like an evanescing spirit of
nighttime.

Invisible on the beach, people say *Ooooo* and *Aaahhh* in unison
and applaud each pop. Their presence is a surprise. We wait for the
next boomp, whoosh and burst, but none occurs. "Oh," I hear someone say in a falling voice. "Shit." "But one was nice," someone says.
"One ain't enough a-nuthin," is the answer.

"That was my first official 'firework' of the holiday," Sally says cheerfully. "That's always very exciting." Where she's looking the sky is smoky and bluish against the black. We are, the two of us, suspended here as though waiting on some other ignition.

"My mother used to buy little ones in Mississippi," I offer, "and let them pop off in her fingers. 'Teensies,' she called them." I'm still leaned amiably on the doorframe, glass dangling in my hand, like a movie star in a celebrity still. Two sips on a mostly empty stomach, and I'm mildly tipsy.

Sally looks at me doubtfully. "Was she very frustrated with life, your Mom?"

"Not that I know of."

"Well. Somebody might say she was trying to wake herself up."

"Maybe," I say, made uncomfortable by thinking of my guileless parents in some revisionist's way, a way that were I only briefly to pursue it would no doubt explain my whole life to now. Better to write a story about it.

"When *I* was a little girl in Illinois, *my* parents always managed to have a big fight on New Year's Eve," Sally says. "There'd always be yelling and things being thrown and cars starting late at night. They drank too much, of course. But my sisters and I would get terribly excited because of the fireworks display at Pine Lake. And we'd always want to bundle up and drive out and watch from the car, except the car was always gone, and so we'd have to stand in the front yard in the snow or wind and see whatever we could, which wasn't much. I'm sure we made up most of what we said we saw. So fireworks always make me feel like a girl, which is probably pretty silly. They *should* make me feel cheated, but they don't. Did you sell a house to your Vermont people, by the way?"

"I've got them simmering." (I hope.)

"You're very skillful at your profession, aren't you? You sell houses when no one else sells them." She rocks forward then back, using just her shoulders, the big rocker grinding the porch boards.

"It's not a very hard job. It's just driving around in the car with strangers, then later talking to them on the phone."

"That's what my job's like," Sally says happily, still rocking. Sally's job is more admirable but fuller of sorrows. I wouldn't get within a hundred miles of it. Though suddenly and badly now I want to kiss her, touch her shoulder or her waist or somewhere, have a good whiff of her sweet, oiled skin on this warm evening. I therefore make my way clump-a-clump across the noisy boards, lean awkwardly down like an oversize doctor seeking a heartbeat with his naked ear, and give her cheek and also her neck a smooch I'd be happy to have lead to almost anything.

"Hey, hey, stop that," she says only half-jokingly, as I breathe in the exotics of her neck, feel the dampness of her scapula. Along her cheek just below her ear is the faintest skim of blond down, a delicate, perhaps sensitive feature I've always found inflaming but have never been sure how I should attend to. My smooch, though, gives rise to little more than one well-meant, not overly tight wrist squeeze and a willing tilt of head in my general direction, following which I stand up with my empty glass, peer across the beach at nothing, then clump back to take my listening post holding up the doorframe, half aware of some infraction but uncertain what it is. Possibly even more restrictions are in effect.

What I'd like is not to make rigorous, manly, night-ending love now or in two minutes, but to have *already* done so; to have it on my record as a deed performed and well, and to have a lank, friendly, guard-down love's afterease be ours; me to be the goodly swain who somehow rescues an evening from the shallows of nullity— what I suffered before my nap and which it's been my magician's trick to save us from over these months, by arriving always brimming with good ideas (much as I try to do with Paul or anybody), setting in motion day trips to the *Intrepid* Sea-Air-Space Museum, a canoe ride on the Batsto, a weekend junket to the Gettysburg battlefield, capped off by a balloon trip Sally was game for but not me. Not to mention a three-day Vermont color tour last fall that didn't work out, since we spent most of two days stuck in a cavalcade of slow-moving leaf-peepers in tour buses and Winnebagos, plus the prices were jacked up, the beds too small and the food terrible. (We ended up driving back one night early, feeling old and tired—Sally slept most of the way—and in no mood even to suffer a drink together when I let her off at the foot of Asbury Street.)

"I made bow ties," Sally says very assuredly, after the long silence occasioned by my unwanted kiss, during which we both realized we are not about to head upstairs for any fun. "That's your favorite, correct? *Farfalline?*"

"It's sure the food I most like to *see*," I say.

She smiles around again, stretches her long legs out until her ankles make smart little pops. "I'm coming apart at my seams, so it seems," she says. In fact, she's an aggressive tennis player who hates to lose and, in spite of her one leg being docked, can scissor the daylights out of a grown man.

"Are you over there thinking about Wally?" I say, for no good reason except I thought it.

"Wally Caldwell?" She says this as if the name were new to her.

"It was just something I thought. From my distance here."

"The name alone survives," she says. "Too long ago." I don't believe her, but it doesn't matter. "I had to give up on that name. He left *me, and* his children. So." She shakes her thick blond hair as if the specter of Weasel Wally were right out in the dark, seeking admission to our conversation, and she'd rejected him. "What I *was* thinking about—because when I drove all the way to New York today to pick up some tickets, I was also thinking it then—was you, and about you being here when I came home, and what we'd do, and just what a sweet man you always are."

This is not a good harbinger, mark my words.

"I *want* to be a sweet man," I say, hoping this will have the effect of stopping whatever she is about to say next. Only in rock-solid marriages can you hope to hear that you're a sweet man without a "but" following along afterward like a displeasing goat. In many ways a rock-solid marriage has a lot to say for itself. "But what?"

"But nothing. That's all." Sally hugs her knees, her long bare feet side by side on the front edge of her rocker seat, her long body swaying forward and back. "Does there have to be a 'but'?"

"Maybe that's what *I* am." I should make a goat noise.

"A butt? Well. I was just driving along thinking I liked you. That's all. I can try to be harder to get along with."

"I'm pretty happy with you," I say. An odd little smirky smile etches along my silly mouth and hardens back up into my cheeks without my willing it.

Sally turns all the way sideways and peers up at me in the gloom of the porch. A straight address. "Well, good."

I say nothing, just smirk.

"Why are you smiling like that?" she says. "You look strange."

"I don't really know," I say, and poke my finger in my cheek and push, which makes the sturdy little smile retreat back into my regular citizen's mien.

Sally squints at me as if she's able to visualize something hidden in my face, something she's never seen but wants to verify because she always suspected it was there.

"I always think about the Fourth of July as if I needed to have something accomplished by now, or decided," she says. "Maybe that was one of my problems last night. It's from going to school in the summers for so long. The fall just seems too late. I don't even know late for what."

I, though, am thinking about a more successful color tour. Michigan: Petoskey, Harbor Springs, Charlevoix. A weekend on Mackinaw Island, riding a tandem. (All things, of course, I did with Ann. Nothing's new.)

Sally raises both her arms above her head, joins hands and does a slinky yoga stretch, getting the kinks out of everything and causing her bracelets to slide up her arm in a jangly little cascade. This pace of things, this occasional lapse into silence, this unurgency or ruminance, is near the heart of some matter with us now. I wish it would vamoose. "I'm boring you," she says, arms aloft, luminous. She's nobody's pushover and a wonderful sight to see. A smart man should find a way to love her.

"You're not boring me," I say, feeling for some reason elated. (Possibly the leading edge of a cool front has passed, and everybody on the seaboard just felt better all at once.) "I don't mind it that you like me. I think it's great." Possibly I should kiss her again. A real one.

"You see other women, don't you?" she says, and begins to shuffle her feet into a pair of flat gold sandals.

"Not really."

"What's 'not really'?" She picks her wine glass up off the floor. A mosquito is buzzing my ear. I'm more than ready to head inside and forget this topic.

"I don't. That's all. I guess if somebody came along who I wanted to see"—"see": a word I hate; I'm happier with "boff" or "boink," "roger" or "diddle"—"then I feel like that'd be okay. With me, I mean."

"Right," Sally says curtly.

Whatever spirit has moved her to put her sandals on has passed now. I hear her take a deep breath, wait, then let it slowly out. She is holding her glass by its smooth round base.

"I think you see other men," I say hopefully. Cuff links come to mind.

"Of course." She nods, staring over the porch banister toward small yellow dots embedded in darkness at an incomprehensible distance. I think again of us Divorced Men, huddled for safety's sake on our bestilled vessel, staring longingly at the mysterious land (possibly at this very house), imagining lives, parties, cool restaurants, late-night carryings-on we ached to be in on. Any one of us would've swum ashore against the flood to do what I'm doing. "I have this odd feeling about seeing other men," Sally says meticulously. "That I *do* it but I'm not planning anything." To my huge surprise, though I'm not certain, I think she scoops a tear from the corner of her eye and massages it dry between her fingers. This is why we are staying on the porch. I of course didn't know she was *actually* "seeing" other men.

"What would you like to be waiting on?" I say, too earnestly.

"Oh, I don't know." She sniffs to signify I needn't worry about further tears. "Waiting's just a bad habit. I've done it before. Nothing, I guess." She runs her fingers back through her thick hair, gives her head a tiny clearing shake. I'd like to ask about the anchor, ball and chain, but this is not the moment, since all I'd do is find out. "Do you think *you're* waiting for something to happen?" She looks up at me again, skeptically. Whatever my answer, she's expecting it to be annoying or deceitful or possibly stupid.

"No," I say, an attempt at frankness—something I probably can't bring off right now. "I don't know what it'd be for either."

"So," Sally says. "Where's the good part in anything if you don't think something good's coming, or you're going to get a prize at the end? What's the good mystery?"

"The good mystery's how long anything can go on the way it is. That's enough for me." The Existence Period par excellence. Sally and Ann are united in their distaste for this view.

"My oh my oh *my*!" She leans her head back and stares up at the starless ceiling and laughs an odd high-pitched girlish *ha-ha-ha*. "I underestimated you. That's good. I . . . never mind. You're right. You're completely right."

"I'd be happy to be wrong," I say, and look, I'm sure, goofy.

"Fine," Sally says, looking at me as if I were the rarest of rare species. "Waiting to be proved wrong, though—that's not exactly taking the bull by the horns, is it, Franky?"

"I never really understood why anybody'd take a bull by its horns in the first place," I say. "That's the dangerous end." I don't much like being called "Franky," as though I were six and of indeterminate gender.

"Well, look." She is now sarcastic. "This is just an experiment. It's not personal." Her eyes flash, even in the dark, catching light from somewhere, maybe the house next door, where lamps have been switched on, making it look cozy and inviting indoors. I wouldn't mind being over there. "What does it mean to you to tell somebody you love them? Or her?"

"I don't really have anybody to say that to." This is not a comforting question.

"But if you did? Someday you might." This inquiry suggests I have become an engaging but totally out-of-the-question visitor from another ethical system.

"I'd be careful about it."

"You're always careful." Sally knows plenty about my life—that I am sometimes finicky but in fact often not careful. More of irony.

"I'd be *more* careful," I say.

"What would you mean if you said it, though?" She may in fact believe my answer will someday mean something important to her, explain why certain paths were taken, others abandoned: "It was a time in my life I was lucky enough to survive"; or "This'll explain why I got out of New Jersey and went to work with the natives in Pago Pago."

"Well," I say, since she deserves an honest answer, "it's provisional. I guess I'd mean I see enough in someone I liked that I'd want to make up a whole person out of that part, and want to keep that person around."

"What does that have to do with being in love?" She is intent, almost prayerful, staring at me in what I believe may be a hopeful manner.

"Well, we'd have to agree that that was what love was, or is. Maybe that's too severe." (Though I don't really think so.)

"It *is* severe," she says. A fishing boat sounds a horn out in the ocean dark.

"I didn't want to exaggerate," I say. "When I got divorced I promised I'd never complain about how things turned out. And not exaggerating is a way of making sure I don't have anything to complain about." This is what I tried explaining to smushed-dick Joe this morning. With no success. (Though what can it mean for one's desideratum to come up twice in one day?)

"You can probably be talked out of your severe view of love, though, can't you? Maybe that's what you meant by being happy to be wrong." Sally stands as she says this, once again raises her arms, wine glass in hand, and twists herself side to side. The fact that one leg is shorter than the other is not apparent. She is five feet ten. Almost my height.

"I haven't thought so."

"It really wouldn't be easy, I guess, would it? It'd take something unusual." She is watching the beach where someone has just started an illegal campfire, which makes the night for this moment seem sweet and cheerful. But from sudden, sheer discomfort, and also affection and admiration for her scrupulousness, I'm compelled to grab my arms around her from behind and give her a hug and a smoochy schnuzzle that works out better than the last one. She is no longer humid underneath her caftan, where she seems to my notice to be wearing no clothes, and is sweeter than sweet. Though her arms stay limp at her side. No reciprocation. "At least you don't need to worry how to trust all over again. All that awful shit, the stuff my dying people never talk about. They don't have time."

"Trust's for the birds," I say, my arms still around her. I live for just these moments, the froth of a moment's pseudo-intimacy and pleasure just when you don't expect it. It is wonderful. Though I don't believe we have accomplished much, and I'm sorry.

"Well," Sally says, regaining her footing and pushing my cloying arms off in a testy way without turning around, making for the door, her limp now detectable. "Trust's for the birds. Isn't it just. That's the way it has to be, though."

"I'm pretty hungry," I say.

She walks off the porch, lets the screen slap shut. "Come in then and eat your bow ties. You have miles to go before you sleep."

Though as the sound of her bare feet recedes down the hall, I am alone in the warm sea smells mixed with the driftwood smoke, a barbecue smell that's perfect for the holiday. Someone next door turns on a radio, loud at first, then softer. *E-Z Listn'n* from New Brunswick. Liza is singing, and I myself drift like smoke for a minute in the music: "Isn't it romantic? Music in the night . . . Moving shadows write the oldest magic . . . I hear the breezes playing . . . You were meant for love . . . Isn't it romantic?"

At dinner, eaten at the round oak table under bright ceiling light, seated either side of the vase sprouting purple irises and white wisteria and a wicker cornucopia spilling summery legumes, our talk is eclectic, upbeat, a little dizzying. It is, I understand, a prelude to departure, with all memory of languor and serious discussion of love's particulars off-limits now, vanished like smoke in the sea breeze. (The police have since arrived, and the firemakers hauled off to jail the instant they complained about the beach being owned by God.)

In the candlelight Sally is spirited, her blue eyes moist and shining, her splendid angular face tanned and softened. We fork up bow ties and yak about movies we haven't seen but would like to (Me—*Moonstruck*, *Wall Street*; she—*Empire of the Sun*, possibly *The Dead*); we talk about possible panic in the soybean market now that rain has ended the drought in the parched Middle West; we discuss "drouth" and "drought"; I tell her about the Markhams and the McLeods and my problems there, which leads somehow to a discussion of a Negro columnist who shot a trespasser in his yard, which prompts Sally to admit she sometimes carries a handgun in her purse, right in South Mantoloking, though she believes it will probably be the instrument that kills her. For a brief time I talk about Paul, noting that he is not much attracted to fire, doesn't torture animals, isn't a bed-wetter that I know of, and that my hopes are he will live with me in the fall.

Then (from some strange compulsion) I charge into realty. I report there were 2,036 shopping centers built in the U.S. two years ago, but now the numbers are "way off," with many big projects stalled. I affirm that I don't see the election mattering a hill of beans to the realty market, which provokes Sally to remember what rates were back in the bicentennial year (8.75%), when, I recall to her, I was thirty-one and living on Hoving Road. While she mixes Jersey blueberries in kirsch for spooning over sponge cake, I try to steer us clear of the too-recent past, talk on about Grandfather Bascombe losing the family farm in Iowa over a gambling debt and coming in late at night, eating a bowl of berries of some kind in the kitchen, then stepping out onto the front porch and shooting himself.

I have noticed, however, throughout dinner that Sally and I have continued to make long and often unyielding eye contact. Once, while making coffee using the filter-and-plunger system, she's stolen a glimpse at me as if to acknowledge we've gotten to know each other a lot better now, have ventured closer, but that I've been acting strange or crazy and might just leap up and start reciting Shakespeare in pig Latin or whistling "Yankee Doodle" through my butt.

Toward ten, though, we have kicked back in our captain's chairs, a new candle lit, having finished coffee and gone back to the Round Hill. Sally has bunched her dense hair back, and we are launched into a discussion of our individual self-perceptions (mine basically as a comic character; Sally's a "facilitator," though from time to time, she says, "as a dark and pretty ruthless obstructor"—which I've never noticed). She sees me, she says, in an odd priestly mode, which is in fact the worst thing I can imagine, since priests are the least self-aware, most unenlightened, irresolute, isolated and frustrated people on the earth (politicians are second). I decide to ignore this, or at least to treat it as disguised goodwill and to mean I, too, am a kind of facilitator, which I would be if I could. I tell her I see her as a great beauty with a sound head on her shoulders, who I find compelling and unsusceptible to being made up in the way I explained earlier, which is true (I'm still shaken by being perceived as a priest). We venture on toward the issue of strong feelings, how they're maybe more important than love. I explain (why, I'm not sure, when it's not particularly true) that I'm having a helluva good time these days, refer to the Existence Period, which I have mentioned before, in other contexts. I fully admit that this part of my life may someday be—except for her— hard to remember with precision, and that sometimes I feel beyond affection's grasp but that's just being human and no cause for worry. I also tell her I could acceptably end my life as the "dean" of New Jersey realtors, a crusty old bird who's forgotten more than the younger men could ever know. (Otto Schwindell without the Pall Malls or the hair growing out my ears.) She says quite confidently, all the while smiling at me, that she hopes I can get around to doing something memorable, and for a moment I think again about bringing up the Marine cuff links and their general relation to things memorable, and possibly dropping in Ann's name—not wanting to seem unable to or as if Ann's very existence were a reproach to Sally, which it isn't. I decide not to do either of these.

Gradually, then, there comes into Sally's voice a tone of greater gravity, some chin-down throatiness I've heard before and on just such well-wrought evenings as this, yellow light twiny and flickering, the summer heat gone off, an occasional bug bouncing off the front screen; a tone that all by itself says, "Let's us give a thought to something a little more direct to make us both feel good, seal the evening with an act of simple charity and desire." My own voice, I'm sure, has the same oaken burr.

Only there's the old nerviness in my lower belly (and in hers too, it's my guess), an agitation connected to a thought that won't go away and that each of us is waiting for the other to admit—something important that leaves sweetly sighing desire back in the dust. Which is: that we've both by our own private means decided not to see each other anymore. (Though "decided" is not the word. Accepted, conceded, demurred—these are more in the ballpark.) There's plenty of everything between us, enough for a lifetime's consolation, with extras. But that's somehow not sufficient, and once that is understood, nothing much is left to say (is there?). In both the long run and the short, nothing between us seems to matter enough. These facts we both acknowledge with the aforementioned throaty tones and with these words that Sally actually speaks: "It's time for you to hit the road, Bub." She beams at me through the candle flicker as though she were somehow proud of us, or for us. (For what?) She's long since taken off her turquoise bracelets and stacked them on the table, moving them here and there as we've talked, like a player at a Ouija board. When I stand up she begins putting them on again. "I hope it all goes super with Paul," she says smilingly.

The hall clock chimes 10:30. I look around as though a closer timepiece might be handy, but I've known almost the exact minute for an hour.

"Yep," I say, "me too," and stretch my own arms upward and yawn.

She's standing now beside the table, fingers just touching the grain, smiling still, like my most steadfast admirer. "Do you want me to make more coffee?"

"I drive better asleep," I say, and produce a witless grin.

Then off I go, rumbling right down the hall past the winking green security panel—which might as well have changed to red.

Sally follows at a distance of ten feet and not fast, her limp pronounced for her being barefooted. She's allowing me to let myself out.

"So, okay." I turn around. She's still smiling, no less than eight feet back. But I am not smiling. In the time taken to walk to the screen door I've become willing to be asked to stay, to get up early, have some coffee and beat it to Connecticut after a night of adieus and possible reconsiderations. I close my eyes and fake a little weaving stagger meant to indicate *Boy, I'm sleepier than I thought and conceivably even a danger to myself and others*. But I've waited too long expecting something to happen *to* me; and if I were to ask, I'm confident she'd simply phone up the Cabot Lodge in Neptune and check me in. I can't even have my old room back. My visit has become like a house showing in which I leave nothing but my card in the foyer.

"I'm real glad you came," Sally says. I'm afraid she might even "put 'er there" and with it push me out the door I came through months ago in all innocence. Worse treatment than Wally.

But she doesn't. She walks up, grasps my short shirtsleeves above my elbows—we are at eye level—and plants one on me hard but not mean, and says in a little breath that wouldn't extinguish a candle, "Bye-bye."

"Bye-bye," I say, trying to mimic her seductive whisper and translate it possibly into hello. My heart races.

But I'm history. Out the door and down the steps. Along the sandy concrete beach walk in the fading barbecue aroma, down sandy steps to Asbury Street at the lighted other end of which Ocean Avenue streams with cruising lovers on parade. I crawl into my Crown Vic; though as I start up I crane around and survey the shadowy cars behind me on both sides, hoping to spy the other guy, whoever he is, if he is, someone on the lurk in summer khakis, waiting for me to clear out so he can march back along my tracks and into my vested place in Sally's house and heart.

But there's no one spying that I can see. A cat runs from one line of parked cars to the one I'm in. A porch light blinks down Asbury Street. Lights are on in most all the houses, TVs warmly humming. There's nothing, nothing to be suspicious of, nothing to think about, nothing to hold me here another second. I turn the wheel, back out, look up briefly at my empty window, then motor on.

6

Up the ink-dark seaboard, into the stillborn, ocean-rich night, my windows open wide for wakefulness: the Garden State, Red Bank, Matawan, Cheesequake, the steep bridge ascent over the Raritan and, beyond, the sallow grid-lights of Woodbridge.

There's, of course, a ton of traffic. Certain Americans will only take their summer jaunts after dark, when "it's easier on the engine," "there're fewer cops," "the gas stations lower the rates." The interchange at Exit 11 is aswarm with red taillights: U-Hauls, trailers, step vans, station wagons, tow dollies, land yachts, all cramming through, their drivers restless for someplace that can't wait till morning: a new home in Barrington, a holiday rental on Lake Memphrémagog, an awkward reunion at a more successful brother's chalet at Mount Whiteface—everyone with kids on board and screaming, a Port-a-Crib lashed to the top carry, desert bag harnessed to the front bumper, the whole, damn family belted in so tight that an easy breath can't be drawn.

And, too, it's that time of the month—when leases expire, contracts are up, payments come due. Car windows in the turnpike line reveal drawn faces behind steering wheels, frowns of concern over whether a certain check's cleared or if someone left behind is calling the law to report furniture removed, locks jimmied, garages entered without permission—a license number noted as a car disappears down a quiet suburban street. Holidays are not always festive events.

Cops, needless to say, are out in force. Up ahead of me on the turnpike, blue lights flash far and near as I clear the toll plaza and start toward Carteret and the flaming refinery fields and cooling vats of Elizabeth. I have had, I realize, one glass of Round Hill too many and am now squinting into the shimmer lights and MERGE LEFT arrows, where road repavers are working late under banks of da-brite spots—our highway taxes at work here too.

It would've been smart, of course, just to pack Sally in with me, lock the house, activate the alarm, inaugurate a new stratagem for the rescue of collapsing love, since I'm at this moment positive that no matter what decision was entered an hour ago, it'll never happen that way. Beyond an indistinct but critical point in life (near my own age, to be sure), most of your latter-day resolves fall apart and you end up either doing whatever's damn well easiest or else whatever you feel strongest about. (These two in fact can get mixed up and cause plenty of mischief.) At the same time it also gets harder and harder to believe you can control anything via principle or discipline, though we all talk as if we can, and actually try like hell. I feel certain, batting past Newark airport, that Sally would've dropped everything and come with me if I'd as much as asked. (How this would go over with Ann would be another bridge to cross.) Paul, I'm sure, would've thought it was fine. He and Sally could've become secret pals in league against me, and who knows what might've been in store for the three of us. For starters, I wouldn't be alone in this traffic-gunk metallurgic air shaft, bound for an empty set of sheets in who knows what motel in who knows what state.

An important truth about my day-to-day affairs is that I maintain a good share of flexibility, such that my personal time and whereabouts are often not of the essence. When poor sweet Clair Devane met her three o'clock at Pheasant Meadow and got pulled into a buzz saw of bad luck, a whole network of alarms and anguish cries bespeaking love, honor, dependency immediately sounded—north to south, coast to coast. Her very *moment* as a lost human entity was at once seismically registered on all she'd touched. But on any day *I* can rise and go about all my normal duties in a normal way; or I could drive down to Trenton, pull off a convenience-store stickup or a contract hit, then fly off to Caribou, Alberta, walk off naked into the muskeg and no one would notice much of anything out of the ordinary about my life, or even register I was gone. It could take days, possibly weeks, for serious personal dust to be raised. (It's not exactly as if I didn't exist, but that I don't exist *as much*.) So, if I didn't appear tomorrow to get my son, or if I showed up with Sally as a provocative late sign-up to my team, if I showed up with the fat lady from the circus or a box of spitting cobras, as little as possible would be made of it by all concerned, partly in order that everybody retain as much of their own personal freedom and flexibility as possible, and partly because I just wouldn't be noticed that much *per se*. (This reflects my own wishes, of course—the unhurried nature of my single life in the grip of the Existence Period—though it may also imply that laissez-faire is not precisely the same as independence.)

Where Sally's concerned, however, I take responsibility for how things went tonight. Since, in spite of other successful adjustments, I have yet to learn to *want* properly. When I've been with Sally for longer than a day—plowing over the Green Mountains, or snug-a-bug in a big matrimonial suite at the Gettysburg Battlefield Colonial Inn, or just sitting staring at oil rigs and trawler lights riding the Atlantic, as we were tonight, what I always think is, Why don't I love you?—which instantly makes me feel sorry for her and, after that, for myself, which can lead to bitterness and sarcasm or just evenings like tonight, when bruised feelings lurk below surface niceties (though still well above *deep* feelings).

But what bothers me about Sally—unlike Ann, who still superintends everything about me just by being alive and sharing ineluctable history—is that Sally superintends nothing, presupposes nothing and in essence promises to do nothing remotely like that (except *like* me, as she admitted she does). And whereas in marriage there's the gnashing, cold but also cozy fear that after a while there'll be no *me* left, only *me chemically amalgamated with another*, the proposition with Sally is that there's *just* me. Forever. I alone would go on being responsible for everything that had me in it; no cushiony "chemistry" or heady synchronicity to fall back on, no *other*, only me and my acts, her and hers, somehow together—which of course is much more fearsome.

This is the very source of the joint feeling we both had sitting on the dark porch: that we weren't waiting for anything to happen or change. What might've seemed like hollow, ritual acts or ritual feelings between us were, in fact, neither hollow nor ritual, but real acts and honest feelings—not nullity, not at all. That was the way we actually felt tonight at the actual time we felt it: simply present, alone and together. There was nothing really wrong with it. If you wanted to you might call our "relationship" the Existence Period shared.

Obviously what I need to do is simply "cut through," make clear and understood what it is I do like about Sally (which is damn plenty), give in to whatever's worth wanting, accept what's offered, change the loaded question from "Why don't I love you?" to the better, more answerable "How can I love you?" Though if I'm successful it would probably mean resuming life at about the point, give or take, where a good marriage would've brought me, had I been able to last at it long enough.

P̲ast Exit 16W and across the Hackensack River from Giants Stadium, I curve off into the Vince Lombardi Rest Area to gas up, take a leak, clear my head with coffee and check for messages.

The "Vince" is a little red-brick Colonial Williamsburg–looking pavilion, whose parking lot this midnight is hopping with cars, tour buses, motor homes, pickups—all my adversaries from the turnpike— their passengers and drivers trooping dazedly inside through a scattering of sea gulls and under the woozy orange lights, toting diaper bags, thermoses and in-car trash receptacles, their minds fixed on sacks of Roy Rogers burgers, Giants novelty items, joke condoms, with a quick exit peep at the Vince memorabilia collection from the great man's glory days on the "Six Blocks of Granite," later as win-or-die Packer headman and later still as elder statesman of the resurgent Skins (when pride still mattered). Vince, of course, was born in Brooklyn, but began his coaching career at nearby Englewood's St. Cecilia's, which is why he has his own rest area. (Sportswriting leaves you with such memories as these.)

As there's a lull at the pumps, I gas up first, then park on the back forty, among the long-haul trucks and idling buses, and hike across the lot and into the lobby, where it's as chaotic as a department store at Christmas yet also, strangely, half asleep (like an old-time Vegas casino at 4 a.m.), with its dark video arcade bing-jinging, long lines at the Roy's and Nathan's Famous and families walking around semi-catatonically eating, or else sitting arguing at plastic tables full of paper trash. Nothing suggests the 4th of July.

I make my visit to the cavernous men's room, where the urinals flush the instant you're done and on the walls, appropriately enough, there're no pictures of Vince. I pass through the "Express Coffee Only" line at Roy's, then carry my paper cup over to the phone bank, which as usual is being held hostage by twenty truckers in plaid shirts with big chained-on wallets, all leaning into the little metal phone cubbies, fingers sealing their ears, maundering to someone time zones away.

I wait till one of them hauls up on his jeans and saunters off like a man who's just committed a secret sex act, then I set up shop and call for my messages, which I haven't heard since three—nearly nine hours and counting. (My receiver holds onto the gritty warmth of the trucker's grip as well as the lime-cologne odor from the rest room dispensers, a smell many women must find it possible to get used to.)

Message one (of ten!) is from Karl Bemish: "Frank, yeah. So's you know. The little Frito Banditos just cruised through. CEY 146. Note that down in case they kill me. Another Mexican's in the back seat this time through. I phoned the sheriff. Nothing to worry about." Clunk.

Message two is another call from Joe Markham: "Look, Bascombe. Goddamn it. 259–6834. Call me. 609 area code. We'll be here tonight." Clunk.

Message three is a hang-up—undoubtedly Joe, going ballistic and becoming speechless.

Message four, though, is from Paul, in a mood of fierce hilarity. "Boss? Hello dere, boss?" His less than perfect Rochester voice. Someone else's squeaky laughter is in the background. "If you needs to get laid, crawl up a chicken's ass and *wait!*" Louder hilarity, possibly Paul's girlfriend, the troubling Stephanie Deridder, though also possibly Clarissa Bascombe, his accomplice. "Okay, okay now. Wait." He's starting a new routine. This is not very good news. "You insect, you parasite, you worm! It's Dr. Rection here. Dr. Hugh G. Rection, calling with your test results. It doesn't look good for you, Frank. Oncology recapitulates ontogeny." He couldn't know what this means. "Bark, bark, bark, bark, bark." This, of course, is very bad, though they're both laughing like monkeys. Change clicks in a pay phone slot. "Next stop the Black Forest. I'll have the torte, pleeeezzz. Bark, bark, bark, bark, bark. Make that two, t-o-o, doc-tah." I hear the sound of the receiver being dropped, I hear them walking away giggling. I wait and wait and wait for them to come back (as though they were really there and I could speak to Paul, as though it wasn't all recorded hours ago). But they don't, and the tape stops. A bad call, about which I feel at a complete loss.

Message five is from Ann (strained, businesslike, a tone for the plumber who fixed her pipes wrong). "Frank, call me, please. All right? Use my private number: 203 526–1689. It's important. Thanks." Click.

Message six, Ann again: "Frank. Call me please? Anytime tonight, wherever you are—526–1689." Click.

Message seven, another hang-up.

Message eight, Joe Markham: "We're on our way to Vermont. So fuck you, asshole. You prick! You try to do—" Clunk! Good riddance.

Message nine, Joe again (what a surprise): "We're on our way to Vermont right now. So stick this message up your ass." Clunk.

Message ten, Sally: "Hi." A long, thought-organizing pause, then a sigh. "I should've been better tonight. I just . . . I don't know what." Pause. Sigh. "But—I'm sorry. I wish you were still here, even if you don't. Wish, wish, wish. Let's . . . umm . . . Sure. Just call me when you get home. Maybe I'll come for a visit. Bye-bye." Clunk.

Except for the last, an unusually unsettling collection of messages for 11:50 p.m.

I dial Ann and she answers immediately.

"What's going on?" I say, more anxious than I care to sound.

"I'm sorry," she says in an unsorry-sounding voice. "It's gotten a little out of hand here today. Paul flipped out, and I thought maybe you could get up here early and take him off, but it's okay now. Where are you?"

"At the Vince Lombardi."

"The fence what?"

"It's on the turnpike." She has in fact used the facilities here. Years ago, of course. "I can make it in two hours," I say. "What happened?"

"Oh. He and Charley got into a fracas in the boathouse, about the right way and the wrong way to varnish Charley's dinghy. He hit Charley in the jaw with an oarlock. I think maybe he didn't mean to, but it knocked him down. Almost knocked him out."

"Is he all right?"

"He's all right. No bones broken."

"I mean is *Paul* all right?"

A pause for adjustment. "Yes," she says. "He is. He disappeared for a while, but he came home about nine—which breaks his court curfew. Has he called you?"

"He left me a message." No need for details: barking, hysterical laughter. (To be great is to be misunderstood.)

"Was he crazy?"

"He just seemed excited. I guessed he was with Stephanie." Ann and I are of one mind about Stephanie, which is that *their* chemistry is wrong. In our view, for Stephanie's parents to send her to a military school for girls—possibly in Tennessee—would be good.

"He's very upset. I don't really know why." Ann takes a sip of something that has ice cubes in it. She has changed her drinking habits since moving to Connecticut, from bourbon (when she was married to me) to vodka gimlets, over whose proper preparation Charley O'Dell apparently exercises total mastery. Ann in general is much harder to read these days, which I assume is the point of divorce. Though on the subject of *why now* for Paul, my belief is that on any given day there're truckloads of good excuses for "flipping out." Paul, in particular, could find plenty. It's surprising we all don't do it more.

"How's Clary?"

"Okay. They've gone to sleep in his room now. She says she wants to look out for him."

"Girls mature faster than boys, I guess. How's Charley? Did he get his dinghy waxed right?"

"He has a big lump. Look, I'm sorry. It's all right now. Where is it you're taking him again?"

"To the basketball and baseball halls of fame." This suddenly sounds overpoweringly stupid. "Do you want me to call him?" My son with his own line, a proper Connecticut teen.

"Just come get him like you planned." She's ill at ease now, itchy to get off.

"How are you?" Comes to my mind that I haven't seen her in weeks. Not so long, but long. Though for some reason it makes me mad.

"All right. Fine," she says wearily, avoiding the personal pronoun.

"Are you spending enough time in skiffs? Getting to see the morning mist?"

"What're you indicating with that tone?"

"I don't know." I actually don't know. "It just makes me feel better."

Phone silence descends. Video arcade and Roy Rogers clatter rises and encapsulates me. Another plaid-shirted, blue-jeaned wavy-haired, big-wallet trucker is now waiting midway of the lobby, glomming a sheaf of businessy-looking papers, staring hatchets at me as if I were on his private line.

"Tell me something that's the truth," I say to Ann. I have no idea why, but my voice to me sounds intimate and means to ask intimacy in return.

I, however, know the look on Ann's face now. She has closed her eyes, then opened them so as to be looking in an entirely different direction. She has elevated her chin to stare next at the lacquered ceiling of whatever exquisite, architecturally *sui generis* room she's occupying. Her lips are pursed in an unyielding little line. I'm actually happy not to see this, since it would shut me up like a truant. "I don't really care what you mean by that," she says in an icy voice. "This isn't a friendly conversation. It's just necessary."

"I just wished you had something important to tell me, or something interesting or wholehearted. That's all. Nothing personal." I'm fishing for a sign of the argument, the one Paul said she'd had with Charley. Nothing more innocent.

Ann says nothing. So I say meagerly, "I'll tell *you* something interesting."

"Not wholehearted?" she says crossly.

"Well . . ." I, of course, have opened my mouth without knowing what words to bring forth, what beliefs to proclaim or validate, what human condition to hold under my tiny microscope. It's frightening. And yet it's what everybody does—learning how you stand by hearing yourself talk. (Locution, locution, locution.)

What I *almost* say is: "I'm getting married." Though I somehow stop myself after "I'm," which sounds enough like "Um." Except it *is* what I want to say, since it announces something important to *do*, and the only reason I don't say it (other than that it's not true) is that I'd end up responsible for the story and later have to invent a series of fictitious "subsequent" events and shocking turns of fate to get me off the hook. Plus I'd risk being found out and looking pathetic to my children, who already have reservations about me.

The hillbilly trucker is still glaring at me. He is a tall, hip-sprung guy with depressed cheekbones and beady sunken eyes. Probably he is another lime-cologne devotee. His watchband, I notice, is formed by linked, gold-plated pull-tabs, and he in fact points to the watch face and mouths the words *I'm late*. I, though, simply mouth some nonsense words back, then turn into the stale little semi-cubicle separating me from the other humans.

"Are you still there?" Ann says irritably.

"Umm. Yeah," my heart whomping once, unexpectedly. I am staring at my undrunk coffee. "I was thinking," I say, still slightly confused (perhaps I'm still buzzed), "that when you get divorced you think everything changes and you shed a lot of stuff. But I don't think you shed a goddamn thing; you just take more on, like cargo. That's how you find out the limits of your character and the difference between *can't* and *won't*. You might find out you're a little cynical too."

"I have to tell you I don't have any idea what you're talking about. Are you drunk?"

"I might be. But what I said is still true." My right eye flutters, along with my heartbeat going bim-bam. I have scared myself.

"Well, who knows," she says.

"Do you feel like a person who was ever married before?" I wedge my shoulder farther up into my little metal phone coffin for whatever quiet there is.

"I don't *feel* like I was married," Ann says, even more irritable. "I was. A long time ago. To you."

"Seven years ago on the eighteenth," I say, though all at once there's the ice-water-down-the-back recognition that *I* am actually *talking* to Ann. Right now. Rather than doing what I do most all the time—*not* talking to her, or hearing recorded messages of her voice, yet having her on my mind. I'm tempted to tell her how peculiar this feels, as a way of trying to woo her back to me. Though after that, what? Then, loud enough to make me jump out of my shoes, *Boom-boom-boom-ding-ding-ding! Crrraaaaaash!* Somebody in the hellhole video chamber across the concourse has hit some kind of lurid jackpot. Other players—spectral, drugged-looking teens—drift nearer for a gander. "I'm beginning not to feel like I used to feel." I say this under the noise.

"And how is that?" Ann says. "You mean you can't feel what it's like to feel married?"

"Right. Something like that."

"It's because you're *not* married. You should *get* married. We'd all feel better."

"It's pretty nice being married to ole Charley, is it?" I'm glad I didn't blub out I was getting married. I'd have missed this.

"Yes, it is. And he's not old. And it's not any of your business. So don't ask me about it, and please don't think because I won't answer you that *that* means anything." Silence again. I hear her glass tinkle and get set firmly down on some solid surface. "My life's private," she says after swallowing, "and it's not that I can't discuss it; I *won't* discuss it. There's no subject to discuss. It's just words. You may be the most cynical man in the world."

"I hope I'm not," I say, with what feels like an idiotic smile emerging unbidden onto my features.

"You should go back to writing stories, Frank. You quit too soon." I hear a drawer open and close wherever she is, my mind ablaze with possibility. "You could have everybody saying what you wanted them to, then, and everything would work out perfectly— for you anyway. Except it wouldn't really be happening, which you also like."

"Do you think that's what I want?" Something like this very thought, of course, is what put me to sleep at Sally's today.

"You just want everything to seem perfect and everybody to seem pleased. And you're willing to let *seem* equal *be*. It makes pleasing anybody be an act of cowardice. None of this is new news. I don't know why I'm bothering."

"I asked you to." This is a sneak frontal assault on the Existence Period.

"You said to tell you something that was the truth. This is simply obvious."

"Or reliable. I'd settle for that too."

"I want to go to sleep. Please? Okay? I've had a trying day. I don't want to argue with you."

"We're not arguing." I hear the drawer open and close again. Back in the gift-shop complex, a man shouts, "I brake for beer," and laughs like hell.

"Everything's in quotes with you, Frank. Nothing's really solid. Every time I talk to you I feel like everything's being written by you. Even my lines. That's awful. Isn't it? Or sad?"

"Not if you liked them."

"Oh, well . . . ," Ann says, as if a bright light had flashed somewhere outside a window in an otherwise limitless dark, and she had been moved by its extraordinary brilliance and for a moment become transported. "I guess so," she says, seemingly amazed. "I've just gotten very sleepy. I have to go. You wore me out." These are the most intimate words she's addressed to me in years! (I have no idea what might've inspired them.) Though sadder than what she thinks is sad is the fact that hearing them leaves me nothing to say, no lines I even can write for her. Moving closer, even slightly, even for a heartbeat, is just another form of storytelling.

"I'll be there in the morning," I say brightly.

"Fine, fine," Ann says. "That'll be fine, sweetheart." (A slip of the tongue.) "Paul'll be glad to see you." She hangs up before I can even say good-bye.

A number of travelers have now cycled out of the Vince heading back to the night, awake enough for another hour of driving before sleep or the police catch up. The trucker who's been fish-eyeing me is now talking to another of his ilk, also wearing a plaid shirt (in green; shirts only available in truck stops). The second guy is gigantic with a huge Milwaukee goiter, red suspenders, a piggy crew cut and an oversize silver-and-gold rodeo-champeen belt buckle to keep his jeans cinched up over his, I'm sure, minuscule private parts. They're both shaking their heads disgustedly at me. Clearly their business is more important than mine—a 900 number for finding out which of their favorite hookers are working the BP lot on Route 17 north of Suffern. I'm sure they're Republicans; I probably seem like the most obvious caller to intimidate.

I decide, though, in a moment of discomposure over Ann, to call the Markhams, since my bet is Joe's all talk about clearing out, and he and Phyllis are right now sitting up stolidly watching HBO, the very thing they lack but yearn for in Island Pond.

The switchboard rings for a long time before it's answered by a woman who was asleep one moment before and who says Sleepy Hollow so it sounds like "slippery olive."

"Those left, I think," she says in an achy, light-in-your-eyes voice. "I saw 'em packin' their vehicle around nine, I guess. But lemme ring it."

And in an instant, Joe is on the line.

"Hi, Joe, it's Frank Bascombe," I say, arch-cheerful. "Sorry to fall out of touch. I've had some family problems I couldn't get out of." (My son poleaxed his mother's hubby with an oarlock, then started barking like a Pomeranian, which has caused us all to drop back a couple of squares.)

"Who do you think *this* is?" Joe says, obviously gloating to Phyllis, who's no doubt parked beside him in a swampy TV glow, bingeing on Pringles. I hear a bell ding on Joe's end and someone jabbering in Spanish. They're apparently watching boxing from Mexico, which has probably put Joe in a fighting mood. "I thought I told you we were gettin' out of here."

"I hoped I'd catch you before you got away, just see if there're any questions. Maybe you'd made a decision. I'll call back in the morning if that's better." I ignore the fact that Joe has called me an asshole and a prick on my machine.

"We already got another realtor," Joe says contemptuously.

"Well, I've shown you what there is out there that *I* know about. But the Houlihan house is worth a serious thought. We'll see some movement there pretty quick if the other agencies are on the case. It may be a good time to make an offer if you thought you wanted to."

"You're talking to yourself," Joe sneers. I hear a bottle clink the rim of a glass, then another glass. "Go, go, go," I hear him say in a brash voice—obviously to Phyllis.

"Let me talk to him," she says.

"You're not going to talk to him. What else do you want to tell me?" Joe says, so I can hear the receiver scrape his dopey goatee. "We're watching the fights. It's the last round. Then we're leaving." Joe's forgotten already about the supposed other realtor.

"I'm just checking in. Your message sounded a little agitated."

"That was three hundred and fifty years ago. We're seeing a new person tomorrow. We would've made an offer six hours ago. Now we won't."

"Maybe seeing someone else is a good strategy at this point in time," I say—I hope—infuriatingly.

"Good. I'm glad you're glad."

"If there's anything I can do for you and Phyllis, you know my number."

"I know it. Zero. Zero, zero, zero, zero, zero, zero."

"In 609. Be sure to tell Phyllis I said good-bye."

"Bascombe sends you warm greetings, dear," Joe says snidely.

"Lemme talk," I hear her say.

"A two letter word ending in *O*." Joe stretches *o* out to a long diphthongal *uhhoouu*, just the way the bozos do in the Beaver Valley.

"You don't have to be such a turd," she says. "He's doing the best he can."

"You mean he's a shithead?" Joe says, partly covering the mouth-piece so I can hear what he's called me but still pretend not to, and he can say what he pleases but pretend not to have said it. After a certain point, which may be a point I've already passed, I don't give a rusty fuck anymore.

Though their situation is pretty much what I imagined this morning: that they'd enter a terrible trial-by-fire period having to do with their sense of themselves, a period which they'd exit disoriented. Afterward they'd wander in a fog until they reached a point of deciding something, which is when I'd wanted to talk to them. As it is, I've called while they're still disoriented and merely *seem* decisive. If I'd waited until tomorrow, they'd both be in straitjackets and ready to roll; inasmuch as what's true for them is true for any of us (and a sign of maturer years): you can rave, break furniture, get drunk, crack up your Nova and beat your knuckles bloody on the glass bricks of the exterior wall of whatever dismal room you're temporarily housed in, but in the end you won't have changed the basic situation and you'll still have to make the decision you didn't want to make before, and probably you'll make it in the very way you'd resented and that brought on all the raving and psychic fireworks.

Choices are limited, in other words. Though the Markhams have spent too long in addlebrained Vermont—picking berries, spying on deer and making homespun clothes using time-honored methods— to know it. In a sense, I provide a service somewhat wider in scope than at first it might seem—a free reality check.

"Frank?" Phyllis is now on the line. Bumping and scraping of motel furniture starts in the background, as if Joe were loading it all in the car.

"Still here," I say, though I'm thinking I'll give Sally a call. Conceivably I can fly her up to Bradley in the morning, where Paul and I could nab her on the way to the Basketball Hall of Fame, then proceed to Cooperstown in a new-dimensional family modality: divorced father, plus son living in another state and undergoing mental sturm und drang, plus father's widowed girlfriend, for whom he feels considerable affection and ambiguity, and whom he may marry or else never see again. Paul would view it as right for our times.

"I guess Joe and I have sort of pulled together on this whole thing now," Phyllis says. Phyllis sounds to me like she's having to exert physical force to talk, as if she's being stuffed in a closet or having to squeeze between big rocks. I imagine her in a pink granny gown, her arms plump above the elbows, possibly wearing socks due to unaccustomed air-conditioning.

"That's just great." *Bing, bing, bingety-bing.* Kids are racking up big numbers on the Samurai Showdown across in the arcade. The Vince operates more like a small-town mall than a part-time sports shrine.

"I'm sorry it's turned out this way after all the work you put in," she says, somehow and with effort freeing herself from whatever's restraining her. Possibly she and Joe are arm-wrestling.

"We'll fight on another day," I say cheerfully. I'm sure she means to tell me her and Joe's complex reasoning for changing boats midstream. Though I'm only willing to hear her spiel it out because telling it will make her feel desperate the instant she's finished. For donkeyish clients like the Markhams, the worst option is having to act on your own advice; whereas letting a paid professional like me tell you what to do is much easier, safer and more comforting, since the advice will always be to follow convention. "Just so you feel like you've made the right decision," I say. I'm still thinking vividly about Sally flying up to meet me: a clear mental picture of her getting in a small plane, in high spirits, carrying an overnight bag.

"Frank, Joe said he could see himself standing in the driveway being interviewed by a local TV reporter," Phyllis says sheepishly, "and he didn't want to be that person, not in the Houlihan house." I must've already talked to Joe about my theory of seeing yourself and learning to like it, since he's now claimed it as his own patented wisdom. Joe has apparently left the room.

"What was he being interviewed about?" I say.

"That didn't matter, Frank. It was the whole situation."

Outside the glass doors in the orange-lit parking lot, a big gold-and-green cruiser bus pulls past the entrance, *Eureka* written on its side in lavish, curving scripted letters. I've seen these buses while driving to Sally's via the Garden State. They're usually crammed with schnockered Canucks headed for Atlantic City to gamble at Trump Castle. They motor straight through, arrive at 1 a.m., gamble forty-eight hours without cease (eats and drinks on the cuff), then hustle back on board and sleep the whole way back to Trois-Rivières, arriving in time for half a day's work on Monday. Someone's idea of fun. I'd like to get on my way before a crew of them comes storming in.

Phyllis, though, has won a round, somehow letting Joe convince himself he's the bad-tempered, tight-fisted old noncompromiser who put the ki-bosh on the Houlihan house. "We also feel, Frank," Phyllis drones, "and I feel this as strongly as Joe, that we don't want to be bossed around by a false economy."

"Which economy is that?" I say.

"The housing one. If we don't get in now, it could be better later."

"Well, that's true. You never get in the river the same place twice," I say dully. "I'm curious, though, if you know where you're going to live by the time school starts."

"Uh-huh," Phyllis says competently. "We think if worse comes to worst, Joe can rent a bachelor place near his work and I can stay on temporarily in Island Pond. Sonja can go right on with her friends in school. We plan to talk to the other relator about that." Phyllis actually says "relator," something I've never heard her say, indicating to me she's reverting to a previous personality matrix— more desperate, but more calculating (also not unusual).

"Well, that's all pretty sound reasoning," I say.

"Do you think that, really?" Phyllis says, undisguised fear suddenly working through her voice like a pitchfork. "Joe says he didn't have a feeling anything significant ever happened in any of the places you showed us. But I wasn't sure."

"I wonder what he had in mind there?" I say. Possibly a celebrity murder? Or the discovery of a new solar system from an attic-window telescope?

"Well, he thinks if we're leaving Vermont we should be moving into a sphere of more important events that would bring us both up in some way. The places you showed us he didn't think did that. Your houses might be better for someone else, maybe."

"They aren't my houses, Phyllis. They belong to other people. I just sell them. Plenty of people do okay in them."

"I'm sure," Phyllis says glumly. "But you know what I mean."

"Not really," I say. Joe's theory of significant events suggests to me he's lost his new finger-hold on sanction. Though I'm not interested. If Joe rents a little *dépendance* in Manalapan, and Phyllis finds "meaningful" work substituting in the Island Pond alternative crafts school, gets into a new "paper group" with a cadre of acid-tongued but spiritually supportive women friends, while Sonja makes the pep squad at Lyndon Academy, marriage Markham-style will be a dead letter by Turkey Day. Which is the real issue here, of course (a profounder text runs beneath all realty decisions): Is being together worth the unbelievable horseshit required to satisfy the other's needs? Or would it just be more fun to go it alone? "Looking at houses is a pretty good test of what you're all about, Phyllis," I say (the very last thing she wants to hear).

"I would've looked at your colored house, Frank—I mean your rental. But Joe just didn't feel right about it."

"Phyllis, I'm at a pay phone on the turnpike, so I better be going before a truck runs over me. But our rental market's pretty tight, I think you'll find." I spy a phalanx of chortling Canadians, most of them in Bermudas, rumbling across the lot, all primed to hit the can, down a gut-bomb, have a sniff at the Vince trophy case, then grab one last en-route catnap before nonstop gaming commences.

"Frank, I don't know what to say." I hear something made of glass being knocked over and broken into a lot of pieces. "Oh, shit," Phyllis says. "This isn't, by the way, a realtor in Haddam. She's more in the East Brunswick area." A portion of central New Jersey resembling the sere suburban scrub fields of Youngstown. It's also where Skip McPherson rents ice time before daylight.

"Well, that'll have a whole new feel for you guys" (the Youngstown feel).

"It's sort of starting over, though, isn't it?" Phyllis says, giving in to bewilderment.

"Well, maybe Joe'll picture himself better up there. And there really isn't any starting over involved, Phyllis. It's all part of your ongoing search."

"What do you think's going to happen to us, Frank?"

The Canadians are now bustling into the lobby, elbowing each other and yucking it up like hockey fans—men and women alike. They are big, healthy, happy, well-adjusted white people who aren't about to miss any meals or get dressed up for no good reason. They break off into pairs and threes, guys and gals, and go yodeling off through the metal double doors to the rest rooms. (The best all-around Americans, in my view, are Canadians. I, in fact, should think of moving there, since it has all the good qualities of the states and almost none of the bad, plus cradle-to-grave health care and a fraction of the murders we generate. An attractive retirement waits just beyond the forty-ninth parallel.)

"Did you hear me, Frank?"

"I hear you, Phyllis. Loud and clear." The last of the laughing Canadian women, purses in hand, disappear into the women's, where they immediately start unloading on the men and gassing about how "lucky" they were to hook up with a bunch of cabbage-heads like these guys. "You and Joe are just overwrought about happiness, Phyllis. You should just buy the first house you halfway like from your new realtor and start making yourselves happy. It's not all that tricky."

"I'm just in a black mood because of my operation, I guess," Phyllis says. "I know we're pretty lucky. Some young people can't even afford a home now."

"Some older people too." I wonder if Phyllis visualizes herself and Joe as among the nation's young. "I gotta get a move on here," I say.

"How's your son? Didn't you tell me he had Hotchkin's or brain damage or something?"

"He's making a comeback, Phyllis." Until this afternoon. "He's quite a boy. Thanks for asking."

"Joe needs a lot of maintenance right now too," Phyllis says, to keep me on the phone. (Some woman in the rest room lets out an Indian whoop that sets the rest of them howling. I hear a stall door bang shut. "Yew-guyz . . . Jeeeeez-us," one of the men answers from next door.) "We've seen some changes in our relationship, Frank. It's not easy to let someone into your inner circle if you're both second-timers."

"It's not easy for first-timers either," I say impatiently. Phyllis seems to be angling for something. Though what? I once had a client—the wife of a church history professor and a mother of three, one of whom was autistic and got left in the car in a restraining harness—who asked me if I had any interest in getting naked with her on the polished floor of a ranch-style home in Belle Mead, a house her husband liked but she wanted a second look at because she felt the floor plan lacked "flow." An instance of pure transference. Though no one in the realty business isn't clued in to the sexual dimension: hours spent alone in close quarters (front seats of cars, provocatively empty houses); the not-quite-false aura of vulnerability and surrenderment; the possibility of a future in the same grid pattern, of unexpected, tingly sightings at the end of the lettuce rack, squirmy, almost-missed eye contact across a hot summer parking lot or through a plate-glass window with a spouse present. There have been instances in these three years and a half when I haven't been a model citizen. Except you can lose your license for that kind of stunt and become a bad joke in the community, neither of which I care to risk as much as I might once have.

Still, for some reason, I find myself imagining fleshy Phyllis not in a pink petunia print but a skimpy slip over her bare underneath, holding a tumbler of warm Scotch while she talks, and peeking out the blinds at the grainy-lit Sleepy Hollow parking lot as the innkeeper's eighteen-year-old half-Polynesian son, Mombo, shirtless and muscles bulging, hauls a garbage bag around to the dumpster outside their bathroom in which sluggo Joe is grouchily tending to more of nature's unthrilling needs behind closed doors. This is the second time today I've thought of Phyllis "in this way," her health situation notwithstanding. My question, however, is: why?

"So you live alone?" Phyllis says.

"What's that?"

"Because Joe had at one time thought you might be gay, that's all."

"Nope. A frayed knot, as my son says." Though I'm baffled. In two hours I have been suspected of being a priest, a shithead and now, a homo. I'm apparently not getting my message across. I hear another round-bell go *ding*, as Joe turns up the TV from Mexico.

"Well," Phyllis says, whispering, "I just wished for a second I was going wherever you were going, Frank. That might be nice."

"You wouldn't have a good time with me, Phyllis. I can promise that."

"Oh. It's just crazy. Crazy, crazy talk." Too bad she can't get on the bus with the Canadians. "You're a good listener, Frank. I'm sure it's a plus in your profession."

"Sometimes. But not always."

"You're just modest."

"Good luck to you two," I say.

"Well, we'll see you, Frank. You be good. Thanks."

Clunk.

*T*he truckers who've been glowering at me have wandered off. And both sets of Canadians now emerge from their comfort stations, hands damp, noses blown, faces splashed, hair wet-combed, shirttails for the moment tucked, yaw-hawing about whatever nasty secrets were shared around inside. They march off into Roy's, their skinny, uniformed bus driver standing just outside the glass doors, having a smoke and some P&Q in the hot night. He cuts his eyes my way, sees me down the phone bank watching him, shakes his head as if we both knew all about it, tosses his smoke and walks out of view.

Without as much as one guarded thought left from dinner, I punch in Sally's number, feeling that I've made a bad decision where she's concerned, should've stayed and wooed my way out of the woods like a man who knows how to get messages across. (This of course may turn out to be a worse decision—tired, half drunk, fretful, not in control of my speech. Though sometimes it's better to make a bad decision than no decision at all.)

But Sally, from her message, must be in a similar frame of mind, and what I'd like to do is turn around and beat it back to her house, scramble into bed with her and have us go slap to sleep like old marrieds, then tomorrow haul her along, and begin instilling proper wanting practices into my life, and fun to boot, and quit being the man holding out. Forty psychics able to find Jimmy Hoffa in a landfill, or to tell you what street your missing twin Norbert's living on in Great Falls, couldn't tell me what's a "better deal" than Sally Caldwell. (Of course, one of the Existence Period's bedrock paradoxes is that just when you think you're emerging, you may actually be wading further in.)

"Uffda, ya goddamn knucklehead," one of the Canadians yorks out as I listen intently to Sally's phone ring and ring and ring.

Though I'm quick to the next decision: leave a message saying I *would*'ve zoomed back but didn't know where she was, yet I stand prepared to charter a Piper Comanche, zoom her up to Springfield, where Paul and I'll pick her up in time for lunch. Zoom, zoom.

But instead of her sweet voice and diversionary, security-conscious message—"Hi! We're not here, but your call is important to us"—I get rings and more rings. I actually picture the phone vibrating all to hell on its table beside her big teester bed, which in my tableau is lovingly turned down but empty. I pound in the number again and try to visualize Sally dashing out of the shower or just coming in from a pensive midnight walk on Mantoloking beach, taking the front steps two at a time, forgetting her limp, hoping it's me. And it is. Only, ring, ring, ring, ring.

An overcooked, nearly nauseating hot dog smell floats across the lobby from Nathan's. "And your mind's a sewer too," one of the Canuck women sounds off at one of the men standing in line.

"So and what's yers, eh? An operating room? I'm not married t'ya, okay?"

"Yet," another man guffaws.

Defeated, I'm nonetheless ready to go, and take off striding right out through the lobby. Gaunt boys from Moonachie and Nutley are straying in toward the Mortal Kombat and Drug War machines, angling for the big kills. New weary-eyed travelers wander through the front doors, seeking relief of some stripe, ignoring the Vince trophy case—too much on a late night. I should, right here and now, buy something to bring Clarissa, but there's nothing for sale but football crap and postcards showing the NJTpk in all four seasonal moods (I'll have to find something tomorrow), and I pass out of the air-conditioning right by the Eureka driver, leaning one leg up on his idling juggernaut, surrounded now by white gulls standing motionless in the dark.

U p again onto the streaming, light-choked turnpike, my dashboard digital indicating 12:40. It's tomorrow already, July 2, and my personal aspirations are now trained on sleep, since the rest of tomorrow will be a testing day if everything goes in all details perfectly, which it won't; so that, I'm determined—late departure and all—to put my woolly head down *someplace* in the Constitution State, as a small token of progress and encouragement to my journey.

But the turnpike thwarts me. Along with construction slowdowns, entrance ramps merging, MEN WORKING, left-lane breakdowns and a hot mechanical foreboding that the entire seaboard might simply explode, there's now even more furious, grinding-mad-in-the-dark traffic and general vehicular desperation, as if to be caught in New Jersey after tonight will mean sure death.

At Exit 18E&W, where the turnpike ends, cars are stacked before, beyond, around and out of sight toward the George Washington Bridge. Automated signs over the lanes counsel way-worn travelers to EXPECT LONG DELAYS, TAKE ALTERNATE ROUTE. More responsible advice would be: LOOK AT YOUR HOLE CARD. HEAD FOR HOME. I envision miles and miles of backup on the Cross Bronx (myself dangled squeamishly above the teeming hellish urban no-man's-land below), followed by multiple-injury accidents on the Hutch, more long toll-booth tie-ups on the thruway, a blear monotony of NO VACANCYs clear to Old Saybrook and beyond, culminating in me sleeping on the back seat in some mosquito-plagued rest area and (worst case) being trussed and maimed, robbed and murdered, by anguished teens—who might right now be following me from the Vince—my body left for crows' food, silent on a peak in Darien.

So, as ill advised, I take an alternate route.

Though there is no truly alternate route, only *another* route, a longer, barely chartable, indefensible fool's route of sailing west to get east: up to 80, where untold cars are all flooding eastward, then west to Hackensack, up 17 past Paramus, onto the Garden State north (again!), though eerily enough there's little traffic; through River Edge and Oradell and Westwood, and two tolls to the New York line, then east to Nyack and the Tappan Zee, down over Tarrytown (once home to Karl Bemish) to where the East opens up just as the North must have once for old Henry Hudson himself.

What on a good summer night should take thirty minutes—the G.W. to Greenwich and straight into a pricey little inn with a moon-shot water view—takes me an hour and fifteen, and I am *still* south of Katonah, my eyes jinking and smarting, phantoms leaping from ditches and barrow pits, the threat of spontaneous dozing forcing me to grip the wheel like a Le Mans driver having a heart attack. Several times I consider just giving in, pulling off, falling over sideways from fatigue, surrendering to whatever the night stalkers lurking on the outskirts of Pleasantville and Valhalla have dreamed up for me—my car down on its rims, my trunk jimmied, luggage and realty signs strewn around, my wallet lifted by shadowy figures in Air Jordans.

But I'm too close. And instead of staying on big, safe, reliable 287 up to big, safe, reliable 684 and pushing the extra twenty miles to Danbury (a virtual Motel City, with maybe an all-night liquor outlet), I turn north on the Sawmill (its homespun name alone makes me sleepy) and head toward Katonah, checking my AAA atlas for the quickest route into CT.

Then, almost unnoticeable, a tiny wooden sign—CONNECTI-CUT—with a small hand-painted arrow seeming to point right out of the 1930s. And I make for it, down NY 35, my headlights vacuuming its narrow, winding, stone-walled, woods-to-the-verge alleyways toward Ridgefield, which I calculate (distances that look long on the map are actually short) to be twelve miles. And in ten minutes flat I'm there, the sleeping village rising into pretty, bucolic view, meaning that I've somehow crossed the state line without knowing it.

Ridgefield, as I drive cautiously up and through, my eyes peeled for cops and motels, is a hamlet that even in the pallor of its barium-sulfur streetlights would remind anyone but a lifelong Ridgefielder of Haddam, New Jersey—only richer. A narrow, English high street emerges from the woodsy south end, leads through a hickory-shaded, lush-lawned, deep-pocketed mansion district of mixed architectural character, each mansion with big-time security in place, winds through a quaint, shingled, basically Tudor CBD of attached shops (rich realtors, a classic-car showroom, a Japanese deli, a fly-tiers shop, a wine & liquor, a Food For Thought Books). A walled war-memorial green lies just at village center, flanked by big Protestant churches and two more mansions converted to lawyers' offices. The Lions meet Wednesday, the Kiwanis Thursday. Other, shorter streets bend away to delve and meander through more modest but still richly tree-lined neighborhoods, with lanes named Baldy, Pudding, Toddy Hill, Scarlet Oak and Jasper. Plainly, anyone living below the Cross Bronx would move here if he or she could pay the freight.

But if you're driving through at 2:19, "town" slips by before you know it, and you're too quick through it and out onto Route 7, having passed no place to stop and ask or caught no glimpse of a friendly motel sign—only a pair of darkened inns (Le Chateau and Le Perigord), where a fellow could tuck into a lobster thermidor across from his secretary, or a veal scarpatti and a baked Alaska with his son from some nearby prep school. But don't expect a room. Ridgefield's a town that invites no one to linger, where the services contemplate residents only, but which makes it in my book a piss-poor place to live.

Exhausted and disappointed, I make a reluctant left at the light onto 7, resigned to sag into Danbury, fifteen miles farther on and by now full to the brim with darkened cars nosed into darkened motel lots. I have done this all wrong. A forceful stand at Sally's or at the very least tarrying in Tarrytown would've saved me.

Yet ahead in the gloom where 7 crosses the Ridgefield line and disappears back into the hinterland of scrub-brush Connecticut, I see the quavery red neon glimmer I've given up hoping for. MOTEL. And under it, in smaller, fuzzier letters, the life-restoring VACANCY. I aim at it like a missile.

But when I wheel into the little half-moon lot (it's the Sea Breeze, though no sea's near enough to offer breezes), there's a commotion in progress. Motel guests are out of their rooms in bathrobes, slippers and tee-shirts. The state police are abundantly present—more blue flashers turning—while a big white-and-orange ambulance van, its strobes popping and its back door open, appears ready to receive a passenger. The whole lot has the backlit, half-speed unreality of a movie set (not what I'd hoped for) and I'm tempted just to drive on, though again that would mean conking out on the car seat and hoping no one kills me.

All the police activity is going on at one end of the lot, in front of the last unit in line; so I park near the other end, beyond the office, where lights are on and a customer counter is visible through the window. If I can be assigned a room away from the action, I may still get one-third night's measure of sleep.

Inside the office the air-conditioning's cranked up high, and a powerful cooking smell from a rear apartment beyond a red drapery makes the air dense and stinging. The clerk is a slender, dull-looking subcontinental whose eyes flicker up at me from a desk behind the counter. He's talking on the phone at a blazing speed and in a language I recognize as not my own. Without pausing, he fingers a little registration card off a stack he has, slides it up onto the glass countertop, where a pen's attached to a little chain. Several hand-lettered and unequivocal instructions have been pressed under the glass, relating to one's use of one's room: no pets, no calls charged, no cooking, no hourly rates, no extra guests, no operation of a business (none of these is currently in my plans).

The clerk, who has on a regulation dirty-collared, short-sleeved white shirt and black slacks, goes right on talking, even becoming at one point agitated and loudly vociferous while I finish filling out the guest card and slide it across with my Visa. At this instant he simply puts the receiver down, clears his throat, stands and starts scribbling on the card with his own ballpoint. My needs are apparently enough like other guests' that we can skip pleasantries.

"So what's happened down at the other end?" I say, hoping I'll hear everything's all over and wasn't any great shakes to begin with. Possibly an on-site demo of police practices for the benefit of the Ridgefield town fathers.

"Don't worry," the clerk says in a fussy voice guaranteed to make anyone worry. "Everything is fine now."

He whips my Visa through the credit-check box, glances at me, doesn't smile, just takes a weary breath and waits for the green numbers to certify I'm a fair risk for $52.80.

"What happened, though?" I feign absolute no-worry.

He sighs. "It's just best to stay away." He's used to answering questions only about room rates and checkout times. He has a long, slender neck that would look much better on a woman, and wisps of little mannish mustache hairs that shadow the corners of his mouth. He does not inspire wide trust.

"Just curious," I say. "I wasn't planning on wandering down there." I look back through the window, where the police and ambulance lights are still buffeting the dark. Several gawker cars have stopped on Route 7, their drivers' faces lit by the flashes. Two Connecticut state troopers in wide Stetsons are conferring beside their cruiser, arms folded, their stiff, tight-fitting uniforms making them seem brawny and stern though unquestionably even-handed.

"Some people maybe got robbed down there," the clerk says, pushing a Visa receipt out for my Frank Bascombe. At this moment a short, round-waisted thick-haired woman in a red-and-black sari and a badgered expression appears at the doorway drapery. She buzzes something to the clerk, then vanishes. For some reason I sense she's been talking via extension to whomever he was talking to, and he's now required again—possibly to catch hell from relatives in Karachi about whatever's happening outside.

"How'd it happen?" I say, putting my name on the dotted line.

"We don't know." He shakes his head, comparing signatures, then pulling the delicate leaves off the receipt, having never even acknowledged the woman who came and left. She, I'm sure, is the person responsible for the venomous cooking smell. "They check in. In a little while some big agitation in there. I don't see what happened."

"Anybody get hurt?" I stare at my Visa receipt in his hand, wishing I hadn't signed it.

"Maybe. I don't know." He hands me my card, receipt and a key. "Get the key deposit when you check out. Ten o'clock is the time."

"Swell," I say, and smile hopelessly, thinking of heading to Danbury.

"It's on the other end, okay?" he says, pointing toward the hoped-for wing, smiling perfunctorily and showing his straight little teeth. He has to be freezing in his short sleeves, though right away he returns to the phone and begins muttering in his tangly tongue, his voice going to a hush in case I might know a word or two of Urdu and spill some important beans.

Back out on the lot, night air feels even more electrified and stoked. Other motel guests have started to drift back, but police radios are crackling, the bugged-up red MOTEL sign hums and an even denser feeling of subsonic noises vibrates off the cruisers and the ambulance and the cars stopped along the highway. Somewhere close by a skunk has been aroused, its hot scent swarming out of the trees beyond the lights. I think of Paul, not so far from here now, and will him to be in bed asleep, as I should be.

The last door in the line of motel doors has been opened now, and harsh lights are on inside, with shadows passing quickly. Several policemen, local Joes, are standing around a two-tone blue Chevy Suburban parked directly in front of the room, all its five doors open, its interior lights on. A Boston Whaler is in tow behind the Suburban and is filled with recreation gear—a bicycle, water skis, some strapped-together lawn furniture, scuba tanks and a wooden doghouse. The local cops are shining flashlights around inside. A big leering Bugs has been stuck to a back side window with suction cups.

"Y'ain't safe no mo' nowhere," a man's thick voice says, and actually makes me jump. I look around fast and find an immense, heavy-breathing Negro standing behind me wearing a green Mayflower moving van uniform. He's holding a black attaché case under his arm, and above his breast pocket, under a red *Mayflower*, the word *Tanks* is stitched within a yellow oval. He's watching what I'm watching.

We're right behind my parked Crown Victoria, and the instant I see him I also notice his Mayflower van parked across Route 7 in the turnout for a seasonal produce stand, closed at this hour.

"What's going on down there?" I say.

"Kids broke on into some people's room owns that Suburban, and robbed 'em. Then they killed the guy. They got 'em both over there"—he points—"in that po-lice car. Somebody oughta just go over there and pop 'em both in the melon and be done with it." Mr. Tanks (first name, last, nickname?) breathes in again momentously. He has a lineman's wide smudge-pot face, a huge big-nostril nose and all but invisible deep-set eyes. His uniform includes ludicrous green walking shorts that barely manage around his butt and thighs, and black nylon knee socks that show off his beefsteak calves. He is a head shorter than me, but it's no chore to feature him bear-hugging an armoire or a new Amana down several flights of stairs.

The two troopers, I determine, are standing guard at their car, which is stopped in the precise middle of the lot with its headlights still on. Through the back window I can make out in the darkness first one white face and then a second one—boys' faces, tilted forward to indicate both are handcuffed. Neither is talking, and both seem to be watching the troopers. The boy I can see more clearly seems to smile in reply to Mr. Tanks's having pointed him out.

The sight of the two faces, though, causes me a sudden jittery interior flutter like a fan blade spinning in my belly. I wonder if I'm about to wince again, but I don't. "How do they know they did it?"

" 'Cause they run, that's why," Mr. Tanks says, confidently. "I was out on number seven. And the police car come around me going a hundred. And two miles on down, here they all were. Two of 'em spread out on the hood. Hadn't been five minutes. Trooper tol' me about it." Mr. Tanks breathes another threatening breath. His thick truckdriver's smell is a nice leathery fragrance mingled with what must be the scent of moving pads. "Bridgeport," he murmurs, making *port* sound like *pote*. "Killin' to be killin'."

"Where are the other people from?" I say.

"I guess Utah." He is silent a moment. Then he says, "Pullin' that little boat."

Just then two male ambulance attendants in red shirts appear in the motel door, horsing a collapsible metal stretcher out into the night. A long black plastic bag that looks like it should hold a set of golf clubs is strapped on top and lumpy from the body inside. A moment later a small, thick-necked, tough-looking white man in a white short-sleeved shirt and tie, and wearing a pistol, and a badge on a string around his neck, escorts a blond woman in a thin blue flowered dress out the door, holding her upper arm as though she were under arrest. They walk quickly toward the state troopers' car, where one of the troopers opens the back door and starts to pull out the boy who's smiled before. But the detective speaks something out in front of him, and the trooper simply stands aside and lets the boy stay put, while the other trooper produces a flashlight.

The detective directs the blond woman to the open car door. She seems very light on her feet. The trooper shines his flash straight into the face of the boy closest. His skin is ghostly and looks damp even from here, his hair buzzed almost bare on the sides but left long in the back. He gazes up into the light as if he's willing to expose everything there is to know about him.

The woman only briefly looks at him, then turns her head away. The boy says something—I see his lips move—and the woman says something to the detective. Then they both turn and walk briskly back toward the room. The troopers quickly close the car door, then climb in the front seat, both sides. Their siren makes a loud *wheep-whoop*, their blue flasher flashes once, and their car—a Crown Vic just like mine—idles forward a few yards before it makes an engine roar, skitters its wheels and shoots out onto 7, where it disappears to the north, its siren coming on again but far out of sight.

"Where *you* tryin' to get?" Mr. Tanks says gruffly. He is now carefully unfolding two sticks of Spearmint, which he inserts into his large mouth both at once. He goes on clutching his attaché case.

"Deep River," I say, nearly silenced by what I've just witnessed. "I'm picking up my son." The jittery flutter has stopped in my stomach.

The watchers out on Route 7 are starting to creep away. The ambulance, now closed, its interior lights out, backs cautiously away from the motel door, then eases off in the direction the troopers have gone—to Danbury is my guess—its silver and red lights turning but with no siren.

"*Then* where you two goin'?" He is crushing his gum wrapper and chewing vigorously. He wears a great chunky diamond-and-gold-crusted ring on his right ring finger, something a large person might design for himself or possibly get by winning the Super Bowl.

"We're going to the Baseball Hall of Fame." I look around at him amiably. "Did you ever go there?"

"Uh-uh," he says, and shakes his head, his mouth emitting a loud Spearminty sweetness. Mr. Tanks's hair is short and dense and black, but doesn't grow on all parts of his head. Islands of his glistening black scalp appear here and there, making him look older than I'm sure he is. We're probably the same age. "What line of work you do?"

The VACANCY sign goes silently off, then the MOTEL sign itself, leaving only a humming red NO illuminated. The clerk lowers the blinds inside the office, switches them closed, and the office lights go almost immediately out.

We aren't socializing here, I realize, only bearing brief dual witness to the perilous character of life and our uncertain presences in it. Otherwise there's no reason for us to stand here together.

"Real estate," I say, "down in Haddam, New Jersey. About two and a half hours from here."

"That's a rich man's town," Mr. Tanks says, still chewing rapidly.

"*Some* rich people live there," I say. "But some folks just sell real estate. Where do you live?"

"Divorced," Mr. Tanks says. "I 'bout live in that rig." He swivels his big midnight face in the direction of his truck.

There in the shadows Mr. Tanks's enormous trailer displays a jaunty good ship *Mayflower* in green, abreast a jaunty sea of yellow. It's the most nearly patriotic sight I've seen in the Ridgefield area. I think of Mr. Tanks snugged up in his high-tech sleep cocoon, decked out (for some reason) in red silk pj's, earphones plugged into an Al Hibbler CD, perusing a *Playboy* or a *Smithsonian* and munching a gourmet sandwich purchased somewhere back down the line and heated up in his mini-micro. It's as good as what I do. Possibly the Markhams should consider long-haul trucking instead of the suburbs. "That must not be so bad," I say.

"It gets old. Cramped gets old," he says. Mr. Tanks must weigh 290. "I *own* a home out in Alhambra."

"Does your wife live there, then?"

"Uh-uh," Mr. Tanks grunts. "My furniture stays out there. I pay it a visit once in a while when I miss it."

Down at the lighted room where a murder has taken place, the local cops shut the Suburban's doors and wander inside, talking quietly, their local-cop hats pushed back on their heads. Mr. Tanks and I are the last observers left. I'm sure it's close to three. I yearn for bed and sleep, though I don't want to leave Mr. Tanks alone.

"Lemme just ask you a question." Mr. Tanks is holding his attaché still under his giant arm and gravely chewing his Spearmint. "Since you're into real estate now" (as if I'd only been in it a couple of weeks). He doesn't look at me. It may embarrass him to address me in terms of my profession. "I'm thinking about selling my home." He stares straight away into the dark.

"The one in Alhambra?"

"Uh-huh." He breathes again noisily through his big nostrils.

"California's holding onto its value is all I hear, if that's what you want to know."

"I bought in seventy-six." Another big sigh.

"Then you're in great shape," I say, though why I'd say that I don't know, since I've never been in Alhambra, don't know the tax base, the racial makeup, the comp situation or the market status. I'll probably visit *the* Alhambra before I visit Mr. Tanks's Alhambra.

"What I'm wonderin' is," Mr. Tanks says and wipes his big hand over his face, "if I oughtn't not to move out here."

"To Ridgefield?" Not an obvious match.

"It don't matter where."

"Do you have any friends and family out here?"

"Naw."

"Is the Mayflower home office out here someplace?"

He shakes his head. "They don't matter where you live. You just drivin' for them."

I look at Mr. Tanks curiously. "Do you like it out here?" Meaning the seaboard, the Del-Mar-Va to Eastport, from the Water Gap to Block Island.

"It's pretty good," he says. His cavey eyes narrow and flicker at me, as if he'd caught a whiff suggesting I might be amused by him.

But I'm not! I understand (I think) perfectly well what he's getting at. If he'd answered in the usual way—that his Aunt Pansy lived in Brockton, or his brother Sherman in Trenton, or if he was positioning himself for a managerial charge inside corporate Mayflower, home offices, say, in Frederick, MD, or Ayer, Mass., and needed to move nearer—that would make sound sense. Though it would be a whole lot less interesting on the human side. But if I'm right, his question is of a much more omenish and divining nature, having to do with the character of eventuality (not rust-belt economics or the downturn in per-square-foot residential in the Hartford-Waterbury metroplex).

Instead, his is the sort of colloquy most of us engage in alone with only our silent selves, and that with the right answers can give rise to rich feelings of synchronicity of the kind I came back from France full of four years ago: when everything is glitteringly about *you*, and everything you do seems led by a warm, invisible astral beam issuing from a point too far away in space to posit but that's leading you to the place—if you can just follow and stay lined up—you *know* you want to be. Christians have their grimmer version of this beam; Jainists do too. Probably so do ice dancers, buckingbronco riders and grief counselors. Mr. Tanks is one of the multitude seeking, with hope, to emerge from a condition he's grown weary of in pursuit of something better, and wants to know what he should do—a profound inquiry.

I'd of course love to help with this alignment of small stars, and without making him worry I'm a loony or a realty shark or a homosexual with polyracial endomorphic appetites. In the most magnanimous sense, such assistance is the heart of the realty profession.

I fold my arms and let myself sway sideways so my thigh pushes against the back bumper of my Crown Victoria. I wait a few seconds, then say, "I think I know exactly what you're getting at."

"What about?" Mr. Tanks says suspiciously.

"About wondering where you ought to go," I say in as unaggressive, unsharky, unhomophilic a way as possible.

"Yeah, but that don't really matter," Mr. Tanks says, instantly shying off the subject now that he's raised it. "But okay," he says, still showing interest. "I'd like to set down someplace else, you know? Like a neighborhood."

"Would you live there?" I say in a helpful, professional voice. "Or would it just be someplace for your furniture to live?"

"I'd live there," Mr. Tanks says, and nods, looking up at the sky

as though wishing to envision a future. "If I liked it, I wouldn't necessarily even mind being in someplace I've lived before. You understand what I mean?"

"Pretty much," I say, meaning "perfectly."

"The East Coast just seems sorta homey to me." Mr. Tanks suddenly looks around at his truck as if he's heard a sound and expects
to see someone scaling the side, ready to break in and steal his TV.
Though there's no one.

"Where'd you grow up?" I say.

He continues staring at his truck and away from me. "Michigan.
Old man was a chiropractor in the U.P. Wasn't too many Negroes
doing that work."

"I bet not. Do you like it up there?"

"Oh yeah. I love it."

There's no use blabbing that I'm an old Wolverine or that we
probably have experiences in common. Divorce, for starters. My
memories, in any case, would probably conflict with his.

"Then why don't you go back and buy a house? Or build one?
That seems like a no-brainer to me."

Mr. Tanks turns and gives me a wary look, as if I might've been
referring to *his* brain. "My ex-wife stays up there now. That don't
work."

"Do you have any children?"

"Uh-uh. That's why I ain't been to the Hall of Fame." His big
eyebrows lower. (What business is it of mine if he has children?)

"Well. I'll just say this." I would still like to encourage Mr.
Tanks with some useful facts offered as data for his search for what
to do next. I in fact feel some anxiety that he doesn't know how
specifically I appreciate how he feels and that I've felt the same way
myself. No disappointment is quite like the failure to share a crucial
understanding. "I just *want* to say this," I begin again, correcting
myself. "I'm selling houses these days. And I live in a pretty nice
town down there. And we're about to see a rise in prices, and I
believe interest rates'll head up by the end of the year and maybe
even before."

"That's too rich down there. I been down there. I moved some
basketball player's mother into some big house. Then moved her
out again a year later."

"You're right, it's not cheap. But let me just say that most experts believe a purchase price two and a half times your annual pre-tax income is a realistic debt load. And I've got houses right now, in the village of Haddam"—all shown to the Markhams, all promptly trashed—"at two-fifty, and I'll have more as time goes on. And I feel like in the long run, whether it's Dukakis or Bush or Jackson"—fat chance—"prices are going to stay up in New Jersey."

"Uh-huh," Mr. Tanks says, making me feel exactly like a realty shark (which is possibly what you are if you're a realtor at all).

Only my view is, if I sell you a house in a town where life's tolerable, then I've done you a big favor. And if I try and don't succeed, then you've got a view you like better (assuming you can afford it). Plus, I don't cotton to the idea of raising the drawbridge, which Mr. Tanks probably has experience with. I mean to guarantee the same rights and freedoms for all. And if that means merchandising New Jersey dirt like dog-nuts so we all get our one sweet piece, then so be it. We'll all be dead in forty years anyway.

I won't (or can't), in other words, be easily shamed. And Mr. Tanks would make a good addition and be as welcome on Cleveland Street as his pocketbook could make him (he'd, of course, have to stash his truck someplace else). And I'm not doing anybody a favor if I don't try to get him interested.

"So what's the worst part about being a realtor?" He's staring around somewhere else again—above the Sea Breeze roofline, where the humpy moon has floated higher and wears a fuzzy halo. Mr. Tanks is now signaling me that he's not ready to buy a house in New Jersey, which is fine. He may conduct conversations like this with everyone—his "thing" being to ramble on dolefully about wishing he could *be* someplace better—and I've spoiled the fun by trying to figure out where and how. He may feel fine dedicating his life to moving other people hither and yon.

"My name's Frank Bascombe, by the way." A gesture of hello and good-bye, poking my hand toward Mr. Tanks's strenuous green belly. He administers a halfhearted little jiggling of just my fingers. Mr. Tanks might look like a guard for old Vince back in the Bart Starr-Fuzzy Thurston gravy days, but he shakes hands like a debutante.

"Tanks," is all he grunts.

"Well, really, I don't know if it has a worst part," I say, addressing the realtor question and feeling a sudden, brain-flattening fatigue and the painful need for sleep. I pause for a breath. "When *I* don't like it so much, I try not to notice it and stay home reading a book. But I guess if it has to have a bad side, it's having clients think I want to sell them a house they don't like, or that I don't care if they like it or not. Which is never true." I pull my hand over my face and push my eyelids up to keep them open.

"You don't like being misinterpreted, is that it?" Mr. Tanks looks amused. He makes an odd gurgly chuckle deep in his throat, which makes me self-conscious.

"I guess so. Or not."

"I figured you guys was all crooks," Mr. Tanks says as though talking about something else *to* someone else. "Like a used-car guy, only 'cept with houses. Or burial insurance. Something like that."

"Some people feel that way, I guess." I'm thinking that we're at this moment two feet away from my trunkful of realty signs, blank offer sheets, earnest money receipts, listing forms, prospect memos, PRICE REDUCED and SORRY, YOU MISSED IT stickers. Burglar's tools, to Mr. Tanks. "Really, a main concern *is* avoiding misrepresentation. I wouldn't want to do anything to you that I wouldn't want done to me—at least as far as realty goes." This did not come out sounding right (due to exhaustion).

"Hunh," is all Mr. Tanks offers. Our time for bearing witness to life's strangeness is nearly over.

Suddenly, at the end of the row of motel units, out the door of the lighted room we've been waiting a vigil over, come two uniformed local police, followed by the tough-nut detective, followed by a uniformed policewoman, holding the arm of the young bluedressed wife who's in turn holding the small hand of a tiny blond girl, who looks apprehensively all around in the dark and back behind her into the room she's left, though suddenly, by dint of memory, she turns and looks up at ole Bugs, stuck to the window of the Suburban, leering his nutty brains out. She's wearing neat little yellow shorts and tennies with white socks, and a hot-pink pullover that has a red heart on the front like a target. She is slightly knockkneed. When she gazes around again and sees no one she recognizes, she fastens her eyes on Mr. Tanks as she's led across the lot to an unmarked vehicle that will take her and her mother elsewhere, to some other Connecticut town, where a terrible-awful thing *hasn't* happened. There, to sleep.

They have left their room standing open, the Whaler jammed with stealable gear somebody should see about locking up or storing. (This I would've waked up and worried about in the middle of the night back in 1984, even if it were my loved one who was killed.)

Though just as the young woman ducks into the dark car, she looks back at her room and at the Suburban and the Sea Breeze and then to the left at Mr. Tanks and me, her companions of a sort, watching her with distant compassion as she encounters grief and confusion and loss all alone and all at once. Her face comes up, light catches it so that I see the look of startlement on her fresh young features. It is her first scent, the first light-glimmer, that she's no longer connected in the old manner of two hours ago but into some new network now, where caution is both substance and connector. (It is not so different from the look on the boy's face who killed her husband.) I, of course, could connect with her—give a word or a look. But it would be only momentary, whereas caution is what she needs now, and what's dawning. To learn a lesson of caution at a young age is not the worst thing.

Her face disappears into the squad car. The door closes hard, and in half of one minute they are all gone—the local boys in their Fairfield Sheriff's cruiser, murmuring ahead, gumball flashing; the unmarked car with the policewoman driving—off in the direction opposite, where the ambulance has gone. Again, when they are all out of sight into the scrub-timber distance, a siren rises. They will not be back tonight.

"I bet they got their insurance paid up," Mr. Tanks says. "Mormons. You know *they're* paid up. Them people don't let nothin' slide." He consults his wristwatch, sunk into his great arm. Time of day means nothing to him. I don't know how he knows they were Mormons. "You know how to keep a Mormon from stealin' your sandwich when you go fishin', don't you?"

"How?" It is an odd moment for a quip.

"Take another Mormon witchyou." Mr. Tanks makes his deep-chested *hunh* noise again. This is his way of resolving the unresolvable.

I, though, have had it in mind—since his position on realtors is that we're first cousins to odometer-spinning car dealers and burial plot scammers—to ask about his views on moving-van drivers. We hear plenty of adverse opinions of *them* in my business, where they're generally considered the loose cannons of the removal industry. But I'm certain he wouldn't have an opinion. I'd be surprised if Mr. Tanks practiced many analytical views of himself. He is no doubt happiest concentrating on whatever's beyond his windshield. In this way he's like a Vermonter.

In the thick trees behind the Sea Breeze I hear a dog barking, perhaps at the skunk, and somewhere else, faintly, a phone ringing. Mr. Tanks and I have not shared much, in spite of my wishing we could. We are, I'm afraid, not naturals for each other.

"I guess I'll hit the hay," I say as if the idea has just come to me. I offer Mr. Tanks a hopeful smile, which awards no closure, only its surface appeal.

"Talk about misinterpreted and not being misinterpreted." Mr. Tanks still has in mind our conversation from before (a surprise).

"Right," I say, not knowing what's right.

"Maybe I'm gon' come down there to New Jersey and buy a big house from you," he announces imperially. I'm beginning to inch away toward my room.

"I wish you'd do that. That'd be great."

"You got some expensive neighborhoods where they'll let me park my truck?"

"That might take some time to find," I say. "But we could work up something." A ministorage up in Kendall Park, for instance.

"We could work on that, huh?" Mr. Tanks yawns a cavernous yawn and closes his eyes as he rolls his big furry head back in the moonlight.

"Absolutely. Where do you park in Alhambra?"

He turns, to notice I'm farther away now. "You got any niggers down there in your part of New Jersey?"

"Plenty of 'em," I say.

Mr. Tanks looks at me steadily, and of course, even as sleepy as I am, I'm awfully sorry to have said that, yet have no way to yank the words back. I just stop, one foot up on the Sea Breeze walkway, and look helpless to the world and fate.

" 'Cause I wouldn't care to be the only pea in the pod down there, you understand?" Mr. Tanks seems earnestly if briefly to be considering a move, committing to a life in New Jersey, miles and miles from lonely Alhambra and lightless, glacial Michigan.

"I bet you'd be happy there," I say meekly.

"Maybe I'll have to call you up," Mr. Tanks says. He, too, is walking away, striding off almost jauntily, his short beer-keg legs prized apart in his green spectator shorts but close together at the knees as if a rolling gait did not come easy for him, his big arms in motion despite his attaché case being mashed under one of them.

"That'd be great." I need to give him my card so he can call me if he rumbles in late, finds no place to park and no one to be helpful. But he is already keying his way in. His room is three away from the murder scene. A light burns inside. And before I can call out and mention my card or say "Good night," or say anything more, he has stepped inside his door and quickly closed it.

*I*n my Sea Breeze double, I run the a/c up to medium, get the lights off and myself into bed as fast as possible, praying for quick sleep, which seemed so overpowering ten minutes or an hour ago. The thought nags me that I should call Sally (who cares if it's three-thirty? I have an important offer to make). But the phone here circuits through the Pakistani switchboard, and everyone there's long asleep.

And then—and not for the first time today but for the first time since my talk with Ann on the turnpike—I think a worrisome, urgent-feeling thought for Paul, under siege at this minute by phantom and real-life woes, and a court date as his official rite of passage into life beyond parent and child. I could want for better. Though I could also want him to stop braining people with oarlocks and blithely stealing condoms and struggling with security guards, to stop grieving for dogs a decade dead, and barking the case for their return. Dr. Stopler says (arrogantly) he could be grieving the loss of whoever we hoped he would be. But I don't know who that boy is or was (unless of course it's his dead brother—which it isn't). My wish has consistently been to strengthen the constitution of whoever he is whenever I meet him—though that is not always the same boy, and because I'm only a part-timer, possibly I have been insufficient at my job too. So that clearly I must do better, must adopt the view that my son needs what only I can supply (even if it's not true) and then try for all I'm worth to imagine just what that something might be.

And then a scant sleep comes, which is more sleep versus unsleep than true rest, but in which for reasons of proximity to death, I dream, half muse of Clair and our sweet-as-tea-cakes winter's romance, commencing four months after she joined our office and ending three months down the road, when she met the older, dignified Negro lawyer who was perfect for her and made my small excitations excess baggage.

Clair was a perfect little dreamboat, with wide liquid-brown eyes, short muscular legs that widened slightly but didn't soften in the high-ups, extra-white teeth with red-lipstick lips that made her smile as much as she could (even when she wasn't happy) and a flipped, meringuey hair configuration she and her roomies at Spelman had borrowed from the Miss Black America pageant that stayed resilient through nights of ardent lovemaking. She had a high, confident, thick-tongued, singsongy Alabama voice, with the hint of a lisp, and wore tight wool skirts, iron-leg panty hose and pastel cashmere sweaters that showed off her wondrous ebony skin so that every time I saw an extra inch of it I squirmed and itched to get her alone. (She in many ways dressed and conducted herself exactly like the local white girls I knew in Biloxi when I was at Gulf Pines back in 1960, and for that sweet reason seemed to me quite old-fashioned and familiar.)

For reasons of her country-style, strict Christian family upbringing, Clair was unswerving in her demand to keep our little attachment just between us two, whereas I lacked a restraining self-consciousness of any kind and especially about being a forty-two-year-old divorced white man smitten to jibbers over a twenty-five-year-old black woman with kids (it's arguable I might've avoided the whole thing for sound professional and crabby small-town reasons, only of course I didn't). To me it was all as natural as grass sprouting, and I floated along on its harmless effusions, enjoying it and myself the way you'd enjoy a high-school reunion where you meet a girl nobody ever thought was beautiful way-back-when, but who now looks like the prettiest girl you ever dreamed of, except you're still the only one who thinks so and therefore get her all to yourself.

To Clair, though, the two of us together bore a "tinge" (her Alabama word meaning bad shadow), which naturally made *us* all the more giddy and distracting to me, but to her made *us* seem exactly wrong and doomed, and an item she absolutely didn't want her ex-husband, Vernell, or her mother, in Talladega, ever getting wind of. So that for our most intimate moments we ended up skulking around on the sly: her blue Civic slipping into my Cleveland Street garage under cover of night, and she slipping in the back door; or worse yet, rendezvousing for dinner plus surreptitious hand-holding and smooching in angst-thick public places such as the HoJo's in Hightstown, the Red Lobster in Trenton or the Embers in Yardley, spiritless venues where Clair felt completely invisible and comfortable and where she drank Fuzzy Navels till she was giggly, then slipped out to the car and made out with me in the dark till our lips were numb and our bodies limp.

Though we also spent plenty of ordinary, cloudy-wintry Sundays with her kids, hauling up and down both sides of the Delaware, treading the towpath, viewing the pleasing but unspectacular river sights like any modern couple whose life of ups and downs had rendered them thus 'n' so, but whose remarkable equanimity in the face of uphill social odds made everyone who saw or sat across from us in Appleby's in New Hope or stood in line behind us at yogurt shops feel good about themselves and all of life in general. I often remarked that she and I were impersonating the very complexly ethical, culturally diverse family unit that millions of liberal white Americans were burning to validate, and that the whole arrangement felt pretty good to me in addition to being hilarious. She, however, didn't like this attitude since it made her feel—in her sweet Talladega lisp—"*thstood*-out." And for that reason (and not that it's a small one) we probably missed a longer run at bliss.

Race, of course, was not our official fatal defect. Instead, Clair insisted my helpless age was the issue that kept us from a real future that I from time to time couldn't keep from wanting in the worst way. We therefore settled ourselves into a little ongoing pocket drama in which I created the role of avuncular but charmingly randy white professor who'd sacrificed a successful but hopelessly stodgy prior life to "work" for his remaining productive years in a (one-student) private college, where Clair was the beautiful, intelligent, voluble, slightly naive but feisty, yet basically kindhearted valedictorian, who realized we two shared lofty but hopeless ideals, and who in the service of simple human charity was willing to woogle around with me in private, hypertensive but futureless (due to our years) lovemaking, and to moon at my aging mug over fish-stick dinners and doughy pancakes in soulless franchise eateries while pretending to everybody she knew that such a thing was absolutely out of the question. (No one was fooled a minute, of course, as Shax Murphy informed me—with a discomforting wink—the day after Clair's memorial service.)

Clair's feeling was ironclad, simple and candidly set out: we were laughably all wrong for each other and wouldn't last the season; though our wrongness served a good purpose in getting her through a bad patch when her finances were rocky, her emotions in a tangle and she didn't know anyone in Haddam and was too proud to head back to Alabama. (Dr. Stopler would probably say she wanted to cauterize something in herself and used me as the white-hot tool.) Whereas for me, fantasies of permanence aside as she demanded, Clair made bachelor life interesting, entertaining and enticingly exotic in a hundred thrilling ways, aroused my keen admiration, and kept me in good spirits, while I acclimated myself to the realty business and my kids being gone.

"Now, when I was back in college, see," Clair once said to me in her high, sweetly monotonous, lispy voice (we were butt naked, lounging in the evening-lit upstairs front bedroom of my former wife's former house), "we all used to *laaaaugh* and laugh about hookin' up with some rich ole white guy. Like some fat bank president or big politician. That was our cruel joke, you know? Like, 'Now, when you marry that ole white fool,' this or that thing was going to happen to you. He was s'posed to try to give you a new car or some trip to Europe, and then you were gonna trick him. You know how girls are."

"Sort of," I said, thinking of course that I had a daughter but didn't know how girls were, except that mine would probably one day be just like Clair: sweet, certain of everything, basically untrusting for sound reasons. "What was so wrong about us ole white guys?"

"Oh well, *you* know," Clair said, raising onto her sharp little elbow and looking at me as if I'd just shown up on the surface of the earth and needed harsh instruction. "Y'all are all boring. White men *are* boring. You're just not as bad as the rest of them. Yet."

"You get more interesting the longer you stay alive, is my view," I said, wanting to put a good word in for my race and age. "Maybe that's why you'll learn to like me more, not less, and won't be able to live without me."

"Uh-huh, you got that wrong," she said, thinking, I'm sure, about her own life, which to date hadn't been that peachy but, I'd have argued, was looking up. It was true, though, she had very little facility for actually thinking about me and never in the time we knew each other asked me five questions about my children or my life before I met her. (Though I never minded, since I was sure some little personal exegesis would only have proved what she already expected.)

"If we didn't get more interesting," I said, happy to belabor a moot point, "all the other crap we put up with in life might drive us right out of it."

"Us Baptists don't believe that, now," she said, flinging her arm across my chest and jamming her hard chin into my bare ribs. "What's his name—Aristotle—Aristotle canceled his class today. He got sick of hearing his own voice and couldn't make it."

"I don't have anything to teach you," I said, thrilled as usual.

"That's *not* wrong," Clair said. "I'm not going to keep you that long anyway. You'll start to get boring on me, start repeating yourself. I'll be right out of here."

Which was not very different from what happened.

One March morning I showed up at the office early (my usual) to type an offer sheet for a presentation later that day. Clair had nearly finished her classes to get her realtor's certification and was at her desk, studying. She was never at ease addressing private-life matters in the office setting, yet as soon as I sat down she got up, wearing a little peach-colored skirt-and-sweater combo and red high heels, came right over to my desk by the front window, took a seat and said very matter-of-factly that she had met a man that week, bond lawyer McSweeny, whom she'd decided to start "dating," and therefore had decided to stop "dating" me.

I remember being perfectly dazed: first, by her altogether firing-squad certainty; and then by how damned unhappy the whole prospect made me. I smiled, though, and nodded as if I'd been thinking along those lines myself (I definitely hadn't) and told her that in my view she was probably doing the right thing, then went on smiling more disingenuously, until my cheeks ached.

She said she'd finally talked to her mother about me, and her mother had immediately told her, in what Clair said were actually "crude" terms, to get as far away from me as possible (I'm sure it wasn't my age), even if it meant spending her nights home alone or moving away from Haddam or finding another job in another city—which I said was too strong a medicine. I would just obligingly step aside, hope she was happy and feel lucky to have had the time with her I'd had, though I told her I didn't think we'd done anything but what men and women had done to and for each other through the ages. My saying this clearly made her aggravated. (She was not well practiced at being argued with, either.) So that I just finally shut up about it and grinned at her again like a half-wit, as a way of saying (I guessed) good-bye.

Why I didn't protest, I'm not exactly sure, since I was stung, and surprisingly near to the heart, and spent days afterward tinkering with convoluted futuristic scenarios in which life would've been goddamned tough but that sheer off-the-map novelty and unlikelihood might've proved the final missing ingredients to true and abiding love—in which case she'd sacrificed to convention a type of mountaintop victory reserved for only the brave and enlightened few. It's, however, undoubtedly true that my idyll with permanence was entirely founded on Clair's being a total impossibility, which means she was finally never more than a featured player in some Existence Period melodrama of my own devising (nothing to be proud of, but not radically different from my cameo in her short life).

After our abrupt sayonara she returned to her desk, resumed studying her realty books—and with this new state of affairs in effect, we stayed on at our desks for another whole hour and a half, doing work! Our colleagues arrived and departed. We both entered into amused, even jocular, conversations with several different individuals. I once asked her about the disposition of a bank foreclosure, and she answered me as equably and cheerfully as you would expect in any well-run office bent on profit. Neither one of us said anything else of moment, and I eventually finished my offer sheet, made a couple of cold client calls, did part of a crossword, wrote a letter, put on my coat and wandered around in it for a few minutes, wisecracking with Shax Murphy, and finally just wandered out and down to the Coffee Spot, after which I did not come back—all the while (I suppose) Clair stayed at her desk, concentrating like a cleric. And basically that was that.

In short order she and lawyer McSweeny became a nice, viable, single-race item in town. (Though she began treating me, in my view, with unneeded correctness in the office, which became, of course, the only place I ever saw her.) Everybody agreed the two of them were lucky to find each other when attractive members of their race were scarce as diamonds. Predictable difficulties came up to prevent their speedy marriage: Ed's grasping grown kids caused a ruckus about Clair's age and financial situation (Ed, naturally, is *my* age, and loaded). Clair's ex-husband, Vernell, declared Chapter 11 in Canoga Park and tried to reopen their divorce decree. Clair's grandmother died in Mobile, her mother broke her hip, her younger brother got put in jail—the usual wearisome inventory of life's encroachments. In the long run it all would've worked out, with Clair and Ed married to the tune of a clearly worded prenuptial agreement. Clair would've moved into Ed's big late Victorian out on Cromwell Lane, would've had a flower garden and a nicer car than a Honda Civic. Her two kids would've grown to like going to school with white children and in time forgotten there was a difference. She would've gone on selling condos and gotten better at it. Ed's grown children would've finally accepted her for the true-hearted, straight-talking, slightly overcertain girl she was, and not as just some hick gold-panner they needed to sic their own lawyers on. She and Ed, in time, would have enjoyed a somewhat isolated suburban existence, with a few but not many people regularly over for dinner, and even fewer close friends—a life spent with each other in a way most people would pay money to know how to pull off but can't because their days are too full of rich opportunity they just can't say no to.

Except that one spring afternoon Clair happened out to Pheasant Meadow and in an entirely professional way got trapped in a bad situation and ended up as dead as the Mormon traveler in the body bag down in room 15.

And as I lie in bed here, still alive myself, the Fedders blowing brisk, chemically cooled breezes across my sheets, I try to find solace against the way this memory and the night's events make me feel, which is: bracketed, limbo'd, unable to budge, as illustrated amply by Mr. Tanks and me standing side by side in the murderous night, unable to strike a spark, utter a convincingly encouraging word to the other, be of assistance, shout halloo, dip a wing; unable at the sad passage of another human to the barren beyond to share a hope for the future. Whereas, had we but been able, our spirits might've lightened.

Death, veteran of death that I am, seems so near now, so plentiful, so oh-so-drastic and significant, that it scares me witless. Though in a few hours I'll embark with my son upon the other tack, the hopeful, life-affirming, anti-nullity one, armed only with words and myself to build a case, and nothing half as dramatic and persuasive as a black body bag, or lost memories of lost love.

Suddenly my heart again goes bangety-bang, bangety-bangety-bang, as if I myself were about to exit life in a hurry. And if I could, I would spring up, switch on the light, dial someone and shout right down into the hard little receiver, "It's okay. I got away. It was goddamned close, I'll tell ya. It didn't get me, though. I smelled its breath, saw its red eyes in the dark, shining. A clammy hand touched mine. But I made it. I survived. Wait for me. Wait for me. Not that much is left to do." Only there's no one. No one here or anywhere near to say any of this to. And I'm sorry, sorry, sorry, sorry, sorry.

7

Eight a.m. Things speed up.

On my way out of the Sea Breeze I remember to hike across, scale the green side of Mr. Tanks's Peterbilt and squeeze a business card under his king-size windshield wiper, with a personal note on the back saying: "Mr. T. Good meeting you. Call up any time. FB." I include my home phone. (The art of the sale first demands imagining the sale.) Strangely enough, when I take a quick curious peek inside the driver's capsule, on the passenger's seat I see a clutter of *Reader's Digest* condenseds and on top of it an enormous yellow cat wearing a gold collar and staring up at me as if I were an illusion. (Pets are not welcome in the Sea Breeze, and Mr. Tanks is no doubt a consummate player-by-the-rules.) I notice also, as I climb down the cab's outer shell, and just in front of the door, a name, painted in ornate red script and set in quotes:*"Cyril."* Mr. Tanks is a man deserving of study.

Back in the lot to leave my key (forgoing my deposit), I see that the Suburban with its Boston Whaler rig is gone now, and yellow "crime scene" tape is stretched across the closed door to #15. And I realize then that I've dreamed about it all: of a sealed room, of a car being towed off in the dark by small, muscular, sweaty white men in sleeveless shirts, shouting, "Come on back, come on back," followed by the sound of scary chains and winches and big motors revving, then someone shouting, "Okay, okay, okay."

*A*t 8:45 I stop bleary-eyed for coffee at the Friendly's in Hawleyville. After consulting my atlas, I decide on the Yankee Expressway to Waterbury and over to Meriden, a jog across and down to Middletown—where adjunct Charley "teaches" Wesleyan coeds to distinguish which column is Ionic and which Doric—then CT 9 straight into Deep River; this instead of drag-assing all the way down to Norwalk and 95 as I meant to do last night, driving east along the Sound with, I'm certain, four trillion other Americans craving a safe and sane holiday, yet doing everything they can to prevent me from having one.

In Friendly's I browse through the Norwalk *Hour* for any mention of last night's tragedy, although I'm sure it happened too late. I learn here, however, that Axis Sally has died in Ohio, aged eighty-seven and an honors graduate of Ohio Wesleyan; Martina has outdueled Chris in three sets; hydrologists in Illinois have decided to draw down Lake Michigan to channel water into the more important and drought-starved Mississippi; and Vice President Bush has declared prosperity to be at "a record high" (though as if to call him a liar there are sidebar reports of declines in prices, mutual funds and CDs, declines in factory orders and aircraft demands—all "pocketbook" issues Dullard Dukakis needs to shanghai or lose his ass in a bucket).

After paying, I make my strategic calls squeezed between the double doors of Friendly's "lobby": one to my answering machine, disclosing nothing—a relief; another to Sally, intending to offer a private charter to anyplace I can meet her—no answer, not even a recording, causing my gut to wrench like someone had tightened a rope around it and jerked downward.

Apprehensively then I call Karl Bemish, first at the root beer palace, where there's no reason for him to be yet, then at his bachelor digs in Lambertville, where he answers on the second ring.

"Everything's jake here, Frank," he shouts, to my inquiry about the felonious Mexicans. "Aw yeah, I should've called you back last night. I called the sheriff instead. I expected some action, really. But. False alarm. They never showed up again, the little fucks."

"I don't want you being in danger down there, Karl." Customers stream in and out beside me, opening the door, jostling me, letting in hot air.

"I've got my alley sweeper, you know," Karl says.

"You've got your what? What's that?"

"A sawed-off twelve-gauge pump," Karl says supremely, and grunts an evil laugh. "A serious piece of machinery."

This is the first I've heard of an alley sweeper, and I don't like it. In fact, it scares me silly. "I don't think it's a good idea to have an alley sweeper at the root beer stand, Karl." Karl doesn't like me to call it root beer, or a "stand," but that's how I think of it. What else is it? An office?

"Well, it beats lying facedown behind the birch beer cooler drinking your brains out of your paper hat. Or maybe I'm wrong about that," Karl says coolly.

"Jesus Christ, Karl."

"Just don't worry. I don't even bring it out till after ten."

"Do the police know about it?"

"Hell, they *told* me where to buy it. Up in Scotch Plains." Karl shouts this too. "I shouldn't have blabbed it to you. You're such a goddamn nervous nelly."

"It makes me goddamn nervous," I say, and it does. "I can't use you dead. I'd have to serve the root beer myself, plus our insurance won't pay off if you're killed with an unlicensed gun in there. I'd probably get sued."

"You just go on and have a holiday with your kid. I'll hold down Fort Apache. I've got some other things to do this morning. I'm not alone here."

There's no more getting through to Karl now. My window's just been shut. "Leave me a message if anything's strange, would you do that?" I say this in an unlikely-to-be-acknowledged voice.

"I plan to be out of touch *all* morning," Karl says, and makes a dumb hardee-har-har laugh, then hangs up.

I immediately dial Sally again, in case she's been out picking up croissants and the *Daily Argonaut*. But nothing.

My last call is to Ted Houlihan—for an update, but also to grill him on the status of our office "exclusive." Making client calls is actually one of the most satisfying parts of my work. Rolly Mounger was right on the money when he said real estate has almost nothing to do with the state of one's soul; consequently a necessary business call is tantamount to an enjoyable game of Ping-Pong. "It's Frank Bascombe, Ted. How's everything going down there?"

"Everything's just fine, Frank." Ted sounds frailer than yesterday, but as happy as he claims. A slow gas leak may create an unbeatable euphoria.

"Just wanted to tell you my clients are taking a day to think about it, Ted. They were impressed with the house. But they've looked at a lot of houses, and they need to push themselves beyond a threshold now. I do think the last house I showed them, though, is the one they ought to buy, and that was yours."

"Super," Ted says. "Just super."

"Anybody else been through to look?" The crucial question.

"Oh, a few yesterday. Some people right after your folks." Followed by not unexpected but still aggravating bad news.

"Ted, I have to remind you that we've got an office exclusive on your house. That's what the Markhams are acting in reliance of. They're under the impression they've got a little time to think without any outside pressure. We got all that stapled down ahead of time."

"Well, I don't know, Frank," Ted says dimly. Conceivably, of course, Julie Loukinen has played down the exclusivity clause for fear Ted would balk, and just put it on the sign anyway. It's also likely Ted's known far and wide as a perpetual "potential," and Buy and Large or whoever else is involved is simply horning in on the chance of splitting a commission; this versus our suing the shit out of them and queering the whole deal—a strategy tantamount to walking in the winning run, something you never want to do. A third possibility is that Ted's as crooked as a corkscrew and wouldn't tell the truth to God in his heaven. The supposedly bum testicle story could be part of the act. (Nothing should surprise anybody anymore.)

"Look, Ted," I say. "Just step out and take a look at that green-and-gray sign and see if it doesn't say 'exclusive.' I'm not going to make a big deal out of it right now, because I'm up in Connecticut. But I'm going to get it straight on Tuesday."

"How is it up there?" Ted says, daffy as a duck.

"It's hot."

"Are you up at Mount Tom?"

"No. I'm in Hawleyville. But if you'd just be considerate enough, Ted, not to show the house to anyone else, maybe we can avoid a big lawsuit. My clients deserve a chance to make an offer." Not that they haven't had ample chance, or that they aren't right now cruising the deserted, lusterless streets of East Brunswick, hoping to find something much better.

"I wouldn't mind that," Ted says, energetic now.

"Great, then," I say. "I'll get back to you in a hurry."

"The people after you yesterday said they'd be coming in with an offer this morning."

"If they do, Ted," and I say this threateningly, "remember my clients have first refusal. It's in writing." Or it should be. Of course this is standard realty baloney, routinely purveyed by both sides: the "bright 'n' early in the morning" offer. In general, people (buyers, usually) who trot out this "promise" are either making themselves feel substantial and will have forgotten it entirely by five o'clock, or else they're deluding themselves by supposing the mere prospect of a fat offer makes everybody feel better. Naturally, only generous offers you can pinch between your thumb and index finger make everybody *actually* feel better. And until one of those comes into view, there's nothing to get excited about (though a rising tide of seller's angst never hurt anybody).

"Frank, do you know what's a very strange thing I've learned," Ted says in a seeming state of goofy wonderment.

"What's that?" Through the window I'm watching a van full of retarded kids off-load in the Friendly's lot—teenage tongue-thrusters, frail cross-eyed girls, chubby Down's survivors of unspecified gender—eight or so, bumbling out onto the hot tarmac in elastic-band shorts of various hues, sneakers and dark blue tee-shirts that have YALE printed on the front. Their counselors, two strapping college girls in matching brown shorts and white pullovers, who look like they go to Oberlin and play water polo, get the van locked up while the kids stand staring in all different directions.

"I've learned that I really enjoy showing people my house," Ted rambles on. "Everyone who's seen it seemed to like it a lot and they all think Susan and I did all right here. That's a good feeling to have. I expected to hate it and feel a lot of grief at having my life invaded. You know what I mean?"

"Yeah," I say. My interest in Ted is dwindling fast since I realize there's a decent chance he's a real estate scammer. "It just means you're ready to move on, Ted. You're ready for Albuquerque and all that sunshine." (And to have your nuts preserved in amber.)

"My son's a surgeon in Tucson, Frank. I'm going out for surgery in September."

"I remember." (I got the city wrong.) The gaggle of afflicted teens and their two big, tan-legged, water-polo-type minders are making for the door now, some of the kids in full charge, and all but a couple wearing plastic crash helmets strapped under their chins like linebackers. "Ted, I just wanted to touch base here, see how your day went yesterday. And I needed to remind you about the 'exclusive.' That's a serious agreement, Ted."

"Okay then," Ted says buoyantly. "Thanks for telling me." I imagine him, white-haired, soft hands, diminutively handsome in his dimpled Fred Waring way, framed in his back window, marveling out at the bamboo wall that has long shielded him from his peaceable prison. It leaves me with a dull feeling that I've gone about this wrong. I should've stayed close to the Markhams, but my instincts said otherwise. "Frank, I'm thinking that if I get this cancer thing behind me I might just give realty a try. I think I might have a gift for it. What do you think?"

"Sure. But it doesn't take a gift, Ted. It's like being a writer. A man with nothing to do finds something to do. I've got to hit the road now. I've got to pick up my son."

"Good for you," Ted says. "Go right on. We'll talk another time."

"You bet," I say darkly, and then that's over.

The kids are clustered at the glass doors now, their counselors wading through them, laughing. One Down's boy is giving the door handle a vicious jerking and making a fierce face at the pane, in which he can no doubt see his reflection. The rest of them are still looking around and up and down and back.

When the first counselor drags the door open with the Down's kid still attached to it, he glares at her and makes a loud, fully uninhibited roar as the door lets hot air right into my face. Then the whole bunch comes scuttling in and past, heading for the second door.

"Oops," the first tall girl says to me with a wondrously bountiful grin. "We're sorry, we're a little clumsy." She moves on by in the current of little feebs in their Eli shirts. Her own shirt has a bright-red shield on its breast that says *Challenges, Inc.* and below that, *Wendy.* I give her a smile of encouragement as she gets shoved past.

Suddenly the little Down's kid whirls left, still attached to the door, and roars again, conceivably at me, his dark teeth clenched and worn to nubs, one little doughboy arm raised, fist balled. I am poised by the phone, smiling down at him, my hopes for the day attempting to scale the ladder of possibility.

"That means he likes you," says the second counselor—*Megan*—inching past at the back of the pack. She's putting me on, of course. What the roar means is: "Stay away from these two honeys or I'll eat your face." (People in many ways are the same.)

"He seems to know me," I say to golden-armed Megan.

"Oh, he knows you." Her face is freckled with sunshine, her eyes as plain brown as Cathy Flaherty's were dazzling. "They look alike to us, but they can pick you and me out a mile away. They have a sixth sense." She smiles without a whit of self-consciousness, a smile to inspire minutes but possibly not hours of longing. The inner door to Friendly's hisses open, then slowly shuts behind her. I head at that moment out into the sunny morning to begin my last leg to Deep River.

*B*y 9:50, feeling late, late, late, I'm larruping down-hill-and-up toward Middletown, Waterbury and Meriden, being already lost in the morning's silvery haze. CT 147 is as verdant, curvy and pleasant as a hedgerow lane in Ireland minus the hedgerows. Tiny pocket reservoirs, cozy roadside state parks, pint-size ski "mountains" perfect for high-school teams, and sturdy frame homes edging the road with satellite dishes out back, show up around every curve. Many houses, I notice, are for sale, and quite a few display yellow plastic ribbons on their tree trunks. I can't now remember what Americans are being held prisoner or where and by whom, though it's easy to conceive *somewhere, somebody* must be. Otherwise the ribbons are wishful thinking, a yearning for another Grenada-type tidy-little-war which worked out so happily for all concerned. Patriotic feelings are much more warming when focused on something finite, and there's nothing like focusing on kicking somebody's ass or depriving them of their freedom to make you feel free as a bird yourself.

My thoughts, though, unwillingly run again to the pathetic Markhams, no doubt at this very minute touring some grisly cul-de-sac, accompanied by a nasal-voiced, thick-thighed residential specialist demoralizing the shit out of them with chatter. An indecent, unprofessional part of me hopes that by day's end, faced with calling me and crawling back to 212 Charity with a full-price offer, they jump for the last house of the day, some standing-empty, dormered Cape whose prior owners gave it to the bank when they transferred-out to Moose Jaw back in '84, some dire shell on a slab, with negative R factors, potential for radon, a seeping septic, in need of emergency gutter work before the leaves fly.

Why, in an otherwise pleasant and profitable summer season, the Markhams would so shadow my mind isn't clear, unless it's that after much finagling, obstruction and idiot discouragement at every level, I have now fashioned the Easter egg, filled it with the right sweet stuff, made the hole and put their eye right to it; and yet I'm afraid they'll never see inside, after which their lives will be worse— my belief being that once you're offered something good, you ought to be smart enough to take it.

Years back, I remember, in the month before Ann and I moved to Haddam, new, happy suburban ethers full in our noses, we got it in mind to buy a practical-sturdy Volvo. We drove out in my mother's old Chrysler Newport to the dealership in Hastings-on-Hudson, kibitzed around the showroom for a hour and a half—chin-rubbing, ear-scratching potential young buyers—fingering the mirror surfaces of some olive-drab five-door job, slipping into and out of its sensible seats, sniffing its chilly perfume, checking out the glove box capacity, the unusual spare tire mounts and jack assembly, finally pretending even to drive it—Ann side by side with me in the driver's seat, both of us staring ahead through the dealership window at a make-believe road to the future as new Volvo owners.

Until, at the end, we simply decided we wouldn't. Who knows why? We were young, spiritedly inventing life by the minute, rejecting this, saying yea to that, completely by whim. And a Volvo, a machine I might even still own and use to transport potting soil or groceries or firewood or keep as a fish car to haul myself to the Red Man Club—a Volvo just didn't suit us. Afterward we drove back into the city toward whatever did suit us, our real future: marriage, parenthood, sportswriting, golf, glee, gloom, death, gyrating unhappiness unable to find a center point, and later, divorce, separation and the long middle passage to now.

Though when I'm in just the right deprived-feeling, past-entangled mood and happen to see one, some brawny-sleek, murmuring black or silver up-to-date-version Volvo, with its enviable safety record, its engine primed to drop out on impact, its boastable storage spaces and one-piece construction, I'm often struck with a heart's pang of *What if?* What if our life had gone in that direction . . . some direction a *car* could've led us and now be emblem for? Different house, different town, different sum total of kids, on and on. Would it all be better? Such things happen, and for as little cause. And it can be paralyzing to think an insignificant decision, a switch thrown this way, not that, could make many things turn out better, even be saved. (My greatest human flaw and strength, not surprisingly, is that I can always imagine anything—a marriage, a conversation, a government—as being different from how it is, a trait that might make one a top-notch trial lawyer or novelist or realtor, but that also seems to produce a somewhat less than reliable and morally feasible human being.)

It's best at this moment not to think much along these lines. Though this I'm sure is another reason why the Markhams come to mind on a weekend when my own life seems at a turning or at least a curving point. Likely as not, Joe and Phyllis know how these things work as well as I do and are scared shitless. Yet, while it's bad to make a wrong move, as maybe I did with the Volvo, it's worse to regret in advance and call it prudence, which I sense is what they're doing roving around East Brunswick. Disaster is no less likely. Better—much, much better—to follow ole Davy Crockett's motto, amended for use by adults: Be sure you're not completely wrong, then go ahead.

*B*y ten-thirty I'm past bland, collegiate Middletown and up onto Route 9, taking in the semi-panoramic view of the Connecticut (vacationers assiduously canoeing, jet skiing, windsurfing, sailing, paraskiing or skydiving right into the drink), and then straight downstream the short distance to Deep River.

My chief hope of a secondary nature here is not to lay eyes on Charley, for reasons I perhaps have brought to light already. With luck he'll be nursing his lumpy jaw out of sight, or else waxing his dinghy or sighting a plumb line or doodling in his sketchbook— whatever rich dilettante architects do when they're not competing in marathon gin rummy matches or tying their bow ties blindfolded.

Ann understands I don't precisely loathe Charley, only that I believe that whenever she tells him she loves him there's an asterisk after "love" (like Roger Maris's home run title), referencing prior, superior attainment in that area, as though I'm certain she'll one day pitch it all and begin life's last long pavane with me and me alone (though neither of us seems to want that).

In nearly all my preceding visits, I've ended up feeling I'd snuck onto the property by way of a scaled fence and left (for wherever I'm taking my children—the mollusk exhibit at Woods Hole, a Mets game, a blustery ferry ride to Block Island for a little stolen quality time) as though I was one step ahead of the law. Ann says I fabricate these feelings. But so what? I still have them.

Charley, unlike me, who thinks everything's mutable, is the sort of man who puts his trust in "character," who muses when alone about "standards" and *bona fides*, "parsing" and "winnowing out men from boys," but who (it's my private bet) stands at the foggy mirror in the locker room at the Old Lyme CC thinking about his dick, wishing he had a bigger one, considering if a rectangular glass doesn't distort proportions, deciding eventually that everybody's looks smaller when viewed by its hypercritical owner and that, in absolute terms, his is bigger than it looks because he's tall. Which he is.

One evening, standing together out below the knoll where his house sits, our shoes nuzzling the pea-gravel path that leads down to his boathouse, beyond which is a dense, pinkly-rose-infested estuarial pond protected from the Connecticut by a boundary of tupelo gums, Charley said to me, "Now, you know, Frank, Shakespeare must've been a pretty damn smart cookie." In his big bony hand he was cradling one of his drop-dead vodka gimlets in a thick, hand-blown Mexican tumbler. (He hadn't offered me one, since I wasn't staying.) "I took a look at everything he wrote this year, okay? And I think history's writers just haven't moved the bar up much since sixteen-whatever. He saw human weakness better than anybody ever did, and sympathetically at that." He blinked at me and rolled his tongue around behind his lips. "Isn't that what makes a writer great? Sympathy for human weakness?"

"I don't know. I never thought a thing about it," I said bleakly but churlishly. I already knew Charley thought it was "odd" that a man who once wrote respectable short stories would "end up" selling real estate. He also had views about my living in Ann's old house, though I never asked what they were (I'm sure they're prejudicial).

"All right, but how *do* you see it?" Charley sniffed through his big Episcopalian nose, furrowing his silver eyebrows as if he were smelling a complex bouquet in the evening's mist that was available only to him (and possibly his friends). He was clad in his usual sockless deck shoes, khaki shorts and a tee-shirt, but with a thick blue zippered sweater I'd seen thirty years ago in a J. Press catalogue and wondered who in the hell would buy. He is of course as fit as a greyhound and maintains some past master's squash ranking for oldsters.

"I don't really think literature has anything to do with moving the bar up," I said distastefully (I was right). "It has to do with being good in an absolute sense, not better." I now wish I could've punctuated this with a shout of hysterical laughter.

"Okay. That's hopeful." Charley pulled on his long earlobe and looked down, nodding as though he were visualizing the words I'd said. His thick white hair glowed with whatever light was left in the twilight. "That's really a pretty hopeful view," he said solemnly.

"I'm a hopeful man," I said, and promptly felt as hopeless as an exile.

"Fair enough then," he said. "Do you suppose in a hopeful way you and I are ever going to be friends?" He half raised his head and looked at me through his metal-rim glasses. "Friend" I knew to be, in Charley's view, the loftiest of lofty human conditions men of character could aspire to, like Nirvana for Hindus. I never wanted to have friends less in my life.

"No," I said bluntly.

"Why's that, do you think?"

"Because all we have in common is my ex-wife. And eventually you'll feel it's okay to discuss her with me, and that would piss me off."

Charley held onto his earlobe, his gimlet in his other hand. "Might be." He nodded speculatively. "You're always coming across something in someone you love that you can't fathom, aren't you? So then you have to ask somebody. I guess you'd be an obvious choice. Ann's not that simple, as I'm sure you know."

He was doing it already. "I don't know," I said. "No."

"You maybe oughta have another go at it, like I did. Maybe you'd get it right this time." Charley rounded his eyes at me and nodded again.

"Why don't you have a go at a flying fuck at whatever's in range," I said moronically, and glared at him, feeling fairly willing to throw a punch irrespective of his age and excellent physical condition (hoping my children wouldn't see it). I felt a chill rise then like a column of refrigerated air right off the pond, making my arm hairs prickle. It was late May. Little house lights had printed up across the silver plane of the Connecticut. I could hear a boat's bell clanging. At that moment I felt not truly angry enough to cold-cock Charley, but sad, lonesome, lost, unhappy and useless alongside a man I wasn't even interested in enough to hate the way a man with character would.

"You know," Charley said, zipping his sweater up to his glunky Adam's apple and tugging his sleeves as if he'd felt the chill himself. "There's something about you I don't trust, Frank. Maybe architects and realtors don't have that much in common, though you'd think we would." He eyed me just in case I might be about to produce guttural sounds and spring at his throat.

"That's fine," I said. "I wouldn't trust me either if I were you."

Charley gently tossed his glass, ice and all, off onto the lawn. He said, "Frank, you can play sharp and play flat but still be in tune, you know." He seemed disappointed, almost perplexed. Then he just strolled off down the gravel path toward his boathouse. "You won't win 'em all," I heard him say to himself, theatrically from out of the dark. I let him walk all the way down, pull aside the sliding door, enter and close it behind him (I'm sure he had nothing to do there). After that I walked back around his house, got in my car and waited for my children, who were soon to be there with me and be happy.

D eep River, as I drive hurriedly through, is the epitome of dozing, summery, southern New England ambivalence. A little green-shuttered, swept-sidewalk burg where just-us-regular-folks live in stolid acceptance of watered-down Congregationalist and Roman Catholic moderation; whereas down by the river there's the usual enclave of self-contented, pseudo-reclusive richies who've erected humongous houses on bracken and basswood chases bordering the water, their backs resolutely turned to how the other half lives. Endowed law profs from New Haven, moneyed shysters from Hartford and Springfield, moneyed pensioners from Gotham, all cruise sunnily in to shop at Greta's Green Grocer, The Flower Basket, Edible Kingdom Meats and Liquid Time Liquors (less often to visit Body Artistry Tattoo, Adult Newz-and-Video or the Friendly Loaner pawn), then cruise sunnily back out, their Rovers heaped with good dog food, pancetta, mesquite, chard, fresh tulips and gin—all primed for evening cocktails, lamb shanks on the grill, an hour of happy schmoozing, then off to bed in the cool, fog-enticed river breeze. It is not such a great place to think of your children living (or your ex-wife).

Nothing extravagant seems planned here for Monday. Droopy bunting decorates a few lampposts. A high-school "Freedom Car Wash" is in semi-full swing out on the fire station driveway, a rake-and-hoe promotion in front of the True Value. Several businesses, in fact, have put up red-and-white maple-leaf flags beside Old Glory, signaling some ancient Canuck connection—a group of hapless white settlers no doubt mercifully if unaccountably spared by a company of Montcalm's regulars back in '57, leaving a residuum of "Canadian Currency OK" sentiment in all hearts. Even Donna's Kut'n Kurl boasts a window sign reading "Time for a trim, eh?" But that's it—as if Deep River were simply saying, "Given our long establishment (1635), the spirit of true and complex independence is observed and breathed here every day. Silently. So don't expect much."

I turn toward the river and head down woodsy Selden Neck Lane, which T's into even woodsier, laurel-choked Brainard Settlement House Way, which curves, narrows and switches back onto American holly and hickory-thick Swallow Lane, the road where Ann's, Charley's and my two children's mailbox resides unnoticeably on a thin cedar post, its dark-green letters indicating THE KNOLL. Beside it a rough gravel car path disappears into anonymous trees, so that an atmosphere of exclusive, possibly less than welcoming habitation greets whoever wanders past: people live here, but you don't know them.

My brain, in the time it's taken me to clear town and wind down into these sylvan purlieus of the rich, has begun to exhibit an unpleasant tightness behind my temples. My neck's stiff, and there's a feeling of tissue expansion in my upper thorax, as if I ought to burp, gag or possibly just split open for relief's sake. I have, of course, slept little and badly. I drank too much at Sally's last night; I've driven too far, devoted too much precious worry time to the Markhams, the McLeods, Ted Houlihan and Karl Bemish, and too little to thinking about my son.

Though of course the most sharp-stick truth is that I'm about to pay my former wife a visit in her subsequent and better life; am about to see my orphaned kids gamboling on the wide lawns of their tonier existence; I may even, in spite of all, have to make humiliating, grinding conversation with Charley O'Dell, whom I'd just as soon tie up on a beach and leave for the crabs. Who wouldn't have a "swelling" in his brain and generalized thoracic edema? I'm surprised it isn't a helluva lot worse.

A small plastic sign I haven't noticed before has been attached to the bottom edge of the mailbox, a little burgundy-colored plaque with green lettering like the box itself, which says: HERE IS A BIRD SANCTUARY. RESPECT IT. PROTECT OUR FUTURE. Karl would be pleased to know vireos are still safe here in Connecticut.

Only directly below the box, on the duffy, weedy ground, lies a bird—a grackle or a big cowbird, its eyes glued shut with death, its stiff feathers swarmed by ants. I peer down on it from behind my window and puzzle: Birds die, we all know that. Birds have coronaries, brain tumors, anemia, suffer bad luck and life's battering, then croak like the rest of us—even in a sanctuary, where nobody has it in for them and everybody dotes on everything they do.

But here? Under their very own sign? Here is odd. And I am, in my brain-tightened unease, suddenly, instantly certain my son's to blame (call it a father's instinct). Plus, animal torture is one of the bad childhood warning signs: meaning he's begun the guerrilla war of spirit-attrition against his foster home, against Charley, against cool lawns, morning mists, matched goldens, sabots, clay courts and solar panels, against all that's happened outside his control. (I don't completely blame him.)

Not that I approve of dispatching blameless tweeties and leaving them by the mailbox as portents of bad things on the wing. I don't approve. It scares me silly. But as little as I hope to be involved in domestic life here, I also believe an ounce of intervention might deter a pound of cure. So, putting my car in park, I shove open my door and climb out into the heat, my brain still expanding, stoop stiffly down, lift the little dull-feathered, ant-swarmed carcass by its wingtip, take a quick look behind me at Swallow Lane curving out of sight, then quick-flip it like a cow chip off into the bushes, where it falls soundlessly, saving my son (I hope) one peck of trouble in a life that may already stretch out long and full of troubles.

Out of ancient habit I quickly raise my fingers for a sniff-check in case I need to go someplace—back up to the Chevron on Route 9—to wash the death smell off. But just as I do, a small dark-blue car (I believe it is a Yugo) with silver lettering and a silver police-shield door decal inscribed with AGAZZIZ SECURITY pulls in to block me where I'm standing beside my car. (Where has *this* come from?)

A slender, blond man in a blue uniform gets quickly out, as though I might just take off running into the trees, but then remains behind his door looking at me with an odd, unhumorous smile—a smile any American would recognize as signifying wariness, arrogance, authority and a conviction that outsiders cause trouble. Possibly he thinks I'm filching mail—ten reggae CD offers, or some prime steaks from Idaho, special for high rollers only.

I lower my fingers—unhappily they *do* smell of feral death—my skull tightened back down into my neck sinews. "Hi," I say, extra cheerful.

"Hi!" the young man says and nods in some unclear sort of agreement. "Whatcha up to?"

I beam probity at him. "I was just going into the O'Dells' here. I've been driving a ways, so I decided to stretch my legs."

"Great," he says, beaming cold indifference back. He is razorish-looking and, although thin, undoubtedly schooled in lethal martial-arts wherewithal. I can't see a firearm, but he's wearing a miniature microphone that allows him to talk to someone in another location by speaking straight into his own shoulder. "You friends of the O'Dells, are ya?" he says cheerfully.

"Yep. Sure am."

"I'm sorry, but what was it you threw over in the trees?"

"A bird. That was a bird. A dead one."

"Okay," the officer says, peering over in that direction as if he could see a dead bird, which he can't. "Where'd *it* come from?"

"It got caught behind the outside mirror of my car. I didn't notice it till I opened the door. It was a grackle."

"I see. What was it?" (Perhaps he thinks my story will change under interrogation.)

"Grackle," I say, as if the word itself might induce a humorous response, but I'm wrong.

"You know, this is a wildlife sanctuary back here. There isn't any hunting."

"I didn't hunt for it. I was just disposing of it before I drove in with it on my car mirror. I thought that'd be better. It'll be okay over there." I look where I'm referring.

"Where you driving from?" His young weak eyes twitch toward my blue-and-cream Jersey plates, then quickly back up at me so that if I claim I've just driven in from Oracle, Arizona, or International Falls, he'll know to call for backup.

"I'm from down in Haddam, New Jersey." I adopt a voice that says I'd be glad to help you in any way I can and would write a letter of commendation to your superiors complimenting you on your demeanor the moment I'm back at my desk.

"And what's your name, sir?"

"Bascombe." And I haven't done a goddamn thing, I say silently, but toss one dead bird in the bushes to save everybody trouble (though of course I've lied about it). "Frank Bascombe." Cool air surrounds me from my open car door.

"Okay, Mr. Bascombe. If I could just look at your driver's license, I'll get out of your way here." The young rent-a-cop seems pleased, as if these words are the standard words and he positively loves saying them.

"Sure thing," I say, and in a flash have my wallet out and license forked from its little slot below my realtor certification, my Red Man Club membership, my Maize and Blue Club alumni card.

"If you'd bring it over here and put it on the hood of my car," he says, giving his shoulder mike an adjustment, "I'll have a look at it while you stand back, then I'll put it back and you can pick it up. Is that all right?"

"It's just great. It seems a little elaborate. I could just hand it to you."

I start in the direction of his Yugo, which has a springy little two-way antenna stuck onto its dumpy top. But he nervously says, "Don't approach me, Mr. Bascombe. If you don't want to show your license"—he's eyeing his shoulder mike again—"I can get a Connecticut state trooper out here, and you can explain your case to him." The blond boy's amiable veneer has, in a heartbeat, disappeared to reveal sinister, police-protocol hardass, bent on construing obvious innocence as obvious guilt. I'm sure his real self is right now trying to figure out how Bascombe is spelled, since it's obviously a Jewish name, remembering that New Jersey's chock-full of Jews and spicks and darkies and towelheads and commies, all needing to be rounded up and reminded of a few things. I see his hands drifting somewhere below window level and around toward his backside, where he probably has his heat. (I have not provoked this. I merely am handing over my license.)

"I don't really have a case," I say, renewing my smile and stepping over to his Yugo and laying my license above the headlight. "I'm happy just to play by the rules." I take a few steps back.

The young man waits till I'm ten steps away, then comes round his door and snakes up my license. I can see his idiotic gold nameplate above his blue shirt pocket. *Erik.* Besides his shirt and blue trousers, he's wearing thick crepe-soled auxiliary-police footwear and a dopey little red ascot. I can also see that he's older than he looks, which is twenty-two. Probably he's thirty-five, has multiple applications in with all the local PDs and been turned down due to "irregularities" in his Rorschachs, even though from a distance he looks like the boy any parent would love and spare no expense in sending off to Dartmouth.

Erik steps around behind his open car door and gives my license thorough study, which includes looking up at me for a mug-shot match. I see now he has an almost colorless Hitler Youth mustache on his pale lip, and something tattooed on the back of his hand—a skull, maybe, or a snake coiled around a skull (no doubt a Body Artistry creation). He is also, I can just make out, wearing a tiny gold earring bead in his right lobe. An amusing little combo for Deep River.

He turns my license over, apparently to see if I'm an organ donor (I'm not), then he walks it back around, lays it on the Yugo's hood and returns to his protective door. I still can't tell if he's packin'.

"There you go," he says, with a remnant of his former warmth. I don't know what he's learned, since it wouldn't say on my license if I was a serial killer. "We just have a lot of strangers drive in here, Mr. Bascombe. People who live in here really don't like being harassed. Which is why we have a job, I guess." He grins amiably. We're friends now.

"I hate it myself," I say, coming over and snugging my license back in my billfold. I wonder if Erik got a whiff of the dead-bird stink.

"You'd probably be surprised the number of wackos come off that I-Ninety-five and end up back in here, roaming around."

"I believe it," I say. "A hundred percent." And then for some reason I am enervated, as if I'd been to jail for days and had just this very moment stepped out into harsh daylight.

"Particularly on your holidays," says Erik the sociologist. "And especially *this* holiday. This one brings out the psychos from *all* over. New York, New Jersey, Pennsylvania." He shakes his head. Those are the states where most lunatics live if you're him. "You old friends with Mr. O'Dell?" He smiles, protected by his door. "I like him a lot."

"No," I say, stepping back to my car, which has cold air still pouring out, making me feel even more enervated.

"You're just business acquaintances, I guess," he says. "You an architect?"

"No," I say. "My ex-wife's married to Mr. O'Dell, and I'm picking up my son to take him on a trip. Does that seem like a good idea?" I can easily imagine wanting to harm Erik.

"Wow, that sounds pretty serious." He leers from behind his open blue door. He's, of course, got me figured now: I'm a defeated, pathetic figure engaged in a demeaning and hopeless mission—not nearly as interesting as a wacko. Though even my kind can cause trouble, can have a trunkful of phosphorous grenades and plastique and be bent on neighborhood mayhem.

"It's not that serious," I say, pausing, looking at him. "It's something I enjoy."

"Is Paul *your* son?" Erik says. He brings his forefinger up to his earring, a small gesture of dominion.

"Yep. You know Paul?"

"Oh yeah," Erik says, smirking. "We're all acquainted with Paul."

"All who? What does that mean?" I feel my brows thicken.

"We've all had contact with Paul." Erik starts lowering himself back into his stupid Yugo.

"I'm sure he hasn't caused you any trouble," I say, thinking that he probably has, and will again. Erik is the kind of monkey Paul would consider a barrel of laughs.

Erik is speaking from the driver's seat now; I can't make his words out. No doubt he's saying something smart-assed he doesn't intend me to hear. Or else he's radioing messages via his shoulder. He drops the Yugo in reverse, scoots back out the drive and wheels around.

I consider saying something vicious, running over and screaming in his window. But I can't afford to get arrested in my ex-wife's driveway. So I only wave, and he waves back. I think he says, "Have a good day," in his policey, insincere way, before heading slowly up Swallow Lane out of my sight.

*M*y daughter, Clarissa, is the first living soul I spy as I drive tired-eyed into compound O'Dell. She is far below the big house, on the ample lawn slope above the pond, committedly whacking a yellow tetherball all by her lonesome, oblivious as a sparrow to me here in my car, surveilling her from afar.

I pull up to the back of the house (the front faces the lawn, the air, the water, the sunrise and, for what I know, the path to all knowledge) and climb wearily out into the hot, chirpy morning, reconciled to finding Paul by myself.

Charley's house is, of course, a glorious erection, chalky-blue-shingled and white-trimmed, with a complex gabled roof, tall paneless windows and a big sashaying porch around three sides that gives onto the lawn down some white steps to the very spot where Charley and I discussed Shakespeare and came to the conclusion we neither one trusted the other.

I wedge in sideways through the row of purple-blooming hydrangeas (contrast my poor dried-up remnants on Clio Street), stagger only slightly, but walk on out onto the hot shadowless grass, feeling light-legged and dazed, my eyelids flickering, my eyes darting side to side to see who might see me first (such entrances are never dignified). I have, to my eternal infamy, forgotten to buy a gift this morning, a love and peace offering to appease Clarissa for not taking her along with her brother. What I'd give for a colorful Vince Lombardi sweatband or a Four Blocks of Granite book of inspirational halftime quotes. It would be our joke. I am lost here.

Clarissa ceases larking with the tetherball when she sees me and stands eyes-shaded, averting her face and waving, though she can't tell it's me she sees—possibly hopes it is and not a plainclothes policeman come to ask questions about her brother.

I wave back, realizing for some reason known only to God that I have begun to *limp*, as though a war had intervened since I last saw my loved ones and I had returned a changed and beaten veteran. Though Clarissa will not notice. Even as rarely as she sees me—once a month nowadays—I am a timeless fixture, and nothing would seem unusual; an eye patch, a prosthetic arm, all-new teeth: none would rate a mention.

"Hi-dee, hi-dee, hi-dee," she sings out when it's clearly me she's waving welcome to. She wears strong contacts and can't see distances well, but doesn't care. She darts and springs barefoot toward me across the dry grass, ready to deliver a big power hug around my aching neck—which every time hurts like a hammerlock and makes me groan.

"I came as soon as I heard the news," I say. (In our makeshift, make-believe life I always arrive just in time to face some dire emergency—Clarissa and I being the responsible adults, Paul and their mother the temperamental kids in need of rescue.) I am still limping, though my heart's going strong with simple pleasure, all tightness in my brain miraculously dispatched.

"Paul's in the house with Mom, getting ready and probably having an argument."

Clarissa, in brilliant red shorts over her blue Speedo suit, jumps up and gives me her hammer hug, and I swing her like a tetherball before letting her sink weak-kneed into the grass. She has a wonderful smell—dampness and girlish perfume applied hours before, now faded. Beyond us is the boathouse crime scene, the pond again dense with pink fleabane and wild callas and, farther on, the row of dense motionless tupelos and the invisible river, above which a squad of pelicans executes a slow and graceful upward soar.

"Where's the man of the house?" I let myself down heavily beside her, my back against the tetherball pole. Clarissa's legs are thin and tanned and golden-sheeny-haired, her bare feet milky and without a blemish. She arranges herself belly-down, chin-propped, her eyes clear behind her contacts and fastened on me, her face a prettier version of my own: small nose, blue eyes, cheekbones more obvious than her mother's, whose broad, Dutch forehead and coarse hair match Paul's looks almost completely.

"He's work-ing now in his studi-o-o." She looks at me knowingly and without much irony. It's life to her, all of this—few tragedies, few great singing victories, everything pretty much good or okay. We are well paired in our family unit.

Charley's studio is half visible beyond a row of deep-green hard-woods that boundaries the lawn and stops at the pond's edge. I see a glint off its tin roof, its row of cypress stilts holding up a catwalk (a project Charley and his roommate doped out as a joke freshman year, back in '44, but that Charley "always wanted to build").

"So how's the weather?" I say, relieved to know where he is.

"Oh, it's fine," Clarissa says noncommittally. A skim of sweat is on her temples from belting the tetherball. My back's already sweaty through my shirt.

"And how's your brother?"

"Weird. But okay." Maintaining her belly-down, she rotates her head around on its slender stem, some routine from dance class or gymnastics, though an unmistakable signal: she is Paul's *buen amiga*; the two of them are closer than the two of us; this all could've been different with better parents, but isn't; do not fail to notice it.

"Is your mom okay too?"

Clarissa stops rotating her head and wrinkles her nose as though I'd announced an unsavory subject, then rolls over on her back and stares skyward. "She's much worse," she says, and looks unconvincingly worried.

"Worse than what?"

"Than you!" She rounds her eyes upward in mock surprise. "She and Charley had a howler this week. And they had one last week too. And one the week before." "Howlers" mean big disputes, not embarrassing verbal miscues. "Hmmmm, hmm, hmm," she says, meaning most of what she knows is being retained silently. I of course can't quiz her on this subject—a cardinal rule once divorce has become the governing institution—though I wish I knew more.

I pluck up a blade of grass, press it between my two thumbs like a woodwind reed and blow, making a sputtery, squawky but still fairly successful soprano sax note, a skill from eons back.

"Can you play 'Gypsy Road' or 'Born in the U.S.A.'?" She sits up.

"That's my whole repertoire on grass," I say, putting my two hands down on both her kneecaps, which are cold and bony and soft all at once. Conceivably she can smell dead grackle. "Your ole Dad loves you," I say. "I'm sorry I have to kidnap Paul and not all two of you. I'd rather travel as a trio."

"He's much needier now," Clarissa says, and drags a blade of grass all her own across the backs of both my hands where they rest on her perfect kneecaps. "I'm way ahead of him emotionally. I'll have my period pretty soon." She looks up at me profoundly, fattens the corners of her mouth and slowly lets her eyes cross and keeps them that way.

"Well, that's good to know," I say, my heart going ker-whonk, my eyes suddenly hot and unhappily moist—not with unhappy tears, but with unhappy sweat that has busted out on my forehead. "And how old *are* you?" I say, ker-whonk. "Thirty-seven or thirty-eight?"

"Thirty-twelve," she says, and lightly pokes my knuckles with the grass blade.

"Okay, that's old enough. You don't need to be any older. You're perfect."

"Charley knows Bush," she says with a sour face. "Did you hear that?" Her blue eyes elevate gravely to mine. This is bottom-line business to her. All that Charley might conceivably have been forgiven is reassigned to him with this choice bit of news. My daughter, like her old man, is a Democrat of the New Deal bent and considers most Republicans and particularly V.P. Bush barely mentionable dickheads.

"I guess I knew that without knowing it." I scour my two fingers on the turf to clean off the death smell.

"He's for the party of money, tradition and influence," she says, way too big for her britches, since Charley's tradition and influence are paying her bills, keeping her in tetherballs, tutus and violin lessons. She is for the party of no tradition, no influence, no nothing, also like her father.

"He has his rights," I say, and add a lackluster "I mean that." I can't help conjuring what Charley's cheek looks like where Paul has whopped him.

Clarissa stares at her blade of grass, wondering, I'm sure, why she has to accord Charley any rights. "Sweetheart," I say solemnly, "is there anything you can tell me about ole Paul? I don't want you to tell me a deep dark secret, just maybe a shallow light one. It would be as-you-know-held-in-strictest-confidence." I say this last to make it halfway a joke and let her feel comradely about providing me some lowdown.

She stares at the thick grass carpet in silence, then angles her head over and squints up at the house with the flowering bushes and the white porch and stairs. Atop the highmost roof pinnacle, in the midst of all the springing angles and gable ends, is an American flag (a small one) on a staff, rustling in an unfelt breeze.

"Are you sad?" she says. In her sun-blond hair I see a tiny red ribbon tied in a bow, something I hadn't noticed but instantly revere her for, since along with her question it makes her seem a person of complex privacies.

"No, I'm not sad, except that you can't go with Paul and me to Cooperstown. And I forgot to bring you anything. That's pretty sad."

"Do you have a car phone?" She raises her eyes accusingly.

"No."

"Do you have a beeper?"

"No, afraid not." I smile at her knowingly.

"How do you keep up with your calls then?" She squints again, making her look a hundred.

"I guess I don't get that many calls. Sometimes there's a message from you on my answering box, though not that often."

"I know."

"You didn't answer me about Paul, sweetheart. All I really want to do is be a good pappy if I can."

"His problems are all stress-related," she says officially. She plucks up another blade of quite green and dry grass and slips it into the cuff of my chinos where I'm cross-legged beside her.

"What stress is he suffering from?"

"I don't know."

"Is that your best diagnosis?"

"Yes."

"How 'bout you? Do you have any stress-related problems?"

"No." She shakes her head, makes a pruny pucker with her lips. "Mine'll come out later, if I have any."

"Who told you so?"

"TV." She looks at me earnestly as though to say that TV has its good points too.

Somewhere high in the firmament I hear a hawk cry out, or possibly an osprey, though when I look up I can't see it.

"What can I do about Paul's stress-related problems?" I say, and, God be gracious, I wish she'd pipe up with a nice answer. I'd put it in place before the sun sets. Somewhere, then, another noise—not a hawk but a thumping, a door slamming or a window being shut, a drawer being closed. When I look up, Ann is standing at the porch rail, watching down on us across the lawn. I sense she's just arrived but would like my chat with Clarissa to come to a close and for me to get on with my business. I make a friendly ex-husband-who-wishes-no-trouble wave, a gesture that makes me feel not so good. "I believe that's your mom," I say.

Clarissa looks up at the porch. "Yeah hi," she says.

"We better dust off our britches here." She will, I see, out of ancient, honorable loyalty, offer no help with her brother. She fears, I suppose, divulging compromising secrets while claiming only to love him. Children are wise to adult ways now, thanks to us.

"Paul might be happier if you could maybe live in Deep River. Or maybe Old Saybrook," she says as if these words require immense discipline, nodding her head slightly with each one. (Parents can break up, fall out of love, get searingly divorced, marry others, move miles away; but as far as kids are concerned, most of it's tolerable if one parent will just tag along behind the other like a slave.)

There was, of course, in the savage period after Ann moved away in '84, a dolorous time when I haunted these very hills and streamsides like a shamus; cruised its middle-school parking lots, its street corners and back alleys, cased its arcades and skating rinks, its Finasts and Burger Kings, merely to be in visual contact with where my children *might* spend the days and afternoons they could've been spending with me. I even went so far as to price a condo in Essex, a sterile little listening post from which I could keep "in touch," keep love alive.

Only it would've made me even more morose, as morose as a hundred lost hounds, to wake up alone in a condo! In Essex! Awaiting my appointed pickup hour with the kids, expecting to take them back where? To my condo? And afterward, glowering back down 95 for a befuddled workweek till Friday, when the lunacy commenced again? There are parents who don't blink an eye at that kind of bashing around, who'd ruin their own lives and everybody's within ten miles if they can prove—long after all the horses are out of the barn—that they've always been good and faithful providers.

But I simply am not one of these; and I have been willing to see my kids less often, for the three of us to shuttlecock up and back, so that I can keep alive in Haddam a life they can fit into, even if precariously, when they will, and meanwhile maintain my sanity, instead of forcing myself into places where I don't belong and making everybody hate me. It's not the best solution, since I miss them achingly. But it's better to be a less than perfect dad than a perfect goofball.

And in any case, with the condo option, they would still grow up and leave in a heartbeat; Ann and Charley would get divorced. And I'd be stuck (worst case) with a devalued condo I couldn't give away. Eventually, I'd sell Cleveland Street as a downsizing measure, perhaps move up here to keep my mortgage company, and grimly pass my last years alone in Essex watching TV in a pair of old corduroys, a cardigan and Hush Puppies, while helping out evenings in some small bookshop, where I'd occasionally see Charley dodder in, place an order and never recognize me.

Such things happen! We realtors are often the very ones called in for damage control. Though thankfully my frenzy subsided and I stayed put where I was and more or less knew my place. Haddam, New Jersey.

"Sweetheart," I say tenderly to my daughter, "if I lived up here, your mother wouldn't like it at all, and you and Paul wouldn't come stay in your own rooms and see your old friends-in-need. Sometimes you can change things and just make them worse."

"I know," she says bluntly. I'm sure Ann hasn't discussed with her Paul's coming to live with me, and I have no idea what her opinion will be. Perhaps she'll welcome it, loyalty aside. I might, if I were her.

She reaches fingers into her yellow hair, her mouth going into a scowl of application. She pulls the little red bow out along the fine blond strands until she frees it still tied, and hands it to me rather matter-of-factly. "Here's *my* latest present," she says. "You can be my bow."

"That's another kind of bow," I say, taking the little frill in my hand and squeezing it. "They're spelled different."

"Yeah, I know. It's okay, though, this time."

"Thanks." Once again, sadly, I have nothing to trade as an act of devotion.

And then she is up and on her bare feet, spanking the seat of her red shorts and shaking out her hair, looking down like a small lioness with a tangled mane. I am less quick but am up too, using the tetherball pole. I look toward the house, where no one's standing on the porch now. A smile is for some reason on my lips, my hand on my daughter's bony bare shoulder, her red bow, my badge of courage, clutched in my other hand, as we start—the two of us— together up the wide hill.

"D id you ever take trips in Mississippi with your father?" Ann asks without genuine interest. We are seated opposite each other on the big porch. The Connecticut River, visible now above the serrated treetops, is a-glitter with dainty sailboats sporting rust-colored sails, their masts steadfast as the wind transports them up the current toward Hartford. All boats of a certain class rising on a rising tide.

"Sure, you bet. Sometimes we went over to Florida. Once we went to Norfolk and visited the Great Dismal Swamp on the way back." She used to know this but has now forgotten.

"Was it dismal?"

"Absolutely." I smile at her in a collegial way, since that is what we are.

"And so did you two always get along great?" She looks away across the lawn below us.

"We got along pretty great. My mother wasn't around to complicate things, so we were on our best behavior. Three was more complicated."

"Women just enjoy disrupting men's lives," she says.

We are fixed firmly in two oversize green wicker chairs furnished with oversize flowery cushions of some lush and complex lily-pad pattern. Ann has brought out an ole-timey amber-glass pitcher of iced tea, which Clarissa has fixed and drawn a fat happy face on. The tea and glasses and little pewter ice bucket are situated on a low table at knee level, as we, the two of us, wait for Paul, who was up late and slow now to rustle his bones. (I notice no warm-hearted carryover from our sentimental sign-off at the Vince last night.)

Ann runs a comb-of-fingers back through her thick, athletically shortened hair, which she's highlighted so sudden blond strands shine from within and look pretty. She's wearing white golfing shorts and an expensive-looking sleeveless top of some earthy taupe color that fits loose and shows her breasts off semi-mysteriously, and tan, sockless tassel shoes that cause her tanned legs to look even longer and stauncher, stirring in me a low-boil sexual whir that makes me gladder to be alive than I ever expected to feel today. I've noticed in the last year a subtle widening of Ann's wonderful derriere and a faint thickening and loosening of the flesh above her knees and upper arms. To my view, a certain tense girlishness, always present (and which I never really liked), has begun subsiding and been replaced by a softer, womanly but in every way more substantial and appealing adultness I admire immensely. (I might mention this if I had time to make clear I liked it; though I see she is wearing Charley's pretentiously plain gold band today, and the whole idea seems ridiculous.)

She has not asked me to come inside to wait, though I'd already decided to stay clear of the glassed-in, malaise-filled "family room," which I can just see into through the long mirror-tinted windows beside me. Charley has of course installed a big antique telescope there, complete with all the necessary brass knobs and fittings, engraved logarithmic calibrations and moon phases, and with which I'm sure he can bring in the Tower of London if he takes a notion. I can also make out the ghostly-white beast of a grand piano and beside it a beaux arts music stand, where Ann and Clarissa almost certainly play Mendelssohn duets for Charley's delectation on many a cold winter's eve. It is a tiresome recognition.

Truth is, the one time I ever waited inside (picking up the kids for a day trip to the fish elevator at South Hadley), I ended up waiting alone for nearly an hour, leafing through the coffee-table library (*Classic Holes of Golf, Erotic Cemetery Art, Sailing*), eventually working my way down to a hot-pink flyer from a women's clinic in New London, offering an enhance-your-sexual-performance workshop, which made me instantly panicky. Prudenter now just to stay on the porch and risk feeling like a grinning high-school kid forced to make deadpan parental chitchat while I await my date.

Ann has already explained to me how yesterday was much worse than I knew, worse than she explained last night when she said I thought "be" and "seem" were the same concept (which may have been true once but isn't now). Not only, it seems, did Paul wound poor Charley with an oarlock from his own damned dinghy, but he also informed his mother in the very living room I won't enter and in front of damaged-goods Charley himself that she "needed" to get rid of "asshole Chuck." After that, he marched out, got in his mother's Mercedes wagon and hit off on a brief tear, barrel-assing unlicensed out the driveway at a high speed, missing the very first curve on Swallow Lane and sideswiping a two-hundred-year-old mountain ash on the neighbor's property (a lawyer, of course). In the process he banged his head into the steering wheel, popped the air bag and cut his ear, so that he had to take a stitch at the Old Saybrook walk-in clinic. Erik, the man from Agazziz, arrived moments after the crash—similar to how he apprehended me—and escorted him home. No police were called. Later he disappeared again, on foot, and came home long past dark (Ann heard him bark once in his room).

She of course called Dr. Stopler, who calmly informed her that medical science knew mighty damn little about how the old mind works in relation to the old brain—whether they're one and the same pancake, two parts of one pancake, or just altogether different pancakes that somehow work in unison (like an automobile clutch). However, distressed family relations were pretty clear bugaboo factors leading to childhood mental illness, and from what he already knew, Paul did have some qualifying preconditions: dead brother, divorced parents, absent father, two major household moves before puberty (plus Charley O'Dell for a stepdad).

He did allow, though, that when he'd conducted his evaluative "chat" with Paul back in May, prior to his Camp Wanapi visit, Paul had failed entirely to exhibit low self-esteem, suicide ideation, neurological dysfunction; he was not particularly "oppositional" (then), hadn't suffered an IQ nosedive and didn't display any conduct disorders—which meant he didn't set a fire or murder any birds. In fact, the doctor said, he'd demonstrated a "real capacity for compassion and a canny ability to put himself in another's shoes." Though circumstances could always change overnight; and Paul could easily be suffering any and every one of the aforementioned maladies at this very minute, and might've abandoned all compassion.

"I'm really just pissed off at him now," Ann says. She is standing, looking out over the porch rail where I first saw her today, staring across the apron of shining river toward the few small white house façades catching the sun from deep in the encroachment of solid greens. Once again I steal an approving look at her new substantial-without-sacrificing-sexual-specificity womanliness. Her lips, I notice, seem fuller now, as if she might've had them "enhanced." (Such surgeries can sweep through the more well-to-do communities like new kitchen appliances.) She rubs the back of one muscular calf with the top of her other shoe and sighs. "You may not know how exactly lucky you've had it," she says, after a period of silent staring.

I mean to say nothing. A careful review of how lucky I am could too easily involve more airing of my "be/seem" misdeeds and tie into the possibility that I'm a coward or a liar or worse. I scratch my nose and can *still* smell grackle on my fingers.

She looks around at where I sit still not very comfortably silent on my lily pad.

"Would you agree to seeing Dr. Stopler?"

"As a patient?" I blink.

"As a co-parent," she says. "*And* as a patient."

"I'm really not based in New Haven," I say. "And I never much liked shrinks. They just try to make you act like everybody else."

"You don't have that to worry about." She regards me in an impatient older-sister way. "I just thought if you and I, or maybe you and I and Paul, went down, we might iron some things out. That's all."

"We can invite Charley, if you want to. He's probably got some ironing out that needs doing. He's a co-parent too, right?"

"He'll go. If I ask him."

I look around at the mirror window behind which sits the spectral white piano and a lot of ultra-modern, rectilinear blond-wood furniture arranged meticulously between long, sherbet-colored walls so as to maximize the experience of an interesting inner space while remaining unimaginably comfy. Reflected, I see the azure sky, part of the lawn, an inch of the boathouse roof and a line of far treetops. It is a vacant vista, the acme of opulent American dreariness Ann has for some reason married into. I feel like getting up and walking out onto the lawn—waiting for my son in the grass. I don't care to see Dr. Stopler and have my weaknesses vetted. My weaknesses, after all, have taken me this far.

Behind the glass, though, and unexpectedly, the insubstantial figure of my daughter becomes visible crossing left to right, intending where, I don't know. As she passes she gazes out at us—her parents, bickering—and, blithely assuming I can't see her, flips one or both of us the bird in a spiraling, heightening, conjuring motion like an ornate salaam, then disappears through a door to another segment of the house.

"I'll think about Dr. Stopler," I say. "I'm still not sure what a milieu therapist is, though."

The corners of Ann's mouth thicken with disapproval—of me. "Maybe you could think of your children as a form of self-discovery. Maybe you'd see your interest in it then and do something a little more wholeheartedly yourself." Ann's view is that I'm a half-hearted parent; my view is that I do the best I know how.

"Maybe," I say, though the thought of dread-filled weekly drives to dread-filled New Haven for expensive fifty-five dread-filled minutes of *mea culpa! mea culpa!* gushered into the weary, dread-resistant map of some Austrian headshrinker is enough to set anybody's escape mechanisms working overtime.

The fact is, of course, Ann maintains a very unclear picture of me and my current life's outlines. She has never appreciated the realty business or why I enjoy it—doesn't think it actually involves *doing* anything. She knows nothing of my private life beyond what the kids snitch about in offhand ways, doesn't know what trips I take, what books I read. I've over time become fuzzier and fuzzier, which given her old Michigan factualism makes her inclined to disapprove of almost anything I might do except possibly joining the Red Cross and dedicating my life to feeding starving people on faraway shores (not a bad second choice, but even that might not save me from pathos). In all important ways I'm no better in her mind than I was when our divorce was made final—whereas, of course, she has made great strides.

Only I don't actually mind it, since not having a clear picture makes her long for one and in so doing indirectly long for me (or that's my position). Absence, in this scheme, both creates and fills a much-needed void.

But it's not all positive: when you're divorced you're always wondering (I am anyway, sometimes to the point of granite preoccupation) what your ex-spouse is thinking about you, how she's viewing your decisions (assuming she thinks you make any), whether she's envious or approving or condescending or sneeringly reproachful, or just indifferent. Your life, because of this, can become goddamned awful and decline into being a "function" of your view of *her* view—like watching the salesman in the clothing store mirror to see if he's admiring you in the loud plaid suit you haven't quite decided to buy, but will if he seems to approve. Therefore, what I'd prefer Ann's view to be is: of a man who's made a spirited recovery from a lost and unhappy union, and gone on to discover wholesome choices and pretty solutions to life's thorny dilemmas. Failing that, I'd be happy to keep her in the dark.

Though in the end the real trick to divorce remains, given this refractory increase in perspectives, not viewing *yourself* ironically and losing heart. You have, on the one hand, such an obsessively detailed and minute view of yourself from your prior existence, and on the other hand, an equally specific view of yourself *later on*, that it becomes almost impossible not to see yourself as a puny human oxymoron, and damn near impossible sometimes to recognize who your self is at all. Only you must. Writers in fact survive this condition better than almost anyone, since they understand that almost everything—e-v-e-r-y-t-h-i-n-g—is not really made up of "views" but words, which, should you not like them, you can change. (This actually isn't very different from what Ann told me last night on the phone in the Vince Lombardi.)

Ann has assumed a seat on the porch railing, one strong, winsome brown knee up, the other swinging. She is half facing me and half observing the red-sailed regatta, most of whose hulls have moved behind the treeline. "I'm sorry," she says moodily. "Tell me where you two're going, again? You told me last night. I forgot."

"We're heading up to Springfield this morning." I say this cheerfully, happy to change the subject away from me. "We're having a 'sports lunch' at the Basketball Hall of Fame. Then we're driving over to Cooperstown by tonight." No use mentioning a possible late crew addition of Sally Caldwell. "We're touring the Baseball Hall of Fame tomorrow morning, and I'll have him in the city at the stroke of six." I smile a reliable, You're in good hands with Allstate smile.

"He's not really a big baseball fan, is he?" She says this almost plaintively.

"He knows more than you think he knows. Plus, going's the *ur*-father-son experience." I erase my smile to let her know I'm only half bluffing.

"So have you thought up some important fatherly things to say to solve his problems?" She squints at me and tugs at her earlobe exactly the way Charley does.

I, however, intend not to give away what I'll say to Paul on our trip, since it's too easy to break one's fragile skein of worthwhile purpose by jousting with casual third-party skepticism. Ann is not in a good frame of mind to validate fragile worthwhile purposes, especially mine.

"My view is sort of a facilitator's view," I say, hopefully. "I just think he's got some problems figuring out a good conception of himself"—to put it mildly—"and I want to offer a better one so he doesn't get too attached to the one he's hanging onto now, which doesn't seem too successful. A defective attitude can get to be your friend if you don't look out. It's sort of a problem in risk management. He has to risk trying to improve by giving up what's maybe comfortable but not working. It's not easy." I would smile again, but my mouth has gone dry as cardboard saying this much and trying to seem what I am—sincere. I drink down a gulp of ice tea, which is sweet the way a child would like it and has lemon and mint and cinnamon and God knows what else in it, and tastes terrible. Clarissa's finger-drawn happy face has droozled down and become a scowling jack-o'-lantern in the heat.

"Do you think you're a good person to instruct him about risk management?" Ann suddenly looks toward the river as if she'd heard an unfamiliar sound out in the summer atmosphere. A fishy breeze has in fact risen offshore and moved upriver, carrying all manner of sounds and smells she might not expect.

"I'm not that bad at it," I say.

"No." She is still looking off. "Not at risk management. I guess not."

I hear a noise myself, unfamiliar and nearby, and stand up to the porch rail and peer over the lawn, hoping I'll see Paul coming up the hill. But to the left, at the edge of the hardwoods, I can see, instead, all of Charley's studio. As advertised, it is a proper old New England seaman's chapel raised ten cockamamie feet above the pond surface on cypress pilings and connected to land by a catwalk. The church paint has been blasted off, leaving the lapped boards exposed. Windows are big, tall, clear lancets. The tin roof simmers in the sun of nearly noon.

And then Charley himself makes an appearance on the little back deck (happily in miniature), fresh from this morning's sore-jawed brainstorms, cooking up super plans for some rich neurosurgeon's ski palace in Big Sky, or a snorkeling hideaway in Cabo Cartouche—Berlioz still booming in his oversized ears. Bare-chested, tanned and silver-topped, in his usual khaki shorts, he is transporting from inside what looks like a plate of something, which he places on a low table beside a single wooden chair. I wish I could crank his big telescope down and survey the oarlock damage. That would interest me. (It's never easy to see why your ex-wife marries the man she marries if it isn't you again.)

I would like, however, to talk about Paul now: about the possibility of his coming down to Haddam to live, so as to stop limiting my fathering to weekends and holidays. I haven't entirely thought through all the changes to my own private dockets that his arrival will necessitate, the new noises and new smells in my air, new concerns for time, privacy, modesty; possibly a new appreciation for my own *moment* and freedoms; my *role*: a man retuned to the traditional, riding herd on a son full time, duties dads are made for and that I have missed but crave. (I could also bear to hear about the howlers Ann and Charley have been conducting, though that isn't my business and could easily turn out to be nothing: mischief Clarissa and Paul dreamed up to confuse everyone's agenda.)

But I'm thwarted by what to say, and frankly inhibited by Ann. (Perhaps this is another goal of divorce—to reinstitute the inhibitions you dispensed with when things were peachy.) It's tempting just to push off toward less controversial topics, like I did last night: my headaches with the Markhams and McLeods, rising interest rates, the election, Mr. Tanks—my most unforgettable character— with his truck, his gold-collared kitty and his Reader's Digest condenseds, a personal docket that makes my own Existence Period look like ten years of sunshine.

But Ann suddenly says, apropos of nothing but also, of course, of everything, "It's not really easy being an ex-spouse, is it? There isn't much use for us in the grand plan. We don't help anything go forward. We just float around unattached, even if we're not unattached." She rubs her nose with the back of her hand and snuffs. It's as if she's seen us outside our real bodies, like ghosts above the river, and is wishing we'd go away.

"There's always one thing we can do." She makes a point of

rarely using my name unless she's angry, so that most of the time I just seem to overhear her and offer a surprise reply.

"And what's that?" She looks at me disapprovingly, her dark brows clouded, her leg twitching in a barely detectable, spasmic way.

"Get married to each other again," I say, "just to state the obvious." (Though not necessarily the inevitable.) "Last year I sold houses to three couples"—two, actually—"each of whom was at one time married, and who got divorced and married, then divorced, then married their original true love again. If you can say it you can do it, I guess."

"We can put that on your tombstone," Ann says with patent distaste. "It's the story of your life. You don't know what you're going to say next, so you don't know what's a good idea. But if it wasn't a good idea to be married to you seven years ago, why would it be a better idea now? *You're* not any better." (This is unproved.) "It's conceivable you're worse."

"You're happily married anyway," I say, pleased with myself, though wondering who the "special someone" will be who'll make decisions about my tombstone. Best if it could be me.

Ann scrutinizes Charley treading long-strided, barefooted, barechested back inside his studio, no doubt to see if his miso is ready and to dig the soy sauce and shallots out of the Swedish mini-fridge. Charley, I notice, walks in a decidedly head-forward, hump-shouldered, craning way that makes him look surprisingly old—he's only sixty-one—but which makes *me* experience a sudden, unexpected and absolutely unwanted and impolitic sympathy for him. A good head shot with an oarlock is more telling on a man his age.

"You like thinking I ought to be sorry I married Charley. But I'm not sorry. Not at all," Ann says, her tan shoe giving another nervous little twitch. "He's a much better person than you are"—grossly unproved—"not that you have any reason to believe that, since you don't know him. He even has a good opinion of you. He tries to be a pal to these children. He thinks we've done a better than average job with them." (No mention of his daughter the novelist.) "He's nice to me. He tells the truth. He's faithful." My ass as a bet on that, though I could be wrong. Some men are. Plus, I'd like to hear an example of some sovereign truth Charley professes—no doubt some self-congratulating GOP Euclideanism: A penny saved is a penny earned; buy low, sell high; old Shakespeare sure knew his potatoes. My unmerited sympathy for him goes flapping away.

"I guess I didn't realize he held me in high esteem," I say (and I'm sure he doesn't). "Maybe we should be best friends. He asked me about that once. I was forced to decline."

Ann just shakes her head, rejecting me the way a great actor rejects a heckler in the audience—utterly and without really noticing.

"Frank, you know when we were all living down in Haddam five years ago, in that sick little arrangement you thrived on, and you were fucking that little Texas bimbo and having the time of your life, I actually put an ad in the *Pennysaver*, advertising myself as a woman who seeks male companionship. I actually risked boredom and rape just to keep things the way you liked them."

This is not the first time I've heard about the *Pennysaver* etc. And Vicki Arcenault was far from a bimbo. "We could've gotten remarried again anytime," I say. "And I wasn't having the time of my life. You divorced *me*, if you can remember precisely. We could've moved back in together. All kinds of things could've happened instead of what did." Possibly I'm about to hear that the most difficult milieu adjustment of my adult life didn't really have to be made (if only I'd been clairvoyant). It's the worst news anyone could hear, and for a nickel I'd pop Ann right in the chops.

"I didn't want to marry you." She keeps shaking her head, though less forcefully. "I just should've left, that's all. Do you even think you know why you and I got unmarried?" She takes a brief, angling look at me—uncomfortably like Sally's look. I'd rather not be delving into the past now, but into the future or at least the present, where I'm most at home. It's all my fault, though, for rashly bringing up the queasy matter of—or at least the word—marriage.

"I'm on record," I say, to answer her fair and square, "as believing our son died and you and I tried to cope with it but couldn't. Then I left home for a time and had some girlfriends, and you filed for divorce because you wanted me gone." I look at her haltingly, as if in describing that time in our life I'd as much as stated a Goya could've easily been painted by a grandmother in Des Moines. "Maybe I'm wrong."

Ann is nodding as if she's trying to get my view straight in her head. "I divorced you," she says slowly and meticulously, "because I didn't like you. And I didn't like you because I didn't trust you. Do you think you ever told me the truth once, the whole truth?" She taps her fingers on her bare thigh, not looking my way. (This is the perpetual theme of her life: the search for truth, and truth's defeat by the forces of contingency, most frequently represented by yours truly.)

"Tell the truth about what?" I say.

"Anything," she says, gone rigid.

"I told you I loved you. That was true. I told you I didn't want to get divorced. That was true too. What else was there?"

"There were important things that weren't being admitted by you. There's no use going into it now." She nods some more as if to ratify this. Though there is in her voice unexpected sadness and even a tremor of remorse, which makes my heart swell and my air passage stiffen, so that for one long festering moment I'm unable to speak. (I've been badly slipped up on here: she is distraught and dejected, and I cannot answer.)

"For a time," she continues, very, very softly and carefully, having slightly recovered herself, "for a long time, really, I knew we weren't all the way *to* the truth with each other. But that was okay, because we were trying to get there together. But suddenly I just felt hopeless, and I saw that truth didn't really exist to you. Though you got it from me the whole time."

Ann was forever suspecting other people were happier than she was, that other husbands loved their wives more, achieved greater intimacy, on and on. It is probably not unusual in modern life, though untrue of ours. But this is the final, belated, judgment on our ancient history: why love failed, why life broke into this many pieces and made this pattern, who at long last is to blame. Me. (Why now, I don't know. I still, in fact, don't know with any clarity what she's talking about.) And yet I so suddenly want to put my hand on her knee in hopes of consoling her that I do—I put my hand on her knee in hopes of consoling her. God knows how I can.

"Can't you tell me something specific?" I say gently. "Women? Or something I thought? Or something you thought I thought? Just some way you felt about me?"

"It wasn't something specific," she says painstakingly. Then stops. "Let's just talk about buying and selling houses now. Okay? You're very good at that." She turns an unpleasant and estimating eye on me. She doesn't bother to remove my warm and clammy hand from her smooth knee. "I wanted somebody with a true heart, that's all. That wasn't you."

"Goddamn it, I have a true heart," I say. Shocked. "And I *am* better. You can *get* better. You wouldn't know anyway."

"I came to realize," she says, uninterested in me, "that you were never entirely there. And this was long before Ralph died, but also after."

"But I loved you," I say, suddenly just angry as hell. "I wanted to go on being your husband. What else from the land of truth did you want? I didn't have anything else to tell you. *That* was the truth. There's plenty about anybody you can't know and are better off not to, for Christ sake. Not that I even know what they are. There's plenty about you, stuff that doesn't even matter. Plus, where the hell was I if I wasn't there?"

"I don't know. Where you still are. Down in Haddam. I just wanted things to be clear and certain."

"I do have a true heart," I shout, and I'm tempted again to give her a whack, though only on the knee. "You're one of those people who think God's *only* in the details, but then if they aren't the precise right details, life's all fucked up. You invent things that don't exist, then you worry about being denied whatever they are. And then you miss the things that *do* exist. Maybe it's you, you know? Maybe some truths don't even have words, or maybe the truth was what you wanted least, or maybe you're a woman of damn little faith. Or low self-esteem, or something."

I take my hand off her knee, unwilling now to be her consoler.

"We don't really need to go into this."

"You started it! You started it last night, about being and seeming, as if you were the world's expert on being. You just wanted something else, that's all. Something beyond what there is." She's right, of course, that we shouldn't go on with this, since this is an argument any two humans can have, could have, have had, no doubt are having at this moment all over the country to properly inaugurate the holiday. It really has nothing to do with the two of us. In a sense, we don't even exist, taken together.

I look around at the long porch, the great blue house on its big lawn, the shimmering windows behind which my two children are imprisoned, possibly lost to me. Charley has not come out onto his little porch again. What I'd thought he was doing—eating his ethical lunch in the ethical sunshine while we two battered at each other far above and out of earshot—is probably all wrong. I know nothing about him and should be kinder.

Ann just shakes her head again, without words accompanying. She eases herself down off the porch rail, lifts her chin, runs one finger from her temple back through her hair, and takes a quick look at the mirror window as if she saw someone coming—which she does: our son, Paul. Finally.

"I'm sorry," I say. "I'm sorry I drove you crazy when we were married. If I'd known I was going to, I wouldn't ever have married you. You're probably right, I rely on how I make things seem. It's my problem."

"I thought you thought how I thought," she says softly. "Maybe that's mine."

"I tried. I should've. I loved you very much all the time."

"Some things just can't be fixed later, can they?" she says.

"No, not later," I say. "Not later they can't."

And that is essentially and finally that.

*W*hy the long face?" Paul says to his mother and also to me. He has arrived, smirking, onto the porch looking far too much like the murder boy from Ridgefield last midnight, as committed to bad luck as a death row convict. And to my surprise he's even pudgier and somehow taller, with thick, adult eyebrows even more like his mom's, but with a bad, pasty complexion—nothing like he looked as recently as a month ago, and not enough anymore (or ever) like the small, gullible boy who kept pigeons at his home in Haddam. (How do these things change so fast?) His hair has been cut in some new, dopey, skint-sided, buzzed-up way, so that his busted ear is evident in its bloody little bandage. Plus, his gait is a new big-shoe, pigeon-toed, heel-scrape, shoulder-slump sidle by which he seems to give human shape to the abstract concept of condescending disapproval for everything in sight (the effects of stress, no doubt). He simply stands before us now—his parents—doing nothing. "I thought of a good homonym while I was getting dressed," he says slyly to either or both of us. " 'Meatier' and 'meteor.' Only they mean the same thing." He smirks, wishing to do nothing out here more than present himself in a way we won't like, someone who's lost IQ points or might be considering it.

"We were just discussing you," I say. I'd meant to mention

something about Dr. Rection, to speak to him via private code, but I don't. I am in fact sorry to see him.

His mother, however, steps right up to him—essentially ignoring him and me—grips his chin with her strong golfer's thumb and index finger, and turns his head to examine his split ear. (He is nearly her height.) Paul is carrying a black gym bag with *Paramount Pictures—Reach Your Peak* stenciled on its side in white (Stephanie's stepfather is a studio exec, so I'm told) and is wearing big black-and-red clunker Reeboks with silver lightning bolts on the sides, long and baggy black shorts, and a long midnight-blue tee-shirt that has *Happiness Is Being Single* printed on the front below a painting of a bright-red Corvette. He is a boy you can read, though he also is someone you'd be sorry to encounter on a city street. Or in your home.

Ann asks him in a private voice if he has what he needs (he has), if he has money (he does), if he knows where to meet in Penn Station (yes), if he feels all right (no answer). He cuts his knifey eyes at me and screws up one side of his mouth as if we're somehow in league against her. (We aren't.)

Then Ann abruptly says, "So okay, you don't look great, but go wait in the car, please. I want to have a word with your father."

Paul wrinkles his mouth into a mirthless little all-knowing look of scorn having to do with the very notion of his mother talking to his father. He has become a smirker by nature. But how? When?

"What happened to your ear, by the way?" I say, knowing what happened.

"I punished it," he says. "It heard a bunch of things I didn't like." He says this in a mechanistic monotone. I give him a little push in the direction he's come from, back through the house and out toward the car. And so he goes.

I'd appreciate it if you'd try to be careful with him," Ann says. "I want him back in good shape for his court appearance Tuesday." She has sought to lead me the way Paul has gone, "back through," but I'm having no part of her sinister house beautiful, with its poisonous élan, spiffy lines and bloodless color scheme. I lead us (I'm still inexplicably limping) down the steps to the lawn and around via the safer grass and through the shrubberies to the pea-gravel driveway, just the way a yardman would. "I think he's injury prone," she says quietly, following me. "I had a dream about him having an accident."

I step through the green-leafed, thick-smelling hydrangeas, blooming a vivid purple. "My dreams are always like the six o'clock news," I say. "Everything happening to other people." The sexual whir I experienced on seeing Ann is now long gone.

"That's fine about your dreams," she says, hands in pockets. "This one happened to be mine."

I don't wish to think about terrible injury. "He's gotten fat," I say. "Is he on mood stabilizers or neuroblockers or something?"

Paul and Clarissa are already conferring by my car. She is smaller and holding his left wrist in both her hands and trying to raise it to the top of her head in some kind of sisterly trick he's not cooperating with. "Come *on*!" I hear her say. "You putz."

Ann says, "He's not on anything. He's just growing up." Across the gravel lot is a robust five-bay garage that matches the house in every loving detail, including the miniature copper weather vane milled into the shape of a squash racket. Two bay doors are open, and two Mercedeses with Constitution State plates are nosed into the shadows. I wonder where Paul's station wagon is. "Dr. Stopler said he displays qualities of an only child, which is too bad in a way."

"I was an only child. I liked it."

"He's just *not* one. Dr. Stopler also said"—she's ignoring me, and why shouldn't she?—"not to talk to him too much about current events. They cause anxiety."

"I guess they do," I say. I am ready to say something caustic about childhood to seal my proprietorship of this day—revive Wittgenstein about living in the present meaning to live forever, blah, blah, blah. But I simply call a halt. No good's to come. All boats fall on a bitter tide—children know it better than anyone. "Do you think you know what's making him worse, just all of a sudden?"

She shakes her head, grips her right wrist with her left hand, and twists the two together, then gives me a small bleak smile. "You and me, I guess. What else?"

"I guess I was wanting a more complicated answer."

"Well, good for you." She rubs her other wrist the same way. "I'm sure you'll think of one."

"Maybe I'll have put on my tombstone 'He expected a more complicated answer.' "

"Let's quit talking about this, okay? We'll be at the Yale Club just for tonight if you need to call." She looks at me in a nose-wrinkled way and slouches a shoulder. She has not meant to be so harsh.

Ann, in amongst the hydrangeas, and for the first time today looks purely beautiful—pretty enough for me to exhale, my mind to open outward, and for me to gaze at her in a way I once gazed at her all the time, every single day of our old life together in Haddam. Now would be the perfect moment for a future-refashioning kiss, or for her to tell me she's dying of leukemia, or me to tell her I am. But that doesn't happen. She is smiling her stalwart's smile now, one that's long since disappointed and can face most anything if need be—lies, lies and more lies.

"You two have a good time," she says. "And please be careful with him."

"He's my son," I say idiotically.

"Oh, I know that. He's just like you." And then she turns and walks back toward the yard, continuing on, I suspect, out of sight and down to the water to have her lunch with her husband.

8

Clarissa Bascombe has snugged something tiny and secret into Paul's hand as we were leaving. And on our way up to Hartford, on our way up to Springfield, on our way to the Basketball Hall of Fame, he has held it without acknowledgment while I've yodeled away spiritedly about what I've thought will break our ice, get our ball rolling, fan our coals—start, via the right foot, what now feels like our last and most important journey together as father and son (though it probably isn't).

Once we swerve off busy CT 9 onto busier, car-clogged I-91, go past the grimy jai alai palace and a new casino run by Indians, I set off on my first "interesting topic": just how hard it is right here, ten miles south of Hartford, on July 2, 1988, when everything seems of a piece, to credit that on July 2, 1776, all the colonies on the seaboard distrusted the bejesus out of each other, were acting like separate, fierce warrior nations scared to death of falling property values and what religion their neighbors were practicing (like now), and yet still knew they needed to be happier and safer and went about doing their best to figure out how. (If this seems completely nutty, it's not, under the syllabus topic of "Reconciling Past and Present: From Fragmentation to Unity and Independence." It's totally relevant—in my view—to Paul's difficulty in integrating his fractured past with his hectic present so that the two connect up in a commonsense way and make him free and independent rather than staying disconnected and distracted and driving him bat-shit crazy. History's lessons are subtle lessons, inviting us to remember and forget selectively, and therefore are much better than psychiatry's, where you're forced to remember everything.)

"John Adams," I say, "said getting the colonies all to agree to be independent together was like trying to get thirteen clocks to strike at the same second."

"Who's John Adams?" Paul says, bored—his pale, bare, beginning-to-be-hairy legs crossed in a concertedly unmanly manner, one

Reebok with its Day-Glo-yellow lacing hiked up threateningly near the gearshift lever.

"John Adams was the first Vice President," I say. "He was the first person to say it was a stupid job. In public, that is. That was in 1797. Did you bring your copy of the Declaration of Independence?"

"Nuhhhn." This may mean either.

He is staring out at the reemerged Connecticut, where a sleek powerboat is pulling a tiny female water-skier, billowing the river's shiny skin. In a bright-yellow life vest, the girl heels *waaaaay* back against her towrope, carving a high, translucent spume out of the crusty wake.

"Why are you driving so eff-ing slow?" he says to be droll. Then, in a mocking old-granny's voice, "Everybody passes me, but I get there just as fast as the rest of 'em."

I, of course, intend to drive as fast as I want and no faster, but take an appraising look at him, my first since we shoved off from Deep River. His ear that wasn't bammed by the Mercedes's steering wheel has some gray fuzzy litter in it. Paul also doesn't much smell good, smells in fact like unbathed, sleep-in-your-clothes mustiness. He also doesn't seem to have brushed his teeth in a while. Possibly he is reverting to nature. "The original framers, you know," I say hopefully, but instantly getting the Constitution's authors muddled up with the signers of the Declaration (my persistent miscue, though Paul would never know), "they wanted to be free to make new mistakes, not just keep making the same old ones over and over as separate colonies and without showing much progress. That's why they decided to band together and be independent and were willing to sacrifice some controls they'd always had in hopes of getting something better—in their case, better trade with the outside world."

Paul looks at me contemptuously, as if I were an old radio tuned to a droning station that's almost amusing. "Framers? Do you mean farmers?"

"Some of them *were* farmers," I say. There's no use trying to haul this business back. I'm not facilitating good contact yet. "But people who won't quit making the same mistakes over and over are what we call conservatives. And the conservatives were all against independence, including Benjamin Franklin's son, who eventually got deported to Connecticut, just like you."

"So are conservatives farmers?" he says, feigning puzzlement but ridiculing me.

"A lot of them are," I say, "though they shouldn't be. What'd your sister give you?" I'm watching his closed left fist. We are quickly coming up into the Hartford traffic bottleneck. Elaborate road construction is on the right, between the interstate and the river—a soaring new off-ramp, a new parallel lane, arrows flashing, yellow behemoths full of Connecticut earth rumbling along beside us, white men in plastic hats and white shirts standing out in the snappy hot breeze, staring at thick scrolls of plans.

Paul looks at his fist as if he has no idea of what it contains, then slowly opens it, revealing a small yellow bow, the twin of the red one Clarissa gave me. "She gave you one," he mutters. "A red one. She said you said you wanted to be her bow, but it was spelled another way." I'm shocked at what a shady, behind-the-scenes con-niver my daughter is. Paul holds the two loose ends of his yellow bow and pulls them tight so the two loops daintily involute and make a knot. Then he puts the whole in his mouth and swallows it. "Umm," he says, and smiles at me evilly. "Good ribbance." (He's constructed this event, including the change in his sister's story, just for a punch line.)

"I guess I'll save mine till later."

"She gave me another one for later." He gives me his slant-eyed look. He is far ahead of me and will, I know, be a struggle.

"So okay, what's the problem with you and Charley?" I am maneuvering us past the Hartford downtown, the little gold-domed capital nearly lost in among big insurance high-rises. "Can't you two be civilized?"

"I can. He's an asshole." Paul is watching out his side as a squad of befezzed Shriners on Harleys comes alongside us. The Shriners are big, overstuffed, fat-cheeked guys dressed in gold-and-green silk harem guard getups with goggles and gloves and motorcycle boots. On their giant red Electra Glides they're as imposing as real harem guards, and of course are riding in safety-first staggered forma-tion, their motor noise even through the closed window loud and oppressive.

"Does braining him with an oarlock seem like a good solution to his being an asshole?" This will be my lone, unfelt concession to Charley's welfare.

The lead Shriner has spied Paul and given him a grinning, gloved thumbs-up. He and his crew are all big, jolly cream puffs, no doubt on their way to perform figure eights and seamless circles within circles for happy, grateful, shopping-center crowds, then hurry off to lead a parade down some town's Main Street.

"It's just *a* solution," Paul says, returning the lead harem guard's thumbs-up, putting his forehead to the window and grinning back sarcastically. "I like these guys. Charley should be one. What do you call them?"

"Shriners," I say, returning a thumbs-up from my side.

"What do they do?"

"It's not that easy to explain," I say, keeping us in our lane.

"I like their suits." He makes a muffled and unexpected little bark, a clipped Three Stooges, testy-terrier bark. He doesn't seem to want me to hear it but can't resist doing it again. One of the Shriners seems to catch on and makes what looks like a barking gesture of his own, then gives another thumbs-up.

"Are you barking again, son?" I sneak a look at him and swerve slightly to the right. An accident here would mean complete defeat.

"I guess so."

"Why is that? Do you think you're barking for Mr. Toby or something?"

"I *need* to do it." He's told me several times that in his view people now say "need" when they mean "want," which he thinks is hilarious. The Shriners drift back in the slow lane, probably nervous after I swerved at them. "It makes me feel better. I don't have to do it."

And frankly there's nothing I feel I can say if greeting the world with an occasional bark instead of the normal "Howzit goin' " or a thumbs-up makes him feel better. What's to get excited about? It might prove a hindrance under SAT testing conditions, or be a problem if he *only* barked and never spoke for the rest of his life. But I don't see it as that serious. No doubt, like all else, it will pass. I should probably try it. It might make *me* feel better.

"So are we going to the Basketball Hall of Fame or not?" he says, as though we'd been arguing about it. His mind is now who knows where? Possibly thinking he's thinking about Mr. Toby and thinking he wishes he weren't.

"We definitely are," I say. "It's coming up pretty quick. Are you stoked for it?"

"Yeah," he says. "Because I have to take a leak when we get there." And that's all he says for miles.

*I*n a hasty thirty minutes we slide off 91 into Springfield and go touring round through the old mill town, following the disappearing brown-and-white BB. HALL OF FAME signs until we're all the way north of downtown and pulled to a halt across from a dense brick housing project on a wide and windy trash-strewn boulevard by the on-ramp to the interstate we were just on. Lost.

Here is a marooned Burger King, attended around the outside by many young black men, and beside it, beyond the parking lot, a billboard showing Governor Dukakis smiling his insincere smile and surrounded by euphoric, well-fed, healthy-looking but poor children of every race and creed and color. No garbage has been picked up here for several days, and a conspicuous number of vehicles are abandoned or pillaged along the streetside. A hall of fame, any hall of fame within twenty miles of this spot, seems not worth the risk of being shot. In fact, I'm willing to just forget the whole thing and head for the Mass Pike, turn west and strike off for Cooperstown (170 miles), which would have us rolling into the Deerslayer Inn, where I've booked us a twin, just in time for cocktail hour.

And yet to bag it would be to translate mere lost directions into defeat (a poor lesson on a voyage meant to instruct). Plus *not* going, now that we're at street level, would be tantamount to temperamental; and in my worst 3 a.m. computations of self and character, temperamental's the thing I'm not, the thing that even a so-so father mustn't be.

Paul, who is ever suspicious of my resolve, has said nothing, just stared at Governor Dukakis through the windshield as if he were the most normal thing in the world.

I therefore execute a fast U-turn back toward town, cruise right into a BP delimart, ask directions out the window from a Negro customer just leaving, who courteously routes us back onto the interstate south. And in five minutes we're on the highway then off again, but this time at a perfectly well marked BBHOF exit, at the end of which we wind around booming freeway pilings and run smack into the Hall of Fame parking lot, where many cars are parked and where a neat little grass lawn with wood benches and saplings for picnickers and reflective roundball enthusiasts borders the Connecticut, sliding by, glistening, just beyond.

When I shut the motor off, Paul and I simply sit and stare through the saplings at the old factory husks on the far side of the river as if we expected some great sign to suddenly flash up, shouting "No! Here! It's over here now! You're in the wrong place! You missed us! You've done it wrong again!"

I should, of course, seize this inert moment of arrival to introduce old Emerson, the optimistic fatalist, to the trip's agenda, haul *Self-Reliance* out of the back seat, where Phyllis had it last. In particular I might try out the astute "Discontent is the want of self-reliance; it is infirmity of will." Or else something on the order of accepting the place providence has found for you, the society of your contemporaries, the connection of events. Each seems to me immensely serviceable if, however, they aren't contradictory.

Paul twists around and frowns back at the metal-and-glass Hall of Fame edifice, which looks less like a time-honored place of legend and enshrinement than a high-tech dental clinic, with its mulberry-colored, fake concrete-slab façade being just the ticket for putting edgy patients at their ease when they arrive for the first-time-ever cleaning and prophylaxis: "Here no one will harm, overcharge or give you bad news." Above these doors, though, are cloth banners in several bright colors, spelling out BASKETBALL: AMERICA'S GAME.

As he looks back, I notice Paul has a thick, ugly, inflamed and unhealthy-looking seed wart on the side of his right hand below his little finger. I also note, to my dismay, what may be a blue tattoo on the inside of his right wrist, something that looks like what a prisoner might do and Paul may have done himself. It spells a word I can't make out, though I don't like it and decide immediately that if his mother can't pay attention to his personal self, I'll have to.

"So what's inside?" he says.

"All kinds of good stuff," I say, postponing Emerson and trying to ignore the tattoo while mounting some roundball enthusiasm, since I want to get out of the car, possibly grab a sandwich inside and make a last-ditch phone plea to S. Mantoloking. "They've got films and uniform displays and photographs and chances to shoot baskets. I sent you the brochures." I'm not making it sound spectacular enough. Driving off might still be easier.

Paul gives me a self-satisfied look, as if a picture of himself shooting a basket were a source of amusement. For half a dollar I'd give *him* a flat-hand pop in the mouth too, for having a goddamned tattoo. Though that would violate, within our first hour together, my personal commitment to quality time.

"You can stand beside a big cutout of Wilt the Stilt and see how you match up sizewise," I say. Our air-conditioning is beginning to dissipate at idle.

"Who's Milt the Stilt?"

This I know he knows. He was a Sixers fan at the time he moved away. We went to games. He saw pictures. A basket in fact is bracketed at this moment to my garage on Cleveland Street. He is now, though, onto complexer games.

"He was a famous proctologist," I say. "Anyway, let's pick up a burger. I told your mother I'd buy you a sports lunch. Maybe they'll have a slam-dunk burger."

His eyes narrow at me across the seat. His tongue flicks nervously into each corner of his mouth. He likes this. His eyelashes, I notice for the first time (also like his mother's), have become ridiculously long. I can't keep up with him. "Are you hungry enough to eat the asshole out of a dead skunk?" he says, and blinks at me brazenly.

"Yeah, I'm pretty hungry." I pop open my door and let stiff dieselly breeze, freeway slam and the gamy river scent all flood inside in one hot, lethal breath. I am also tired of him already.

"Well, you're pretty hungry, then," he says. He has no good follow-up, so that all he can say is: "Do you think I have symptoms that need treatment?"

"No, I don't think you have any symptoms, son," I say down into the car. "I think you have a personality, which may be worse in your case." I should ask him about the dead bird but can't bring myself to.

"A-balone," Paul says. I stand and gaze over the hot roof of my car, over the Connecticut, over the green west of Massachusetts, where soon we'll be driving. I feel for some reason lonely as a shipwreck. "How do you say 'I'm hungry' in Italian?" he says.

"Ciao," I say. This is our oldest-timiest, most reliable, jokey way of conducting father-son business. Only today, due to technical difficulties beyond all control, it doesn't seem exactly to work. And our words get carried off in the breeze, with no one to care if we speak the intricate language of love or don't. Being a parent can be the worst of discontents.

"Ciao," Paul says. He has not heard me. "Ciao. How soon they forget." He is climbing out now, ready for our trip inside.

*O*nce in, Paul and I wander like lost souls who have paid five bucks to enter purgatory. (I have finally quit limping.)

Strategically placed, widely modern staircases with purple velvet crowd-control cords move us and others, herd-like, all the way up to Level 3, where the theme is basketball-history-in-a-nutshell. The air, here, is hypercleaned and frigid as Nome (to discourage lingering), everyone whispers like funeral-parlor guests, and lights are low to show off various long corridors of spotlit mummy-case artifacts preserved behind glass only a multiple-warhead missile could penetrate. Here is a thumbnail bio of inventor Naismith (who turns out to have been a Canadian!), alongside a replica of the old Doc's original scrawled-on-an-envelope basketball master plan: "To devise a game to be played in a gymnasium." (Success was certainly his.) Farther on is a black-and-white picture display featuring Forrest "Phogg" Allen, beloved old Jayhawks chalkboard wizard from the Twenties, and next to that, a replica of the "original" peach basket, along with a tribute to YMCAs everywhere. On all the walls there are grainy, treasured period photos of "the game" being played in shadowy wire-window gyms by skinny unathletic white boys, plus two hundred old uniform jerseys hung from the dark rafters like ghosts in a spook house.

A few listless families enter a dark little Action Theatre, which Paul avoids by hitting the can, though I watch from the doorway as the history of the game unfolds before our preprandial eyes, while the action sounds of the game are piped in.

In eight minutes we progress briskly down to Level 2, where there's more of the same, though it's more up-to-date and recognizable, at least to me. Paul expresses a passing spectator's interest in Bob Lanier's size 22 shoe, a red-and-yellow plastic cross-section model of an as-yet-unmangled human knee, and a film viewable in another little planetarium-like theater, dramatizing how preternaturally large basketball players are and what they can all "do with the ball," in contrast to how minuscule and talentless the rest of us have to suffer through life being. In this way it is a true shrine—devoted to making ordinary people feel like insignificant outsiders, which Paul seems not to mind. (The Vince was in fact more welcoming.)

"We played at camp," he says flatly as we pause outside the amphitheater, both of us looking in as huge, muscular, uniformed black men ram ball after ball through hoop after hoop on a mesmerizing four-sided screen, to the crowd's rapt amazement and smattered applause.

"And so were you a major force," I ask. "Or an intimidator, possibly a franchise or an impact player?" I'm happy to have unfreighted exchange on any subject, though I stare at his shorts, tee-shirt and skinhead and don't like any of it. He seems to me to be in disguise.

"Not really," he says, absolutely earnest. "I can't jump. Or run. Or shoot, and I'm a lefty. And I don't give a shit. So I'm not really cut out for it."

"Lanier was a lefty," I say. "So was Russell." He may not know who they are, even though he'd recognize their shoes. The audience in the jam-o-rama amphitheater makes a low "Ooooo" of utter reverence. Other men with their boys stand beside us, looking in, uninterested in sitting down.

"We weren't really playing to win anyway," Paul says.

"What were you playing for? Fun?"

"Thur-uh-py," he says to make a joke of it, though he seems unironic. "Some of the kids would always forget what month it was, and some of them talked too loud or had seizures, which was bad. And if we played basketball, even stupid basketball, they all got better for a while. We had 'share your thoughts' after every game, and everybody had a lot better thoughts. For a while at least. Not me. Chuck played basketball at Yale." Paul's hands are in his shorts pockets as he stares at the ceiling, which is industrial modern and shadowy, with metal girders, trusses, rafters, sprinkling-system pipes, all painted black. Basketball, I think, is American's postindustrial national pastime.

"Was he any good?" I may as well ask.

"I don't know," he says, digging a finger into his mossy ear and creasing the corner of his mouth like a country hick. A second loud "Ooooo" comes from inside. Someone, a woman, shouts out, "Yes! I swear to God. Look at that!" I don't know what she saw.

"You know the one thing you can do that's truly unique to you and that society can't affect in any way?" he says. "We learned this in camp."

"I guess not." People out here with us are starting to stray away.

"Sneeze. If you sneeze in some stupid-fuck way, or in a loud way that pisses people off in movies, they just have to go along with it. Nobody can say, 'Sneeze a different way, asshole.' "

"Who told you that?"

"I don't remember."

"Does that seem unusual?"

"Yes." Gradually he lets his eyes come down from the ceiling but not to me. His finger quits excavating his ear. He is now uncomfortable for being unironic and a kid.

"Don't you know that's the way everything is when you get to be old? Everybody lets you do anything you want to. If they don't like it, they just don't show up anymore."

"Sounds great," Paul says, and actually smiles, as if such a world where people left you alone was an exhibit he'd like to see.

"Maybe it is," I say, "maybe it isn't."

"What's the most misunderstood automotive accessory?" He's ready to derail serious talk, alert to the dangers inherent in my earnest voice.

"I don't know. An air filter," I say, as the dunk-o-rama film gets over in the auditorium. I have seen no big cutout of Milt the Stilt, as was promised.

"That's pretty close." Paul nods very seriously. "It's a snow tire. You don't appreciate it until you need it, but then it's usually too late."

"Why does that make it misunderstood? Why not just underappreciated?"

"They're the same," he says, and starts walking away.

"I see. Maybe you're right." And we both walk off then toward the stairs.

*O*n Level 1, there's a busy gift boutique, a small room dedicated to sports media (zero fascination for me), an authentic locker room exhibit, a vending machine oasis, plus some gimmicky, hands-on exhibits Paul takes mild interest in. I decide to make my call to Sally before we hit the road. Though I have yet to see a legitimate snack bar, so that Paul wanders off in his new heavy-gaited, pigeon-toed, arm-swinging way I hate, to the vending-machine canteen with money I've supplied (since his is evidently for some other uses—a possible kidnap emergency) and my order to bring back "something good."

The phone area is a nice, secluded, low-lit little alcove beside the bathrooms, with thick, noise-muffling wall-to-wall covering everything, and the latest black phone technology—credit card slits, green computer screens and buttons to amplify sound in case you can't believe what you're hearing. It is an ideal place for a crank or ransom call.

Sally, when I punch in her 609 number, answers thrillingly on the first jingle.

"So where in the world are *you*?" she says, her voice tingly and happy but also a voice that's taking a reading. "I left you a long and poignant message last night. I may have been drunk."

"And I tried to call you right back all this morning, to see if you'd fly up here in a chartered Cessna and come to Cooperstown with us. Paul thinks it'd be great. We'd have some fun."

"Well. My goodness. I don't know," Sally says, acting happily confused. "Where are you right now?"

"Right now I'm in the Basketball Hall of Fame. I mean we're visiting it—we're not enshrined here. Not yet anyway." I feel the most buoyant good spirit expand in my chest. All is not pissed away.

"But isn't that in Ohio?"

"No, it's in Springfield, Mass, where the first peach basket was nailed to the first barn door and the rest is history. Football's in Ohio. We don't have time for that."

"Where *are* you going, again?"

She is enjoying all this, possibly relieved, acting breathless and appealed to. Plans might still spring to life. "Cooperstown, New York. One hundred seventy miles away," I say enthusiastically. A woman several nooks down leans back and glowers at me as if I were making a call that amplified my voice in her receiver. Possibly she feels at risk being near a person in legitimately high spirits. "So whaddaya say?" I say. "Fly up to Albany right now, and we'll pick you up." I *am* talking too loud and need to put a lid on it before a Hall of Fame SWAT team is summoned. "I'm serious," I say, more modulated, but more serious too.

"Well, you're very sweet to ask."

"I *am* very sweet. That's right. But I'm not letting you off the hook." I say this a bit too loud again. "I just woke up this morning and realized I was crazy as hell last night and that I'm crazy about you. And I don't want to wait till Monday or whenever the hell." For a nickel I'd muster Paul right back to the car and beat it back down to South Mantoloking along with all the other beach yahoos. Though I'd be a bad man for doing so. Being willing to invite Sally in on our sacred hombre-to-hombre is already bad enough—though like anybody else, Paul'd have more fun being along on something technically illicit. The world, as I told him, lets you do what you want if you can live with the consequences. We're all free agents.

"Could I ask you something?" she says, two jots too serious.

"I don't know," I say. "It may be too serious. I'm not a serious man. And it can't be about you not coming up here."

"Would you tell me what you find so enthralling now that you didn't notice last night?" Sally says this in a self-mocking, good-natured way. But important info is being sought. Who could blame her?

"Well," I say, my mind suddenly whirring. A man exits the bathroom, so that I get a stern whiff of urinal soap. "You're a grown-up, and you're exactly the way you seem, at least as far as I can tell. Everybody's not like that." Including me. "And you're loyal and you have a quality of straight-talking impartiality"—this sounds wrong—"that isn't inconsistent with passion, which I *really* like. I guess I just have a feeling some things have to be investigated further between you and me or we'll both be sorry. Or *I* will anyway. Plus, you're just about the prettiest woman I know."

"I'm just about *not* the prettiest woman you know," Sally says. "I'm pretty in a usual way. And I'm forty-two. And I'm too tall." She sighs as though being tall made her tired.

"Look, just get on a plane and come up here, and we'll talk all about how pretty you are or aren't while the moon sets on romantic Lake Otsego and we enjoy a complimentary cocktail." While Paul goes who knows where? "I just feel a tidal attraction to you, and all boats rise on a rising tide."

"Your boat seems to rise most when I'm not around," Sally says with distinctly diminished good nature. (It's possible I'm not providing convincing answers again.) The woman in the far phone nook

snaps closed an immense black patent-leather purse and goes striding quickly out. "Do you remember saying you wanted to be the
'dean' of New Jersey realtors last night? Do you even remember
that? You talked all about soybeans and drought and shopping centers. We drank a lot. But you were in a state of some kind. You also
said you were beyond affection. Maybe you're still in some state." (I
should probably toss off a couple of barks to prove I'm nuts.) "Did
you visit your wife?"

This is not the wisest tack for her to take, and I should actually
warn her off. But I simply stare at my little black phone screen,
where it states in cool green letters: *Do you wish to make another call?*

"Right. I did," I say.

"And how was that—was that nice?"

"Not particularly."

"Do you think you like her better when she's not around?"

"She's not 'not around,' " I say. "We're divorced. She's remarried to a sea captain. It's like Wally. She's *officially* dead, only we still
talk." I'm suddenly as deflated by a thought of Ann as I was happy to
be thinking of Sally, and what I'm tempted to say is, "But the real
surprise is she's leaving ole Cap'n Chuck, and we're getting married
again and moving to New Mexico to start up an FM station for the
blind. That's really the reason I'm calling—not to invite you to
come up here, just to give you my good news. Aren't you happy for
me?" There's an unwieldy silence on the line, after which I say: "I
really just called up to say I had a good time last night."

"I wish you'd stayed. That's what my message said, if you haven't
heard it yet." Now she is mum. Our little contretemps and my little
rising tide have gone off together in a stout, chilly breeze. Good
spirits are notoriously more fragile than bad.

A tall, big-chested man in a pale-blue jumpsuit comes strolling
down the phone alcove, holding a little girl by the hand. They stop
along the opposite phone bank, where the man begins to make a
call, reading off a paper scrap as the little girl, in a frilly pink skirt
and a white cowboy shirt, watches him. She looks at me across the
shadowy way—a look, like mine, of needing sleep.

"Are you still there?" Sally says, possibly apologetic.

"I was watching a guy make a phone call. I guess he reminds me
of Wally, though he shouldn't, since I don't think I ever saw Wally."

Another mum pause. "You really have very few sharp angles, you know, Frank. You're too smooth from one thing to the next. I can't keep up with you very well."

"That's what my wife thinks too. Maybe you two should discuss it. I think I'm just more at ease in the mainstream. It's my version of sublime."

"And you're also very cautious, you know," Sally says. "And you're noncommittal. You know that, don't you? I'm sure that's what you meant last night about being beyond affection. You're smooth and you're cautious and you're noncommittal. That's not a very easy combination for me." (Or a good one, I'm sure.)

"My judgments aren't very sound," I say, "so I just try not to cause too much trouble." Joe Markham said something like this yesterday. Maybe I'm being transformed into Joe. "But when I feel something strong, I guess I jump in. That's how I feel right now." (Or did.)

"Or you seem to anyway," Sally says. "Are you and Paul having lots of fun?" A shift back in the direction of rising spirits, speaking of smooth.

"Yeah. Loads and loads. You would too." I get a faint but putrid sniff of the dead grackle still on my receiver hand. Apparently it's to be on my skin forever and ever. I intend to ignore this last remark about *seeming* to jump in.

"I'm sorry you don't think your judgment's very sound," Sally says, falsely perky. "That doesn't bode very well for how you say you feel about me either, does it?"

"Whose cuff links were those on the bed table?" This, of course, is rash and against all good judgment. But I'm indignant, even though I have no good right to be.

"They were Wally's," Sally says, perky but not falsely. "Did you think they belonged to somebody else? I just got them out to send to his mother."

"Wally was in the Navy, I thought. He almost got blown up in a boat. Isn't that right?"

"He did. But he was in the Marines. Not that it matters. You just made up the Navy for him. It's all right."

"Okay. Yeah, I was callin' about this house you got for rent on Friar Tuck Drive," I hear the big man say across the alcove. His little girl is staring up at her dad/unc/abductor as if he'd told her he needed some moral support and she should focus all her thoughts his way. "What's the rent on that one?" he says. He is a southwest-erner, possibly a twangy Texan. Though he isn't wearing dusty old Noconas but a pair of white Keds no-lace low-tops of the male-nurse/minimum-security-prisoner variety. These are Texans with-out a ranch. My guess is he's busted out of the oil patch, a new-age Joad moving his precious little brood up to the rust belt to set life spinning in a new orbit. It occurs to me the McLeods may likewise be in hot financial water and be in need of a break but are too stub-born to say so. That would change my attitude about the rent, though not totally.

"Frank, did you hear what I said, or have you just drifted off into space?"

"I was watching the same guy trying to rent a house. I wish I had something I could show him in Springfield. Of course, I don't live here."

"Okay-yay," Sally says, ready for our conversation to float off too. I have registered whose cuff links they were, though they aren't any of my business. The Navy-Marine mixup I can't explain. "Is it pretty up there?" she asks brightly.

"Yeah, it's beautiful. But really," I say, suddenly picturing Sally's face, a winning face, worth wanting to kiss. "Don't you want to come up here? I'm popping for everything. Your money's no good. All you can eat. Double stamps. Carte blanche."

"Why don't you just call me some other time, okay? I'll be home tonight. You're very distracted. You're probably tired."

"Are you sure? I'd really like to see you." I should mention that I'm not beyond affection, because I'm not.

"I'm sure," she says. "And I'm just going to say good-bye now."

"Okay," I say. "Okay."

"Good-bye now," she says, and we hang up.

The little cowgirl across the alcove gives me a fretful look. Possi-bly I was talking too loud again. Her big Texan daddy swivels half around to look at me. He has a big tough-jawed face, unruly dark hair and enormous pipe-fitter's mitts. "No," he says decisively into the phone. "No, that ain't gonna work, that's way outa line. Forget that." He hangs up, crumpling his little scratch of paper, which he drops on the carpet.

He fishes in his breast pocket, pulls out a pack of Kools, takes one out with his mouth, still holding little Suzie's hand, lights up one-handed with a thick, mean-looking Zippo. He blows a big, frustrated, lung-shuddering drag right at the international NO SMOKING insignia attached to the carpeted ceiling, and I immediately expect to be drenched in cold chemicals, for alarms to trigger, security people to skid around the corner on the dead run. But nothing happens. He gives me an antagonistic look where I'm lost in front of my phone screen. "You got a problem?" he says, fishing back in his cigarette pocket for something he doesn't find.

"No," I say, grinning. "I just have a daughter about your daughter's age"—a total fabrication, followed hard by another one—"and she just reminded me of her."

The man looks down at the child, who must be eight and who looks up at him smiling, charmed by being noticed but unsure exactly how to be charmed. "You want me to sell this one to you?" he says, at which moment the little girl throws her head back and lets her whole self go limp so she's hanging off his big mitt, smiling and shaking her pretty head.

"Nope, nope, nope, nope, nope," she says.

"They're too expensive for me," he says in his Texas accent. He raises his child off the ground, limp as a carcass, and gives her a dainty little swing out.

"You cain't sell me," she says in a throaty, bossy voice. "I'm not for sale."

"You're for sale big time, that's whut," he says. I smile at his joke—a helpless fatherish way of expressing love to a stranger in a time of hardship. I should appreciate it. "You don't have a house to rent, do you?"

"Sorry," I say. "I'm not from Springfield. I'm just here for a visit. My son's running around in here someplace."

"You know how long it takes to get up here from Oklahoma?" he says, his cigarette in one side of his big mouth.

"It's probably not that quick."

"Two days, two nights straight. And we been in the KOA for three damn days. I got a highway job starts up in a week, and I can't find anything. I'm gonna have to send this orphan back."

"Not me," the little girl says in her bossy voice and lets her knees give way, hanging on. "I'm not an orphan."

"You!" the big guy says to his daughter and frowns, though not angrily. "You're my whole damn problem. If I didn't have you with me, *somebody* would've been considerate of me by now." He gives me a big leer and a roll of the eyes. "Stand up on your feet, Kristy."

"You're a redneck," his daughter says, and laughs.

"I might be, and I might be worse than that," he says more seriously. "You think your daughter's like this outfit?" He's already starting to walk away, holding his daughter's tiny hand in his great one.

"They're both pretty sweet when they want to be, I bet," I say, watching his child's quick knock-kneed steps and thinking of Clarissa giving Ann and me, or possibly just me, the finger. "The holiday'll probably change everything." Though I don't know how. "I'll bet you find someplace to stay today."

"It's that or drastic measures," he says, walking away toward the lobby.

"What's that mean?" his daughter says, hanging onto his hand. "What's drastic measures?"

"Being your ole man, for starters," he says, as they go out of sight. Then he adds, "But it might mean a whole lot of things too."

*P*aul, when I walk out to find him, is not waiting with an armload of vending-machine provisions but has taken up an observer position alongside "The Shoot-Out" exhibit, which dominates one whole wall-side of Level 1 and where a lot of visitors have already become noisy participators.

"The Shoot-Out" is nothing more than a big humming people-mover conveyor belt, just like in an airport, but built right alongside and at the same level as a spotlit arena area, full of basketball backboards, hoops and posts, at varying heights and distances from the belt—ten feet, five yards, two feet, ten yards. Along beside the moving handrail and between the little arena and the people-mover itself, a trough of basketballs is continuously being replenished through a suction tube under the floor, exactly in the manner of a bowling alley rack. A human being getting on the moving floor (as many already are) and traveling at approximately one half of one mile an hour, can simply pick up ball after ball and shoot basket after basket—jump shots, hooks, two-hand sets, over the back, one's whole repertoire—until he reaches the other end, where he steps off. (Such a screwy but ingenious machine has undoubtedly been invented by someone with a dual major in Crowd Control and Automated Playground Management from Southern Cal, and anybody in his right mind would've fought to get ground-floor money in on it. In fact, if the Hall of Fame management didn't insist that you first mull past murky old Phogg Allen pictures and replicas of Bob Lanier's dogs, everyone would spend his whole visit right down here where the real action is, and the rest of the building could go back to being a dentist's office.)

A pocket-size grandstand has been built just on the other side of the conveyor, and plenty of spectators are up there now, noisily ya-hooing and razzing their kids, brothers, nephews, stepsons who're taking the ride and trying to shoot the eyes out of all the baskets.

Paul, who's on the sidelines by the entrance gate, where there's a line of kids waiting to get on, seems on the alert, as though he were running the whole contraption. He is, however, watching a scrappy, thick-thighed white kid in a New York Knicks uniform, who's hustling around among the backboards, kicking trapped balls toward the suction tube gutter, tipping stuck balls out of the nets, snapping vicious passes back at kids on the conveyor and occasionally taking a graceless little short-armed hook shot, which always goes in, no matter what basket he shoots at. No doubt he's the manager's son.

"Did you try out your patented two-hand set yet?" I say, coming up right behind Paul and over the noise. I instantly smell his sour sweat smell when I put my hand on his shoulder. There's also, I can see, a thick scabby jag in his scalp, where whoever authored his skint haircut made a mistake. (Where are such things done?)

"That'd be good, wouldn't it," he says coldly, going on watching the white kid. "That nitwit thinks because he works here his game's gonna improve. Except the floor's tilted and the baskets aren't regulation. So he's actually fucked." This seems to make him satisfied. He has purchased no food that I can see.

"You better give it a try," I say over the basketball clatter and the thrum the giant machine's making. I feel exactly like a dad among other real dads, encouraging my son to do what he doesn't want to do because he's afraid he'll be bad at it.

"D'you always dribble before you shoot?" someone in the bleachers shouts out at the moving conveyor. A short bald man who's about to try a precarious hook shot yells back without even looking: "Why don't you try eating me," then wings a shot that misses everything and causes other people in the bleachers to laugh.

"You do it." Paul snorts a disparaging little snuffle. "I saw some Nets scouts in the crowd." The Nets are his favorite team to belittle, because they're no good and from New Jersey.

"Okay, but then *you* have to do it." I cuff his shoulder in an unnatural comradely way, catching another unappetizing look at his offended ear.

"I don't *have* to do anything," he says without looking at me, just watching the bright, indoor air a-throng with orange balls.

"Okay, you just watch me, then," I say lamely.

I step around him and into line and am quickly right up to the little gate behind a small black kid. I take a look back at Paul, who's watching me, leaning an elbow on the plywood fence that separates the arena from the waiting line, his face completely unawed, as if he expects to see me do something stupid beyond all previous efforts.

"Check out how my balls rotate," I call back at him, hoping it'll embarrass him, but he doesn't seem to hear me.

And then I'm up on the rumbling belt, moving right to left as the rack of balls and the little forest of stage-lit baskets, backboards and poles begins quickly gliding past in the opposite way. I'm instantly nervous about falling down, and don't make a move toward a ball. The black kid in front of me has on a huge purple-and-gold team jacket that says *Mr. New Hampshire Basketball* on the back in sparkling gold letters, and he seems able to handle at least three balls at any one time, virtually spewing shots at every goal, every height, every distance, and with each shot emitting a short, breathy *whoof* like a boxer throwing a punch. And of course everything goes spinning in: a bank, a set, a one-hander, a fall-away, a short-arm hook like the ball boy's—everything but an alley-oop and a lean-in power jam.

I lay hands on my first ball halfway through the ride, still not confident about my balance, my heart suddenly starting to beat fast because other shooters are behind me. I frown out toward the clutter of red metal posts and orange baskets, set my feet as well as I can, cock the ball behind my ear and heave up a high arching shot that misses the basket I expected to hit, strikes a lower one, bounces out and nearly drops in the very lowest goal, which I hadn't actually seen.

I quick grab another ball as Mr. New Hampshire Basketball is putting up shot after shot, making his stagy little *whoof* noise and hitting nothing but net. I take similar aim at a medium-height basket at a medium distance, hoist my shot off one-handed, though well gyroed by a good rotation I learned from watching TV, and come pretty damn close to making it, though one of Mr. Basketball's shots hisses through just ahead and knocks mine down off into the gutter. (I also lose my balance and have to grab the plastic escalator handrail to keep from falling over sideways and causing a pileup.) Mr. B. flashes me a suspicious look over his gigantic purple roll collar, as if I'd been trying to mess with his head. I smile at him and mutter, "Lucky."

"You're supposed to dribble *before* you shoot, you cluck," the same idiot yorks out again amid a lot of other shouting and metallic hum and machinery smell. I turn around and take a squinty look at the crowd, which is essentially invisible because of the bright lights on the baskets. I don't really give a shit who yelled at me, though I'm sure it's not someone whose son is in the audience, smirking.

I complete one more wayward shot before I'm to the end—a lumpy, again off-balance one-hander that clears everything and drops behind the baskets and the wooden barrier, where basketballs aren't supposed to go. "Good arch!" the little wiseacre gym-rat kid cracks as he climbs back to retrieve my ball. "Wanna play horse for a million bucks?"

"Maybe I'll have to start trying, then," I say, my heart pounding as I step off the belt onto terra firma, all the excitement over now.

Mr. New Hampshire Basketball is already walking away toward the sports-media gallery with his father, a tall black man in a green silk Celtics jacket and matching green leisure pants, his long arm over the boy's scrawny shoulders, no doubt laying out a superior strategy for rubbing off the screen, picking up the dribble, taking the J while drawing the foul—all just words to me, a former sportswriter, with no practical application on earth.

Paul is staring at me down the length of the conveyor. Conceivably he's been barking his approval while I've been shooting but doesn't want it known now. I have in fact enjoyed the whole thing thoroughly.

"Take your best shot!" I shout through the loud crowd noise. The ball boy, off to one side now, is chatting up his chunky, ponytailed blond sweetheart, laying his two meaty hands on her two firm shoulders and goo-gooing in her eyes like Clark Gable. For some reason, having I'm sure to do with queuing theory, no one is on the conveyor at the moment. "Come on," I shout at Paul with false rancor. "You can't do any worse than I did!" Only a few spectators remain in the darkened grandstand. Others are heading off to other exhibits. It is the perfect time for Paul. "Come on, Stretch," I say— something I vaguely remember from a sports movie.

Paul's lips move—words I just as well can't hear. A jocose "Up your ass" or a lusty "Why don't you eat shit"—his favorite swear words from another, antique vintage (mine). He looks behind him, where there's now mostly empty lobby, then just ambles slowly up to the entrance in his clumsy, toes-in gait, pauses to look down toward me again with what appears to be disgust, stares for a moment at the spotlit baskets and stanchions, and then simply steps on, completely alone.

The conveyor moves him seemingly much more slowly than I myself was moved, and certainly leisurely enough to get off six or seven good shots and even to dribble before he shoots. The ball boy takes a casually demeaning look to where Paul is moving along in his garbage-pail shoes and sinister haircut, hands fixed oddly on his hips. He cracks a nasty grin, says something to his girlfriend so she'll look, which she does, though in a kinder, more indulgent older-girl's way at the goony boy who can't help being goony but has a big heart and racks up top math scores (which he doesn't).

When he comes to the end—having faced the baskets the whole way, never once looking at me, just staring into the little arena like a mesmerist, never taking a shot or even touching a ball, only gliding—he just wobbles off on the carpet and walks over and stands by me, where I've been watching like any other dad.

"High fives," a straggler shouts in a ridiculing voice from the grandstand.

"Next time think about trying a shot," I say, ignoring the shout, since I'm happy with his efforts.

"Are we coming back here anytime soon?" He looks at me, his small gray eyes showing concern.

"No," I say. "You can come back with *your* son." Another batch of adults is invading the bleachers, with more sons and daughters plus a few dads beginning to line up at the gate, checking out how the whole gizmo works, calculating the fun they're about to have.

"I liked that," Paul says, looking at the stage-lit posts and baskets. I hear the surprising voice of some boy he once was (seemingly only a month ago, now disappeared). "I'm thinking I'm thinking all the time, you know? Except when I was on that thing I quit. It was nice."

"Maybe you should do it again," I say, "before it gets crowded." Unhappily, there's no way for him to stay on The Shoot-Out for the rest of his days.

"No, that's okay." He's watching new kids glide away from the gate, new balls arching into the vivid air, the first inevitable misses. "I don't usually like things like that. This was an exception. I don't usually like things I'm supposed to like." He stares at the other kids empathetically. This cannot be a simple truth to admit to your father—that you don't like the things you're supposed to like. It is adult wisdom, though most grown men would fail of it.

"Your ole man isn't very good at it either. If it makes you feel any better. He'd like to be. Maybe you can tell me what you liked about it that made you quit thinking you're thinking."

"You're not that old." Paul looks at me peevishly.

"Forty-four."

"Umm," he says—a thought possibly too fretsome to speak. "You could still improve."

"I don't know," I say. "Your mother doesn't think so." This doesn't qualify as a current event.

"Do you know the best airline?"

"No, let's hear it."

"Northwest," Paul says seriously. "Because it flies to the Twin Cities of Minneapolis and Saint Paul." And suddenly he's trying to suppress a big guffaw. For some reason this is funny.

"Maybe I'll take you out there sometime on a camping trip." I watch basketballs fill the interior air like bubbles.

"Do they have a hall of fame in Minnesota?"

"Probably not."

"Okay, good," he says. "We can go anytime, then."

On our way out we make a fast foray through the gift boutique. Paul, at my instruction, picks out tiny gold basketball earrings for his sister and a plastic basketball paperweight for his mother—gifts he feels uncertain they'll like, though I tell him they will. We discuss a rabbit's foot with a basketball attached as an olive branch gesture for Charley, but Paul goes balky after staring at it a minute. "He has everything he wants," he says grudgingly, without adding "including your wife and your kids." So that after buying two tee-shirts for ourselves, we pass back out into the parking lot with Charley ungifted, which suits both of us perfectly.

On the asphalt it is full, hot Massachusetts afternoon. New cars have arrived. The river has gone ranker and more hazy. We've spent forty-five minutes in this hall of fame, which pleases me since we got our fill, exchanged words of hope, encountered specific subjects of immediate interest and concern (Paul thinking he's thinking) and seem to have emerged a unit. A better start than I expected.

The big, jumpsuited Oklahoman is sprawled out with his tiny daughter under one of the linden saplings by the river's retaining wall. They are enjoying their lunch from tinfoil packets spread on the ground, and drinking out of an Igloo cooler, using paper cups. He has his Keds and socks off and his pants rolled up like a farmer. Little Kristy is as pristine as an Easter present and talking to him in a confidential, animated way, wiggling one of his toes with her two hands while he stares at the sky. I'm tempted to wander over and offer a word of parting, talk to them twice because I've talked to them once, act as a better welcome committee for the Northeast Corridor, dream up some insider dope "I just thought about" and am glad to find him still here to share—something in the realty line. As always, I'm moved by the displacement woes of other Americans.

Only there's nothing I know that he doesn't (such is the nature of realty lore), and I decide against it and just stand at my car door and watch them respectfully—their backs to me, their modest picnic offering this big, panoramic, foreign-seeming river as comfort and company, all their hopes focused on a new settlement. Some people do nicely on their own and by the truest reckoning set themselves down where they'll be happiest.

"Care to guess how hungry I am?" Paul says over the hot car roof, waiting for me to unlock his side. He is squinting in the sun, looking unsavory as a little perpetrator.

"Let's see," I say. "You were supposed to get us something from the fucking vending machines." I say "fucking" just to amuse him.

The freeway pounds along behind us—cars, vans, U-Hauls, buses—America on a move-in Saturday afternoon.

"I guess I just fucked up," he says to challenge me back. "But I could eat the asshole out of a dead Whopper." An insolent leer further disfigures his pudgy kid's features.

"Soup'd be better on an empty brain," I say, and pop his door lock.

"Okay, doc-taaah! Doc-tah, doc-tah, doc-tah," he says, snapping open his door and ducking in. I hear him bark in the car. "Bark, bark, bark, bark." I don't know what this is to signify: happiness (like a real dog)? Happiness's defeat at the hands of uncertainty? Fear and hope, I seem to remember from someplace, are alike underneath.

From the linden tree shade, Kristy hears something in the afternoon breeze—a dog barking somewhere, my son in our car. She turns and looks toward me, puzzled. I wave at her, a fugitive wave her bumpkin father doesn't see. Then I duck my own head into the hot-as-an-oven car with my son and we are on our way to Cooperstown.

*A*t one o'clock, we pull in for a pit stop, and I send Paul for a sack of Whalers and Diet Pepsis while I wash dead grackle off my hand in the men's. And then we're off spinning again down the pike, past the Appalachian Trail and through the lowly Berkshires, where not long ago Paul was a camper at Camp Unhappy, though he makes no mention of it now, so screwed down is he into his own woolly concerns—thinking he's thinking, silently barking, his penis possibly tingling.

After a half hour of breathing Paul's sour-meat odor, I make a suggestion that he take off his *Happiness Is Being Single* shirt and put on his new one for a change of scenery and as an emblematic suiting-up for the trip. And to my surprise he agrees, skinning the old fouled one off right in the seat, unabashedly exposing his untanned, unhairy and surprisingly jiggly torso. (Possibly he'll be a big fatty, unlike Ann or me; though it doesn't make any difference if he will simply live past fifteen.)

The new shirt is Xtra large, long and white, with nothing but a big super-real orange basketball on its front and the words *The Rock* underneath in red block letters. It smells new and starched and chemically clean and, I'm hoping, will mask Paul's unwashed, gunky aroma until we check into the Deerslayer Inn, he can take a forced bath and I can throw his old one away on the sly.

For a while after our Whalers, Paul again grows moodily silent, then heavy-eyed, then slips off to a snooze while green boilerplate Massachusetts countryside scrolls past on both sides. I turn on the radio for a holiday weather and traffic check and conceivably to learn the facts of last night's murder, which, for all the time and driving that's elapsed, occurred only eighty miles south, still well within the central New England area, the small radar sweep of grief, loss, outrage. But nothing comes in on AM or FM, only the ordinary news of holiday fatality: six for Connecticut, six for Mass., two for Vermont, ten for NY; plus five drownings, three boating *per se*, two falls from high places, one choking, one "fireworks related." No knifings. Evidently last night's death was not charged to the holiday.

I "seek" around then, happy to have Paul out of action and for my mind to find its own comfort level: a medical call-in from Pittsfield offers "painless erection help"; a Christian money-matters holiday radiothon from Schaghticoke is interpreting the The Creator's views on Chapter 13 filings (He thinks some are okay). Another station profiles lifers in Attica selling Girl Scout cookies "in the population." "We *do* think we shouldn't be totally prevented from adding to the larger good"—laughter from other cons—"but we don't go around knocking on each other's cells wearing little green outfits either." Though a falsetto voice adds, "Not this afternoon anyway."

I turn it off as we get into the static zone at the New York border. And with my son beside me, his scissored and gouged head against his cool window glass, his mind in some swarming, memory-plagued darkness which causes his fingers to dance and his cheek to twitch like a puppy's in a dream of escape, my own mind bends with unexpected admiration toward meisterbuilder O'Dell's big blue house on the knoll; and to what a great, if impersonal, true-to-your-dreams *home* it is—a place any modern family of whatever configuration or marital riggery ought to feel lamebrained not to make a reasonably good go of life in. A type of "go" I could never quite catch the trick of, even in the most halcyon days, when we all were a tidy family in our own substantial house in Haddam. I somehow could never create a sufficiently thick warp and woof, never manufacture enough domestic assumables that we could get on to assuming them. I was always gone too much with my sportswriting work; never felt owning was enough different from renting (except that you couldn't leave). In my mind a sense of contingency and the possibility of imminent change in status underlay everything, though we stayed for more than a decade, and I stayed longer. It always seemed to me enough just to know that someone loved you and would go on loving you forever (as I tried to convince Ann again today, and she rejected again), and that the *mise-en-scène* for love was only that and not a character in the play itself.

Charley of course is of the decidedly *other* view, the one that believes a good structure implies a good structure (which is why he's so handy with plain truth: he has the mind of a true Republican). It was fine with him, as I happen to know via discreet inquiries, that his old man owned a seat on the commodities exchange, kept an unadvertised pied-à-terre on Park Avenue, supported an entire Corsican second family in Forest Hills, was barely a gray eminence whom young Charles hardly ever saw and referred to only as "Father" when he happened to catch a glimpse (never Dad or Herb or Walt or Phil). All was jake as long as there was a venerable old slate-roofed, many-chimneyed, thickly pillared, leaded-glass-windowed, deep-hedged, fieldstone Georgian *residence* reliably there in Old Greenwich, reeking of fog and privet and boat varnish, brass polish, damp tennies and extra trunks you could borrow in the poolhouse. This, in Charley's view, constitutes life and no doubt truth: strict physical moorings. A roof over your head to prove you have a head. Why else be an architect?

And for some reason now, tooling along westward with my son in tow—and not because either of us gives a particular shit about baseball, but because we simply have no properer place to go for our semi-sacred purposes—I feel Charley might just not be wrong in his rich-boy's manorial worldview. It might *be* better if things were more anchored. (Vice President Bush, the Connecticut Texan, would certainly agree.)

Though there's something in me that's possibly a little off and which I'm sure would make finding firm anchorage a problem. I'm not, for instance, as optimistic as one ought to be (relations with Sally Caldwell are a good example); or else I'm much too optimistic (Sally qualifies again). I don't come back from bad events as readily as one should (or as I used to); or else the reverse—I'm too adept at forgetting and don't remember enough of what it is I'm supposed to resume (the Markhams serve here). And for all my insistent prating that they—the Markhams—haul themselves into clearer view, I've never seen myself all that exactly, or as sharing the frame with those others I might share it with—causing me often to be far too tolerant to those who don't deserve it; or, where I myself am concerned, too little sympathetic when I should be more. These uncertainties contribute, I'm sure, to my being a classic (and possibly chickenshit) liberal, and may even help to drive my surviving son nutty and set him barking and baying at the moon.

Though specifically where he is concerned, I dearly wish I could speak from some more established *place*—the way Charley would were he the father of the first part—rather than from this constellation of stars among which I smoothly orbit, traffic and glide. Indeed, if I could see myself as occupying a fixed point rather than being in a process (the quiddity of the Existence Period), things might grow better for us both—myself and barking son. And in this Ann may simply be right when she says children are a signature mark of self-discovery and that what's wrong with Paul is nothing but what's wrong with us. Though how to change it?

Spiriting on across the Hudson and past Albany—the "Capital Region"—I am on the lookout now for I-88, the blue Catskills rising abruptly into view to the south, hazy and softly solid, with smoky mares' tails running across the range. Following his nap Paul has fished into his Paramount bag and produced a Walkman and a copy of *The New Yorker*. He's inquired moodily about the availability of tapes, and I've offered my "collection" from the glove compartment: Crosby, Stills and Nash from 1970, which is broken; Laurence Olivier reading Rilke, also broken; *Ol' Blue Eyes Does the Standards*, Parts I and II, which I bought one lonely night from an 800 number in Montana; two sales motivation speeches all agents were given in March and that I have yet to listen to; plus a tape of myself reading *Doctor Zhivago* (to the blind), given as a Christmas gift by the station manager who thought I'd done a bang-up job and ought to get some pleasure from my efforts. I've never put it on either, since I'm not that much for tapes. I still prefer books.

Paul tries the *Doctor Zhivago*, tunes it in on his Walkman for approximately two minutes, then begins looking at me with an expression of phony, wide-eyed astoundment and eventually says, his earphones still on, "This is very revealing: 'Ruffina Onissimovna was a woman of advanced views, entirely unprejudiced and well disposed toward everything that she called positive and vital.' " He smiles a narrow, belittling smile, though I say nothing, since for some reason it embarrasses me. He clicks in the Sinatra then, and I can hear Frank's tiny buzzy-bee voice deep inside his ear jacks. Paul picks up his *New Yorker* and begins reading in stony silence.

But almost the instant we're south of Albany and out of sight of its unlovely civic skyscrapers, all vistas turn wondrous and swoopingly dramatic and as literary and history-soaked as anything in England or France. A sign by a turnout announces we have now entered the CENTRAL LEATHERSTOCKING AREA, and just beyond, as if on cue, the great corrugated glacial trough widens out for miles to the southwest as the highway climbs, and the butt ends of the Catskills cast swart afternoon shadows onto lower hills dotted by pocket quarries, tiny hamlets and pristine farmsteads with wind machines whirring to undetectable winds. Everything out ahead suddenly says, "A helluva massive continent lies this way, pal, so you better be mindful." (It's the perfect landscape for a not very good novel, and I'm sorry I didn't bring my four-in-one Cooper to read aloud after dinner and once we're staked out on the porch. It would beat being taunted about *Doctor Zhivago*.)

In my official view, absolutely nothing should be missed from here on, geography offering a natural corroboration to Emerson's view that power resides in moments of transition, in "shooting the gulf, in darting to an aim." Paul could do himself a heap of good to set aside his *New Yorker* and try contemplating his own status in these useful terms: transition, jettisoning the past. "Life only avails, not having lived." I should've bought a tape of it and not a book.

But he's locked down in a bit-lip sound cocoon of "Two sweethearts in the summer wind," and reading "Talk of the Town" with his lips moving, and couldn't give a sweet rat's fart about what interesting movie's playing outside his window. Traveling *is* finally a fool's paradise.

I make a brief scenic turnout below Cobleskill to stretch my back (my coccyx has now begun aching). Leaving Paul in the seat, I climb out into the little breezy lot and walk to the sandstone parapet beyond which the luminous Pleistocene valley leaps out stark and vast and green and brown-peaked with the animal grandeur of an inland empire any bona fide pioneer would've quaked before trying to tame. I actually climb onto the wall and take several deep clean breaths, do several strenuous jumping jacks and squat thrusts, touch my toes, pop my fingers, rotate my neck as the sweet odors float in on the watery air. Beyond me hawks soar, martins dip, a tiny airplane buzzes, a distant hang glider like a dragonfly wheels and sways in the rising molecules. A door in a far-off, invisible house slams audibly shut, a car horn blows, a dog barks. And visible on the hillside opposite, where the sun paints a yellow square upon the western gradient, a tractor, tiny but detectably red, halts its progress in an emerald field; a tiny, hatted figure climbs down, pauses, then starts on foot back up the hill he's tractored down. He moves for a long, slow ways above and away from his machine, turns and goes a distance along a curved rim top, then resolutely, undramatically goes over, disappears at his own pace to whatever world's beyond. It is a fine moment to savor, even alone, though I wish my son could break loose and share it. You can lead a horse to water, but you can't make him sing opera.

I stand and stare a while at nothing in particular, my exercise ended, my back loosened, my son entombed in the car reading a magazine. The yellow square begins gradually to fade on the opposite hillside, then moves mysteriously left, darkens the green hayfield instead of lighting it, and I decide—satisfied and palpably enlivened—to pack it in.

Somebody has left a plastic bag of Styrofoam "popcorn" half out of the trash can—the pale-green kernels that Christmas wreaths or your repaired Orvis reel comes boxed in. A new warm afternoon breeze is shifting wispy kernels here and there around the lot. I stop before climbing in to jam the bag down farther and to police up what bits I can with two hands.

Paul looks up from his *New Yorker* and stares at me where I'm tidying up the asphalt around the car. I merely look back at him from my side of the window, my hands full of clingy green stuff. He fingers his cut ear under his Walkman, blinks, then slowly makes his fingers into a pistol, points it at his temple, produces a silent little "boom" sound with his lips, throws his head back in terrible mock death, then goes back to reading. It's scary. Anyone would think so. Especially a father. But it's also funny as hell. He is not so bad a boy.

S hort-term destinations are by far the best.

Paul and I skirt the outskirts of Oneonta a little past five, turn north on Route 28 along the newly rose Susquehanna, and in truth are almost there. (Geography, while instructive, is also the North-east's soundest selling point and best-kept secret, since in three hours you can stand on the lapping shores of Long Island Sound, staring like Jay Gatz at a beacon light that lures you to, or away from, your fate; yet in three hours you can be heading for cocktails damn near where old Natty drew first blood—the two locales as unalike as Seattle is to Waco.)

Route 28 takes a pretty hickory-and-maple-shaded course straight upriver through tiny postcard villages, past farms, woodlots and single-family roadside split-levels and ranches. Here is a cut-ur-own Xmas tree lot, a pick-ur-own raspberry patch and apple orchard, a second-echelon B&B tucked into a hillside sugarbush; an attack-dog academy, an ugly clear-cut bordered by a low-yield hay meadow with Guernsey cows grazing to the edge of a gravel pit.

Here you'd expect to find no planning boards, PUDs, finicky building codes, septic standards, sidewalk ordinances or ridgetop laws; just an as yet unspoilt place to site your summer cabin or mobile home where and exactly how you want it, right down the road from a good Guinea restaurant, with its own marinara and Genesee on tap, and where a 10 a.m. night owl's mass is still cele-brated Sundays at St. Joe's in Milford. It's the perfect mix, in other words, of small-scale Vermont atmospherics with unpretentious, upstate hardscrabble, all an afternoon's drive from the G.W. Bridge. (Dark rumors may now and then surface that it's also a prime loca-tion for big-city muscle to off-load their mistakes, but no place is without a downside.)

Meanwhile, my spirits have taken a strong upward turn and I'd now like to try hauling Paul into a planned off-the-cuff give-and-take squarely on the notion of Independence Day itself, and to point out that the holiday isn't just a moth-bit old relic-joke with men dressed up like Uncle Sam and harem guards on hogs doing circles within circles in shopping-mall lots; but in fact it's an observance of human possibility, which applies a canny pressure on each of us to contemplate what we're dependent on (barking in honor of dead basset hounds, thinking we're thinking, penis tingling, etc.) and after that to consider in what ways we're independent or might be; and finally how we might decide—for the general good—not to worry about it much at all.

This may be the only way an as-needed parent can in good faith make contact with his son's life problems; which is to say sidereally, by raising a canopy of useful postulates above him like stars and hoping he'll connect them up to his own sightings and views like an astronomer. Anything more purely parental—wading in and doing some stern stable-cleaning about stealing rubbers, wrecking cars, kicking security personnel, braining stepfathers (who might even deserve it), torturing innocent birds, eventually hauling up his court appearance and how that might correlate inversely with coming to Haddam to live with me and after that with his chances of ever getting into Williams on a "need scholarship"—simply wouldn't work. In the dizzyingly brief time we have together, he would only retreat into raucous barking, furtive smiles and sullener silences, ending up with me in a fury and in all likelihood ferrying him back to Deep River, feeling myself to be (and being) a ruinous failure. I don't, after all, know what's wrong him, am not even certain anything is, or that *wrong* isn't just a metaphor for something else, which may itself already be a metaphor. Though probably what's amiss, if anything, is not much different from what's indistinctly amiss with all of us at one time or another—we're not happy, we don't know why, and we drive ourselves loony trying to get better.

Paul has stashed his Walkman back in his bag and set his *New Yorker* on the dash, where it reflects distractingly in the windshield, but he has also grabbed up the slender green-jacketed Emerson off the back seat, where it's been on top of my red REALTOR windbreaker, and begun giving it a look. This is better than I could've planned, though it's clear he hasn't cracked the copy I mailed him.

"Do you think you'd rather have a child with Down's syndrome or a child with just regular mental illness?" he says, leafing casually backward through *Self-Reliance* as if it were *Time*.

"I'm pretty pleased with how you and Clarissa turned out. So I guess I'd rather have neither one." A mental mug shot of the little feral Mongoloid back in Friendly's hours ago opens a cruel vein of awareness that Paul may think he's that or heading that way.

"Choose," Paul says, still leafing. "Then give me your reasons."

On the right, outside pretty little Federalist Milford, we cruise by the Corvette Hall of Fame, a shrine Paul, if he saw it, would vigorously insist on touring since, for reasons of Charley's Old Greenwich tastes, he's claimed the Corvette as his favorite car. (He likes them, he says, because they'll melt.) Only he doesn't see it because he's looking through Emerson! (Plus, I'm now headed for the barn and a tall, stiff drink and an evening in a big wicker rocker made by native artisans working with local materials.)

"Ordinary mental illness, then," I say. "You can sometimes cure that. Down's syndrome you're pretty much stuck with."

Paul's eyes, his mother's slate-gray ones, flicker at me astutely, acknowledging something—I'm not certain what. "Sometimes," he says in a dark voice.

"Do you still want to be a mime?" We have passed out along the little Susquehanna again—more postcard corn patches, blue and white silos, more snowmobile repairs.

"I didn't *want* to be a mime. That was a joke at camp. I *want* to be a cartoonist. I just can't draw." He scratches his scalp with the warty side of his hand and sniffs, then makes a seemingly involuntary little *eeeck* noise back in his throat, grimaces, then stations both hands in front of his face, palms out, doing the man-in-the-glass-box and, looking over at me, still grimacing, silently mouthing "Help me, help me." He then quits and immediately begins flipping Emerson pages backward again. "What's this supposed to be about?" He stares down at the page he happens to have opened. "Is it a novel?"

"It's a terrific book," I say, uncertain how to promote it. "It's got—"

"You've got a lot of things underlined in it," Paul says. "You must've had it in college." (A rare reference to my having had a life prior to his. For a boy in the clench of the past, he has little interest in life before his own. My or his mother's family history, for instance, lack novelty. Not that I entirely blame him.)

"You're welcome to read it."

"Wel-come, welcome," he says to mock me. "And that's the *way* it is, Frank," he says, reverting to his Cronkite voice again, staring down at *Self-Reliance* on his lap as though it interested him.

Then almost surprisingly we are on the south fringes of Cooperstown, coming in past a fenced sale lot packed with used speedboats, another lot with "bigfoot" trucks, a prim white Methodist church with a VACATION BIBLE SCHOOL sign, right in line with a smattering of neat, overpriced, Forties-vintage mom and pop motels with their lots already full of luggage-crammed sedans and station wagons. At the actual village limits sign, a big new billboard demands the passerby "Vote Yes!" However, I see no signs for the Deerslayer or the Hall of Fame, which simply means to me that Cooperstown doesn't put its trust in celebrity or glamour but prefers standing on its own civic feet.

" 'The great man,' " Paul reads in a pseudo-reverent Charlton Heston voice, " 'is he who in the midst of the crowd keeps with perfect sweetness the independence of solitude.' Blah, blah, blah, blah-blah, blah, blah. Glub, glub, glub. 'The objection to conforming to usages that have become dead to you is that it scatters your force. It loses your time and blurs the impression of your character.' Quack, quack, quack, quack. I am the great man, the grape man, the grapefruit, I am the fish stick—"

"To be great is usually to be misunderstood," I say, watching traffic and looking for signs. "That's a good line for you to remember. There're some other good ones."

"I've got enough things I remember already," he says. "I'm drowning. Glub, glub, glub." He raises his hands and makes swimming-drowning motions, then makes a quick, confidential *eeeck* like an old gate needing oiling, then grimaces again.

"Reading it's good enough, then. There's not going to be a test."

"Test. Tests make me really mad," Paul says, and suddenly with his dirty fingers rips out the page he's just read from.

"Don't do that!" I make a grab for it, crunching the green cover so that I dent its shiny paper. "You have to be a complete nitwit asshole to do that!" I stuff the book between my legs, though Paul still has the torn page and is folding it carefully into quarters. This qualifies as oppositional.

"I'll keep it instead of remembering it." He maintains his poise, while mine's all lost. He sticks the folded page into his shorts pocket and looks out his window the other way. I am glaring at him. "I just took a page from your book." He says this in his Heston voice. "Do you by the way see yourself as a complete failure?"

"At what?" I say bitterly. "And get this fucking *New Yorker* off the dashboard." I grab it and wing it in the back. We're now encountering increased vehicular traffic, entering shady little bendy-narrow village streets. Two paperboys sit side by side on a street corner, folding from stacks of afternoon papers. Outside, the air—which of course I can't feel—looks cool and moist and inviting, though I'm sure it's hot.

"At anything." He makes his little *eeeck* sound far down his throat, as if I'm not supposed to hear it.

My chest feels emptied with outrage and regret (over a page in a book?), but I answer because I'm asked. "My marriage to your mother and your upbringing. These haven't been the major accomplishments in my current term. Everything else is absolutely great, though." I am gaunt with how little I want to be in the car alone with my son, only barely arrived upon the storied streets of our destination. My jaw has gone steely, my back aches again and the interior feels thick and airless, as if I'm being gassed by fearsome dread. I wish to a lonely, faraway and inattentive god that Sally Caldwell were in this car with us; or better yet, that Sally was here and Paul was back in Deep River, torturing birds, inflicting injuries and dispensing his smoky dread within the population there. (The Existence Period was patented to ward off such unwelcome feelings. Only it isn't working.)

"Do you remember how old Mr. Toby would be if he hadn't gotten run over?"

I'm just about to ask him if he's been snuffing grackles for fun. "Thirteen, why?" My eyes are fast seeking any DEERSLAYER INN sign.

"That's something I can't quit thinking about," he says for possibly the thirtieth time, as we come to the center-of-town intersection, where some kids dressed exactly like Paul are slouching delinquently on the corner curb, playing idiotic Hacky Sack right in among the passersby. Town seems to be a little brick and white-shuttered village, shaded by big scarlet oaks and hickories, all as charming and snappily tended to as a well-kept cemetery.

"Why do you think you think about that?" I say irritably.

"I don't know. It seems like it ruined everything that was fixed back then."

"It didn't. Nothing's fixed anyway. Why don't you try writing some of it down." For some reason I feel aggravated by the story of my mother and the nun on Horn Island and wanting (God knows why) more children.

"You mean like a journal?" He eyes me dubiously.

"Right. Like that."

"We did that at camp. Then we used our journals to wipe our asses and threw them in bonfires. That was the best use for them."

Around and down the cross street I now unexpectedly see the Baseball Hall of Fame, a pale-red-brick Greek Revival, post-office-looking building, and I make a quick, hazardous right off what was Chestnut and onto what is Main, postponing my drink for a drive-by and a closer look.

Full of baseball vacationers, Main Street has the soullessly equable, bustly air of a better-than-average small-college town the week the kids come back for fall. Shops on both sides are selling showcases full of baseball *everything*: uniforms, cards, posters, bumper stickers, no doubt hubcaps and condoms; and these share the street with just ordinary villagey business entities—a drugstore, a dad 'n' lad, two flower shops, a tavern, a German bakery and several realty offices, their mullioned windows crammed with snapshots of A-frames and "view properties" on Lake So-and-so.

Unlike stolid Deep River and stiff-necked Ridgefield, Coopers-town has more than ample 4th of July street regalia strung up on the lampposts and crossing wires, stoplights and even parking meters, as if to say there's a right way to do things and this is it. Posters on every corner promise a "Big Celebrity Parade" with "country music stars" on Monday, and all visitors strolling the sidewalks seem glad to be here. It seems in fact and on first blush like an ideal place to live, worship, thrive, raise a family, grow old, get sick and die. And yet: Some suspicion lurks—in the crowds themselves, in the too-frequent street-corner baskets of redder-than-red geraniums and the too-visible French *poubelle* trash containers, in the telltale sight of a red double-decker City of Westminster bus and there being no *mention* of the Hall of Fame *anywhere*—that the town is just a replica (of a legitimate place), a period backdrop to the Hall of Fame or to something even less specific, with nothing authentic (crime, despair, litter, the rapture) really going on no matter what civic illusion the city fathers maintain. (In this way, of course, it's no less than what I imagined, and still a potentially perfect setting in which to woo one's son away from his problems and bestow good counsel—if, that is, one's son weren't an asshole.)

We cruise slowly by the unimpressive little brick-arched entryway to the Hall, with its even more post-office-ish, Old-Glory-on-a-pole look and a single flourishing sugar maple out front. Several noisy citizens seem to be parading in a little circle on the sidewalk, doing their best, it looks like, to get in the way of paying customers who have walked over from nearby inns or hotels or RV parks and want to get inside for a quick evening tour. These circlers all have placards and signs and sandwich boards and, when I let Paul's window down to hear, are chanting what sounds like "shooter, shooter, shooter." (It's hard to know what could be worth picketing in a place like this.)

"So who're those morons?" Paul says, and makes a quick *eeeck* followed by a look of dismay.

"I got here when you did," I say.

"Hooter, hooter, hooter, hooter," he says in a gruff, giant's voice. "Neuter, neuter, neuter, neuter."

"That's the Baseball Hall of Fame right there, though." I'm disappointed, to be honest, but with no right to be. "You've seen it now, so we can go home if you want to."

"Hooter, hooter, hooter," Paul says. "Eeeck, eeeck."

"Do you want to just get it over with? I'll get you back to New York early tonight. You can stay at the Yale Club."

"I'd rather stay up here a whole lot longer," Paul says, still watching out his window.

"Okay," I say, deciding he means he'd rather not go to New York. Though the air of anger flushes right out of me then, and I see my job as father once again to be a permanent, lifelong undertaking.

"What actually supposedly happened here? I forgot." He is musing out at the milling sidewalk traffic.

"Baseball was supposedly dreamed up here in 1839, by Abner Doubleday, though nobody really believes that." All info courtesy of brochures. "It's just a myth to allow customers to focus their interests and get the most out of the game. It's like the Declaration of Independence being signed on the Fourth of July, when it was actually signed some other time." This, of course, is straight from avuncular old Becker and probably a waste of time now. Though I mean to persist. "It's a shorthand to keep you from getting all bound up in unimportant details and missing some deeper point. I don't remember what the point is with baseball, though." A second wave of deep fatigue suddenly descends. It's tempting to pull over and go to sleep on the seat and see who's here when I wake up.

"So this is all just bullshit," Paul says, watching out.

"Not exactly. A lot of things we think are true aren't, just like a lot of things that are, you don't have to give a shit about. You have to make your own assessments. Life's full of little potted lessons like that."

"Why, thank you, then. Thank you, thank you, thank you, thank you." He looks at me with amusement, but he is scornful. I could easily pass out.

Though I'm still not to be turned aside, under the syllabus topic of separating the wheat from the chaff, or possibly it's the woods from the trees. "You shouldn't get trapped by situations that don't make you happy," I say. "I'm not always very good at it. I fuck up a lot. But I try."

"I'm trying," he says—to my great and heart-wrenching surprise—moved by something. A platitude. The strength of a simple platitude. What else do I offer? "I don't really know what I'm supposed to do."

"Well, if you're trying, that's all you can do."

"Eeeck," he says quietly. "Hooter."

"Hooter. Right," I say, and we motor on.

I drive us farther down Main into the tree-thick neighborhood of expensive and familiar Federalist and well-preserved Greek Revivals—all in primo condition and shaded by two-hundred-year-old beeches and red oaks—which in Haddam would cost a million eight and never come on the market (friends sell to friends to keep us realtors out of it). A couple here, though, have signs on their lawns, one with a JUST REDUCED sticker. Another paperboy is here, walking his route, swinging his swag sack full of afternoon dailies. An older man, in bright-red jackass pants and a yellow shirt, is standing in a yard behind a picket fence, holding an icy drink and raising his free hand for the boy to throw him a paper, which he does, and which the man snags. The boy turns toward us idling past, waves a furtive little wave at Paul, mistaking him for someone he knows, then quickly douses it and looks off. Paul, though, waves back! As though he thought, like a good dreamer, that if we all still lived in Haddam and life was revised back to what it should be, this boy would be him.

"Do you like my clothes?" he says, closing his window with the button.

"Not much," I say, steering the curve around onto another shaded street, where there's a blue HOSPITAL sign, and women in nurses' garb and men in doctors' smocks with dangling stethoscopes are walking down the sidewalk, headed for home. "Do you like mine?"

Paul looks me over seriously—chinos, Weejuns, yellow socks, Black Watch plaid short-sleeve from Mountain Eyrie Outfitters in Leech Lake, Minnesota, clothes I've worn as long as he's known me, the same as I wore the day I stepped off the New York Central in Ann Arbor in 1963 and am at home in still. Generic clothing.

"No," Paul says.

"But see," I say, the crunched *Self-Reliance* still under my thigh, "in my line of work I'm supposed to dress in a way that makes clients feel sorry for me, or better yet superior to me. I think I accomplish that pretty well." Paul looks over at me again with a distasteful look that might be ready to slide into sarcasm, only he doesn't know if I'm making fun of him. He says nothing. Though what I've just told him, of course, is merely true.

I steer us back now through a nice but less nice neighborhood of red- and green-shuttered houses on narrower streets, thinking by this route to wind back to 28 and find the Deerslayer. Plenty's for sale here too. Cooperstown, it seems, is up for grabs.

"What's your new tattoo say?"

Paul instantly holds his right wrist up for me to see, and what I make out upside down is the word "insect," stained in dull-blue Bic-pen-looking ink right into his tender flesh. "Did you think that up by yourself," I say, "or did someone help you?"

Paul sniffs. "In the next century we're all going to be enslaved by the insects that survive this century's pesticides. With this I acknowledge being in a band of maladapted creatures whose time is coming to a close. I hope the new leaders will treat me as a friend." He again sniffs, then worries his nose with his dirty fingers.

"Is that a lyric from some rock song?" I'm getting us back into the traffic flow, heading toward the center of town again. We have made a circle.

"It's just common knowledge," Paul says, rubbing his knee with his wart.

Almost immediately I see a sign I missed when Paul and I were arguing: a tall, rail-thin, buckskin-and-high-moccasined pioneer man in profile, holding a flintlock rifle, standing on a lakeshore with triangular pine trees in the background. DEERSLAYER INN STRAIGHT AHEAD. A blessed promise.

"Don't you have a better view of human progress than that?" I push right out across Main among the late-Saturday traffic and trolley vans shunting tourists hither and yon. Lake Otsego is unexpectedly straight out ahead—lush, Norwegian-looking headlands miles away on its far shore, lumping north into the hazy Adirondacks.

"Too many things are bothering me all the time. It gets to be old."

"You know," I say, ignoring him, "those guys who founded this whole place thought if they didn't shake loose of old dependencies they'd be vulnerable to the world's innate wildness—"

"By place do you mean Cooperstown?"

"No. I don't. I meant something else."

"So who was Cooperstown named after?" he says, facing toward the sparkling lake as if it were space he was considering flying off into.

"James Fenimore Cooper," I say. "He was a famous American novelist who wrote books about Indians playing baseball." Paul flashes me a look of halfway pleasant uncertainty. He knows I'm tired of him and may be making fun of him again. Though I can also see in his features—as I have other times, and as the dappled light passes over them—the adult face he'll most likely end up with: large, grave, ironic, possibly gullible, possibly gentle, but not likely so happy. Not my face, but a way mine could've been with fewer coping skills. "Do you think *you're* a failure?" I say, slowing across from the Deerslayer, ready to turn up the drive through two rows of tall spruces beyond which is the longed-for inn, its Victorian porches shaded deep in the late day, the big chairs I've daydreamed about occupied by a few contented travelers, but with room for more.

"At what?" Paul says. "I haven't had enough time to fail yet. I'm still learning how." I wait for traffic to clear. Lake Otsego is beside us now, flat and breezeless through an afternoon haze.

"I mean at being a kid. An ass-o-lescent. Whatever it is you think you are now." My blinker is blinking, my palms gripping the wheel.

"Sure, Frank," Paul says arrogantly, possibly not even knowing what he's agreeing to.

"Well, you're not," I say. "So you're just going to have to figure out something else to think about yourself, because you're not. I love you. And don't call me Frank, goddamn it. I don't want my son to call me Frank. It makes me feel like your fucking stepfather. Why don't you tell me a joke. I could use a joke. You're good at that."

And then a sudden stellar quiet settles on us two, waiting to turn, as if a rough barrier had been reached, tried, failed at but then briskly gotten over before we knew it or how. I for some reason sense that Paul might cry, or at least nearly cry—an event I haven't witnessed in a long time and that he has officially ceased yet might try again just this once for old times' sake.

But in fact it's my own eyes that go hot and steamy, though I couldn't tell you why (other than my age).

"Can you hold your breath for fifty-five seconds straight?" Paul says as I swing up across the highway.

"I don't know. Maybe."

"Do it," Paul says, looking straight at me, deadpan. "Just stop the car." He is opaque and gloating with something hilarious.

And so, in the shady drive to the Deerslayer, I do. I hit the brakes. "All right, I'm holding it," I say. "This better be really funny. I'm ready for a drink."

He clamps his mouth shut and closes his eyes, and I close mine, and we wait together in the a/c wind and engine murmur and thermostat click while I count, one-one-thousand, two-one-thousand, three-one-thousand . . .

When I closed my eyes the dashboard digital read 5:14, and when I open them it reads 5:15. Paul has his open, though he seems to be counting silently like a zealot speaking some private beseechments to God.

"Okay. Fifty-five. What's the punch line? I'm in a hurry." My foot is easing off the brake. " 'I didn't know shit could hold its breath so long?' Is it that good?"

"Fifty-five is how long the first jolt lasts in the electric chair. I read that in a magazine. Did you think it seemed like a long time or a short time?" He blinks at me, curious.

"It seemed pretty long to me," I say unhappily. "And that wasn't very funny."

"Me too," he says, fingering his bunged-up ear rim and inspecting his finger for blood. "It's supposed to knock you out, though."

"That'd be a lot better," I say. Parents, of course, think about dying day and night—especially when they see their children one weekend a month. It's not so surprising their children would follow suit.

"You just lose everything when you lose your sense of humor," Paul says in a mock-official voice.

And I'm back in gear then, tires skidding on pine needles and up into the cool and (I hope) blissful removes of the Deerslayer. A bell is gonging. I see an old belfry stand in the side yard being clappered by a smiling young woman in a white tunic and chef's hat, waving to us as we arrive, just like in some travelogue of happy summer days in Cooperstown. I wheel in feeling as if we were late and everybody had been distracted by our absence, only now we've arrived and everything can start.

9

The Deerslayer is as perfect as I'd hoped—a wide, rambling, spavined late Victorian with yellow scalloped mansards, spindle-lathed porch railings, creaky stairs leading to long, shadowy, disinfectant-smelling hallways, little twin pig-iron bedsteads, a table fan, and a bath at the end of the hall.

Downstairs there's a long, slumberous living room with ancient-smelling slipcovered couches, a scabbed-up old Kimball spinet, a "take one, leave one" library, with dinner served in the shadowy dining room between 5:30 and 7:00 ("No late diners please!"). There is, however and unfortunately, no bar, no complimentary cocktails, no canapés, no TV. (I have embellished it some, but who could blame me?) And yet it still seems to me a perfect place where a man can sleep with a teenage boy in his room and arouse no suspicions.

Drinkless, then, I stretch out on the too-soft mattress while Paul goes "exploring." I relax my jaw sinews, twist my back a little, unlimber my toes in the table-fan breeze and wait to let sleep steal upon me like a bushman out of the twilight. To this end I again braid together new nonsense components, which seep into my mind like anesthesia. *We better dust off our Sally Caldwell . . . I'm sorry I drove your erection you putz . . . Phogg Allen, the long face . . . eat your face . . . You musta been a beautiful Doctor Zhivago, you stranger in the Susquehanna . . .* And I'm gone off into tunneling darkness before I can even welcome it.

And then, sooner than I wanted, I'm emerged—lushly, my head spinning in darkness, alone, my son nowhere near me.

For a time I lie still, as a cool lake breeze circulates thickly around the spruce and elms and into the room through the soft fan whir. Somewhere nearby a bug zapper toasts one after another of the big north-woods Sabre-jet mosquitoes, and above me on the ceiling a smoke detector beams its little red-eye signal out of the dark.

Floors below I hear fork and plate noises, chairs scraping, muffled laughter followed by footfalls trudging up the stairs past my door, the sound of a door closing and soon a toilet-flush—water skittering, splashing through pipes. Then the door reopens and more heavy footfalls fade into night.

Through a wall I hear someone sawin' 'em off just the way I must've been—stertorous, diligent, thorough-sounding breaths. Someone's playing "Inchworm" on the spinet. I hear a car door open in the gravel lot below my window—the muffled *ping, ping, ping* of the interior "door open" bell—then a man and a woman talking in low voices, affectionately. "It's dirt cheap here, really," the male says in a whisper, as if others needed to be kept in the dark.

"Yeah, but then what?" the female says, and giggles. "What would we do?"

"What d'ya do anywhere?" he says. "Go fishing, play golf, eat dinner, fuck your wife. Just like home."

"I choose window number four," she says. "There's not enough of *that* back home." She giggles again. Then thump, the trunk is slammed; chirp, a car alarm activated; crunch, their feet cross the gravel headed toward the lake. They are talking houses. I know. Tomorrow they'll do some window-browsing, check with an agent, look through some listing books, see one house, maybe two, to get a feel, discuss a feasible "down," then wander dreamily off down Main Street and never think one thought of it again. Not that it's always that way. Some guys write out whopper checks, ship their furnishings, establish whole new lives in two weeks—and *then* think better of it all, after which they list the house again with the same realtor, take a beating on the carrying charges, shell out a penalty for early pay-off, and in this way, in the process of mistake and correction, the economy remains vibrant. In that sense real estate is not about finding your dream house but getting rid of it.

I give a wistful thought to Paul and wonder where he could be in a strange but peril-free town after dark. Possibly he and the Hacky Sack gang from Main and Chestnut have forged lifelong bonds and removed to a dingy diner for cottage fries, waffles and burgers at his expense. He may, after all, lack precise peer grouping in Deep River—where everyone's at least old enough to be an adult. In Haddam he'll do better.

"Jeepers," I hear someone—a woman's nasally voice say, mounting the creaky stairs to floor three. "I told Mark"—Merk—"why can't she just move to the Cities, where we can keep an eye on her, then Dad won't have to drive so far for his dialysis? He's completely helpless without her."

"So then what'd Mark say to that?" another woman's equally nasally voice says without true interest—heavy treading down the hall away from my door.

"Oh, you know Mark. He's such a clod." A key in a lock, a door opening back. "He didn't say too much." Slam.

Since I have napped in my clothes (an irresistible luxury), I change only my shirt, slip on shoes, stretch my spine backward and forward, tramp woozily down to the communal bathroom for a visit and a face washing, then amble downstairs to have a look at things, locate Paul and get a tip on dinner; I've by now missed the inn's: spaghetti, salad, garlic bread, tapioca, all highly praised on the "Weekly Score Card" left on my dressertop ("Mmmmmm," one penciled-in comment by a previous guest).

In the long, brown-carpeted parlor all the old parchment lamps are burning cheerily and several guests are engrossed in gin games or Clue or reading newspapers or books out of the library, but saying little. A too-strong cinnamon candle is somewhere smoldering, and above the cold fireplace hangs a shadowy six-foot-tall portrait of a man in full leather gear with a silly, compromised expression on his U-shaped face. This is the Deerslayer himself. A big, elderly, long-eared, ham-handed Swede-looking guy is yakking away to a Japanese man in confidential tones about "invasive surgeries" and the extremes he'd be willing to suffer to avoid them. And across the room a horsey, middle-aged southern-sounding woman in a red-and-white polka-dot dress is seated at the piano, talking too loudly to another woman, in a foam neck brace. The polka-dot woman's eyes roam the long room, wanting to know who might be listening and being wildly entertained by what she's yammering about, which is whether you can ever trust a handsome man married to a not-so-pretty woman. "Clampin' a big padlock on my china cabinet'd be my first official move," she says in a loud voice. She spies me in the doorway contentedly watching the tableau of easygoing inn life (exactly how any prospective proprietor would fantasize it: every room filled, everybody's credit card slip salted away in the safe, no refunds offered, everybody in bed by ten). Her eyes snap at me. She offers me a long-toothed, savage stare and waves my way as if she knew me from Bogalusa or Minter City—maybe she simply recognizes a fellow southerner (something in the submissive, shruggy set of my shoulders). "Hey, you! All right! Come on down here, I see you," she shouts toward the door, rings flashing, bracelets banging, dentures a-twinkle. I wave good-naturedly, but fearing I'll end up piano-side having my brains turned to suet, I step discreetly back and out of the doorway, then hustle down the front under-the-stairs hallway to make some calls.

I would certainly like to call Sally and *should* call for messages. The Markhams could've come back from around the bend, and there might be an all-clear from Karl. These subjects have blessedly slipped my mind for several hours, but I haven't noticed much relief in the bargain.

Someone (no doubt the old southern number) has begun playing "Lullaby of Birdland" at a slow, lugubrious pace, so that the whole atmosphere on floor one suddenly feels calculated to drive everyone to bed.

I wait for messages, staring at a diagram illustrating the five steps that will save someone from choking, and fingering a stack of pink tickets from a dinner theater in Susquehanna, PA. *Annie Get Your Gun* is playing this very night, and the stack of playbills on the telephone table rings with the critics' kudos: "Everybody's first rate"— Binghamton *Press & Sun Bulletin*; "Move over 'Cats'"—Scranton *Times*; "This baby's got legs under her"—Cooperstown *Republican*. I can't help conjuring up Sally's review: "My team of death's-door opening-nighters simply couldn't get enough of it. We laughed, we cried, we damn near died"—*Curtain Call Newsletter*.

Beeeeep. "Hello, Mr. Bascombe, this is Fred Koeppel calling again from Griggstown. I know it's a holiday weekend, but I'd like to get a little action going on my house right away. Maybe show it on Monday if we can get the commission worked out. . . ." Click. Ditto.

Beeeeep. "Hello, Frank, it's Phyllis." Pause while she clears her throat, as though she's been asleep. "East Brunswick was a *total* nightmare. Total. Why'n't you tell us, for God's sake? Joe got depressed after one house. I think he may be headed for a big cave-in. So anyway, we've reconsidered about the Hanrahan place, which I'm ready to change my mind about it, I guess. Nothing's forever. If we don't like it we can just sell it. Joe liked it anyway. I'll get over worrying about the prison. I'm at a phone booth here." A deepening change comes into her voice (signifying what?). "Joe's asleep. Actually I'm having a drink at the bar at the Raritan Ramada. Quite a day. *Quite* a day." Another long pause, representing possible stock-taking within the Markham ménage. "I wish I could talk to you. But. I hope you get this message tonight and call us up in the morning so we can get our offer over to old man Hanrahan. I'm sorry about Joe being such a butt. He's not easy, I realize that." A third pause, during which I hear her say, "Yeah, sure," to someone. Then: "Call us at the Ramada. 201-452-6022. I'm probably going to be up late. We couldn't stand that other place anymore. I hope you and your son are getting to share a lot." Click.

Except for the boozy longing (which I ignore), there's no shocker here. East Brunswick's well known for dreary, down-market, cookie-cutter uniformity. It is not a viable alternative even to Penns Neck, though I'm surprised the Markhams came around so soon. It's too bad they couldn't have taken the evening, shot up to Susquehanna for *Annie* and chicken piccante. They'd have laughed, they'd have cried, and Phyllis could've found ways to start getting over worrying about the prison in her back yard. Of course, it won't surprise me if "old man Hanrahan's" house is realty history by now. Good things don't hang around while half-wits split hair follicles, even in this economy.

I instantly put in a call to Penns Neck, to get Ted on the alert for an early-morning offer. (I'll get Julie Loukinen to deliver it.) But the phone rings and rings and rings and rings. I repunch it, taking care to mentally picture each digit, then let it ring possibly thirty times while I stare down the front hall past the old grandfather clock and the portrait of General Doubleday and through the open screen door into the night and farther through trees to the diamond-twinkle lights of another, grander inn across on the lakeshore, a place I didn't see this afternoon. All the ranked windows there are warmly lit, car headlights coming and going like some swank casino in a far-off seaside country. Out on the Deerslayer's porch the high backs of the big Adirondack rockers are swaying as my fellow guests snooze away their spaghetti dinners, murmur and chuckle about the day—something bust-a-gut hilarious somebody's son has piped up with in front of the Heinie Manusch bust, something else about the pros and cons of opening a copy shop in a town this size, something further about Governor Dukakis, whom someone, probably a fellow Democrat, laughingly refers to as "that Beantown Jerkimo."

But nothing in Penns Neck. Ted may have slipped off to an Independence Day open house across the fence.

I try Sally's number, since she said to call and since I intend to renew our amorous connections the instant I let Paul off in Gotham, a time that now feels many miles and hours from now but isn't. (With one's children everything happens in a flash; there's never a now, only a then, after which you're left wondering what took place and trying to imagine if it can take place again so's you'll notice.)

"Hello-o," Sally says in a happy, airy voice, as if she'd just been in the yard, pinning up clothes on a sunny line.

"Hi," I say, relieved and cheered for an answer somewhere. "It's me again."

"Me again? Well. Good. How are you, Me? Still pretty distracted? It's a wonderful night at the beach. I wish you could distract yourself down to here. I'm on the porch, I can hear music, I ate radicchio and mushrooms tonight, and I've had some nice Duck's Wing fumé blanc. I hope you two're having as splendid a time wherever you are. Where are you?"

"In Cooperstown. And we are. It's great. You should be here." I picture one long, shiny leg, a shoe (gold, in my mind) dangling out over her porch banister into darkness, a big sparkling glass in her lounging hand (a banner night for women tipplers). "Have you got any company?" Apprehension's knife enters my voice; even I hear it.

"Nope. No company. No suitors scaling the walls tonight."

"That's good."

"I guess," she says, clearing her throat just the way Phyllis did. "You're extremely sweet to call me. I'm sorry I asked you about your old wife today. That was indiscreet and insensitive of me. I'll never do it again."

"I still want you to come up here." This is not literally true, though it's not far from true. (I'm certain she won't come anyway.)

"Well," Sally says, as though she were smiling into the dark, her voice going briefly weak, then coming back strong. "I'm thinking very seriously about you, Frank. Even though you were very rude or at least odd on the phone today. Maybe you couldn't help it."

"Maybe not," I say. "But that's great. I've been thinking seriously about you."

"Have you?"

"You bet. I thought last night you and I came to a crossroads, and we went in the wrong direction." Something in the South Man-toloking background makes me think I hear surf sighing and piling onto the beach, a blissful, longed-for sound here in the steamy Deerslayer hallway—though conceivably it's only weak batteries in Sally's cordless phone. "I think we need to do some things a lot differently," I say.

Sally has a sip of her fumé blanc right by the receiver. "I thought over what you said about loving someone. And I thought you were very honest. But it seemed very cold too. You don't think you're cold, do you?"

"No one ever told me I was. I've been told about plenty of other faults." (Some quite recently.) Whoever's playing "Lullaby of Birdland" in the living room stops and switches straight into "The Happy Wanderer" at an allegretto clip, the heavy bass notes flat and metallic. Someone claps along for two bars, then quits. A man out on the porch laughs and says, "I think I'm a happy wanderer myself."

"So I've just had this odd feeling all afternoon," Sally says. "About what you said and what I said to you, about being noncommittal and smooth. That *is* how you are. But then if I have strong feelings about you, shouldn't I just follow them? If I have a chance? I believe I could figure things out better when I was younger. I certainly always thought I could alter the course of things if I wanted to. Didn't you say you had a tidal something or other about me? Tides were in it."

"I said I had a tidal attraction to you. And I do." Possibly we can move beyond smooth and noncommittal here. Someone—a woman—starts loudly singing "Balls-de-reee, balls-de-rah" in a quavery voice and laughing. Possibly it's the loudmouth in polka dots who gave me the barbarous eyeball.

"What does that mean, tidal attraction?" Sally says.

"It's hard to put into words. It's just strong and persistent, though. I'm sure of that. I think it's harder to say what you like than what you don't."

"Well," Sally says almost sadly. "Last night I thought I was in a tide pulling me toward you. Only that isn't what happened. So I'm not very sure. That's what I've been thinking about."

"It's not bad if it's pulling you toward me, is it?"

"I don't think so. But I got nervous about it, and I'm not used to being nervous. It's not my nature. I got in the car and drove all the way to Lakewood and saw *The Dead*. Then I had my radicchio and mushrooms by myself at Johnny Matassa's, where you and I had our first encounter."

"Did you feel better?" I say, fingering up two *Annie* ducats, wondering if a character in *The Dead* reminded her of me.

"Not completely. No. I still couldn't understand if the unchangeable course was toward you or away from you. It's a dilemma."

"I love you," I say, totally startling myself. A tide of another nature has just swirled me into very deep, possibly dark water. These words are not untrue, or don't feel untrue, but I didn't need to say them at this very moment (though only an asshole would take them back).

"I'm sorry," Sally says, reasonably enough. "What is it? What?"

"You heard me." The living room pianist is playing "The Happy Wanderer" much louder now—just banging away. The Japanese man who's been hearing all about invasive surgeries walks out of the living room smiling, but immediately stops smiling when he hits the hall. He sees me and shakes his head as if he were responsible for the music but now it won't stop. He heads up the front stairs. Paul and I will be happy to be on floor 3.

"What's that mean, Frank?"

"I just realized I wanted to say it to you. And so I said it. I don't know everything it means"—to put it mildly—"but I know it doesn't mean nothing."

"But didn't you tell me you'd have to make somebody up to love them? And didn't you say this was a time in your life you probably wouldn't even remember later?"

"Maybe that time's over, or it's changing." I feel jittery and squeamish saying so. "But I wouldn't make you up anyway. It isn't even possible. I told you that this afternoon." I'm wondering, though, what if I'd said "don't" in front of the verb? Then what? Could that be the way life progresses at my age? A-stumble *into* darkness and *out* of the light? You discover you love someone by trying it without "don't" in front of the verb? Nothing vectored by your *self* or by what *is*? If so, it's not good.

There's a pause on the line, during which Sally is, understandably, thinking. I'm mightily interested in asking if she might love me, since she'd mean something different by it, which would be good. We could sort out the differences. But I don't ask.

"The Happy Wanderer" comes to a crashing end, followed by complete, relieved silence in the living room. I hear the Japanese man's feet treading the squeaky hall above me, then a door click closed. I hear pots being banged and scrubbed beyond the wall in the kitchen. Out on the dark porch the big rockers are rocking still, their occupants no doubt staring moodily across at the nicer inn that's too ritzy for them and probably not worth the money.

"It's very odd," Sally says, clearing her throat again as though changing the subject away from love, which is okay with me. "After I talked to you today from wherever you were, and before I went to see *The Dead*, I walked up the beach a while—you'd asked me about Wally's cuff links, and I just got this idea in my head. And when I came home I called his mother out in Lake Forest, and I demanded to know where he is. It just occurred to me for some reason that she'd always known and wouldn't tell me. That was the big secret, in spite of everything. And I've never even been a person who thought there *was* a big secret." (Unlike, say, Ann.)

"What did she tell you?" This would be an interesting new wrinkle in the tapestry. *Wally: The Sequel.*

"She didn't know where he was. She actually started crying on the phone, the poor old thing. It was terrible. *I* was terrible. I said I was sorry, but I'm sure she doesn't forgive me. I certainly wouldn't forgive me. I told you I can be ruthless sometimes."

"Did you feel better?"

"No. I just have to forget it, that's all. You can still see your ex-wife even if you don't want to. I don't know which is better."

"That's why people carve hearts on trees, I guess," I say, and feel idiotic for saying it, but for a moment also desolate, as if some chance has been once again missed by me. Ann seems all the more insubstantial and distant for being substantial and not even very distant.

"I sound very un-smart to myself," Sally says, ignoring my remark about trees. She takes a drink of wine, bumping the phone with the glass rim. "Maybe I'm undergoing the early signs of something. Self-pitying failure to make a significant contribution in the world."

"That's not true a bit," I say. "You help dying people and make them happier. You make a hell of a contribution. A lot more than I make."

"Women don't usually have midlife crises, do they?" she says. "Though maybe women who're alone do."

"Do you love me?" I say rashly.

"Would you even like that?"

"Sure. I'd think it was great."

"Don't you think I'm too mild? I think I'm very mild."

"No! I don't think you're mild. I think you're wonderful." The receiver for some reason is tightly pinned to my ear.

"I think I'm mild."

"Maybe you feel mild about me." I hope not, and my eyes fall again upon the little stack of pink dinner-theater tickets. They are, I see, for July 2, 1987—exactly a year ago. "If it's free, how good could it be?"—F. Bascombe.

"I *would* like to know something." She could very well want to know plenty.

"I'll tell you anything. No holding back. The whole truth."

"Tell me why you're attracted to women your own age?" This harks back to a conversation we had on our gloom-infested fall excursion to Vermont to peep at leaves, eat overcooked crown roasts and wait in stationary lines of bus traffic, later to retreat homeward in a debrided, funky silence. On the way up and in soaring early spirits, I explained, off the cuff and unsolicited, that younger women (who I'd had in mind I can't remember, but somebody in her middle twenties and not very smart) always wanted to cheer me up and sympathize with me, except that finally bored the socks off me, since I didn't want to be sympathized with and was cheerful enough on my own. We were whizzing up the Taconic, and I went on to say it seemed like a textbook definition of adulthood that you gave up trying to be a cheerleader for the person you loved and just took him or her on as he or she was—assuming you liked him (or her). Sally made no reply at the time, as though she thought I was just making something up for her benefit and wasn't interested. (In fact, I might already have been coaching myself against making *people* up for the purpose of loving them.)

"Well," I say, aware I could blow the whole deal with an inept turn of phrase, "younger women always want everything to be a success and have love depend on it. But some things can't be a success and you love somebody anyway."

Silence again intervenes. Again I think I hear surf languidly sudsing against the sandy shingle.

Sally says, "I don't think that's exactly what you said last fall."

"But it's pretty close," I say, "and it's what I meant and what I mean now. And what do you care? You're my age, or almost. And I don't love anybody else." (Except my ex-wife, which is a non-issue.)

"I guess I'm concerned that you're making me up different from how I am. Maybe you think there's only one person in the world for anybody, and so you keep making her up. Not that I mind being improved on, but you have to stick to my particular facts."

"I have to forget about making people up," I say guiltily, sorry I ever gave utterance to the idea. "And I don't think there's just one person for anybody. At least I hope to hell not, since I haven't done so well yet."

"We have some more fireworks out on the water here," Sally says dreamily. "That's very nice. Maybe I'm just feeling susceptible tonight. I felt good when you called."

"I *still* feel good," I say, and suddenly the bony, horse-face woman who's been banging the piano to death strides out into the foyer and looks down the hall straight at me, where I'm leaning on the wall above the phone table. She's in step with the plump woman in the neck brace, whom she's no doubt been making sing "Balls-dereee, balls-de-rah." She issues me another savage-eyebrowed look, as if I was where she knew I'd be and up to my pants pockets in the deceit of some angelic and unsuspecting wifey. "Look. I'm in a public phone here. But I feel a lot better. I just want to see you tomorrow if I can't see you in ten minutes."

"Where?" Sally says smally, still susceptible.

"Anywhere. Name it. I'll come down there in a Cessna." The two women stay standing in the lighted foyer, unabashedly ogling me and listening in.

"Are you still taking Paul to the train in New York?"

"By six o'clock," I say, wondering where Paul could be at this minute.

"Well, I could take a train up there and meet you. I'd like that. I'd like to spend the Fourth of July with you."

"You know, it's my favorite holiday of a non-religious nature." I am enthused to hear her even warily agreeable, though she can seem more agreeable than she is. (I have to tabulate all the declarations and forswearings I've committed to in the last ten minutes.) "You didn't answer my question, though."

"Oh." She sniffs once. "You're not really very easy to fix on. And I don't think I'd be a good long-term lover or a wife for somebody like that. I had a husband who was hard to fix on."

"That's all right," I say. Though surely I'm not as elusive as Wally! The Wally who's been gone for damn near twenty years!

"Is that all right? For me to be a not very good lover or wife?" She pauses to think about this novel idea. "Don't you care, or are you just not putting any pressure on me to do anything?"

"I care," I say. "But I'd actually just be happy to hear any good words."

"Everything isn't just about how you say it," Sally says, very formally. "And I wouldn't know what to say anyway. I don't think we mean the same things when we say the same things." (As predicted.)

"That's fine too. As long as you're not sure you *don't* love me. I read a poem someplace that said perfect love was not knowing you weren't in love. Maybe that's what this is."

"Oh my," she says, and sounds sorrowful. "That's too complicated, Frank, and it's not very different from how it was last night. It's not very encouraging to me."

"It's different because I get to see you tomorrow. Meet me at seven at Rocky and Carlo's on Thirty-third and Seventh. We'll start new from there."

"Well," she says. "Are we making a business deal to be in love? Is that what's happening?"

"No, it's not. But it's a good deal, though. Everything's up front for a change." She laughs. And then I try to laugh but can't and have to fake laughing.

"Okay, okay," she says, in a not very hopeful voice. "I'll see you tomorrow."

"You better believe it," I say in a better one. And we hang up. Though the instant she's off I depress the plunger and shout into the empty line, "And so you're nothing but a fucking asshole, are you? Well, I'll have you killed before Labor Day, and that's God's promise." I snap a vicious look around at the two women, framed by the screen door, peering at me. "I'll see you in hell," I say into the dead line, and slam the phone down as the women turn and head hastily upstairs to their beds.

I take a quick peek out onto the porch to see if Paul's there. He's not—only one of the gin players is left, asleep but managing to rock his rocker anyway. I make an investigative turn through the smelly dining room, where the light's still on and the big boarding-house lazy Susan table is cleared and shining dully from being wiped with a greasy rag. Through the two-way kitchen door open at the back I see the young woman who was clanging the dinner bell, wearing a chef's hat and waving when Paul and I arrived. She's seated at a long metal table in the brackish light, smoking a cigarette and flipping through a magazine, her hand around a can of Genny, her chef's hat in front of her. Clearly she's immersed in her own well-earned and private quality time. But nothing would make me happier than a warmed-up plate of dinner spaghetti with a couple of cold-as-they-may-be slabs of garlic bread and maybe a brew of my own. I'd eat right here, standing up, or sneak a plate to my room by the back stairs so no other guests would have to know about it. ("The next thing, everybody'll want to eat late, and we'll be serving dinner from now to Christmas. It's hard to know where to draw the line in these things"—which of course is true.)

"Hi," I say in through the kitchen door, one room into the next, sounding meeker than I want to sound.

The young woman—who's still wearing a chef's boxy-looking white tunic, institutional baggy pants and a red neckerchief—turns and gives me a skeptical, unwelcoming look. A round tin ashtray sits on the table in front of her, beside a package of Winstons. She looks back and flicks her smoke on the ashtray's rim.

"What can I do you for?" she says without looking up at me. I take a couple of minuscule steps nearer the doorframe. In fact, I hate to be the one asking for special treatment, who wants his dinner late, his laundry returned without his ticket, who can't find his stub for his prints, has to have his tires rotated *this* afternoon because he needs to drive to Buffalo in the morning and the left front seems to be wearing a little unevenly. I prefer my regular place in line. Only tonight, after 10 p.m., worn uneven myself from a long, befuddling day with my son, I'm willing to bend the rules like anyone else.

"I thought I might get a good tip on dinner somewhere," I say, with a you-know-what-I-really-mean look. My tired eyes dart around to what I can see of the kitchen: a giant cold box, a black eight-burner Vulcan, a bulky silver pot-washer, its door open, four big tub-sinks, dry as a desert, all utensils—pots, pans, skillets, whisks, spatulas—dangling like weaponry from a rack on the rear wall. Nowhere do I see a still-warm pot of spaghetti with a metal spoon handle poked up over the top. Nothing's doing here food-wise.

"I guess the Tunnicliff's kitchen shuts off at nine." The lady chef glances at her wristwatch and shakes her head without looking up. "You just missed that by an hour. I'm sorry to break the news."

She is a harder-boiled piece of business than I guessed. Frizzy blond hair, pallid indoor skin, blotchy where I can't now see, thick little wrists and neck, and wandering breasts not well captained inside her chef's getup. She is twenty-nine, no doubt, with a kid at home she's slow getting back to, and in all likelihood rides a big Harley to work. (Almost certainly she's the innkeeper's squeeze.) Though whatever her arrangements, they haven't left her easy to win over.

"Got any better ideas?" My stomach produces an audible querking noise as if on cue.

She takes a drag on her Winston and turns her head slightly to the side and blows smoke the other way. I can see the magazine she's reading is *Achieve Super Marital Sex* (something you might get mail order). I can also see she's not wearing a wedding ring, though that's not my business. "If you want to drive down to Oneonta, there's a Chinese stays open till midnight. Their egg drop's almost edible." She yawns and stifles it halfway.

"That's a pretty fur piece," I say, grinning witlessly. I sniff a gamy pilot light/old stale food smell reminiscent of Ted Houlihan's house. I of course hate egg drop soup, know no one who actually likes it, and hold my ground.

"Twenty-five air miles." She flips the pages of her magazine to one that has pictures I'm not close enough to see.

"Nothing else open in town, then, huh?" I am less convincing, I can tell.

"Bars. This is just a little hick burg. It pretends different. But what else is new." She flips another page nonchalantly, then leans forward to get a better look at something—possibly a defter "mounting strategy" or some fancy new penetration protocol, a tricky Swedish "apparatus" for manipulating previously undiscovered parts and zones, ingenuity for making life better than ever. (My own parts, I realize dimly, have not been manipulated in a coon's age, except in the age-old way; I wonder bleakly if Paul might not be somewhere in the menaceless warp of Cooperstown, having his own parts ardently worked over while I'm here begging a little supper.)

"Look," I say, "you think there's any chance I could get a little leftover spaghetti? I'm as hungry as a bear, and I'd be glad to eat it cold. Or I'd eat something else that was handy. Maybe some tapioca or a sandwich." I edge in the door to make my presence more a feature in the room.

She shakes her frizzy head and thumps her Genny, still intent on her sex magazine. "Jeremy hangs a big lock on the fridge so nobody can come down for Dagwoods, which used to happen, especially with the Japanese. They're apparently always starving. But I'm not trusted with the combination, 'cause I'd just stand back and let you have it all."

I look to the dimly shining Traulsen cold box, and indeed there's a hasp and bail soldered right onto it, and a big impregnable-looking lock—something it'd be a lot of trouble to jimmy off.

I'm close enough, though, to see the diagram that's captured the chef's special attention: a full page of four-panel drawings showing a man and woman, both naked, and painted using translucent, unprurient pastels, in front of a completely nonsexual pea-green background of hazy bedroom details (all emblematic of marriage). Fido-style is the theme here. In panel #1 they're both on their knees; in #2 "he's" standing and "she's" half draped off a bed, fully "offered"; in #3 they're both standing, and I can't see #4, though I'd like to.

"You finding some new recipes in there?" I leer down at her.

Her head twists around and up, and she gives me a brazen, pouty-mouth look that says: Mind your own business or I'll mind it for you. It makes me immediately like her, even if she won't unlock the fridge and build me up a Dagwood. This, I think, is the end of dinner, though my bet is she's got the combination committed to memory.

"I thought you wanted a sandwich," she says, looking back, amused at the canine escapades of two idealized pastel versions of married people who look like us. "Whatta you think she's saying?"

She points her short finger, which has some flour dried on its fingernail, at #1, in which the female is looking back around at the already hooked-up male, as if she's just had a good new idea. " 'Knock, knock, Who's there?' " the chef says. " 'Did you hear the garage door?' or 'Do you mind if I balance my checkbook?' " She tours her tongue roguishly around in her cheek and looks mock-disgusted, as if this were all just shameless.

"Maybe they're talking about a sandwich," I say, experiencing a gradual resituating of my own little-thought-of below-decks apparatus.

"Maybe they are," she says, leaning back again while she smokes. "Maybe she's sayin', 'Now, did you remember to buy Bibb lettuce, or did you get that old iceberg again?' "

"What's your name?" I say. (My talk with Sally has been more serious and relieving than actual fun.)

"C-h-a-r, Char," she says. She has a pop of her Genny and swallows it down. "Which is short for Charlane, not Charlotte and not Charmayne. My older sisters are blessed with those."

"Your pop must've been named Charles."

"You know him?" she says. "Great big loud guy with a tiny little brain?"

"I don't think so." I'm waiting for her to flip another page, interested to see what else our panelists come up with.

"Funny," she says, putting her Winston between her teeth so the smoke makes her squint, and pushing the bulky chef's sleeves above her fragile elbows. She is more delicate on second notice. Her outfit is what makes her look chunky and tough. The "chef look" is not a good look for her.

"How'd you get to be a chef?" I say, happier, even just for a moment, to be here in the lighted kitchen with a woman rather than scrounging a burger in the dark or struggling to make contact with my son.

"Oh, well, first I attended Harvard and got a Ph.D.—let's see— in, ah, can opening. Then I did my postdoctoral work in eggs and toast buttering. That must've been at MIT."

"I bet it's harder than English."

"You *would* think so." She lays the page over to reveal more pastel panels, this time spotlighting fellatio, with some vivid but tasteful close-ups showing everything you'd ever want to know from a picture. The female panelist, I notice, now has her hair tied back in an accommodating ponytail. "My, my," Char says.

"You a subscriber?" I say archly. My stomach makes another deep, organic-sounding grumble-gurgle.

"I just read what the guests leave after meals. That's all." Char pauses longer at the fellatio panels. "This was left under one of the chairs. I'll be interested by who asks about it tomorrow. My guess I'll get to keep it."

I picture ole horseface stealing down after lights-out to give the room a tumble.

"Listen," I say, with the sudden realization (again) that I can do anything I want (except get a plate of spaghetti). "Would you like to strike out to one of those bars and let me buy you another beer while I have a gin and maybe a sandwich? My name's Frank Bascombe, by the way." I give her a smile, wondering if we should shake hands.

"And by the way?" Char says, mocking me. She snaps the magazine shut back-to-front, and on the back is a full-page color ad for a thick, pink, anatomically audacious but rather fuzzily photographed dildo that some comical prior reader has drawn a red Happy Face on the business end of. "Well, hel-lo," Char says, peering down at the pink appendage grinning back off the tabletop. "Aren't *we* happy?" The dildo is referred to in the ad as "Mr. Standard Pleasure Unit," though I'm dubious about what it has to do with the standard marriage realities. Under standard circumstances, "Mr. Pleasure" would be a hard act to follow. "He" in fact doesn't have a particularly good effect on my own enthusiasm and leaves me oddly glum.

"Maybe I'll let you walk me over to the Tunnicliff," Char says, sliding the magazine out across the slick tabletop, rejecting Mr. Pleasure Unit as pie in the sky. She pushes back in her metal chair and turns her attention finally to me. "That's halfway home. And we'll say good night at that point."

"Great. That's great," I say. "That'll be a good end to the night for me."

She stays seated, however, squeezes her eyes shut, then pops them open as if she's just emerged from a trance, then woggles her head around to loosen everything up at the end of a long day's hard chefing. "What line of work you in, Frank?" She's not quite ready to get up, possibly deciding she needs more background on me.

"Residential realty."

"Where at?" She fingers her Winston hard pack as though she's thinking about something else.

"Down in Haddam, in New Jersey. About four hours from here."

"Never hoid of it," she says.

"It's a pretty well-kept secret."

"You in the Millionth Dollar Club? I'd be impressed if you were." She raises her eyebrows.

"Me too," I say. (In Haddam, of course, the Millionth Dollar Club had better be joined by Valentine's Day, or you're out of business by Easter.)

"I prefer to rent," Char says, staring inertly at the distant *Achieve Super Marital Sex* where she's shoved it away, with Mr. Standard Pleasure Unit's happy face turned up. "Actually I want to get into a condo, but a car costs what a house *used* to cost. And I'm still paying off my car." (Not a Harley.)

"You can rent these days," I say cheerfully, "for about half the cost of buying and save money to boot." (There's in fact no use telling her that at her age—twenty-eight or thirty-three—she's looking at a life of more of the same unless she robs a bank or marries a banker.)

"Well," Char says, suddenly motivated by something—an idea, a memory, a determination not to bellyache to a stranger. "I guess I just need to find a rich husband." She raps both sets of knuckles hard on the tabletop, grasps her pack of smokes and stands up (she is not very tall). "Let me get out of my Pillsbury doughgirl outfit." She's walking slowly away toward a little door off the kitchen, which when she opens it and snaps on the light within reveals a tiny, fluorescent-lit bathroom. "I'll meet you out on the piazza later," she says.

"I'll be there," I say at the door as it closes and goes locked.

I wander back out into the foyer to wait in the cool breeze through the screen. The old bucket-eared Swede is now hunched over the tiny phone where I'd been, his big, rough finger jammed in his other cavernous ear for better hearing. "Well, what makes you a saint, ya satchel-ass sonofabitch?" I hear him say. "For starters, tell me that. I'd like to get that straight tonight."

I look out through the screen, where all the chairs are now

empty—everyone safe in bed, plans in motion for an all-out Sunday morning assault on the Hall of Fame.

From the darkness of new-mown grass I hear the distant yet close harmonies of a barbershop quartet, singing what sounds very much like *"Michelle, ma belle, sont des mots qui vont très bien ensemble, très bien ensemble."* And back among the spruces and elm trunks I see a couple materializing in light-colored summery clothes, arms around, walking in step, returning (I'm certain) from a wonderful five-course dinner in some oak-paneled lakeside *auberge* now closed and locked up tight as Dick's hatband. They're laughing, which makes me realize that it is a good time of night to feel good, to be where you've been headed all day, blissful hours with a significant other still in front of you, half surprised that the day's gone this well, inasmuch as the 4th is the summer's pivotal day, when thoughts turn easily to fall and rapid change and shorter days and feelings of impendment that won't give way till spring. These two are ahead of the game.

They come into view now, in the inn's reflected window glow: he wearing white bucks, seersucker pants, a yellow jacket slung over his shoulder foreign-correspondent style; she in a flimsy pastel-green skirt and a pink Peter Pan blouse. By their flat Ohio vowels I recognize them as the couple from the parking lot back when I lay dozing and their interests lay in property values. Now they have other interests to pursue above floors.

"I ate way too much," he says. "I shouldn't have ordered that Cajun linguine. I'll never get to sleep."

"That's no excuse," she says. "You can sleep when you get home. I've got plans for you."

"You're the expert," he says, not at all eager enough by my standards.

"You're damn right I am," she says, then laughs. "Hah."

I want to be well out of their way when they come through—the lacquer of sex being suddenly too thick around me in the night air—want not to be standing behind the screen with a knowing, Now-you-two-have-a-real-good-sleep smirk on my mug. So, as their shoes hit the steps, I slip back into the living room to wait for my "date."

Two red-shaded lamps have been left on in the long, warm, overfurnished, cinnamon-scented parlor. The Ohioans troop by without seeing me, their voices falling, becoming more intimate as they reach the first landing and then the hallway above. They are full silent as their key enters the lock.

I cruise around the old wainscoted parlor lined with oak bookshelves, a full complement of cast-off butler and drumhead tables, slipcovered couches, wobbly hassocks, nautical-looking brass lamps—all scavenged at antique fairs and roadside flea markets in the Cortland-Binghamton-Oneonta triangle. The scented candle has been extinguished, and bulky shadows encompass the wall art, which includes, in addition to Natty Bumppo himself, a framed, yellowed topo from the Twenties, showing "Lake Otsego and Environs," several portraits of bewhiskered "founders"—doubtless all shopkeepers dressed up to look like presidential candidates—and a sampler hung over the main door, with good advice for the spiritual wanderer: "*Confidences are easy to give, but hard to get back.*"

I mouse over the various tabletops, fingering the reading matter—stacks of old MLS booklets for guests whose vacation idea is to consider putting down roots in an alien locale (the Ohioans, for example). The price of the fancy Federalist pile Paul and I passed this afternoon is eye-poppingly low by Haddam standards at 530K (something has to be wrong with it). Plenty of old *People*s and *American Heritage*s and *National Geographic*s are stacked up on the long library table by the back window. I browse down the shelf containing stiff bound editions of *New York History*, the Otsego *Times*, *The Encyclopedia of Collectibles*, *American Cage Bird* magazine, *Mechanix Illustrated*, Hersey's *Hiroshima* in three different editions, two whole yards of matched Fenimore Coopers, a *Golden Treasure of Quotable Poetry*, two volumes of *Rails of the World*, surprisingly enough another *Classic Holes of Golf*, a stack of recent Hartford *Courant*s—as if somebody had moved here from Hartford and wanted to stay in touch. And to my wonderment and out of all account, among the loose and uncategorized books, here is a single copy of my own now-old book of short stories, *Blue Autumn*, in its original dust jacket, on the front of which is a faded artist's depiction of a 1968-version sensitive-young-man, with a brush cut, an open-collared white shirt, jeans, and an uncertain half smile, standing emblematically alone in the dirt parking lot of a country gas station with an anonymous green pickup (possibly his) visible over his shoulder. Much is implied.

I flinch as always when I see it, since in a panicky time-crunch the artist elected to paint *my* face from my author's photo right onto the cover of my book, so that I see my young self now, made to look perplexed, forever staring out alone from the front of my very first (and only) literary effort.

And yet I cart the book over to one of the red-shaded lamps, full of unexpected thrill. The boxful that I own, shipped to Haddam when the book was remaindered, was left in the attic on Hoving Road, untouched since its arrival and of no more interest to me than a box of clothes that no longer fit.

But *this* book, this *specimen*, sparks interest—since it is after all still "out there," in circulation, still official if somewhat compromised, still striving to the purposes I meant it to: staging raids on the inarticulate, being an ax for the frozen sea within us, providing the satisfactions of belief in the general mess of imprecision. (Nothing's wrong with high-flown purposes, then or now.)

A cake of fine house dust covers the top, so it's clear none of tonight's Clue players has had it down for pre-bedtime sampling. The old binding makes a dry-leaves crackle as I open it back. Pages at the front, I see, are yellow and water-stained, whereas those in the middle are milky, smooth and untouched. I take a look at the aforementioned author photo, a black-and-white taken by my then-girlfriend, Dale McIver: again a young man, though this time with a completely unwarranted confidence etched in his skinny mouth, ludicrously holding a beer and smoking a cigarette (!), an empty sun-lit (possibly Mexican) barroom and tables behind, staring fixedly at the camera as though he meant to say: "Yep, you just about have to live out here on the wild margins to get this puppy done the way God intended. And *you* probably couldn't hack it, if you want to know the gospel." And I, of course, *couldn't* hack it; chose, in fact, a much easier puppy on a much less wild margin.

Though I'm not displeased to view myself thus—fore and aft, as it were, on my own book, two sides of the issue; not queasy in the hollow of my empty stomach where most of life-that-might've-been finally comes to rest. I carried that sandpaper regret around in me for a time back in 1970, then simply omitted it the way I'd have Paul omit the nightmares and dreads of his child's life stolen away by bad luck and unconscionable adults. Forget, forget, forget.

Nor is this the first time I've happened onto my book *blind*:

church book sales, sidewalk tables in Gotham, yard sales in unlikely midwestern cities, one rain-soaked night on top of a trash can behind the Haddam Public Library, where I was groping around in the dark to find the after-hours drop-off. And once, to my dismay, in a friend's house shortly after he'd blown his brains out, though I never thought my book played a part. Once published, a book never strays so far from its author.

But without thinking a thought about its absolute worth, I intend to put my book in Char's hands the moment she arrives and to speak the words I can't now wait to speak: "Who do you think wrote *this*, that I found right here on the shelf below Natty Bumppo's portrait and hard by the J. F. Coopers?" (My two likenesses will be my proof.) And not that it'll have any important favorable effect on her. But for *me*, finding it still in "use" is high on the manifest of writerly thrills longed for—along with seeing someone you don't know hungrily reading your book on an overland bus in Turkey; or noticing your book on the shelf behind the moderator on *Meet the Press* next to *The Wealth of Nations* and *Giants in the Earth*; or seeing your book on a list of overlooked American masterpieces compiled by former insiders in the Kennedy administration. (None of these has been my good luck yet.)

I blow the dust off and run my finger over the page ends to uncover the original red stain, then flip to the front and survey the contents page, twelve little titles, each as serious as a eulogy: "Words to Die By," "The Camel's Nose," "Epitaph," "Night Wing," "Waiting Offshore," all the way down to the title story— considered my "chance" at something to expand into a novel and thereby break me into the big time.

The book doesn't in fact seem ever to have been opened (only rained on). I turn past the dedication—"To My Parents" (who else?)—back to the title page, ready to greet crisp "Frank Bascombe," "*Blue Autumn*" and "1969," set out in sturdy, easy-on-the-eyeball Ehrhardt, and to feel the old synchronicity extend to me in the here and now. Except what my eye finds, scrawled over the title page in blue, and in a hand I don't know, is: "For Esther, remembering that really *bleu* autumn with you. Love ya, Dwayne. Spring, 1970," every bit of which has been x-ed through with a smeary lipstick and below it written: "Dwayne. Rhymes with pain. Rhymes with fuck. Rhymes with the biggest mistake of my life. With contempt for you and your cheap tricks. Esther. Winter, 1972." A big red smooch has been plastered on the page below Esther's signature, and this connected by an arrow to the words "My Ass," also in lipstick. This is a good deal different—by virtue of being a great deal less—than what I'd expected.

But what I feel, dizzily, is not wry, bittersweet, ain't-life-strange amusement at poor Dwayne and Esther's hot flame gone smoking under the waves, but a totally unexpected, sickening void opening right in my stomach—right where I said it wouldn't two minutes ago.

Ann, and the end of Ann and me and everything associated with us, comes fuming up in my nostrils suddenly like a thick poison and in a way it never has even in my darkest seven-year despairings, or in the grim aftermath of my periodic revivals of hope. And instead of bellowing like a gored Cyclops, what I instinctively do is whap my book shut and sling it side-arm whirligig across the room, where it smacks the brown wall, knocks loose a crust of Florida-shaped plaster and hits the floor in the crumbles and dust. (Many fates befall books other than being read and treasured.)

The chasm (and what else is it?) between our long-ago time and this very moment suddenly makes yawningly clear that all is now done and done for; as though she was never *that* she, me never *that* me, as though the two of us had never embarked on a life that would lead to this queer librarial moment (though we did). And rather than being against all odds, it's in precise accordance with the odds: that life would lead to here or someplace just as lonely and spiritless, no less likely than for Dwayne and fiery, heartbroke Esther, our doubles in love. Gone in a hiss and fizzle. (Though if it weren't that tears had just sprung stinging to my eyes, I'd accept my loss with dignity. Since after all I'm the man who counsels abandonment of those precious things you remember but can no longer make hopeful use of.)

I drag my wrist across my cheeks and dab my eyes with my shirt-front. Someone, I sense, is coming from somewhere in the house, and I hustle over, snake up my book, refit its cover, flatten the pages I've busted and carry it back to its coffin slot, where it can sleep for twenty more years—this just as Char appears at the front door, looks out, then sees me standing here like a teary immigrant and saunters in smelling of cigarettes and appley sweetness applied just on the off chance I might be the guy to buy her that condo.

And Char is not the Char of ten minutes ago. She's dressed now in some shrunk-tight jeans with red cowboy boots, a concha belt, a sleeveless black tank top that reveals strong, round, bare athletic shoulders and the breasts I've already envisioned (now in *much* plainer view). She has done "something" to her eyes, and also to her hair, which has made it frizzier. There's rose color in her cheeks, and what seems like glistening lubricant on her lips, so that she's recognizable from when she was a chef, but only just. Though to me she's not nearly as comely as in her boxy whites, when less of her was in view.

But neither am I in the same "place" emotion-wise as ten minutes ago, nor am I exactly used to women with their tits on such nautical display. And I'm now no longer looking forward to being hauled through the door of the Tunnicliff—a place I can all too perfectly picture—and filling the slot as one of "Char's guys from the inn" while the locals grab off their nightly geeze at those hogans, while writing me off as the doofus I am.

"All right, Mr. Pleasure Unit, you ready to roll? Or are you still reading the instructions?" Char's new eyelashes bat closed and open, her small hazel eyes roguishly fixing me. "What's wrong with your eyes? You been in here crying? Is that what I'm getting into?"

"I looked at a book and got dust in my eyes," I say ludicrously.

"I didn't know anybody ever *read* those books. I thought they were just to make the room look cozy." She surveys the shelves, unimpressed. "Jeremy buys 'em by the metric ton from some recycler up in Albany." She sniffs, detecting some of the cinnamon redolence. "Pew. P-U," she says. "Smells like an old folks' home at Christmas in here. I'm in need of a Black Velvet." She fires me off a challenging smile. A smile with a future.

"Great!" I say, thinking I'd feel better if I could just take a walk by myself down to the soggy lakeshore and hear the tinkly, liquid sounds of faceless, nameless others enjoying themselves gaily in long, red-walled rooms lit by crystal chandeliers. Not much to ask.

But I can't back out on something as unfreighted as a simple walk and a drink, especially since it's me did the asking. Canceling will make me out to be a weepy, cringing nutcase who can't go a step without scuttling back three for fear and shame.

"Maybe I'll just have to break down and cook you a fried-egg sandwich à la Charlane. Since you're so starved." She's moving toward the front screen, her hard butt encased in denim like a rodeo wrangler's, her thighs chunky and taut.

"I should try to find my son eventually, I guess," I mutter not quite loud enough to be heard, following onto the porch, where little town lights twinkle in through the trees.

"Say what?" Char gives me a head-cocked look. We're in the solid porch darkness here now.

"My son Paul's here with me," I say. "We're going to the Hall of Fame in the morning."

"Did you leave Mom at home this time?" She rolls her tongue around inside her cheek again. She has heard a warning signal.

"In a sense I did. I'm not married to her anymore."

"So who *are* you married to?"

"Nobody."

"And where's your son gone?" She glances out around at the dark lawn, as if he's there. She runs a finger under her tank top strap, attempting to seem noncommittal. I sniff apple perfume again. That would have to go.

"I don't know where he is," I say, trying to sound both at ease and concerned. "He sort of took off when we got here. I had a nap."

"When was this?"

"I guess five-thirty or a quarter to six. I'm sure he'll be coming back pretty soon." I've lost all heart for everything now—a walk, the Tunnicliff, a drink, *oeufs à la Charlane.* Though my failure is a part of human mystery I understand, even have sympathy for. "I should maybe stick around here. So he can find me." I smile cravenly at her in the darkness.

Out on the highway a dark car rumbles past, its windows open or its top down, loud rock music blaring and thumping through the silent trees. I can make out one scalding phrase only: "Get wet, go deep, take it all." Paul could be there, in the act of disappearing forever, to be seen by me only on milk cartons or grocery store bulletin boards: "Paul Bascombe, 2–8–73, last seen near Baseball Hall of Fame, 7–2–88." It is not a relaxing thought.

"Well, whatever stokes your flame the hottest, I guess," Charlane says, already I hope thinking of something else. "I gotta take off, though." She's leaving down the steps right away, concluding I'm more trouble than I'm worth, though also probably embarrassed for me.

"Do you have any children?" I say just to say something.

"Oh yeah," she says, and half turns back.

"Where's he right now?" I say. "Or she. Or they?"

"*He's* at wilderness survival."

I hear a faint cry then, a woman's high-pitched voice, brief and ululating, from somewhere above. Char looks up and around, a little smile crossing her lips. "Somebody's enjoying her fireworks early."

"What's your son learning to survive?" I say, trying not to think about the Ohioans right above us. Char and I are descending back through the stages of familiarity and in a minute will once again be unknown to each other.

She sighs. "He's with his dad, who lives out in Montana in a tent or a cave someplace. I don't know. I guess they're surviving each other."

"I'm sure you're a great mom," I say, apropos of nothing.

"Eastern religion," she says in a wise-cracky voice. "Motherhood's as close as I come to it." She raises her small nose toward the warm, spruce-scented air and sniffs. "I smelled a lilac just then, but it's too late for lilacs. Musta been somebody's perfume." She squints down hard at me as though I've suddenly moved far, far away and am moving farther (which I am). It's a friendly squint, full of sympathy, and makes me want to come down off the porch and give her a bustly hug, but which would only confuse matters. "I assume you'll find your son," she says. "Or he'll find you. Whatever."

"We will," I say, holding my ground. "Thanks."

"Yep," Char says, and then, as though she's embarrassed by something else, adds, "They don't usually stay gone long. Not long enough, really." Then she hikes off into the trees alone, gone out of sight well before I can manage an audible good-bye.

"*Très amusant*," a voice familiar to me speaks out of the summer's wicking darkness. "*Très, très amusant*. Your most important sexual organ is between your ears. Eeeck, eeeck, eeeck. So use it."

Down the porch, in the last rocking chair in line, Paul is slouched barely visible behind his drawn-up knees, his *The Rock* shirt giving out the only light hereabouts. He's been overhearing my

cumbersome parting, no doubt wondering if I'll get around to finding our dinner.

"Howz ur health?" I say, walking down the line of rockers, laying
a palm on the smooth spindled back of his and giving it a small,
fatherly push.

"Fine 'n' yours?"

"Is that Dr. Rection's anatomy advice?" I am, God knows, full
of airy relief he's not departed for Chicago or the Bay Area in the
blaring-music car, or not off getting his ashes perilously hauled,
or, worse, stretched out in the Cooperstown ER with a wound
drip-drip-dripping on the tiles, waiting for some old turkey-neck
GP, woozy from the Tunnicliff, to shake his head clear. (If I intend
to have him home with me, I'll need to be more vigilant.)

"Was that my new mom?"

"Almost. Did you eat anything?"

"I got a mocktail, some mock turtle soup and a piece of mock
apple pie. Don't mock me, please." These are all holdovers from
childhood. If I could see his face, it would be worked into a look of
secret satisfaction. He seems, however, completely calm. I might be
making progress with him and not realizing it (every parent's dearest hope).

"Do you want to call your mother and say you got here safely?"

"Ix-nay." He's tossing a little Hacky Sack up and down in the
dark, barely making movement but suggesting he's less calm than
seems. I have an aversion to Hacky Sacks. My view is that its skills
are perfect only for the sort of brain-dead delinquents who whonked
me in the head on my way home from work this spring and sent me
sprawling. I understand from it, though, that Paul may have made a
connection with the towny kids on the corner.

"Where'd you get that thing?"

"I purchased it." He still hasn't looked around. "At the local
Finast." I would still like to ask him if he killed the helpless, driveway grackle, only it now seems too unwieldy a subject. It also seems
preposterous to think he could be guilty. "I've got a new question to
ask you." He says this in a more assertive voice. Conceivably he's
spent the last four hours in a badly lit diner studying Emerson, fingering his Hacky Sack and mulling issues such as whether nature
really suffers nothing to remain in her kingdom that can't help
itself; or whether every true man is a cause, a country and an age.
Good issues for anyone to mull.

"Okay," I say just as assertively, not wanting to seem as eager and encouraged as I am. From across the lawn the tart odor not of lilac but of a car's exhaust reaches my nostrils. I hear an owl, invisible on a nearby spruce bough. *Who-who, who-who, who-who.*

"Okay, do you remember when I was pretty little," Paul says very seriously, "and I used to invent friends? I had some talks with them, and they said things to me, and I'd get pretty involved doing it?" He stares fiercely forward.

"I remember it. Are you doing it again?" This is not about Emerson.

He looks around at me now, as if he wants to see my face. "No. But did it make you feel weird when I did that? Like make you mad or sick and want to puke?"

"I don't think so. Why?" I'm able to make out his eyes. I'm certain he thinks I'm lying.

"You're lying, but it's okay."

"I felt odd about it," I say. "Not any of those other things, though." I am not willing to be called a liar and have no defense in the truth.

"Why were you?" He doesn't seem angry.

"I don't know. I never thought about it."

"Then think. I *need* to know. It's like one of my rings." He shifts back around and trains his gaze across toward the windows of the fancier inn across the road, where fewer warm and yellow room lights are on now. He wants my voice in his ears perfectly distilled. The waning moon has laid a silken, sparkling path dead across the lake, and above its luminance is arrayed a feast of summer stars. He makes, and I vaguely hear it, another tiny *eeeck*, a self-assuring sound, a little rallying *eeeck*.

"It made me feel a little weird," I say uncomfortably. "I thought you were getting preoccupied with something that maybe was hurtful in the long run." (Innocence, what else? Though that word seems not exactly right either.) "I wanted you not to get tricked. I guess maybe it wasn't very generous of me. I'm sorry. Maybe I'm wrong too. I could've just been jealous. I am sorry."

I hear him breathe, air hitting his bare knees where he has them hugged up to his chest. I feel a small loosening of relief, mixed of course with shame for ever making him feel his preoccupations mattered less than mine. Who'd have thought we'd talk about this?

"It's all right," he says, as if he knew a great, great deal about me.

"Why'd this come to mind?" I say, a warm hand still on his rocking chair, his back still turned to me.

"I just remember it. I liked doing it, and I thought you thought it was bad. Don't you really think something's wrong with me?" he says—unbeknownst to him, fully within his own command now, an adult for just this moment.

"I don't think so. Not especially."

"On a scale of one to five, with five being hopeless?"

"Oh," I say. "One, probably. Or one and a half. It's better than me. Not as good as your sister."

"Do you think I'm shallow?"

"What do you do that's shallow?" I wonder where he's been to come back with these questions.

"Make noises sometimes. Other things."

"They aren't very important."

"Do you remember how old Mr. Toby would be now? I'm sorry to ask that."

"Thirteen," I say bravely. "You did ask me about that today already."

"He could still be alive, though." He rocks forward, then back, then forward. Maybe life will seem better when Mr. Toby reaches the end of his optimum life span. I hold his chair steady. "I'm thinking I'm thinking again," he says as if to himself. "Things don't fit down together right for very long."

"Are you worried about your court hearing?" I pinch his chairback hard between my fingers and hold it nearly still.

"Not especially," he says, copying me. "Were you supposed to give me some big advice about it?"

"Just don't try to be the critic of your age, that's all. Don't be a wise-ankle. Let your best qualities come through naturally. You'll be fine." I touch his clean cotton shoulder, ashamed again, this time for waiting till now to touch him lovingly.

"Are you coming up with me?"

"No. Your mother's going."

"I think Mom's got a boyfriend."

"That's not interesting to me."

"Well, it should be." He says this completely without commitment.

"You don't know. Why do you think you remember everything and think you're thinking?"

"I don't know." He stares out at headlights that are curving along the road in front of our inn. "That stuff just comes back around all the time."

"Do the things seem important to you?"

"Importanter than what?"

"I don't really know. Importanter than something else you might do." The debating club, getting your Junior Life Saver's certificate, anything in the here and now.

"I don't want to have it forever. That'd be completely fucked up." His teeth click down once and grind together hard. "Like today for a while, back at the basketball thing, it went away for a while. Then I got it back."

We pause in silence again. The first adult conversation a man can have with his son is one in which he acknowledges he doesn't know what's good for his own child and has only an out-of-date idea of what's bad. I don't know what to say.

Through the trees now there comes into view a medium-size brown-and-white dog, a springer, loping toward us, a yellow Frisbee in his mouth, his collar jingling, his breath exaggerated and audible. Somewhere out behind him, a man's hearty voice, someone out for a walk in the parky darkness. "Keester! Here, Keester," the voice says. "Come on now, Keester. Fetch it! Keester—here, Keester." Keester, on a mission of his own, stops, looks at us in the porch shadows, sniffs us, his Frisbee clenched tight, while his master strolls on, calling.

"Come on now, Keester," Paul says. "Eeeck, eeeck."

"It's Keester, the wonder dog," I say. Keester seems happy to be just that.

"I was bewildered when I saw I'd turned into a dog—"

"Named Keester," I say. Keester stares up at us now, uncertain why we strangers would know his name. "I guess my thinking is," I say, "you're trying to keep too much under control, son, and it's holding you back. Maybe you're trying to stay in touch with something you liked, but you have to keep going. Even if it's scary and you screw up."

"Uh-huh." He leans his head back toward me and looks up. "How can I not be a critic of my age? Is that something you think's pretty great?"

"It doesn't have to be great," I say. "But for instance, if you go in a restaurant and the floor's marble and the walls are oak, you wouldn't wonder if it's all fake. You'd sit down and order tournedos and be happy. And if you don't like it, or you think it's a mistake to eat there, you just don't come back. Does that make any sense?"

"No." He shakes his head confidently. "I probably wouldn't stop thinking about it. Sometimes it's not that bad to think about it. Keester," he says in a sharp command voice to poor old baffled Keester. "Think! Think, boy! Remember your name."

"It *will* make sense," I say. "You don't have to fight to get everything right, that's all. Sometimes you can relax." I notice two more yellow window squares go dark in the big inn across the way. *Who-who*, goes the owl. *Who-who. Who-who*. He's got Keester in his sights, standing stupidly with his yellow Frisbee, waiting for us to get interested in throwing it, as we always do.

"If you're a tightrope walker in the circus, what's your best trick?" Paul looks up at me, smiling cruelly.

"I don't know. Doing it blindfolded. Doing it naked."

"Falling," Paul says authoritatively.

"That's not a trick," I say. "It's a fuck-up."

"Yeah, but he can't stand the straight and narrow another minute, because it's so boring. And nobody ever knows if he falls or jumps. It's great."

"Who told you about that?" Keester, finally disappointed by us, turns and trots off through the trees, becoming a paler and paler hole in the dark, then is gone.

"Clarissa. She's worse than I am. She just doesn't show it. She doesn't act out anything, because she's sneaky."

"Who says?" I am absolutely certain this isn't true, certain she's just as she seems, flipping the bird behind her parents' backs like any normal girl.

"Dr. Lew D. Zyres sez," Paul says, and suddenly bounds up, with me still clinging to his chairback. "My session's over tonight, Doctah." He starts off toward the front screen, his big shoes noisily clunkety-clunking on the porch boards. He is again trailing a sour smell. Possibly it is the smell of stress-related problems. "We need some fireworks," he says.

"I've got bottle rockets and sparklers in the car. And this wasn't a session. We don't have sessions. This was you and your father having a serious talk."

"People are always shocked at me when I say"—the screen swings open and Paul tromps in out of sight—"ciao."

"I love you," I say to my son, slipping away, but who should hear these words again if only to be able to recall much later on: "Somebody said that to me, and nothing since then has really seemed quite as bad as it might have."

10

"You know, Jerry, the truth is I just began to realize I didn't care what happened to me, you know? Worry and worry about making your life come out right, you know? Regret everything you say or do, everything seems to sabotage you, then you try to quit sabotaging yourself. But then *that's* a mistake. Finally you just have to figure a lot's out of your control, right?"

"Right! Thanks! Bob from Sarnia! Next caller. You're on *Blues Talk*. You're on the air, Oshawa!"

"Hi, Jerry, it's Stan. . . ."

Out my window a tall, blond, bronze-skinned, no-shirt, chisel-chest hombre of about my own age is working a big chamois cloth over a red vintage Mustang with what looks to be red-and-white Wisconsin plates. For some reason he's wearing green lederhosen, and it is his loud and blarey radio that has shaken me awake. Crackling morning light and leafy shadow spread across the gravel and the lawns of neighborhood houses behind the inn. It's Sunday. The lederhosen guy's here for the "Classic Car Parade," which rolls tomorrow, and doesn't want the dust and grime to get ahead of him. His pretty plump-as-a-knödel wife is perched on the fender of *my* car, sunning her short brown legs and smiling. They've hung their bright red floor mats off my bumper to dry.

Another American—Joe Markham, for instance—might snarl out at them: "Getyerfuckinmatsoffyaasshole." But that would spoil a morning, wake the world too early (including my son). Bob from Sarnia has already put it well enough.

By eight I've shaved and showered, using the clammy, tiny-windowed, beaverboard cubicle, already hot and malodorous from the previous user (I spied the woman with the neck brace slipping in, slipping out).

Paul is twisted into his covers when I rouse him with our oldest reveille: "Time's a wastin' . . . miles to go . . . I'm hungry as a bear . . . hop in the shower." We've checked out when we checked in and now have only to eat and beat it.

Then I'm down the stairs, hearing church bells already, as well as the muffled sumptuary noises of belly-buster breakfasts being eaten in the dining room by a group of total strangers who have only the Baseball Hall of Fame in common.

I'm eager to call Ted Houlihan (I forgot to try again last night), and get him ready for a miracle: the Markhams have crumbled; my strategy's borne fruit; his balls are as good as gone. Though the choking-man diagram, here again above the phone as I listen to ring after ring, reminds me unerringly of what realty's all about: we—the Markhams, the bad apples at Buy and Large, Ted, me, the bank, the building inspectors—we're all hankering to get our hands around somebody's neck and strangle the shit out of him for some little half-chewed piece of indigestible gristle we identify as our "nut," the nitty gritty, the carrot that makes the goat trot. Better, of course, to take a higher road, operate on the principle of service and see if things don't turn out better. . . .

"Hello?"

"Hey, good news, Ted!" I shout straight into the receiver. The breakfast club in the next room falls hushed at my voice—as if I'd gone hysterical.

"Good news here too," Ted says.

"Let's hear yours first." I am instantly wary.

"I sold the house," Ted says. "Some new outfit down in New Egypt. Bohemia, or something, Realty. They got it off the MLS. The woman brought a Korean family over last night around eight. And I had an offer in hand by ten." When I was gabbing with Paul about whether or not he's truly hopeless. "I called you around nine and left a message. But I really couldn't say no. They put the money in their trust account night deposit."

"How much?" I say grimly. I experience a small, tight chill and my stomach goes corked.

"What's that?"

"How much did the Koreans pay?"

"Full boat!" Ted says exuberantly. "Sure. One fifty-five. I jewed the girl a point too. She hadn't done anything to earn it. You'd done more by a long shot. Your office gets half, of course."

"My clients just don't have anyplace to live now, Ted." My voice has lowered to a razor-thin whisper. I would be happy to choke Ted with my hands. "We had an exclusive listing with you, we talked about that yesterday, and at the least you were going to get in touch with me so I could put a competitive offer in, which is what I've got authorized." Or nearly. "One fifty-five. Full boat, you said."

"Well." Ted pauses in a funk. "I guess if you want to come back at one-sixty, I could tell the Koreans I forgot. Your office would have to work it out with Bohemia. Evelyn something's the girl's name. She's a little go-getter."

"What I think is, Ted, we're going to have to probably sue you for breach of contract." I say this calmly, but I'm not calm. "Have to tie your house up for a couple of years while the market drops, and let you convalesce at home." All baloney, of course. We've never sued the first client. It's business suicide. Instead, you simply bag your 3%, of which I get half, exactly $2,325, maybe make a worthless complaint to the state realty board, and forget about it.

"Well, you have to do what you have to do, I guess," Ted says. I'm sure he's standing once again at the rumpus room window in a sleeveless sweater and chinos, mooning out at his pergola, his luau torches and the bamboo curtain he's just breached in a big way. I wonder if the Koreans even bothered to walk out back last night. Although a big lighted prison might've made them feel safer. They aren't fools.

"Ted, I don't know what to say." The noisy eaters in the next room have started back tink-tink-tinking their flatware, mouths full of pancakes, blabbing about how the berm-improvements work between here and Rochester'll "impact" on driving times to the Falls. Suddenly my chill is over and I'm hot as a sauna bath.

"You might just feel happy for me, Frank, instead of suing me. I'll probably be dead in a year. So it's good I sold my house. I can go live with my son now."

"I really just wanted to sell it for you, Ted." I am made lightheaded at the unexpected arousal of death. "I've *got* it sold, in fact," I say faintly.

"You'll find them another house, Frank. I didn't think they much liked it here."

I push my fingertips hard onto the stack of year-old *Annie Get Your Gun* tickets. Someone, I see, has slid the copy of *Achieve Super Marital Sex* underneath the stack, with old Mr. Pleasure Unit's happy face peeking upward. "They liked it a lot," I say, thinking about Betty Hutton in a cowboy hat. "They were cautious, but they're sure now. I hope your Koreans are that reliable."

"Twenty thousand clams. No contingencies," Ted says. "And they know there's other parties interested, so they'll follow up. These people don't throw money away, Frank. They own a sod farm down around Fort Dix, and they want to move up in the world." He would like to burble on about his good fortune now that he's started, but doesn't out of politeness to me.

"I'm just really disappointed, Ted. That's all I can say." Though I'm inventorying my mind for an acceptable fallback, sweat beginning to prickle out of my forehead. I'm to blame for this, for getting diverted from standard practices (though I don't know that I have any practice I could class as standard).

"Who you voting for this fall?" Ted says. "You guys all pull for business, I guess, don't you?" I'm wondering if some computer wizard at Bohemia has hacked into our office circuitry. Or possibly Julie Loukinen, who's new, is double-dipping on our potentials list. I try to remember if I've ever seen her with a scruffy Eastern European–looking boyfriend. Though most likely Ted just listed his house as "exclusive" with everybody who came to the door. (And who can be surprised in a free country? It's laissez-faire: serve your granny to the neighbors for brunch.) "You know neither Dukakis or Bush wants to put out a budget. They don't want to deliver any unhappy news in case it might offend somebody. I'd much rather they told me they were about to fuck me so I wouldn't tense up." Randy new lingo for Ted, the successful house seller. "You want me to take that sign down, by the way?"

"We'll send somebody out," I say glumly.

Then suddenly my line to Penns Neck goes loud with fierce papery static so that I can barely hear Ted jibbering on, half gassed, about fin de siècle qualms and something or other, I don't know what.

"I can't hear you now, Ted," I say into the old gunk-smelling receiver, frowning at the stick-figure man signaling me he's choking, his own hands at his throat, a look of rounded dismay on his balloon face. Then the static stops and I can hear Ted starting in about Bush and Dukakis not being able to tell a good joke if their asses depended on it. I hear him laugh at the whole idea. "So long, Ted," I say, sure he can't hear me.

"I read where Bush accepted Christ as his personal savior. Now there's a joke . . . ," Ted's saying extra loud.

I set the receiver gently in its cradle, understanding this bit of life—his and mine—is now over with. I'm almost grateful.

*M*y sworn duty is of course to call the Markhams in a timely manner and break the news, which I try to do, though they're not in their room at the Raritan Ramada. (No doubt they're going through the brunch buffet a second time, cocky for making the right decision—too late.) No one comes on the line after twenty-five rings. I call back to leave a message, but a recording puts me on hold, then leaves me out in murky "hold" purgatory, where an FM station is playing "Jungle Flute." I count to sixty, my hands getting clammy, then decide to call back later since nothing's at stake anymore.

There are other calls I should make. A hectoring, early-bird "business" call to the McLeods, with an innuendo of unspecified pending actions regarding matters of rent irrespective of personal financial pinches; a call to Julie Loukinen just to let her know "somebody" has let Ted swim through the net. A call to Sally to reaffirm all feelings and say whatever comes into my head, no matter how puzzling. None of these, though, do I feel quite up to. Each seems too complicated on a hot morning, none likely to be rewarding.

But just as I turn to go shake Paul loose from his dreams again, I feel a sudden, flushed, almost breathless urge to call Cathy Flaherty in Gotham. Plenty of times I've considered just how welcome (and gratifying) it would be were she just to appear on my doorstep with a bottle of Dom Perignon, demanding an instant barometer reading on me, take my temperature, get the lowdown on how I've *really* been since we last made contact, having naturally enough thought about me no fewer than a million times, with multiple what-ifs embedded everywhere, finally deciding to hunt me down via the Michigan Alumni Association and show up unannounced but "hopefully" not unwelcome. (In my first-draft of the script, we only talk.)

As I was thinking in my room at Sally's two days ago, few things are as pleasing as being asked to do basically nothing but having all good things come to you as if by right. It's exactly what poor Joe Markham wanted to happen with his Boise "friend," except she was too smart for him.

As it happens, I still have Cathy's number committed to memory from the last time I heard her voice, after Ann announced four years ago that she and Charley were tying the knot and taking the kids, and I was tossed for several loop-the-loops, landing me in the realty business. (Back then I only heard Cathy's recorded message and couldn't think of one of my own to leave other than to shout "Help, help, help, help!" and hang up, which I decided against.)

But almost before I know it, I've dialed the old number in old 212—a place once guaranteed to work a strange, funkish, double-whammy of low self-regard on me when I worked there as a sports-writer and life was coming unglued the first time. (Now it seems no stranger than Cleveland; such are the freeing, desanctifying fringe benefits of selling real estate.)

More avid cafeteria-eating noises, commingled with mirthless laughter, rise and ebb from next door. I wait for the 212 circuits to lock in on a ring and an answer to occur to someone—honey-haired, honey-skinned Cathy, I'm happily hoping, by now a bona fide M.D., doing her something-or-other, highly competitive specialty whatchamacallit up at Einstein or Cornell, and conceivably willing (it's also my hope) to take me on for a few moments' out-of-context, ad hominem–pro bono phone "treatment." (I'm actually counting on reverse spin here, by which the sound of Cathy's voice will at once make me feel smart—as can happen—but also feel that I'd better get cracking or face being plowed under by advancing generations with ice water in their veins.)

Ring-ring-ring-a-jing. Ring-ring-ring. Then click. Then a brusque mechanical whir, then another click. It's not promising. Then, finally, a voice—male, young, smug, as yet undisappointed, an insufferable smart aleck for whom outgoing messages are nothing but chances to gloatingly entertain himself, while demonstrating what an asshole he is to us blameless callers-in. "Hi. This is Cathy and Steve's answering mechanism. We're not home now. Really. I promise. We're not lounging in bed making faces and laughing. Cathy's probably at the hospital, saving lives or something like that. I'm probably down at Burnham and Culhane, slicing out a bigger piece of the pie for myself. So just be patient and leave us a message, and when time permits one of us will call you back. Probably it'll be Cathy, since answering machines really kind of bug me. See ya. Bye. Of course wait for the beep."

Beeeeeeeeeeeeeeeeeeeeep, click, then the yawning, paralyzing opportunity to leave the most appropriate of messages. "Hi, Cathy?" I say, exhilarated. "It's Frank." (Less exhilarated.) "Um. Bascombe. Nothing special, really. I'm, uh, it's the Fourth of July, or right about then. I'm just up here in Cooperstown, just happened to think about you." At 8 a.m. "I'm glad to know you're at the hospital. That's a good sign. I'm pretty fine. Up here with my son, Paul, who you don't know." A long pause while the tape's running. "Well, that's about it. By the way, you can tell Steve for me that he can kiss my ass, and I'd be happy to beat the shit out of him any day he can find the time. Bye." Click. I stand a moment, the receiver in my sweaty hand, assessing what I've just done in terms of how it has left me feeling, and also in terms of its character as a small but rash act, possibly foolish and demeaning. And the answer is: better. Much better. Unaccountably. Some idiotic things are well worth doing.

I hike back upstairs to pack, roll Paul out and get the day whacking, since at least for my main purpose (the Markhams aside) it still has some rudiments of promise based on last night's edgy rapprochement and in any case will end soon enough far from here, with Sally at Rocky and Carlo's.

Paul meets me at the head of the stairs, hauling along his Paramount bag and wearing his Walkman ear calipers on his neck. He's groggy and wet-haired, but he's put on fresh baggy maroon shorts, fresh Day-Glo-orange socks and a big new black tee-shirt that for reasons I know nothing of says *Clergy* in white on the front (possibly a rock group). When he sees me coming up he offers me his fat-cheeked, impassive expression, as if knowing about me was one thing but seeing me quite another. "I'm surprised to see a fart-smeller like you up here," he says, then makes a little throaty *oink* and passes on down the stairs.

In five minutes, though, after making a check for telltale wetness in Paul's sheets (nothing), I'm back downstairs with my suit bag and my Olympus, ready for breakfast, except the big dining room is still packed with poky breakfasters and Paul is standing at the doorway, staring in with amused disdain. Charlane, in a tight tee-shirt and the same faded jeans from last night, is serving more plates of flapjacks and bacon and bowls of steaming instant scrambled. She looks at me but seems not to recognize me. So that I quickly decide there's no use waiting (and being ministered to spitefully by Charlane) when we can just as well stash our gear in the car, hike to Main and scare up breakfast for ourselves before the Hall of Fame opens at nine. In other words, let the old Deerslayer sink into history.

Though it hasn't been that bad a place, lack of an honor bar notwithstanding. Inside its walls, I may have ended the seemingly unendable with Ann, dodged a ricochet with Charlane and, possibly, set things on the rails with Sally Caldwell. Plus, Paul and I have skirmished nearer each other's trust, and I have been able at least to speak a few of the way-pointing words I'd prepared for that purpose. All noteworthy accomplishments. With only slightly better luck, the Deerslayer could've become a hallowed and even sacred place where, say, early next century, Paul could come back alone or with a wife or girlfriend or his own troublesome brood, and tell them this was a place he "used to come with his late dad," where life-altering wisdom that made all the difference in later life was passed along—though he might not be able to say with complete certainty what the wisdom was.

Several munching breakfasters (I see no one I recognize) have raised wintry eyes up from their plates to where Paul and I are standing at the dining room door, briefly transfixed by deep currents of good coffee, smoked sausage, hash browns, sticky buns, pancake syrup, scrapple and powdered eggs. Their guarded eyes say, "Hey, we won't be hurried." "We've paid for this." "We're entitled to our own pace." "It's our vacation." "Waitchyerturn." "Isn't that the joker who was shouting on the phone?" "What about this 'Clergy' shirt?" "Something's fishy here."

Paul, though, his Paramount bag slung to his pudgy shoulder, suddenly sets both his hands palms out against the invisible wall and begins sliding them place to place, here and there, up, down, side to side, a look of empty-mouthed horror contorting his sweet boy's face, and whispering "Help me, help me. I don't want to die."

"So I don't think there's room at the inn for us, son," I say.

"Please don't let me die," Paul continues softly, so only I can hear. "Just don't drop the tablet in the acid. Please, warden." He *is* a sweet, tricky boy and after my heart—my ally just when (or almost when) I feel most in need.

He turns his dying-man's face of hollow-yap horror up to me, his hands now to his cheeks in silent, stricken astonishment. No one in the room has the will to look at him now, their noses back in their vittles like jailbirds. He makes two plainly audible *eeeck*s that seem to come out of the bottom of a shallow well. "Alias Sibelius," he says.

"What's that mean?" I hike my suit bag up, ready to roll.

"It's a good punch line. I can't think of the joke, though. Mom puts arsenic in my food since she got a boyfriend. So my IQ's dropping."

"I'll try to talk to her," I say, and then we are off, no one noticing as we step together out into the morning's hot brilliance, bound for the Hall of Fame.

*C*hurch bells now clang and clatter all over town, rounding 'em up for morning worship. Well-dressed, pale-faced family groups of three, four and even six march two abreast down every village sidewalk, veering this way toward the Second Methodist, that way toward the Congregationalists, across to Christ Church Episcopal and the First Prez. Others, less well turned out—men in clean but unpressed work khakis and polo shirts, women in red wraparounds, no stockings and a scarf—exit cars to dash into Our Lady of the Lake for a brief and breathless brush with grace before heading off to a waitress job, a tee time or an assignation in some other village.

Paul and I, on the other hand, fit in well with the pilgrim feel of things temporal—nonworshipful, nonpious, camera-toting dads and sons, dads and daughters, in summery togs, winding our certain but vaguely embarrassed way toward the Hall of Fame (as if there were something shameful about going). Cars are moving by us, the Gay Nineties trolleys toting "senior groups" to the town's other attractions—the Fenimore House and the Farmers' Museum, where there are displays and demos of things as they used to be when the world was better. Plus, all the shops are open, ice cream's for sale, music's in the air, the lake's full of water, nothing a visitor could want wouldn't be taken into at least partial account by somebody.

We have parked our gear in the car behind the inn and hiked by dead reckoning down to the marina and into a booth in a little aquablue eatery with oversize windows called The Water's Edge, built right out over the water like Charley's studio, only on creosote pilings. Inside, though, it's so rigidly cold that the cheese fries and Denver omelet aromas seem as dank as the inside of an old ice chest, making me feel, in spite of scenic lake views, that we would've been smarter to wait for a place where we'd already paid.

Paul, on our walk over through the short, lakeside back streets lined with homey blue-collar abodes, has raised himself to the best good humor of the trip, and once we're in our red booth has commenced a wide-ranging discourse of what it'd be like to live in Cooperstown.

Working over his Deluxe Belgian, piled with canned whipped cream and gelid strawberries, he declares that if we were to move here he would definitely invest in a "big paper route" (in Deep River, he says, this is an industry bossed over by "Italian greasers" who kick ass on whitebread kids who try to horn in). He likewise says, all sarcasm gone, gray eyes sparkling while he eats, that he'd feel obligated to visit the Hall of Fame once a week until he had it memorized—"Why else live here?"—and that he would eat here at The Water's Edge "religiously every Sunday morning," just like now, would find out all about the Cardiff Giant (another local attraction) and the Farmers' Museum, possibly even work there as a guide, and would probably go out for baseball and football. He also surprisingly informs me, while I'm plowing through my own fast-congealing "Home Run Plate" and occasionally gazing out at a flock of mallards mooching popcorn from boat dock tourists, that he's decided to read all of Emerson when he gets home, since he'll probably be on probation and have more time for reading. He muddles his liquefying whipped cream around over his waffle cleats, getting it conscientiously into all sectors while explaining to me, head down, his Walkman still on his neck, that as a "borderline dyslexic" (this is news to me) he notices more than most people in his age bracket, since he doesn't "process" things as fast and ends up having more opportunity to consider (or get completely derailed by) "certain subjects," which is why he reads the labor-intensive *New Yorker*—"klepto'd out of Chuck's crapper"—and why in fact he's come to believe I need to ditch the realty business—"not interesting enough"—and move away from New Jersey—ditto—possibly to "a place sort of like this one," and maybe get into a business like furniture stripping or bartending, something hands-on and low-stress, and "maybe get back to writing stories." (He has always respected the fact that I was briefly a writer and keeps a signed copy of *Blue Autumn* in his room.)

My heart, needless to say, leaps to him. Beneath the turmoiled surfaces he means everyone everywhere all the best, security guards included. Cooperstown, even before he's stepped through the doors of its magical Hall of Fame, has won a magical victory over him by inducing a stress-free idyll of small-pond-big-fish ordinariness he would dearly love to be his. (Seemingly all his bad-fitting rings have spun down into happy congruence.) Though I can't help wondering if this brief flight of empire-sketching might not be the happiest moment of his life, and in a twinkling he may look back on it with no clarity, no grasp of the details. It may in fact turn out to cause him even greater anxiety and wider warping since he'll never summon up such an idyll again in just this way and yet will never completely forget it or stop wondering about where it's gone. This is the cautionary view I took when he was small and talked to people who weren't there, a view I might've thought would protect him. I should've known, however, as I know now and as it ever is with kids and even those who're older: nothing stays as it is for long and, once again, there's no such thing as a false sense of well-being.

I should raise my Olympus now and snap his picture in this official happy moment. Only I can't risk breaking his spell, since soon enough he'll look again on life and conclude like the rest of us that he used to be happier but can't remember exactly how.

"But look," I say, staying in the spell with him, my hands cold, gazing at the top of his gouged head while he studies his waffle, his mind springing and lurching, his jaw muscles dedicatedly seeking the best alignment for his molars. (I love his fair, delicate scalp.) "I like real estate a lot. It's both forward-thinking and conservative. It was always an ideal of mine to combine those two."

He does not look up. The old skinny-armed fry cook, wearing a stained tee-shirt and a dirty sailor's topper, leers at us from behind the row of empty counter stools and salt-and-pepper caddies. He senses we're locking horns—over a divorce, a change in private schools, a bad report card, a drug bust, whatever visiting dads and sons usually bicker over within his earshot (usually *not* a father's midlife career choices). I flash him a threatening look that makes him shake his head, hang a damp cigarette from his snaggly mouth and reconsider his grill.

Only three other diners are here with us—a man and woman who aren't talking, merely sitting by a window staring at the lake over coffee, and an older, bald man in green pants and green nylon shirt playing an illegal poker machine in the dark and farthest corner, once in a while scoring a noisy win.

"You know the tightrope walker act? About falling off and having that be your great trick?" Paul is ignoring what I've declared about the delicate balance between progressivism and conservatism, with the fulcrum being the realty business. "That was just a joke." He looks up at me, narrows his eyes over his three-quarters scarfed waffle and blinks his long lashes. He is a smarter boy than any.

"I guess I knew that," I lie, clamping eye contact back on him. "But I took you seriously, though. I was just pretty sure you knew that making wild changes didn't have much to do with real self-determination, which is what I want you to have, and which is really pretty much a natural sort of thing. It's not that complicated." I smile at him goonily.

"I've decided where I want to go to college." He inserts one finger in the slick residue of maple syrup, which he's moated all around his waffle, drawing a circle, then licking the sweet off with a pop.

"I'm all leers," I say, which makes him give me an arch look; one more of our jokes from the trunk of lost childhood, *Take it for granite. A new leash on life. Put your monkey where your mouse is.* He, like me, is drawn to the fissures between the literal and the imagined.

"There's this place in California, okay? You go to college and work on a ranch and get to brand cows and learn to rope horses."

"Sounds good," I say, nodding, wanting to keep our spirit level high.

"Yep, it is," he says, a young Gary Cooper.

"You think you can study astrophysics on a cayuse?"

"What's a cayuse?" He's forgotten about being a cartoonist. "Aren't we going fishing?" he says, and quickly moves his gaze outward to where the big lake extends from the boat slips toward folded indistinct mountain headlands. On the dock's edge a girl is seated wearing a black bathing suit and an orange float vest, a pair of short water skis fastened to her feet. A sleek speedboat with her friends inside, two boys and a girl, rocks at idle fifty feet out, its motor gurgling. All in the boat are watching her on the dock. Suddenly the girl flags her hand up and wide. One boy turns and guns the boat, which even through our window glass gurgles loudly, then roars, seems for an instant to hesitate, then surges, almost leaps to life, its nose up, its rear sunk in foam, catching the thick rope-slack and yanking the girl off the dock and onto her skis, lariating her forward over the water's mirror top away from us, until she is—faster than would seem possible—small upon the lake, a colorless dot against the green hills. "That'd be the butt, Bob," Paul says, watching fiercely. He has seen this, almost exactly, on the Connecticut yesterday, but offers no sign of remembering.

"I guess we're not going fishing," I admit reluctantly. "I don't think we've got time now. I had a big imagination. I just thought we had forever. We may have to miss Canton, Ohio, and Beaton, Texas, too." It doesn't matter to him, I think, though I wonder bleakly if one day he'll be my guardian and do a better job. I also wonder just as bleakly if Ann actually has a boyfriend, and if so where she meets him, and what she wears and if she lies to truth-teller Charley the way I used to lie to her (my guess is she does).

"How many times do you think you'll get married?" Paul says, still watching the faraway skier, not wanting to trade eyes with me on this subject—one he does care about. He looks quickly around behind the grill at the big wall-size color photo of a hamburger on a clean white plate, with a bowl of strangely red soup and a fountain Coke, all coated with grease enough to hold a fly captive till Judgment Day. He has asked me this question as recently as two days ago, I think.

"Oh, I don't know," I say. "Eight, nine times before I'm good 'n' done, I guess." I shut my eyes, then slowly open them so he is in dead center. "What the hell do you care? Have you got some old bag in the stripping business you want me to meet down in Oneonta?" He, of course, knows Sally from our visits to the Shore but has remained significantly silent about her, as he should.

"It doesn't matter," he says almost inaudibly, my fear—the ordinary and abiding parent's fear that he'll miss his childhood—clearly unfounded, given the look on his face. Though Ann's fear, of harm and of his frailty, rises to my mind's view like a warning—a boating mishap, a collision at a bad intersection, a kid's punch-out whereby his tender forehead kisses a curb. Letting him sly away into the dark unguarded last night would definitely be frowned on by the experts, might possibly even be seen as abusive.

He is pick-picking at the duct tape that holds together The Water's Edge's ancient plastic booths. "I wish we could stay here another day," he says.

"Well, we'll have to come back." I'm out with my camera then in half a second. "Lemme make yer pitcher to prove you really came." Paul quickly looks behind him as if to find out who'll mind having his picture taken. The coffee drinkers have slipped away and wandered off down the dock. The poker player has his back humped over his machine. The cook is occupied whipping up a breakfast of his own. Paul looks back at me across the little table, his eyes troubled by a wish for something more, for more to get in the picture—me, possibly. But that's not possible. He is all there is.

"Tell me another good joke," I say in behind my Olympus, through which his girlish boy's face is small but fully captured.

"Have you got the hamburger in the picture?" he says, and looks stern.

"Yeah," I say, "the hamburger's in." And it is.

"That's what I was worried about," he says, then brightly, wonderfully smiles at me.

And that is the picture I will keep of him forever.

U p the welcomingly warm morning hill we trudge, side by each, bound finally for the Hall of Fame. It's 9:30, and time is in fact a-wastin'. Though when we round the corner onto sunny Main, a half block from the Hall—red brick, with Greek pediments and dubious trefoils on the gable ends, an architectural rattlebag resembling the building-fund dream of some overzealous flock of Wesleyans—something again is amiss. Out front, on the sidewalk, another or possibly the same cadre of men and women, boys and girls, is marching a circle, hoisting placards, sporting sandwich boards and chanting what from here—the red-white-and-blue-buntinged corner by Schneider's German Bakery—sounds again like "shooter, shooter, shooter." Though there seem to be more marchers now, plus an encircling group of spectators—fathers and sons, larger families, assorted oldsters, alongside normal every-Sunday parishioners just sprung by Father Damien down at Our Lady—all crowding and observing the marchers and spilling back into the street, slowing traffic and jamming the building entry, the exact coordinates Paul and I are vectored for.

"What's this happy horseshit again?" he says, scowling at the crowd and its nucleus of noisy protesters, which suddenly blossoms into two circles rotating in opposite directions, so that ingress to the Hall is essentially stoppered.

"I guess something *is* worth protesting at the Hall of Fame," I say, admiring the protesters, their (from here) illegible signs jutting in the air and their chants becoming louder as stronger-voiced marchers rotate our way. To me it all has a nice collegial feel of my Ann Arbor days (though I was never involved back then, being a scared-stiff, Dudley Doright frat-rat possessor of a highly revocable NROTC scholarship). Yet it feels laudable today that a spirit of manageable unrest and disagreement can be alive still on the fruited plain, even if it's not associated with anything important.

Paul, however, doesn't know what to say in the face of other people's dissension, accustomed only to his own. "So okay, what're we supposed to do—wait?" he says, and crosses his arms like an old scold. Potential new Hall visitors are drifting past us but stopping soon to take in the spectacle. Some Cooperstown police are standing across Main Street, two bulky men and two small, blue-shirted, terrier women, thumbs in their belts, amused by the whole event, now and then pointing toward something or someone they think is especially comical.

"Protests never last very long, in my experience," I say.

Paul says nothing, only scowls and raises his hand to his teeth and gives his wart a delicate but incisive bite. All this is making him uneasy; his good-kid spirit has gone with the dew. "Can't we just go in around 'em?" he says, tasting his own flesh and blood.

No one, I notice, is getting through or even trying. Most of the spectators, in fact, are looking entertained and talking at the protesters, or taking their pictures. It's nothing too serious. "The idea is for us to be inconvenienced a while, then they'll let us go on in. They have some point they want to make."

"I think the cops oughta arrest 'em," Paul says. He makes one emphatic little *eeeck* midway down his throat and grimaces. (Clearly he has spent more time with Charley than is healthy, since his human-rights attitude favors bulldozer privilege: faced with a blind beggar suffering an epileptic seizure in the revolving door of the University Club, you damn well find a way to bowl through for your court time in the sixty-and-over double-elimination consolation round.) I could easily pose a canny analogy to our nation's early days, in which legitimate grievances were ignored and a crisis followed, but it would fall on uncaring ears. However, I mean to respect the protestors' line even without knowing what it's about. There's time enough for the little we hope to do.

"Let's take a walk," I say, and set my hand on my son's shoulder like a regular ole dad and guide us both out into crowded Main toward the Cooperstown Fire and Rescue station, where glistening yellow vehicles sit out in the driveway on Sunday display, uniformed firefighters and paramedics lounging around the bay doors watching *Breakfast at Wimbledon*. More church cars and several packed Gay Nineties trolleys are stacking up noisily, a few drivers willing to lean on their horns and poke heads irritably out windows to find out what's what. Paul, I can see, is plainly troubled by this delay and mix-up, and I'd like to get us out of the action and avoid another run-in of our own. So I proceed us up the sidewalk against the pedestrian traffic, past more storefronts with sports paraphernalia and trading cards, two open-early taprooms showing nonstop World Series games from the Forties, a movie theater and the tweedy realty office I saw yesterday from the car, with snazzy color snapshots in the window. Where we're headed, I don't know. But unexpectedly as we walk across an open side alley, there, straight left and down the narrow passageway, which widens out at the other sunny end, sits Doubleday Field, hallowed and deep green and decidedly vest pocket in the midmorning light—a most perfect place to see and play a ball game (and distract your bad-tempered son). From somewhere nearby and right on cue, a tooting steam organ begins to play "Take Me Out to the Ball Game," as if our aimless activities were being watched.

"What's that for, Little League?" Paul says, still disapproving and unavailable, done in by his simple failure to gain the Hall of Fame on the first try, though in no time we'll be inside, soaking up the full wonderment: cruising its exhibits, roaming its pavilions, ogling Lou Gehrig's vanity license plate, the Say-Hey Kid's actual glove, Ted Williams's illustrated strike zone and the United Emirates baseball stamp display, while chuckling at Bud and Lou doing "Who's on First" (again)—just the way we did it back in Springfield, only much, much better.

"It's Doubleday Field," I say, warmly admiring it. "Those brochures I sent you explained the whole deal. It's where the Hall of Fame game's played when the new inductees are enshrined in

August." I try to think of who'll be ushered in next month, but can't think of any baseball name but Babe Ruth. "It holds ten thousand people, was built in 1939 by the WPA when the country was on its knees and the government was helping to find jobs, which would be nice if it'd do today."

Paul, however, is staring at three public batting cages that are just outside the grandstand wall and from which we both can hear a sharp Coke-bottle *poink* of aluminum meeting horsehide. A small black kid employing a Joe Morgan elbow-trigger stance is at the plate and making repeated, withering contact in what is probably the "fast" cage. It occurs to me, as I'm sure it occurs to Paul, that it is Mr. New Hampshire Basketball again, lording it over everybody in yet another sport, in another town, and that he and his dad are on the same well-intentioned father-son circuit as we two and are having much more fun. Here, though, he's Mr. New Hampshire *Baseball*.

Though of course it's not. This kid has buddies, white and black, hanging on the cage rungs outside, jeering and insulting in a comradely way, encouraging him to miss so they can jump in and take their big-time cuts. One of these is a skinny, bad-posture Hacky Sack punk from yesterday—one of the lowlifes I imagined Paul bonding with last night over cheese fries and burgers. They seem much older than Paul now, and I'm certain he wouldn't know how to address them (unless they communicated by barking).

We walk a ways down the widening alley to the point behind the old brick buildings on Main, where it turns into the Doubleday Field parking lot and where several men—men my age—dressed in new-looking big-league uniforms are departing cars with their gloves and bats, hurrying on noisy cleats toward the open grandstand tunnel, as though they were showing up late for a twin bill. Two teams' uniforms are in evidence: the flashy yellow and unappetizing green of the Oakland A's, and the more conservative red, white and blue of the Atlantas. I look for a number or a face I recognize from my years in the press box—somebody who'd be flattered to be remembered—but no one looks familiar.

In fact, two "A's" who pass right by us—*R. Begtzos* and *J. Bergman* stitched to their backs—have sizable Milwaukee goiters and seam-splitting butts, which argue against their having played anytime in recent memory.

"I'm clueless," Paul says. His own outfit is no more appetizing than Bergman's and Begtzos's.

"It's an important part of the whole Cooperstown experience to take a look inside here." I begin moving us toward the tunnel behind the "players." "It's supposed to be good luck." (This I've made up on the spot. But his euphoria has now burned off like ether, and I'm back to conflict-containment drills and getting through our last hours as friendly enemies.)

"I've got a train to catch," he says, following along.

"You'll make it," I say, less friendly myself. "I've got plans of my own."

When we walk through to the end of the tunnel we could easily stroll straight out onto the field where the players are, or else turn and climb steep old concrete steps into the grandstand. Paul shies off from the field as though warned against it and takes the steps. But to me it's irresistible to walk a few yards into the open air, cross the gravel warning track and simply stand on the grass where two teams, ersatz Braves and ersatz A's, are playing catch and limbering stiff, achy joints. Gloves are popping, bats cracking, voices sailing off into the bright air, shouting, "I could catch it if I could see it," or "My leg won't bend that way anymore," or "Watch it, watch it, watch it."

Un-uniformed, I venture far enough that I can see up to the blue sky from within my shadow and all the way out to the right-field fence, where the numbers spell "312," and bleacher seats and tree-tops and neighborhood rooflines are beyond, and above that a shining MOBIL sign revolves like a radar dish. Heavy, capless men in uniforms sit in the grass below the fence palings, or lie back staring up, taking in moments of deliverance, carefree and obscure. I have no idea what's up here, only that I would love to be them for a moment, complete with a suit and no son.

Paul sits alone on an old grandstand bench, affecting timeless boredom, his Walkman earphones clutching his neck, his chin on a pipe railing. Little is afoot here, the place being mostly empty. A few kids his age are far up in the drafty back rows, cackling and cracking wise. A scattering of chatty wives are below in the reserved seats—women in pantsuits and breezy sundresses, sitting in pairs and threes, viewing the field and players, laughing occasionally, extolling a good catch or merely occupying themselves with the neutral subjects they each are at ease with. And happily—happy as linnets in a warm and gentle wind, with nothing better to do than twitter.

"What'd the bartender say to the mule when he ordered a beer?" I say, coming down the row of seats. I feel I have to break new ground again.

He turns his eyes to me disparagingly without moving his chin off the pipe rail. This won't be funny, his look indicates. His "insect" tattoo is visible. An insult. "Clueless," he says again to be rude.

" 'I'm sorry, sir, what seems to be bothering you?' " I sit beside him, wanted or unwanted, and muse off down the first-base line in silence. A tiny, antique man in a bright white shirt, shoes and trousers is pushing a chalk wheel down the base path. He stops midway and looks where he's been in estimation of his trueness, then resumes toward the sack. I raise my camera and take his picture, then squeeze one off at the field and the players seemingly readying themselves to play, and finally one of the sky with the flag raised but motionless above the "390" sign in center.

"What good is it to come to some beautiful place?" Paul says broodily, his chin still resting on the green pipe, his heavy, downy-haired legs splayed so as to reveal a scar on his knee, a long and pink and still scabby thing of unknown origin.

"The basic idea, I guess, is you'll remember it later and be a lot happier." I could add, "So if you've got some useless or bad memories this'd be a great place to start off-loading them." But what I mean is obvious.

Paul gives me the old dead-eye and shuffles his Reeboks. The hatless ballplayers who have been running sprints and stretching in the outfield are walking in together now, some with their caps on backward, some with arms on each other's shoulders, a couple actually walking backward and clowning it up. "Come ahnnn, Joe Louis!" one of the wives shouts, getting her sports and heroes confused. The other wives all laugh. "Don't yell like that at Fred," one says, "you'll scare him to death."

"I'm sick of not liking stuff," Paul says, seeming not to care. "I'm ready for a big change."

News not unwelcome, since a move to Haddam may be on his horizon. "You're just getting started," I say. "You'll find a lot of things to like."

"That's not what Dr. Stopler says." He stares out at the wide, mostly vacant ballyard.

"Well, fuck Dr. Stopler, then. He's an asshole."

"You don't even know him."

I fleetingly consider telling Paul I'm moving to New Mexico and opening an FM station for the blind. Or that I'm getting married. Or that I have cancer.

"I know him well enough," I say. "Shrinks are all alike." Then I sit silent, resentful of Dr. Stopler for being an authority on all of life—mine included.

"What is it I'm supposed to do again if I'm not supposed to be a critic of my age?" He's been studying this subject since last night. The thought of a whole new leash on life might in fact have inspired his short-lived euphorics.

"Well," I say, watching the players coalesce into two rival but friendly "teams," as a hugely fat man with a tripod and box camera emerges slowly out of the runway, his one leg stiff. The cameraman appraises the sun, then starts to set up in accordance. "I'd like you to come live with me a while, maybe learn to play the trumpet, later go to Bowdoin and study marine biology; and not be so sly and inward while you're there. I'd like you to stay a little gullible and not worry too much about standardized tests. Eventually I'd like you to get married and be as monogamous as possible. Maybe buy a house near the water in Washington State, so I could come visit. I'll be more specific when I have time to direct your every waking movement."

"What's monogamous?"

"It's something like the old math. It's a cumbersome theory nobody practices anymore but that still works."

"Do you think I was ever abused?"

"Nothing I was personally involved in. Maybe you can remember a few minor cruelties. Your memory's pretty good." I stare at him, unwilling to be amused, since his mother and I love him more than he (of all people) will ever know. "Do you want to file a complaint? Maybe talk to your ombudsman about it on Tuesday?"

"No, I guess not."

"You know, you shouldn't think you're not supposed to be happy, Paul. You understand that? You shouldn't get used to not being happy just because you can't make everything fit down right. Everything doesn't fit down right. You have to let some things go, finally." Now would be the moment to bring to light what a quirky old duck Jefferson was—the practical idealist *qua* grammarian—his whole life spent gadgeting out the mysteries of the status quo in quest of a firmer foothold on the future. Or possibly I could borrow a baseball metaphor having to do with some things that happen inside the white lines and those that happen out.

Only I am suddenly stopped cold. Not what I'd planned.

The A's and Braves have formed two team-photo groups down the third-base line, taller men behind, shorter men kneeling (Messrs. Begtzos and Bergman are shorter). The kneeling men have their gloves and a fan of wooden bats arranged prettily on the grassy foreground. A low, portable signboard has been wheeled out and placed in front of them. O'MALLEY'S FAN-TASY BASEBALL CAMP, it says in red block letters, and below it, in temporary lettering: "Braves vs. '67 Red Sox—July 3, 1988." The sign makes all the Braves laugh. None of the Red Sox seem to be present.

Pictures are quickly snapped. The man who has chalked the base paths supervises wheeling the sign over to the canary-suited A's, where he jiggers the letters to read O'MALLEY'S FAN-TASY BASEBALL CAMP: "Athletics vs. '67 Red Sox—July 3, 1988."

All clap when the pictures are done, and players begin straying toward the dugout and down the baselines, or just wandering out onto the infield in their too-tight uniforms, looking as if something wonderfully memorable had just happened but they'd missed it or it wasn't enough, this even though the *big game* with the BoSox, the whole megillah, what it's all about, is still to come. "You look great, Nigel," a husky-voiced wife shouts out from the stands in a yawky Aussie accent. Nigel, who's a big, long-armed and bearded "Brave," with a thick middle and turned-in toes that make him seem shy, pauses on the dugout steps and lifts his blue Atlanta cap like ole Hank on his glory day. "You look damn good," she shouts out. "Damn good on you." Nigel smiles introspectively, nods his head, then ducks into the shadows along the bench with his mates. I should've taken his picture.

For, how else to seize such an instant? How to shout out into the empty air just the right words, and on cue? Frame a moment to last a lifetime?

A dead spot now seems to be where these two days have delivered us—not even inside the Hall of Fame yet, but to an unspectac-

ular moment in a not exactly bona fide ballpark, where two spiritually wrong-footed "clubs" make ready to play a real team whose glo-
ries are all behind them, and where by some system of inner weights
and measures I have just run out of important words, but before I've
said enough, before I've achieved a desired effect, before the
momentum of a shared physical act—strolling the hallowed halls,
viewing the gloves, license plates, strike zones—can take us up and
carry us to a good end. Before I've made of this day a memory worth
preserving.

I'd have done better to have us wait with the crowd until the
doors were cleared, instead of seeking one more chance at quality
time and risking this flat-footed feeling of nothing doing, with our
last point of significant agreement being that I had probably not
abused my son. (My trust has always been that words can make most
things better and there's nothing that can't be improved on. But
words *are* required.)

"People my age are on a six-month cycle," Paul says in a reflective adult voice. The "A's" and the "Braves" mill the sidelines, wanting something to happen, something they've paid good money for. I
still wouldn't mind joining them. "Probably the way I am now will
be different by Christmas. Adults don't have that problem."

"We have other problems," I say.

"Like what?" He looks around at me.

"Our cycles last a lot longer."

"Right," he says. "Then you croak."

I almost say, "Or worse." Which would send his mind off inventorying Mr. Toby, his dead brother, the electric chair, being fed
arsenic, the gas chamber—on the hunt for something new and terrible in the world to be obsessed by and later make jokes about. And
so I say nothing. My face, I suspect, bears promise of some drollery
about death and its too, too little sting. But as I said, I've said all I
know.

I hear the steam organ begin tootling away on "Way down upon
the Swanee River." Our little ballpark has a lazy, melancholy carnival fruitiness afloat within it now. Paul looks at me shrewdly when I
don't answer as expected, the corners of his mouth flickering as if he
knows a secret, though I know he doesn't.

"Why don't we head back now?" I say, leaving death unchal-
lenged.

"What are those guys doing down there?" he says, looking quickly to the level playing field, as if he'd just now seen it.

"They're having a great time," I say. "Doesn't it look like fun?"

"It looks like they're not doing anything."

"That's how adults have fun. They're really having the time of their lives. It's just so easy they don't even have to try."

And then we go. Paul first, down the aisle behind the wives, then struggling over the stumpy steps to the runway; and I, having a last fond look at the peaceful field, the men at loose ends but still two teams with games on tap.

We walk through the tunnel's shadows and out into the sunny parking lot, where the steam-organ music seems farther away. Up on Main Street cars are moving. I'm certain the Hall of Fame is open, its morning crises resolved.

The batting cage boys have now shoved off, their metal bats leaned outside the fence, all three cages empty and inviting.

"I believe we have to take a few chops, whatta you think?" I say to Paul. I am not at full strength but am ready, suddenly, for *something*.

Paul estimates the cages from a distance, his clumsy feet turned out now, as slew-footed as the least athletic of boys, heavy and uninspirable.

"Come on," I say, "you can coach." Possibly he makes a tiny double *eeeck* or a fugitive bark; I'm not certain. Though he comes.

Like a militant camp counselor, I lead us straight across to the fenced cages, which are fitted out with fifty-cent coin boxes and draped inside with green netting to keep careening balls from maiming people and injuring the pitching machines, which are themselves big, dark-green, boxy, industrial-looking contraptions that work by feeding balls from a plastic hopper through a chain-drive circuitry that ends with two rubber car tires spinning in opposite tangency at a high rate of speed and from between which each "pitch" is actually *expelled*. Signs posted all around remind you to wear a helmet, protective glasses and gloves, to keep the gates closed, to enter the cage alone, to keep small children, pets, bottles, anything breakable including wheelchair occupants out—and if none of these warnings is convincing, all risk is yours anyway (as if anybody thought different).

The three metal bats leaning on the fence are identically too short, too light, their taped grips much too thin. I tell Paul to stand clear while I "test" one bat, holding it up in front of me like a knight's sword, sighting down its blue aluminum shaft (as I used to do long ago when I played in military school) and for some reason waggling it. I turn sideways of Paul—my camera still on my shoulder—cock the bat behind my ear in a natural-feeling Stan Musial knees-in stance and peer straight at him as though he were Jim Lonborg, the old BoSox righty, ready to rare, kick and fire.

"This is how Stan the Man used to stand in there," I say over my left elbow, my eyes hooded. I trigger a wicked swing, which feels clumsy and ridiculous. Some necessary leverage between my wrists and shoulders feels sprung now, so that my swing could only possibly contact the ball with a slapping motion that wouldn't drive a fruit fly out of the phone booth but would absolutely make me look like a girl.

"Is that how Stan the Man swung?" Paul says.

"Yeah, and it went a fuckin' mile," I say. I hear shouts, a chorus of "I got it, I got it," from inside Doubleday Field. I look around and above the grandstand where we were five minutes ago; white balls arch through the sky, two and three at once, all to be caught but invisible to us here.

Each cage has a title to colorfully reflect the speed of its pitches: "Dyno-Express" (75 mph). "The Minors" (65 mph). "Hot Stove League" (55 mph). I have no reservations about trying my skills in the "Dyno-Express" and so give Paul my camera and two quarters, leaving the batting helmets on their fence hook. I step right inside, close the gate, walk to the batter's box and look out toward the mean green machine as I seek out solid footing a bat's length from the outside corner of the regulation rubber plate that's planted between two scruffy rectangular AstroTurf pads put there to make things look authentic. I once again assume my Musial stance, make a slow, measuring pass of the bat barrel through my putative strike zone, square my knuckles on the handle, rotate the trademark back and line my deck-shoe toes with the center-field flag (though of course there is no flag, only the pitching machine itself and the protective netting, behind which is a sign that says "Home Run?"). I take and release a breath, once more deliberately extend the bat over the plate, then slowly bring it back.

"What time is it?" Paul says.

"Ten. There's no clock in baseball." I glimpse him over my shoulder through the diamond fence wires. He is looking up at the sky and back at the grandstand entrance, where a few fantasy players and their young-looking wives are strolling happy-go-lucky into the sunshine, gloved hands draped over soft shoulders, ball caps turned sideways, everyone ready for a beer, a bratwurst and a few yucks before the big game with Boston.

"Weren't we supposed to do something else?" he says, and looks at me. "Something about a hall of fame?"

"You'll get there," I say. "Trust me."

I again have to establish my stance and settle on a proper balance and repose. But once I'm fixed I say loudly to Paul, "Slap the money in the box," and he does, after which and for a long moment there is calm as the machine radiates a kind of patient human immanence, though this is broken after several seconds by a deep mechanical humming during which a heretofore unnoticed red bulb begins to brighten on top, after which the plastic hopper full of balls begins to vibrate. The machine gives no other sign it means business, but I stare riveted at the black confluence of rubber tires, which have not moved.

"Those greaseballs fucked it up," Paul says behind me. "You wasted your money."

"I don't think so," I say, keeping my balance and stance, my calm intact, bat back, eyes to the machine. My palms and fingers squeeze the bat tape, my shoulders stiffen, though I feel my wrists begin to bend back in a way Stan would deplore but that feels necessary for the raised bat barrel to descend quickly enough to the plane of the ball for me to avoid the girlish *slap* motion I don't want to be "my swing." I hear someone shout out, "Look at that asshole," and can't resist a quick look to see who's being referred to but see no one, then quickly return my gaze to the machine and the two tires, where there's still nothing happening to indicate a "pitch." Until I slightly relax my shoulders to avoid "binding," and it's then the machine makes a more portentous, metallic whirring noise. The black tires start to spin at an instantly great rate. A single ball teeters in full view down a previously unremarked metal channel, then goes "underground" into a smaller slot, after which it or one just like it is viciously spit from between the spinning rubber rings and crosses the plate at a speed so fast and at a distance so easily reachable that I don't even swing, merely let the ball whang the fence behind me and bound back through my legs and out toward an unobserved concrete bunker in front of me whose duty is to route balls back to the hopper. (The basketball version was much jazzier.)

Paul is silent. I do not even turn his way, refixing instead like a sniper on what is my opponent, the slit between the spinning tires. Another interior whirring sound becomes audible. I watch as another ball wobbles down the metal track, disappears and then is shot through space, hissing across the plate directly under my fists and again whanging the fence behind me, untouched and unswung at.

Paul again says nothing. Not "Strike two" or "It sounded high" or "Just try and make contact, Dad." No chuckle or raspberry or fart noise. Not even a bark of encouragement. Only adjudicating silence.

"How many do I get?" I say, merely to hear a sound.

"I just got here," he says.

Though just as I'm picturing the numeral five as the likeliest number, another orange-stitched ball comes rocketing across the plate and rattles the screen, suggesting the machine has possibly quick-pitched me.

Sweat has now appeared upward of my hairline. For ball number four, I extend the stubby bat barrel like a gate barrier straight out into my strike zone and hold it there stiff until the machine generates another pitch, which hits the bat and ricochets off the metal sweet spot with a *dink-poink*, and fouls off against one of the warning signs, finally bouncing back and actually striking me on the heel.

"Bunt," Paul says.

"Fuck you, bunt. Bunt when it's your turn. I'm up here to hit." I'm not looking at him.

"You should be wearing your windbreaker," he says. "You're a windbreaker."

I frown out into the now sinister black crease, twist my fists into the tape, straighten my wrists into a properer Stan-like trigger cock, shift my balance to the ball of my right foot, and ready my left to rise and stride toward contact. The machine whirs, the red light glows, the ball teeters down its metal chase, drops from view, then spanks out from between the rings fast and in full view, at which instant I lunge, flail the blue barrel down into the ordained space, hear my wrists "snap," actually *see* my arms extend, my elbows nearly meet, feel my weight shift as my breath gushes—all just as my eyes squeeze tightly shut. Only this time the ball (unseen, of course) squalls off the bat straight up into the netting, pinballs off two rankled fence surfaces, then falls back to the asphalt in front of me and drains off toward the bunker, leaving me with a ferocious handful of bees I'm determined not to acknowledge.

"Strike five, you're history," Paul says, and I glare back at him as he snaps my picture with my camera, disdainful concentration on his plummy lips. (I can't help seeing what I'll look like: bat slumped to the side, my cheeks sprouting sweat, my hair awry, face distressed by a frown of failure endured in a dopey cause.) "The Sultan of Squat," Paul says, snapping another picture.

"Since you're the expert, you need to try it," I say. Bees are burning my hands.

"Right." Paul shakes his head as though I'd spoken the most preposterous of words. We are completely alone here, though more ersatz players and their real-life wives and kids are strolling carefree and happy across the hot parking lot, their voices crooning praise and good motives. Balls still rise above and arc down upon Doubleday Field. This is the small, consoling music of baseball. For a man to entice his son into a few swings would not be mistreatment.

"What's the matter?" I say, letting myself out of the cage. "If you miss it you can say you meant to miss it. Didn't you say that was the best trick?" (He has already denied this, of course, but for some reason I don't mean to let him.) "Don't you eat stress for lunch?"

Paul holds my camera at belly level below "Clergy" and takes another picture, with an evil smile.

"You're the daredevil tightrope walker, aren't you?" I say, leaning the bat back against the fence, the big green machine now silent behind me. A warm breeze kicks up a skiff of parking lot grit and sweeps it by my sweaty arms. "I think you're walking way too narrow a line here, you need to find a new trick. You have to swing if you're going to hit." I'm wiping sweat off my forearms.

"Like you said." His smile becomes a smirk of dislike. He is still snapping my camera at me, one picture after the next—the same picture.

"What was that? I don't remember."

"Fuck you."

"Oh. Fuck me. Sorry, I did forget that." I come toward him suddenly, pity and murder and love each crying for a time at bat. It is not so rare a fatherly lineup. Children, who sometimes may be angels of self-discovery, are other times the worst people in the world.

When I get in reach of him, I don't know why but I grapple him behind his head, my fingers achy from squeezing my bat, my shoulders weightless as if my arms were nothing. "I just thought," I say, strenuously holding him, "you and me could experience a common humiliation and go off with our arms draped over our shoulders and I'd buy you a beer. We could bond."

"Fuck you! I can't drink. I'm fifteen," Paul says savagely into my chest, where I'm still clutching him.

"Oh, of course, I forgot that too. I'd probably be abusing you." I pull him in even more harshly, finding his rough buzzed hairline, his Walkman earphones and his neck tendons, forcing his face into my shirtfront so his nose pokes my breastbone and his warty fingers and even my camera push and dig my ribs in rejection. I don't entirely know what I'm doing, or what I want him to do: change, promise, concede, guarantee me something important will be better or pan out, all expressed in language for which there are no words. "And why are you such a little prick?" I say with difficulty. I may be hurting him, but it's a father's right not to be pushed, so that I squeeze him even harder, intent on keeping him till he gives up the demon, renounces all, collapses into hot tears only I can minister to. Dad. His.

But that is not what happens. The two of us begin awkwardly scuffling on the pavement beside the batting cages, and almost immediately, I realize, to attract the interest of tourists and church-goers out for a Sunday stroll, plus lovers of baseball on their way, as we should be, to the famous shrine—except that we're struggling here. I can almost hear them murmur, "Well, hey now, what's all this about? This can't be good and wholesome. We need to call somebody. Better call. Go ahead and call. The cops. 911. What's the goddamned country coming to?" Though of course they don't speak. They only stop and gaze. Abuse can be mesmerizing.

I loose my grip on my son's neck and let him break away, his fleshy face gray with anger and disgust and shame. My grip has ridden into his cut ear and got it bleeding again, its little bandage rucked off. When I see it, I look in my hand and there is beet-red blood down my middle finger and smeared in my palm.

Paul gapes at me, his left hand—the other's still holding my camera, with which he has gored me in the ribs—gone fiercely into the pocket of his baggy maroon shorts as if he is trying to look casual about being furious. His eyes grow narrow and shiny, though his pupils widen with me in their sight.

"All in fun. No big deal," I say. I flash him a lame, hopeless grin. "High fives." One hand is up for a slap, the other, bloody, one finding my own pocket. Sunglassed tourists continue observing us from forty yards out in the parking lot.

"Gimme the cocksucking bat," Paul seethes and, ignoring my high fives, goes tromping past me, grabbing the blue bat off the fence, kicking the gate open and entering the cage like a man come to a task he's put off for a lifetime. (His Walkman earphones are still on his neck, my camera now lumped in his shorts pocket.)

Inside the "Dyno-Express" cage he stalks to the plate, the bat slung back over his shoulder, and peers down as if into a puddle of water. He suddenly turns back to me with a face of bright hatred, then looks at his toes again as though aligning them with something, the bat still sagging in spite of one attempt to keep it up. He is not a hitter to inspire fear. "Put in the fucking money, Frank," he shouts.

"Bat left, son," I say. "You're a southpaw, remember? And back off a little bit so you can get a swing at it."

Paul gives me a second look, this time with an expression of darkest betrayal, almost a smile. "Just put the money in," he says. And I do. I drop two quarters in the hollow black box.

This time the green machine comes alive much more readily, as if I had previously wakened it, its red top light beaming dully in the sun. The whirring commences and again the whole assembly shudders, the plastic hopper vibrates and the rubber tires start instantly spinning at a high speed. The first white pill exits its bin, tumbles down the metal chute, disappears then at once reappears, blistering across the plate and smacking the screen precisely where I'm standing so that I inch back, thoughtful of my fingers, though they're stuffed in my pockets.

Paul, of course, does not swing. He merely stands staring at the machine, his back to me, his bat still slung behind his head, heavy as a hoe. He is batting right-handed.

"Step back a bit, son," I say again as the machine goes into its girdering second windup, humming and shuddering, and emits another blue darter just past Paul's belly, again thrashing the fence I'm now well back of. (He has, I believe, actually inched in closer.) "Get your bat up to the hitting position," I say. We have performed hitting rituals since he was five, in our yard, on playgrounds, at the Revolutionary War battlefield, in parks, on Cleveland Street (though not recently).

"How fast is it coming?" He says this not to me but to anyone, the machine, the fates that might assist him.

"Seventy-five," I say. "Ryne Duren threw a hundred. Spahn threw ninety. You can get a swing. Don't close your eyes" (like I did). I hear the steam organ playing: "No use in sit-ting a-lone on the shelf, life is a hol-i-day."

The machine goes again into its Rube Goldberg conniption. Paul leans over the plate this time, his bat *still* on his shoulder, gazing, I assume, at the crease where the ball will originate. Though just as it does, he sways an inch back and lets it thunder past and whop the screen again. "Too close, Paul," I say. "That's too close, son. You're gonna brain yourself."

"It's not that fast," he says, and makes a little *eeeck* and a grimace. The machine circuits then into its next-to-last motion. Paul, his bat on his shoulder, watches a moment, and then, to my surprise, takes a short ungainly step forward onto the plate and turns his face to the machine, which, having no brain, or heart, or forbearance, or fear, no experience but throwing, squeezes another ball through its dark warp, out through the sprightly air, and hits my son full in the face and knocks him flat down on his back with a terrible, loud *thwock*. After which everything changes.

In time that does not register as time but as humming motor noise solid in my ear, I am past the metal gate onto the turf and beside him; it is as if I had begun before he was hit. Dropped to my knees, I grab his shoulder, which is squeezed tight, his elbows into his sides, both his hands at his face—covering his eyes, his nose, his cheek, his jaw, his chin—underneath all of which there is a long and almost continuous *wheeee* sound, a sound *he* makes bunched on the plate, a hard, knees-contracted bundle of fright and lightning pain centered where I can't see, though I want to, my hands busy but helpless and my heart sounding in my ears like a cannon, my scalp prickly, damp, airy with fear.

"Let's see it, Paul"—my voice a half octave too high, trying to say it calmly. "Are you all right?" I am hit by ball number five, a sharp blow like a punch off the back of my neck and scalp, skipping smartly on into the netting.

"Wheeee, wheeee, wheeee."

"Let's see, Paul," I say, the air between him and me oddly red-tinted. "Are you all right? Let's see, Paul, are you all right?"

"Wheeee, wheeee, wheeeeee."

People. I hear their footsteps on the concrete. "Just call right now," someone says. "I could hear it halfway to Albany." "Oh boy." "Ohhh boy." The cage door clanks. Shoes. Breathing. Trouser cuffs. Someone's hands. An oiled-leather ball-glove smell. Chanel No. 5.

"Ohhhh!" Paul says in a profound exhalation conceding hurt, and writhes sideways, his elbows still pinned to his sides, his face still covered by his hands, his ear still bleeding from my having grabbed him too hard.

"Paul," I say, all the air still reddish, "let me see, son," my voice giving way slightly, and I am tapping his shoulder with my fingers as if I could wake him up and something else could happen, something not nearly as bad.

"Frank, there's an ambulance coming," someone says from among the legs, hands, breaths all around me, someone who knows me as Frank (other than my son). A man. I hear other footsteps and look up and around, frightened. Braves and A's are outside the fence, gawking in, their wives beside them, their faces dark, troubled. "Wasn't he wearing his helmet?" I hear one inquiry. "No, he wasn't," I say out loud to anyone. "He wasn't wearing anything."

"Wheeee, wheeee," Paul cries out again, his face covered with his hands, his brown head of hair resting squarely on the filthy white plate. These are cries I don't know, cries he has never cried in my hearing.

"Paul," I say. "Paul. Just be still, son." Nothing feels like it's happening to bring help. Though not very far away I hear two sharp *bwoop-bwoop*s, then a heavy engine roar, then *bwoop-bwoop-bwoop*. Someone says, "Okay, great." I'm aware of more feet scuffling. I have my hands pressed tight into Paul's shoulder—his back is to me—feeling how hard his body has become, how unambiguously concentrated on injury it is. Someone says, "Frank, let's let these people try to help. They'll help him. Let them get where you are."

This. This is the worst thing ever.

I stand dizzily and step backward among many others. Someone has my upper arm in his big hand, assisting me gently back, while a stumpy white woman in a white shirt, tight blue shorts, with a huge butt, and then a thinner man in the same clothes but with a stethoscope on his neck, slip past and get onto their hands and knees on the AstroTurf and begin to practice on my son procedures I can't see but that make Paul scream out "Nooooo!" and then "Wheeee" again. I push forward and find myself saying to the people who are here now all around, "Let me talk to him, let me talk to him. It'll be all right," as if he could be persuaded out of being hurt.

But whoever it is here who knows me—a large man—says, "Just stay here a second, Frank, stay still. They'll help. It'll be better if you just stand back and let them."

And so I do. I stand in the crowd as my son is avidly worked on and helped, my heart battering its walls, right to the top of my belly, my fingers cold and sweating. The man who has called me Frank holds onto my arm even yet, says nothing, though I suddenly turn to him and look at his long, smooth-jawed Jewish face, large black eyes with specs and a slick tanned cranium, and say as if I had a right to know, "Who are you?" (Though the words do not actually sound.)

"I'm Irv, Frank. Irv Ornstein. Jake's son." He smiles apologetically and squeezes my arm more tightly.

Whatever has turned the air red now ceases. Here is a name—Irv—and a face (changed) from far away and past. Skokie, 1964. Irv—the good son of my mother's good husband #2, my stepbrother—gone after my mother's death, with his father in tow, to Phoenix.

I do not know what to say to Irv, and simply stare back at him like a specter.

"This is not the best time to meet, I know," Irv says to my voiceless face. "We just saw you on the street this morning, over by the fire station, and I said to Erma: 'I know that guy.' This must be your son who got hurt." Irv is actually whispering and casts a fretful eye now at the medics kneeling over Paul, who screams "Noooo!" again from beneath their efforts.

"That's my son," I say, and move toward his cry, but Irv reins me in once more.

"Just give 'em a couple minutes more, Frank. They know what

they're doin'." I look to my other side, and here is a dishy, tiny, wheat-haired woman in her thirties, wearing a tight yellow-and-peach plastic-looking single-piece outfit that resembles a space suit. She has a grip on my other elbow as if she knows me as well as Irv does and the two of them have agreed to prop me up. Possibly she's a weight lifter or an aerobics instructor.

"I'm Erma," she says, and blinks at me like a hatcheck girl. "I'm Irv's friend. I'm sure he's going to be fine. He's just scared, poor thing." She too looks down at the two medics huddled over my son, and her face goes doubtful and her lower lip discreetly extends sympathy. Hers is the Chanel I whiffed.

"It's the left eye," I hear one of the medics say. Then Paul says, "Ohhhh!"

Then I hear someone behind me say, "Oh, ugh." Some of the Braves and A's are already starting to back away. I hear a woman say, "They said it's his eye," and someone else say, "Probably wasn't wearing protective eye covering." Then someone says, "It says 'Clergy.' Maybe he's a minister."

"Where are you now, Frank?" Irv says, still whispering confidentially. His hand seems to encircle my upper arm, his hold on me firm. He is a big, tanned, hairy-looking engineer type, wearing blue designer sweatpants with red piping and a gold cardigan with no shirt under. He is much bigger than I remember him when we were college age, me at Michigan, he at Purdue.

"What?" I hear my own voice sounding calmer than I feel. "New Jersey. Haddam, New Jersey."

"Whaddaya do down there?" Irv whispers.

"Real estate," I say, then look at him again suddenly, at his broad forehead and full, liver-lipped but sympathetic mouth. I remember him absolutely and at the same time have no idea who in the hell he is. I look at his hairy-fingered hand on my arm and see that it has a diamond pinkie ring on its appointed finger.

"We were just coming over to speak to you when your boy got hit," Irv says, giving Erma an approving nod.

"That's good," I say, staring down at the wide, maxi-brassiered back of the fireplug female medic, as if this part of her would be the first to indicate something significant. She struggles to her feet at this very moment and turns to search among us and the two or three others who are still gathered around.

"Anybody responsible for this young man?" she says in a wiry, south Boston *nyak* accent, and extracts a large black walkie-talkie out of her belt holster.

"I'm his father," I say, breathless, and pull away from Irv. She holds her walkie-talkie up toward me as if she expects me to want to speak into it, her finger on the red Talk button.

"Yeah, well," she says in her tough-broad voice. She is a woman of forty, though perhaps younger. Her belt has a blizzard of medical supplies and heavy gear fastened on. "Okay, here's the thing," she says, gone totally businesslike. "We need to get him down to Oneonta pretty fast."

"What's wrong with him?" I say this too loudly, terrified she's about to say his brain has been rendered useless.

"Well, what—did he like get hit with a baseball?" She clicks her walkie-talkie trigger, making it produce a scratchy static sound.

"Yes," I say. "He forgot his helmet."

"Well, he got hit in the eye. Okay? And I can't really tell you if he's got much vision in it, because it's swollen already and got blood all in it, and he won't open it. But he needs to see somebody pretty quick. We take eye injuries down to Oneonta. They've got the staff."

"I'll drive him." My heart makes a bump-a-bump. Cooperstown: not a *real* town for *real* injuries.

"I'd have to get you to sign a form if you take him now," she says. "We can get him down in twenty minutes—it'd take you longer—and we can get him stabilized and monitored." I see her name on her silver nameplate: *Oustalette* (something I need to remember).

"Okay, great. Then I'll just ride with you." I lean to the side to see Paul, but can see only his bare legs and his lightning-bolt shoes and orange socks and the hem of his maroon shorts behind the other paramedic, who's still kneeling beside him.

"Our insurance won't permit that," she says, even more all-business. "You'll have to travel by separate vehicle." She clicks her red Talk button again. She is itchy to go.

"Great. I'll drive." I smile awfully.

"Frank, lemme drive you down," Irv Ornstein says from the side and with full authority, gripping my arm again as if I were about to escape.

"Okay," Ms. Oustalette says, and instantly begins talking tough into her big Motorola without even turning away. "Cooperstown Sixteen? Transporting one white male juvenile ADO to A.O. Fox. Ophthalmic. BP. . . ." There is a moment when I can hear the motor idling on her ambulance, hear two bats pop in quick succession from over the fence in the ballpark. Then all at once five immense jet planes come cracking in over us, low and ridiculously close together, their wings steady as knife blades, their *smack-shwoosh* eruption following a heart's beat behind. All present look up, shocked. All the planes are deep blue against the morning blue sky. (Would anyone believe it was still morning?) Ms. Oustalette doesn't even look up as she awaits her confirmation.

"Blue Angels," Irv says into my deafened ear. "Pretty close. They've got a show here tomorrow."

I step away from Irv's grip, my ears hollowed, and move toward Paul, where the other medic has just left and he is on his back alone, pale as an egg, his hands covering his eyes, his soft stomach, bare beneath his *Clergy* shirt, rising and settling heavily with his breath. He is making a low, throaty grunt of deep pain.

"Paul?" I say, the Blue Angels roaring off in the distance over the lake.

"Uhn," is all he says.

"That was just the Blue Angels that flew over. This is gonna be okay."

"Uhn," he says again, not moving his hands, his lips parted and dry, his ear not bleeding now, his "insect" tattoo the thing I can see best—his concession to the next century's mysteries. Paul smells like sweat, and he is sweating freely and is cold, as I am.

"It's Dad," I say.

"Uhn-nuh."

I reach into his shorts pocket and delicately slide my camera out. I consider removing his Walkman phones but don't. He makes no motion, though his shoes waggle one way and the other on the phony turf. I put my fingers on the blond-fleeced tan line of his thigh. "Don't be afraid of anything," I say.

"I'm fine now," Paul says woozily from under his covering hands, but distinctly. "I'm really fine." He takes a deep breath through his nose and holds it a long, painful moment, then slowly lets it go. I can't see his smacked eye and don't want to, though I would if he asked. Dreamily he says, "Don't give Mom and Clary those presents, okay? They're too shitty." He is too calm.

"Okay," I say. "So. We're going to the hospital in Oneonta. And I'm going down there, too. In another car." No one, I assume, has told him he's going to Oneonta.

"Yep," he says. He removes a hand from one damp gray eye, the one not injured, and looks at me, his other eye still guarded from light and my view. "You have to tell Mom about this?" His one eye blinks at me.

"It's okay," I say, feeling lifted off the ground. "I'll just make a joke out of it."

"Okay." His eye closes. "We're not going to the Hall of Fame now," he says indistinctly.

"You never can tell," I say. "Life's long."

"Oh. Okay." Behind me I hear creaky-squeaky sounds of a stretcher and Irv's deepened official voice saying, "Give 'em some room, give 'em some room, Frank. Let 'em do their job now."

"You just hang on there," I say. But Paul says nothing.

I stand up and am moved back, my Olympus in hand. Paul goes out of sight again as Ms. Oustalette begins to slide a litter board under him. I hear her say "All right?" Irv again is pulling me back. I hear Paul say "Paul Bascombe" to someone's question, then "No" to the subject of allergies, medications and other diseases. Then he is somehow up onto the collapsible stretcher and Irv is still hauling me farther out of the way, clear to the side of the batting cage we are still in. There are but a few people now. A "Brave" and his wife look in at me warily from outside the cage. I don't blame them.

Someone says, "Okay? Let us out."

And then Paul is on his way out, under a blanket, one hand still covering his damaged eye like a war casualty, through the cage door and across the asphalt to the blinking, clicking yellow Life Line ambulance—a Dodge Ram Wagon with antennas, flashers, lights rotating all over.

I watch with Irv as the stretcher is loaded, the doors go closed, both attendants walk around and enter in no great rush. Two more loud *bwoop-bwoop*s sound as their stand-clear, then the engine makes a deep reverberant rumble, lurches into gear, more lights go sharply on, the whole immense machine inches forward, stops, wheels turn, then it is going again, gathering itself, and is quickly gone in the direction of Main without benefit of siren.

11

Irv-the-solicitous is concerned with how to keep my mind off my woes and so drives us back down Route 28 as slowly as a funeral cortege, trusting to cruise control in his blue renter Seville and talking about whatever would take his mind off *his* woes and turn anyone like him toward the bright side. He is wearing big rattan sandals which, with his swarthy balding head and gold cardigan over his hairy chest make him look like nothing as much as a Mafia capo out for a drive. Though in truth he's in the simulator business out in the Valley of the Sun, his particular mission being to design flight simulators where the pilots for all the big airlines learn their business, a skill he acquired along with aeronautical engineering at Cal Tech (though I'm sure I remember him being a Boilermaker).

Irv, however, doesn't want to get into "six-degree freedom, or any of that," which he lets me know to be the high and guiding principle of the simulator racket (roll, pitch, yaw, up, side, backward). "It has to do with what your middle ear's telling you, and it's all pretty routine." He's interested instead in him and me "getting back on track after lo these blows," which involves telling me unexpectedly what a wonderful woman my mother was and what a "real character" his dad was, too, and how lucky they were to find each other in their waning years, and how his dad had confided to him that my mother always wished she could be closer to me after she remarried, but Irv figured she understood pretty well that I could take care of myself and that I was over in Ann Arbor preparing for a damn good career in whatever walk of life I selected (she might be surprised today), and how he'd tried several times over the years to contact me but had never "gotten through."

It occurs to me as we're cruising airily along by the factory sweater outlets and undercoating garages on Route 28, and farther yet past the sugar houses and corn patches and pristine hardwood hillsides rememberable from our trip up yesterday, that Erma, Irv's lady friend, has somehow disappeared and hasn't even been mentioned. And indeed she is a palpable loss, since I'm sure Irv would drive faster if she were in the back seat, and they would talk to each other and defer to my particular woes in silence.

Irv, though, starts spieling about Chicago, which he pronounces *Shu-caw-guh*, telling me he's giving some thought to moving back there, possibly to Lake Forest (near Wally Caldwell's relations), since the aircraft industry's about to take it right in the center hole, in his view. He, along with every other licensed and still-breathing engineer in the world, is a Reagan man, and he's right now expecting to "go with" Bush, yet feels Americans don't like indecisiveness, and Bush doesn't seem much good on that front, only to his mind he's better than any of the "mental dwarfs" my party's currently sponsoring. He hasn't, however, totally ruled out the protest vote or an independent candidate, since the Republicans have sold out the everyday wage earner the way the Nazis sold out "their friends the Czechs." (He does not strike me as a likely Jackson supporter.)

I basically stay silent, thinking sorrowfully of my son and of this day, both of which seem bitter and bottomless losses with absolutely no hope of recovery. There is no *seeming* now. All is *is*. In a better world, Paul would've snagged a line drive bare-handed off the bat of one of the ersatz A's, gone trooping off to the Hall of Fame with a proud, satisfyingly swollen mitt, had a satisfactory but not overly good time nosing around through Babe Ruth's locker, taking in the Johnny Bench "out at second" video and hearing the canned crowd noises from the Thirties. Later we could've walked out into the shimmery sunshine of Sunday, caught-ball in hand, gone for a Gay Nineties malt, found some aspirin, had our caricatures drawn together wearing vintage baseball suits, had some well-earned laughs, played Frisbee, set off my bottle rockets along a deserted inlet of the lake and ended the day early, lying in the grass under a surviving elm, with me explaining the ultimate value of good manners and that a commonsense commitment to progress (while only a Christian fiction) can still be a good, pragmatic overlay onto a life that could get dicey and long. Later on, motoring south, I'd have turned off on a back road and let him practice driving, after which we'd forge a plan, once his legal problems are settled, for his coming down to Haddam for school in the fall. A day, in other words, when the past got pushed further away and neutralized, when a promising course was charted for a future based on the postulate that independence and isolation were not the same, when all concentric rings would've snapped down and into place, and a true youthful (bark-less, *eeeck*less) synchronicity might've flourished as only in youth it can.

But instead: Remorse. Pain. Reproach. Blindness (or, at the very least, corrective lenses). Gloom. Tedium (involving lengthy, lonely drives up to New Haven and the final failure of progress to mean more than avoidance and denial)—nothing we couldn't have accomplished by staying home or revisiting the fish elevator. (He'll never come to live with me now, I'm sure of it.)

Irv, grown mute out of respect or boredom, crests the last hill above I-88, and through the tinted windshield I can see a long, river-sinuous cornfield opening down the narrow valley of the Susquehanna just where the two roadways meet. There a pheasant bursts out of the high green stalks, flashes just above the tassel tops, sets its wings at a fence row and sails halfway across the four-lane and settles into the median-strip grass.

Who or what scared it, I wonder? Is it safe there in the middle? Can it possibly survive?

"You know, Frank, you can get hooked up to too commanding a metaphor in my business," Irv says, finally sick of being silent and just starting in on whatever he happens to be thinking about as we turn west toward the bricky old town of Oneonta. It is the habit of a man too much alone. I know its symptoms. "Nothing else seems as interesting as simulation when you're in it. Everything seems simulatable. Except," he adds, and looks at me for serious emphasis, "the people who do it best are the people who leave their work at the office. Maybe they're not always the geniuses, but they see simulation as one thing and life as another. It's just a tool, really." Irv gives his own tool a little two-finger nudge inside his sweatpants for comfort's sake. "You get in trouble when you confuse the two."

"I understand, Irv," I say. Irv, who has traveled to Cooperstown for one of O'Malley's Fan-tasy games tomorrow (with the '59 White Sox), is, in fact, a good and sweet man. I wish I knew him better.

"You married, Frank?"

"Not these days," I say, feeling my arms and shoulder joints already stiffening and getting sore, as if I'd been in an accident or had aged twenty years in an hour. I'm also grinding my teeth and will, I'm sure, lose more precious angstroms of enamel by morning.

I point out to Irv the important blue sign with a white "H," and we begin following its direction down into town, where church is in session everywhere and few cars are on the move.

"Erma's trying out as my third wife," Irv says soberly, seeming to reflect conscientiously on the whole concept of wives (though not on Erma's whereabouts). "You see a big ugly guy like me, Frank, with a pretty gal like Erma, you know everything's just luck. Totally luck. That and being a good listener." He slightly pooches out his thick smooth lips like Mussolini, giving the impression he'd be willing to start listening now if there was anything worth listening to. "Did you guys get a chance to get into the Hall of Fame?"

"We were about to, Irv." I'm watching for another "H" sign but not seeing one, and am nervous we've passed it and will end up at the other end of town and back out on the interstate headed the wrong way, just like in Springfield. Precious time lost.

"You really oughta get back there when this is over. It's a treat. It's an education in itself, really, more than you can take in in a day. Those guys, those early guys, they played because they wanted to. Because they *could*. It wasn't a career for them. It was just a game. Now"—Irv looks disapproving—"it's a business." His voice trails off. I know he's heard himself doing his level best for his long-lost not-quite brother, whom he may remember now in finer detail and have figured out he never liked much and would be happy never to see again, though he still can simulate good cheer and be of service in the way he would to a crippled hitchhiker in a snowstorm, even if the hitchhiker was a convicted felon. "Incidents we can't control make us what we are—eh, Frank?" Irv says, changing subjects as he suddenly takes a sweeping left straight into an unnoticed but landscaped driveway that leads back to a crisp new three-story glass-and-brick hospital building with blinking antennae and microwave dishes on top. The A. O. Fox Hospital. Irv has been paying careful attention; I have been lost in a funk.

"Right, Irv," I say, not catching it all. "At least you can see it that way."

"I'm sure Jack's fine," Irv says, guiding us one-handed through a circular, shrub-lined drive, following the red EMERGENCY signs and stripes. The yellow Cooperstown Life Line ambulance is just swaying back out the drive, its flashers off, its cargo hold dark, as though something deathly has occurred. Ms. Oustalette is at the wheel and talking animatedly while smoking a cigarette, her nameless male partner barely visible in the shadowy passenger's seat.

"Home sweet hospital," Irv says, as he pulls alongside a bank of sliding glass doors designated simply as "Emergency." "Just hop on in, Franky," he says and smiles as I'm already leaving. "I'll park this beast and find you inside."

"Okay." Irv is radiating limitless sympathy, which has nothing to do with liking me. "Thanks, Irv," I say, leaning a moment back down into the door, where it's cool, and out of the hot, gunmetal sunlight.

"Simulate calm," Irv says, hiking one big blue-clad knee up on the leather seat. A tiny bell starts gonging inside.

"He'll probably have to wear glasses, that's all," I say. I shake my head at these wishful words.

"Wait and see. Maybe he's in there right now laughing his ass off."

"That'd be nice," I say, thinking how nice it *would* be and how, if so, it would also be the first time in a long time.

*B*ut that is not the case at all.

Inside at the long apple-green admissions desk I am told by the receptionist that Paul has "gone right in"—which means he is out of my reach behind some thick, shiny metal doors—and that an ophthalmologist has been "called in specially" to have a look at him. If I would take a seat "over there," the doctor will be out pretty soon to talk to me.

My heart has begun whompeting again at the antiseptic hospital colors, frigid surfaces and the strict, odorless, traffic-flow yin-yang of everything within sight and hearing. (All here is new, chrome-looking and hard plastic and, I'm sure, owes its existence to a big bond issue.) And *everything's* lugubriously, despairingly *for* something; nothing's just for itself or, better, for nothing. A basket of red geraniums would be yanked, a copy of *American Cage Bird* magazine tossed like an apple core. A realty guide, a stack of *Annie Get Your Gun* tickets—neither would last five minutes before somebody had it in the trash. People who end up here, these walls say, take no comfort from grace notes.

I sit nervously midway down a row of connected cherry-red high-impact plastic chairs and peer up at a control-less TV, bracketed high and out of reach and where Reverend Jackson in an opened-collared brown safari shirt is being interviewed by a panel of white men in business suits, who're beaming prudish self-confidence at him, as if they found him amusing; though the Reverend is exhibiting his own brand of self-satisfied smugness plus utter disdain, all of it particularly noticeable because the sound's off. (For a time this winter I considered him "my candidate," though I finally decided he couldn't win and would ruin the country if he did, and in either case would eventually tell me everything bad was my fault.) His goose is cooked anyway, and he's only on TV today to be humored.

The glass doors to the outside sigh open, and Irv strolls casually through in his blue sweats and sandals and yellow cardigan. He looks around without seeing me, then turns and walks back out onto the hot sidewalk as the doors shut, as if he'd come in the wrong hospital. A ticker running under Reverend Jackson's shiny brown mug reveals that the Mets defeated Houston, Graf defeated Navratilova, Becker defeated Lendl but is losing to Edberg, and while we're at it that Iraq has poisoned hundreds of Iranians with gas.

Suddenly both metal ER doors swing back, and a small young lemon-haired woman with a scrubbed Scandinavian face and wearing a doctor's smock comes striding out holding a clipboard. Her eyes fall directly on my worried face, alone here in the red relatives' alcove. She walks to the admissions desk, where a nurse points me out, and as I stand already smiling and overgrateful, she heads over with a look—I have to say—that is not a happy look. I would hate for it to be the look that spoke volumes about me, though of course in every way it does.

"Are you Paul's father?" she starts even before she gets to me, flipping pages on her silver clipboard. She's wearing pink tennis shoes that go *squee-kee-gee* on the new tiles, and her smock is open down the front to reveal a crisp tennis dress and short legs as brown and muscled out and thick as an athlete's. She seems totally without makeup or scent, her teeth as white as brand-new.

"Bascombe," I say softly, still grateful. "Frank Bascombe. My son's Paul Bascombe." (A good attitude can oft-times, Gypsies believe, deflect bad news.)

"I'm Dr. Tisaris." She consults her chart again, then fixes me with perfectly flat blue eyes. "Paul's had a very, *very* bad whack to the eye, I'm afraid, Mr. Bascombe. He's suffered what we call a dilation to the upper left arc of his left retina. What this essentially means is—" She blinks at me. "Was he hit with a baseball?" This she simply can't believe; no eye protection, no helmet, no nothing.

"A baseball," I say, possibly inaudibly, my good attitude and Gypsy hope gone, gone. "At Doubleday Field."

"Okay. Well," she says, "what this means is the ball hit him slightly left of center. It's what we call a macula-off injury, which means it drove the left front part of his eye back into the retina and basically flattened it. It was a very, very hard blow."

"It was the Express cage," I say, squinting at Dr. Tisaris. She is pretty, svelte (if short) but sinewy, a little athletic Greek, though she's wearing a wedding ring, so conceivably it's her husband the gastroenterologist who's the Greek and she's as Swedish or Dutch as she looks. Anyone but a fool, however, would feel complete confidence in her, even in tennis clothes.

"At the moment," she says, "he has okay vision in the eye, but he's having bright light flashes, which are typical of a serious dilation. You should probably have a second doctor take a look at him, but my suggestion is we repair it as soon as possible. Before the day's out would be best."

"Dilation. What's a dilation?" I am instantly as cold as mackerel flesh. The nurses at the admissions desk are all three looking at me oddly, and either I've just fainted or am about to faint or have fainted ten minutes ago and am recovering on my feet. Dr. Tisaris, however, model of rigorous antifainting decorum, doesn't seem to notice. So that I simply do not faint but grip my ten toes into the soles of my shoes and hang onto the floor as it dips and sways, all in response to one word. I hear Dr. Tisaris say "detachment" and feel certain she's explaining her medical-ethical perspective toward serious injury and advising me to act in a similar manner. What I hear myself saying is, "I see," then I bite the inside of my cheek until I taste dull, warm blood, then hear myself say, "I have to consult his mother first."

"Is she here?" Clipboard down, a look of unbelief on Dr. Tisaris's face, as if there is no mother.

"She's at the Yale Club."

Dr. Tisaris blinks. There is no Yale Club in Oneonta, I think. "Can you reach her?"

"Yes. I think so," I say, still staggered.

"We should try to get on with this." Her smile is indeed a detached, sober, professional one containing many, many strands of important consideration, none specific to me. I tell her I'd be grateful for the chance to see my son first. But what she says is, "Why don't you make your call, and we'll put a bandage on his eye so he won't scare you to death."

I look down for some reason at her curving, taut thighs beneath her smock and do not speak a word, just stand gripping the floor, tasting my blood, thinking in amazement of my son scaring me to death. She glances down at her two legs, looks up at my face without curiosity, then simply turns and walks away toward the admissions desk, leaving me alone to find a telephone.

*A*t the Yale Club on Vanderbilt Avenue, Mr. or Mrs. O'Dell is not in. It is noon on a bright Sunday before the 4th of July, and no one, of course, *should* be in. Everyone *should* be just strolling out of Marble Collegiate, beaming magisterially, or happily queuing for the Met or the Modern, or "shooting across to the Carlyle" for a Mozart brunch or up to some special friend's special duplex "in the tower," where there's a hedged veranda with ficuses and azaleas and hibiscus and a magical view of the river.

An extra check, though, uncovers Mrs. O'Dell has left behind a "just-in-case" number, which I punch in inside my scrubbed, green-and-salmon hospital phone nook—just as stout-fellow Irv wanders in again, scans the area, sees me waving, gives a thumbs-up, then turns, hands in his blue sweatpants' pockets and surveys the wide world he's just come from through the glass doors. He is an indispensable man. It's a shame he's not married.

"Windbigler residence," a child's musical voice says. I hear my own daughter, bursting with giggles, in the background.

"Hi," I say, unswervingly upbeat. "Is Mrs. O'Dell there?"

"Yes. She is." A pause for whispering. "Can I say who's calling, plee-yuzzz?"

"Say it's Mr. Bascombe." I am cast low by the insubstantial sound of my name. More concentrated whispers, then a spew of laughter, following which Clarissa comes on the line.

"Hel-*lo*," she says in her version of her mother's lowered serious voice. "This is Ms. Dykstra speaking. Can I be of any use to you, sir?" (She means, of course, Can I be of any service.)

"Yes," I say, my heart opening a little to let a stalk of light enter. "I'd like to order one of the twelve-year-old girls and maybe a pizza."

"What color would you like?" Clarissa says gravely, though she's bored with me already.

"White with a yellow top. Not too big."

"Well, we only have one left. And she's getting bigger, so you'd better place your order. What kind of pizza would you like?"

"Lemme speak to your mom—okay, sweetheart? It's sort of important."

"Paul's barking again, I bet." Clarissa makes a little schnauzer bark of her own, which drives her friend into muffled laughter. (They are, I'm certain, locked away in some wondrous, soundproof kids' wing, with every amusement, diversion, educational device, aid and software package known to mankind at their fingertips, all of it guaranteed to keep them out of the adults' hair for years.) Her friend makes a couple of little barks too, just for the hell of it. I should probably try one. I might feel better.

"That's not very funny," I say. "Get your mom for me, okay? I need to talk to her."

The receiver goes *blunk* onto some hard surface. "That's what he does," I hear Clarissa say unkindly about her wounded brother. She barks twice more, then a door opens and steps depart. Across the waiting room, Dr. Tisaris emerges again through the emergency room door. She has her smock buttoned now and baggy green surgical trousers down to her feet, which are sheathed in green booties. She is ready to operate. Though she heads over to the admissions desk to impart something to the nurses that makes them all crack up laughing just like my daughter and her friend. A black nurse sings out, "*Giiirl*, I'm tellin' you, I'm tellin' *you* now," then catches herself being noisy, sees me and covers her mouth, turning around the other way to hide more laughter.

"Hello?" Ann says brightly. She has no idea who's calling. Clarissa has kept it as her surprise secret.

"Hi. It's me."

"Are you here *already*?" Her voice says she's happy it's me, has just left a table full of the world's most interesting people, only to find even better pickings here. Maybe I could cab over and join in. (A conspicuous sea change from yesterday—based almost certainly on the welcome discovery that something has finally ended between us.)

"I'm in Oneonta," I say bluntly.

"What's the matter?" she says, as if Oneonta were a city well known for cultivating trouble.

"Paul's had an accident," I say as quickly as I can, so as to get on to the other part. "Not a life-threatening accident"—pause—"but something we need to confer about right away."

"What happened to him?" Alarm fills her voice.

"He got hit in the eye. By a baseball. In a batting cage."

"Is he blind?" More alarm, mixed with conceivable horror.

"No, he's not blind. But it's serious enough. The doctors feel like they need to get him into surgery pretty quick." (I added the plural on my own.)

"Surgery? Where?"

"Here in Oneonta."

"Where *is* it? I thought you were in Cooper's Park."

This, for some reason God knows but I don't, makes me angry. "That's down the road," I say. "Oneonta's a whole other city."

"What do we have to decide?" Cold, stiffening panic now; and not about the part she can't control—the unexplained wounding of her surviving son—but about the part she realizes, in this instant, she *is* accountable for and must decide about and damn well better decide right, because I am not responsible.

"What's wrong with him?" I hear Clarissa spout out officiously, as if she were accountable for something too. "Did he get his eye blown out with fireworks?"

Her mother says, "Shush. No, he did not."

"We have to decide if we want to let them do surgery up here," I say, peevishly. "They think the sooner the better."

"It's his eye?" She is voicing this as she's understanding it. "And they want to operate on it up there?" I know her thick, dark eyebrows are meshed and she's tugging the back of her hair, picking up one strand at a time, tugging and tugging and tugging until she feels a perfect pin-stick of pain. She has done this only in recent years. Never when I lived with her.

"I'm getting another opinion," I say. Though of course I haven't yet. But I will. I gaze at the TV above the waiting-area chairs. Reverend Jackson has vanished. The words "Credit No Good?" are on the screen against a bright blue background. Irv, when I look around, is still inside the sliding doors, Dr. Tisaris gone from the admissions desk. I'll need to find her pronto.

"Can it wait two hours?" Ann says.

"They said today. I don't know." My anger, just as suddenly, has gone.

"I'm going to come up there," she says.

"It takes four hours." Three, actually. "It won't help." I begin thinking of the clogged FDR, holiday inbounds. Major backups on the Triborough. A traffic nightmare. All things I was thinking about on Friday, though now it's Sunday.

"I can get a helicopter from the East River terminal. Charley flies down all the time. I should be there. Just tell me where."

"Oneonta," I say, feeling strangely hollowed at the prospect of Ann.

"I'm going to get on the phone right now on the way and call Henry Burris. He's at Yale–New Haven. They're in the country this weekend. He'll explain all the options, tell me exactly what's wrong with him."

"Detachment," I say. "They say he has a dilated retina. There's no need to come right this second."

"Is he *in* the hospital?" I have the feeling Ann is writing everything down now: *Henry Burris. Oneonta. Detachment, retina, batting cage? Paul, Frank.*

"Of course he's in the hospital," I say. "Where do you think he is?"

"What's the exact name of the hospital, Frank?" She's as deliberate as a scrub nurse; and I a merely dutiful next of kin.

"A. O. Fox. It's probably the only hospital in town."

"Is there an airport there?" Clearly she has written down *airport.*

"I don't know. There should be, if there isn't." Then a silence opens, during which she may in fact have stopped writing.

"Frank, are you all right? You sound not very good."

"I'm not very good. I didn't have my eye knocked out, though."

"He didn't have his eye knocked out really, did he?" Ann says this in a pleading voice of motherhood that can't be escaped.

From the door Irv turns toward me with a worried look, as if he's overheard me say something bitter or argumentative. The black admissions nurse is looking at me too, over the top of her computer terminal.

"No," I say, "he didn't. But he got it knocked. It's not very good."

"Don't let them do anything to him. Please? Until I get there? Can you?" She says this now in a sweet way that is tuned to the helplessness we share and that I would improve if I could but can't. "Will you promise me that?" She has not yet mentioned her dream of injury. She has done me that kindness.

"Absolutely. I'll tell the doctor right now."

"Thank you so much," Ann says. "I'll be there in two hours or less. Just hold on."

"I will. I'll be right here. And so will Paul."

"It won't be very long," Ann says half brightly. "All right?"

"All right."

"Okay then. Okay." And that is all.

*F*or two hours that turn into three hours that turn into four, I walk round and round the little color-keyed lobby, while everything is on hold. (Under better circumstances this would be a natural time to make client calls and take my mind off worrying, but it's not possible now.) Irv, who's decided to toss in the afternoon "drinks party" with the '59 Sox and keep me company, heads out at two and forages a couple of fat bags of Satellite burgers, which we eat mechanically in the plastic chairs while above us on TV the Mets play the Astros in audio-less nontime. Now is not an action period for the ER. Later, when the light fails and too much beer's been guzzled on the lake, an extra base attempted with bone-breaking results, or when somebody who knows all about Roman candles doesn't quite know enough—*then* resources here will be put to the test. As it is, one possibly self-inflicted minor knife wound, an obese woman with unexplained chest pains, one shirtless, shaken-up victim of a one-car rollover come through, but not all at once, and without fanfare (the last chauffeured in by the Cooperstown crew, who frown at me on their way back out). Everyone is eventually set free under his or her own power, all emerging stone-faced and chastened by the sorry outcome of their day. The nurses behind the admissions desk, though, stay in jokey spirits right through. "Now you wait'll tomorrow 'bout this time," one of them says with a look of amazement. "This place'll be jumpin' like Grand Central Station at rush hour. The Fourth's a *biiig* day for hurtin' yourself."

At three, a fat young crew-cut priest passes by, stops and comes back to where Irv and I are watching silent TV, asks in a confessional whisper if everything's under control, and if not, is there anything he can do for us (it's not; there isn't), then heads smilingly off for the ICU wing.

Dr. Tisaris cruises through a time or two, seemingly without enough to do. Once she stops to tell me a "retina man" from Binghamton who did his work at "Mass Eye" has examined Paul (I never saw him arrive) and confirmed a retinal rupture, and "if it'd be okay we'd like to prep him for when your wife gets here, after which we can shoot him in. Dr. Rotollo"—the Binghamton hired gun—"will do the surgery."

Once again I ask if I can see Paul (I haven't since the ambulance left Cooperstown), and Dr. Tisaris looks inconvenienced but says yes, though she needs to keep him still to "minimalize" bleeding, and maybe I might just peek in unbeknownst, since he's had a sedative.

Leaving Irv, I follow her, *squee-kee-gee, squee-kee-gee*, through the double doors into a brightly lit, mint-colored bullpen room smelling of rubbing alcohol, where there are examining bays around on all four walls, each hung with a green hospital curtain. Two special rooms are marked "Surgical" and have heavy, push-in doors with curved handles, and Paul is housed in one of these. When Dr. Tisaris cautiously shoves back the noiseless door, I see my son then, on his back on a bed-on-wheels equipped with metal sidebars, looking very bulky with both his eyes bandaged over like a mummy, but still in his black *Clergy* shirt and maroon shorts and orange socks, minus only his shoes, which sit side by side against the wall. His arms are folded on his chest in an impatient, judicial way, his legs out straight and stiff. A beam of intense light is trained down on his bandaged face, and he's wearing his earphones plugged into a yellow Walkman I've never seen before, and which is resting on his chest. He seems to me in no particular pain and to all appearances except the bandages seems unbothered by the world (or else he's dead, since I can't detect rise or fall in his chest, no tremor in his fingers, no musical toe twitch to whatever he's tuned in to). His ear, I see, has a new bandage.

I would of course dearly love to bound across and kiss him. Or if that couldn't be, at least to do my waiting in here, unacknowledged amongst the instrument trays, oxygen tubes, defibrillator kits, needle dumps and rubber glove dispensers: sit a vigil on a padded stool, be a presence for my son, "useful" at least in principle, since my time for being a real contributor seems nearly over now, in the way that serious, unraveling injury can deflect the course of life and send it careering an all new way, leaving the old, uninjured self and its fussy familiars far back in the road.

But neither of these can happen, and time goes by as I stand with Dr. Tisaris simply watching Paul. A minute. Three. Finally I see a hopeful sigh of breath beneath his shirt and suddenly feel my ears being filled by hissing, so much that if someone spoke to me, said "Frank" again, out loud from behind, I might not hear, would only hear hiss, like air escaping or snow sliding off a roof or wind blowing through a piney bough—a hiss of acceptance.

Paul, then, for no obvious reason, turns his head straight toward us, as if he's heard something (my hiss?) and knows someone is watching, can imagine me or someone through a red-black curtain of molten dark. Out loud, in his boy's voice, he says, "Okay, who's here?" He fiddles sightlessly with his Walkman to kill the volume. He may of course have said it any number of times when no one was present.

"It's Dr. Tisaris, Paul," she says, utterly calm. "Don't be frightened."

All hissing ceases.

"Who's frightened?" he says, staring into his bandages.

"Are you still having flashes of light or vivid colors?"

"Yeah," he says. "A little. Where's my Dad?"

"He's waiting for you." She lays a cool finger upon my wrist. I am not to speak. I am the virus of too much trouble already. "He's waiting for your Mom to get here, so we can fix your eye up." Her starchy smock shifts against the doorframe. I catch a first faint scent of exotica from underneath its folds.

"Tell my dad he tries to control too much. He worries too much too," Paul says. With his warty, tattooed hand he gropes down at his pleasure unit and gives it a delving scratch just like Irv, as though all lights were out and no one could see anyone. Then he sighs: great wisdom conferring great patience.

"I'll see he gets that message," Dr. Tisaris says in an echoless, professional's voice.

And it is *this* voice that makes me wince, a not-small, mouth-skewing wince up from my knees, sudden and forceful enough that I have to clear my throat, turn my head away and gulp. Here is the voice of the *outer* world become primary: "I'll see he gets that message; I'm sorry, that job's filled; we'd like to ask you some questions; I'm sorry, I can't talk to you now." And so on, and so on, and so on all the way to: "I'm sorry to tell you your father, your mother, your sister, your son, your wife, your dog, your-*anybody*-you-might-ever-know-and-love-and-want-to-survive has left, disappeared, been called away, injured, maimed, expired." While mine—the silenced voice of worry, love, patience, impatience, comradeship, thoughtlessness, understanding and genial acquiescence—is the small voice of the old small life losing ground. The Hall of Fame—impersonal but shareable—was meant as the staging ground for a new life's safe beginning (and nearly, nearly was) but instead has had itself pre-empted by a regional hospital full of prognoses, voices without echoes, cheery disinterest, cold hard facts impossible to soften. (Why is it we're never quite prepared, as I'm not now, for our plans to work out wrong?)

"Do you have any kids?" Paul asks sagely to his tanned doctor in a voice as echoless as hers.

"Nope," she says, smiling jauntily. "Not yet."

I should stay now, hear his views on child rearing, a subject he has unique experience with. Only my feet won't hear of it and are inching back, shifting direction, then shoving off, getting out of range fast across the bullpen, headed for the doors, much as when I heard him years ago conferring ardently with his made-up "friends" at home and couldn't bear it either, was made too weak and sick at heart by his inspired and almost perfect sufficiency.

"If you have any," I hear him say, "don't ever—" Then that's it, and I am quickly out through the metal doors and back into the cool watery room for relatives, friends, well-wishers, where I now belong.

*B*y four Ann has not arrived, and Irv and I elect a walk out of the hospital, across the lawn and onto the summery afternoon streets of Oneonta, a town I never once for all my travels imagined myself in; never dreamed I'd be a worried father-in-waiting in, though that has been my MO for moons and moons.

Irv has blossomed into even wider good spirits, the net effect of awaiting dire events that aren't truly dire for him, that will make him sorry if things go bad but never truly bereaved. (Much like your Aunt Beulah's second husband, Bernie from Bismarck, who takes it on himself to tell jokes at your grandfather's funeral and in doing so makes everyone feel a lot better.)

We troop purposefully out across the tonsured Bermuda grass and onto the warm sidewalk where hilly Main drops quickly toward town and is now much busier than when church was going. Here great shagbark hickories and American chestnuts, descendants of our central hardwood forest primeval, have bulged their roots through the aged, crumbly concrete and made strolling a challenge. Ranked along the descending street are old sagging frame residences built on the high ground above retaining walls, going gray and punky from the years and soon to be settling (if work's not done and done soon) into perfect valuelessness. Some are deserted, some have American flags flying, a couple show familiar yellow ribbons, while others show signs that say FOR RENT. FOR SALE. FREE IF YOU MOVE IT. In my trade these are "carpenter's specials," "starter homes for newlys," "not for everyone" homes, "mystery abounds" homes, "make offer" homes—the downward-tending lingo of loss.

Irv, being Irv, means to take up an issue, and in this case the issue is "continuity," which is what his life at least seems to him to be "all about" these days—recognizing, he willingly admits, that his concern may be "tied to" his Jewishness and to the need to strive, to the pressure of history and to a certain significant portion of his life spent on a kibbutz after his first marriage went down the tubes and wrecked continuity big-time, and where he harrowed the dry and unforgiving Bible land, read the Torah, served six nerve-racking months in the Israeli army and eventually married another kibbutznik (from Shaker Heights), a marriage that also didn't last long and ended in scalding, vituperative, religiously dispiriting divorce.

"I learned a lot in the kibbutz, Frank," Irv says, his rattan sandals slapping the split pavement as we head down Main at a good clip. We seem by no particular design to be aiming toward a red Dairy Queen sign below on the Oneonta strip-commercial, a neighborhood where the houses stop and possibly it's unsafe for strangers (a neighborhood in transition).

"Everybody I know who went over there says it was pretty interesting, even if they didn't like it much," I say. I actually know no one but Irv who ever admitted to living on a kibbutz, and all I *do* know I read in the Trenton *Times*. Irv, though, is not a bad advertisement for the life, since he's decent and thoughtful and not at all a pain in the ass. (I've now recalled Irv's boyhood persona: the exuberant, accommodating, gullible-but-complex "big" boy who needed to shave way too early in life.)

"You know, Frank, Judaism doesn't have to be practiced just in the synagogue," Irv says solemnly. "Growing up in Skokie, I didn't always have that impression. Not that my family was ever devout in any way." *Slap-slap, slip-slap, slip-slop.* Local toughs with local sweethearts notched under their bulging biceps are cruising East Main in hot-looking Trans Ams and dark, channeled S-10s. (No Monzas.) Irv and I stand out here like two Latvian rustics in native attire, which isn't that uncomfortable since it's our own country. (A common language alone *should* assure us entry-level acceptance anywhere within a two-thousand-mile radius of Kansas City, though pushing your luck could mean trouble, just like on a kibbutz, and we are now and then glared at.)

"You have any kids, Irv?" I say, not at ease—continuity aside—with religious talk today, happier to be led elsewhere.

"No kids," Irv says. "Didn't want kids, which is what shot my deal with the second wife. She remarried right away and had a bunch. I don't even have any contact with her, which is too bad. They shunned me. You wouldn't think that would happen." Irv seems amazed but sorrowfully willing to accept life's mysteries.

"Self-sufficient thinking's always in short supply in those kinds of places, I guess. Just like with the Baptists and the Presbyterians."

"I guess Sartre said freedom isn't worth a nickel unless you can act on it."

"That sounds like Sartre," I say, thinking all over again what I've always thought about hippie communes, Brook Farms, kibbutzes, goofball utopian ideals of every stripe: let one real independent emerge, and everybody turns into Hitler. And if a good egg like Irv can't make it work for him, the rest of us may as well stay where we are. I don't know what this has to do with continuity, though I'm sure I should.

We pass along by an old building with a dirty junk-store window display piled and jumbled with dented teakettles, wooden hotel coat hangers, busted waffle irons, bits of saddlery, snow tires, empty picture frames, books, lamp shades, plus a whole lot more crap heaped back on a shadowy concrete floor—stuff the last owner couldn't give away when he went bust and just left. In the glass, though, I unexpectedly and unhappily see myself, in brighter colors than the junk but still dim and, to my surprise, a good half a head shorter than Irv and walking along in a semi-*stooped* posture, as if grasping forces were tightening strings and sinews in my gut, causing me to bunch up, humping my shoulders in a way I sure as hell never imagined myself and, now that I see, am shocked by! Irv, of course, is oblivious to his reflection. But I sternly brace back my shoulders and stiffen up like a clothes dummy, take a deep chest breath, give myself a good erective stretching and work my head around like a lighthouse (not very different from what I did standing on the wall overlooking the Central Leatherstocking Region yesterday, but now with more cause). Irv meanwhile goes back to elaborating on his continuity concerns as we reach the bottom of the hill, passing a low-rent, two-desk real estate office, City of Hills Realty, whose name I don't recognize from the signs I saw farther back.

"Anyway," Irv says, tramping right along, not noticing my furious stretching, opening a button on his gold cardigan to cool off in the warm afternoon. "Do you have a lot of friends?"

"Not too many," I say, my neck worked back, my shoulders squared.

"Same here. Simulators only socialize as a group, but I'd rather take off for a long walk in the desert alone, or maybe go camping."

"I've become an amateur trout fisherman." I walk a little faster now. Moving my shoulders and neck have also awakened an achiness where I was whacked by the baseball.

"See? There you are," meaning what I'm not sure. "How 'bout a girlfriend? You fixed up there?"

"Well," I say, and think an awkward thought about Sally for the first time in too long. I should definitely call South Mantoloking before she gets on the train. Recalculate our plans; aim for tomorrow. "I'm pretty set there, Irv."

"How 'bout marriage plans?"

I smile at Irv, a man with two wives down and one on deck, a man who hasn't seen me in twenty-five years yet who's trying hard to console me against bad events by the honest application of his simple self to mine. Much of human goodness is badly undersold, take it from me. "I'm a bachelor these days, Irv."

Irv nods, satisfied that we're in the same semi-seaworthy boat. "I didn't really explain what I meant about continuity," he says. "It's just my Jewish thing. With other people it's probably different."

"I guess so." I'm picturing the ten separate digits of Sally's phone number, counting the possible rings and her sweet voice in answer.

"I'd think in the realty business you'd get a pretty good exposure to everybody's wish for it. I mean in the community sense."

"What's that?"

"Just continuity," Irv says, smiling, sensing some resistance and maybe considering just letting the subject go (I would). We're across the street from the DQ now, having homed in here through some mutual understanding we haven't needed to voice.

"I don't really think communities are continuous, Irv," I say. "I think of them—and I've got a lot of proof—as isolated, contingent groups trying to improve on an illusion of permanence, which they fully accept as an illusion. If that makes any sense. Buying power is the instrumentality. But continuity, if I understand it at all, doesn't really have much to do with it. Maybe realty's not that commanding a metaphor."

"I guess that makes sense," Irv says, pretty certainly not buying a word of it, though he ought to be satisfied since my definition of community fits right into a general notion of simulation as well as his personal bad experience on the kibbutz. ("Community" is actually one of those words I loathe, since all its hands-on implications are dubious.)

I am braced up straighter now, almost as erect and tall as Irv, though he's meatier from all his months with a Galil strapped to his back while hoeing the dry ground and keeping an eagle eye out for murderous, uncommunity-oriented Arabs.

"Does that seem like enough, though, Frank? The *illusion* of permanence?" Irv says this committedly. It is a subject he no doubt wrangles over with everybody, and may be his *true interest*, one that makes his happy life a sort of formal investigation of firmer stuff beyond the limits of simulation; rather than like mine, a journey toward someplace yet to be determined but that I have good hope for.

"Enough for what?"

We've crossed to the DQ, which true to the old town is an

"oldie" itself, in lackluster disrepair since Oneonta has yet to blossom into a destination resort. It's nowhere as nice as Franks, though there are enough similarities to make me feel at home standing in front of it.

"It's still all tied up in my mind with continuity," Irv says, arms folded, reading the hand-lettered menu board from where we're stopped at the back of a short queue of native Oneontans. I scan down for a "dipped" cone, my all-time fave, and feel for just this fleeting moment incongruously happy. "I was remembering while I was waiting for you at the hospital"—Irv allows a look of goodwilled perplexity to pass over his big Levantine mouth—"that you and I were around Jake's house together while our parents were married. I was right there when your mother died. We knew each other pretty well. And now twenty-five years of absence go by and we bump into each other up here in the middle of the north woods. And I realized—I realized it pacing around up there worried about Jack and his eye—that you're my only link to that time. I'm not gonna get all worked up over it, but you're as close to family as anyone there is for me. And we don't even know each other." Irv, even as he's making his ice cream choice, and without actually looking at me, lays his big, fleshy, hairy, pinkie-ringed hand heavily onto my shoulder and shakes his head in wonderment. "I don't know, Frank." He looks at me furtively, then stares hard at the big menu. "Life's screwy."

"It is, Irv," I say. "It's screwy as a monkey." I put my smaller hand on Irv's shoulder. And though we don't splutter forward and glom onto each other at the end of the DQ line, we do exchange a number of restrained but unambiguous shoulder pats and glance squeamishly into each other's faces in ways that on any other day but this odd one would set me off up the hill at a dead run.

"We've probably got a lot of things to talk about," Irv says prophetically, keeping his heavy hand where it is, so that I feel forced to keep mine where *it* is, in a sort of unwieldy, arms-length non-embrace. Several Oneontans waiting in front of us have already cast threatening now-just-don't-get-me-involved-in-this frowns our way, as though dangerously unsuppressed effusions were about to splash on everybody like battery acid, with violence a likely outcome. But this is as far as it's going; I could easily tell them as much.

"We might, Irv," I say, not knowing what those things could be.

A shadowy someone inside the Dairy Queen slides back the rickety glass on the SORRY CLOSED window and says from inside, "I can help you down here, folks." The Oneontans all give us a hesitant look as if Irv and I might suddenly rush the other window, though we don't. They turn back toward their own original window, consider it skeptically, then as a group all shift over to number two, giving Irv and me a straight shot to the front.

On our way back up the hill we walk side by side, as solemn as two missionaries, I with my fast-dissolving "dip," Irv with a pink "strawberry boat" that snugs perfectly into the palm of one big hand. He seems to be elated but containing his feelings of transcendence owing to the sober protocol of Paul's (Jack's) injury.

He explains to me, though, that lately he's been going through an "odd passage" in life, one he associates with getting to be forty-five (instead of being Jewish). He complains of feeling detached from his own personal history, which has eventuated in a fear (kept within boundaries by his demanding simulator work) that he is diminishing; and if not in an actual physical sense, then definitely in a spiritual one. "It's hard to explain in literal terms and make it seem really serious or clear," he assures me.

I look upward when he says this, my sticky napkin squeezed into a tight dry ball in my palm, my jaw beginning to ratchet tight again after our respite. High above us, sea gulls circle dizzyingly and in great numbers on the clear afternoon air waves, framed by the old green hardwood crowns up the hillside, high enough to seem to make no sound. Why gulls, I wonder, so far from a sea?

Fear of diminishment of course is a concept I know plenty about under the title "fear of disappearance," and would be happy to know not much more. Though in Irv's case it has occasioned what he calls the "catch of dread," a guilty, hopeless, even deathly feeling he experiences just at the moment when anyone else in his right mind might expect to feel exultation—upon seeing sea gulls in dizzying great numbers on a matte of blue sky; or upon stealing an unexpected glimpse down a sun-shot river valley (as I did just yesterday) to a shimmering glacial lake of primordial beauty; on seeing unreserved love in your girlfriend's eyes and knowing she wants to dedicate her life only to your happiness and that you should let her; or just smelling a sudden, heady perfume on a timeworn city sidewalk as you turn a crumbling corner and spy a bed of purple loosestrife and Shasta daisies in full bloom in a public park you had no reason to expect was there. "Little things *and* large," Irv says, referring to whatever has made him feel first wonderful, then terrible, then lessened, then potentially canceled altogether. "It's crazy, but I feel like some bad feeling is sort of eating away at me on the edges." He jabs with his plastic spoon at the bottom of his corrugated pink boat and furrows his big-lug brows.

To tell the truth, I'm surprised to hear this kind of dour talk out of Irv. I'd have guessed his Jewishness plus native optimism would've sheltered him—though of course I'm wrong. Native optimism is that humor most vulnerable to sneak attacks. About Jewishness I don't know.

"My view of marriage"—Irv has earlier admitted a strange unwillingness to tie the knot and make little hard-body Erma Mrs. Ornstein #3—"is that I'm still ready to go whole hog and lose myself in it, but really since about '86 or so I've had this feeling, and this goes along with the dread, of just losing myself period, and in Erma's case of maybe losing myself into the wrong person and being eternally sorry." Irv looks over at me to see, I assume, if I've changed in appearance, having now heard his bitter admissions. "And I do love her, too," he adds as a capper.

We are nearly back to the hospital lawn. The old, settling houses up above the sidewalk behind aged hickories and oaks seem less decrepit now for having been viewed twice in different moods and lights. (A cornerstone principle for your hard-to-sell listing: make 'em see it twice. Things can look better.) I turn and gaze back down the hill and over town. Oneonta seems like a sweet and homey place—admittedly not a place I'd want to sell real estate, but still a fine place to live once your family has gone off and left you to your own devices for combating loneliness. The gulls I've seen have suddenly vanished, and the afternoon air above the treetops is now swept through by evening swifts, taking insects and filling the sky like motes. (I should call the Markhams, as well as Sally, but these needs recede, each as they are counted.)

"Any of that stick to your wall?" Irv says earnestly, knowing he's blathered on like a mental patient and I've said zilch, except it's allowable now since we're brothers.

"All of it does, Irv." I smile, hands down deep in my pockets, letting the warm breeze lave me before I turn back toward the hospital. Naturally, I've felt what Irv is feeling five hundred times over and have no single solution to offer, only the general remedies of persistence, jettisoning, common sense, resilience, good cheer—all tenets of the Existence Period—leaving out the physical isolation and emotional disengagement parts, which cause trouble equal to or greater than the problems they ostensibly solve.

Someone from a passing pickup, a tee-shirted white kid with a mean red mouth and a plump, sneering girlie with her hands parked behind her head, shouts out his window something that sounds like *honi soit que mal y pense* but isn't, then floors it, laughing. I wave at him good-naturedly, though Irv is captained by his probs.

"I guess I'm sort of surprised to hear you say all that, Irv," I resume, to try and be a help. "But I think a small act of heroism might be to go ahead and try saying yes to Erma. Even if you get whacked. You'll get over it, just like you got over the kibbutz." (I'm a big talker when it's somebody else getting whacked.) "How long ago were you over there, by the way?"

"Fifteen years ago. It left a major impression. But that's interesting for the future," Irv says, nodding, and meaning again that it's *not* interesting at all but the goddamn craziest thing he's ever heard of, though he'll pretend it isn't because he feels sorry for me. (I'd have thought the kibbutz experience was last September, not 1973!) Irv sniffs the air, as if seeking a fragrance he recognizes. "Now's maybe not the time to take that kind of chance, Frank. I'm thinking about the continuity I was boring you with, about getting a clearer sense of where I've come from before I try to find out where I'm going. Just take the pressure off the moment, if you see my point." He looks at me, nodding judiciously.

"How're you going to do that? Get some genealogical charts made up?"

"Well, for instance, today—this afternoon—this has meant something to me along those lines."

"Me too." Though again I'm not completely sure what. Possibly it's something on the order of what Sally said about not ever getting to see Wally and having to get used to it, only in reverse: I *am* getting to see Irv, and I like it, but it doesn't have a profound effect.

"But that's a good sign, isn't it? Someplace in the Torah it says something about beginning to understand long before you know you understand."

"I think that's in *Miracle on 34th Street*," I say, and smile again at Irv, who is kind but goofy from too much simulation and continuity. "I'm pretty sure it says it in *The Prophet* too."

"Never read it," he says gravely. "But let me just show you something, Frank. This'll surprise you." Irv goes groping in his sweatpants' back pocket and comes out with a tiny wafer wallet that probably cost five hundred dollars. Concentrating downward, he thumbs through his credit cards and papers, then fingers out something that appears softened by time. "Take a look at that," he says, handing it forward. "I've carried that for years. Five years now. Tell me why."

I turn the card and hold it so the daylight's behind me. (Irv has gone to the trouble of laminating it as a seal of its importance.) And it's not a card at all but a photograph, black and white, encased in layers and re-layers of plastic and for that reason is fogged and dim as memory. Here are four humans in a stately family pose, two parents, two adolescent boys, standing out on some front porch steps, squinting-smiling apprehensively at the camera and into a long-ago patch of light that brightens their faces. Who are these? Where are they? When? Though in a moment I see it's Irv's once-nuclear family in the greenage days in Skokie, when times were sweet and nothing needed simulating.

"Pretty great, Irv." I look up at him, then admire the photo again for politeness' sake and hand it back, ready to re-commence my own parenting tasks, put the pressure back on the moment.

Not far off I hear the wet *thwop-thwop-thwop* and realize the hospital has a helipad for such emergencies as Paul's, and that this is Ann arriving.

"It's us, Frank," Irv says, and looks at me amazed. "It's you and Jake and your mom and me, in Skokie, in 1963. You can see how pretty your mom is, though she looks thin already. We're all there on the porch. Do you even remember it?" Irv stares at me, damp-lipped and happy behind his glasses, holding his precious artifact out for me to see once more.

"I guess I don't." I look again reluctantly at this little pinch-hole window to my long-gone past, feel a quickening torque of heart pain—unexceptional, nothing like Irv's catch of dread—and once again proffer it back. I'm a man who wouldn't recognize his own mother. Possibly I should be in politics.

"Me either really." Irv looks appreciatively down at himself for the eight jillionth time, trying to leech some wafting synchronicity out of his image, then shakes his head and re-snugs it among his other wallet votives and crams it all back into his pocket, where it belongs.

I survey the sky again for a sight of the chopper but see nothing, not even the swifts.

"I mean, no great big deal, of course." Irv is squaring up his expectations to my rather insufficient response.

"Irv, I better get inside now. I'm pretty sure I hear my wife's helicopter arriving." (Is this a sentence one *usually* says? Or is it me? Or the day?)

"Hey, don't be crazy." Irv's heavy hand is again right up on my shoulder like a gangplank. (My heart has in fact gone rapid with its own *thwopetty-thwop*.) "I wanted to show you what I meant about continuity. It's nothing dangerous. We don't have to cut our arms and mingle blood or anything."

"I might not agree with you about everything, Irv, but I—" and then for an instant I lose my breath entirely and almost gasp, which makes me panic that I'm choking and need a quick Heimlich (if Irv knows how and would oblige). I've done wrong by taking this Dairy Queen walk and letting myself be hoodwinked just like Paul, by cozy, small-town plenitude, lured to think I can float free again against all evidence of real gravity. "But I want you to know," I say just before a second, less terrifying gullet stop, "that I respect how you see the world, and I think you're a great guy." (When in doubt fall back on the old Sigma Chi formula: Ornstein = Great Guy. Let's pledge him, even if he is a Hebe.)

"I don't think I've miscalculated you, Frank," Irv says. He is the stalwart project leader over in the yaw-pitch-and-roll lab now: always flying level even if the rest of us aren't. Though I've been him (more than once) and won't be caught again. Irv is entering his own Existence Period, complete with all the good and not-so-good trimmings, just as it seems I'm exiting it in a pitch-and-tumble mode. We have passed in daylight; we have interfaced, given each other good and earnest feedback. But ours is not life coterminous, though I like him fine.

I start off then toward the hospital doors, my heart popping, my jaw going stiff as an andiron, leaving Irv with my best words for our future as friends. "We'll try to go fishing sometime." I look around for emphasis. He is poised, one long, sandaled foot on the edge of the grass, one off, his bright cardigan catching the sunlight. He is, I know, silently wishing us both clear sailing toward the next horizon.

12

Ann is standing in the emergency room lobby all alone, in her buttoned-up tan trench coat, bare-legged, wearing worn white running shoes. She looks as if her mind is full of worries, none of which can be solved by seeing me.

"I've been standing here watching you through those doors as you crossed the lawn. And it wasn't until you got to the door that I realized it was you." She smiles at me in a daunted way, takes her hands out of her trench coat pockets, holds my arm and gives me a small kiss, which makes me feel a small bit better (though not actually good). We are less joined than ever now, so much that a kiss can't matter. "I brought Henry Burris with me. That's why I'm so late," she says, immediately all business. "He's already looked at Paul and his chart, and he thinks we ought to fly him down to Yale right away."

I simply stare at her in confoundment. I have indeed missed everything important: her arrival, a new examination, a revised prognosis. "How?" I say, looking hopelessly around the apple-green-and-salmon waiting room walls, as if to say, Well, you can see what *I* bring to the table: Oneonta. It may be a funny name, it may not even be the best, but by God, it's reliable and it's where we are.

"We've already got another helicopter coming that can transport him. It's maybe already here." She looks at me sympathetically.

Behind the admissions desk there is a new crew: two tiny, neat-as-pins Korean girls in high Catholic-nursing-school caps, working over charts like actuaries, plus a listless young blond (a local), engrossed by her computer monitor. None of these knows of my case. It would encourage me to have Irv waltz in, take a seat in the back row and be my ally.

"What does Dr. Tisaris say?" I'm wondering where she is, wishing she would get in on this powwow. Though possibly Ann has already dismissed her and Dr. Rotollo both, put her own surgical team in place while I was out having my "dip." I'll need to apologize to her for a lack of faith.

"She's fine about releasing him," Ann says, "especially to Yale. We just sign a form. I've already signed one. She's very professional. She knows Henry from her residency" (natch). Ann is nodding. Suddenly, though, she peers directly up at my eyes, her gray, flecked irises gone perfectly round and large, shining with straight-ahead imploring. She is not wearing her wedding ring (possibly for the wit's-end, nerves-stripped-bare look). "Frank, I'd just like to do this, okay? So we can get him down to New Haven in fifty minutes? Everything's all set there. It's a half hour to get him prepped and an hour or so in surgery. Henry'll supervise it. Then the best that can happen will." She blinks at me dark-eyed, not wanting to say more, having played the big card first—though she can't help herself. "Or he can be operated on in Oneonta by Dr. Tisaris or whoever, and she may be fine."

"I understand," I say. "What's the risk to him of flying?"

"Smaller than the risk, in Henry's opinion, of doing retinal surgery here." Her features soften and relax. "Henry's done two thousand of these."

"That oughta be enough," I say. "Is he a classmate of Charley's?"

"No. He's older," she says curtly and then is silent. Possibly Henry's our mystery mister; they almost always fill innocent roles as cover. Older, in this case; experienced in treating the ravaged victims of human suffering (such as Ann); uncannily bears Ann's father's name as a karmic asset. Plus, once he saves Paul's vision (days of soulful waiting for the bandages to be removed and sight to re-dawn), it'll be a snap to lay it all out to Charley, who'll wryly, maybe even gratefully, stand aside, outmaneuvered round the final buoy. Charley's a sport, if nothing else. I am much less of one.

"Do you want to know what happened?" I say.

"He got hit with a batting cage, you said." Ann produces a business-size envelope from her trench coat pocket and moves back a step toward the admissions desk, indicating I should come with her. It is another release form. I am releasing my son into the world. Too early.

"He got hit with a baseball, *in* a batting cage," I say.

Ann says nothing, just looks at me as if I'm being overly fastidious about these large-scale events. "Wasn't he wearing a helmet of some kind?" she says, inching back, drawing me on.

"No. He got mad at me and just ran in the cage, and stood there for a couple of pitches, then he just let one hit him in the face. I put the money in for him." I feel my eyes, for the third time in less than twenty-four hours, cloud with hot tears I don't want to be there.

"Oh," Ann says, her envelope in her left hand. One of the Oriental micro-nurses looks up at me in a nose-high, nearsighted way, then goes back to charting. Tears mean nothing in the emergency room.

"I don't think he *wanted* to put his eye out," I say, my eyes brimming. "But he may have wanted to get whacked. To see what it felt like. Haven't you ever felt that way?"

"No," Ann says, and shakes her head, staring at me.

"Well, I have, and I wasn't crazy." I say this much too loudly. "When Ralph died. And after you and I got divorced. I'd have been happy to take a hard one in the eye. It would've been easier than what I *was* doing. I just don't want you to think he's nuts. He's not."

"It was probably just an accident," she says imploringly. "It isn't your fault." Though she is meticulous, her own eyes go shiny against all effort and instinct. I am not supposed to see her cry, remember? It violates the divorce's creed.

"It *is* my fault. Sure it is," I say, terribly. "You even dreamed about it. He should've been wearing protective eye covering and a suit of armor and a crash helmet. You weren't there."

"Don't feel that way," Ann says and actually smiles, though bleakly. I shake my head and wipe my left eye, where there seem to be too many tears. Her seeing me cry is *not* an issue in my code of conduct. There is no issue between us. Which is the issue.

Ann takes a deep unassured breath, then shakes her head as a signal of what I'm not supposed to do now: make things worse. Her left, ringless hand rises as if by itself and places the envelope on the green plastic admissions counter. "I don't think he's crazy. He just may need some assistance right now. He was probably trying to make you notice him."

"We all need assistance. I was just/trying to make him *do* something." I am suddenly angry with her for knowing but knowing wrongly what everybody's supposed to do and how and why. "And I *will* feel this way. When your dog gets run over, it's your fault. When your kid gets his eye busted, that's your fault. I was supposed to help manage his risks."

"Okay." She lowers her head, then steps to me and takes one

sleeve again as she did when she gave me one small kiss and talked me into agreeing for my son to fly to Yale. She lets her face go sideways against my chest, her body relaxed as a way for me to know she's trying—trying to slip back between the walls of years and words and events, and listen to my heartbeat as a surety that we are both now alive, if we're nothing else, together. "Don't just be mad," she says in a whisper. "Don't be so mad at me."

"I'm not mad at you." I am whispering too, into her dark hair. "I'm just so something else. I don't think I know the word. There's not a word for it, maybe."

"That's what you like, though. Isn't it?" She's holding my arm now, though not too tight, as the nurses behind us politely turn their faces.

"Sometimes," I say. "Sometimes it is. Just not now. I'd like to have a word now. I'm in between words, I guess."

"That's okay." I feel her body grow taut and begin to pull away. She would have a word for it. It's her precise way of truth. "Sign this paper now, won't you? So we can get things going? Get him all fixed up?"

"Sure," I say, letting go. "I'll be glad to."

And of course, finally, I am.

*H*enry Burris is a dapper, white-thatched, small-handed, ruddy-cheeked little medico in white duck pants, more expensive deck shoes than mine and a pink knit shirt straight—in all probability—from Thomas Pink. He is sixty, has the palest, clearest limestone-blue eyes and when he talks does so in a close, confidential South Carolina low-country drawl, while keeping a light grip on my wrist as he tells me everything's going to be all right with my son. (Zero chance, I now believe, that he and Ann are playing sexual shenanigans, owing chiefly to his height, but also because Henry is famously attached to a highly prized, implausibly leggy and also rich wife named Jonnee Lee Burris, heiress to a gypsum fortune.) Ann has in fact told me, while we waited together like old friends in an airport, that the Burrises are the touchstones for everyone's glowingest marital aspirations there in otherwise divorce-happy Deep River; and likewise in New Haven, where Henry runs Yale-Bunker Eye Clinic, having given up Nobel Prize–caliber research in favor of selfless humanitarian service and family time—not an obvious candidate for a roll in the hay, though who's ever not a candidate?

"Now, Frank, lemme tell ya, I once had to perform a procedure just like the one I'm going to do on young Paul when I was down at Duke twelve years ago. Visiting Professor of Ophthalmology." Henry has already drawn me an impressive freehand picture of Paul's eye but is spindling it now like an unwanted grocery store circular while he's talking (secretly condescending, of course, since I'm his friend's second wife's first husband and probably a goofball with no Yale connections). "It was on a big fat black lady who'd somehow been hit in the eye by some damn kids throwing horse apples right out in her yard. Black kids too, now, not a racial matter."

We are on the back lawn of the hospital, out beside the blue-and-white square landing pad, where a large red Sikorsky from Connecticut Air Ambulance is resting on its sleds, its rotor gliding leisurely around. From out here, a modest hilltop and perfect setting for a picnic, I can see the shaded Catskills, their hazy runnels plowing south to blue sky and, in the intermediate distance below, a fenced cube of public tennis courts, all in use, beyond which I-88 leads to Binghamton and back up to Albany. I can hear no traffic noise, so that the effect on me is actually pleasant.

"And so this black lady said to me, just as we were about to shoot her up with anesthetic, 'Doctah Burris, if today was a fish, I'd sho th'ow it back.' And she grinned the biggest old snaggle-tooth grin, and off she went to sleep." Henry rounds his eyes out wide and tries to suppress a whooping laugh with a phony mouth-shut grimace— his usual bedside performance.

"What happened to her?" Gently I free my wrist and let it dangle, my eyes drawn helplessly back to the copter thirty yards away, where Paul Bascombe is right now being professionally on-loaded by two attendants, in advance of waving good-bye.

"Oh, golly, I'm tellin' you," Henry Burris says, whispering and raising his voice both at once. "We fixed her *right* up like we're going to do Paul today. She can see as clear as you can, or at least she could then. I'm sure she's dead now. She was eighty-one."

I have complete faith in Henry Burris, due to our talk. He in fact reminds me of a younger, vigorous, more intelligent and no doubt less slippery Ted Houlihan. I have no reluctance about letting him darn away on my son's retina, no sense of this being a terrible blunder or that regret will rise in me like molten metal and harden forever. It is the right thing to do in all ways and, for that reason, rare. "Discretion," Henry Burris has said to me, "is our best route here, since what we worry about in these things are the problems we *can't* see." (Much like a house purchase.) "We've got some doctors who've seen it all down at Yale." (Which I'll bet is true; possibly I should ask what causes wincing.)

My problem is only that I don't know where to attach my own eyes to Henry, can't *sense* him, and not even that I can't tell you what makes him tick. Eyes make him tick: how you fix 'em, what's wrong with 'em, what's good about 'em, how they make us see and sometimes fail to (similar to Dr. Stopler's contrast between the mind and the brain). But what I can't tell, not that it even matters except for my comfort, is what and where his mystery is, the part you'd discover if you knew him for years, learned to respect him professionally, wanted to discover even more and so decided to take a dude-ranch vacation with him up to the Wind Rivers, or went on a twosome freighter trip around the world or a canoe exploration to the uncharted headwaters of the Watanuki. What are his uncertainties, the quality of his peace made with contingency, his worries about the inevitability of joy or tragedy out in the unknown where we all plow the seas: his rationale, based on experience, for the *advisability* of discretion? I know it about Irv, by God, and you could know mine in 8.2 seconds. But in Henry, where a clue would speak volumes and satisfy much, no clue's in sight.

It's possible, of course, that he lacks a specific rationale; that for him it's just eyes, eyes and more eyes, and secondarily a commanding wife with a statuesque bank account, all topped off by his own damn positive attitude. Discretion, in other words, is a standard, not optional, feature. His is the same glacially suitable, semi-affable medical emanation I sensed around Dr. Tisaris, though there was in Dr. T. that whiff of something *else* under her doctor smock. However (and I'm quitting thinking about it now), this is undoubtedly the very emanation you want in a healthcare provider, particularly when your son's in need of serious fixing and you're sure never to see the guy again.

Ann is waiting a few yards away beneath the helipad's red wind sock, talking overattentively to Irv, who's still in his sandals and gold Mafia sweater and is all curled up in his own folded arms and a slightly feminine hip-in, knees-out posture, as if he feels in need of protection from the likes of Ann. They have discovered some mutual cronies from the "Thumb," who went to the same glockenspiel camp in northern Michigan in the Fifties and frolicked like monkeys on the dunes before they were bulldozed to make a park, on and on. For Irv, today is a banner day for continuities, and he seems as engrossed as an Old Testament scholar, although conscious that Ann's and my continuity is kaput and he should therefore hold some measure back (his snapshot, for instance).

Ann has continued to pass a weather eye my way as I've stood with Henry, occasionally signaling me with a faint and faintly puzzled smile, once even a little one-finger wave, as if she suspected me of plotting a last-second dash in under the rotors to save my son from being saved by her and others, and hoped a twinkle in her eye would be enough to head me off. Though I'm not so stubborn and am a man of my word, if allowed to be. She may only want a small gesture of faith. But I feel a change is now in motion, a facing of fact long overdue, so that my good act toward her will be my faithful forbearance.

I have, of course, had a last chance to reenter Paul's brightly lit hospital room and say my good-byes. He lay, as before, seemingly painless and in resolute spirits, his eyes still patched and taped, his feet spraddled over the end of his gurney—a boy grown too big for his furnishings.

"Maybe when I get out of the hospital and if I'm not on probation, I'll come down and stay with you a while," he said, blindly facing the light and as if this were an all-new subject he'd dreamed up in his sedative daze, though it made me light-headed, my arms featherish and tingling, since chances seemed iffy.

"I'm looking forward to it if your mom thinks it's a good idea," I said. "I'm just sorry we didn't have a very good time today. We didn't get into the Hall of Fame, like you said."

"I'm not hall of fame material. It's the story of my life." He smirked like a forty-year-old. "Is there a Real Estate Hall of Fame?"

"Probably," I said, my hands on the bars of his bed.

"Where would it be? In Buttzville, New Jersey?"

"Or maybe Chagrin Falls. Or Cape Flattery, B.C. Maybe Sinking Springs, PA. One of those."

"Do you think they'd let me in school in Haddam in a pirate's patch?"

"If they'll let you in with what you've got on today, I guess so."

"Do you think they'll remember me?" He exhaled with the tedium of injury, his mind flickering with vivid pictures of school commencing in an old/new town.

"I think you cut a pretty wide swath down there, if I remember it right." I looked studiously down at his nose, wrinkled by the bandage, as if he could know I was concentrating on him.

"I was never really appreciated down there." And then he said, "Did you know more women attempt suicide than men? But men succeed more?" A smirk fattened his cheeks under his bandage.

"It's good to be worse at some things, I guess. You didn't try to kill yourself, did you, son?" I stared even harder at him, feeling my posture suddenly sink with the awful weight of fearsome apprehension.

"I didn't think I was tall enough to get hit. I screwed up. I got taller."

"You're just too big for your britches," I said, hoping he wouldn't lie—to me anyway. "I'm sorry I made you stand up there. That was a big mistake. I wish I'd gotten hit instead."

"You didn't make me." He squinted at the light he couldn't see but could feel. "HBP. Runners advance." He touched his bandaged ear with his warty finger. "Ouch," he said.

I put my hand on his shoulder and pressed down again, as I did in the batting cage, my fingers still bearing a scuff of his blood from my rough-up of this very ear. "It's just my hand," I said.

"What would John Adams say about getting beaned?"

"Who's John Adams?" I said. He smiled a sweet self-satisfied smile at nothing. "I don't know, son. What?"

"I was trying to make up a good one. I thought maybe not seeing would help."

"Are you thinking you're thinking now?"

"No, I'm just thinking."

"Maybe he'd say—"

"Maybe he'd say," Paul interrupted, fully involved, " 'You can lead a horse to water, but you can't make him blank.' John Adams would say that."

"What?" I said, wanting to please him. "Swim? Water-ski? Windsurf? Alias Sibelius?"

"Dance," Paul said authoritatively. "Horses can't dance. When John Adams got beaned, he said, 'You can lead a horse to water, but you can't make him dance.' He'll only dance if he feels like it." I expected an *eeeck* or a bark. Something. But there was nothing.

"I love you, son, okay?" I said, suddenly wanting to clear out and in a hurry. Enough was enough.

"Yep, me too," he said.

"Don't worry, I'll see you soon."

"Ciao."

And I had the feeling he was far out ahead of me then and in many things. Any time spent with your child is partly a damn sad time, the sadness of life a-going, bright, vivid, each time a last. A loss. A glimpse into what could've been. It can be corrupting.

I leaned and kissed his shoulder through his shirt. And it was, luckily, then that the nurses came to make him ready to fly far, far away.

R otors, rotors, rotors, turning now in the warm afternoon. Strange faces appear in the open copter door. Henry Burris shakes my hand in his small trained one, ducks and goes stooping across the blue concrete to clamber in. *Thwop-thwop, thwop-thwop, thwop-thwop.* I give a thought to where Dr. Tisaris might be now— possibly playing mixed doubles on one of the cubed courts below. Well out of it.

Ann, bare-legged in her buttoned-up trench coat, shakes hands like a man with Irv. I see her lips moving and his seeming to mouth it all back verbatim: "Hope, hope, hope, hope, hope." She turns then and walks straight across the grass to where I stand, slightly stooped, thinking about Henry Burris's hands, small enough to get inside a head and fix things. He's got a head for eyes and the hands to match.

"Okay?" Ann says brightly, indestructible. I no longer fear or suppose she could die before I die. I am not indestructible; do not even wish to be. "Where will you be tonight so I can call you?" she says over the *thwop-thwop-thwop.*

"Driving home." I smile. (Her old home.)

"I'll leave a number on your box. What time will you get there?"

"It's just three hours. He and I talked about his coming down with me this fall. He wants to."

"Well," Ann says less loudly, tightening her lips.

"I do great with him almost all the time," I say in the hot, racketing air. "That's a good average for a father."

"We're interested in *him* doing well," she says, then seems sorry. Though I am delivered to silence and perhaps a small catch of dread, a fear of disappearance all over again, a mind's snapshot of my son standing with me on the small lawn of my house, doing nothing, just standing—canceled.

"He'd do great," I say, meaning: I hope he'd do great. My right eye flickers with fatigue and, God knows, everything else.

"Do you really *want* to?" Her eyes squint in the rotor wash, as if I might be telling the biggest of all whoppers. "Don't you think it'd cramp your style?"

"I don't really have a style," I say. "I could borrow his. I'll drive him up to New Haven every week and wear a straitjacket if that's what you want. It'll be fun. I know he needs some help right now." These words are not planned, possibly hysterical, unconvincing. I should probably mention the Markhams' faith in the Haddam school system.

"Do you even like him?" Ann looks skeptical, her hair flattened by the swirling wind.

"I think so," I say. "He's mine. I lost almost everybody else."

"Well," she says and closes her eyes, then opens them, still looking at me. "We'll just have to see when this is over. Your daughter thinks you're great, by the way. You haven't lost everybody."

"That's enough to say." I smile again. "Do you know if he's dyslexic?"

"No." She looks out at the big rumbling copter, whose winds are beating us. She wants to be there, not here. "I don't think he is. Why? Who said he was?"

"No reason, really. Just checking. You should get going."

"Okay." She quickly, harshly grabs me behind my head, her fingers taking my scalp where I'm tender and pulling my face to her mouth, and gives me a harder kiss on my cheek, a kiss in the manner of Sally's kiss two nights ago, but in this instance a kiss to silence all.

Then off she goes toward an air ambulance. Henry Burris is waiting to gangway her in. I, of course, can't see Paul on his strapped-in litter, and he can't see me. I wave as the door slides slap-shut and the rotors rev. A helmeted pilot glances back to see who's in and who's not. I wave at no one. The red ground lights around the concrete square suddenly snap on. A swirl and then a pounding of hot air. Mown grass blasts my legs and into my face and hair. Fine sand dervishes around me. The wind sock flaps valiantly. And then their craft is aloft, its tail rising, miraculously orbiting, its motor gathering itself, and like a spaceship it moves off and begins swiftly to grow smaller, a little, and then more, then smaller and smaller yet, until the blue horizon and the southern mountains enclose it in lusterless, blameless light. And everything, *every thing* I have done today is over with.

Streets away, in the summoning, glimmery early-morning heat, a car alarm breaks into life, shattering all silences. *Bwoop-bwip! Bwoop-bwip! Bwoop-bwip!* On the front steps of 46 Clio Street, reading my paper, I gaze up into the azure heavens through sycamore boughs, take a breath, blink and wait for peace.

I am here before nine, again in my red REALTOR jacket and my own *The Rock* shirt, awaiting the Markhams, currently on their way down from New Brunswick. Though unlike most of my previous intercourse with them, this time there is not a long story. Possibly there is even a hopeful one.

At the end of yesterday's bewildering if not completely demoralizing events, Irv was good enough to chauffeur me back up to Cooperstown—a drive during which he talked a mile a minute and in an almost desperate way about needing to get out of the simulator business, except that in his current view and based on careful analysis, the rah-rah, back-slap, yahoo days in his industry were all done, so that a policy favoring a career move seemed foolhardy, whereas holding his cards seemed wise. Continuity—an earnest new commanding metaphor—was applicable to all and was taking up the slack for synchronicity (which never carries you far enough).

When we arrived long into the shaded dewy hours of early evening, the Deerslayer lot was jammed full of new vacationer cars and my Ford had been towed away, since inasmuch as I was no longer a paying guest my license number was no longer on file. Irv and I and the resurrected Erma then sat in the office at the Mobil station behind Doubleday Field and waited until the tow-truck driver arrived with keys to the razor-wire impoundment, during which time I decided to make my necessary calls before paying my sixty dollars, saying good-bye and turning homeward alone.

My second call and inexcusably late was to Rocky and Carlo's, to leave a message with Nick the bartender. Sally would receive this when she got in from South Mantoloking, and among its profuse apologies were instructions to go straight to the Algonquin (my first call), where I'd reserved a big suite for her, there to check in and order room service. Later that night, from the village of Long Eddy, New York, halfway down the Delaware, we spoke and I told her all about the day's lamentable happenings and some odd feeling of peculiar and not easily explainable hope I'd already started to revive by then, after which we were able to impress each other with our seriousness and the possibilities for commitment in ways we admitted were "dangerous" and "anxious-making" and that we had never quite advanced to in the solitary months of only "seeing" each other. (Who knows why we hadn't, except there's nothing like tragedy or at least a grave injury or major inconvenience to cut through red tape and bullshit and reveal anyone's best nature.)

Joe and Phyllis Markham, when I reached them, were as meek as mice on hearing they'd missed their chance on the Houlihan house, that I was now fresh out of good ideas and a long way from home, that my already afflicted son had been poleaxed playing baseball and was at that moment in ominous surgery at Yale–New Haven and would probably lose his vision. In my voice, I know, were the somber tonalities and slow, end-stop rhythms of resignation, of having run the course, made the valiant try in more ways than ten, endured imprecation, come back from the trash heap with no hard feelings, and yet in a moment or two I would say good-bye forever. ("Realty death" is the industry buzzword.)

"Frank, look," Joe said, annoyingly tapping a pencil lead on the receiver from within his medium-priced double at the Raritan Ramada and seeming as clearheaded, plainspoken and ready to own up to reality as a Lutheran preacher at the funeral of his impoverished aunt. "Is there any way Phyl and I could get a peek at that colored rental property you mentioned? I know I got away from myself a little on Friday when I flared up that way. And I probably owe you an apology." (For calling me an asshole, a prick, a shithead? Why not, I thought, though that was as close as we got.) "There's one colored family in Island Pond who's been there since the Underground Railroad. Everybody treats 'em like regular citizens. Sonja goes to school right beside one of them every day."

"Tell him we want to look at it tomorrow," I heard Phyllis say. Changes had occurred aloft, I realized, a storm pushed on out to sea. In the realty business, change is good; from 100 percent *for* to 150 percent *against*, or vice versa, are everyday occurrences and signs of promising instability. My job is to make all that seem normal (and, if possible, make every nutty change in a client's mind seem smarter than anything I myself could've advised).

"Joe, I'll be home tonight around eleven, God willing." I leaned wearily against the window glass at the Mobil, the *da-ding, da-ding, da-ding* of the customer bell going constantly. (There was no use picking up the racial cudgels to try explaining to Joe that it was not "a colored house" but *my* house.) "So if I don't call you, I'll meet you on the porch at forty-six Clio Street at nine a.m. tomorrow."

"Four-six Clio, check," Joe said militarily.

"When can we move in?" Phyllis said from the background.

"Tomorrow morning if you want to. It's ready to go. It just needs airing out."

"It's ready to go," Joe said brusquely.

"Oh, thank God," I heard Phyllis say.

"I guess you heard that," Joe said, brimming with relief and craven satisfaction.

"I'll see you there, Joe." And in that way the deal was sealed.

The car alarm goes just as suddenly silent, and quiet morning reconvenes. (These almost never herald an actual robbery.) Down the block some kids are hovering around what looks like a red coffee can they've set in the middle of the street. No doubt they're following through on plans for an early-morning detonation to alert the neighbors that it's a holiday. Fireworks, of course, are unthinkably illegal in Haddam, and once the explosion blows, it's automatic that a cruiser will idle through the neighborhood, an HPD officer inquiring if we've heard or seen people shooting or carrying guns. I've noticed Myrlene Beavers twice behind her screen, her walker glinting out of the murk. She seems not to notice me today but to concentrate her vigilance on the boys, one of whom—his little face shiny and black—is sporting a bright Uncle Sam costume and will no doubt be marching in the parade later on (assuming he's not in jail). There is yet no sign of the Markhams, or for that matter the McLeods, whom I also have business with.

Since arriving at eight, I've mowed the small front yard with the (supplied) hand mower, watered the parched grass and sprayed the metal siding using my hose from home. I've cut back the dead hydrangea branches and the spirea and the roses, hauled the refuse to the back alley and opened windows and doors front and back to get air flowing inside the house. I've swept the porch, the front walk, run the tap in all the sinks, flushed the commode, used my broom to jab any cobwebs out from the ceiling corners and finished up by taking down the FOR RENT sign and stowing it in my trunk just to minimize the Markhams' feelings of displacement.

As always, I've noticed an awkward, flat-footed sensation involved with showing my own rental house (though I've done it several times since the Harrises left). The rooms seem somehow too large (or small), too drab and unhopeful, already used up and going nowhere, as though the only thing to truly revive the place would be for me to move in myself and turn it homey with my own possessions and positive attitudes. It's possible, of course, that this reaction is only compensatory for some wrong *take* a potential renter might fall victim to, since my underlying feeling is that I like the house exactly the way I liked it the day I bought it almost two years ago, and the McLeods' house the same. (I've seen a curtain twitch there now, but no face shows behind it—someone observing me, someone who doesn't enjoy paying his or her rent.) I admire its clean, tidy, unassuming adequacy, its sturdy rightness, finished off by the soffit vents, the new wrought-iron banister on the stoop, even the flashing to prevent ice dams and water "creep" during January thaws. It would be my dream house if I were a renter: tight, shipshape, cozy. A no-brainer.

In the Trenton *Times* I find holiday news, most of it not good. A man in Providence has sneaked a peek down a fireworks cannon at the most imperfect of moments and lost his life. Two people in far distant parts of the country have been shot with crossbows (both times at picnics). There's a "rash" of arsons, though fewer boating mishaps than might seem likely. I've even found a squib for the murder I stumbled upon three nights back: the vacationers *were* from Utah; they *were* bound for the Cape; the husband *was* stabbed; the alleged assailants *were* fifteen—the age of my son—and from Bridgeport. No names are given, so that all seems insulated from me now, only the relatives left to bear the brunt.

On the briefer, lighter side, the Beach Boys are at Bally's grandstand for one show only, flag-pole sales have once again skyrocketed, harness racing is celebrating its birthday (150) and a kidney transplant team (five men and a black Lab) is at this hour swimming the Channel—their foreseeable impediments: oil slicks, jellyfish and the twenty-one miles themselves (though not their kidneys).

Though the most interesting news is of two natures. One pertains to the demonstration at the Baseball Hall of Fame yesterday, the one that diverted Paul and me off our course and onward to what fate held in store. The demonstrators who blocked the Hall's doors for an important hour were, it turns out, rising in support of a lovable Yankee shortstop from the Forties, who deserved (they felt) a place, a plaque and a bust inside but who in the view of the sportswriter pundits was never good enough and had come by his obscurity honestly. (I side with the protesters on the principle of *Who cares anyway?*)

Yet of even more exotic interest is the "Haddam story," the discovery by our streets crew of a whole human skeleton unearthed, so the *Times* says, Friday morning at nine (on Cleveland Street, the 100 block) by a backhoe operator trenching our new sewer line under the provisos of our "well-being" bond. Details are sketchy due to the backhoe operator's poor command of English, but there's speculation by the town historian that the remains could be "very old, indeed, by Haddam standards," though another rumor has it that the bones are a "female Negro servant" who disappeared a hundred years ago when the Presidents Streets were a dairy farm. Still another theorizes an Italian construction worker was "buried alive" in the Twenties when the town was replatted. Local residents have already half-seriously named the bones "Homo haddamus pithecarius," and an archaeological team from Fairleigh Dickinson is planning to have a look. Meanwhile, the remains are in the morgue. More later, we think, and hope.

*W*hen I arrived last night at eleven, having beaten it home in four hours to an odd day-within-night indigo luminance down the quiet streets of town (many house lights were still lit), a message was waiting from Ann, declaring that Paul had come through his surgery "okay" and there was reason for hope, though he would probably develop glaucoma by fifty and need glasses much sooner. He was "resting comfortably" in any event, and I could call her anytime at a 203 number, a Scottish Inn in Hamden (the closer-in New Haven places already filled again with holiday voyagers).

"It was funny, almost," Ann said drowsily, I supposed from bed. "When he came out of it he just jabbered on and on about the Baseball Hall of Fame. All about the exhibits he'd seen and the . . . I guess they're statues. Right? He thought he'd had a splendid time. I asked him how you'd liked it, and he said you hadn't been able to go. He said you'd had a date with somebody. So . . . some things are funny."

A languor in Ann's voice made me think of the last year of our marriage, eight years ago nearly, when we made love half waking in the middle of the night (and only then), half aware, half believing the other might be someone else, performing love's acts in a half-ritual, half-blind, purely corporal way that never went on long and didn't qualify as much or dignify passion, so vaguely willed and distant from true intimacy was it, so inhibited by longing and dread. (This was not so long after Ralph's death.)

But where had passion gone? I wondered it all the time. And why, when we needed it so? The morning after such a night's squandering, I'd wake and feel I'd done good for humanity but not much for anyone I knew. Ann would act as if she'd had a dream she only remotely remembered as pleasant. And then it was over for a long time, until our needs would once more rise (sometimes weeks and weeks later) and, aided by sleep, our ancient fears suppressed, we would meet again. Desire, turned to habit, allowed to go sadly astray by fools. (We could do better now, or so I decided last night, since we understand each other better, having nothing to offer or take away and therefore nothing worth holding back or protecting. It is a kind of progress.)

"Has he done any sort of barking?" I asked.

"No," Ann said, "not that I've heard him. Maybe he'll quit that now."

"How's Clarissa?" Emptying my pockets, I'd found the tiny red bow she'd presented me out of her hair, companion to the one Paul had eaten. No doubt, I thought, it's she who'll decide what goes on my tombstone. And she will be exacting.

"Oh, she's fine. She stayed down to see *Cats* and the Italian fireworks over the river. She's interested in taking care of her brother, in addition to being slightly glad it happened."

"That's a dim view." (Although it was probably not a far-fetched one.)

"I feel just a little dim." She sighed, and I could tell, as used to be true, she was in no rush to get off now, could've talked to me for hours, asked and answered many questions (such as why I never wrote about her), laughed, gotten angry, come back from anger, sighed, gotten nowhere, gone to sleep on the phone with me at the other end, and in that way soothed the rub of events. It would've been a perfect time to ask her why she hadn't worn her wedding ring in Oneonta, whether she had a boyfriend, if she and Charley were on the fritz. Plus other queries: Did she really believe I never told the truth and that Charley's dull truths were better? Did she think I was a coward? Didn't she know why I never wrote about her? More, even. Only I found that these questions had no weight now, and that we were, by some dark and final magic, no longer in the other's audience. It was odd. "Did you get anything interesting accomplished in two days? I hope so."

"We didn't get around to any current events," I said to amuse her. "I heard most of his views. We talked over some other important things. It might be better. *He* might be better. I don't know. His accident cut everything short." With my tongue I touched the sore, bitten inside of my mouth. I did not mean to talk specifics with her.

"You two are so much alike, it makes me sad," she said sadly. "I can actually see it in his eyes, and they're *my* eyes. I think I understand you both too well." She breathed in, then out. "What are you doing for the holiday?"

"A date." I said this too forcefully.

"A date. That's a good idea." She paused. "I've become very impersonal now. I felt it when I saw you this afternoon. You seemed very personal, even when I didn't recognize you. I actually envied you. Part of me cares about things, but part doesn't really seem to."

"It's just a phase," I said. "It's just today."

"Do you really think I'm a person of little faith? You accused me of that when you got mad at me. I wanted you to know that it worried me."

"No," I said. "You're not. I was just disappointed in myself. I don't think you are." (Though it's possible she is.)

"I don't want to be," Ann said in a mournful voice. "I certainly wouldn't like it if life was just made up of the specific grievances we could answer all strung together and that was it. I decided that's what you meant about me—that I was a problem solver. That I just liked specific answers to specific questions."

"Liked them instead of what?" I said. Though I guessed I knew.

"Oh. I don't know, Frank. Instead of being interested in important things that're hard to recognize? Like when we were kids. Just life. I'm very tired of some problems."

"It's human nature not to get to the bottom of things."

"And that doesn't ever get uninteresting to you, does it?" I thought she might be smiling, but not necessarily happily.

"Sometimes," I said. "More recently it has."

"A big forest of fallen trees," she said in a dreamy way. "That doesn't seem so bad today."

"Don't you think I could bring him down here in September?" I knew this was not the best time to ask. I had asked seven hours before. But when was the best time? I didn't want to wait.

"Oh," she said, staring I was sure out a frosted air-conditioned window at the small lights of Hamden and the Wilbur Cross, a-stream with cars bound for less adventuresome distances, the holiday almost over before the day even arrived. I would miss it with my son. "We'll have to talk to him. I'll talk to Charley. We'll have to see what his ombudsman says. In principle it might be all right. Isn't that okay to say now?"

"In principle it's fine. I just think I could be some use to him now. You know? More than his ombudsman."

"Ummm," she said. And I couldn't think of anything else to say, staring at the mulberry leafage, my reflection cast back: a man alone at a desk by a telephone, a table lamp, the rest dark. The complex odors of backyard cooking over with hours before still floated out of the evening. "He'll want to know when you're coming to visit him." She said this without inflection.

"I'll drive up Friday. Tell him I'll visit him wherever he's in custody." Then I almost said, "He bought you and Clarissa some presents." But true to my word, I forbore.

And then she was silent, taking time to assess. "Doing anything wholeheartedly is rare. That's probably why you said that. I was shitty the other night, I'm sorry."

"That's okay," I said brightly. "It's harder, that's for sure."

"You know, when I saw you today I felt very good about you. That was the first time in a long time. It seemed very strange. Did you notice it?"

I couldn't answer that, so I just said, "That's not bad, though, is it?" my voice still bright. "That's an advance."

"You always seem like you want something from me," she said. "But I think maybe you just want to make me feel better when you're around. Is that right?"

"I *do* want you to feel better," I said. "That's right." It is part of the Existence Period—and I think now not a good part—to seem to want something but then not to.

Ann paused again. "Do you remember I said it's not easy being an ex-spouse?"

"Yes," I said.

"Well, it's not easy not being one, either."

"No," I said, "it's not," and then I said nothing.

"So. Call up tomorrow," she said cheerfully—disappointed, I knew, by some more complicated, possibly sad, even interesting truth she had heard herself speak and been surprised by but that I hadn't risen to. "Call the hospital. He'll need to talk to his Dad. Maybe he'll tell you about the Hall of Fame."

"Okay," I said softly.

"Bye-bye."

"Bye-bye," I said, and we hung up.

*B*lam!
  I watch the red coffee can spin high as the rooftops, become a small, whirly shadow on the sky, then lazily sink back toward the hot pavement.

All the kids hightail it down the street, their feet slapping, including Uncle Sam, holding for some reason the top of his head, where he has no tall hat.

"You gon git yo eye put out!" someone shouts.

"Wooo, wooo, wooo, got *damn*!" is what they say in answer. Across Clio Street a young black woman in astonishing yellow short shorts and a yellow buxom halter top leans out over her porch rail, watching the boys as they scatter. The can hits the pavement in front of her house, torn and jagged, bounces and goes still. "Ah-mo beat ya'll butts!" she shouts out as Uncle Sam rounds the corner onto Erato on one hopping, skidding foot, still holding his bare head, and then is gone. "Ah-mo call the cops 'n' *they* gon beat ya'll butts too!" she says. The boys are laughing in the distance. There is,

I see, a FOR SALE sign in front of her house, conspicuous in the little privet-hedged and grassy postage-stamp yard. It is new, not ours.

With her hands on the banister, the woman turns her gaze my way, where I'm seated on my porch steps with my paper, gazing back in a neighborly way. She is barefooted and no doubt has just been waked up. " 'Cause ah-mo be *glaaad* to git outa *this* place, y'unnerstan?" she says to the street, to me, to whoever might have a door open or a window ajar and be listening. " 'Cause it's *noisy* up here, ya'll. Ah'm tellin ya'll. Ya'll be nois*eee!*"

I smile at her. She looks at me in my red jacket, then throws her head back and laughs as if I was the silliest person she ever saw. She puts her hand up like a church witness, lowers her head, then wanders back inside.

Crows fly over—two, six, twelve—in ragged, dipping lines, squawking as though to say, "Today is not a holiday for crows. Crows work." I hear the Haddam H.S. band, as I did Friday morning, early again on its practice grounds, rich, full-brass crescendos streets away, a last fine-tuning before the parade. "Com-onna-my-house-my-house-a-com-on" seems to be their rouser. The crows squawk, then dive crazily through the morning's hot air. The neighborhood seems unburdened, peopled, serene.

And then I see the Markhams' beater Nova appear at the top of the street, a half hour late. It slows as though its occupants were consulting a map, then begins again bumpily down my way, approaches the house with my car in front, veers, someone waves from inside, and then, at last, they have come to rest.

O h, we got into such a bind, Frank," Phyllis says, not quite able to portray for me what she and Joe have been forced through. Her blue eyes seem bluer than ever, as if she has changed to vivider contacts. "We felt like we were strapped to a runaway train. She just wouldn't quit showing us houses." *She*, of course, refers to the horror-show realty associate from East Brunswick. Phyllis looks at me in dejected wonderment for the way some people will act.

We're on the stoop of 46 Clio, paused as though to defeat a final reluctance before commencing our ritual walk-thru. I've already pointed out some improvements—a foundation vent, new flashing— noted the convenience of in-town shopping, hospital, train and schools. (No mention has been made by them of other races in close proximity.)

"I guess she was going to make us buy a house if it killed her," Phyllis says, bringing the Other Realtor story to a close. "Joe sure wanted to murder her. I just wanted to call *you.*"

It is of course foregone that they will rent the house and move in as early as within the hour. Though in the spirit of lagniappe I am acting as if all is not yet quite settled. Another realtor might adopt a supercilious spirit toward the Markhams for being hopeless donkeys who wouldn't know a good deal if it grabbed them by the nuts. But to me it's ennobling to help others face their hard choices, pilot them toward a reconciliation with life (it's useful in piloting toward one's own). In this case, I'm helping them believe renting is what they should do (being wise and cautious), by promoting the fantasy that each is acting in his own best interest by attempting to make the other happy.

"Now, I can tell this is a completely stable neighborhood," Joe says with more of an off-duty military style now. (He means, though, no Negroes in evidence, which he takes to be a blessing.) He's remained on the bottom step, small hands inserted in his pockets. He's dressed entirely in Sears khaki and looks like a lumberyard foreman, his nutty goatee gone, his pecker shorts, flip-flops and generic smokes all gone, his little cheeky face as peaceable and wide-eyed as a baby's, his lips pale with medicated normalcy. (The "big cave-in" has apparently been averted.) He is, I'm sure, contemplating the front bumper of my Crown Vic, where sometime in the last three days Paul—or someone like Paul—has affixed a LICK BUSH sticker which, also in the spirit of lagniappe, I'm leaving on.

Joe senses, I'm sure, his gaze carrying across the newly mown lawn and down Clio Street, that this neighborhood is a close replica writ small of the nicer parts of Haddam he was offered and mulishly turned down, and of nicer parts he wasn't offered and couldn't afford. Only he seems happy now, which is my wish for him: to put an end to his unhappy season of wandering, set aside his ideas of the economy's false bottom or whether a significant event ever occurred in this house, to be a chooser instead of a bad-tempered beggar, to view life across a flatter plain (as he may be doing) and come down off the realty frontier.

Though specifically my wish is that the Markhams would move

into 46 Clio, ostensibly as a defensive holding action, but gradually get to know their neighbors, talk yard-to-yard, make friends, see the wisdom of bargaining for a break in the rent in exchange for minor upkeep responsibilities, join the PTA, give pottery and papermaking demonstrations at the block association mixers, become active in the ACLU or the Urban League, begin to calculate their enhanced positive cash flow against the dour financial imperatives of ownership in fashioning an improved quality of life, and eventually stay ten years—after which they can move to Siesta Key and buy a condo (if condos still exist in 1998), using the money they've saved by renting. In other words, do in New Jersey exactly what they did in Vermont—arrive and depart—only with happier results. (Conservative, long-term renters are, of course, any landlord's dream.)

"I think we're damn lucky not to have got sucked into that Hanrahan house." Joe looks at me with a bully's self-assurance, as if he's just figured this out by staring down the street—though of course he's only angling for approval (which I'm happy to supply).

"I don't think you ever saw yourself in that house, Joe. I don't really think you liked it." He's still staring off from the bottom step, waiting, I take it, for nothing.

"I didn't like having a prison in my back yard," Phyllis says, fingering the doorbell, which chimes a distant, lonesome two tones back in the empty rooms. She is dressed in her own standard roomy, hip-concealing pleated khakis and sleeveless white ruffle-front blouse that makes her appear swollen. In spite of trying to act plucky, she looks hollow-cheeked and spent, her face too flushed, her fingernails worked down, her eyes moist as if she might start crying for no reason—though her red mushroom cut is as ever neat, clean and fluffy. (Possibly she's experiencing recurrent health woes, though it's more likely her last few days on earth have simply been as rigorous as mine.)

And yet despite these diminishments, I sense an earnest, almost equable acceptance is descending on both the Markhams: certain fires gone out; other, smaller ones being ignited. So that it's conceivable they're on the threshold of unexpected bliss, know it instinctually like a lucky charm but can't quite get it straight, so long has their luck been shitty.

"My view's simple," Joe says, apropos of the lost Hanrahan option. "If somebody buys a house you think you want before you can get it, they just wanted it more than you did. It's no tragedy." He shakes his head at the sound wisdom of this, though once again it's verbatim "realtor's wisdom" I provided long months ago but actually don't mind hearing now.

"You're right there, Joe," I say. "You're really right. Let's take a look inside, whaddaya say?"

A walk-thru of an empty house you expect to rent (and not buy and live in till you croak) is not so much a careful inspection as a half-assed once-over in which you hope to find as little as possible to drive you crazy.

The Harrises' house, in spite of opened doors, raised windows and every single tap run for at least a minute, has clung to its unwelcoming older-citizen odor of sink traps and mouse bait, and generally stayed dank and chilly throughout. As a consequence, Phyllis lingers noncommittally near the windows, while Joe heads right off for the bathroom and a quick closet count. She touches the nubbly plaster walls and looks out through the blue blinds, first at the close-by McLeods', then down at the narrow side yard, then into the back, where the garage sits locked up in the morning sunshine, surrounded by a bed of day lilies weeks past bloom. (I've left the push mower against the garage wall where they can notice it.) She tries one sink faucet, opens one cabinet and the refrigerator (which I have somehow failed to inspect but am relieved to find doesn't stink), then walks to the back door, leans and looks out its window, as if in her mind right outside should be a verdant mountain pinnacle in full view, where she could hike today and take a drink from a cold spring, then lie faceup in gentians and columbines as pillowy clouds scud past, causing no car alarms to go off. She has wanted to come here, and now here she is, though it requires a specific moment of wistful renunciation, during which she may once again be seeing *backward* to today from an uncertain future, a time when Joe is "gone," the older kids are even more scattered and alienated, Sonja is with her own second husband and his kids in Tucumcari, and all she can do is wonder how things took the peculiar course they did. Such a view would make anyone but a Taoist Sage a little abstracted.

She turns to me and smiles actually wistfully. I am in the arched doorway connecting the small dining room with the small, neat kitchen, my hands in my red windbreaker pockets. I regard her companionably while fingering the house keys. I am where a loved one would wait below a mistletoe sprig at Christmas, though my reverie of a physical Phyllis has become another holiday statistic.

"We *did* think about just staying permanently in a motel," she says almost as a warning. "Joe considered becoming an independent contractor at the book company. The money's so much better that way, but you pay for your own benefits, which is a big consideration for me now. We met another young couple there who were doing it, but they didn't have a child, and it's hard to go off to school from a Ramada. The clean sheets and cable are attractive to Joe. He even called some nine hundred number at two o'clock this morning about moving to Florida. We were just beyond making sense."

Joe is in the bathroom, studiously testing the sink and both faucets, checking out the medicine cabinet. He does not know how to rent a house and can only think in terms of permanence.

"I expect you all to keep right on looking," I say. "I expect to sell you a house." I smile at her, as I have in other houses, in direr straits than now, which in fact are not so dire but pretty damn good at $575.

"We were burning our candle at both ends, I guess," she says, standing in the middle of the empty red-tiled kitchen. It is not the right trope, but I understand. "We need to burn one end at a time for a while."

"Your candle lasts longer that way," I say idiotically. There isn't much that really needs saying in any case. They're renting, not buying, and she is simply not used to it either. All is fine.

"Bip, bip, bip, bip, bip, bip, bip," Joe can be heard saying back in the bedroom, seizing his chance to check the filters on the window unit.

"How's your son?" Phyllis looks at me oddly, as if it has occurred to her at this very second that I'm not at his bedside but am here showing a short-term rental on the 4th of July with my child on the critical list. A sense of shared parental responsibility but also personal accusation clouds her eyes.

"He came through the surgery real well, thanks." I fidget the keys in my pocket to make a distracting sound. "He'll have to wear glasses. But he's moving down here with me in September." Perhaps in a year, as a trusted older boy, he can even escort Sonja on a date to a mall.

"Well, he's lucky," Phyllis says, swaying a little, her hands judgmentally down in her own generous pockets. "Fireworks are dangerous no matter whose hands they're in. They're banned in Vermont." She now wants me out of her house. In the span of sixty seconds she's assumed responsibility for things here.

"I'm sure he's learned his lesson," I say, and then we stand saying nothing, listening to Joe's footsteps in the other rooms, the sound of closet doors being cracked open and reopened to check for settling, light switches clicked up and down, walls thumped for studs—all activities accompanied by the occasional "Bip, bip, bip" or an "Okay, yep, I get it," now and then an "Uh-oh," though most often "Hmm-hmmm." All, of course, is in perfect, turn-key condition; the house was gone over by Everick and Wardell after the Harrises left, and I have checked it myself (though not lately).

"No basement, huh?" Joe says, appearing suddenly in the hall doorway, from which he takes a quick look around the ceiling and back out toward the open front door. The house is warming now, its floors shiny with outside light, its dank odors shifting away through the open windows. "I'll have to improvise a kiln somewhere else, I guess." (No mention of Phyllis's papermaking needs.)

"They just didn't build 'em in this neighborhood." I nod, touch my sore, bitten cheek with my tonguetip, feel relieved Joe isn't planning to fire pots on site.

"You can bet it's a groundwater consideration," Joe says in a spurious engineer's voice, going to the window and looking out as Phyllis did, straight into the side of the McLeods' house, where my hope is he doesn't come eye-to-eye with a shirtless Larry McLeod aiming his 9-mm. across the side yard. "Anything really bad ever happen in this house, Frank?" He scratches the back of his bristly neck and peers down at something outside that has caught his eye—a cat, possibly.

"Nothing I know about. I guess all houses have pasts. The ones I've lived in all sure did. Somebody's bound to have died in some room here sometime. I just don't know who." I say this to annoy him, knowing he's out of options, and because I know his question is a two-bit subterfuge for broaching the race issue. He doesn't want credit for broaching it, but he'd be happy if I would.

"Just wondering," Joe says. "We built our own house in Vermont, is all. Nothing bad ever happened there." He continues staring down, inventorying other gambits. "I guess this is a drug-free zone." Phyllis looks over at him as if she'd just realized she hated him.

"S'far's I know," I say. "It's a changing universe, of course."

"Right. No shit." Joe shakes his head in the fresh window light.

"Frank can't be held responsible for the neighbors," Phyllis says crabbily (though it's not completely true). She has been standing under the arch with me, looking at the empty walls and floors, possibly envisioning her lost life as a child. Only her mind's made up.

"Who lives next door?" Joe says.

"On the other side, an elderly couple named Broadnax. Rufus was a Pullman porter on the New York Central. You won't see them much, but I'm sure you'll like them. Over on the other side is a younger couple" (of miscreants). "She's from Minnesota. He's a Viet vet. They're interesting folks. I own that house too."

"You own 'em both?" Joe turns and gives me a crafty, squint-eyed look, as if I'd just grown vastly in his estimation and was probably crooked.

"Just these two," I say.

"So you're holdin' onto 'em till they're worth a fortune?" He smirks. For the moment he has begun speaking in a Texas accent.

"They're already worth a fortune. I'm just waiting till they're worth two fortunes."

Joe adopts an even more ludicrous, self-satisfied expression of appreciation. He's always had my number but now sees we are much more of a pair and a lot sharper cookies than he ever thought (even if we are crooked), since socking away for the future's exactly what he believes in doing—and might be doing if he hadn't plunged off on a two-decade *Wanderjahr* to the land of mud season, black ice, disappointing perk tests and feast-or-famine resales, only to reenter the real world with just the vaguest memory of which coin a quarter was and which was a dime.

"It's all still a matter of perception, idn't it?" Joe says enigmatically.

"It seems to be, *these* days," I say, thinking perhaps he's talking about real estate. I more noisily jingle the keys to signal my readiness to get a move on—though I have little to do until noon.

"Okay, well, I'm pretty satisfied here," Joe says decisively, Texas accent gone, nodding his head vigorously. Through the window he's been looking out, and across the side yard, I see little Winnie McLeod's sleepy face behind the thin curtain, frowning at us. "Whaddaya think, baby doll?"

"I can make it nicer," Phyllis says, her voice moving around the empty room like a trapped spirit. (I've never imagined Phyllis as "baby doll" but am willing to.)

"Maybe Frank'll sell it to us when we come into our inheritance." Joe gives me a little tongue-out, sly-boots wink.

"Two inheritances," I say and wink back. "This baby'll cost ya."

"Yeah, okay. Two, then," Joe says. "When we make two fortunes we can own a five-and-a-half-room house in the darky section of Haddam, New Jersey. That's a deal, isn't it? That's a success story you can brag to your grandkids about." Joe rolls his eyes humorously to the ceiling and gives his shiny forehead a thump with his middle finger. "How 'bout the election? How d'ya choose?"

"I'm joined at the hip with the tax-and-spenders, I guess." Joe wouldn't be asking if he weren't at this very moment vacating long-held principles of cultural liberalism in favor of something leaner and meaner and more suitable to his new gestalt. He expects me to sanction this too.

"You mean joined at the wallet," Joe says dopily. "But hell, yes. Me too." This to my absolute surprise. "Just don't ask me. My old man"—the Chinese-slum king of Aliquippa—"had a wide streak of social conscience. He was a Socialist. But what the fuck. Maybe living here'll pound some sense in my head. Now Phyllis, here, she's the mahout, she rides the elephant." Phyllis starts for the door, tired and unamused by politics. Joe fastens on me a gaping, blunt-toothed, baby-faced smile of philosophical comradeship. These things, of course, are never as you expect. Anytime you find you're right, you should be wrong.

*I*t is good to stand out on the hot sidewalk with the two of them under the spreading sycamore, and encouraging to see how quickly and tidily permanence asserts its illusion and begins to confer a bounty.

In fifteen minutes the Markhams have become longtime residents, and I their unwieldy, unwished-for guest. An invitation to come back, have lemonade, sit out back on nylon lawn chairs is definitely not forthcoming. They both squint from the pavement to the sun and the untroubled beryl sky as though they judge a good soaking rain—and not my paltry, unremarked watering—to be the only thing that'll do their yard any good.

We have painlessly agreed on a month-to-month, with three months in advance as a security blanket for me—though I've consented to remit a month if they find a house worth buying in the first thirty days (fat chance). I've passed along our agency's "What's The Diff?" booklet, spelling out in layman's terms the pros and cons of renting vs. buying: "Never pay over 20 percent of gross income on housing," although "You always sleep better in a place you own" (debatable). There's nothing, however, about needing to "see" yourself, or securing sanction or the likelihood of significant events ever having occurred in your chosen abode. Those issues are best dealt with by a shrink, not a realtor. Finally we've agreed to sign the papers tomorrow in my office, and I've told them to feel free to haul in their sleeping bags and camp out in their "own house" tonight. Who could say nay?

"Sonja's going to find it real eye-opening here," Phyllis the Republican says with confidence. "It's what we came down here for, but maybe we didn't know it."

"Reality check," Joe says stonily. They're both referring to the race issue, albeit deviously, while holding each other's hand.

We are beside my car, which gleams blue and hot in the ten o'clock sun. I have the Harrises' accumulated junk mail and the Trenton *Times* tucked under my arm, and have handed over their keys.

I know that filtering up like rare and rich incense in both the Markhams' nostrils is the up-to-now endangered prospect of life's happy continuance—a different notion entirely from Irv Ornstein's indecisive, religio-ethnic-historical one, though he might claim they're the same. An abrupter feeling is the Markhams', though, tantamount to the end of a prison sentence imposed for crimes they've been helpless to avoid: the ordinary misdemeanors and misprisions of life, of which we're all innocent and guilty. Alive but unrecognized in their pleased but dizzied heads is at least now the *possibility* of calling on Myrlene Beavers with a hot huckleberry pie or a blemished-second "gift" pot from Joe's new kiln; or of finding common ground regarding in-law problems with Negro neighbors more their age; of letting little dark-skinned kids sleep over; of nurturing what they both always knew they owned in their hearts but never exactly found an occasion to act on in the monochrome Green Mountains: that magical sixth-sense understanding of the other races, which always made the Markhams see themselves as out-of-the-ordinary white folks.

A police cruiser, our lone Negro officer at the wheel, finally passes slowly by, on the lookout for the Clio Street bombers. He waves perfunctorily and continues on. He is now their neighbor.

"Look, when we get all our shit moved in, we'll get you over here for a meal," Joe says, turning loose Phyllis's hand and trussing a short proprietary arm even more closely about her rounded shoulders. It is obvious she's informed him of her newest medical sorrows, which may be why he came around to renting, which may be why she told him. Another reality check.

"That's a meal I'm happy to wait for," I say, wiping a driblet of sweat off my neck, feeling the touchy spot where I was struck by a baseball in a far-off city. I have expected Joe to bring up the lease-purchase concept at least once, but he hasn't. Possibly he still harbors subconscious suspicions I'm a homosexual, which makes him standoffish.

I take a guarded look up at the old brick-veneer facade and curtained windows at #44, where there is no movement though I know surveillance is ongoing, and where I feel for an uneasy moment certain my $450 is being held hostage to the McLeods' ingrown convictions regarding privacy and soleness, having nothing to do with financial distress, lost jobs or embarrassment (which I would know how to cope with). I am, in fact, less concerned for my money than with the prospect of my own life's happy continuance with this problem unresolved. And yet I'm capable of making more of anything than I should, and I might just as well take a more complex approach to the unknown—such as *never* asking them for another goddamned nickel and seeing what effect that produces over time. Today, after all, is not only the fourth, but the Fourth. And as with the stolid, unpromising, unlikable Markhams, real independence must sometimes be shoved down your throat.

On a street we cannot see, a car alarm (possibly the same one as before) sets off loudly, and at hectic intervals, *bwoop-bwip, bwoop-bwip*, just as the bells at St. Leo's begin tolling ten. It makes for a minor cacophony: thirteen clocks striking at the same second. Joe and Phyllis smile and shake their heads, look around at the heavens as if they were breaking open and this was the only signal they would hear. Though they have decided to try being happy, are in a firm acceptance mode and would agree at this moment to like anything. It must be said, at last, that I admire them.

I take a parting glimpse at Myrlene Beavers's, where the silver bars of her walker are visible behind the screen. She is watching too, phone in her quaverous grip, alert to fresh outrage. "Who are *these* people? What do they hope to achieve? If only Tom were alive to take care of it."

I'm shaking Joe Markham's hand almost without knowing it. It is good to leave now, as I have done the best I can by everyone. What more can you do for wayward strangers than to shelter them?

I take a morning's ride up into town now, bent on nothing special—a drive-by of my hot-dog stand on the Green, a pass of the parade's staging grounds for a sniff of the holiday aromas, a cruise (like a tourist's) down my own street to inspect the site of Homo haddamus pithecarius, whose appearance, irrespective of provenance—M or F, human or ape, freedman or slave—I have a certain natural interest in. Who of us, after all, would be buried minus the hope of being returned someday to the air and light, to the curious, the tentative and even affectionate regard of our fellow uprights? None of us, I grant you, would mind a second appraisal with the benefit of some time having passed.

I in fact enjoy such a yearly drive through town, end to end, without my usual purposes to spur me (a property-line check, a roof and foundation write-up, an eleventh-hour visit before a closing), just a drive to take a *look* but not to touch or feel or be involved. Such a tour embodies its own quiet participation, since there is sovereign civic good in being a bystander, a watcher, one of those whom civic substance and display are meant to serve—the public.

Seminary Street has a measly, uncrowded, preparade staticness to it all around. The town's new bunting is swagged on our three stoplights, the sidewalk flags not flying but lank. Citizens on the sidewalks all seem at yawing loose ends, their faces wide and uncommunicative as they stop to watch the parade crew blocking the curbs with sawhorses for the bands and floats that will follow, as if (they seem to say) this *should* be a usual Monday, one *should* be getting other things done and started. Skinny neighborhood boys I don't recognize slalom the hot middle stripes on skateboards, their arms floating out for balance, while at the Virtual Profusion and the former Benetton and Laura Ashley (now in new personas as Foot Locker and The Gap) clerks are shoving sale tables back to their storefronts, preparing to wait in the cool indoors for crowds that may finally come.

It is an odd holiday, to be sure—one a man or woman could easily grow abstracted about, its practical importance to the task of holding back wild and dark misrule never altogether clear or provable; as though independence were *only* private and too crucial to celebrate with others; as though we should all just get on with *being* independent, given that it is after all the normal, commonsensical human condition, to be taken for granted unless opposed or thwarted, in which case unreserved, even absurd measures should be taken to restore or reimagine it (as I've tried to do with my son but that he has accomplished alone). Best maybe just to pass the day as the original signers did and as I prefer to do, in a country-like setting near to home, alone with your thoughts, your fears, your hopes, your "moments of reason" for what new world lies fearsomely ahead.

I cruise now out toward the big unfinished Shop Rite at the eastern verge of town, where Haddam borders on woodsy Haddam Township, past the Shalom Temple, the defunct Jap car dealer and the Magyar Bank, up old Route 27 toward New Brunswick. The Shop Rite was scheduled to be up and going by New Year's, but its satellite businesses (a TCBY, a Color Tile and a Pet Depot) began dragging their feet after the stock market dip and the resultant "chill" in the local climate, so that all work is at present on hold. I, in fact, wouldn't be sad or consider myself an antidevelopment traitor to see the whole shebang fold its tents and leave the business to our merchants in town; turn the land into a people's park or a public vegetable garden; make friends in a new way. (Such things, of course, never happen.)

Out on the wide parking lot, fairly baking in the heat, waits most of our parade, its constituents wandering about in unparade-like disorder: a colonial fife-and-drum band from De Tocqueville Academy; a regiment of coonskin-cap regulars in buckskins, accompanied by several burly men in Mother Hubbards and combat boots (dressed to show independence can be won at the cost of looking ridiculous). Here is a brigade of beefy, wired-up wheelchair vets in American-flag shirts, doing weaves and wheelies while passing basketballs (others simply sit smoking and talking in the sunshine). Waiting, too, is another Mustang regatta, a female clown troupe, some local car dealers in good-guy cowboy hats, ready to chauffeur our elected officials (not yet arrived) in the backs of new convertibles, while a passel of political ingenues are all set to ride behind on a flatbed truck, wearing oversize baby diapers and convict clothes. A swank silver bus parked all by itself under the shadeless Shop Rite sign contains the Fruehlingheisen Banjo and Saxophone Band from Dover, Delaware, most of whose members have postponed coming out. And last but not least, two Chevy bigfoots, one red, one blue, sit mid-lot, ready to rumble down Seminary at parade's end, their tiny cabs like teacups above their giant cleated wheels. (Later on there're plans for them to crush some Japanese cars out at the Revolutionary War Battlefield.) All that's lacking, in my view, are harem guards, who would make Paul Bascombe happy.

From where I stop out on the shoulder for a look, nothing yet seems inspired or up to parade pitch. Several tissue-paper floats are not yet manned or hitched up. The centerpiece Haddam High band has not appeared. And marshals in hot swallowtail coats and tricorne hats are hiking around with walkie-talkies and clipboards, conferring with parade captains and gazing at their watches. All in fact seems timeless and desultory, most of the participants standing alone in the sun in their costumes, looking off much as the fantasy ballplayers did in Cooperstown yesterday, and much, I'm sure, for the same reasons: they're bored, or else full of longing for something they can't quite name.

I decide to make a fast swerve through the lot entrance, avoid the whole parade assemblage and continue back out onto 27 toward town, satisfied that I've glimpsed behind the parade's façade and not been the least disappointed. Even the smallest public rigmarole is a pain in the ass, its true importance measurable not in the final effect but by how willing we are to leave our usual selves behind and by how much colossal bullshit and anarchy we're willing to put up with in a worthwhile cause. I always like it better when clowns seem to try to be happy.

Unexpectedly, though, just as I make my turn around and through the Shop Rite entrance, bent on escape, a man—one of the swallowtail marshals in a hat, red sash and high-buttoned shoes, who's been consulting a clipboard while talking to one of the young men wearing diapers—starts hurriedly toward my moving car. He waves his clipboard as if he knows me and has an aim, means to share a holiday greeting or message, perhaps even get me in on the fun as someone's substitute. (He may have noticed my LICK BUSH sticker and thinks I'm in the mood for high jinks.) Only I'm in another mood, perfectly good but one I'm happy to keep to myself, and so continue swerving without acknowledging him, right back onto 27. There's no telling, after all, who he might be: someone with a lengthy realty complaint, or possibly Mr. Fred Koeppel of Griggstown, who "needs" to discuss a negotiated commission on his house, which'll sell itself anyway (so let it). Or possibly (and this happens with too great a frequency) he's somebody from my former married days who happened to be in the Yale Club just yesterday morning and saw Ann and wants to report she looks "great," "super," "dynamite"—one of those. But I'm not interested. Independence Day, at least for the daylight hours, confers upon us the opportunity to act as independently as we know how. And my determination, this day, is to stay free of suspicious greetings.

I drive back in on sunny and fast-emptying Seminary, where the actual civic razzmatazz still seems a good hour off—past the closed PO, the closed Frenchy's Gulf, the nearly empty August Inn, the Coffee Spot, around the Square, past the Press Box Bar, the closed Lauren-Schwindell office, Garden State S&L, the somnolent Institute itself and the always officially open but actually profoundly closed First Presbyterian, where the WELCOME sign out front says, *Happy Birthday, America! * 5K Race * HE Can Help You At The Finish Line!*

Though farther on and across from Village Hall on Haddam Green there is action, with plenty of citizens already arrived in musing good spirits. A red-and-white-striped carnival marquee has been put up in the open middle sward, with our newly refurbished Victorian bandstand shining whitely in the elms and beeches and crawling with kids. Many Haddamites are simply out here strolling around as they might on some lane in County Antrim, though wearing frilly pastel dresses, seersuckers, white bucks, boaters and pink parasols, and looking—many of them—like self-conscious extras in a Fifties movie about the South. Out-of-place country-yokel music is blaring from a little glass-sided trailer owned by the station where I read *Doctor Zhivago* to the blind, and the police and fire departments have their free exhibits of flameproof suits, bomb-defusing shields and sniper rifles set up side by side under the big tent. The CYO has just begun its continuous volleyball game, the hospital its free blood pressure testing, the Lions and AA their joint free-coffee canteen, while the Young Democrats and Young Republicans are in the process of hosing down a mudhole for their annual tug-of-war. Otherwise, various village businesses, with their employees turned out in white aprons and red bow ties, have joined forces behind long slug-bucket grills to hawk meatless leanburgers, while some costumed Pennsylvania Dutch dancers perform folk didoes on a portable dance floor to music only they can hear. Later on, a dog show is planned.

Off to the left, across from the lawn of Village Hall, where seven years ago I achieved the profound and unwelcome independence of divorce, my silver "Firecracker Weenie Firecracker" cart sits in the warm witch hazel shade, attracting a small, dedicated crowd including Uncle Sam and two other Clio Street bombers, a few of my neighbors, plus Ed McSweeny in a business suit and a briefcase and Shax Murphy wearing a pair of pink go-to-hell pants, a bright-green blazer and running shoes—and looking, despite his Harvard background, like nothing so much as a realtor. Wardell and Everick's gleaming onyx faces are visible back inside the trailer under the awning. Dressed in silly waiters' tunics and paper caps, they are dispensing free Polish dogs and waxed-paper root beer mugs and occasionally rattling the "Clair Devane Fund" canisters Vonda has made up in our office. I have tried now on three occasions to sound out the two of them about Clair, whom they adored and treated like a rambunctious niece. But they have avoided me each time. And I've realized, as a consequence, that what I probably wanted was not to hear words about Clair at all but to hear something life-affirming and flattering about *myself*, and they are merely wise to me and have chosen not to let me get started. (Though it's also possible that they've been stung to silence now by the two days when they were held by the police, treated harshly and then released without comment or ceremony—deemed, after all and as they are, entirely innocent.)

And yet, all is as I've expected and modestly planned it: no great shakes, but no small shakes either—a fine achievement for a day such at this, following a day such as that.

I pull unnoticed to the curb on the east edge of the Green, just at Cromwell Lane, let down my window to the music and crowd hum and heat, and simply sit and watch: millers and strollers, oldsters and lovers, singles and families with kids, everyone out for a morning's smiley look-see, then an amble up Seminary for the parade, before hearkening to the day's remains with a practical eye. There is the easeful feeling that the 4th is a day one can leave to chance; though as the hours slide toward dark it will still seem best to find oneself at home. Possibly it's too close to Flag Day, which itself is too close to Memorial Day, which is already too damn close to Father's Day. Too much even well-motivated celebration can pose problems.

I of course think of Paul, cased in gauze and bandages in not-so-far-away Connecticut, who would find something funny to say at the day's innocent expense: "You know you're an American when you . . ." (get socked in the eye). "They laughed at me in America when I . . ." (barked like a Pomeranian). "Americans never, or almost never . . ." (see their fathers every day).

Surprisingly, I have not thought of him at length since early dawn, when I woke up in a gray light and cold from a dream in which, on a lawn like the Deerslayer's, he was dragged to earth by a dog that looked like old Keester and torn bloody, while I stood on the porch nuzzling and whispering with an indistinct woman wearing a bikini and a chef's hat, whom I couldn't break away from to offer help. It is a dream with no mystery—like most dreams—and merely punctuates our puny efforts to gain dominion over our unbrave natures in behalf of advancing toward what we deem to be right. (The complex dilemma of independence is not so simple a matter, which is why we fight to be known by how hard we try rather than by how completely we succeed.)

Though where Paul is concerned I've only just begun trying. And while I don't subscribe to the "crash-bam" theory of human improvement, which says you must knock good sense into your head and bad sense out, yesterday may have cleared our air and accounts and opened, along with wounds, an unexpected window for hope to go free. A *last* in some ways, but a first in others. "The soul becomes," as the great man said, by which he meant, I think, slowly.

*L*ast night, when I stopped in the moon-shot river village of Long Eddy, New York, a TOWN MEETING TONITE sign had been posted in both directions. "Reagan Cabinet Minister to Explain Things and Answer Questions" was their important agenda, there on the banks of the Delaware, where just below town single fishermen in ghostly silhouette stood in the darkly glittering stream, their rods and lines flicking and arcing through the hot swarms of insects.

At a pay phone on a closed-up filling station wall, I made a brief reconnaissance call down to Karl Bemish, to learn if the menacing "Mexicans" had had their fates sealed at the business end of Karl's alley sweeper. (Not, I prayed.)

"Oh well, jeez, hell no, Franky. Those guys," Karl said merrily from his cockpit behind the pop-stand window. It was nine. "The cops got them three skunks. They went to knock over a Hillcrest Farms over in New Hope. But the guy runnin' it was a cop himself. And he came out the front blazin' with an AK-47. Shot out the glass, all the tires, penetrated the engine block, cracked the frame, shot all three of 'em in the course. None of them died, though, which is sort of a shame. Did it standing right on the sidewalk. I guess you need to be a cop to run a small business these days."

"Boy," I said, "boy-oh-boy." Across silent, deserted Highway 97, all the windows in the belfried town hall were blazing and plenty of cars and pickups sat parked out front. I wondered who the "Reagan Minister" might've been—possibly someone on his way to prison and a Christian conversion.

"I bet you're having a bang-up time, aren't you, with your kid?" Mugs were clanking in the background. I could hear muffled, satisfied voices of late-night customers as Karl opened and shut the window slide and the cash register dinged. Good emanations, all.

"We had some problems," I said, feeling numbed by the day's menu of sad events, plus the driving, plus my skull and all my bones beginning to ache.

"Ahh, you prolly got your expectations jacked up too high," Karl said, preoccupied yet annoying. "It's like armies moving on their bellies. It's slow going."

"I never thought that's what that meant," I said, good emanations rising away into the mosquitoey darkness.

"D'you think he trusts you?" Clink, clink, clink. "Thanks, guy."

"Yeah. I think he does."

"Well, but you can't tell when you're getting anyplace with kids. You just have to hope they don't grow up like these little Mexican twerps, pulling stickups and getting shot. I take myself out to dinner and drink a toast to good luck every third Sunday in June."

"Why didn't you have any kids, Karl?" A lone citizen of Long Eddy, a small man in a pale shirt, stepped out the front door to the top of the town hall steps, lit a cigarette and stood drinking in the smoke and considering the evening's sweet benefactions. He was, I supposed, a disgruntled refugee from the cabinet minister's explanations—possibly a moderate—and I felt envy for whatever he might've had on his mind just at that instant, the mere nothing-much of it: the satisfactions of optional community involvement, a point of honest disagreement with a trusted public servant, a short beer later with friends, a short drive home, a quiet after-hours entry to his own bed, followed by the slow caressing carriage to sleep at the hands of a willing other. Could he know, I wondered, how lucky he was? There was hardly a doubt he did.

"Oh, Millie and I tried our best," Karl said drolly. "Or I *guess* we did. Maybe we didn't do it right. Let's see now, first you put it in, then . . ." Karl was obviously in a mood to celebrate not being robbed and murdered. I held the receiver out in the dark so I wouldn't have to hear his rube's routine, and in that splitting instant I missed New Jersey and my life in it with a grinding, exile's poignancy.

"I'm just glad you're all right down there, Karl," I broke back in, without having listened.

"We're pretty damn busy down here," he brayed back. "Fifty paid customers since eleven a.m."

"And no robberies."

"What's that?"

"No robberies," I said more loudly.

"No. Right. We're actually geniuses, Frank. Geniuses on a small scale. We're what this country's all about." Clink, clink, clink, mugs colliding. "Thanks, pal."

"Maybe," I said, watching the pale-shirted man flick away his smoke, spit on the porch steps, run both hands back through his hair and reenter the tall door, revealing a coldly brilliant yellow light within.

"You can't tell me ole Bonzo's uncle's *that* fulla shit," Karl said vehemently, referring to our President of the moment, whose cabinet minister was only yards away from me. "Because if he's that fulla shit, *I'm* fulla shit. And I'm not fulla shit. That's what I know. I'm *not* fulla shit. Not everybody can say that." I wondered what our customers could be thinking, hearing Karl bellowing away behind his little sliding screen about not being fulla shit.

"I don't like him," I said, though it made me feel debilitated to say so.

"Yeah, yeah, yeah. You believe God resides in all of us, nobility of man, help the poor, give it all away. Yakkedy, yakkedy, yak. I believe God resides in heaven, and I'm down here selling birch beer on my own."

"I *don't* believe in God, Karl. I believe it takes all kinds."

"No it don't," he said. Karl might've been drunk or having another small stroke. "What I think is, Frank, you *seem* one way and *are* another, if you want to know the gospel truth, speaking of God. You're a conservative in a fuckin' liberal's zoot suit."

"I'm a liberal in a liberal's zoot suit," I said. Or, I thought, but certainly didn't admit to Karl, a liberal in a conservative's zoot suit. In *three* days I'd been called a burglar, a priest, a homosexual, a nervous nelly, and now a conservative, none of which was true. (It was not an ordinary weekend.) "I do like to help the poor and displaced, Karl. I sure as hell in fact dragged you to the surface when you were tits-up."

"That was just for sport," he said. "And that's why you have so much effing trouble with your son. Your message is all mixed up. You're lucky he'll have anything to do with you at all."

"Why don't you bite my ass, Karl?" I shouted, standing in the dark, wondering if there wasn't some simple, legal way to put Karl out on the street, where he'd have more time to practice psychology. (Spiteful thoughts are not unique to conservatives.)

"I'm too busy to gas with you now," Karl said. I heard the cash register ding again. "Thanks a million. Hey, pardon me, ladies, you want your change, don't you? Two cents is two cents. Next. Come on, don't be shy, sweetheart." I waited for Karl to blast back something else infuriating, something more about my message being mixed. But he simply put the phone down without hanging it up, as if he meant to return, so that for a minute I could hear him going about his business serving customers. But in a while I put my receiver back on the hook and just stared out at the sparkling, alluring river beyond me in the dark, letting my breathing come back to normal.

*M*y call to the Algonquin and Sally had a completely different, unexpected and altogether positive result, which, when I got home and found out Paul had weathered his surgery as well as could be hoped, allowed me to crawl in bed with all the windows open and the fan on (no more thought of reading Carl Becker or *drifting* to sleep) and to swoon off into profound unconscious while the cicadas sang their songs in the silent trees.

Sally, to my surprise, was as sympathetic as a blood relative to my long story about Paul's getting beaned, our never making it into the Hall of Fame, my having to stay in Oneonta, then heading home late rather than pounding down to NYC to share the night with her, and instead dispatching her to the nicest place I could think of (albeit for another night alone). Sally said she thought she could hear something new in my voice, and for the first time: something "more human" and even "powerful" and "angular," whereas, she reminded me, I had seemed until this weekend "pretty buttoned up and well insulated," "priestly" (this again), often downright "ornery and exclusive," though "down deep" she'd always thought I was a good guy and actually not cold but pretty sympathetic. (I had thought most of these last things about myself for years.) This time, though, she said, she thought she heard worry and some fear in my voice (buzzy timbres familiar, no doubt, from her dying clients' critiques of *Les Misérables* or *M. Butterfly* on their chatty return trips to the Shore, but apparently not incompatible with "powerful" or "angular"). She could tell I'd been "vitally moved" by something "deep and complicated," which my son's injury may have been "only the tip of the iceberg for." It may, she said, have everything to do with my gradual emergence from the Existence Period, which she actually said was a "simulated way to live your life," a sort of "mechanical isolation that couldn't go on forever"; I was probably already off and running into "some other epoch," maybe some more "permanent period" she was glad to see because it boded well for me as a person, even if the two of us didn't end up together (which it seemed might be the case, since she didn't really know what I meant by love and probably wouldn't trust it).

I, of course, was simply relieved she wasn't sitting back with her long legs parked on a silken footrest, ordering tins of Beluga caviar and thousand-dollar bottles of champagne and calling up everybody she knew from Beardsville to Phnom Penh and regaling them at length about what a poor shiftless specimen I was—really just pathetic when you got right down to it—and actually comical (something I'd already admitted to), given my idiotic and juvenile attempts to make good. Just such narrowly missed human connections as this can in fact be fatal, no matter who's at fault, and often result in unrecoverable free fall and a too-hasty conclusion that "the whole goddamn thing's not worth bothering with or it wouldn't be so goddamn confusing all the goddamn time," after which one party (or both) just wanders off and never thinks to look toward the other again. Such is the iffiness of romance.

Sally, however, seemed willing to take a longer look, a deeper breath, blink hard and follow her gut instincts about me, which meant looking for good sides (making me up with the brighter facets out). All of which was damn lucky for me since, standing there by the dark gas station in Long Eddy, I could sense like a faint, sweet perfume in the night the *possibility* of better yet to come, only I had no list of particulars to feel better about, and not much light on my horizon except a keyhole hope to try to *make* it brighter.

And indeed, before I finally climbed back in my car and headed off into the lush night toward Jersey, she began talking at first about whether or not it would ever be possible for *her* to get married after all these years, and then about what kind of permanent epoch might be dawning in *her* life. (Such thoughts are apparently infectious.) She went on to tell me—in much more dramatic tones than Joe Markham had on Friday morning—that she'd had dark moments of doubting her own judgment about many things, and that she worried about not knowing the difference between risking something (which she considered morally necessary) and throwing caution to the winds (which she considered stupid and, I supposed, had to do with me). In several electrifying leaps and connections that made good sense to her, she said she wasn't a woman who thought other adults needed mothering, and if that's what I wanted I should definitely look elsewhere; she said that making her up (which she referred to then as "reassembling") just to make love appealing was actually intolerable, no matter what she'd said yesterday, and that I couldn't just keep switching words around indefinitely to suit myself but needed instead to accept the unmanageable in others; and finally that while she might understand me pretty well and even like me a lot, there was no reason to think that necessarily meant anything about true affection, which she again reminded me I'd said I was beyond anyway. (These accounted, I'm sure, for the feelings of congestion she experienced early Friday morning and that prompted her call to me while I was in bed snuffling over my Becker and the difference between making history and writing it.)

I told her, raptly watching while the last of the night's anglers waded back across the ever darker but still brilliant surface of the Delaware, that I once again had no expectations for reassembling her, or for mothering either, though from time to time I might need a facilitator (it didn't seem necessary to give in on everything), and that I'd thought in these last days about several aspects of an enduring relationship with her, that it didn't seem at all like a business deal, and that I liked the idea plenty, in fact felt a kind of whirring elevation about her and the whole prospect—which I did. Plus, I had a strong urge to make her happy, which didn't seem in the least way smooth (or cowardly, as Ann had said), and wished in fact she'd take the train to Haddam the next day, by which time the Markhams and the parade would be in the record books and we could resume our speculations into the evening, lie out in the grass on the Great Lawn of the Institute (where I still had privileges as temporal consultant without portfolio) and watch Christian fireworks, after which we might ignite some sparks of our own (a borrowed idea, but still a good one).

"That all sounds nice," Sally said from her suite on West Forty-fourth. "It seems reckless, though. Doesn't it to you? After the other night, when it seemed all so over with?" Her voice suddenly sounded mournful and skeptical at once, which wasn't the tone I'd exactly hoped for.

"Not to me it doesn't," I said out of the dark. "To me it seems great. Even if it *is* reckless it seems great." (Supposedly *I* was the one tarred with the "caution" brush.)

"Something about all those things I said to you about myself and about you, and now taking the train down and lying in the grass watching fireworks. It's suddenly made me feel like I don't know what I'm getting into, like I'm out of place."

"Look," I said, "if Wally shows up, I'll do the honorable thing, assuming I know what it is or who he is."

"Well, that's sweet," she said. "You're sweet. I know you'd try to do that. I'm not going to think about Wally showing up anymore, though."

"That's a good idea," I said. "That's what I'm doing too. So don't worry about feeling out of place. That's what I'm here for."

"That's an encouraging start," she said. "It *is*. It's always encouraging to know what you're here for."

And in that way last night it all began to seem promising and doable, if lacking in long-term specifics. I finished our talk by telling her not that I loved her but that I wasn't beyond affection, which she said she was glad to hear. Then I beat it back down the road toward Haddam as fast as humanly possible.

*O*ut in the unshaded center of the Haddam green, I notice all citizens beginning to look up. Young moms with prams and jogger pairs in Lycra tights, cadres of long-haired boys with skateboards on shoulders, men in bright braces wiping sweat off their brows, all gaze into heaven's vault beyond linden, witch hazel and beech limbs. The Dutch dancers stop their bustle and hurry off the floor, the police and firemen step out of their tent to the grass, seeking to see. Everick and Wardell, Uncle Sam and I (fellow townsman, alone in my car with the sunroof back), each raise eyes to the firmament, while the honky-country music comes to a stop, just as if there were one special moment of portent in this day, to be overseen by some infallible Mr. Big with a knack for coincidence and surprises. Not so far away, still on their practice field, I hear the Haddam band lock down on one sustained note in perfect major-key unison. Then the crowd—as random minglers, they have not precisely *been* a crowd—makes a hushed, suspiring "Ohh" like an assent to a single telepathic message. And suddenly down out of the sky come four men *en parachute!* smoke canisters bracketed to their feet—one red, one white, one blue, one (oddly) bright yellow like a caution to the other three. They for a moment make me dizzy.

The helmeted parachutists, wearing stars 'n' stripes, jumpsuits and cumbersome packs binding their torsos and backsides, all come careening to earth within five seconds, landing semi-gracefully with a hop-skip-jump close by the Dutch dance floor. Each man—and I only guess they're men, though reason would have it they're not *just* men; conceivably they're also kidney-transplant survivors, AIDS patients, unwed mothers, ex-gamblers or the children of any of these—each *apparent* man promptly flourishes a rakish hand like a circus performer, does a partly-smoke-obscured but still stylish star turn to the crowd and, after a smattering of stunned and I can only say is sincere and relieved applause, begins strenuously reefing in his silks and lines, and sets about getting the hell on to the next jump, in Wickatunk—all this before my momentary dizziness has really begun to clear. (Possibly I'm more drained than I thought.)

Though it is wonderful: a bright and chancy spectacle of short duration enhancing the day's modest storage of fun. More of this would be better all around, even at the risk of someone's chute not opening.

The crowd begins straying apart again, becoming single but gratified minglers. The dancers—skirts bunched in front like frontier women—return to their dance floor, and someone reignites the hillbilly music, with a strutting fiddle and steel guitar out ahead and a throaty female singing, "If you loved me half as much as I loved you."

I climb out of my car onto the grass and stare at the sky to glimpse the plane the jumpers have leaped free of, some little muttering dot on the infinite. As always, this is what interests me: the jump, of course, but the hazardous place jumped *from* even more; the old safety, the ordinary and predictable, which makes a swan dive into invisible empty air seem perfect, lovely, the one thing that'll do. *This* provokes butterflies, ignites danger.

Needless to say, I would never consider it, even if I packed my own gear with a sapper's precision, made friends I could die with, serviced the plane with my own lubricants, turned the prop, piloted the crate to the very spot in space, and even uttered the words they all must utter at least silently as they go—right? "Life's too short" (or long). "I have nothing to lose but my fears" (wrong). "What's anything worth if you won't risk pissing it away?" (Taken together, I'm sure it's what "Geronimo" means in Apache.) I, though, would always find a reason not to risk it; since for me, the wire, the plane, the platform, the bridge, the trestle, the window ledge—these would preoccupy me, flatter my nerve with their own prosy hazards, greater even than the risk of brilliantly daring death. I'm no hero, as my wife suggested years ago.

Nothing's up there to see anyway, no low-flying Cessna or Beech Bonanza recircling the drop site. Only, miles and miles high, the silver-glinting needle's-eye flash of a big Boeing or Lockheed inches its way out to sea and beyond, a sight that on most days would make me long to be anywhere but where I am, but that on this day, with near disaster so close behind me, leaves me happy to be here. In Haddam.

And so I continue my bystander's cruise around town for the purpose of my own and civic betterment.

A loop through the Gothic, bowery, boxwood-hedged Institute grounds and out the "backs" and around and down onto the Presidents Streets—oak-dappled Coolidge, where I was bopped on the head, wider and less gentrified Jefferson, and on to Cleveland, where the search is under way for signs of history and continuance in the dirt in front of my house and the Zumbros'. Though no one's digging this morning. A yellow "crime scene" tape has been stretched around two mulberries and the backhoe, and serves to define the orange-clay hole where evidence has been uncovered. I look down and in from my car window, for some reason not wanting to get out but willing to see something, anything, conclusive—my own dwelling being just to starboard. Yet only a cat stands in the open trench, the McPhersons' big black tom, Gordy, covering up his private business with patience. Time, forward and back, seems suddenly not of the essence on my street, and I ease away having found out nothing, but not at all dissatisfied.

I take a sinuous drive across Taft Lane and up through the Choir College grounds, where it's tranquil and deserted, the flat brick buildings shut tight and echoless for the summer—only the tennis courts in use by citizens in no humor for a parade.

A slow turn then past the high school, where the sixty-member Hornet band is wandering off the practice field, sweltering red tunics slung over their sweaty shoulders, trombones and trumpets in hand, the brawnier instruments—bass drums, sousaphones, cymbals, a bracketed Chinese gong and a portable piano—already strapped atop their waiting school bus, ready for the short trip to the Shop Rite.

On down Pleasant Valley Road along the west boundary fence of the cemetery, wherein tiny American flags bristle from many graves and my first son, Ralph Bascombe, lies near three of the "original signers," but where I will not rest, since early this very morning, in a mood of transition and progress and to take command of final things, I decided (in bed with the atlas) on a burial plot as far from here as is not totally ridiculous. Cut Off, Louisiana, is my first choice; Esperance, New York, was too close. Someplace, though, where there's a peaceful view, little traffic noise, minimum earthly history and where anyone who comes to visit will do so just because he or she means to (nothing on the way to Six Flags or Glacier) and, once arrived, will feel I had my head on straight as to location. Otherwise, to be buried "at home," behind my own old house and forever beside my forever young and lost son, would paralyze me good and proper and possibly keep me from maximizing my remaining years. The thought would never leave me as I went about my daily rounds of house selling: "Someday, someday, someday, I'll be right out there. . . ." It would be worse than having tenure at Princeton.

The strongest feeling I have now when I pass along these streets and lanes and drives and ways and places for my usual reasons—to snapshot a listing, dig up a comp for a market analysis, accompany an appraiser to his tasks—is that holding the line on the life we promised ourselves in the Sixties is getting hard as hell. We want to *feel* our community as a fixed, continuous entity, the way Irv said, as being anchored into the rock of permanence; but we know it's not, that in fact beneath the surface (or rankly all over the surface) it's anything but. We and it are anchored only to contingency like a bottle on a wave, seeking a quiet eddy. The very effort of maintenance can pull you under.

On the brighter side, and in the way that good news can seem like bad, being a realtor, while occasionally rendering you a Pollyanna, also makes you come to grips with contingency and even sell it as a source of strength and father to true self-sufficiency, by insisting that you not give up the faith that people have to be housed and will be. In this way, realty is the "True American profession coping hands-on with the fundamental spatial experience of life: more people, less space, fewer choices." (This, of course, was in a book I read.)

*T*wo, make that *two*, full-size moving vans are parked prominently in front of two houses, side by side, on Loud Road this late holiday morning, just around the corner from my old once-happily married house on Hoving. One, a bullish green-and-white Bekins is open at all ports; the other, a jauntier blue-and-white Atlas, is unloading off the back. (Regrettably there's no green-and-yellow Mayflower.) Signs in front of each house have identical YOU MISSED IT! stickers plastered over FOR SALE. Neither is our listing, though neither are they Bohemia or Buy and Large or some New Egypt outfit, but the reputable local Century 21 and a new Coldwell Banker just opened last fall.

Clearly it is a good day for a fresh start, coming or going. My new tenants must feel this spirit in the air. All neighborhood lawns mowed, edged and rolled, many facades newly painted, trimmed and bulwarked since spring, foundations repointed, trees and plantings green and in full fig. All prices slightly softened. Indeed, if I didn't rue the sight of them and didn't mind risking a facedown with Larry McLeod, I'd drive down Clio Street, see how things have progressed since ten and wish the Markhams well all over again.

Instead I make my old, familiar turn down fragrant, bonneted Hoving Road, a turn I virtually never make these days but should, since my memories have almost all boiled down to good ones or at least to tolerable, instructive ones, and I have nothing to fear. Appearances here have remained much the same through the decade, since it is in essence a rich street of hedges and deep, shadowed lawns, gazebos in the rear, well-out-of-sight pools and tennis courts, slate roofs, flagstone verandas, seasonal gardens somehow always in bloom—country estates, really, shrunk to town size but retaining the spirit of abundance. Farther up at #4, the Chief Justice of the NJ Supreme Court has died, though his widow stays actively on. The Deffeyes, our aged next-door neighbors from day one, have had their ashes mingled (though on two foreign shores). The daughter of a famous Soviet dissident poet, who arrived before I left, seeking only privacy and pleasant, unthreatening surroundings, but who found instead diffidence, condescension and cold shoulders, has now departed for home, where she is rumored to be in an institution. Ditto a rock star who bought in at #2, visited once, wasn't welcomed, didn't spend the night—then went back permanently to L.A. Both listings were ours.

The Institute has done its very best to keep alive a homey, lived-in feel at my former home, now officially the Chaim Yankowicz Ecumenical Center, and straight ahead amid my old and amiable beeches, red oaks, Japanese maples and pachysandra. Yet as I pull to a halt across the street for a long-overdue reconnoitering, I cannot help but register its more plainly institutional vibes—the original half-timbers replaced and painted a more burnished mahogany, new security windows and exterior low lights on the neater, better-kept lawn; the driveway resurfaced, leveled and converted to semi-circular; a metal fire escape on the east side, where the garage was but isn't now. I've heard from people in my office that there's also a new "simplified" floor plan, a digital sprinkler-and-alarm matrix and glowing red EXIT lozenges above every exterior door—all to insure the comfort and security of foreign religious dignitaries who show up, I'm sure, with nothing more weighty in mind than a little suburban R&R, some off-the-record chitchat, and a chance to watch cable.

For a while after I sold out, a group of my former neighbors laid siege to the planning board with complaints and petitions about increased traffic flow, spot zoning, "strangers on the block" and weakened price structures should the Institute put its plans in gear. An injunction was even briefly obtained and two "old families" who'd been here forty years moved out (to Palm Beach in both cases, both selling to the Institute for choker prices). Eventually the furor burned down to embers. The Institute agreed to remove its barely noticeable sign from the head of the driveway and install some expensive landscaping (two adult ginkgoes trucked in and added to one property line; my old tulip tree sacrificed). As a final settlement, the Board of Overseers bought the house of the lawyer who filed the injunction. After which everyone got happy, except for a few founder types who hold it against me and bluster at cocktail parties that they knew I couldn't afford to live here and didn't belong way back in '70, and why didn't I just go back to where I came from—though they're not sure where that is.

And yet and yet, do I sense, as I sit here, a melancholy? The same scent of loss I sniffed three nights ago at Sally's and almost shed a tear over, because I'd once merely been *near* there in a prior epoch of life and was in the neighborhood again, feeling unsanctioned by the place? And so shouldn't I feel it even more *here*, because my stay was longer, because I loved here, buried a son nearby, lost a fine, permanent life here, lived on alone until I couldn't stand it another minute and now find it changed into the Chaim Yankowicz Center, as indifferent to me as a gumdrop? Indeed, it's worth asking again: is there any cause to think a place—any place—within its plaster and joists, its trees and plantings, in its putative essence *ever* shelters some spirit ghost of us as proof of its significance and ours?

No! Not one bit! Only other humans do that, and then only under special circumstances, which is a lesson of the Existence Period worth holding onto. We just have to be smart enough to quit asking places for what they can't provide, and begin to invent other options—the way Joe Markham has, at least temporarily, and my son, Paul, may be doing now—as gestures of our God-required but not God-assured independence.

The truth is—and this may be my faith in progress talking—my old Hoving Road house looks more like a funeral home now than it looks like my house or a house where any past of mine took place. And this odd feeling I have is of having passed on (not in the bad way) to a recognition that ghosts ascribed to places where you once were only confuse matters with their intractable lack of corroborating substance. I frankly think that if I sat here in my car five more minutes, staring out at my old house like a visitant to an oracle's flame, I'd find that what felt like melancholy was just a prelude to bursting out laughing and needlessly freezing a sweet small piece of my heart I'd be better off to keep than lose.

Now look here, would you buy a used house from this man?" I hear a sly voice speak, and bolt around startled out of my wits to find the flat, grinning moon face of Carter Knott outside my window. Carter's head is cocked to the side, his feet apart, arms crossed like an old judge. He's in damp purple swimming trunks, wet parchment sandals and a short purple terry-cloth cabana jacket that exposes his slightly rounded belly, all of which means he's gotten out of his pool down at #22 and snuck this far just to scare the piss out of me.

I would in fact be embarrassed as hell if anybody else had caught me twaddling away out here like a nutcase. But Carter is arguably my best friend in town, which means he and I "go back" (to my solitary, somber year in the Divorced Men's Club in '83) and also that we regularly bump into each other in the lobby at United Jersey and discuss bidnus, and that we're willing to stand in most any weather outside Cox's News, arms folded around our newspapers, yakking committedly about the chances of the Giants or the Eagles, the Mets or the Phils, whatever exchange won't take longer than ninety seconds, after which we might not see each other for six months, by which time a new sports season and a new set of issues will have taken up. Carter, I'm positive, couldn't tell me where I was born, or when, or what my father's job was, or what college I attended (he would probably guess Auburn), though I know he attended Penn and studied, of all things, classics. He knew Ann when she still lived in Haddam, but he may not know we had a son who died, or why I moved from my old house across the street, or what I do in my spare time. It is our unspoken rule never to exchange dinner invitations or to meet for drinks or lunch, since neither of us would have the least interest in what the other was up to and would both get bored and depressed and end up ruining our relationship. And yet in the way known best to suburbanites, he is my *compañero*.

After the Divorced Men disbanded (I left for France, one member committed suicide, others just drifted off), Carter put together a good post-divorce rebound and was living a freewheeling bachelor's life in a big custom-built home with vaulted ceilings, fieldstone fireplaces, stained-glass windows and bidets, out in some newly rich man's subdivision beyond Pennington. Somewhere about 1985, Garden State Savings (which he was president of) decided to turn a corner and get into more aggressive instruments, which Carter couldn't see the wisdom in. So that the other stockholders bought him out for a big hunk of change, after which he went happily home to Pennington, got to tinkering with some concepts for converting invisible-pet-fence technology into sophisticated home-security applications. And the next thing he knew, he was running another company, had fifteen employees, four million new dollars in the bank, had been in operation two and a half years and was being wholly bought out by a Dutch company interested in only one tiny microchip adaptation Carter'd been wily enough to apply for a patent on. Carter once again was only too happy to cash out, after which he took in another eight million and bought an outlandish, all-white, ultra-modern, Gothic Revival neighborhood nightmare at #22, married the former wife of one of the aggressive new S&L directors and essentially retired to supervise his portfolio. (Needless to say, his is not the only story in Haddam with these as major plot elements.)

"I figured I'd caught you out here pullin' on old rudy in your red jacket and gettin' teary about your old house," Carter says, hooding his lower lip to look scandalized. He is small and tanned and slender, with short black hair that lies stiffly over on both sides of a wide, straight, scalp-revealing part. He is the standard for what used to be known as the Boston Look, though Carter actually hails from tiny Gouldtown in the New Jersey breadbasket and, though he doesn't look it, is as honest and unpretentious as a feed-store owner.

"I was just doping out a market analysis, Carter," I lie, "getting set to take in the parade. So I'm happy to have you startle the crap out of me." It's evident I have no such appraisal paperwork on the seat, only the Harrises' junk mail and some leftovers from my trip with Paul, most of which are in the back: the basketball paperweight and earring gifts, the crumpled copy of Self-Reliance, his Walkman, my Olympus, his copy of The New Yorker, his odorous Happiness Is Being Single tee-shirt and his Paramount bag containing a copy of the Declaration of Independence and some brochures from the Baseball Hall of Fame. (Carter, though, isn't close enough to see and wouldn't care anyway.)

"Frank, I'm gonna bet you didn't know John Adams and Thomas Jefferson died on the very same day." Carter mimps his regular closed-mouth smile and spreads his tanned legs farther apart, as if this was leading up to a randy joke.

"I didn't," I say, though of course I do, since it came up in the reading for my just completed trip and now seems ludicrous. I'm thinking that Carter looks ludicrous himself in his purple ensemble, standing actually out *in* Hoving Road while he quizzes me about history. "But let me try a guess," I say. "How 'bout July 4th, 1826, fifty years exactly after the signing of the Declaration, and didn't Jefferson say as his last words, 'Is it the Fourth?' "

"Okay, okay. I didn't realize you were a history professor. And Adams said, 'Jefferson still lives.' " Carter smiles self-mockingly. He loves this kind of stagy palaver and kept us all in stitches in the Divorced Men. "My kids let me in on it." He flashes his big straight teeth, which makes me remember how much I like him and the nights with our bereft compatriots, hunched around late tables at the August Inn or the Press Box Bar or out fishing the ocean after midnight, when life was all fucked up and, as such, much simpler than now, and as a group we learned to like it.

"Mine too," I lie (again).

"Both your rascals in fine fettle up in New London or wherever it is?"

"Deep River." Carter is more in the know than I'd have guessed, though a retailing of yesterday's events would cloud his sunny day. (I wonder, though, how he knows.)

I look up Hoving Road as a black Mercedes limo appears and turns right into the semicircular driveway of my old house and passes impressively around to the front door, where I have stood six thousand times contemplating the moon and mare's tails in a winter's sky and letting my spirits rise (sometimes with difficulty, sometimes not) to heaven. A surprising pang circuits through me at this very mind's image, and I'm suddenly afraid I may yield to what I said I wouldn't yield to over a simple domicile—sadness, displacement, lack of sanction. (Though by using Carter's presence I can fight it back.)

"Frank, d'you ever bump into ole Ann?" Carter says soberly for my sake, sticking his two hands up his opposite cabana coat sleeves and giving his forearms a good rough scratching. Carter's calves are as hairless as a turnip, and above his left knee is a deep and slick-pink dent I've of course seen before, where a big gout of tissue and muscle were once scooped violently out. Carter, despite his Boston banker's look and his screwy cabana suit, was once a Ranger in Vietnam, and is in fact a valorous war hero and to me all the more admirable for not being self-conscious about it.

"Not much, Carter," I say to the Ann question and blink my reluctance up at him. The sun is just behind his head.

"You know, I thought I saw her at the Yale–Penn game last fall.

She was with a big crowd of people. How long you two been kaput now?"

"Seven years, almost."

"Well, there's your biblical allotment." Carter nods, still scratching his arm like a chimp.

"You catchin' any fish, Carter?" I say. It is Carter who has sponsored me for the Red Man Club, but now never goes himself since his own kids live in California with their mom and tend to meet him in Big Sky or Paris. To my knowledge I'm the only member who regularly plies the Red Man's unruffled waters, and soon expect to do more of it with my son, if I'm lucky enough.

Carter shakes his head. "Frank, I never go," he says regretfully. "It's a scandal. I need to."

"Well, gimme a call." I'm ready to leave, am already thinking about Sally, who's coming at six. Carter's and my ninety seconds are up.

Where the Mercedes has drawn to a halt in front of my former front door, a small, liveried driver in a black cap has jumped out and begun hauling bulky suitcases from the trunk. Then out from the back seat emerges a stupendously tall and thin black African man in a bright jungle-green dashiki and matching cap. He is long and long-headed, splendid enough to be a prince, a virtual Milt the Stilt when he reaches his full elevation. He looks out at the quiet, hedge-bound neighborhood, sees Carter and me scoping him out, and waves a great, slow-moving, pink-palmed hand toward us, letting it wag side to side like a practiced blessing. Carter and I rapidly—me in my car, him out—raise ours and wave back and smile and nod as if we wished we could speak his lingo so he could know the good things we're thinking about him but unfortunately we can't, whereupon the limo driver leads the great man straight into my house.

Carter says nothing, steps back and looks both ways down the curving street. He was not part of the injunction junta but came along afterward and thinks, I'm sure, that the Ecumenical Center is a good neighbor, which is what I always felt would be the case. It's not true that you can get used to anything, but you can get used to much more than you think and even learn to like it.

Carter, it's my guess, is now inventorying his day's thoughts, jokes, headlines, sports scores, trying to determine if there's anything he can say to interest me that won't take over thirty more seconds yet still provide him an exit line so he can go plop back in his pool. I, of course, am doing the same. Save when tragedies strike, there's little that really needs to be said to most people you know.

"So any news about your little agent's murder?" Carter says in a businesslike voice, choosing a proper tragedy and replanting his paper-clad feet even farther apart on the smooth pavement and assuming an expression of dogged, hard-mouthed, law 'n' order intolerance for all unwanted abridgments of personal freedoms.

"We're offering a reward, but not that I know of," I say, hard-mouthed myself, thinking once again of Clair's bright face and her sharp-eyed, self-certain sweetness, which cut me no slack yet brought me to ecstasy, if but briefly. "It's like she got struck by lightning," I say, and realize I'm describing only her disappearance from my life, not her departure from this earth.

Carter shakes his head and makes of his lips a pocket of compressed air, which causes him to look deformed before he lets it all out with a *ptttt* noise. "They oughta just start stringin' those kinda guys up by their dicks and lettin' 'em hang."

"I think so too," I say. And I do.

Because there is truly nothing more to say after this, Carter may be about to ask me my view of the election and its possible radiant lines into the realty business and by that route snake around to politics. He considers himself a "Strong Defense—Goldwater Republican" and likes treading a line of jokey, condescending disparagement toward me. (It is his one unlikable quality, one I've found typical of the suddenly wealthy. Naturally he was a Democrat in college.) But politics is a bad topic for Independence Day.

"I heard you reading *Caravans* on the radio last week," Carter says, nodding. "I really enjoyed that a lot. I just wanted you to know." Though his thinking is suddenly commandeered by a whole new thought. "Okay, now look," he says, his eyes turned intent. "You're our words guy, Frank. I'd think a lot of things these days might make you want to go back to writing stories." Having said this, he looks down, cinches his purple belt tight around his belly and peers at his small feet in their paper sleeves as if something about them has changed.

"Why do you think that, Carter? Does now seem like a dramatic time to be alive? I'm pretty happy with it, but it hasn't to me. I'd find it encouraging if you thought so." The limo is now swinging around to leave, its heavy pipes murmuring against the driveway surface. I'm frankly flattered Carter knows anything about my prior writing life.

My fingers, delving half-consciously between my seat and the passenger's, come up with the tiny red bow Clarissa gave me. Along with Carter's personal crediting of my long-ago and momentary life as a writer, finding this makes me feel measurably better, since my spirits had drooped over thoughts of Clair.

"It just seems to me like a lot more things need explaining these days, Frank." Carter is still peering at his toes. "When you and I were in college, ideas dominated the world—even if most of them were stupid. Now I can't even think of a single new big idea, can you?" He looks up, then down at Clarissa's red bow, which I'm holding in my palm, and wrinkles his nose as though I were presenting him with a riddle. Carter, I sense, has been sitting too long on the sidelines counting his money, so that the world seems both simple and simply screwed up. He may, I'm afraid, be on the brink of voicing some horseshit, right-wing dictum about freedom, banning the income tax, and government interventionism in a free-market economy—"ideas" to feed his need for some certitude and whole-heartedness between now and cocktail hour. He of course is not interested in my former writing career.

But if Carter were to ask me—as a man once did on a plane to Dallas back when I was a sportswriter—what I thought he ought to do with his life now that he'd come into a bank vault full of loot, I'd tell him what I told that man: dedicate your life to public service; do a tour with VISTA or the Red Cross, or hand-deliver essential services to the sick and elderly in West Virginia or Detroit (the man on the Dallas flight wasn't interested in this advice and said he thought he might just "travel" instead). Carter indeed would probably like to be put in touch with Irv Ornstein, once he's retired from his fantasy baseball career. Irv, panting to get free of the simulator business, could tempt Carter with the big new commanding metaphor of *continuity*, and the two of them could start cooking up some sort of self-help scheme to franchise on television and make another fortune.

Or I could suggest he come down just the way I did and have a talk with our crew at L & S, since we have yet to replace Clair but soon must. Stepping into her shoes could satisfy his unsatisfied needs by championing the "idea" of doing something for others. He's at least as qualified as I was, and in some of the same ways— except that he's married.

Or possibly *he* should take up words, pen some stories of his own to fling out into the void. But as for me on that score—I've been there. The air's too thin. Thanks, but no thanks.

I muse up at Carter's small, delicate features, which seem added on to a flat map. I mean to look as though I can't imagine a single idea, good or bad, but know there to be plenty floating around loose. (My most obvious idea would be misconstrued, turned into a debate I don't care to have, ending us up in the politics of stalemate.)

"Most important ideas still probably start with physical acts, Carter," I say (his friend). "You're an old classicist. Maybe what you need to do is get off your butt and stir up some dust."

Carter stares at me a long moment and says nothing, but is clearly thinking. Finally he says, "You know, I *am* still in the Active Reserves. If Bush could get a little conflict fired up when he gets in, I could be called up for serious midlife ass kicking."

"There's an idea, I guess." My daughter's red bow is attached to my little finger like a reminder, and what I'm reminded of is my LICK BUSH sticker, which I'm sorry Carter hasn't seen. Though this is enough, and I ease my car down into gear. The limo's taillights brighten at Venetian Way, swing left and glide from sight. "You might arrange to get yourself killed doing that."

"I-BOG is what we used to say in my platoon: In a blaze of glory." Carter mugs a little and rolls his eyes. He's no fool. His fighting days are long over, and I'm sure he's glad of it. "You relatively happy with your current life's travails, ole Franko? Still planning on staying in town?" He does not exactly mean "travails" but something more innocent, and smiles at me with purest, conversation-ending sincerity built upon the rock of lived life.

"Yep," I say, with goodwill in all ways equal to his. "You already know I believe home's where you pay the mortgage, Carter."

"I'd think real estate might get a little tiresome. About as ridiculous as most jobs."

"So far, not. So far it's fine. You oughta try it, since you're retired."

"I'm not *that* retired." He winks at me for reasons that aren't clear.

"I'm headed for the parade, ole Knott-head. You endure a fine Independence Day."

Carter snaps up a crisp, absurd little army salute in his colorful poolside attire. "Ten-four. Go forth and do well, Cap'n Bascombe. Bring back glory and victory or at least tales of glory and victory. Jefferson still lives."

"I'll do my best," I say, slightly embarrassed. "I'll do my best." And I motor off into my day, smiling.

*A*nd that is simply that. The whole nine yards, that which *it* was all about for a time, ending well, followed by a short drive to a parade.

There is, naturally, much that's left unanswered, much that's left till later, much that's best forgotten. Paul Bascombe, I still believe, will come to live with me for some part of his crucial years. It may not be a month from now or six. A year could go by, and there would still be time enough to participate in his new self-discovery.

It is also possible that I will soon be married, following years supposing I never could again, and so would no longer view myself as the suspicious bachelor, as I admit I sometimes still do. The Permanent Period, this would be, that long, stretching-out time when my dreams would have mystery like any ordinary person's; when whatever I do or say, who I marry, how my kids turn out, becomes what the world—if it makes note at all—knows of me, how I'm seen, understood, even how I think of myself before whatever there is that's wild and unassuagable rises and cheerlessly hauls me off to oblivion.

Up Constitution Street, from my car seat, I now can see the marchers passing beyond crowded spectators' heads, hear the booms of the big drums, the cymbals, see the girls in red and white skirtlets high-prancing, batons spinning, a red banner held aloft ahead of flashing trumpets borrowing the sun's spangly light. It is not a bad day to be on earth.

I park behind our office and beside the Press Box Bar, lock up and then stand out in the noon heat below a whitening sky and begin my satisfied amble up to the crowd. "Ba-boom, ba-boom, ba-boom, ba-boom! Hail to the victors valiant, hail to the conquering heroes . . ." Ours is a familiar fight song, and everyone up ahead of me applauds.

Late last night when I was dead asleep and the worst of my day's events were put to rest after a long trial-by-error followed by the reemergence of some small hope (which is merely human), my phone rang. And when I said hello from the darkness, there was a moment I took to be dead silence on the line, though gradually I heard a breath, then the sound of a receiver touching what must've been a face. There was a sigh, and the sound of someone going, "Ssss, tsss. Uh-huh, uh-huh," followed by an even deeper and less certain "Ummm."

And I suddenly said, because someone was there I felt I knew, "I'm glad you called." I pressed the receiver to my ear and opened my eyes in the dark. "I just got here," I said. "Now's not a bad time at all. This is a full-time job. Let me hear your thinking. I'll try to add a part to the puzzle. It can be simpler than you think."

Whoever was there—and of course I don't know who, really—breathed again two times, three. Then the breath grew thin and brief. I heard another sound, "Uh-huh." Then our connection was gone, and even before I'd put down the phone I'd returned to the deepest sleep imaginable.

And I am in the crowd just as the drums are passing—always the last in line—their *boom-boom-boom*ing in my ears and all around. I see the sun above the street, breathe in the day's rich, warm smell. Someone calls out, "Clear a path, make room, make room, please!" The trumpets go again. My heartbeat quickens. I feel the push, pull, the weave and sway of others.

RANDOM HOUSE AUDIOBOOKS

INDEPENDENCE DAY

Richard Ford's
Pulitzer Prize–winning novel is available on cassette from Random House Audio

Read by John Rubinstein

Running time: 3 hours, abridged • 2 cassettes

At your bookstore or call TOLL FREE 1-800-793-2665

*When calling or ordering by mail, please indicate tracking code: 026-40

Please send me the audiocassette_____ (0-679-44380-0) of
***Independence Day* by Richard Ford**

_____ @ $18.00   = _____
(Quantity)

Shipping/Handling*   = _____

Subtotal   = _____

Sales Tax (where applicable)   = _____

Total Enclosed   = _____

*Please enclose $4.00 to cover shipping and handling (or $6.00 if total order is more than $20.00).

☐ If you wish to pay by check or money order, please make it payable to Random House Audio Publishing.

☐ To charge your order to a major credit card, please fill in the information below.

Charge to   ☐ American Express   ☐ Visa   ☐ MasterCard

Account No._____ Expiration Date_____

Signature_____

Name_____

Address_____

City_____ State_____ Zip_____

Send your payment with the order form above to:

Random House Audio Publishing, Dept. CC, 25-1, 201 East 50th Street, New York, NY 10022.
Prices subject to change without notice. Please allow 4-6 weeks for delivery.

For a complete listing of Random House AudioBooks, write to the address above.